# CAPTIVES OF MORE THAN LOVE

**Madelaine**—the French seductress who had adored the Count Saint-Germain for her two hundred years as the reigning beauty of the undead

**Irina**—the Russian duchess whom Saint-Germain had rescued from the flames of the Russian Revolution to take a place in his kingdom of devotees

**Rudi**—the proud German noblewoman whose world of unbending propriety melted in a night of fulfillment that only Saint-Germain could offer

**and Laisha**—the lovely and innocent girl-woman who made Saint-Germain desperately fight his own growing desire.

**All would do anything for the most irresistible vampire ever to hold a woman in thrall—just as he would do anything to save them from the greatest evil ever to shadow the earth.**

# TEMPTING FATE

## More SIGNET Bestsellers

# Chelsea Quinn Yarbro

# TEMPTING FATE

A SIGNET BOOK
NEW AMERICAN LIBRARY
TIMES MIRROR

NAL BOOKS ARE AVAILABLE AT QUANTITY DISCOUNTS WHEN USED
TO PROMOTE PRODUCTS OR SERVICES. FOR INFORMATION PLEASE
WRITE TO PREMIUM MARKETING DIVISION. THE NEW AMERICAN
LIBRARY. INC.. 1633 BROADWAY. NEW YORK. NEW YORK 10019.

SIGNET TRADEMARK REG. U.S. PAT OFF. AND FOREIGN COUNTRIES
REGISTERED TRADEMARK—MARCA REGISTRADA
HECHO EN CHICAGO. U.S.A

SIGNET, SIGNET CLASSICS, MENTOR, PLUME, MERIDIAN AND NAL BOOKS
are published by The New American Library, Inc.,
1633 Broadway, New York, New York 10019

First Signet Printing, November 1982

1  2  3  4  5  6  7  8  9

PRINTED IN THE UNITED STATES OF AMERICA

As with the other books in this series, every reasonable effort has been made to recreate the time of the action as it was. The early part of this century is still within living memory; journalistic, personal, photographic, cinematic, academic, and diplomatic documentation is available for most of the action and locales of this novel.

Time and history have not yet judged the latter half of the nineteenth century, let alone the twentieth, and opinions are varied and emotionally charged. Memoirs of this period have the insight that comes in retrospect rather than in the event, and for that reason I have approached them with caution, drawing from many sources rather than a few.

Of course there are errors, most of them inadvertent, a small number of them demanded by the course of the plot, for this is, after all, a work of fiction, and the story it tells, although occurring in recognizable places and concerned with real events, is the product of the writer's imagination and should not be construed as representing or intending to represent any actual persons living and dead.

The writer wishes to thank the following persons for their generous help and assistance in the preparation of this book:

Ron Bounds

Sarah Chambers

Sharon McDaniel

David Nee

Edward Nicholls

Dr. and Mrs. Karl Schalfrant

Dan Nobuhiko Smiley

Natalie Wendruff

Errors in language and history are those of the writer, not of these expert advisers, whose memories and skills have been invaluable.

# PART I

## Laisha Vlassevna

Text of a letter from the American journalist James Emmerson Tree, to his cousin Audrey in Denver.

*Portsmouth*
*September 21, 1917*

*Dear Audrey:*

*There were two more delays in London, which didn't surprise me. You know what it's been like so far, trying to get to Europe. Those reporters with the Associated Press have been having a little better luck, but those of us simply on assignment are at the bottom of the heap. Every time the question of passage comes up, it seems that the last men they have room for are reporters like me. I was talking to a man from Chicago, over here for the Sun, a couple of days ago, who said he'd been waiting for almost a month to get a space on a boat. He told me that he was getting so discouraged that he was thinking of renting a dinghy and getting himself across. However, as you see from the heading, I've made a little progress, and if all goes well, we'll leave the day after tomorrow on a boat bound for Brest. Originally they were going to take us to Le Havre, but they think Brest is safer, because it's about as far away as they can get us from the fighting and still land us in France. There'll be five journalists and a couple of dozen nurses on the boat, so if I'm seasick again, it probably won't matter.*

*Someday, when this war is finally over, you've got to get Uncle Ned to bring you over here to England. I knew it would be a revelation, but I never realized how much is crammed into this little place. It isn't just in London that you keep tripping over history, you can find it everywhere. If Crandell will let me, I'm going to do some pieces on England and Europe that he can run when the war winds down, not just to say what's happened since the Germans busted loose, but everything that went on before. If he isn't interested, I know I can sell articles to magazines. Maybe* Century Magazine *or* Atlantic Monthly *would be interested if Crandell says no.*

    *There's a lot of rumors floating around London right now, and sitting in the pubs, you can hear most of them. I haven't sent any back to Crandell, of course, because most of it's just the usual run of wartime boasts and worries. Here in Portsmouth it isn't as extreme, but London is alive with gossip. Everyone tells everyone else that they shouldn't pass on rumors, but . . . and then they come out with the latest story. They can get pretty wild, sometimes. Since I'm from the other side of the Atlantic, and America's just gotten into the war, many of the men I meet seem to think it's okay to mention things to me. I told one man that I work for a newspaper and it might be wiser to keep his information to himself, since he couldn't know what use I'd make of it. He smiled and said, "But it's an* American *paper, isn't it?" and then came up with a real whopper about machines that will blow all the poison gas back at the Huns. I let him rattle on about it for a while, and then I went back to Grantley's place in Bloomsbury, which is where I've been staying since my hotel got taken over by a bunch of visiting European generals or adjutants, or whatever they are. My mail's taking a little longer to get to me because of the move, so I haven't had any letter from you since the one you sent August 2, which arrived yesterday.*

    *In that letter, you said you were thinking about stopping your French lessons. Don't you do it! You know how I used to grouse about learning it, and how it was silly and there was no point to it, and Madame Courante was a real witch, and all the rest of it. Well, let me tell you, Audrey, the last two months, I've been more grateful than I can say to that impossible old bat. It isn't just that I can speak French that makes so many of the Europeans take a shine to me in spite of the fact that I'm an uncouth and uncultured American, but that I can speak it* right. *Aunt Myra's doing you a favor, making you take those classes. I know it's hard work and most of the kids in school think it's a crazy thing to do, but take it from your Cousin James, you'll be way ahead of the game if you stick with it.*

    *I found out the other night that they've outlawed ab-*

sinthe in France, so I won't be able to tell you how it tastes, after all.

It's a real pity about the censors in New York suppressing the Dreiser book; I finally got a copy of it, and it's damned good. Fellow from Boston, of all places, brought it with him, and he's staying at Grantley's too, for the same reason I am. And if you ever tell Aunt Myra or Uncle Ned that I said "damned" to you, you better be wearing three pair of bloomers next time I see you.

It's about time Uncle Ned got rid of that old Model A. I know it's been a great automobile, but the last time I rode in it, it sounded like a goat digesting a load of tin cans. You need something that's going to hold up through the winter. It may also surprise you to know that I think you ought to learn to drive. Aunt Myra doesn't want to, and with Paul going into the army, there ought to be someone there other than Uncle Ned who can drive. Aunt Myra may want to shoot me for saying that, but I'd hate to think of you people being stranded out there, twelve miles from town. Even with the telephone in, it would be a help to have a second driver around.

Sorry, but I haven't been able to find out anything about Tom McMillian, except what we already know, that he's somewhere in France. From what I hear, Americans aren't doing much fighting yet, so the chances are he's safe. I'll ask around some more when I get there, but don't get your hopes up. It's a huge war, and if what we've been told is accurate, it's being botched by the people who shouldn't make those kinds of mistakes. I know we're not supposed to talk that way, or think that way, but I went to a hospital near here (and this is not to be repeated, young lady; this part is just between us, because it has to be) and I saw some of the men who've been at the Front, and I've learned what happened to them—those who could still talk sense told me about it—and that's one of the reasons I really want to get over there. I know about soldiers' bitterness, from what old Colonel Hurst said about Andersonville that time. Fifty years had gone by, almost, and he still couldn't talk about the place without blaspheming. So I'm not sure that these are the men I should be listening to. That's not to say I think we should forget them: everyone ought to know what it's cost to hold the Huns back, not only in dead, but those who have had *their lives taken away from them without the release of death.*

*Once I get to France, it's going to be harder to send you letters. Most of my writing is going to have to be for the Post-Dispatch, and not for the family. If I make good over here, then it could mean I'll have the career I want. They sent me over because I'm pretty expendable. If I get hurt, they can still pick up stories from American Associated Press. I haven't kidded myself about that. But I'm going to make myself indispensable to them. So if you don't hear from me for a while, don't worry. I'll do my best to write to you once a month, and trust that some of the letters get through. If anything bad happens, you'll know about it. Remember that when my mother and Aunt Myra start thinking I've been shot.*

*You remember that reporter from Seattle I told you about? He got passage to Sweden and had arrangements made to get into Russia. He actually went through with it. Europe may be at war, but Russia's exploding. He told us a little about what he'd found out from his contacts, and I tell you, that's one place I'm staying out of until the dust really and truly settles. Don't you fear for me unless you find out I'm being sent to Moscow.*

*Tell Aunt Myra and Uncle Ned I think about them often and fondly, and remember that I'm on your side, Audrey. This will have to be Happy Thanksgiving, too, I think, because I doubt you'll hear from me again before Christmas. If you're still saying prayers, say a few for me when you think of it, and for those poor soldiers in the trenches.*

*Until I write again, be good to each other.*

*Your loving cousin,*
*James*

*P.S. You might tell Madame Courante that I'm not as hopeless as she thought. I had a talk with a Captain in the French Army and he complimented me on the way I speak. He said I have a fine accent. She did a good job. But don't let her give you a bad time. If France is anything like England, I can see why she might find Denver a bit of a comedown.*

# 1

Petrograd was burning. The wind from the city was filled with soot and cinders and the greasy odor of charring things. Dark, close clouds hung low in the sky, molten with the lurid reflection of the flames. At this distance it was impossible to know what buildings were being destroyed: perhaps the palaces along the Nevsky Prospekt, or the Fortress and Cathedral of Saints Peter and Paul on the far side of the Neva.

The Monastery of the Victory was not far from Konstantinovka, nearer to Krasnoye Selo than to Petrograd, situated a fair distance from the road on a wide, treeless stretch of ground where the Imperial Guard had held maneuvers. It was an ancient building, with thick walls and small, barred windows. This made it an ideal prison.

Some twenty Cossacks held the monastery, guarding twice that number of prisoners. It had been a heady pleasure at first, but more than a week had passed and the excitement was beginning to pall. Now, with the last chaos of October 24 fading, most of the men had turned to the mundane business of securing billets with the villagers of Konstantinovka, leaving only their three officers to tend the monastery and the men incarcerated there.

Most of the wine kept in the monastery cellar had been drunk, and so the remaning men regaled themselves with raw vodka which the villagers had provided. They had all the vast Pilgrims' Hall to themselves, though they did not stray far from the enormous hearth, for the stark winter chill permeated the place and the fire made little progress against it. Most of the tables and benches which had filled the Hall had been broken up to provide wood for the hearth, but a glance revealed that this was insufficient fuel for more than another two days, and so the vodka augmented the fire.

The youngest officer, an overgrown boy of seventeen, was Acting Captain Yuri Yureivich Garin. He was bored as well as drunk, and was trying to alleviate the first and deny the second with an impromptu display of Cossack dancing. He jumped into the air, determined to click the heels of his scuffed boots, and before he could try a second time, fell heavily to the floor.

"Ah, Comrade Garin," Acting Colonel Dmitri Mihialovich Rubashek chided the youngster, wagging his half-empty bottle instead of a finger. "That is not worthy of an officer. No. Not at all. You must let me, for I am older and more experienced, show you how . . ."—he got unsteadily to his feet—"it is to be done."

Yuri Yureivich had not bothered to get up. He wedged his arm under his head and stared up, making a halfhearted salute before he remembered that he was now an officer and did not have to offer this courtesy to Rubashek. "You're in no condition . . ." he warned, but the other man was already essaying a hopping turn on one leg.

The third man, well into his thirties and of a more somber disposition, put the mouth of his vodka bottle to his lips and tilted his head back, letting the clear, potent liquid run into him. He paid no attention to his companions. As Acting Colonel Dmitri Mihialovich stumbled and fell onto the feebly protesting Acting Captain Yuri Yureivich, this third man, Nikolai Ivanevich Rozoh, rose and made his way from the Pilgrims' Hall, muttering to the bottle he held tucked into the curve of his arm. His rank was now Acting Major, but he continued to think of himself as Corporal Rozoh.

The corridor he entered was poorly lit and dank, the thick stones clammy to the touch. Behind him he could hear the other two arguing noisily, and he muttered imprecations at them only he could hear.

"Who's there?" a desperate, cracked voice cried from behind one of the closed wooden doors of the cells that lined the hallway. "For the love of God!"

"Help! You must help!" another, weaker cry joined the first.

Acting Major Rozoh paid no attention to the pleas, nor to the others that echoed them from the other barred doors. He marched steadily down the passage toward the kitchen.

It was a large room, quite deserted, and all but one of the stoves was cold. Nikolai Ivanevich put his bottle down on the worn planking of the table and tried to marshal his thoughts. He was hungry, he was fully aware of that, and no one was left to make him a meal. It was as bad as being a Corporal still. He made his way around the kitchen, pulling open cupboards that revealed ominously few provisions. The significance of this discovery escaped him for the moment, though there was a small, sober part of his mind that became alarmed. Vaguely he recalled that he and his two fellow-officers had been mandated to provide for the prisoners. No one had told them how this was to be done. Corporal . . . no, Acting Major Rozoh sighed. Insects had got into the flour, so it was not possible to make bread. Nothing was left of the salt pork that had been brought a week ago. There had been fish, but the last of it had turned bad. A little fruit was left, and there were perhaps ten pounds of potatoes in the bins, most of which had sprouted. The people of Konstantinovka had promised to keep the monastery in supplies, but now, with most of the soldiers billeted there, it was not likely that they would continue to bring food. Nikolai Ivanevich sat down on the edge of the nearest table and stared gloomily at the far wall. During the next hour he did little other than finish the vodka.

At sunset Acting Colonel Dmitri Mihialovich ambled uncertainly into the kitchen and blinked at Rozoh. "You here?"

"Yes." The vodka bottle lay in pieces at his feet, and he felt quite remotè from his surroundings.

"Did you feed the prisoners?" He made erratic progress to where Nikolai Ivanevich was sitting.

"No. There's no food."

"Ah." He hoisted himself up onto the table beside the Acting Major. "No food. Pity."

"Um."

"General Svenyets will be angry." The very thought was chastening. "We have to give them something. We'll be flogged."

"Where's Yuri?" Nikolai Ivanevich asked.

Dmitri Mihialovich wagged his hand in the direction of the corridor. "Asleep. The boy can't drink." He ruined this condemnation with a loud belch. "Spawn of the devil, we've got to give the prisoners *something*, or . . ."

". . . we'll be flogged," Nikolai Ivanevich finished for him.

The two men said nothing. Dmitri Mihialovich swung his legs back and forth, occasionally setting his heels against a table leg and humming unidentifiable scraps of melody.

"Well, perhaps one of us should ride into Konstantinovka and remind the villagers that there are still men here," Dmitri Mihialovich said more than ten minutes later.

"There's just the two horses left, and one of them is lame," Nikolai reminded him.

"Damn!" He scowled, and then his expression lightened. "It might be possible to put sufficient provisions for tonight on one horse. You'd have to go back in the morning, but tonight would be taken care of. Those prisoners are supposed to eat. So are we."

The "*you'd* have to go back in the morning" was not lost on Nikolai. He looked hard at his companion. "You're in no condition to ride."

"I'm a Cossack!" Dmitri announced with sudden belligerence. "I can ride anything at any time. Drunk or sober. Summer or winter. Naked or clothed." His outburst faded. "You're no better off than I am."

"True."

Several more minutes passed; then Nikolai sighed and stood up, hardly swaying at all. The kitchen was almost totally dark, and he had to grope his way to the one warm stove. He rummaged blindly in the woodbox for a bit of kindling, and finally pulled out a long, dry stick, which he thrust into the dying coals of the stove. At last the stick caught fire, and Nikolai withdrew it, shielding the flame with his hand. He made his way to the nearest of the hanging kerosene lamps and lifted the smoke-dulled glass chimney to light the wick, which was poorly trimmed and sputtered often.

"Splendid," Dmitri said as he lay back on the table, his knees up, his hands laced behind his head. "What time is it?"

"Between six and seven, I should guess," Nikolai answered, attempting to adjust the flame. He shook the lamp gently and heard the fuel slosh in the tin reservoir. "We'll need more kerosene tomorrow night."

"Ask the villagers. They're not issuing fuel at headquarters for another four days, they said. Most of the materials are being shunted off to Petrograd, in any case." He yawned. "It will be colder tonight. Do you think we should break up the benches in the sanctuary?"

"We'll have to." Nikolai sighed. He had had a religious upbringing, and though he had long since turned from the practice of his faith, the vestiges of superstition and respect had not deserted him.

"Get Yuri to do it. He's younger than either of us." Dmitri braced one heel against his raised knee. "Build up the fire, will you? It's turning damned cold."

"There isn't any wood left in the box," Nikolai told him, thinking that it was typical of their fortunes that these tasks should fall to them.

"Well, then have some chopped. Get out one or two of the prisoners to do it, if you don't want to," Dmitri suggested.

"I wouldn't want to be around one of them if he had an ax in his hand," Nikolai remarked, dismissing the idea. "Besides, headquarters requisitioned most of the logs. We'd have to cut down one of the trees, and they're too far away."

Dmitri hummed again for a while as Nikolai busied himself with smashing two footstools into pieces sufficiently small for the stove. The fitful lamplight grew less effective as the night deepened until it was augmented by the faint glow from the tinderbox of the stove.

"It's warming up," Nikolai said when he was satisfied with the fire he had built.

"Wouldn't want it to get any colder," Dmitri said as he rolled onto his side. "This time of year . . . Poor turds in the cells. They're oppressors of the people and enemies of the revolution and reactionary criminals, but it's too bad they have to freeze to death."

"Or starve," Nikolai added. He looked around for more usable wood and considered the low bench where the monks had sat to hull peas or peel potatoes. He picked it up and brought it down against the massive cutting table. The bench broke apart and one length of wood very nearly hit Dmitri Mihialovich as it flew across the kitchen.

"By Saint Vladimir! . . ." Dmitri swore as he quickly rolled off the table. "Watch what you're doing, Nikolai Ivanevich."

Nikolai did not respond. He worked steadily at breaking up the planking, oblivious of the sections of wood sailing around the room. Only when he was through did he give a pleased grunt and speak to his fellow-officer. "Keep out of range, if you don't want to help."

"Oh-ho, so that's how it is," Dmitri said as he crawled out from under the table. "Thinking to scare me into cooperating with you, is that it?" He got to his feet. "Maybe I should take the horse and go into Konstantinovka to get food."

"It's dark now," Nikolai reminded him. "And the horse couldn't make it, being lame." He made his way around the kitchen, picking up the broken sections of wood and stacking them beside the warm stove.

"One of them's sound. A couple of bagfuls of bread would be something. A roast doesn't take up much room, and isn't too heavy. If I rode the horse, I could carry a meal for us." He was warming to the idea, now that hunger was vying with drink for his attention.

"And the prisoners?" Nikolai asked, with a touch of pity for the men in the cells.

"I could bring enough to give them all a little something,"

Dmitri said, dismissing the matter. "There's a good amount of vodka left, and we might as well distribute it to them—help to keep out the cold and make them forget their troubles." He came over to the stove and rubbed his hands over it.

"They're hungry," Nikolai reminded him.

"So are we." His manner turned surly. "That's the army for you, never paying any attention to its enlisted men."

"We're officers now," Nikolai pointed out, but his sarcasm was lost on Dmitri.

"They should pay attention to officers. But instead, they send the rest of the men off to bunk in the village with food and women and drink and festivities. We're left here in the dark with a handful of stinking aristocrats, and what good is that to us? We could go into Konstantinovka ourselves. The prisoners aren't going anywhere. The walls here are thirty inches thick, the windows are barred and the doors are a foot thick and stapled and hinged with heavy iron. As long as we make sure the bars are in place, we could leave them here, and come back in the morning." He waved his hand in a vague way. "What do you say, Comrade? Do we go into Konstantinovka?"

Nikolai did not respond to this heartiness. "We'd be shot if it were ever found out."

"Who's to tell them?" Dmitri said, punching Nikolai in the shoulder with rough good-fellowship. "You? Me? Yuri Yureivich? The prisoners? They'll all be dead in a week."

"The General is at Krasnoye Selo. He might send a messenger here, or come himself," Nikolai said darkly, recalling just such an unpleasant occasion when Petrograd was still St. Petersburg and the Czar had held court there at the Winter Palace.

"Not with the city in flames. He won't budge from Krasnoye Selo until that whole place is calm again. If he does anything else, he might become the next target for one of the revolutionary committees, and that would not suit him at all." Dmitri was bitterly amused at his own assessment of the current predicament. "Come on. Let's go get the horses. We can leave the lame one here for Yuri Yureivich, if he wants to make use of it. It's not far to Konstantinovka. We'll ride double and—"

Nikolai interrupted him. "Acting Colonel Rubashek," he said to Dmitri with great formality, "if you wish to ride to Konstantinovka tonight, there's nothing I can do to stop you. I intend to remain here, with the prisoners. Those were my orders and until they are countermanded, I will obey them." He folded his arms and stared at the other man impassively.

"Ach!" Dmitri stamped his foot and glared at Nikolai. "Very

well. You and the boy can remain here. I will ride into Konstantinovka and in the morning, I will bring provisions and another horse. Then we can butcher the lame one for meat, if you like." He stamped toward the corridor on which the cells were located. "Why do we bother to feed them, when they're going to be shot? What does it matter? Why don't we leave them alone?" He had no answer for his questions, and Nikolai was adding more wood to the stove. Dmitri stood at the limits of the lanternlight and pointed at Nikolai. "Acting Major Rozoh, if you ever report this to the General or to anyone else, I will deny your accusation and tell them that you sought to protect these enemies of the people from their just punishments. And that will be the end of you, Nikolai Mihialovich."

"I will say nothing," Nikolai assured him, and continued to stoke the tinderbox as Dmitri left the kitchen. A few minutes later he heard the heavy side door open, and then close with the resounding solidity of foot-thick planks. Nikolai sighed once and began to break up another bench.

The kitchen was tolerably warm when Acting Captain Yuri Yureivich Garin stumbled into it. His young face was mottled and his eyes red-rimmed and blurry. "Where's supper?" he asked, slurring the words, as he blinked at Nikolai.

"There isn't any."

"But I'm hungry," the young man protested, then lurched suddenly against the nearest table. "Got to eat. Tell Rubashek."

"Rubashek's gone," Nikolai told him. He was gathering up what little was left and slicing the few vegetables into a pot.

"Gone where?" Yuri asked, but without any genuine interest.

"Into Konstantinovka. He'll be back in the morning, with food." Privately he doubted this, but it was not his place to say more. Fifteen years of army life had taught him a degree of prudence. He added more water to the vegetables in the pot and reached for a wooden spoon to stir the mess with.

"Damn," the youth said listlessly. He dropped down, cross-legged, near the warm stove. "What have you there?"

"Vegetables. That and the vodka are all that's left." He went on with the very simple cooking, paying little heed to Yuri. In half an hour the young man was asleep, and Nikolai went in search of the wooden bowls in which the prisoners were given their meals. When he had found them and the large tin spoons the monks had used, he put five of them on the largest tray and ladled out small portions of the steaming, tasteless stew.

The first round of serving went uneventfully. Acting Major Rozoh asked the questions he was required to ask, and received, as always, stony silence from the men in the little, cold cells. The next ten were much the same as the first five. Count Piotyr Pavlovich, in the twenty-third cell, threw the bowl at Nikolai and cursed him roundly. Former Major Viktor Sergeivich, in cell thirty-five, was shaking with ague, his white mustaches wet and drooping, his face gray but for the two hectic fever spots in his sunken cheeks. Seeing him, Nikolai suppressed the urge to pray for the old man.

Acting Major Rozoh always saved the thirty-sixth cell for last. That was where the foreigner was, the only man among the prisoners at the monastery who had the ability to disturb him. Nikolai hesitated before turning the massive key in the old lock and lifting the heavy iron bar.

Predictably, the foreigner rose; he was commanding but without hauteur, and though less than middle height, he had a presence about him that had little to do with his lack of inches. Only he, of all the men in the cells, had contrived to stay neat: only he did not complain of rats.

"Foreigner," Nikolai said uneasily, holding out the bowl of now-cold vegetable stew.

"Tovarich." The foreigner inclined his head slightly and favored his jailer with a fleeting, ironic smile.

"You did not eat the food I brought this morning." It was more than an accusation, for the foreigner had steadfastly refused all the meals he had been provided.

"Nyet, Tovarich."

"Will you want this?" Nikolai asked, proffering the bowl again.

"Nyet, Tovarich."

Nikolai sighed. "There is vodka. Do you want some?"

"Nyet, Tovarich."

He made one last effort. "There may be one or two bottles of sacramental wine still left in the cellar, if that would do as—"

"I do not drink wine."

"It's going to be very cold tonight," Nikolai persisted, uncertain of how to deal with this prisoner who did not behave as the others, who did not seem to realize how desperate his circumstances were.

"That is, of course, unfortunate." There was one rickety chair in the cell, and the foreigner sat on it. His suit of fine black wool was a little rumpled, and he had removed his wilted collar and in its place had tied a stock of black silk, fixing the knot with a ruby stickpin.

"If you do not take care, you will freeze to death." Nikolai wished that this announcement would cause some alteration in the foreigner's implacable demeanor.

"And cheat the firing squad?" the foreigner suggested gently.

Nikolai could not meet those dark, penetrating eyes. "Yes; you are condemned. It's decided . . . But—"

"I trust," the foreigner interrupted pleasantly, urbanely, "that your marksmen will take careful aim. I should hate to have them make"—he turned his head away—"a mess of it."

"That isn't likely," Nikolai said, beginning to feel foolish as the simple flour thickening began to congeal around the cold bits of vegetable in the bowl he still held.

"It isn't?" He looked at Nikolai. "Tell me, Corporal Rozoh, why should it matter whether I starve or freeze or fall to an executioner's bullet?"

"There is the question of justice," Nikolai said rather obliquely, not knowing himself what he meant.

"But if it is merely my death that is required, why not leave me to whatever winter brings? Why not simply lock the door to the cell and walk away?" His mouth turned at the corner; a wry smile.

It was a moment before Nikolai could answer, and when he did, the words came out with stiff formality. "We are not like the old order was. We are not willing to practice such inhumanity. We care for those in our custody. It is not our intention to be cruel, only just."

"Naturally," the foreigner agreed. "Which is why you keep us here in unheated cells with a column of soldiers to guard us night and day. Surely the walls are thick enough that half a dozen men might tend to the forty of us."

"That is not the issue," Nikolai said, thinking of Yuri Yureivich lying in a stupor in the kitchen, of Dmitri Mihialovich riding toward Konstantinovka. "Every man imprisoned here has demonstrated himself to be an enemy of the people, and for that reason, it is necessary that measures be taken."

"And what particular crimes have you attributed to me? It is true that I own three houses and a palace in Russia, but when have you ever heard that I abused my servants? Perhaps it is the factories I started, Corporal. I did provide schooling for my workers. Is that my crime?" His voice dropped. "I won't press you for an answer."

"Your way of life . . ." Nikolai burst out.

"Ah. I am accused of being rich. There I must admit I am guilty." He shook his head. "Soldiers are hardly necessary to protect the world from my wealth. And, as I understand it, my monies and lands have been taken from me. Why then the troops, and the firing squad?"

"The troops are not here tonight," Nikolai snapped, eager to silence the disturbing questions the foreigner asked. As soon as he had spoken, he regretted it.

"Indeed? On orders or simple desertion?" He waved his own question away with one small, beautiful hand. "You needn't answer that."

In spite of his doubts about this prisoner, Nikolai was driven to defend his men. "We do not desert. Our loyalty has never been in question."

"Not even by the Czar? How providential."

Nikolai's face reddened. "That was not a question of loyalty."

Quite affably the prisoner said, "Certainly not. Yet if your men are not here, they must be busy elsewhere. There is a paper mill at Krasnoye Selo, isn't there? It would be quite a prize for the counterrevolutionary forces."

"There are more than two hundred men posted there. My troops are much nearer than that," Nikolai assured him, feeling smug.

"Konstantinovka." He read assent in Nikolai's rugged features. "I see."

"They are gathering provisions, so that none of you here will be forced to starve as so many of us have starved." He almost flung the contents of the bowl across the cell, but controlled the impulse.

"That does not particularly impress me," the foreigner said, giving a pointed look to the untouched gruel left over from the morning.

In a surge of baffled rage, Nikolai demanded, "Why don't you eat? Aren't you hungry?"

The foreigner regarded him evenly. "If it is any consolation to you, I am famished."

"But why . . . ?" Nikolai began, then stopped, not knowing why he felt so abashed by this prisoner.

"Nevertheless, the others will doubtless be gratified to hear that more provisions are being fetched."

"By tomorrow morning," Nikolai declared with shaky confidence, "there will be ample rations in the kitchen."

"I should hope so, if that"—he indicated the bowl Nikolai still held—"is any indication of your current supplies."

"Unlike the decadent and corrupt nobility, we do not neglect . . ." He stopped this pompous speech as abruptly as he had begun it.

"Yes?" the foreigner said when Nikolai had been silent for more than a minute.

"There will be supplies in the morning. Not that such information would seem to matter to you." He was about to leave the cell when the foreigner said, "Do you know, it does matter to me."

Behind Nikolai half a dozen light, powerful steps sounded, and before he could turn to see the prisoner, he felt two small, strong hands seize his shoulders, and heard the well-bred, gentle voice speak in his ear.

"You must forgive me, Nikolai Ivanevich: this opportunity will not come again."

Nikolai struggled against the foreigner and was astonished to find that he could not break free of the smaller man. Nothing in his experience had prepared him for the force that dragged him back into the cell and with a deceptively gentle blow drove consciousness from his mind.

The foreigner stood over Acting Major Rozoh. He knew that Nikolai would not recover for more than an hour, and he hoped that would buy him sufficient time to make his escape. He bent and took the pistol from the Acting Major's belt, and was not entirely surprised to discover that it was not loaded. After a moment's hesitation he put the weapon into his pocket; he might still find a use for it. He had a small valise tucked under the straw of the pallet that served him for a bed, and this he pulled out before dragging Nikolai onto the straw. Carefully he arranged Nikolai's limbs in a posture suggesting sleep, and then dragged the two thin blankets allotted to him over the recumbent man. Such a minor deception would not survive even the most trivial scrutiny—Acting Major Rozoh was at least eight inches taller than the prisoner and his hair was fulvous brown—but it might delay pursuit a few crucial minutes more than if he had left the Acting Major in a heap. He had learned over the years that just such little advantages as this could make an essential difference in survival.

Marginally satisfied with his efforts, the foreigner stepped back. He had a black coachman's cloak with a sable collar hung on the peg that had previously held a crucifix. He and the other prisoners had been allowed to keep their coats because of the unrelieved cold of the monastery, and now he was grateful for it. Deciding not to hamper himself with wearing the heavy garment at the moment, he dropped it over his arm and lifted the valise as he left the cell.

In the door he paused long enough to glance first toward the Pilgrims' Hall and then toward the kitchen. Both rooms were nearly dark, but a low, fitful light in the kitchen warned him that however many men were left to guard the monastery, they were more likely to be found near the cooking stoves than in the drafty Hall. He pulled the cell door closed behind him, dropped the iron bar into place, and turned the key in the lock, hearing the old wards fall. He was about to place the key in his pocket with the pistol when he noticed the unmistakable sound of pacing from the thirty-first cell. He hesitated, knowing that every second he lingered increased his risk of discovery. In an instant he had made up his mind: walking lightly, he went to the door of the thirty-first cell and tried the key in the lock, wincing at the scrape of metal on rusty metal, fearing that it was loud as cannon fire and knowing that the pacing within was louder.

The footfalls stopped. "I have not changed my mind, Rozoh," warned the voice inside.

"Be quiet," the foreigner whispered, stopping his work.

On the other side of the door the footsteps faltered, then came nearer. "Rozoh, if this is a new ploy . . ."

"It's not Rozoh," the foreigner said quietly. "Keep walking." He was secretly grateful to hear the footsteps resume. With a final tug, he turned the key, and the lock grated open. Slowly he lifted the lock and bent to set it on the floor, then rose to lift the bar from its braces.

"What's happening out there?" the voice from within demanded with some urgency.

"Your door is open. You'll be able to swing it back. The key is in the lock. Wait three minutes and let yourself out, and open one of the other doors." It was all he could do.

"Who . . . ?" The prisoner's voice had sunk to a murmur, he was obviously standing pressed against the thick planking.

But the foreigner moved away, silent and agile in spite of the burden of valise and cloak. He went swiftly toward the Pilgrims' Hall, unhampered by the darkness. There was a small door that led to the neglected monastery garden, he remembered, and now he hoped that it, like the rest of the building, would be carelessly guarded, if guarded at all. His quiet steps echoed softly in the Hall, and reminded him unpleasantly of the scuttle of rats. He thought of the hours he had spent trapping the rodents in his cell, disgust surging through him as intense as nausea.

The garden door gasped on its hinges, then balked. The foreigner slipped through the narrow opening out into the frost-spangled night. Now he stopped to pull on the black, tiered cloak, fastening the frogs from knee to neck. At his back he heard the distant groaning of a cell door opening, and knew it was time to be gone. He took up his valise again and ran toward the stables.

Franchot Ragoczy was free. His hunger was terrible.

Text of a broadsheet tacked up throughout the city of Riga in Latvia.

TO ALL TRUE AND LOYAL LATVIANS:

*Long enough have we listened to the lies and promises of those who tell us that we must destroy in order to build. Each of you has struggled in his heart to find the justice that is truly desired by all Latvians. The chaos in Petrograd should convince you all that this new order which has been promised us is more disastrous than the most oppressive Czar we have ever known. These men who claim to have taken control of the government have declared themselves to be the champions of the workers and the toilers in the factories, mills, and fields. Yet who has seen his children go hungry to bed, but those same workers in the fields and mills and factories?*

DO NOT BE DECEIVED!

*Those of us who remain loyal to our country, our Czar, and our church know that the bulletins coming from the usurpers of the Winter Palace are lies and dastardly calumnies sent to trick you into betraying your honor. The despair that fills you is the product of the mendacious enemy, intended to confuse and isolate us each from the other, so that in the ensuing disruption, the agents of the regicidal tyrants may install themselves in places of power so that their conquest of all the Russias, their Dukedoms and Protectorates, may be facilitated by the very disheartened morale they themselves inspire.*

HAVE COURAGE!

*Your loyalty is not in vain. You are not forgotten. When this disorderly rabble has been suitably rewarded for treachery, then you who have remained staunch in your trust will be acknowledged as the valued and much-loved children of our Little Father, who has lived his whole life for our benefit. Who among you would be*

*willing to stand beside the Czar today, to face his wife
and his daughters and the blessed Czarevich and give an
account of himself? If you cannot say that you would do
this with pride, then it is you who harbor the vile and
pestilential contamination of revolution within your breast,
and it is you who have joined with the conspirators to
bring war, famine, and disaster to our country. Let no
one excuse himself for any action he may take at this
time. You have heard tales of the October Atrocities in
Petrograd. Be reminded that such events can occur here
as well, if we are not vigilant and faithful to our country
and our cause!*

## LATVIANS!

*Pray for strength in this time of turbulence and trial!
Surely God, who has kept the Czar in His heart, will
lavish blessings upon those who strive to live true to His
Will! Let every one of you examine himself to be certain
that his faith is firm and his heart constant in love of God
and the sainted Little Father. Ignore the prating of those
who seek to bring revolution and change to us, and instead
search for the guidance of those who have long provided
it: the clergy, the aristocracy, and the elders who attend
to justice. When you appear before the Throne of God,
there will be no room for the lies of the self-proclaimed
heralds of the new order, there will only be the stern and
triumphant judgment of Our Lord.*

Scrawled across this broadsheet in red ink:

REACTIONARY SODOMIZERS OF INFECTED SWINE!

## 2

Monbussy stood in an elbow of the Marne, halfway between
Chaumont and Langres. Its central tower dated back to the
thirteenth century, but the rest of the château had been built
in the sixteenth century, which resulted in an uneasy cross-
breeding of architectural styles. The remnants of a moat

could be seen on the north side of the structure, now ice-rimmed on this sleety day after Christmas.

Captain Timbres waited in the drawing room, staring at the pine sprays that framed the tall windows. These were the only festive indications in this elegantly-appointed chamber, but the scent of the house—a curious mixture of evergreen and incense—indicated the holiday season in spite of the restraint he saw around him. The room itself was chill, but the Captain did not pay much heed: he was cold, his clothes were damp, and he was in that remote frame of mind that comes after too many shocks. He was vaguely aware that he had tracked mud onto the fine turquoise-and-olive carpet; it was unimportant to him.

The woman who entered the room was startlingly young, dressed with elegant restraint and in woolens that were more warm than wholly fashionable. Her coffee-colored hair was shoulder-length and simply coiffured. She came across the drawing room toward him, her hand extended to him, her violet eyes meeting his frankly. "Captain; my housekeeper said you wished to speak to me?"

"You're Madame de Montalia?" he asked, having imagined a much older woman to be mistress of this château.

"Yes, I am. And you are . . ." she persisted politely.

"Captain Phillippe Timbres, at your service." There was a time, not much more than a year ago, when he would have introduced himself with polish and address, but war had rid him of his courtesy. He took her hand as if uncertain what to do with it, and after a moment, let it go.

Madelaine de Montalia studied him a moment, then indicated one of the velvet-covered sofas near the fireplace. "Won't you sit down, Captain Timbres, and tell me what brings you to my home?"

He did not respond at once, but gestured at his damp, mud-spattered uniform. "Do you think . . . ?"

"Pray don't let it bother you, Captain. I am sure that these walls have witnessed far worse things than your state of dress." She herself had taken a beautiful Louis XV chair and pulled it near the sofa. As she sat down, she motioned the Captain to do the same. "I'm sorry I have so little to offer you on this occasion, but, as you know far better than I, there is little to be had."

"Of course," he answered mechanically. His head ached, his eyes were sore, and he had been coughing for three days. He pulled his stained handkerchief from his pocket and held it to his mouth.

"Still, if you will allow me, I will have wine or cognac served, whichever you prefer." She had already reached for the silver bell that stood on a table at the end of the sofa. It's single melodic note sounded on the cold air.

"It's not necessary—" he began.

"But of course it is," she interrupted him with such a cordial smile that he was startled. "My fields have provided some food, but there has been so little else I could do. This is a minor thing, yet it would please me if you would accept my hospitality."

While Captain Timbres tried to think of a reason to refuse, Madelaine de Montalia turned to the elderly servant who entered the drawing room. "Claude," she said pleasantly, "please bring a bottle of cognac from the cellar. The Captain is cold."

Claude bowed and departed with no change of expression whatever.

"Believe me, Madame, this is not necessary." He was nonplussed at having to deal with so young a woman. The other landowners in the area had been respectably middle-aged, not so glowingly attractive.

"But it would be churlish of you to refuse," she reprimanded him gently. "Now, while we wait for Claude to bring the cognac, perhaps you will be kind enough to tell me what it is I am to have the pleasure of doing for you."

He did not answer her at once. "You are aware of the current state of the war?"

"Not absolutely, no, but I have paid a great deal of attention to all the announcements and dispatches which have come through the valley." Her self-possession was alarmingly genuine. "I realize that recent advances along the Front have been . . . unhappy for France. I am also aware that there is fear of further aggression. That is what you've come to tell me, isn't it?"

Captain Timbres regarded Madelaine with puzzlement. From the look of her, Madame de Montalia could not be more than twenty; her face was fresh, her figure admirably deep-bosomed and sleekly curved, strangely reminiscent of the portraits he had seen of Madame de Pompadour. Yet she had the manner and confidence of a very experienced woman, and there was something about her eyes that had little to do with youth. He was suddenly aware of the silence between them. "Yes. Yes, that's why I've come, Madame de Montalia. It's about this château."

"One of the generals has need of it?" she inquired. There was no fear or anger in her.

"In part, yes," the Captain admitted. His clothes, very damp and far from clean, seemed to create their own presence. He looked at her as he touched the buttons of his tunic. "I apologize for my . . . condition. You must understand that it is not my habit to call in such—"

Madelaine interrupted him, a compassionate smile on her lips. "Captain, you are an officer fighting a war for my country. You have nothing to be ashamed of." She paused. "On the other hand, you may wish to refresh yourself, and if you do, let me have a bath drawn for you and a bed prepared. You may find that an hour or two of rest will do a great deal to restore you, and during that time my staff will do something about your uniform."

Captain Timbres was fatigued to the point of total exhaustion, so his hostess' suggestion seemed an invitation to Paradise. At thirty-eight he was not immune to Madelaine's attractions, but he had no intentions beyond a certain remote appreciation. He stared down at his mud-caked boots and stained gaiters. His gray-blue trousers were filthy, he realized, and his tunic was as bad. The greatcoat he had left with the servant who had admitted him was in even poorer repair. "It would be pleasant to have a respite," he said cautiously.

"Excellent," Madelaine said at once, rising. "I'll instruct my household and will return to you in a moment. I believe we have a bit of ham left in the pantry. I'm afraid I don't concern myself overmuch with food, but when you have rested, no doubt we can scrape together some sort of a meal for you."

This was all going much too fast for Captain Timbres. He held up his hand to stop her. "Madame de Montalia, perhaps you don't realize that I have come with the unpleasant task of informing you that you must release this château to the use of the Army. You will not be allowed to stay here. There's a great deal of danger, and for you, some of it would certainly come from our own soldiers. It is not a happy admission for me to make, but many of them have been at war for a long time and they have forgot . . . their manners. It is necessary that you leave, you and your staff, within forty-eight hours." Having said it, he wished there were some way to soften the impact of his orders.

"I am sure we can manage to accommodate you, Captain," Madelaine said, as unruffled as ever.

"We cannot provide you transportation or alternate housing elsewhere. If you have relatives or others you might stay with . . ." He had little hope of this, for few families were willing to take in those homeless in the land because of the scant supply of food and other essentials.

"I have a house in Provence which I have not visited in some time. The Army has taken my two automobiles, but we have a few horses left and a few outmoded carriages that will do very well. I can assure you that you need not fear my resistance to your request, Captain." She had gone to the door and called out, "Félicité, prepare a bath for the Captain and see that the bed is made up in the green bedchamber."

"I am grateful, Madame, however . . ." he began.

"It is little enough to do for you, Captain Timbres," she said as she came back to her chair. "We here at Monbussy we are aware of some of the privations those in the trenches have suffered. A bath, a meal, some cognac are nothing in comparison."

The Captain shook his head. "No. That's not what I had intended to say, Madame de Montalia. I wished to caution you about going into Provence. I cannot promise you that there will be no fighting there. Most of the fighting in Italy has been in the northeast, but . . ."

Madelaine filled in the awkward silence with an easy smile. "Captain, I am convinced that Les Diables Bleus will be able to protect me." She used the nickname for the Chasseurs Alpins deliberately and was pleased to see the slight nod Captain Timbres gave in agreement.

"I feel I should try to dissuade you from going there. Have you no one in the west of France, perhaps near Bordeaux?"

"I could perhaps hide in what's left of the forests," she said thoughtfully. "No, Captain, to answer your question, I cannot call upon relatives there. Those of my blood live . . . elsewhere." Her jaw tightened for an instant as she said it, for it brought with it an intense longing for her first and most treasured lover. She had had no word of him for more than a year, which distressed her greatly when she allowed herself to think of it.

"It is unfortunate, Madame," the Captain said, and looked up to see Claude enter the room carrying a silver tray and a smoke-colored dusty bottle with a faded label.

"The cognac, Madame," Claude said, and put the tray down

on the table where the bell lay. "Félicitié is preparing the bath for the Captain. She asks that she be allowed thirty minutes."

"Thank you, Claude. Tell Felicitie that will be quite satisfactory." She motioned dismissal to the butler and gave her attention once again to Captain Timbres. "These old châteaux resist the modern ways, I am afraid. There is a pump in the kitchen which we are using currently because of the fear of typhus in the district. I trust that the delay will not inconvenience you." As she spoke, she reached over and picked up the cognac bottle, inspecting it critically. "Yes, this will do," she said, and opened the shallow drawer in the table to take out a small penknife with which she stripped away the wax sealing the bottle.

Captain Timbres was very divided in his mind. He knew that if he interpreted his orders strictly, he should thank this woman and leave her château at once so that he could speak to the farmers and other landholders nearby. But this was the first taste he had had of a proper gentleman's life in more than a year, and he desired the luxury of fine cognac, a hot bath, and a proper meal as ardently as he suddenly realized he desired his hostess. He put one hand to the stubble on his face and hoped he had not flushed. "This is very kind of you, Madame."

"Nonsense." She had the bottle open now and sniffed at the cognac before pouring it into the single crystal snifter on the silver tray.

"But you . . ." he said, fearing now that he was depriving her of the last of her cellar.

She held the snifter out to him. "You must excuse me, Captain Timbres. I have a curious intolerance for spirits. It gives me a great deal of pleasure to be able to offer them to those who do not have this aversion."

The cognac was excellent; fragrant, potent, tracing his tongue with warmth. "Superb, Madame."

Madelaine smiled. "How good of you to say so, Captain. I hope you will not be reticent if you wish more." Again she rose. "If you don't mind, I will leave you for a moment while I see how matters stand in the kitchen."

He half-stood with remembered courtesy, mumbling a polite phrase he had not used in over a year. The cognac's fire began to seep through him, heating his veins.

Claude was standing just behind the large entrance hall, his elderly face worried. "Madame?" he asked in an undervoice as Madelaine approached him.

"Yes, it is what we have been expecting, Claude, and I fear that we will have to move more quickly than we anticipated at first. We have been given forty-eight hours."

"That is not much time, Madame." His face relaxed as he said it, as this was longer than he had assumed they would be given.

"It is sufficient. We are to use the carriages. That means you must send David to Jacques Dandeau and buy those four Percherons. I know that the Army should have first chance at them, but if they are going to take over my château, they cannot begrudge me four horses." She was still as self-possessed as she had been with Captain Timbres, but with a greater air of command. Clearly she expected her instructions to be carried out without delay or excuse. "I will want to leave at night, of course, for that will mean that I can ride. See that the two heavy hunters are readied for the journey. We must take feed with us, since I doubt there will be much opportunity to forage along the way. Have David attend to that, as well."

"Certainly, Madame." He took strength from her determination, confident that she had the situation well in hand.

"The Captain will require a meal after his rest. If there is not ham enough, then tell Nanette to kill a brace of ducks and do what she can with them. While he is resting there is a great deal that must be done. I am sure that you have already opened the vault in the cellar."

"Yes, Madame. And Félicitié has started setting aside the silver and gold to be stored in it," he reported eagerly.

"Fine. Take care to put most of the paintings there, as well, and the best of the furniture. I know it is not the intention of the Generals to ruin the houses where they stay, but it inevitably seems to happen." She brushed her hair back from her face, and made an exasperated frown. "I had hoped that Monbussy was remote enough to allow us to remain undisturbed, but that is no longer possible. Well, you have much to do and I will not keep you."

"Very good, Madame." Claude bowed and turned away.

"Oh, one thing more, Claude," Madelaine said to him. "If it should happen that the Captain notices that furniture and pictures and similar ornaments are gone, he is to be told that I have suffered severe financial reverses because of the war. It is credible enough, and not uncommon."

Claude nodded. "I will tell the others, as well. Is there any way we can explain the Percherons?"

It was only an instant before Madelaine had an answer. "Do not go out of your way to show them to Captain Timbres, but if he should learn of them, say that they were given in lieu of rent by one of the farmers who feared he would not be able to feed them in any case. And inform David that he must tell the same tale to Jacques Dandeau."

"Will he agree?" Claude had long been familiar with the stubbornness of the farmers in the valley.

"He will. If he does not, he will dishonor himself, and I don't think he would do that." She tugged at the hem of her jacket and nodded once to Claude. "We shall manage, good friend. You will see this is so."

"Yes, Madame," Claude said before heading off toward the kitchens and the stableyard beyond.

Captain Timbres was on his second tot of cognac when Madelaine came back into the withdrawing room. He was feeling cheerier than he had in months, and welcomed the return of his sense of gallantry. "Madame, I was beginning to fear you had forgotten me."

Madelaine had assessed his condition as she came into the room and decided that a bantering tone would be more successful than any other. "Impossible, Captain. When you have brought so much excitement to my life, how could I forget you?"

At this he was chagrined. "It is not my desire to send you away from here, but that I would be filled with regret to know that you were needlessly exposed to danger."

"I will keep that in mind on my way to Provence," she said as she sat down. "My household has set to work with packing, and so you must forgive them if your wishes are not attended to as promptly as you or I might wish. We can take little, and it is a difficult matter to know what to choose."

"My General asked me to inform you that he would not countenance any damage to your property or acts of vandalism by his troops. You have only to store your more prized possessions in a room designated for that purpose and you may be confident that they will be safe."

"But so much is precious to me, Captain, and my circumstances here are already reduced . . ." She shook her head, and her brown hair shone with subtle topaz lights in the dim room. "Do not trouble yourself about such matters. Compared to the ordeals you have endured, this must seem surprisingly inconsequential."

"No, no, Madame. It is for precisely this reason that we

fight to defend our homeland from les Boches. You are not to think that your plight does not concern me." He stared at her fixedly as he spoke, and then quickly downed the last of the cognac in his glass.

"Let me give you some more." The bottle was proffered, but Captain Timbres waved it away.

"I thank you, but no. I haven't been much in the habit of drinking fine cognac these last several months, and I fear that if I have any more it will go more to my head than it has already, and then I might behave in a way that *you* would find odious, and *I* would deeply regret." He put his hand to the front of his tunic and contrived to appear more worldly than he felt.

"As you like, Captain. I certainly don't want to distress you. But, if you wish, I will have this bottle delivered to your bedchamber." Her suit was reminiscent of a riding habit, functionally tailored, and included a neckcloth not unlike a stock. She paused to give the muslin a twitch. "If you are ready, I will show you to the bath now, so that you may make whatever preparations you prefer. The heated water will be brought up in less than ten minutes. I am certain that we can lend you a razor, if you intend to shave.

He came promptly to his feet and was rocked by a moment's dizziness. "You're most gracious, Madame." As she walked toward the second door to the withdrawing room, she passed quite near him and he was again struck with her very youthful appearance. How old was she? he asked himself, and was the title "Madame" indicative of marriage or widowhood or simply ownership of Monbussy? He could think of no tactful way to inquire.

Madelaine paused in the door, her hand outstretched. "Come, Captain. The stairs are just ahead on the left."

Captain Timbres nodded and put the snifter down before falling into step a discreet three paces behind her.

The staircase, he noticed, had been carpeted once but was not now. What he did not know was that the magnificent Ottomans with their jewel-bright colors and furlike density were rolled and stored in a sealed cupboard in the attic, where they had been since the outbreak of the war. On the landing there was a seventeenth-century Flemish table with a large porcelain vase standing on it. Captain Timbres was sorry that Madame de Montalia would have to leave these behind.

The green bedchamber was so-called for the spread and hangings of the huge, old bed that dominated it, and for the draperies which were a paler version of them. The spread and blankets had been turned back on sheets of embroidered white linen. Looking at this, Captain Timbres was possessed of the most voluptuous fatigue. It would be so easy to succumb to the promise of that bed.

"I hope this is to your satisfaction, Captain?" Madelaine said politely.

"Yes. Oh, yes."

"Very good. The bath is across the hall, the second door down. I believe there is a robe in the armoire that you may use. If you will excuse me, I will see to the ordering of your supper." Her smile was almost audacious as she turned and left the room, closing the door behind her.

Claude met Madelaine on the stair; he was lifting the porcelain vase from the table. "The Captain?"

"He's getting ready to bathe, and after that I think he'll sleep for three or four hours. See that the cognac is delivered to the green bedchamber." She rubbed her hands together once and admitted that as inconvenient as this move was, she could not help but enjoy the sudden, secret flurry of activity.

"David has gone to see about the horses." He held the vase in both arms and began his precarious descent.

"Fine. Have the carriages been inspected? Have they been readied for travel? Is the harness in good condition?" She walked beside her servant, reaching out once to steady him as he faltered with his burden.

"David has been keeping them ready," Claude reminded her, panting a little. "We will be able to depart as soon as you wish."

"Fine." They had reached the foot of the stair and Madelaine glanced at the ticking clock that stood in an alcove by the hall. "I will want reports from the household every hour. If there are any difficulties at all, I expect to be informed at once. Delays at this time are critical."

"Of course," Claude said, preparing to start down toward the cellar and the vault.

Madelaine glanced toward the narrow windows. "I hope the weather does not worsen," she said quietly, and went to stare intently out into the sleet.

It was quite dark when Captain Timbres came reluctantly down from the green bedroom. His face, clean-shaven, was not unattractive, though the hardships of war had chiseled his mouth to a grim line bracketed by bitter, deep-cut folds. His uniform had been tended, and it was almost presentable. As he was not familiar with Monbussy, he went to the withdrawing room where he had been earlier in the day.

Gas-lights filled the room with their soft luminescence, and a small fire in the hearth gave some warmth to the room. Captain Timbres sat before the fire, wondering if he ought to ring for one of the servants, and had just lifted the little bell from the table when Madelaine came into the room.

She had changed her clothes and was in a beautiful silk gown over a robe of brocade, five years gloriously out of fashion. The waist was high and the crossover bodice had a square neck. The skirt was not cut in the extreme of the hobble, but achieved the same effect by the artful pleating and crossing of the gown which revealed the long narrow panels of the robe beneath. Her hair was brushed back and secured with a jeweled comb, which was her only jewelry. She held her hand out to the Captain and allowed him to kiss it. "You're looking refreshed," she said to him as he released her fingers.

"I can't thank you enough. I was more tired than I knew, and now I feel reborn." He was being deliberately extravagant, eager to have her respond to him.

"How kind of you to say so," she said. "Come. The fare is not very exciting, but I am fairly confident that you will have a tolerable meal. It's actually past the usual dinner hour here, and so you will excuse me if I only enjoy your company."

Captain Timbres thought that this was a courteous lie, and that in all probability he was being given the last food in the larder. By all the dicta he had ever been taught, he should politely insist that she join him, or not eat himself. Sixteen months in the trenches had changed that in him, and he could not bring himself to utter the formal phrases. He was hungry. He had been hungry for more than a year. He offered Madelaine his arm. "Madame, I will feast on your presence as much as on the meal provided."

So as Captain Timbres sat at the antique satinwood dining table and regaled himself on soup, stuffed mushrooms, and duck, Madelaine smiled at him and made sure that his glass stayed filled, while in the rest of the château, the last of the treasures were stowed in the vault and the four Percherons were brought to draw the carriages that would carry Madelaine and her five servants away from Monbussy and the privations of war.

Text of a letter from Roger, manservant to Franchot Ragoczy, Count of Saint-Germain, to Sir William Graddiston in London.

*Stockholm, Sweden*
*9 February, 1918*

*Sir William Graddiston*
*92 Cadogan Square*
*London, England*

*Sir William:*

*My employer, Franchot Ragoczy, requested that upon my arrival in Stockholm I contact you on his behalf, with the enclosed authorization for the transfer of funds from his account. The amounts are indicated in the accompanying letter, and the specific wishes of the Count are expressed therein: he is confident that his long association with your bank will be taken into consideration by you and your staff as you carry out his instructions.*

*At the moment, my employer's whereabouts is not known, and for that reason it is all the more important that you act with alacrity so that the monies requested will be available to him immediately upon his arrival. Most of his Russian holdings have been seized by the new government and whatever wherewithal he had there is now no longer at his disposal. When the political situation there is somewhat more regular, it is my employer's intention to petition for at least token acknowledgments of the transfer of his various enterprises and holdings to the ownership and control of the emerging government. In the meantime, he is confident that the arrangements he suggests to you will not require him to make any drastic changes in his business commitments.*

*On behalf of my employer, Franchot Ragoczy, Count of
Saint-Germain, believe me to be*

Most sincerely yours,
Roger

*3*

In the past the dasha had been staffed by sixteen servants,
but now there were only three: a groom, a carpenter, and a
frightened Swiss nanny who kept to her rooms adjoining the
empty nursery. Throughout the country house cold and neglect held gelid control. Only the year before there had been a
midwinter duck hunt, with two dozen guests. Then the halls
had been alive, the rooms rollicking and filled with New Year
merriment, and the family had bustled with happy pride. Now
the dasha was abandoned, as forlorn as a ruin.

Duchess Irina Andreivna Ohchenov sat in her dressing room,
her hands folded in her lap, her eyes on the framed photograph to the right of the mirror. She no longer wept, for the
shocks of the last five months had driven the tears out of her.
The images of four children, insubstantial as ghosts, smiled
back at her, and one of them, the youngest, her Piotr, who
would have been six, lifted his hand to wave. Ilya's collar was
askew, Ludmilla had mud on her frilled skirt from fishing with
her brothers, and Evgeny still held his buggy whip after
driving the rest of the family to a picnic earlier that day. Irina
Andreivna turned toward the frosted windows. That day had
been so warm, smelling of summer. The only thing that had
marred it was Leonid's hasty departure on urgent summons
from Ergli. She remembered the way he had told her he
would have to leave for a few days, his affability turned to
testiness at the thought of dealing with rebellious Latvians.
As he embraced and kissed her, she thought again how fortunate she was to have married him; so many of her friends had
been disappointed in the husbands their families had found for
them, but Leonid was a treasure. He had looked so impressive
in his Guards' uniform, and he had bent over her, whispering a
promise to make up to her the days he would be gone. Then he

had mounted his rawboned bay gelding and rode out through the tall wooden gates. The next time she had seen him, he was lying amid the refuse in the corridor of a wrecked hospital. His face was wizened with pain and he was so far gone in fever that he did not truly know her. She had wiped his brow, speaking softly to him, ignoring the hideous smell of his blackened, shattered hands. One of the sergeants who had served with Leonid and respected him had escorted her back to the dasha and later had tried to bring her husband's body to her for burial, but could not get permission. The graves near the house did not hold Leonid or their children.

Irina rose and began methodically to remove her clothes. They hung on her now, almost as shapeless and as colorless as the garments worn by the market women. She shivered in the cold, wishing for a moment that she could share the warmth of a snug, crowded izba that housed the peasants who worked her land. She had been in one of those two-room cottages last year and had thought then that it was a poor place to be, and had felt sympathy for the poor farmer whose family lived there. Now, that isba seemed desirable as the citadels of Heaven. She laid her bodice aside and unhooked her skirt; taking it up from the floor, she placed it over the back of her chair. Until last October, she had never picked up any garment; there had been maids to do such work. For a few weeks these minor chores had been curiously comforting, providing her small tasks that demanded little of her, yet kept her from thinking too much. In time the novelty had worn off and the care of her clothes, along with the preparation of diminishing amounts of food, the drawing of water for washing and occasional bathing, the clearing away of ice and snow around the house, and the chopping of the last few cords of wood, had become part of the mindless, irritating routine that could no longer block her memories or offer solace in escape.

Her nightgown felt clammy, subtly contaminated by the damp that seeped through the dasha. Irina reached for her velvet housecoat and pulled that on as well. The small fire in the grate would be cold before morning and she would be grateful for the extra warmth of the heavy garment. She turned back the covers, smoothing the grayed sheets and wishing that she had more soap and another bottle of bluing to spare for all her linen. There were stains on the sheets, and she frowned as she did a quick calculation: her courses would come again in a week, and she had no rags to spare for it. She looked at the sheet and sighed. Perhaps it would be best to tear up this sheet so that the others might be spared. Irina got into bed slowly, reaching for her brush on the nightstand as she settled back against the pillows and began to loosen her hair.

When she had completed sixty strokes, she became aware of a tapping at the window. Apprehensively she told herself that it was a frozen branch on the glass, nothing more. The tapping resumed, this time in distinctly three-four rhythm. TONK-tap-tap TONK-tap-tap. Irina put her brush aside and peered at the windows. It was quite dark out, and even the little light the low-burning kerosene lantern provided turned the windows to mirrors. She could see nothing but the occasional bright reflection from the frost-ferns climbing the panes. TONK-tap-tap TONK-tap-tap TONK-tap-tap.

Stilling the muted shriek of fear in her mind, Irina got out of bed. Surely, she thought, no one seeking to break into the house would announce himself in waltz time. She crossed the room toward the window where she heard the sound, and was startled as she recalled that this was the one window that did not have trees or flowers growing beside it. For an instant she faltered, tempted to return to her bed, blow out the light, and rush away through her empty, freezing house. The impulse was gone almost at once. She reached the window and her hand closed on the stiff latch. "Who's there?" she called softly.

"Ragoczy," was the answer.

Irina stifled a gasp. Leonid's foreign friend! She pressed her hand to the window. "A moment. Just a moment. The latch is hard to open. It's . . ." She took the latch in both hands, pushing against the little curved lever.

Ragoczy nodded and half-waved to indicate he understood, then clung to the rickety trellis beside the window. He would have liked to have the remnants of vines on the fan-shaped wooden structure for what little extra stability they might lend, but apparently there had been nothing planted below for several seasons and the trellis was bare. His face stung and his hands were febrilely cold in the icy rain mixed with snow blowing on the sharp gusts out of the north. His coachman's cloak was torn at the shoulder, its sable collar bedraggled, his high black boots scuffed and muddied. He closed his dark eyes and leaned his forehead against the nearest pane of glass, his whole body quivering with fatigue.

The latch grated, wailed, then popped open and the window swung outward on protesting hinges. Irina held out her hand to him. "Count. You must come in." Fleetingly she tried to imagine how he had got there, on the trellis outside this second-story window, but this passed. It was obvious that he was there, and certainly he would not have attempted so risky a climb if he were not desperate. She took a step back, astonished at the force of the wind, and waited, thinking that in happier times she would have been affronted to find this man in her room.

"I am grateful, Duchess," he said as he came into the room, then reached to pull the window shut again. "You're very good to let me in. I would have understood if you had decided not to."

She tried to match his aplomb. "I doubt that soldiers would go to the trouble of knocking on my window." Her mouth pulled down at the corner, but she extended her hand to him.

He raised her fingers to his lips. "I am aware that this is an unorthodox manner to pay a visit, but the circumstances . . ."

She was able to smile a bit at this ironic gallantry, and her fear of him subsided. "These are unorthodox times, Count." She recalled seeing a village church in flames, its onion dome like a falling comet; her smile faded.

He bowed to her, wholly correct. "Irina Andreivna, I thank you from my heart. I had not expected to see any kindness in any part of this chaotic land. You surprise me."

"I have seen little kindness as well, Count. It is rarer than I used to suppose." She clasped her hands, then, with a conscious effort, let them fall. "Would you mind if I asked why you came here?"

"What right have I to mind?" He said it lightly enough, but there was an unspoken distress in his words. "I have been traveling for a considerable time, and it was becoming difficult to go on. I hoped that I might find some sort of refuge here, but I did not know you had the same notion."

"This is hardly a refuge, Count," she said, making no attempt to conceal her bitterness. "At best, it is a tomb."

Ragoczy gave her a single, intent look. "And you are walled up in it?"

"I have told myself that what I've wanted is to keep safe until the worst is over, but that's not so." She sighed, the air shuddering out of her, as she lifted her hands, partly in supplication, partly in resignation. "What else can I do? Where is there left to go?"

"You have friends, Irina."

"And where are they, these friends? They are hiding, as I

am. They are trapped, timorous, afraid. How might they welcome me? I have nothing to offer them but helplessness."

"You took me in," he pointed out with such gentleness that she could hardly bring herself to look at him.

"That's a different matter. You're not . . ." She turned away from him, staring at the kerosene lantern, thinking that she would soon have to use candles at night, and then, when they were gone, there would be darkness.

"Leonid?" It was tactless to ask, and Ragoczy knew it. If the Duchess had not mentioned her husband, it was because he was missing or dead. He could not bring himself to keep silent. "What of him?"

She shook her head, the tiniest motion. "After he left, when he did not come back, word was sent that we should return to St. Petersburg—I will *not* call it Petrograd. He was hurt. He could not come with us, and I found that I could not leave. None of the trains were running properly, and then, after Evgeny went to help the Guards and . . . was shot . . ." Her mouth trembled.

"Your son and Leonid?" Ragoczy said, his dark, compassionate eyes on her. "I had not known. I am truly, deeply sorry, Irina Andreivna."

"Oh, not just Evgeny and Leonid. All of them. They're all dead. Ludmilla, Ilya, and Piotr, too. Ludmilla and Ilya died of fever and congested lungs. There was no physician to tend them, only a nurse, and she said that this disease is becoming common. For her there was nothing unusual in their deaths. After they became ill, I could not move them." She was speaking faster, her voice hushed, as if by keeping her private disasters a secret she might lessen them. "Piotr was taken by soldiers. I had sent him away from the house because of Ludmilla—Ilya wasn't really ill yet—and a troop of revolutionary irregulars came upon him. Sasha, my groom, found him that evening. They had . . . spitted him on their sabers." Automatically she crossed herself. Her face was vacant now, and she could not bear to look at her husband's foreign friend.

"I have never learned anything to say at these moments," Ragoczy said after Irina fell silent. "No words are adequate. For what little consolation it may be, I share your grief."

Her hands clenched abruptly. "How can you?" The rage that swept through her was more startling to her than to him. "*How can you?* What were they to you that you can say that?" She rushed at him, hand up, fingers hooked, grief-driven. She seized handfuls of his wet hair, tugging at them in her frenzy.

They were much the same height, and her assualt might have toppled them, but Ragoczy was more powerful than might be supposed, and he held her up as she screamed. She was hardly aware of him at all as she railed at her dead for their desertion, and she did not resist his strength. Gently he pulled her fingers from his hair, then put his arms around her, holding her as her shrieks turned to shattering sobs. "Weep for them, Irina," he whispered to her, stroking her tumbled hair. "I envy you your tears: I have only sorrow."

Gradually her outburst passed. The cold room, desolate in the dim light, once more closed in around her. She wiped ineffectually at her eyes and then noticed that Ragoczy's cloak was soaking wet and that her housecoat was damp. "Forgive me," she muttered, her voice thickened in the aftermath of her crying. "I don't know what . . ."

"There is nothing to forgive, Irina Andreivna," he assured her quickly, and opened his arms to release her.

This was the time for a few socially correct phrases that would absolve them from any possible embarrassment, but Irina was too worn to utter them. She took a few steps away from Ragoczy, then turned back to him. "You're welcome here, Count, for as long as—"

Ragoczy interrupted her. "Irina Andreivna, you need not trouble yourself. I do not want to intrude." He shrugged. "I had hoped that this house would be empty, and then my coming might not disturb anyone. Clearly that's not the case."

"These are hardly times for standing on ceremony." Her face was wan and her voice listless. "You said it has been difficult."

He did not know what he should tell her. The cell in the Monastery of the Victory where he had been imprisoned would provide her no comfort. His escape—a fluke—was not a tale for a woman with so much to mourn. The details of his uncertain journey: the horse he had stolen was lame and it had taken all his special concentration to master the animal and give it the impetus to go on. After two days, the gelding's suffering had been too much, and Ragoczy had put a bullet into its head once the worst of his hunger had been assuaged. The rest of the way he had come on foot, through marshland and fens, avoiding villages and other settlements, crossing rail lines only at night, surviving on the few stray farm animals he had come across or had been able to attract. What point was there in telling this bereaved woman any of that? He held out his hand to her. "I have come through much worse, Irina."

"Then my heart aches for you," she said in a stifled tone. "As it aches for my family." She made her way across the room with the caution of a blind person, feeling her way with care. When she reached the old-fashioned chaise, she sank down upon it, one hand held against her face to shield herself from his eyes.

"Duchess," Ragoczy began, not approaching her, "tell me what you would prefer: I will leave, if that is what you wish, but I admit that I hope you will let me remain, at least for a little time."

Irina lifted one shoulder.

"Do not let me offend you, Irina," he said more forcefully. "You have already done me great service and it is lamentable that I should require more."

"We all require more," she said as she turned toward him. "I am very much alone here. Most of the servants are gone, and those that remain are less than useless. I have nothing to offer you, except the shelter of the roof. If that is enough . . . I confess that I long for company." Her laughter was brief and shaky. "Absurd, is it not, Count, that at such time I should wish for the banter I used to deplore. No one would think it strange if I wanted to retire to a convent for the rest of my days, but I don't think I could endure that. Leonid always said that you are erudite and intriguing. Would it be too much to ask of you that you remain here—it needn't be long, if that is your concern—and converse with me?" She was weak with wanting him to agree. Until she saw him, she had been drowning in sadness; now she felt the first, tenuous stirrings of life in her. "If I keep to myself much longer, I may well go mad." It was a danger she had not admitted, even to herself.

Ragoczy listened to her, studying her as she spoke. "If you truly desire my company, I will be most honored to oblige you, Duchess, and believe myself remarkably fortunate." He reached up to unfasten the frogs of his cloak.

"I would prefer that the rest of the household . . ." she said impetuously, and broke off in confusion.

". . . be unaware of my presence?" he finished for her as he draped the sodden cloak over the end of her dresser.

"Yes." She was pleased he said it for her, as it saved her the shame, but felt compelled to explain further. "In these times, well, the danger . . . it is not a matter of discretion, precisely, but I am fairly certain we are watched, and if it were known that . . ."

Ragoczy nodded. "I saw a man on patrol near the izbi. I

didn't recognize the uniform, but he had an insignia on his sleeve and he carried a rifle." He did not add that the man had been half-drunk and whistling as he made his rounds this freezing night.

Irina put shaking hands to her head. "Oh, God! What more do they want of me? They have had so much. If they want my life, then let them come and take it, and be done with it."

"Irina Andreivna," Ragoczy said as he pulled her arms down, "no, you must not do this. Believe me, this no longer has anything to do with you, only with the chance of your birth and station. If you were a shopkeeper or a peasant or an artisan, you might be as mean of spirit and abusive as you liked and have approbation of those climbing to power. But you were born to rank, and nothing can excuse that: it is your rank that is being punished—you are innocent."

"Am I?" She let her fingers close around his. "I thought I was, but when I read the accusations against us . . . There was such a document delivered, just before Ilya . . ." She pulled away from him and went unsteadily across the room. "I never intentionally deprived any of our household of bread or a decent place to sleep or fuel for warmth or had the grooms knouted for my amusement—what a horrible thing!" She took a deep breath. "I have never felt the lash, but I remember the rods of the instructresses at Smolny Institute, and I would not find it amusing to see others used so. As for the knout . . ."

"It isn't pleasant," Ragoczy interjected quietly, remembering the times he had had his back laid open.

"No. But," she went on in a smaller voice, "none of those things, the food and fuel and punishments, mattered to me very much. I did not concern myself with them. My servants were well-treated because any other usage is folly, but poorly-handled servants are not willing and cheerful, and it is impossible for work to get done. It may be, then, that I am truly as bad as the worst of rank. I was not kind out of any sense of humanity, but for my own convenience. I have thought about it a great deal, Count," she said seriously, meeting his dark eyes and then looking away. "At first I decided that the complaints were absurd, but in the last few days, I see there may have been good reason for them to accuse me."

Ragoczy did not approach her. "It would not matter what you did," he said. "You might have been the harshest aristocrat here, or the most humble and pious, the denouncement would have come in either case. You say that you treated your servants well because it was convenient. That's not an unworthy motive. The world may dismiss it, but it is as laudable as any other."

"You sound so . . . certain," she said.

"Think of France, Duchess. Their Revolution was intended at first merely to redress egregious wrongs. Look what it became. Not only aristocrats, but teachers and poets and seamstresses lost their heads for no more terrible crimes than a word of disagreement, or imagined disagreement with those jockeying for power. There have been other instances when similar—"

"It is an outrage!" Irina cried out. "They are dead, and for what? These accusations defame my husband's memory: I will not have him mocked! He died for them, and they . . . they . . ." She gave a deep sob and sank to her knees. "Saints protect me. I am at the end of my strength." She crossed herself and tried to pray.

Ragoczy copied her gesture, but in the Roman manner, left to right shoulder. "Irina . . ." He came to her side and went down on his knee. "Irina, it is not a fault in you that you mourn. Do not think it."

"I keep believing that this isn't true," she said unsteadily. "I wait to awaken, when I am certain I will find my children alive and well and Leonid sympathetic and amused by my fancies. It won't happen, will it? They are gone, aren't they?"

"They are gone," he said with such poignance and compassion that she could no longer comfort herself with her illusions. He saw her face change as anguish possessed her; he braced her with his arm and stayed close to her as she keened for everything she had lost.

When at last she was quiet, she kept still for several minutes, her long, disarrayed hair concealing her face. Finally she looked toward the stranger beside her. "I will be all right now."

"You're certain?" His compelling eyes searched her pale, mottled face.

"Yes." She pushed back from him, feeling faintly queasy now that she was past her greatest outburst. She moistened her lips and wiped her face with trembling hands. It was difficult not to be angry with Ragoczy, for he had seen too mu~h of her inmost suffering. Without being obvious, she moved away from him as she got to her feet again. "It was good of you to—"

"You wish to curse me, Irina," he interrupted her, not accusing her or showing indignation. He rose, watching her.

"Yes," she murmured. "I would curse the whole world if it would lessen my pain. But nothing will." Her dressing table was near and she sat in the velvet-upholstered chair in order to keep from stumbling, as she feared she would if she tried to walk the dozen steps to her bed. The few crystal vials were dusty, and the mirror had not been cleaned in months. Looking into the glass, she was shocked to see how altered her face was. Her cheeks were gaunt and her eyes sunken and the flesh under her chin had started to sag. She braced her elbows on the table and leaned her head on her hands. Nothing was left of the world she had known; not even her own body remained. Now there was a starved and haunted wraith where she had been a woman of warm and opulent beauty.

"Irina," Ragoczy said quietly. He did not move toward her yet, sensing that she did not want to have him near her.

The Duchess looked up, her eyes on the mirror, to the place where Ragoczy's reflection should have been. At first she was puzzled, for there was no sign of him. She turned around, thinking that perhaps he had moved. "You—"

"I know," he said, lifting a hand to stop her. "It is my nature, Irina Andreivna."

"Your nature?" She stared at him, then glanced back in the mirror. "How? How is . . . this your nature?"

He did not answer her directly. "Your husband knew me as a foreigner and was nonetheless my friend. Yet my . . . alienness is greater than he supposed." The last time he had seen his own face reflected, he had been thirty-three years old; his mirror had been a shield of polished copper. It was an effort to remember that day, so very long ago.

"Do Europeans have no reflections?" she asked lightly, feeling suddenly as if she had been catapulted once more into the world of her dreams.

"You know those who do not have reflections," he said gravely.

Irina laughed once, a little wildly. "That's a fable, a tale for children and English novelists. Peasants believe such things."

Ragoczy said nothing. He saw her face in the mirror as her expression changed again, though she could not see him.

"It's ridiculous," she insisted. "It must be a skill, like those magicians who are forever turning women into lions and back into women again. You must not trick me this way, Count. I . . . I am not able to . . . appreciate such humor at the moment."

"It is no trick," Ragoczy said.

"No trick? But it must be." She wanted to sleep, to shut out the treasonous world, where all her family could die in less than four months and this foreign guest cast no reflection. She reached for the small golden crucifix on the chain around her neck and was momentarily reassured by it. "You crossed yourself," she said impetuously as she recalled this.

"Yes." He held out his small hand. "Place holy water here, or any blessed thing. I will not flinch, or turn into a puff of smoke. Had I been able to do that, they could not have held me in prison," he added grimly, unable to smile.

"Of course not," she agreed, fighting hideous laughter. "Nor would you have had to climb up the trellis to my window." All at once she clapped her hands over her mouth and turned away from him, not knowing whether it was hysteria or nausea that threatened her. She bent over, her head brushing her knees, her mind in turmoil, so that she did not notice Ragoczy's approach, nor the assuasive touch of his hand on her shoulder.

"Irina, do not fear me; I will not harm you." His voice was at once so calming and so sad that she dared to lift her head and look at him.

"I'm not afraid, not of you. You're nothing, compared to . . ." She could not continue.

"Do you still wish me to stay? If you'd rather I left, I will want to be away before too much time goes by." He paused. "I am . . . somewhat exhausted and it is . . . easier to travel at night."

To her own amazement, she heard herself say, "You needn't go. I don't want you to go."

He bowed to her. "For that, Irina Andreivna, I am more grateful than you will ever know." Then he lifted her hands and kissed them.

"Count . . ." She did not know what she wanted to tell him, for the confusion of this night almost overwhelmed her. Inwardly she was aware of the attraction of this man—for surely he could be called nothing else—which was born as much from his kindness as from her response to his superb manner. His dark, arresting eyes held hers, and she had the dizzying sensation of falling into them. Frightened by this intensity, she drew back.

"Ah, no, Irina," he said, dropping her hands; his gaze never wavered from her face. "Perhaps I should leave, after all." He said this almost to himself, so softly that Irina was not certain she heard him speak at all.

The prospect of passing the night alone, however, terrified

her, and she clutched at his sleeve. "No. No, you must stay. Please."

Ragoczy looked down at her hand. "As you wish, Duchess."

"And you?" Her boldness came from her fear; she did not care how censorious her friends would be—her friends were in flight, in hiding, or dead.

"I? This is a welcome haven, Irina Andreivna," he said in a carefully neutral tone. "It would not be . . . pleasant to go out in that"—he cocked his head toward the ice-shiny windows—"again."

"No," she said, subdued. It was an effort for her to release his sleeve, but she did so, joining her hands together so that she would not be tempted to touch him. "I am glad you will stay, and not only because I don't want to think of you out there."

"I'm flattered, Irina," he replied rather distantly. He watched her with growing speculation, wondering what it was she wanted of him.

"There's no food to spare . . ." Wisely, she made no attempt to apologize for this lack.

"I have . . . other requirements," he said.

"Oh. Yes." Her hands tightened around themselves.

"Do not concern yourself with me; I shall manage." He stepped back from her. "Is there a dressing room, or a pallet that I may lie on, Irina Andreivna?"

She stared at him, uncomprehending. "A pallet?"

"Yes, Irina. Even I must sleep." His wry half-smile took the sting out of his words. "I'm not fussy."

"But a pallet?" To her dismay, her thoughts had anticipated a different course for her tonight, and until he dashed them with his sensible request, she had not permitted herself to be aware of what she desired. Her face suffused with color and she got up from the dressing table so that she would not be so close to him. "A Count on a pallet?"

His response chided her amiably. "A Duchess without heat in the winter? Be assured, Irina, that I have slept on less enticing beds than any you might provide." The memories of many of those places he had rested danced through his mind: prisons, temples, fields, mountain trails, ditches, burrows . . . "My own bed," he added truthfully, "is narrow and quite hard. A pallet will not distress me." He did not mention that the thin, down-filled mattress on his bed lay over a chest of his native earth.

"But . . ." Her courage nearly deserted her. "My bed is

largé. Surely . . ." There; she had said as much as she was able, and was quite shocked with herself.

Ragoczy did not speak for the better part of a minute. "What is it you want of me, Irina?"

"Companionship," she answered at once. "I have had only the thoughts of my losses to keep me company. If you are not offended, I would welcome someone beside me."

"Is that all?" He unbuttoned his longish suit jacket. "I do not wish to offend you, either."

Irina was unable to say more. She paced the length of the room, pausing once less than an arm's length from him. "No, that is not all," she said in a tense, hushed voice. "You were Leonid's friend. You knew my children. I . . ." She faced him squarely. "Must I say it? Isn't it awkward enough that I must ask at all? What can you think of me, now?"

Ragoczy chose to answer the last of her questions first. "I think you are brave, Irina, and alone. If you want me to lie with—"

"*Want?* Oh, no, Count. I *need* you to hold me in your arms, to drive away the ghosts." She reached out to him, certain she would die if he did not accept her.

He enfolded her, his arms secure about her. "Irina, I have a need, as well." His lips brushed her cheek, touched the corner of her mouth, the angle of her jaw, her throat.

She made a small, choking sound, then tangled her hands in his dark, loose curls, tugging him close against her. How shameful she felt, and how restored! Nothing prepared her for the delirious tumult of her senses, for the spurt of her pulse, the warmth that burned through her, the heady ignition of her desire. Her ill-fitting robe fell away from her, and she felt herself being lifted with easy strength, carried across the bedchamber.

The sheets were musty, but neither of them noticed. Ragoczy drew the covers up around Irina, then paused long enough to remove his jacket before pulling off his boots. At last he sank down beside her, sensing the urgency of her ardor. He took her face in his hands and kissed her mouth so slowly, so lingeringly, that she was quieted, capable of pleasure instead of frenzy. Now his kisses came quickly, lightly, like the caress of a butterfly's wing. One arm slipped beneath the covers to hold her, then the other.

Irina was stirred now, her passion growing without urgency, and for the first time in years, perhaps in her life, she relinquished her avidity and was doubly fulfilled. Her body, warmed with the probing of his hands and mouth, exulted, so that she wept again, but not for grief or pain.

Only once in that dazzled night did she realize that he had given all the coverings to her, as a kind of soft cave to warm her where he could not. "But you haven't a blanket . . ." she protested, suddenly concerned for him.

His dark eyes were luminous. "I am not cold."

Text of a report from Former Acting Major, Former Corporal Nikolai Ivanevich Rozoh to his commanding officer, Colonel Alexei Sergeivich Genadov.

Petrograd
27 March, 1918

Colonel Alexei Sergeivich Genadov
Ahkno Palace
Nevsky Prospekt, Petrograd

Colonel Genadov:

You have already had the reports of the rest of the company left to guard the prisoners at the Monastery of the Victory at Konstantinovka, and doubtless you agree that the escape of nineteen of the men guarded there was inexcusable. I do not wish to dispute that, because I believe that such a judgment is fair. However, I wish to protest the death sentence given to all the men in the company. Those who were billeted in the village were unaware of what was happening at the monastery and therefore should not be held responsible. Only Acting Captain Yuri Yureivich Garin, Acting Colonel Dmitri Mihialovich Rubashek and I were at the monastery when the escape occurred, and it is only the three of us who ought to bear the responsibility for it.

It is the stated policy of the new government to mete out justice with true impartiality, and if that is the case, then I ask that this sentence be reviewed so that men who were in no way involved with the escape be exonerated. Without doubt the three of us who were there are guilty and deserve the penalty. The rest have no share in it, and it is wrong that they pay the price of our inexcusable neglect.

You yourself have stated that it is the intention of the military court to make an example of our little garrison.

47

*If that is in fact what you intend, then make an example of those officers responsible, and do not condemn blameless soldiers to die for the errors of their leaders.*

*I would also like to take this opportunity to point out that one of the reasons so much of the garrison was in Konstantinovka rather than at the monastery was that our supplies had run so low that if the men had remained at the monastery, there would not have been sufficient food to provide sufficient meals for half of them, let alone for the prisoners. As it is, of those prisoners who did not escape, two froze to death, one died of the fever, and six starved. The supplies promised us were never delivered, and the villagers, after two grantings of food and drink, refused further assistance because of the inadequacy of their own stores. If the prisoners who had escaped had remained at the monastery, many of them would have died, as there would have been no way to feed them.*

*As you have been informed, of the nineteen prisoners who escaped, sixteen have been accounted for: the other three have probably perished, since the winter storms interfered with our pursuit. Such a hunt should not have been necessary, and it is our fault that it was, but those three men might have got away in the course of moving the prisoners to Petrograd, as was planned.*

*I beseech you to have the men who were in Konstantinovka attend the execution of Garin, Rubashek, and myself, but spare them. You will have better and more dedicated service from them if you do, and I will not feel that I have unwittingly brought about the deaths of my men.*

*In gratitude for your attention, I most respectfully sign myself*

                               *Nikolai Ivanevich Rozoh*

An appended memo in Colonel Alexei Sergeivich Genadov's hand reads:

*Rozoh's point is well-taken. The firing squad for Garin and Rubashek and the full Parade of Dishonor for Rozoh, all the men of the Monastery of the Victory garrison attending. Rozoh can then be sent to one of the regiments on the Polish border in as menial a capacity as we can contrive. A man willing to do so much for his soldiers should have some recognition. When the hostilities are over, Rozoh can be sent to join the other pioneers at one of the Siberian outposts.*

*Has there been any more learned about the three prisoners still missing?*

# 4

Frost had hardened the ground, spangling the dried stalks of plants so that they glistened under the moon. Wind sloughed in the branches of the distant trees and fanned the last of the embers into winking red eyes before passing on across the ice-girded lake. Wraiths of smoke slipped out of the ruined stables, fleeing the burned buildings as the horses had done more than twelve hours ago. Spring had made only the most tentative headway here, although April was half over.

Ragoczy rode out of the woods where he had waited since sundown, his dark eyes impassive as he looked at the destruction around him. He had seen a great deal of it in the last five days—ruined bridges, rails twisted like party ribbon, blackened and gutted buildings, barges overturned on the riverbanks like beached fish, always accompanied by carnage. Since he left the dasha with Duchess Irina Andreivna Ohchenov, two weeks ago, he had felt himself condemned to Dantean hell, and the deepest pit not yet reached.

He drew in his horse as he thought of Irina. With any luck she would be in Poland now, in the company of her cousin and his family. He told himself again that it was the wisest course for her; he could not offer her the protection her cousin did. At first Irina had been reluctant to accompany her relatives, insisting that she would be safe at the dasha as long as Ragoczy was with her, but they both knew this was not so. Spring would signal the return of revolutionary forces, and then there would be no protection for any of them. Irina had asked Ragoczy to go with her, but he had explained gently that this was not possible. Kiril Lukovsky might welcome his widowed cousin Irina, but it was unlikely that he would be as generous with her foreign lover. Finally Irina had consented after demanding that Ragoczy make every effort to contact her once he was out of danger. She already knew that her cousin intended to go to Paris, and so she quite optimistically said she could be found there within the year. Whatever his private opinion—and he was inclined to doubt her assurances that the journey would be easy once Russia and her territories were left behind—he gave her his word, kissed her hand and embraced her with passion one last time before they parted. He looked at the smoking wreckage and wondered if the *dasha* still stood.

More than burning and vengeance had been done here: the stables had been robbed of all but two ancient plows before the fires were started. Only one rickety cart with the characteristic Russian bowed yoke still leaning against the wooden planks of the driver's seat remained, obviously left behind by the raiding party that had visited the estate. No livestock were left in the pens, and gates standing ajar gave mute testimony to the fate of the missing animals: the revolutionary band was large and the men were hungry. Even the chicken coops, with walls punched out of them to give access to the rabbit hutches on the far side, had not been neglected.

The manor, some little distance from the stable, was a charred hulk now, collapsed on the west side where crude bombs had been hurled through dining-room windows. It had been left to burn, for the revolutionaries were still zealous enough to look with contempt on the gauds of the nobility. That, Ragoczy knew from long experience, would not last. In time, very little time, the insurgents would deck themselves as lavishly as their former overlords had done.

Ragoczy touched his mount's flanks lightly with his heels, and the chestnut gelding started forward cautiously, his ears pricking, his nostrils distended. He whickered nervously, ready to bolt the moment Ragoczy relinquished his masterful hold on the reins or the firm pressure of his knees.

He was almost past the chicken coops when Ragoczy heard a high, thin wail, piercingly intense but not very loud. The chestnut jerked his head up in alarm, muscles bunching for a sprint. Ragoczy steadied him and looked around, scowling in sudden concentration.

The sound came again, more loudly, in angry gasps, and Ragoczy realized that it was the sound of a child crying.

The chestnut sidled and almost bucked as Ragoczy dismounted. His withers darkened with sweat, but Ragoczy paid little attention. He led the gelding to an iron pole which had once formed part of the support for the block-and-tackle rig to the hayloft. Carefully Ragoczy secured the reins to the pole, knotting them twice. He took time to pat the horse, to blow in his nostrils and calm him before turning toward the chicken coops and the high, hysterical sobs of the child.

As he stepped into the coop, the smell of chickens and blood almost made him dizzy. Ragoczy lifted one arm and steadied himself against the low beam. The mangled bodies of two cocks had been flung against the wall and were now crumpled bundles of feathers in the straw. It was the only evidence of waste that Ragoczy had seen on this estate.

Near the far door, there was a small figure half-covered in straw. At the sound of Ragoczy's approaching footsteps the child screamed and was echoed by the nervous whinny of the tethered chestnut outside.

Ragoczy stopped. "No, no, child," he said soothingly, first in Russian, then in Polish. He waited, listening, until the shriek died away. "I will not harm you, child. I won't hurt you." He took two cautious steps forward. He could see more clearly now. "You have nothing to fear from me."

Quite abruptly the child fell silent. A face poked out of the straw and large eyes as brown as Dutch chocolates grew huge with terror. The child whimpered once, then trembling, attempted to burrow into the straw.

This pathetic gesture filled Ragoczy with sorrow. He stood still as he spoke to the youngster. "I have said I will not hurt you." He repeated his words in Polish, then went back to Russian. "I am alone. I will not hurt you." He could not say that he was unarmed because there was a knife tucked into the top of his boot and a pistol in his sleeve.

The child scrambled in the straw, huddling closer to the wall of the chicken coop.

"Be still, child," Ragoczy murmured, and in two swift, silent strides was beside the cringing figure. He went down on one knee. "I will not harm you. You are safe with me. Believe this." Then, very deliberately, very shyly, he put his hand on the child's back.

At this the child stopped moving, almost stopped breathing.

"I will not harm you," Ragoczy said again, making no further movement. Under his long, small fingers he could feel the child's breath in shallow panting. He realized with some surprise that the child was wearing an ill-fitting dress of ornate brocades. They remained thus—Ragoczy with his hand resting lightly on the child's back, the child half-hidden in the straw—for more than a quarter of an hour. Then the child turned a filthy, blotched face up to Ragoczy.

"Who are you?" she asked in excellent, aristocratic Russian.

"Franchot Ragoczy, Count of Saint-Germain," he answered at once.

"You're not with them?" Her voice quavered and she dragged an embroidered cuff over her upper lip.

"No."

"Are they still here?"

He shook his head. "They've been gone since before sunset."

"Oh." She got unsteadily to her knees. "Is anyone left?"

Regretfully he told her the truth. "I didn't see anyone: I don't think so."

This information made very little impression on the girl. She shook her head, frowning. "I ran. Everyone did." She struggled to her feet, tugging at the brocade dress that did not fit her. It was of fine quality, a light shade of teal, Ragoczy judged, though in this gloom even he could not be sure. There was embroidery on the sleeves, the bodice, and the hem, and the waist and neck were sewn with patterns of seed pearls. It had been made for a girl of twelve or thirteen; the child who wore it was no more than seven. Her feet were bare and badly scraped. There was one jeweled comb in her tangled blonde hair. She stared at the far wall. "I don't remember . . ."

"It's not important now," Ragoczy said, knowing how many times great shocks were lost to the mind. "What's your name?"

She looked up at him as if she did not understand the question. "Laisha Vlassevna?"

He heard the uncertainty in her voice. "Is that all?"

She considered a moment, then nodded. "Laisha Vlassevna."

No last name. It would make finding her family—if any of them remained—quite difficult. He could not leave her here, and if what he had seen was any indication, there were few havens here on the edge of Poland. "Where do you come from, Laisha Vlassevna?"

"Here?" She trembled again.

He decided not to pursue the matter. Perhaps later, when she was less frightened, when she was able to recall more of her identity, he would find out where she lived and whose child she was. "I will have to leave here soon, Laisha Vlassevna. Do you want to come with me?" He could not abandon her, and had already made up his mind that he must take her away from this ruin and the danger that was all around them. Yet he did not want to add to the fright that already overwhelmed her, so he waited while she thought about what he asked her.

More than three minutes later she asked him, "Where are you going?"

"Away from here. Westward." He had not yet decided which of his houses would be best, though he was fairly certain his château in France, located near Béthincourt in la Forêt du Mort-Homme, had not fared well in the war. It might be wisest to go to his Schloss on the west side of Schliersee: he would not be far from his house in München, and his estate outside Wien would be within reach.

"Is that far?" Her smile was tentative, disoriented.

"A fair distance, yes." Wherever he went, it would be far away from this place.

"Oh." She pulled at a long strand of pale hair, humming a little. "I don't know. If I leave, someone might . . ." Her face contorted at once and fresh tears spilled from her eyes.

Ragoczy picked her up and held her, saying nothing until the worst was over. He had little experience of children, but the plight of this girl filled him with pity. "Laisha Vlassevna," he said quietly, hoping that it actually was her name, and not simply a name she remembered out of her past.

She put her hands on his shoulder and pushed away, but when he tried to set her down, she shrieked and clung to the collar of his coat. "No. No! No!"

"Then you must come with me, Laisha Vlassevna." He began to pick his way across the floor of the chicken coop. As he neared the door, Laisha grabbed him around the neck and squirmed in his grasp. "What is it?" he asked as calmly as he could, stopping while she hid her head against his shoulder.

"They're out there. I hear them. They're waiting. *I can't.*" She was not speaking clearly or loudly, her fear turning her to an infant. Her mouth was wet.

"No, Laisha," he said quietly. "We're alone. My horse is tied up, and we'll ride away on him. No one is here but the two of us."

She was crying again, but with silent resignation. Her arms were limp around his neck and she seemed possessed of no more vitality than a doll. She slumped in his grasp; for a moment Ragoczy wondered if she had lost consciousness. Her fingers caught in his collar, which slightly reassured him, but she paid no heed to the few kind words he said to her as he once again started toward the door. Inside the overlarge dress she felt even smaller than she was; her brown eyes were half-closed.

"See, Laisha? My horse is over there. He's a chestnut gelding, that's an Austrian hussar's saddle on his back," Ragoczy said as he stepped out into the wasteland of the farmyard. He did not dare stop talking, for he sensed that the girl would be overwhelmed by her fear if he did. "We're going to get onto his back, and then we'll ride him out of here. He's strong, Laisha. He'll carry us a long way." He wished now that he knew how to reach Duchess Irina Andreivna, for she might wish to have a child to care for again. In all his long years, Ragoczy had done so only twice, and those instances were far in the past, and neither of the children had been like this one.

"It's gone," she whispered, although she did not look directly at any of the destruction around her. "Gone, gone."

Ragoczy's gaze traveled over the gutted buildings and empty pens. "Yes." He felt the despair of the child he held and it was anguish to him as he recalled other times when catastrophe had prostrated a family or a town or a city or a nation. Whether it was nature's destructive caprice or human venality, there was more devastation in his memories than he could easily face. He held the child closer. To be so young and endure this . . . But then, he told himself sardonically, almost all the world, compared to him, was young.

The chestnut brought his head up sharply, eyes rolling, as Ragoczy came toward him. He chafed at the bit and tried to jerk his reins free of the post where they were secured. As Ragoczy came up to him, he stamped nervously, not calming until Ragoczy caught his rein and drew his head down to blow in his nostrils and pat his neck with his free hand. The chestnut gave a low, unhappy whinny, but stood still.

"Laisha, this is my horse," Ragoczy said as he moved to the side. "He's sixteen-hands-three—that's taller than I am. His chest is deep, and you can tell by his shoulders that he has Orlov blood in him." It was ludicrous to tell the girl such things, but he could think of no other way to diminish her fright. He put his hand on the stirrup. "I'm going to put you on his back, in the saddle. You must hang on. I'll have to get the reins before I mount. Have you ever been on a horse before?"

"I don't know," she answered dreamily. "Maybe."

He sighed inwardly. "Do you think you can hang on? . . . Laisha?"

She stared at the saddle. "Hang on?"

"Here." Ragoczy put his hand on the pommel. "You can hang on here." He lifted her so that she could touch where his hand was. "You can hold that, can't you?"

She nodded uncertainly.

"You'll have to tuck your skirts up. Keep your legs down. Will you do that?" He did not want to think about getting onto the chestnut holding the child as he did so. The horse was apprehensive enough. "If you're ready, Laisha, I'm going to put you into the saddle."

"I'm ready," she said in a voice that quavered with uncertainty. She let go of him and pulled at the heavy brocade of her dress.

"Good." Ragoczy boosted her onto the chestnut's back, keeping his hand firmly on the stirrup leather as the child settled herself in the saddle, hands gripping the pommel. He smiled a little, knowing what an effort it was for her; he liked her courage. "Are you settled?"

"Yes," she said grimly.

He went to the chestnut's head and freed the reins, brought them over the head with practiced ease and had his foot in the stirrup before the chestnut was quite aware that he had been released. The chestnut wheeled as Ragoczy swung his leg over and found his seat almost on the cantle. He gathered the reins and brought his hands in close to the child. "You won't fall, Laisha. I'll hold you."

The girl wiped her eyes with one grubby hand. "I'll hang on."

"Good for you." He had been checking the chestnut but now let him have his head. The horse swang away and Laisha cried out as she lurched back against Ragoczy behind her. "You won't fall," he said once more, adding, "You can hold on to my wrists, if you like. You don't have to keep gripping the saddle." The chestnut had settled into a canter, keeping to the middle of the long road that led from the main coachway to the estate and its farmyard.

Laisha turned once to look back at the desolation behind her, and her face set: she did not cry.

At the coach road, Ragoczy pulled the chestnut to a walk and set his face toward the west. The horse was getting tired, and was certainly hungry. Ragoczy knew that he would have to find fodder for the chestnut before morning came, and perhaps a place to rest for several hours. Absently he turned to touch the leather duffel bag strapped behind the cantle. There was the familiar, sustaining comfort of his native earth, and he would need to rest with it before the coming day was over. Then he looked down at the pale-haired child dozing in the saddle before him. She would need food. Undoubtedly it had been more than twelve hours since she had eaten. Where was he to find a meal for her? What did children her age eat? Ragoczy could fend for himself easily enough, but the girl would need something more than a stray sheep. "Dear me," he said softly, "this is apt to be awkward."

Laisha stirred at the sound of his voice, but did not wake up. She tried to change her position in the saddle, then settled back into half-slumber.

The coach road was quite empty, which Ragoczy knew was fortunate. Yet he began to look for peasant dwellings—outlying farms or little churches—where it would be possible to buy bread and cheese for the girl. Perhaps he could learn who the girl was, as well. He discarded that thought as quickly as it occurred to him: with all the insurrectionist troops in the area, a child of the aristocracy—if she was a child of the aristocracy—might expect brutal treatment at the hands of the rebels. It would be best to say that she had taken the gown she wore, since it so obviously did not fit her. Looting would be understood, even indulged.

With a snort the chestnut brought his head up, stopping, poised and alert, in the middle of the coach road. His flanks quivered once and his tongue pressed at the bit, but he did not run.

"What is it?" Ragoczy asked in an undervoice. "What do you hear?" Then he heard it, too—the distant growl of an engine.

Laisha opened her eyes and swiveled around to look up at Ragoczy. "Where are we?"

"On the coach road," he said truthfully.

"Why aren't we moving?"

"Because I think there is an automobile coming," he answered, his eyes narrowed as he peered through the darkness.

"I've been in an automobile," she announced proudly. Then she touched her skirt where it was rolled up, and her shoulders slumped. Her voice grew small with embarrassment. "I've wet myself."

"It's not important," Ragoczy said.

"You didn't," she said petulantly, refusing to be absolved.

"But I'm older than you are." How could he tell her, now or ever, that the difference in their ages was measured in millennia? He was pleased that she accepted his statement without questioning it. "We'll take care of it later."

The sound of the engine was louder, and then Ragoczy could make out two trembling lights he was certain were the side lanterns of the automobile. It had to be an older vehicle, then, for most of the more recent automobiles had true headlights and not side lanterns. Ragoczy could feel the chestnut tense and he drew in the reins for more control.

Ten minutes later the automobile came up to them. It was an old, much-used Wartbergwagon, the caning long since broken away and patched with bits of canvas. There were two men in the automobile, one sitting on the low front seat and facing backward, the other in the higher driver's seat. Both men were armed.

"Good night to you, gentlemen," Ragoczy said in Polish, trusting that this was the language of the men in the Wartbergwagon.

The driver had braked the automobile and his passenger swung his rifle around to aim it at Ragoczy. "Who are you, and where might you be bound?"

"Franchot Ragoczy," he answered at once. "And my ward, Laisha."

"Foreign name," the man facing backward said to the driver.

"Hungarian, I think," the driver said.

The first man glared at Ragoczy. "That doesn't explain anything. Why are you here?"

As Ragoczy began to improvise, he hoped that Laisha would not challenge him or contradict his various inventions. "It was not my choice, gentlemen. Believe this. It was my intention to visit friends in"—he thought for a distant town—"Ignalina, and we were to take the train to Białystok. We were staying at an inn outside Łomża when we were told that the tracks had been blown up."

The driver of the automobile nodded and relaxed a little. "You're far from Białystok," he said, slightly suspiciously but with a degree of concern.

"Yes," Ragoczy agreed at once. "I was told that we might be able to get a carriage near here, but I see that most of this district has suffered . . . misfortunes."

The passenger put the rifle aside. In his heavy driving coat and eye guards he looked to be impressively huge, but as he stood it became apparent that he was a slight man, no longer young, and very tired. "Misfortunes," he repeated. "Indeed. This poor country has been subjected to every indignity. But that is not of importance to you, is it?" He stared at Ragoczy a moment. "We are going to Ciechanowiec and cannot ask you to come with us. Doubtless you understand." This was a courtesy; his tone made it clear that he did not care if Ragoczy understood or not.

"Of course," Ragoczy said, equally polite. "My ward and I are more anxious to go west, in any case. It is apparent to me that it would be folly to try to continue to Ignalina. If it were possible to find transportation other than this poor horse . . ."

"We had word that there are coaches for hire at Rózan. Try there. You should be able to reach it by noon tomorrow if you make good time and there are no . . . delays." He regarded Ragoczy quizzically. "A strange traveling dress for your ward."

"Most improper," Ragoczy said. "She would try on the gift we were bringing to her cousin, and then insurgent forces reached the inn . . ." He left the rest to the two men's imagination.

"I have children of my own," the driver said unexpectedly. "Five of them. They adore mischief." He studied Ragoczy a bit longer. "There was a Prince by your name, wasn't there?"

"Not recently," Ragoczy said wryly.

"It isn't wise to be too well-born in these times." It was a warning. The driver released the brake and the automobile started to roll. "We'll have to report you, but we'll wait until we've had a meal and a bath." He waved slightly as the old Wartbergwagon gathered speed and rattled away into the night.

When Ragoczy had given the chestnut his head again, Laisha craned her neck to look up at him. "Is that what happened?"

"What?" He was taken aback by the innocence of her question.

"Were we at an inn, and all that you said?" She looked mildly distracted, and had begun to pull at a tendril of hair again.

Ragoczy looked down at her, feeling suddenly a great compassion for the child. "No," he said as kindly as he could. "I made that story up. I hope you will remember it, though, because we may have need of it again."

"I'm not your ward?" she asked tremulously, brown eyes slick with terror.

"Oh, that's true enough," Ragoczy said as he smoothed her pale hair. He smiled as she sighed and leaned back against him, already drifting into sleep once more.

"Are we going to Rózan?" Her words slurred.

"No. I'm not quite sure where we are going, but not to Rózan." He turned in the saddle to looked at the eastern horizon. The sky was still dark. He wished that the few high clouds would part so that he could see the stars. He guessed it to be between three and four in the morning. In less than two hours farm chores would begin and he would have to find shelter for them, and food for Laisha and the horse. "We're going west."

"West," she murmured. One of her hands closed around his wrist.

They had gone no more than two miles when Ragoczy heard gunfire behind them, in the distance. The sounds were faint but distinctive, and he reined in the chestnut to listen. Half a dozen shots, then another one, separate, and the thick, muffled blow of an explosion. Ragoczy thought of the two men in the old Wartbergwagon, hurrying at night to Ciechanowiec. The driver had said he had five children. Ragoczy brought one beautiful, small hand up to Laisha's tangled, pale hair, then urged the chestnut into a weary trot.

Text of a letter from Maximillian Altbrunnen to his sister, Gudrun Ostneige.

My dearest sister;

How marvelous to hear from you. In this place, we count ourselves lucky to get news once a week, and the way things are in München, we believe less than a third of what we're told. The Reds are sure to be tossed out, but what chaos in the meantime.

It's a pity about Jürgen, but everyone's got some losses from this horrible war. You must tell him for me that I applaud his bravery. He's an honorable man, and no doubt you are proud of his accomplishments. If only we had not been subverted by our own bureaucrats, then we might have taught all Europe a needed lesson. Look whom we've trusted in! It's not worth the effort to complain however, and Jürgen will tell you the same thing, I know.

I would be delighted to come to Hausham and live with you. From what I remember, it is a most pleasant location, and isolated enough that we need not fear being invaded by opportunistic officers at every opportunity. You say that Jürgen has enough to put the place back in order, which is necessary. I'm no good at that kind of thing, but with Jürgen so badly hurt, you'll be grateful to have a man about, I'd imagine. If that little gamekeeper's cottage at the far side of the stream is still standing, I might take that over as my personal retreat, for you won't want me underfoot all the time, and this way I can do my own entertaining without trespassing on your hospitality or making trouble with Jürgen. I'm not the sort to live chaste as a monk, you know, but I know better than to *expect you to be able to enter into the spirit of fun with your husband so ill.*

*Poor Hildegard is in a terrible way. Both her brothers are dead, one shot for failing to respond to commands. According to the letter she had from a physician serving on the Front, August was suddenly seized with coward-ice, sat in a niche of the trench, refused to speak to anyone and screamed when he heard gunfire. Luckily the father is dead, though Hildegard's mother is appalled by the disgrace. She has said that she will not have August buried in the family vault, but Hildegard thinks that she is being too hard on him. August, as you remember, was only nineteen, and Hildegard believes that he was not sufficiently prepared for the rigors of battle. The rest of the family refuse to discuss it (and you can hardly blame them), and so Hildegard has been telling me about it for days on end. She said that the English have decided that such cowardice is a disease and not a despicable lack of courage and dedication. It is clear that attitudes of this sort have weakened the entire British nation and Empire. How could an army exist, I ask you, if all a soldier need say in order not to fight is that he has contracted a disease that immobilizes him? I can't help but sympathize with Hildegard, but at the same time I wish she would not go on about it so.*

*You recall I mentioned the new club I had been asked to join? (Well, it is not a club precisely, but more of a brotherhood, and no, I promise you, my too-careful sis-ter, they are not Freemasons.) I have attended two meetings, and if I am accepted by the senior members of the group, then they will welcome me into their numbers with all the privileges that they bestow. I'm not supposed to disclose the nature of the organization, but I know that the men I have met through it are all of the highest moral and patriotic tone. All of them are afraid of what this war will mean for Deutschland because of the traitors among us who have led us from certain victory to the likelihood of defeat. It is their purpose to find the way to assure Deutschland's proper place in the world. Already there are officers and men of high position who are active in this organization. It is more than a simple matter of false trust—there are those in this country whose very exis-tence saps the spiritual strength of this nation, like loath-some parasites. Through this Bruderschaft and those other organizations which are sponsored by it, the evil will be identified and rooted out.*

*Well, that's for the future. At the moment, it is a true joy to think of seeing you again and I am looking forward to living at Wolkighügel. I will do what I can to help you ease your burdens, but it might not be possible for me to be always at your beck and call.*

*Should you hear any reliable news from München, send Otto to me with word of it. I'm sure you can spare him for a day or so, and at the moment, time is of the essence. Don't trust the phone lines or the telegraph, for anyone might have access to your information. Besides, the phone lines here are few, and the doddering old fool who takes the telegraphs is a worse gossip than the village priest. Barring events in München, I anticipate arriving at Wolkighügel in three weeks. I will be needed here until then, but with a little expeditious work on my part, I doubt I'll be delayed longer than that. I'll get you word in plenty of time as to when you are to expect me. If you still have the Daimler, have Otto meet me at the train station so that I won't have to arrange with the carter to get my luggage up to the schloss. I will bring my goods in stages, of course, but in such uncertain times, I don't want to leave four or five trunks of books and clothes on the station platform, for I might not see them again. Otto will understand, without doubt.*

*My regards to you and your husband, my dear sister, and my gratitude to you for this invitation.*

*Fondly,*
*Maxl*

# 5

A thin, watery sun submerged in high clouds made the small cluster of houses at Chambrecy look insubstantial; James Emmerson Tree, riding uncomfortably with six other men in a ten-year-old Fiat, expected the little village to disappear as they approached. They had left Meaux at four-thirty that morning, and it was close on noon. James had a cramp in one leg and the other had gone to sleep. For the first hour or so he and the other men—three of them journalists like himself, the other two medical personnel—had traded stories and boasts, but that had palled and for the last two hours all had been silent.

The driver pulled the Fiat up at the gates to a small country château, very much the worse for wear. Part of the roof had been demolished by artillery fire and most of the windows were gone. "This is your destination, m'sieurs," the driver said, breaking the silence. Now that the motor was off, the sounds of the countryside rushed in: birds, livestock, the rustles of leaves and grasses. This was offset by the occasional sound of gunfire and the presence of soldiers.

An unshaven, gray-faced Sergeant looked at the new arrivals. "Your documents," he said in a gravelly bass.

Each of the men proffered his credentials. Rather than the usual cursory glance that these had been accorded in the past, the Sergeant examined them with care. Finally he grunted. "You may go in. You will wait in the first room on your left after you enter the château. You are not to go elsewhere. If you do, you will be imprisoned. You are in a war zone, and we cannot allow anything to jeopardize our men." He had said this many times before and now rattled the warning without inflection or thought, his hard, stricken eyes fixed on the middle distance. When he was finished, he pulled the gate open and stood aside for the six men. The driver bobbed his head once and climbed back into his Fiat as he asked the Sergeant if there were anywhere he could get petrol, adding hastily that he had a requisition permit.

James went with the rest, looking about him with less

curiosity than he would have shown a month ago; then he had been with Horne's troops at Bethune, fifteen miles south of the Lys, where the Huns had launched their second offensive. That artillery-tattered April sky! He had talked to one of the dispatch riders from Plumer and had been hideously awed by what he heard. He had not been able to rid himself of the sight of shattered men lying in filth-ridden trenches. The sounds of their suffering were louder in his ears now than the noise of the guns had been. And the smell, so vile, so richly rotten . . . He forced himself to stare at the broken château ahead of him.

A private opened the door for the six men and indicated the room on their left. "You understand that the officers cannot spare a great deal of time for you."

"We appreciate this much," said the exquisitely-mannered Gregory Roper from London. He began to unbutton his long canvas driving coat. "Gentlemen. . . ?"

They followed him into the room on the left. It had been quite a pretty salon at one time, but four years of war had changed that. The fine rosewood furniture was broken and scarred, the Aubusson carpet was threadbare and so dirty that it was almost impossible to make out its floral pattern. Four chairs, two of them spilling out horsehair from rents in the upholstery, were placed near the hearth, and a sagging chaise longue had been shoved against the wall under the broken oriel windows. Douglas from New York took one of the better chairs; he had removed his hat, revealing a grimy, exhausted face. "Christ! What they don't ask you to do."

The medicos stood near the door, deliberately apart from the journalists, as if they feared contamination. Thomas McClaren, the younger of the two, was shy of these impressive men; Henri Montnoir was contemptuous of them, thinking them vultures feeding on the devastation.

The fourth journalist, a taciturn man of the old, scrappy school of inflammatory reportage, dropped onto the chaise. He was coughing still, and no longer apologized.

"One of you should have a look at old Whitstowe," Gregory Roper suggested to the medicos. "He really does not look well."

"Neither do the men in battle," snapped Montnoir. He made no move to approach the journalist.

"I don't want them fussing over me," Vaughn Whitstowe said at once, losing the last of his words in another bout of coughing.

James studied the man, wondering why someone in his fifties should undertake so arduous an assignment. It was harrowing enough for young men, like himself, but for Whitstowe it was crushing. He went across the room to the chaise. "Can I get you anything?"

Whitstowe turned his red-rimmed eyes on James. "No; thanks, lad. Unless you have some cognac on you."

Feeling angry for no very clear reason, James shook his head.

"I'm tired, that's all. Got a bit of a chill. It'll go off." He attempted an uncaring gesture, but broke it.

"Let him be," Harry Douglas said from his chair. "My ankles must be the size of cantaloupes. We should have come on the train."

"The train is being used solely for troops and supplies to Paris," Roper reminded him gently.

"There's always room for reporters," Douglas insisted. "Then we could have stretched out. Henry Ford be damned, automobiles are the very devil to ride in, except for the enclosed tourers. But those Fiats! A man spends a couple hours in one of those things, he isn't fit for anything." He rubbed at his calves through his dusty trouser legs.

"General Gallieni used taxis to get his men to the Front in 1914," James said, recalling the night when an exhausted French Corporal told him the story of the Taxis of the Marne.

"Did they tip the drivers?" Douglas asked sarcastically.

James was about to rebuke Douglas; he was acutely embarrassed by the other American's callousness, but Roper intervened. "Considering the hour, I think we might all benefit from a meal. Shall I see if there is anyone about who can tend to that?"

All six men were as hungry as they were tired, and the diversion was quite successful. Montnoir pointed out that it was entirely possible that all the food would be held for the fighting men and not for opportunistic newspapermen.

As Roper was about to step into the hall there came a sound from somewhere within the château, a deep, gurgling howl, mindlessly loud. The six men exchanged uneasy glances.

"It might be an amputation," McClaren ventured after the sound had died away. "They say there isn't enough morphine—"

"There isn't enough of anything," Montnoir cut in.

"There was no mention of a field hospital here," McClaren said to himself. "We were told that . . . But in war things change so fast . . ." He touched the medical bag he carried as if seeking confidence from it.

A second, longer, deeper scream echoed through the château.

"Sometimes soldiers go mad," McClaren said before the sound died away. "They're at the Front too long."

Roper was frowning. "I trust there is an explanation for it," he said doubtfully.

James said nothing; he was remembering the agony he had seen three weeks before. Then he had been in a trench and had seen a putrescent arm and hand protruding from the earthen wall. When he had stopped, appalled, the Corporal with him explained that the men who died in the winter had occasionally been lost in the mud, and that parts of such bodies were sometimes recovered. No cloth was left on the decayed limb—it was impossible to know what army he had been with. One of the men in the trench, seeing the hand, had decided it belonged to his missing brother and had tried to dig the corpse out of the trench wall with his bare hands. The cries of that man were as heartrending, as mad, as the ones that rang through this château.

"They've probably got one of the Huns down there," Douglas said laconically. "Paying him back a bit." He began to whistle through his teeth, and James was startled to realize it was "You Made Me Love You," which had been popular three or four years before. It angered him that Harry Douglas should be whistling a silly, sentimental song while a man shrieked in pain.

The door to the room opened to admit three officers, two French and one British. All three men looked exhausted.

"Good afternoon, gentlemen," said the British Captain as he regarded each of them in turn. "Which of you are the journalists?"

There was a ragged, identifying chorus and the Captain continued, "If the two medicos will go with the Lieutenant . . ." —he waited until McClaren and Montnoir had left the room—"then, gentlemen, we will do our best to spare you a little time. You've come a long way, we appreciate that."

Vaughn Whitstowe began to cough again, but managed to stifle it well enough. "Beg pardon, Captain."

The Captain nodded. "Wars always spread sickness, gentlemen, and this one is no exception. Have one of the nurses give you a draft for that if it hangs on." He shifted his stance. "I want to introduce Major Phillippe Timbres and Captain

Reynard Dos. These men will do their best to answer your questions as far as is practicable, given our current situation—"

The cry this time was shuddering and ended breathlessly.

"—our current situation," the Captain went on with deliberate calm, "and our need for security. When you have finished your reports, you will bring them to me for review."

"What about us?" Harry Douglas asked in his brashest tone. "You're not in a position to give orders to any civilian, let alone an American."

"My dear sir," the Captain said blandly, "there are American soldiers—doughboys, if you will—in the trenches along with British and French men. If you wish to endanger their lives as well as the freedom of Europe, then, by all means, act as you see fit."

Douglas got out of the chair. "You're trying to bluff me, Captain, and I don't like that. We've got freedom of the press where I come from."

"Douglas, for God's sake . . ." James said urgently.

"You're letting them bully you, kid, if you take this kind of guff from them." He folded his arms and glared at the British Captain. "You're trying to use us. That's why you let us come out here—so that we could tell the kind of story you want us to. Am I right?"

"Of course you are," the Captain said quietly. "It may surprise you that I don't wish you to lie. But there are sensitive areas that could mean a great deal—"

"Sensitive areas," Douglas repeated. "That's censorship, Captain."

"Would you rather be sent back to Paris with no story at all?" The Captain accepted Douglas' challenge sadly.

"You can't stop me from reporting what I saw coming here today, or what you're telling me." He planted his feet a little farther apart. "And if you try—"

Major Timbres interrupted. "You are not in America, you are in France, and France is a country at war. We cannot afford to tolerate those who hamper us in the defense of our country." His English was heavily accented and spoken in French cadences which might have earned him a few indulgent smiles had this been a social gathering, but on this occasion no one was amused.

Douglas gave a truculent sigh. "One way or another, you make sure we do it your way. All right." He pulled a notebook from his pocket. "What have you got to say?"

"It will not work quite that way, gentlemen. Two of you will go with Major Timbres, and two with Captain Dos. Both men are reasonably proficient in English and you should have no trouble with them. Both Captain Dos and Major Timbres have dealt with journalists before and have been in action quite quite recently and so are well aware of the way things stand at present. I would recommend that you divide up, one Briton and one American with each officer, as there are questions that might otherwise go unasked."

"Why bother, when you'll disallow the answers they give us in any case?" Douglas demanded, wholly unmoved by the British Captain.

"Because we would prefer to keep the British and the Americans informed on the course of the war if such information does not add to the danger of our fighting men. You mayn't believe me, but you have my word that it is the truth." He turned to the two men with him and spoke quickly in French. James listened with great interest, deciding that he would not admit he was fluent in the language. He had already mentioned that he had studied French in high school but was aware that in most cases this meant nothing.

"Can you follow that?" Whitstowe asked James in an undervoice.

"Some," he answered, frowning.

The Captain addressed the journalists once more. "If you're ready?"

Gregory Roper, who had been listening to all this with very little change of expression, spoke up. "I would prefer to share my interview with Mr. Tree." He ignored the angry glance from Douglas.

Major Timbres inclined his head. "Come with me. There is a sitting room at the back of the château." He stepped out into the hall, not waiting to see if the two journalists were following him.

In the hall the scream was louder, more hollow, coming now in sharp gasps.

"Major," James said, "what is that?"

"A German," Major Timbres answered shortly.

"But . . ." James did not know what next to say. That the man was in terrible pain was beyond doubt.

"Mr. . . ."

"Tree," James supplied.

"Tree," the Major repeated, a little surprised. "Mr. Tree, for the last two weeks we have had reason to believe that the Germans are planning to extend their offensive to the south, but we have had no way to discover more than our suspicions tell us. Have you seen what has happened north of here?"

"Yes," James said quietly.

"Then you can understand why we don't wish to have the same thing occur here. It has been several days since that man was captured and we are desperate." He spoke matter-of-factly, showing no inclination to offer justification.

"But torture . . ." James began as the Major opened the door to a small parlor looking out on what had once been a garden.

"We have an amusing sophistry we practice with this man," Major Timbres said with no trace of humor. "He is in the hands of two women. One of them was raped by Germans two years ago, very badly hurt by them. She walks with a cane now. The other woman has lost all her family—husband, father, and six children—to German guns. We have left the man in their keeping and have given our word not to interfere if they will get us information."

Roper chose an overstuffed love seat. "Don't you think that you're bending the rules a little too much, Major?"

The French officer stood still, looking at the ruined windows. "Very likely," he said after a moment. "I sometimes wonder how I will feel when the war is over, if I am alive. This is not the first man I have heard scream. Most of them were Frenchmen, gassed or shot to pieces by the Huns."

James and Roper exchanged glances. It was James who spoke. "You are supposed to be telling us about the progress of the war."

Major Timbres came as close to smiling as he was able. "Yes. It is good of you to remind me. I suppose you're aware," he added apologetically, "that what you have heard about the German in the cellar cannot be reported?" He waited until both journalists acknowledged this. "Later, perhaps, when memoirs are written, some of this will be exposed. But that is for history gentlemen." He looked at the peeling wallpaper of blue stripes and rose garlands. "This must have been a very pretty room, once," he said, without thinking that he had spoken aloud.

"Yes," Roper said. "I've been in several houses and châteaux in the last two years. It is very quite to see what has become of so many of them." He cleared his throat. "Tell us, Major, how do you evaluate the current military dangers?"

He did not answer at once, and when he did, he approached the question obliquely. "Last October there was an assault on

Italy using tactics which the Germans had up until then used only on the Russian Front, called 'Hutier tactics.' These are characterized by short, intense artillery barrages, and then fast, mobile advance units penetrate the lines, engaging in little hard-pressed combat, seeking out the weakest points and in that manner breaking up the defensive line. It was 'Hutier tactics' that allowed von Below to pursue Cadorna to the Piave River. If we had not sent men to aid the Italians . . ." He fell silent. "We fear a similar assault here. The Germans have been very successful so far with these tactics. There is little reason to suppose that they will not be so again." He folded his grimy hands. "In another week, May will have ended. We are worried that the Germans might be determined to begin June with another offensive."

For the better part of a minute neither Roper nor James responded. Each man was alone with his private nightmare of what could happen here. The German lines were less than three miles east of Rheims, and their two offensives in the north had gained a great deal of ground for them. James looked at Major Timbres. "Was that what they used at Bethune, on the Lys?"

"The German Sixth Army used them, yes. Hutier led his men at the Somme, but luckily France has more heavy artillery than Italy and the advances were not as great as Germany had hoped. We have artillery here, but the Germans are already adapting their tactics to accommodate this." His exhausted face was resigned. "We must fight. Any other course is unthinkable. We have held them off for a time, but . . ." He shrugged in that eloquent way that is uniquely French.

"Are you suggesting that we be prepared to lose the war?" Roper asked in a completely neutral tone.

"No," Major Timbres said, recovering himself. "German losses have been heavy, and they are as damaged by that as we are. They cannot continue indefinitely."

James turned his head, hearing a bird singing in the wreckage of the garden. The song was pure and liquid, joyous. He let the delicious sound ripple through him, invigorating as good wine.

When the German prisoner screamed again, it was more of a bellow, full of hatred as well as irremedial hurt.

"Good God, Major, isn't there something you can do?" Roper burst out. "That man—"

"—need only tell us what we wish to know, and we'll release him from his suffering," Major Timbres said, his face starting to sweat. "The women have said that they will not let him linger once he has told them—"

The last sound was short and high, more like metal scraping on stone than a human voice.

James could feel his pulse hard against his collar and could not bring himself to look at the Major. He said to his companion, "Roper, I don't think . . ."

Roper gestured. "I trust it is over, Major Timbres."

"I trust so, too," was the devout answer. "If there is no information, then . . ." He clenched his teeth so that the muscles stood out on the side of his jaw. "If we cannot learn what it is that the Germans are planning, we stand to take enormous losses. When you think of the number of men already sacrificed to this war, then the death of one German soldier . . . It is a soldier's lot to die for his country." The defiance in his tone was startling.

"Major," Roper said heavily, "I'm not so naive that I don't know such things happen in wars, but I had hoped that it was not the French or the British or any of the Allies who indulged in these practices. In your place, however, I would find it most difficult to resist the temptation if it were presented to me."

The Major said nothing, but the expression in his eyes was eloquent.

James gave a diplomatic cough and searched for another approach. "Major, the people who own this château, what will become of them after the war?"

"Assuming we win?" Major Timbres asked sadly. "They will be given the building back, of course, and there is talk of compensation, but the costs of the war have been high, very high. This family, I know, has a house in Paris where they are living now. They are in what I think the British call 'reduced circumstances' "—he raised an eyebrow toward Roper—"and I am not sure they will be able to restore this place. They may not want to. It was one of the real jewels before the war; as you can see, it is fourteenth-century with a few seventeenth-century additions. Most of the time this region is fairly prosperous and the châteaux in the area have reflected that."

"Then it will be left a ruin?" Roper asked with ill-disguised incredulity.

"They can no doubt find a buyer for it, if that is their wish. One or two of the other families whose châteaux have been hurt by the war have said that they would prefer that the buildings be left as they are as monuments to the valor of

France." The Major took a turn about the room. "Many of us on this part of the Front have had to go to these old châteaux and ask that the owners leave them. I have done that myself. It is one of the least gratifying things I have done." He stopped beside a small, sagging gate-legged table. "You see, we must always assure the owners that we will do everything in our power to see that no part of the property is damaged, but you need only look around you . . ."

"Where do the owners of these châteaux go? You said that the owners of this one have a house in Paris, but not all of them do, do they?" James was thinking of doing a story, one that would be uniquely his, on the plight of those driven out of their homes by war. He had already seen a few articles on the usual refugees, the displaced people who had been farmers or innkeepers or grocers, but no one had written about those owning land and extensive homes, whose heritage as well as their property was falling to the ruin of war.

"Not all of them, no," Major Timbres said uneasily. "A few have refused to leave and they have paid the full price for that. The rest have gone to other parts of the country. We have encouraged them to consider the Atlantic coast. That way, if we fail, there will be a chance for them."

James regarded the Major with steady eyes. "Would you be willing to give me the names and current addresses of some of them?"

"Why?" Major Timbres inquired, though he knew the answer.

"I want to write about them. My paper would be interested." He had not asked Crandell about the story, for he had thought of it only in the last ten minutes, but he was confident that he would be able to convince his editor that there was merit in the idea.

"Another of 'The Plight of the French' stories?" Major Timbres asked bitterly.

"I don't do sob-sister stuff," James said a little stiffly. "Look, Major, America may be sending you troops but there aren't any Germans dug in outside Philadelphia. A lot of people in my country don't realize what's going on over here. They don't know what it's like to have an invader on their soil. The Civil War was us versus us, and that's not the same thing. If one family has owned this place since the fourteenth century, it means a lot more to lose it than if a guy in Atlanta has to give up his ten-year-old house and move to Chicago."

Roper gave James a long, measuring look. "You're likely to do well in this business, Tree," he said, as if to himself.

Timbres considered what James had said. "You understand that it is quite possible that none of these people will want to talk to you. Loss of an estate such as this is more than painful."

"I figured that." James nodded. "I won't insist that anyone see me. But I'd like to ask. And I'm hoping a few of them will want the rest of the world to know how much they've had to give up." If some of the names used to have titles, James thought, it would be even better. There was nothing Americans liked better than tarnished aristocrats. He watched the Major as he slowly paced the length of the room.

"Very well," Major Timbres said. "I will give you a dozen names. A few of them I do not have addresses for, but with a little diligence you should be able to find them. When you do, you must say that it was Captain, not Major Timbres who provided information on them. I had not been promoted when I was asked to discharge that unpleasant duty. I warn you that several of the families were barely cordial. They may receive you in the same way."

"Were any of them helpful?" James said, refusing to be daunted.

"Grudgingly. There was one, quite a young woman, really, who was gracious and hospitable. She gave me an excellent meal, good cognac, and a few hours' sleep in a clean bed. I . . ."—he very nearly laughed—"I was half in love with her by the time I left her château."

"Who is this paragon?" James asked. "Do you think she'd talk to me?"

"Probably. She has another estate, I believe. In Provence, if I recall correctly. She mentioned Les Diables Bleus. I'm fairly sure she went there. Her name is Madelaine de Montalia." He did not want to say her name and both journalists knew it.

"Don't worry, Major. I won't abuse her good nature," James said as he reached for a notepad. "Any idea *where* in Provence?"

"No. Doubtless there are records in Paris. Another you will wish to speak to, assuming he agrees, is Henri-Gilbert Griffe. He is very old, with a large family. He has endured much through this war, but he is not bowed down by it. Currently he is living with one of his grandsons near Beauvais. He will be quite willing to speak to you if he is convinced of your sincerity."

James had taken his dog-eared notebook from his pocket and was scribbling in it. "Henri-Gilbert Griffe and Madelaine de Montalia. Anyone else?" He had also written a few indicative notes to himself: *Griffe—old, feisty, big family. De Montalia—young, Provence, something special.* He began to think he was really on to a story.

"There is also Louis Creusée, who had not one but two châteaux destroyed in 1914. He is working in Paris now, studying codes. He speaks seven languages, and so is very much needed." Timbres did not like Louis Creusée, who was always demanding that his losses be recognized. His conversation consisted entirely of demands for recompense and declarations that the Germans had caught the French napping and it would serve France right if Germany won. The last time Major Timbres had seen Creusée, he had come close to hitting him.

"A large family as well?" James asked.

"Not particularly. They say he has the Eng . . ." Major Timbres stopped suddenly, with a guilty look toward Gregory Roper.

"The English Vice?" Roper said at his most mild. "That is what it's called here, isn't it? We have other names for it, as you might expect. Just as we consider syphilis the French Disease."

Timbres accepted this without demur. "Creusée has that reputation," he said, thinking that had he liked the man, he would not have mentioned this about him. Major Timbres knew that if he wanted to embarrass Creusée, this was one way to do it.

"I don't think I'll put that in my story," James said with much more aplomb than he would have had six months ago.

"There's two families from near Verdun: one of them is now at Fontainebleau and the other at La Rochelle. I will get their names for you. We had to evacuate a convent near Metz. The nuns are now at a hospital in Caen. The Abbess will have a great deal to tell you. Gaspard Froidmain had quite a sizable estate not far from Fumay, where he raised draft horses. He's moved his family to Tours and is working with supply and transportation departments. There are others, some much less resourceful than these. There were two very old sisters in a huge château about ten miles outside of Commercy who had nowhere to go and now the château is in ruins, and all that they had in it. The war has made them destitute and they have only a niece left to them, who is a widow." His eyes were growing hard with his recounting of these losses. "I have no idea where the sisters are now. Shall I go on, Mr. Tree, or will a list be sufficient?"

"A list will be much appreciated, Major," James said, knowing that he had enough to give Crandell. Perhaps he could even get a series of articles. And once the war was over, he might stay on, doing more stories about how various people put their lives back together. It was suddenly vitally important that Crandell approve of this; it would give him his ticket to stay in Europe. So caught up in his own burgeoning plans was James that he did not hear the question Roper asked the Major, and was startled to hear the answer.

"That is what we hope. If there are more incidents of the same sort in the German ranks, it will be to our advantage." The Major had folded his arms.

"I thought Jew-baiting went out with Captain Dreyfus," Roper observed.

"And Disraeli," Major Timbres said sharply. "Neither of those men had any great influence on Germany. We know of four instances already and we have reason to assume there will be more." He paused, giving Roper a thoughtful look. "As far as I am aware, no one has said much about this. It might be wise to point it out, but it might also be divisive, if there is dissatisfaction over Jews in your country."

"I'll have to weigh the issues and ask for instructions from my employers." He returned the Major's look. "There are always difficulties, Major."

There was a knock at the door, and Major Timbres excused himself to answer it. A young Corporal stood waiting for him, and after saluting, addressed the Major in low, rapid words. Major Timbres heard him out with increasing gravity. When the young man had finished, he saluted and left, his hurried footsteps loud as he went down the uncarpeted hallway. The Major closed the door slowly.

"You must forgive me, gentlemen," Major Timbres said abruptly, wanting to conceal the urgent apprehension that quickened his pulse. "It seems that the German did say something before the end. It may be important. Colonel Tranche has asked that all his officers attend him at once. I must go. You will understand, of course."

"Of course," Roper said.

"Sure," said James.

"Then excuse me." He left the room in long strides which retreated down the hall, joined by several others, moving equally quickly.

When the two journalists had been alone for several minutes, Roper turned to his American colleague. "What did you get of that?"

"Most of it. There's a major offensive building up, to begin on the twenty-seventh or twenty-eighth, in another attempt to reach Paris. The Germans are bringing up more heavy artillery. Air surveillance will be increased from Rheims to Soissons. I think it's the Seventh Army and one other. I didn't hear it clearly." James spoke in his most conversational manner and rather quietly.

"You have a better command of French than I," Roper said with some surprise. "You won't mind my saying that's rare in an American. I thought you studied it in high school."

"I did. My teacher was Madame Courante." James could not entirely keep from smiling.

"I see." Roper turned to a new page in his notebook. "What have you got there?"

"Mostly the names of people who have lost their estates." He was a bit guarded with the English journalist, for he had come to know that the competition in this profession was ruthless.

"That's not much use to me, but I'll tell you, I believe you've hit upon something worthwhile there. I think you're right about Americans and their lack of comprehension." He went on in a more clipped tone. "You don't want to go back to the trenches, do you?"

James closed his eyes in a futile attempt to keep from remembering what he had seen and heard and touched and smelled. "No."

"No. No more do I." He sighed. "I hope the other two have got something to share with us."

"If the Major lets us use any of it. With that new offensive, they might put a stop to stories coming out of this area." He had had that happen twice before.

"I'll risk it," Roper said. "I wonder how long they'll keep us here?"

It was more than an hour later when the same young Corporal who had spoken with Major Timbres came to the room and said in very poor English that the two journalists were to leave now.

Roper got out of his chair and stretched. "And another dreadful ride, I suppose. We'll be lucky if they allocate us an oxcart."

Douglas and Whitstowe were waiting for them just inside

the front door. There were soldiers with them, stern men holding rifles.

"What'd they tell you?" Douglas asked. "That Dos is one smooth-talking bastard; nothing but tactics and ordnance."

Vaughn Whitstowe looked worse than he had earlier; his eyes were glazed, feverish. He had to clear his throat to speak above a whisper. "I'm worried," he said.

Before he could clarify this statement, the door was opened and all four men sighed as they saw a battered but serviceable Panhard Levassor turn in through the gates.

Text of a letter fron Irina Andreivna Ohchenov to her uncle Pavel Ilyevich Yamohgo.

*Rotterdam*
*June 16, 1918*

*Dear Uncle Pavel;*

*As you must realize from this letter, I am in the Netherlands. I have been in the company of Kiril Lukovsky—you may remember him: he is my cousin on my father's side, the second son of my father's oldest sister—and his family. They are intending to live in France, but at the moment Kiril's wife, Tania, and two of their children are ill, and their physician has advised them that it would be unwise to attempt to travel at this time.*

*Leonid is dead, and all the children. I don't know what has happened to my brothers or their families; no one I have met can tell how I might find out. It is so very disheartening. I have brought some of my jewels, but not all of them, and getting to the Danish ship in order to leave Poland took the diamond-and-ruby necklace that was so treasured by Leonid and his mother. I have now a fair amount of jewelry left, but I am giving the emerald bracelet to Kiril, for he has been my good angel and he has little to support his family in their illness.*

*What I hope, my uncle, is that you will be willing to take me into your house. I know you and my mother did not get along well and that she spoke harshly of you when you decided to live in Paris. She was not always as charitable as could be wished, but there was little anyone could do. My father loved her with great devotion, and that is always rare. If the sins of my mother must be visited on me, then so be it, and all I ask is that you tell me, if you will, where I must try to live and how much money will be necessary for my well-being. My jewels are all I have and when they are gone, then I will have to find a way to earn my living. I would gladly give the jewels to you rather than sell them if you would be willing to let me stay with you while I seek some sort of training for earning my living. At the moment my only real skills are for languages and tapestrywork. Since France has some of the best weavers in the world and there is little call for Russian, Greek, Czech, and Polish, except at universities where they already have such scholars, I suppose I must learn from the beginning. I have an aptitude for figures, and they are one area where language is no difficulty. Two plus two will equal four in Russian, Chinese or Hottentot.*

*If it is not possible, either because of past injuries from my mother or because the war has made such demands on you that you cannot receive me or guide me, then I hope that you will allow me to leave my address, wherever I come to live, with you, so that any of the rest of our family who may live through that terrible upheaval at home will be able to find me. You have lived away from us for so long that it might not mean a great deal to you. For me, with my own family gone, finding just one nephew or aunt would give me real hope again.*

*It will be some little time before I am able to travel, and therefore you may reach me at this hotel for at least six more weeks. We have been advised that the fighting in France is currently very bad, and it is probably unwise to try to get there until the worst is over. You may be pleased to know that the belief here is that France will beat back the invaders and emerge triumphant. These people are good-hearted but cautious and they say little. We have been told that in spite of their neutrality, it is feared that Germany might not honor this if they were much provoked. Yet sympathy is with France, and if that gives you heart, then think of it, my uncle, and be proud.*

*I have had to break off, for the physician was here again. Tania is much worse and the physician has said that he is afraid she has the influenza which is spreading so quickly. He has prescribed willow-bark tea and hearty broth to give her strength, but has admitted to Kiril that the outlook is not good. This influenza has shown itself to be deadly, and as Tania is already weakened, he can make no promises for her recovery. The three children are another matter. Sasha is already feeling a bit better—one*

*can tell because of the whining. It is too soon to know
with Olga and Boris. Olga, being the youngest, is sadly
worn down and she is not often fully aware of her surroundings. Kiril has been sitting alone by the window. To
have come so far and lost so much and then to be faced
with this! I feel his affliction deeply, and yet I know that
I am helpless; I cannot comfort him. If this influenza is
truly as dangerous as we have been told, what will happen when the war is over and the soldiers go home? Will
they carry it with them? I can think of nothing but death.*

*We have been told that there is a wireless report from
Paris and so I am going down to the lounge to listen to it.
I will mail this at the desk when I do. For your sake, and
my own, I hope that the news is good. It would be wonderful to learn of something—anything—that is not another
disaster.*

*If I do not have a letter from you in the next six weeks,
I will suppose that I am not welcome with you, and will
do what I can to fend for myself. I hope you will choose to
have me. You may fear that others will make similar
demands, and are therefore reticent. I cannot blame you
for that, but I must tell you that I hope some of the family
will approach you for aid, for it will mean that they are
alive, and that far outweighs any other consideration.*

*With my prayers and my gratitude, no matter what
your response may be, this from your loving niece,*

*Irina Andreivna Ohchenov*

## 6

Jürgen Ostneige glared up from his hunched place in his wheel-
chair, his hands clenched in impotent rage, and muttered at
his wife.

"Yes, darling, I know," she said woefully as she looked
around the front hall of Wolkighügel.

The carpets were viciously ripped, there were obscene words
scrawled on the walls, the beautiful fixtures for the gas lights
were smashed, and most of the furniture was gone. Gudrun

did not know if she could stand to see the rest of the little Schloss if the front hall was like this. Her shoes crunched fragments of broken glass.

"Animals!" Jürgen spat, his mouth working with emotion. There was a line of foam on his lower lip.

Seeing this, Gudrun was recalled to herself. "You must not let this disturb you," she said, biting back a laugh at the absurdity of it all. "The doctor has said that you must stay calm, Jürgen. It's very bad for you to be upset." Rather desperately she added, "Last time they had to tie you to the bed. Do you remember that, my darling?" She managed to keep her voice from rising, but it left her feeling faintly breathless. Unlike many of her countrywomen, Gudrun Ostneige was not a Walküre. She was tall and slender, in the fragile, willowy style. Her blonde hair was confined at the neck in a sensible, braided bun and her woolen suit was of a conservative cut and dove-gray shade which washed out the color of her eyes and the delicate hue in her cheeks. She had the manner of a matron of thirty-five; she was twenty-six. She turned to the man behind them. "Walther, I think it might be better if you take my husband up to his room and give him his medication now."

Walther Stoff did not quite salute her, but his grizzled head bent in agreement. "That I will, Frau Ostneige." He bent over his employer who had been his commanding officer. "It will be better when I've had a chance to clean it up, Mein Herr."

Jürgen's speech was always garbled when he was aroused, and neither Walther nor Gudrun could make out what he was trying to say. At last he thumped the arms of his chair and sobbed twice before going limp and allowing Walther to push him toward the stairs.

"I will have a look around," Gudrun said, dreading the thought. "When Walther comes down, he and I will make a catalog of the damage and will work out a plan of how to repair it." She said this last wistfully, for she knew it would be her inheritance that would pay for the restoration of Wolkighügel. She sighed. It had seemed like such a huge sum four years ago, but now it was much diminished in her eyes and she was very much afraid that her brother Maximillian had already run through his share of it. Dear Maxl, she said to herself with a touch of annoyance. Dear, kind, handsome, idealistic, irresponsible, arrogant, thoughtless, charming Maxl. She wondered if she had really invited him to live here with her because she would feel more comfortable with a male

member of her family about, or whether what she intended
was to keep an eye on him.

These speculations were driven from her mind as she walked
into the main reception room. If the front hall had been a
shambles, then this was a ruin. Nothing had been left intact.
All the windows were smashed, the draperies pulled down,
the furniture upended and the upholstery slit open. Rain had
got in and there were dreadful white, shrunken streaks on the
tall wainscoting, like scars on well-tanned skin. She put her
hands to her eyes and tried to weep.

The dining room was as bad. Deep gouges ran the length of
the hundred-year-old mahogany table that was long enough to
seat twenty guests in comfort and the deeply-carved legs had
been shattered by repeated wanton blows with a heavy
instrument, probably a hammer, for there was no chipping of
the wood, only bludgeoning. The elaborate petit-point chair
seats and backs had all been repeatedly slashed, the fine
needlework totally effaced and the canvas beyond restoration.
Mud and other noxious substances had been smeared across
the two pier glasses that remained intact. They stood between
the tall smashed windows. The carpeting had been set afire in
several places.

Gudrun wandered through the rooms, a somnambulist caught
in a nightmare. The wreckage ceased to mean anything to her,
and she felt strangely unmoved as she stared down at a tuft
of kapok spilling out of a number of tears in a hassock, as she
touched the filth-stained damask of a Louis XIV settee, as she
scuffed at the spreading mildew on a fine old Turkish carpet.
These were simply the culmination of all the horrors of her
life: this Schloss where she had planned to retreat from the
disasters of war and loss was as bad as what she had left behind
in München.

She was not surprised to discover the pantry had been
raided. Here, at least, there was little destruction. Whoever
had sacked her home had been sufficiently hungry to treat the
larder with a modicum of respect. The pungent, sour smell
that pervaded the place warned her that the wine cellar had
not fared as well. As she opened the door at the head of old
stone steps the odor of spilled vintages rushed up at her,
palpable, melancholy, and intoxicating. She lit the candle in
the sconce by the door and stared down. About half the bottles
had been broken, which was not as bad as her worst fears.
Some of the cellar would be salvaged. She thought it was

absurd to have dozens of bottles of old wines and nothing left in the Schloss to eat.

When she had examined the library—some books had been snatched from the shelves, piled in the center of the room along with three desks and an antique inlaid table and set alight, others were strewn about the floor—she went in search of Walther.

"He's quiet now, Frau Ostneige. I have given him his medication and he is no longer so overcome." Walther kept his voice low, and his wrinkle-fretted eyes were filled with concern. "Is it very bad?"

"All of a piece," she said, putting a hand to her brow, which was the only indication of weakness she would permit herself. "It will take time to bring a semblance of order to the place, and it has to be done before autumn comes; my husband must avoid the cold, you know . . . ." She was aware that Walther was as familiar with Jürgen's physician's instructions as she was, but it gave her a sense of purpose to repeat them. "We ought to keep that in mind."

"The Schloss will be repaired." Walther made the statement as if it could not possibly be contradicted. Any other course was unthinkable.

"Yes. And I will see that it is. You need not worry about that, Walther. I have enough of my inheritance for this, and a bit more." She felt an odd, numb pain as she spoke, and hurried on. "But with the war and so few men available to work, it may be more difficult than we anticipate now. Something should be done quickly, and for that we must have laborers. How much damage is there on this floor, have you looked?" Before she could assess her requirements, she had to know how vast a problem faced her.

"There is some breakage. The hangings on Herr Ostneige's bed have been pulled down and the dresser is badly scratched. I think they must have taken a gardener's trowel to it. I've been in four of the other rooms, and they are in similar condition. Nothing is anywhere near as bad as the . . . disaster on the ground floor. I haven't been up into the attic rooms yet, but it may be that they confined themselves to the first two floors." Although he had been out of uniform for almost a year, Walther Stoff still spoke like the soldier he had been and he stood at attention. He unbent enough to favor Gudrun with a paternal smile. "It is not impossible, Frau Ostneige. We will accomplish it. A few of the men who served with mein Herr will be pleased to discharge their obligations to him by helping to put the Schloss in order again. That way, too, they will be usefully employed and will not be tempted to listen to the Spartacists or that Red riffraff from Wien. Working men are not discontented with their lot. Let me inquire. If you will give me permission to do so, I will write to four or five of them immediately."

"Yes. Do as you think best." Gudrun was already planning: she could house the workers in the attic rooms, assuming they were fit enough to be used for that purpose. It would also be necessary to hire a cook to provide good meals for the men. One of the inns might be able to recommend someone reliable. Doubtless the men who worked here would require a day to visit their families, and Sunday was the traditional day for such things. That would mean six days of work from each of them. Nine, ten, at the most a dozen who were willing to work until the first snows—the Schloss could be made habitable again in that time, and it would not be necessary to subject her husband to further discomfort. "Write to them, by all means."

Walther conditionally approved of Herr Ostneige's wife, and so he very nearly saluted her. "I will bring the letters to you when I have finished with them."

"I'm sure they'll be fine," Gudrun said, not wanting to have to go over the letters, but Walther took this as another indication of her ability to deal well with her inferiors. He decided to make mention of her quality and the devotion she had shown her crippled husband. The men would respond to her duty.

"Is there anything more, Frau Ostneige?" He would have liked to be able to do something for her, something that would show her how much he respected her.

"Nothing now, thank you. But I think I should mention that my brother will be here later. We sent him a telegram when we left München, and if he left Rosenheim this afternoon, he should be here before too long." She anticipated seeing her brother with mixed emotions but masked this from Walther.

"Your brother. This is Altbrunnen, isn't it?" He had met the young man once and held him in contempt because Maximillian was not in uniform. There had been some excuse about being medically unfit and he remembered that Herr Ostneige had mentioned a serious illness in youth, but to Walther's mind, any young man who was fit should have been fighting for Deutschland, not spending his days in questionable company or living off of his sister.

"My brother has told me he would prefer to make his quarters in the gamekeeper's cottage. Would you hike over to it and see if it has been damaged, and if so, how badly?" If there was an answer, she did not hear it. She opened the door to the muniment room and was relieved to see that the vandals who had been there had contented themselves with smearing mud on the various rolled documents. She picked one up, handling it gingerly. With a little care, she thought, it would be possible to save most of them. The parchment was heavy, and if it were sponged, it should come reasonably clean. She began to pull the long rolls from their niches.

When Walther returned from the gamekeeper's cottage, he brought a terrified old man with him. He was not pleased with his discovery and wondered, as he had wondered on the walk back from the cottage, if he should have summoned the authorities.

They found Gudrun once more in the library, sorting out the books which had been pulled from the shelves but not burned. She was down on her knees—it distressed both men to see her there, for each believed that women of her rank should not be doing servant's work—with a number of tall piles of volumes around her. As the door closed, she looked up with the semblance of satisfaction on her face. "You're back," she said, then stopped and gave a little shriek of recognition. "Otto! Gott im Himmel!" She stumbled to her feet, oversetting two stacks of books in her haste, and very nearly ran into the old man's arms. "Otto, you're alive."

He patted her awkwardly. "Nein, Rudi, don't cry. You are the Gnädige Frau now, and not my little friend Rudi." There were tears in his eyes as he stepped away from her.

"Oh, Otto. When I saw the Schloss, I thought you must have been hurt or killed. I knew you wouldn't be driven off." She reached out to take his hand, but hesitated and did not. She could see relief in Walther's eyes.

"I hid, Gudrun. I can't justify it. There were so many of them that I . . ."

"How many?" Walther asked. He had not allowed Otto to speak to him while they had walked side by side back to the schloss.

"I counted nine," Otto said defensively. "I did not stay to find if there were more, not after they shot out all but two of the front windows. They caught one of the goats and killed it, but I buried the poor animal after they were gone."

"Who were they?" Gudrun inquired with a calm that surprised her.

"I don't know. I didn't recognize any of them. They may have been Spartacists, because one of them kept shouting about how the people had cast off their chains in Russia." He looked around the library. "I had my gun, but not very many bullets. You understand, if I had had enough, I would have done anything to prevent this." His tired old eyes grew shiny with tears.

Gudrun smiled gently. "Then I would have had to face worse than this. Your death would only have added to the loss and solved nothing." She was also aware that his sight had been growing weaker in the last few years, and she doubted he would have been able to aim well.

"You're kind, Frau Ostneige." Otto bowed properly.

"Oh, Otto, don't behave this way. I'm still Rudi. It's no different than when I was a child here. My father did not leave this Schloss to me so that I could be a stranger in it. You're all the tie I have left to those days, you and Maxl. If you behave as if you do not know me, it will be cruel of you." She had not intended to say so much, and was shocked to hear the loneliness in her tone.

Otto nodded a number of times. "My little one, yes. But it is not the same. If we are alone you are still Rudi, but otherwise, you are Frau Ostneige, and that is how it should be."

Walther was fast revising his opinion of Otto, deciding now that the old man had very properly refused to give information to an unknown man. Loyalty was rare, he reminded himself, and for that reason it could be unrecognized when encountered. He lamented the familiarity that Frau Ostneige showed the old man, but if she had known him since childhood, it could be excused: Otto was well aware of what respect was due his lady, and that was important. Without looking at Frau Ostneige again, he began to restack the books she had overturned.

"When did this happen, Otto?" Gudrun extended her hand in such a way that it included the whole Schloss.

"More than a month ago. It's rained twice since they were here, and I've seen the damage the water did. They rampaged all through this area. You know Schloss Saint-Germain? It was treated the same way. The Blau Pferd near Gmud was burned to the ground and the innkeeper badly beaten. Two large houses at Fischbachau were broken into and wrecked. I've heard that Schloss Schafhorn was burned day before yesterday, but there has been no confirmation. Everyone here is afraid, Rudi. They have seen what can become of them and it is terrifying. You must not think ill of them."

"I don't," she said, aghast at what she was told. A large inn, and four or more Schlosses vandalized! "Isn't the war enough for them?" she demanded of the air.

Otto lowered his head. "The stationmaster at Hausham has said that we may use the telegraph and the telephone if we need to." It was no easy thing for Otto to say. "We have to get there, but it isn't very far."

"We have an automobile," Gudrun said. She took unwarranted pride in the Hispaño-Suiza double phaeton she had been able to get so cheaply a year ago because it was not a German car. Jürgen had not been entirely happy with her purchase, but she had pointed out that at the time their 1911 model was made, the cars were still being built in Spain rather than France, and further, in 1911, the two countries were not at war. Jürgen had allowed himself to be persuaded because he quickly came to appreciate the convenience of the large, elegant vehicle.

"The red-and-white one I saw on the road?" Otto asked, revealing more delight than he wished to.

"Yes. My only concern is fuel. Where does one get petrol here?" The thought had occurred to her as they had driven out of Dürnbach, and it still worried her.

"There is fuel to be had at Miesbach, but it is also possible to order it. I have heard that Sigfried von Grünstrasse has small tanks of it delivered to him. It's difficult to get now, with the Army having priorities, but because of Herr Ostneige, it may be that allowances will be made for him." As Otto said it, it seemed to him to be an excellent idea. "If you wish, I will make inquiries."

"Yes. Do that, Otto," Gudrun said gratefully, having envisioned an entire week spent attempting to make proper arrangements. "Let me know what the cost will be and what is required. The road here is not in the best repair . . ."

"I will mention that." He again made that movement that was half a nod, half a bow. "Is there anything else, Frau Ostneige?"

Gudrun sighed. "Yes, Otto," she said, resigned to the change in their relationship. "My brother will be arriving sometime this afternoon. Would you meet him at the depot? Do we still have the horses, or were they killed?" She had not thought of that earlier, and hoped that she would not have to buy horses as well as fuel for the automobiles, another light carriage, and finance the restoration of the Schloss. She envisioned her inheritance reduced to nothing.

"One was hurt. Hässlich and Wahnsinn are all right," he told her, with an affectionate smile for the two big Holsteins. "Stürmisch had to be put down last winter—he got an illness and the farrier could do nothing. Von Grünstrasse's groom had a look at him as well, but both said he couldn't be saved." He did not like telling her this, because Gudrun had ridden the splendid Prussian Trakehnen for almost seven years and loved the animal. "Dumm is being cared for at von Grünstrasse's."

With a gesture to show she did not blame Otto for the loss of her Trakehnen, she said, "Then you'd best harness up Hässlich and Wahnsinn and leave for the train station in the next hour. I gather that my brother"—she was not certain if she should call him "Maxl" to Otto any longer—"will be bringing a fair amount of baggage."

"Very good, Frau Ostneige," Otto said, and prepared to leave.

"You may have to buy food for us, as well. Here, let me find my purse. You'll know better than I what we need until I find a cook." She glanced once at Walther. "Will you look in on my husband shortly, Walther? He ought to be resting, but it isn't certain that he is." She saw Walther give a modified salute as she followed Otto out of the library. It was odd, she thought as she went across the hall. She had lived with servants most of her life, but always her father or husband had taken care of the management of them. In München Walther had attended Jürgen and she had shared the services of a housekeeper with another couple. Now she did not have that luxury. Here she was mistress, and the realization baffled her. She trusted that Otto or Walther would be willing to guide her in her responsibilities.

Otto held the door for her, and she went into the sitting room where Walther had brought her trunks. "I put it down here. It is disgraceful, isn't it, to see such ruin?" She found her purse and opened it. How much would Otto need for the food? She had no idea. She handed him four or five banknotes, saying, "This should do for the moment. All I ask is you remember that my husband must have a simple and very sustaining diet."

"Fine," Otto said emotionlessly, then added in rather cautious accents, "The second cook from the Blau Pferd is out of work, and I know he is good at his job. Would you wish me to ask him to call upon you in a day or so?"

For the first time that day, Gudrun actually smiled without inner pain. "Yes. Oh, yes, Otto. I would be delighted to see him. I was afraid I would have to hire the stationmaster's sister or someone else horrid. Ask him if tomorrow afternoon is too soon."

"With pleasure, Rudi," he said as he took the money from her. "I will be back in two or three hours if the train is on time. That is not always the case, especially now." He faltered. "They say the war is going badly."

Gudrun did not answer at once, and when she did, her mouth was a thin line. "When has war gone well?" She dashed her hand across her eyes. "Never mind. Whatever happens, we will hear of it soon enough. I cannot take time to think of France and Italy and Poland and Bulgaria. My home is in ruin, my husband is an invalid and that is all that matters to me now."

Otto's expression was sympathetic, but he kept a proper distance. "I will bring your brother from the train station and I will see that there is food. I'll let the cook from the Blau Pferd know you wish to interview him tomorrow." He had learned years ago to repeat the orders he was given, and did it for Gudrun as if he had done it always.

When Otto was gone, Gudrun sat down on the largest of her cases and gave way to tears. It was so difficult and never-ending. She had talked at length with Jürgen's physician and was aware that it was most unlikely that he would recover much more than he had done, but that if it was to happen at all it would be in the most relaxed surroundings she could provide, which is why she had elected to return to Wolkighügel rather than sell the Schloss. To have arrived expecting so much and be greeted by this! Her sobs were more bitter for being almost silent. She wished she still kept the faith of her childhood, but during the last four years her willingness to place trust in God had drained away. Her confessor had listened to her doubts and her hopelessness, and rather than give her the warmth she craved, had castigated her, reminding her that despair was a great sin, according to some priests, one of the Seven Deadly Sins, more damning than sloth. And so she turned away from Catholicism and had not been able to put anything in its place. If she had had any faith left, she would have believed that these trials were punishment for her doubts, but that fear had faded with her faith. When she looked down at her hands she saw that one of the nails was torn, and this brought on a fresh torrent of tears even as she chided herself for silliness. What was a torn fingernail here? But her weeping did not stop, and she ceased to resist it. This once, she told herself. She would indulge herself now and put it behind her.

By the time Otto returned, she was dry-eyed and curiously composed. She had changed into a dark brown faille peg-top dress. Her hair was still in a braided bun, but she had changed her shoes to a pair of high-heeled kid slippers. In the last hour she and Walther had cleared away the greatest part of the mess in the afternoon reception salon, and Gudrun had asked that one of the tables be brought down from the attic. It was not much, but she had to begin somewhere, so she had changed her clothes in order to appear as a proper hostess, no matter what the vandals had done to her Schloss.

Maximillian Altbrunnen grinned at her as he came through the main hall. "Otto warned me. You've got your work cut out for yourself, Rudi, dear." He embraced her enthusiastically and gave her a perfunctory peck on the cheek. "It's been more than a year. What have you done to yourself? You look like somebody's widow!" Immediately he said it he flushed and gave a conscience-stricken glance toward Otto, who was dragging the larger of his two chests through the door. "I didn't mean that the way it sounded, Rudi. You must believe me. I wasn't thinking. I'm just not used to thinking of Jürgen being . . ." He broke off vaguely and let her assume the rest for herself. Standing there, he was quite astonishingly handsome. Tall, well-built, with strikingly deep blue eyes and a shock of silver-blond hair that always demanded attention. His features were regular, almost classical, and at twenty-four he was lacking in the experience that stamps character over beauty. He was dressed in a long, light coat and carried an alpiner's hat in one hand.

"How are you, Maxl?" Gudrun asked as she linked her arm through her brother's. It was like old times, before the war, when their parents were alive and neither of them had a care in the world. She could not help comparing the wreckage of her husband to this glorious youth, and felt a pang of remorse. She scolded herself for treachery.

"I'm well enough. You know what the times are, but all things considered, I manage well enough." He looked around the hall. "Is the rest like this?"

"Some of it is worse, some not so bad. Most of the damage is on this floor. The attic rooms are practically untouched." She nudged him in the direction of the salon. "Come, let me give you some tea. That's about all I can offer you until Otto shows me what he's brought from Hausham."

"Tea's fine. I've got a bottle of brandy in my bags, and I persuaded one of the innkeepers I know to part with a cask of dark beer. Otto will be bringing that in with him." Maximillian's easy smile made it almost impossible for Gudrun to rebuke him.

"I wish you'd brought three or four chickens and a ham, as well." She was apologetic, but the wish was genuine.

"If what Otto said is accurate—and you know he does exaggerate, Rudi—I wish I had, too." He entered the salon and his lips tightened for a moment in distaste. "I don't think I want to see the rest of the rooms. I'll go out to the gamekeeper's cottage when we've had tea." He took one of the hard wooden chairs and drew it up to the dusty old table that Gudrun and Walther had dragged down from the attic an hour ago.

"I won't be able to flee," she said, more sharply than she wished to, for it was foolish to blame Maxl for the destruction here. She decided to make amends. "You mentioned a brotherhood of some sort in your letter. Are you still part of that group?"

"Oh, yes. It's been a busy time. I told you a little about them, didn't I? Well, it looks as if I'm going to be accepted into it." The frown that had been deepening between his brows was banished by his enthusiasm. He put his elbows on the table, heedless of the dust and grime on the old wood. "It's pretty much a sure thing. There were a few moments that had me worried, the Geselschaft has very high standards for its members; but Ulrich told me just yesterday that if Eckart gives his approval, it's settled."

"How wonderful for you," Gudrun said, smiling in spite of herself. Her brother had always been able to lift her spirits, even when she had been determined he could not. "You're proud of it, aren't you?"

"Of course. Not everyone is accepted, and Eckart isn't the sort to be too lenient, for all that he looks like someone's indulgent uncle. He's got a sharp mind and he is truly aware of what's been going wrong in the world. Part of the purpose of the Geselschaft and Bruderschaft is to help put things right again. Rudi, I can't tell you what a difference it's made since I met Eckart. Before then, I was convinced that it was useless to do anything, that I might as well fritter away my time because nothing could be done anymore." His blue

eyes shone with purpose; to his doting sister he looked like
an angel. "Just when I thought it was over for Deutschland,
Eckart showed me how we were betrayed, and told me what
could be done about it."

"Can you tell me, Maxl?" Gudrun asked, hoping that Walther would bring in the tea soon.

"Not really. It is a secret brotherhood, and in general we're
not supposed to advertise our association with it. Ulrich explained it all to me." He got up from the table and went to the
door. "I hope Otto isn't having too much trouble with the
trunks."

"If he is, he will ask Walther to help him," Gudrun said with
a complacency she was far from feeling.

"Who's Walther?" Maximillian inquired, with minimal interest.

"Well, strictly speaking, he's Jürgen's servant. He served
with him in the war and takes care of him now. He's been the
greatest comfort and I trust him completely. He's already
made a few suggestions about taking care of the Schloss and—"

"Be careful about that," Maximillian interrupted her. "You
never know with servants. They worm their way into your
confidence and then try to take over your life. That maid Aunt
Frida had was that sort. You don't want that happening."

"I'm sure that Walther isn't that kind of man," Gudrun said
stiffly, disliking her brother's tone. What would she do without Walther? she asked herself. How could she care for Jürgen
herself?

"They're all that kind," Maximillian said wearily. "But if he
served with Jürgen, then he might feel he owes some sort of
obligation to him. Soldiers are like that."

Gudrun's hands closed into fists in her lap, but she was
spared any more embarrassment by the arrival of Walther
himself, with a tray of tea and sweet biscuits. She indicated
the table, and as Walther set this tray down, she said, "This is
my brother, Herr Altbrunnen. He is going to be staying
here."

"Very good, Gnädige Frau," Walther said as he set out the
cups.

"How is my husband doing, Walther?" This last question
was as much for Maximillian's benefit as for any information.

"He's still resting, Frau Ostneige. Otto brought bones from
the butcher and I am taking the liberty of preparing a broth
for him." He stepped back from the table. "Will that be all?"

"Yes, thank you, Walther." She sighed as the servant withdrew, then turned a challenging eye on her brother.

"Looks well enough," Maximillian observed, and reached for one of the biscuits, saying nonchalantly before he bit into it, "I told Ulrich before I left that you'd be delighted to invite Eckart to stay for a while, if he wished."

"What! Here?" Gudrun stared at Maximillian. "Invite him? With the Schloss in disrepair and Jürgen confined to his bed?"

Maximillian finished the biscuit and reached for another. "From what I hear," he temporized lightly, "Jürgen is apt to be there until the day he dies, and you're too young to shut yourself up in the tomb with him. You need to have friends around you, Rudi. I don't know how you've stood it without them. And look at you—you're positively haggard! And the Schloss? Otto said that you're going to have it restored, so where is the difficulty?" He poured a cup of tea and dunked a third biscuit into it.

"It isn't right, Maxl. You don't understand the difficulties. I don't know the first thing about Herr Eckart. What does he do? What sort of person is he?" This was a desperate ploy on her part, and she waited, knowing that Maximillian would not tolerate being disappointed.

"He's a fine man. He owns a newspaper. And he's not a foolish child. Have Otto or that Walther make inquiries in München if you're not willing to trust what I tell you." He drew up his shoulder and sulked as he had when a child.

"Oh, Maxl," Gudrun said, capitulating. She felt so lonely, so wholly isolated that it seemed petty of her to deny Maximillian this pleasure, particularly since she was reasonably certain that the owner of the newspaper would not take long holidays away from his work, and might even give her a chance to keep up with the life she had left behind. "Very well, if Jürgen is willing. But first do let me have the repairs made."

Maximillian beamed. "Of course, Rudi. Mein Gott, you don't think I'd ask a man like Dietrich Eckart to stay while the place looks like this, do you?" He gave one of his robust bursts of laughter. "You're house-proud, my dear Rudi, and all I can say is . . . thank goodness."

It was an effort to answer his smile with one of her own, but Gudrun managed, all the while reassuring herself that it was the fatigue and disappointment of her trip that made her so suddenly frightened.

Text of a letter from Madelaine de Montalia to James Emmerson Tree.

Montalia
August 5, 1918

James Emmerson Tree
16, Rue des les Frères Gris
Faubourg Saint-Germain-des-Prés
Paris

My dear Mr. Tree:

You did me the kindness of writing to me in French, so I will return the compliment and write this in English; it is excellent practice for me. Should I commit any grotesque error, I hope you will forgive me.

I have your letter of last month finally, as it took more than four weeks to get here. I see that you are interested in discussing the plight of those deprived of their homes through this dreadful war. I am more than willing to speak with you, if that is what you wish, but I must warn you that you are not going to find a tale of woe at Montalia. My château here is a glorious old pile which has been in my family for centuries; indeed, this is where I was born and grew up, so I have a sense of restoration here, of continuity. If you search for those driven into proverty and homelessness, this is not the place to find one.

My home on the Marne, Monbussy, I have been informed by the Army, has fared badly in the war. That saddens me a great deal, Mr. Tree. Monbussy was added to my family holdings not long after the Revolution, and it has been much treasured. To know that it has been bombarded by artillery distresses me greatly, yet I know there is little I can do but hope that when all is over I will be allowed to go there once again and see it put in order.

*You tell me that a Major Phillippe Timbres recommended you contact me. How kind of him. I must tender him my congratulations on his promotion. He called upon me at the time I had to leave Monbussy and was most kind in discharging his duties.*

*Let me suggest that in coming here, you travel first to Avignon, which is a most interesting place, as well as being the quickest route to Montalia. There is a train to Digne you may take, or if you plan to drive an automobile, I must inform you that the only other dedicated automobilist in this area is myself. It is difficult to get petrol in the best of times, and with the shortages of war, you will find something of a hazard in getting petrol. I would also urge you to carry a full set of replacement tires, as these roads are primitive and there are few places that can provide proper repairs. I keep a small supply of petrol here at my château, so once you arrive there will be little problem, but you may experience some inconvenience getting here. On the coast it is otherwise, and I confess there are times it seems to me that those living here in the mountains often take delight in rejecting all that is popular near the ocean.*

*But to continue your directions. Once you reach Digne, take the road to Saint-Jacques-sur-Crête, then take the east road toward Estfalaise. There is a fine waterfall you will see after the crossroad for Sage Disparu, and just beyond that there is a long, high meadow, almost a plateau; near the end of it, you will find a stone gate on your left. That is the entrance to my home. The château is some little distance along the road, but the drive is not steep, for there was a time when carriages instead of automobiles used this road, and the horses, after dragging the coach up such rugged slopes, were in need of a rest.*

*The winter is severe in these mountains and I would not advise you to come any later than the end of October, unless you are inclined to pass the New Year at my château, which you are welcome to do, but might not suit you, as I have heard that there is hope that the war will be ended with the year. A man in your profession doubtless hears more than I, and you must be in a better position to weigh the merit of such rumors, but if it should be that you cannot get here until spring, I will quite understand.*

*The constabulary at Saint-Jacques-sur-Crête has a telephone, and should you need to get a message to me, you may call there and ask that one of the postmen bring it with my mail. This has been done in the past and will certainly be done until such time as I have telephone lines strung to Montalia.*

*One thing I feel I should tell you: I am an archeologist, and if the war in the Middle East should be resolved in the next few months, I will make application to go there to resume my studies at various excavations. My last expedition was in the Sudan, and it is my fervent hope that it has not been too much disturbed by the fighting. Think of lying buried in sand for three thousand years, brought to light at last only to be destroyed by bullets and bombs. Should my request be approved, I will leave as soon as preparations are made, but I will make every effort to see you before I leave. As much as I have dreaded the destruction of Monbussy, I have felt a far greater fear for the dig in the Sudan.*

*I look forward to your visit, Mr. Tree, and trust that after such enterprise you will not be too disappointed.*

> *It is my pleasure to be*
> *Most sincerely yours,*
> *Madelaine de Montalia*

## 7

"I'm hungry," Laisha whined as she pulled on Ragoczy's hand. She was shivering, though the night was warm.

"Yes, I know," he responded kindly, suppressing the desire to speak sharply to her. It had been more than a day since he had found food for her and she had done her best not to complain. "It will have to be a bit longer, Laisha. It's hard to wait, but you'll do it."

"How long?" Her huge eyes glowered up at him accusingly.

"Another hour, perhaps a little more." He was waiting for the windows of the houses to go dark, but he did not tell her that. Since sunset they had lain at the edge of the field, alert to everything around them. In the distance a dozen farmhouses clustered together around a wooden church with a steeple like a witch's hat. Most of the windows were bright, and there was still movement in the little village. Ragoczy had seen enough to know that the farmers were aiding the insurrectionists, but was relieved to discover few signs of activity.

"An hour?" From her tone, she felt it was eternity.

"That's not very much, Laisha. An hour is a tiny thing." But as he said it, the memory of other hours came back to him, and each stretched on forever: hours in the full enervating power of the sun outside Babylon, hours in plague-maddened Thebes, hours in Salonika as the earth shook, hours in a cell under the Circus Maximus, in a slave caravan outside Tunis, on the cliffs near Ranegonda's castle, in a flooded temple, in an abandoned Crusaders' stronghold, at a bedside in Careggi on a Passion Sunday, in a burning cellar in Paris . . .

"It's not," Laisha stated, putting her fist to her mouth and biting rebelliously. Her face was smudged with dirt, her hair was tangled, and the loose-fitting trousers and shirt he had found for her three days before were already stained and torn at the knees. He supposed that he did not look much better.

"Perhaps not," he agreed, touching her head lightly. "But if we don't wait, it might be very . . . unpleasant."

She drew away from him a little, not quite pouting.

Without speaking, he took her hands in his and crouched down beside her, waiting until she deigned to meet his eyes. "Laisha, do you recall the men with the guns at Kielice, and how difficult it was to get away from them? Five people were shot that night, and two of them were children. Do you remember?"

"Yes." She nodded solemnly. "You tricked them."

"I tricked them," he agreed. "But it was a desperate chance and there's little likelihood that we would be lucky again. The nearer we get to Breslau, the more danger we're going to encounter. There isn't just one war going on here, Laisha, but many, and it would be bad for us to be caught up in any of them. I know you're hungry and thirsty and tired," he went on, warmth in his tone. "We've had to take too many risks, and that has made it impossible to live sensibly. You've been brave and cheerful. I know it isn't easy for you, hiding out and making do with straw beds and scraps of cheese, but it's the only way to get through this to safety."

Laisha sniffed. "I don't know why I can't get something to eat. The men were having sausages . . ." She looked wistfully toward the distant houses. "I saw them."

"And so did I," he said. His voice was soft, but there was a quality of command in it that made her look at him once more. "I also saw they had guns with them. It is better to be hungry than dead, my child. You'll have supper before the night is too far gone, and you will eat in safety."

"But how? Where?" Her eyes were awash with tears and she thumped her legs with her fists.

Ragoczy smiled slightly. "Why, in church. Where else should we find charity?"

His irony was lost on the child. "Will the priest feed us?"

"I don't think we'll ask him," Ragoczy said. "There is a side entrance to the sanctuary, and if we go in there, we will do well enough. That's where the tithing basket is kept and at this time of year, it is well-filled. If you wish sausages, Laisha, you'll have them. We'll bring a few with us, as well."

She ran her tongue around her lips. "And bread?"

"Certainly." He dropped back down onto the ground. "We have only to wait a bit. Be comfortable. We may not have much rest tonight."

"Why not?" The question had little importance to her and she did not wait for an answer but curled up beside him, her head pillowed on his arm. She twisted uncomfortably once, settled, and lay still, her fatigue bringing her sleep almost at once.

Ragoczy watched her with a contemplative expression that was not quite a smile. There were so many complications since he had become Laisha's *ipso facto* guardian. Guardian. He turned the word over in his mind in several languages. Guardian he had been before many times, but not with a ward. He was childless, after the manner of his kind, yet now he had a child. His eyes were no longer sardonic and he kept still so that he would not disturb her rest.

It was almost two hours later when Ragoczy gently shook Laisha awake. Her eyes opened quickly, fright-wide, but changed at once as she saw him. "Is it time?" she asked apprehensively.

"Yes." He braced his head on his hand. "We have to go quickly once we begin to move. There are dogs in the village, but if I have a little time I can quiet them for as long as it will take us to raid the tithing basket. Then we must hurry."

Laisha stared at him. "How will you quiet the dogs?"

He looked away. The questions would come, and they would have to be answered, he told himself. But what if that trusting face should turn from him in dread? Ragoczy's dark eyes were enigmatic as he turned back toward her. "Those of my blood have certain gifts, Laisha. One of them is a limited control of animals. It is strenuous, and cannot be used on the run. But if I lie still here, I can influence the dogs, and for a while each will be in a stupor. When I become active, I won't be able to keep that control, but with luck the dogs will take a few minutes to wake up." He waited for the revulsion he had seen so many times before to show in her face, but to his surprise, the child grinned.

"Can you teach me how?" she asked eagerly.

Ragoczy shook his head. "No. It's not a thing that's taught: it's . . . acquired. And it isn't always safe to use. Here, with very little to watch but the fields, I can take the risk, but if there were others here, or if we had to move suddenly, then it would not be wise for me to try it." He doubted that she understood, but he hoped she would have some sense of the particular difficulties of this manipulation and would not regard it as an ability available at any caprice.

An owl drifted overhead and suddenly plummeted down to seize a hapless mouse. There was a single shrill squeak from the mouse, and then the owl was flying off silently with supper held tightly in its talons.

"What happens?" Her dark eyes were sparkling.

"You won't notice much," he said kindly, amused at her absurd disappointment. "I'll just lie here. You're not to disturb me. I will know when it's done."

She glared at him, obviously convinced that he was deliberately withholding a treat from her. "Why shouldn't I disturb you?"

"Because that would cause a great deal of confusion in me and the dogs would be aware that something was wrong, and we would not get the sausages in the tithing basket." There were greater, more subtle dangers, but these he did not mention, knowing that this girl would be distressed by them, as so many others were.

"I wish we still had the horse," she said quietly.

"So do I, Laisha. It would be . . . helpful." They had left the horse at the last inn they had used. Soldiers had come with orders to arrest all foreign travelers; Ragoczy and Laisha had had less than five minutes to escape out a window and slip into the wood before the terrified innkeeper opened their rooms to the armed men. Ragoczy had paused only to grab his bag and a small leather pouch containing a few gold coins; then he climbed down the two stories to the ground.

"Could we get another one?" She looked woefully down at the ruined knees of her trousers.

"Perhaps." He handed her the bag he had carried. "Hold on to this for me, will you? If something goes wrong and we must run, I will be a bit . . ."—he did not want to frighten her with stories of the disorientation he felt when brought suddenly out of his special concentration—"confused. If I am, I'm depending on you to make sure we keep this. It's very important. All right?"

She took the leather bag onto her lap. She was plainly in awe of it.

"Will you remember?" He had never put his trust in anyone so young, and it troubled him. "It will be very bad for me if I don't have the bag, Laisha." He watched her duck her head, and decided that he had done all he could to impress upon her how necessary the bag was to him without telling her everything about himself, which he had no desire to do. He sighed once and moved back from her. "Once I lie down, you must not talk to me or disturb me in any way unless there is real danger. If the bushes rustle, don't be concerned. On the other hand, if you see a farmer approaching, or hear an automobile or an aeroplane, then tell me. I will not respond easily, but shake me until I do. Will you do that, Laisha?"

"Yes," she promised, not daring to look away from him.

"All right." He gave her what he hoped was an encouraging pat, then stretched out on the ground, his hands locked behind his head. It was never easy to achieve that first, drifting state of mind, and this time was harder than usual. He looked up into the night sky, watching stars and the curve of the moon. Slowly his breath deepened, and his eyes closed. There were dogs, several of them, fierce and loyal. Each in turn was lulled from watchfulness to curled ease to dreamless slumber. One of the dogs whined as Ragoczy's influence touched him, but this did not last, and the animal was soon asleep. When he was satisfied that the dogs would rest, he brought his concentration back to himself and opened his eyes.

Laisha was staring at him. "You looked so strange, so still. You were away." She did not realize that seeing him then she had touched some essential part of his great age; her own youth guarded her from recognition.

"Yes," he said, rising awkwardly, extending his hand to her.

She misunderstood the gesture and offered the leather bag, upset by his quick frown. "You told me . . ."

"So I did," he relented. "But first let's get you on your feet." His fleeting smile dispelled her anxiety, and she took his hand at once, letting him lift her several inches into the air before standing. He picked up the bag and motioned for her to follow him. "We must stay low and speak very little once we start across the fields. The dogs can still be roused by a real disturbance. Are you ready?"

She tugged at the tail of her shirt and bit her lip, but wagged her head. Then she bent over to demonstrate her readiness to do as he had bade her.

"Excellent," he murmured, tapped her shoulder, and began to move forward quickly. So swift and powerfully controlled was his crouching run that he seemed to drift over the ground, a shadow detached from all other shadows. Behind him, Laisha struggled to keep up, and did not know that when she did come abreast of him, it was because he had slowed down for her.

The houses in the village were of stone and planking with wattle roofs and tiny, unglazed windows. At the backs of the dwellings were pigpens and sheepfolds, and the shelter for the various dogs of the peasants; all remained silent as Ragoczy and Laisha approached. At one end of the village, near the church, was the midden, redolent from the warmth of the day. At the other end of the village, away from the holy building, was the bathhouse where the families went once a week to scrub themselves clean of their grime and enjoy the faint and pleasurable frisson of doing something wicked. Ragoczy slipped between two houses with little more than a startled bleat from a ewe, and into the open space around the village well. He paused a moment, holding out his hand to Laisha.

"Are you thirsty?" he whispered.

"Um." She was afraid to speak aloud, so adamant had he been about the need for silence.

He reached for the bucket beside the well and dropped it down, hoping that the handle would not squeak too much. He brought the water up as quickly as he dared and held the bucket for her as she drank eagerly from it. "Don't talk," he cautioned her when he pulled it away. "You won't be able to run if you do."

Conscientiously she wiped her hands on her shirt, studying her toes. "I'm ready," she muttered.

He turned away from the well and slipped gratefully into the shadow of the church's steeple. He pressed against the wall, listening, but no sound came from within. The priest was not keeping vigil, chanting prayers as some did. Ragoczy was grateful. He went along the side of the building toward the sanctuary door, feeling the pull on his jacket from where Laisha had grabbed it. His hand closed on the latch. Delicately he lifted it, and to his relief it opened with little more than a pop. Long experience had taught him the folly of pressing his luck, and so he waited until he had counted three hundred before stepping through the door.

The tithing basket hung in the narrow passageway. It was made of heavy wicker and was secured to the rafter above it by an old, rusty chain. When Ragoczy pressed it, the basket resisted the swing; Ragoczy smiled. The basket was full.

Laisha was tugging at his coat, holding back her panting with an effort. She blurted out one word: "Sausage."

Ragoczy did not reprimand her for this. He pressed her hand, and then reached into the basket, pulling out two long links of sausages in greasy casings. He touched apples and what felt like onions, and pulled out three items at random. "Here," he said in a voice so low that it was nearly inaudible. "Put them in your shirt. Now."

Laisha sniffed as she obeyed. The sausages felt peculiar next to her skin, and the apples were intrusive lumps, but she knew that no matter how alien they seemed now, they were food. She swallowed impatiently and thrust another length of sausage into her shirt as Ragoczy handed it to her.

"That's enough, I think," he said in that very quiet tone.

She had to resist the urge to protest, but her emotion was plain in her face.

"No, mahya dotch," he chided her affectionately. "Any more, and we could not carry them. As it is, I fear the dogs will be able to smell our trail for the better part of a week."

She accepted this, fear closing around her again. As his small hand touched her shoulder in sympathy, she straightened up, determined not to be cast down.

Then a sound caught his attention, and he turned, lifting a hand in warning. He had let himself become dangerously inattentive while he stole from the tithing basket, he told himself harshly. It was the sort of error he had not made in centuries.

The hollow sound of horses coming into the village grew louder.

"Three," Ragoczy whispered.

From outside there came a shout. "Andrzej! Stefan! Casimir! Zygmunt! Where are you?" This was followed by a few indistinct words; then another voice called out, "This is Wladyslaw! Come out!"

At the far end of the village a door opened and there was a jumble of voices. One old man demanded querulously what had become of the dogs, that men could ride into the village without a warning being sounded.

"That's it," Ragoczy said resignedly. His influence on the animals would cease as soon as their masters called them. He reached around and grabbed Laisha by the waist. "We must run now, just as the dogs begin to bark, or we will be chased."

"But . . ." She was baffled by this change, and her terror was growing stronger.

He lifted her onto his shoulders, ignoring her protests and admonishing her to be silent. "Hold on to my hair," he said, letting the increasing noise in the village square cover the sound of his voice. "Once I begin to run, you must keep steady and still or I will fall and it is likely we will be caught. That would not be wise."

"I will," she said.

"Here." He gave her his bag again, adding, "Put your arms through the handles. You'll balance better that way."

The first hysterical barking erupted in the night, and the farm animals responded with bleats and grunts and crowings. Another dog awoke and did its best to make up for its earlier failure. Doors were banging open.

Ragoczy stood in the shadow of the church at the sanctuary door for as long as he dared, then sprinted away across the fields, moving westward from the village. The weight of the child, the food, and his bag was annoying, and once he faltered at an obstacle he would usually have jumped with ease. But the manipulation of the dogs had tired him, and the added weight made him cautious; he struck out away from the low stone boundary marker, toward a line of brush, hoping that he would be able to get through the thicket without hurting the girl on his shoulders.

A light came on in the church and sliced through the night bright as a polished sword. "Demons!" cried a voice in a better accent than any other Ragoczy had heard in the village. He feared the priest had seen him.

Another man ran up to the robed figure in the sanctuary door and looked where the trembling arm pointed. Then both crossed themselves, for they knew that anything moving at that speed and of so unnatural a shape must be sent by the powers of Hell.

Ragoczy had heard the yelling and recognized what they had been called, and his heart lightened. The villagers would waste no time chasing supernatural beings. For the moment they had escaped and were free.

The woods loomed ahead and he moved even lower, his speed increasing as he used more of his great strength for a last dash into the stand of brush. They would, he knew, leave a most undemonlike hole in their passing, but at night it would not be seen, and by morning, he and Laisha would be a good distance away.

Twigs snapped around his head and branches whipped them. Laisha yelled once, her hands twisting his hair painfully; then she lowered her head so that it was close against the leather bag, and hung on as Ragoczy plunged on until they came to a marshy glade, where he allowed himself the chance to rest.

"Can you get down?" he asked the girl, whose hands were wrapped around his neck.

"I don't know," she answered, then did her best to release him. "I'll try."

"It's just like getting off a horse," Ragoczy coaxed her, his breath ragged as he spoke. "Only not so far to the ground."

She wriggled, then slid off him, the bag falling beside her. She reached for it, holding it in her arms, attempting to ignore the discomfort she now felt from the sausages and fruit inside her shirt.

Ragoczy took the bag and stood up straight, feeling just for a moment that he had nearly reached his limits. "You did well," he told Laisha. "You did very well."

At first she could say nothing; then she met his dark eyes for a moment. "I was frightened."

His laughter was brief and not entirely pleasant. "My child, so was I." As he spoke he looked away over the glade. At the far end there was stagnant water, which made him frown. He did not want to chance crossing water in his currently weakened state. The earth in the soles of his shoes—his native earth—insulated him to a degree, but he would have preferred not to have to deal with water just now. He glanced across the clearing and saw the suggestion of a path, too well-maintained to be an animal's trail. That would mean another village close by. There was nothing for it: they would have to cross water.

"What's wrong?" Laisha asked. She had already reached into her shirt and pulled out an apple. "Do you want one?" Her face was set into a well-mannered smile, but her eyes begged him to refuse.

"No thank you," he responded, equally politely, thinking that there would come a time when the girl would ask him why he did not eat. He wanted to postpone that moment as long as possible.

Smiling gratefully, she bit into the apple and then found it difficult to swallow the fruit; she was too near weeping. At last she choked the first mouthful down, and then her hunger took over. She gobbled the apple, attempting to lick the juice from her chin between bites.

Ragoczy watched her, delighted at her pleasure, and was reluctant to intrude on it. "Laisha, when you are through," he said at last when there was little left of the apple but the core, "we must move on. In the morning the peasants may have second thoughts about the demons, and if they do, we must not be here for them to find."

"Why?" Now that she had eaten, she was touched with the onset of sleep; her eyelids felt as sticky as her fingers.

"Because it could go badly for us." He wanted to give her a more complete answer, but this was not the time for it. "If you want to talk about it, we'll do that later, when we're away from here and have found shelter. Can you walk now?"

Laisha was terribly hungry, for the apple had only whetted her appetite. She hung back, her lower lip forward and sleepiness making her eyes heavy. "Can I have a sausage?"

"While we walk," he said in a tone that would not tolerate opposition. He held out his hand to her. "Come, Laisha."

She scuffed her toe in the spongy grass. "I'm hungry."

There was no softening of the order now. "Come, Laisha," he repeated, his dark eyes on hers.

Although she was not precisely afraid of him, still she did not want to argue, not when his voice grew so quiet and uncompromising. She reached into her shirt and pulled out a sausage. "I'll eat this," she announced, refusing his hand.

"All right. We will go across the marsh"—he pointed toward the far end of the glade, hoping as he did that there would be a reasonably well-marked path through the hummocks and reeds—"and then turn more to the south." He took three or four steps away from her and waited as she tagged along petulantly. "Laisha?"

"Oh, well." With an exaggerated show of compliance she fell into step beside him, pausing now and again to chew on the sausage she held in her hand.

The ground underfoot was less firm, and water shone blackly in the night. Ahead of them something small scuttled and splashed away from them, and a little later the low, eerie shape of a water bird skimmed over the marsh less than ten strides ahead of them. There was the marsh sound all around them, like an old man sucking on false teeth.

There was an irregular sort of path marked across the worst of the marsh, and Ragoczy thought he would not like to have to follow it if he had not had his remarkable vision: even a man who knew the way well would be hard-put to follow it at night.

Laisha hesitated as she looked from one patch of reeds to the next. For her, they were indistinct shapes in the dark water. She wished now she had held on to Ragoczy's hand. He was two steps ahead of her, then three. Her features tightened into a grimace as she tried not to call out to him. She was terrified of being left alone in the marsh, but her pride would not allow her to make a sound.

Then, five long steps away from her, Ragoczy turned, staring back over the brackish water. "Laisha?"

She had a panic-filled moment when she feared he would not see her, that she would be another mound in a multitude of mounds; he would pass her by. Desperately, illogically, she dug her fingers into the sausage she held. It was impossible for her to make a sound.

"Are you all right?" he asked her, mild apprehension sharpening his question. He had come directly to her and stood beside her on the uneven footing of the hummock.

"I was lost," she said when she dared to look at him, expecting ire.

"No." He reached down and lifted her to his back again. "Just hold on, Laisha," he said as he pulled her legs around his waist and caught her knees in the crooks of his arms. "Don't strangle me this time." He was startled to discover how worried he had been about her when he had not heard the scamper of her feet behind him; and then the relief when he had seen her, frightened, silent, and defiant among the reeds, had put his irritation to flight. He walked more slowly, picking his way over the marsh. The place was discomforting to him, as water always was. Once he caught the shine of a reflection and saw, to his amusement, a sleeping child apparently suspended in the air, arms and legs around empty space. He was secretly glad that Laisha did not see it, and began to go more quickly; he wanted to be away from the water before the sun rose and sapped his strength even more.

Text of a letter from Roger, manservant to Franchot Ragoczy, Count of Saint-Germain, to Sir William Graddiston.

*Christiania, Norway*
*August 20, 1918*

*Sir William Graddiston*
*92 Cadogan Square*
*London, England*

*Sir William:*

*While I fully understand your apprehension about my employer, I can assure you that there is no reason to fear for his safety. Current difficulties in Eastern Europe make contact with him sporadic, but I have no reason to believe that he has suffered any injury or other mishap.*

*At the time I left St. Petersburg, or if you prefer, Petrograd, he was making plans for his own departure. As you may be aware, my employer has an aversion to traveling by water and does it only when no other option is open to him. At that time he had secured passage by train, and from what I have been told, that was one of the last trains to leave for Warsaw. There were several members of his household who accompanied me on my journey, as my employer is not the sort of master who leaves others to fend for themselves.*

*If I have had no word from him by the first of next year, then I will follow his instructions and begin investigating records for his present location.*

*Your concern for his safety is appreciated and he will doubtless be most gratified to learn of it. You specifically state that you are apprehensive about the various out-of-hand executions and imprisonments that have occurred in Russia of late. I share your sentiments, but not in regard to my employer's fate.*

*It is my assumption that when this tragic war is ended my employer may well establish himself in Switzerland, Austria, or Germany. Recent work done in those countries in the area of organic chemistry has most profoundly intrigued my employer, who has a long-abiding interest in such studies. For you, so deeply committed to this war and so obdurate an opponent of the current German government, such a decision may appear inexcusable, but let me give you my word that my employer has no sympathy with aggression of the sort that Germany has visited upon the world these last four years. Therefore, I trust you will not delay your transfer of funds, as requested, to the bank and account indicated in the enclosed authorization.*

*As soon as I have word from my employer, I will contact you, and request that my employer do the same. I have been in Saint-Germain's service for some considerable time and it has been my experience that he lands on his feet more often than not. In his time he has been in positions more precarious than this one and has won through.*

*On behalf of my employer, Franchot Ragoczy, Count of Saint-Germain, believe me, Sir William, to be*

*Most sincerely yours,*
*Roger*

## 8

At the other end of the trench there was stagnant water; two corpses lay in it, one of them already turning slightly green. A rifle barrel protruded from under the nearer body: possibly the weapon was still clutched in the dead hand in the water.

This first day of September it was hazy, and at another time the men in the trench might have spared a moment to look about them and enjoy the morning, but none of them did.

"It's going to be like Montdidier," one of the men said, too resigned to complain. He patted his pocket automatically, forgetting he had run out of cigarettes two days before. He cursed without much feeling, and expected no reaction from the other men with him.

"What do you suppose they're thinking now? Ludendorff's going to order another retreat, they say." The speaker was the youngest man of the eight of them, a fair-haired, blue-eyed boy of seventeen.

"Paul," one of the older men said, "the Canadians and the Australians have broken through north of here, and there are British divisions from Arras to Lassigny. They're using those new tanks, too . . ."

"Whippets," one of the others supplied. "Christ."

"And air support. Ludendorff must fall back. What else can he do?"

The youngest soldier looked at his companions as if he did not speak their language. "He can fight."

"Oh, there'll be fighting, don't doubt that." The speaker had been silent until now, nursing his right arm that hung in a hastily-made sling.

"There hasn't been much use for artillery," Paul protested unconsciously touching the black braid ng his dark blue sleeve. "Three months ago we were blasting them to bits."

"We're low on ammunition," the oldest of the men reminded him, adding, "We're low on everything else."

"Supply has said as soon as we have an established line, then . . ." The man with his arm in a sling did not continue as the other seven stared at him.

"When do we move out?" one of the others asked. All of them avoided looking at the far end of the trench.

"No word yet," the oldest said. "No word on anything."

It was impossible to be comfortable in the trench. It was clammy, crumbling, and vile, more like an open sewer than a defense. The men did not touch the earthen walls unless they absolutely had to, and it was not the mud that revolted them.

"It's like standing in a grave," the man with the sling said a bit later, voicing the opinion of the rest. An uneasy silence fell over the men.

"Does anyone know what happened to Colonel Stark?" one of the men asked impartially of the others.

"He died," the oldest said. "Yesterday afternoon sometime."

"He was a good man," the man with his hand in the sling said, which was all the eulogy anyone could give him. "Do you know who's going to replace him?"

"No," the oldest answered. "They've sent word to his family. He has . . . had a wife and three children. Both his brothers were killed last year."

"Julius, that can be said of half the men in this brigade," the man with his arm in a sling pointed out.

"That makes it no better, Edmund," Julius Quelle shot back.

"No," Edmund Falls said quietly, looking covertly at the other men. There was no one here who had not lost a brother, father, cousin, or friend to the war.

Again no one spoke. In the distance there was the snap of rifle fire and all eight men turned automatically to listen, each tense as they waited, then drooping with relief when it was certain that the shots were distant.

"They haven't brought up the big guns yet," the tallest man remarked for what little comfort they could take from that.

"They won't have the chance, not if we move tonight," Julius said.

Paul was least pleased, and he flushed. "We should fight," he demanded.

"Don't be a fool," the tallest man, Lukas, admonished him. "You want to prove your bravery? Hunt a wild boar unarmed. It's safer than this is."

The flush deepened but Paul did not challenge the other soldier. Soon his restlessness got the best of him again. He nudged the man beside him. "What's wrong with Wildenloch?" he asked, pointing to one of their number who stood a little apart from the rest.

"His Lisa died a week ago, from the influenza. He only learned of it today." It was plain that none of the others wanted to discuss Gilbert Wildenloch's grief, but Paul could not contain himself.

"Influenza! Here we are," he went on rather loudly, "being killed by the thousands for the protection of our loved ones, and at home they are dying from this influenza. It's all wrong, Christian," he insisted to the man beside him.

"Naturally," Christian murmured, then turned to Edmund Falls. "When you were getting your arm dressed, did they tell you when we were going to be fed? Did you talk to Mantel?"

He shook his head. "No. Mantel wasn't around. Since Colonel Stark died . . . I was only told that we would be given rations sometime today."

Christian scoffed and clapped his mud-crusted hands together. "They said that yesterday and all I got was a crust of bread and watery soup that hadn't seen meat for a week. They promised pork but we never got any."

"Well," Arnold said, trying to be philosophical, "it's not as if we're being singled out. All the rest of the battalion has the same problem. The officers say they're helpless."

"What they mean," Gilbert Wildenloch put in, "is that they do not want to be held accountable. Colonel Stark did his best for us, but there are incompetents in charge."

"Now, wait," Paul objected. "You don't know what they're up against at headquarters. With the situation changing every hour, they're being kept very busy. We're not the only men in the field. I heard that there's a critical shortage of wagons and horses, and that means moving any distance at all—"

"Stop it," Julius told them flatly. "It doesn't matter one way or the other. We're here, there's no food and no ammunition, so whether the officers understand the situation, it makes no difference to us."

Gilbert and Paul both choked on retorts. They had gone too far, but neither knew how to take back his words.

"Did you get a chance to find out about the new officers?" Arnold asked Edmund, in a deliberate effort to keep Paul from bickering with another one of them.

"No. There are supposed to be two new Majors, but I wasn't told who. The first-aid station was too busy for idle chatter." His dark eyes were sunken in his face, and the injection he had been given for pain was fading. He hoped he would not have to fight until he had been given another injection. In his current condition he doubted he could aim at anything smaller than a château.

"Who might we talk to? I don't like not knowing the officers," Julius said. "We had that happen at the beginning, and it was deadly for us."

His words stilled the questions the others were going to ask. Each man retreated into his own thoughts.

A large shell exploded some little distance away and for several minutes the faint mists were lurid as they caught the light of burning, but the fire died quickly and there were no more shells.

"They're as low on ammunition as we are," Christian remarked without expecting an answer.

"Then we should attack now," Paul insisted at once.

"With what?" Edmund stared at the young man until the blue eyes slid away from his.

Arnold pulled out a pocketknife and began to whittle at a

piece of root he had found. Christian let his head drop forward in the vain hope that he might be able to rest for a bit.

Ten minutes later there came another short volley of rifle fire, nearer but not close enough to cause any concern. The eighth man, who had a long, fresh scar on his face, gripped convulsively at his rifle, then with a visible effort relaxed his hold on the weapon.

"It's going to be a long day, I think," Arnold said with the appearance of unconcern.

Not far away there came the sound of horses; they were moving at a steady trot, and for that reason the eight men straightened up and looked toward the sound. Most of the horses available could hardly walk. Sound animals meant some-one of importance.

A Lieutenant none of the men could remember seeing before approached on a well-bred mare. He stopped near the edge of the trench and leaned over. "Artillery?"

Paul held up his sleeve, which was the cleanest of any of the men's. "Artillery."

"Under Colonel Stark?" It was an unnecessary question, for all the units along this stretch of trenches were under the late Colonel Ferdinand Stark.

"Of course." Julius had given the Lieutenant a lackadaisical salute and without being actually insubordinate, made it ap-parent that he was not impressed with the Lieutenant. He and his companions sagged.

"I'm bringing you a new officer. He's with me. Stand to attention, you men." This announcement brought the men in the trench to their feet, at which the Lieutenant's mouth twitched.

"New officer," Arnold said softly as he reached over to prod Christian. "Stand up."

"Very well." Christian grumbled, and pulled at his tunic in a futile effort to look a bit more presentable.

"Soldiers," the Lieutenant announced, "this is Major Hel-mut Rauch. Stand to attention."

There was a firm tread, and a figure, colossal to the men in the trench, loomed over them. His uniform, if not immaculate, was clean, his boots had been recently polished and his face was free of stubble. He returned the salute of his men. "Name and rank," he ordered at once.

"Private Paul Reinald," he said, proud to be the first.

"Private Christian Zuflucht."

"Corporal Gilbert Wildenloch."

"Private Bernhard Ulmedach."

"Private Arnold Teichfrost."

"Private Lukas Jetzt."

"Corporal Julius Quelle."

"Corporal Edmund Falls. The two men there"—he pointed to the corpses at the far end of the trench—"are Privates Wilhelm Fuchspfote and Udolph König. Their names haven't been recorded yet."

"Lieutenant," Major Rauch snapped, "make a note of those names. And see that their families are notified." He did not bother to look to see if the Lieutenant had done as ordered, for there was not a doubt in his mind that he would be obeyed. "I don't suppose I have to tell you that there is going to be another retreat." He spat the words out, his brow darkening.

"We've been told very little, sir," Edmund said respectfully.

"That's what I've heard all up and down the line." He frowned. "Why haven't you extended the trench any farther? You're supposed to join up with Sergeant Klinge's unit—"

"I realize that, sir," Edmund interrupted, meeting Rauch's hard stare evenly. "We discovered we were digging through bodies. A great many of them. Colonel Stark ordered us to stop, and then he was killed."

Major Rauch rubbed at his lower lip thoughtfully. "Colonel Stark left no mention of it. Well." He shrugged impatiently. "Continue the digging. We'll be moving by tomorrow, but there's no reason why we should not conduct ourselves as soldiers. If any of the bodies are our men save what you can of them."

"I beg your pardon, sir," Julius Quelle said, "but there's almost nothing left of the uniforms."

"In that case," Helmut Rauch said more decisively, "do what you must. This is not a time to be squeamish. And be prepared to evacuate this position on twenty minutes' notice." He brought up his hand sharply and scowled at the slowness of the men's response. As he turned away from the trench, he made an impatient gesture. "Lieutenant Bischof, so far all the men I have seen have been ill-fed, ill-equipped, and ill-mannered."

"Yes, sir," the Lieutenant said, not sure how to respond to this criticism.

"How does that come about?" He had reached the side of his chestnut Beberbeck, and was making a routine check of the girth as he asked.

"Sir, it's that way everywhere. It's not just the retreat, it's all of it. There's not enough food, or ammunition, or medicine, or petrol, or . . . any of the rest of it. There's not enough soap to wash, and no strops for the razors . . ." He opened his hands before taking the reins of his big Schleswig mare's bridle.

Major Rauch had swung into the saddle. "It's inexcusable," he declared. "Someone is responsible for this debacle, and I intend to find out who it is. We should be winning this war, Lieutenant Bischof, and we're not." He clapped his heels to the Beberbeck's sides and they started off again in the direction of Sergeant Klinge's unit.

"But, Major Rauch," the Lieutenant protested as he followed the man, "without food or ammunition, how can we fight? How can we win?"

"The French haven't food or ammunition, and the English have lost most of their officers. They're in worse condition than we are." He looked down with distaste at the shattered remains of a laden wagon. It had been drawn by two mules, and three men had been on it. "Isn't there time to bury these unfortunates?"

"No," Lieutenant Bischof said with real bitterness. "No, Major Rauch, there isn't. And if there were, there is no place to bury them. This whole area is thick with bodies. If you dig down any way at all, you'll find them."

Major Rauch clicked his tongue in disapproval, but put the matter aside as Lieutenant Bischof brought him up to the next section of trench where Sergeant Klinge's men huddled between the damp, fetid walls.

At the end of his inspection, Major Helmut Rauch was thoroughly disgusted. The troops, as he told Lieutenant Bischof at length, were in lamentable condition, the morale was inexcusable, and the preparedness of the Army was disgraceful. His harangue took up the better part of half an hour as he returned to the temporary headquarters for this zone.

"I intend to make a full report, Lieutenant, and it will not be the sort of pleasant nothings that they are used to hearing in Berlin. When I read the report of General Groener, I thought he was exaggerating, but I am beginning to think that he was understating the case."

Lieutenant Bischof had heard rumors about General Groener's report, but had not read it, being too junior an officer to have access to it. "He was upset at the industrialists, wasn't he, sir? He accused them of making extreme profits . . ."

"Oh, indeed he did. The War Office found one instance of a

private company turning a profit of more than thirty million.
And that was not the only instance. That's what comes of
letting foreign businessmen into our . . ." He drew up as they
reached the tent of Lieutenant Colonel Gotthard Aufenthalt.
Major Rauch was a little less meticulous than he had been
when he set out that morning, and it irked him to have to
report to his commanding officer in less than parade-ground
perfection. He tossed the reins to Lieutenant Bischof, saying,
"See that he's fed and watered. I brought along a supply of
oats, which are in my tent."

Lieutenant Bischof stared after Major Rauch, the amiable
expression he had managed to keep on his face so far that day
faded to one of fatigue and impotence. The last thing the men
needed now was a martinet, but from the look of it, that was
what they would have. He nudged his mare to a walk, leading
the Beberbeck toward Major Rauch's tent. He put all thoughts
of Major Helmut Rauch out of his mind for the moment, and
instead concentrated on the very real problem of getting something to eat.

Lieutenant Colonel Gotthard Aufenthalt was reading through
a number of dispatches, and shaking his head. He was not a
young man, and the war had aged him cruelly. His hair was
white; his light blue eyes, once described as dreamy were now
haunted and seemed to be hiding in the fretwork of lines that
surrounded them. He was quite tall and wire-lean. He returned Major Rauch's salute in an abstracted way and motioned the younger man to be seated.

"I would prefer to stand," Major Rauch declared.

Lieutenant Colonel Aufenthalt sighed. "We're not conduct-
ing an exercise here, Major. You will find that it is wise to
take rests when they are offered to you. Sit down." He was no
longer looking at Rauch, but at a casualty list that sickened
him. "Heilige Engel, will it never end?"

"Sir!" This single word was as much of a reprimand as
Major Rauch dared to give his superior. He cleared his throat.
"I have made the inspection you requested, Lieutenant Colo-
nel, and I wish to report my findings to you."

"Must you say it aloud, Major? I will accept it in writing."
Aufenthalt was exhausted, and the prospect of whatever complaints this stiff-backed young officer had to make—and he
must surely have complaints, if his overly-correct posture was
any indication—would be an additional burden he did not want
to shoulder.

"I think it best be kept between the two of us, Sir." Major

Rauch turned his hard brown eyes on the Lieutenant Colonel with earnest zeal. "There is a great deal to be done, and little time to do it."

"I'm aware of that, Major," Aufenthalt said in an attempt to forestall him. "That is why I cannot give you my full attention just now."

"But you must," Major Rauch insisted. "Sir, this whole line is intolerable. I have to tell, as shamed as I am to say it, that I believe our forces here are close to surrender."

Whatever reaction Helmut Rauch expected, he did not get it. Lieutenant Colonel Aufenthalt nodded slowly. "I'm not surprised. That they've held out this long is a miracle. If we had fresh troops, that would be different, but these men have been in the trenches, some of them, for two and three years. *Two and three years, Major!*" He brought his hand down on the tabletop for emphasis. "Do you know what they've gone through? You think today was distressing, do you? You should see it when it's raining, when the mud of the road comes up to your knees and men who fall from exhaustion suffocate in the mud and sink without a trace. Today is pleasant. There is some sunshine, but it isn't so hot that the smell is overpowering. These trenches are the worst of the charnel house and the latrine, Major. Now, what is it you want to tell me?" There was a little color in his face, and his voice had risen. His hands were trembling, and it took him a little time to master himself sufficiently to speak in a calm, reasonable tone. "I can understand why you are . . . disappointed, Major Rauch. You would like to think that Deutschland has men who are unstoppable, or who lose with grace and honor. Instead, you see these poor wretches living where you would not kennel a rabid dog." He wiped a hand over his face. "It has been a very long day, Major. I did not sleep last night, I have not eaten since noon yesterday. It is still four hours until sunset and there is much to do. Now, if you have anything that you feel cannot wait, I will listen."

Major Rauch had stood unflinching through the Lieutenant Colonel's outburst, his face set in a stoic mask. "If the Lieutenant Colonel will forgive me, there are a few matters that should be discussed now."

Aufenthalt let out a long, whistling breath. "Very well, Major. What is it that can't wait?"

"First, Sir, if you will pardon me for speaking of it, your own attitude is deplorable. How can you expect these men to rally and stop the Allied advance if you do nothing but bemoan their fate? You should exhort them to turn defeat into victory. Then, the men should be set to work when they are not actually fighting. Some of the problems of morale come from idleness. If they were set to repairing wagons and reinforcing gun installations, then they would believe they stood a chance to win. And with sufficient preparation, we might turn this appalling retreat into a successful assault. It would also be wise to set some of these men to foraging, since the food supplies appear to be dreadfully low."

"I see." Lieutenant Colonel Aufenthalt tapped the table with the edge of the casualty report. "First, I have not set the men to work because they haven't the strength for it. They're hungry, Major, and tired. Most of them will have to be on the march before another day goes by, and I don't want to lose any more of them than I must. There's little point in building up emplacements that will simply have to be abandoned, and that would leave necessary supplies behind for the Allied forces to use themselves. As for foraging, I believe that every acre of ground between here and Saint Quentin has been picked clean. These men are more desperate than goats, Major Rauch. They would eat hemlock if we allowed it, only to have something inside them." He pushed his chair back and was about to rise when he caught sight of another figure in the door.

"Lieutenant Colonel Aufenthalt," said the newcomer with a crisp salute, "I am Captain Aaron von Rathenau." He held out his orders to Aufenthalt.

"Captain von Rathenau," Lieutenant Colonel Aufenthalt said, his gelid eyes warming slightly, "it is an honor." He took the orders and glanced over them. "I see that you were supposed to report to Colonel Stark, but I imagine you have heard that he is dead."

"Yes, Sir," Captain von Rathenau said quietly. He was shorter than the other two men, with tanned skin and dark hair. His eyes were olive-green and intelligent. Without doubt he had left his university studies for the war, for he could not have been more than twenty-one.

"And for the moment you must report to me," Aufenthalt said. "We're not doing too well here in artillery, but there are still a number of options left to us . . ."

Major Rauch had been studying Captain von Rathenau in silence, his expression gradually becoming more contemptuous. Now he interrupted the Lieutenant Colonel again. "Von

Rathenau. Are you related to Walther von Rathenau of Allgemeine Elektrizitaetsgesellschaft?"

"And the War Ministry, yes," the Captain said immediately. "He is my uncle."

Puzzled by the Major's behavior, Lieutenant Colonel Aufenthalt tried to smooth the awkward moment over. "A fine family. They've done a great deal for Deutschland. You must be proud to know—"

"They are traitors!" Major Rauch burst out. "They're the ones who have lost this war for us, if it is lost. They're devouring our country whole! Bureau Haber, all of them have been working for our destruction!" His complexion had darkened and his voice rose to an overwhelming shout.

At first Captain von Rathenau had stood, baffled, at this outburst, but as the accusations continued, he drew himself up very straight.

"Major . . ."—he realized he did not know his antagonist's name—"Major, you have no reason to speak so. My family has given its money, its children, its facilities to Deutschland. If not for my uncle, there would have been no chance at all to win this war—"

"You're subtle, Captain, and a liar!" Major Rauch drew back his arm to strike the Captain, but Lieutenant Colonel Aufenthalt lunged across the table at iam, knocking his arm aside. His face was pale with fury.

"Now then, Major Rauch! You will account for this to me and to Captain von Rathenau at once or tell me why you should not face Court-Martial in the morning." There was a quiver in his cheek, and he spoke softly, as if he did not dare give vent to his feelings.

"Account!" Major Rauch got to his feet and spat. "Damned Jewish swine!" He faced Captain von Rathenau. "You're sly, you Jews. But there are a few of us left who are not blind. You say that you've given so much to Deutschland, but you're only exacting profits in the guise of patriotism." He started to turn away, but with insulting courtesy saluted Lieutenant Colonel Aufenthalt, then strode out of the tent.

Lieutenant Colonel Aufenthalt stared after the Major as he straightened up. "Captain, I extend my apology for . . . that."

Aaron von Rathenau was breathing more quickly than usual and his hands were tight at his sides. "You did nothing, Lieutenant Colonel. It was Major . . . Rauch, is it?"

"Major Helmut Rauch," Aufenthalt supplied. "I had no idea

he would . . ." He gestured his confusion as he once more took his seat.

"He is not the only one who feels that way," von Rathenau said with undisguised anger. "It is popular in certain circles to blame the Jews for what is happening. That way none of them need feel tainted by failure." He stared at the Lieutenant Colonel. "We're going to lose. We all know it, but no one wants to say so. The Kaiser does not want to believe it, and therefore we all pretend that it isn't so. The Kaiser will not admit it, and those who do not agree are well-advised to be silent. You might have me Court-Martialed for what I have just said, Lieutenant Colonel Aufenthalt." He studied the white-haired officer in front of him.

"I wish it were over," Aufenthalt whispered. "I wish it would stop." He met von Rathenau's eyes. "And that could get *me* Court-Martialed, Captain."

Von Rathenau permitted himself a tentative smile. "I am grateful, Lieutenant Colonel. To be honest with you, I have had such encounters before, but none of them here."

"Yes." Aufenthalt leaned back in his chair. "It's difficult to know what to do with him." He saw the ire kindle in Aaron von Rathenau's eyes again. "I share your sentiments, Captain, although you may not credit it. But as you yourself have said, he is not alone in his opinion, and if this were to be brought out now, there would be many who would take his part. That would mean more disruption than we have already endured. We are retreating, Captain, and are losing men in the most irresponsible fashion. To bring Major Rauch's outburst to the attention of the men would cause a greater disunity . . ." He picked up the pile of dispatches. "He need not get off entirely. I must send in a report in any case, and I will explain in detail what occurred here this afternoon."

"Will you recommend that any action be taken against him?" There was a dangerous politeness in the young officer's attitude.

"Yes. When the worst of this is over. First I must get as many of my men as I can home. Then I will appeal to the General Staff for action. Will that satisfy you, Captain, or must you have vengeance now?" He favored von Rathenau with a long, even stare.

With an unpleasant grimace, Captain von Rathenau shrugged. "The men must come first. I won't oppose you for that."

There was a sudden rush of air, and then a nearby explosion buffeted the tent. There were shouts at once, and screams of the wounded. Both men hesitated a moment.

"By the time this is over," the Lieutenant Colonel said carefully, "there may not be any need for action. Not every man here will survive these next few months."

"Truly," von Rathenau said quietly.

Another shell exploded, a bit farther away.

"I must see to the damage," Lieutenant Colonel Aufenthalt said as he got unsteadily to his feet. "This is a rearguard action, Captain, and that imposes certain truths on all of us. The English and the Americans are determined, the French are fanatical, and there are not many of us left with the heart to fight. Major Rauch has the will to continue the battle, and for that reason I need him."

"Yes," Captain von Rathenau said, standing aside to allow the other officer to pass him.

When Lieutenant Colonel Aufenthalt was gone, Aaron von Rathenau stood for a minute or two by himself in the tent. Although he had managed to conceal it well, resentment smoldered in him as hot and deadly as the Allied shell that had fallen. His uncle had warned him, and Aaron had promised him that he would not give vent to his indignation. It had been an easy assurance to give, but he was discovering that it would be difficult to honor his word.

"Captain von Rathenau!" came the cry from outside. "We need an officer with Sergeant Klinge's unit. There's no one there."

"At once!" von Rathenau answered, saluting the Lieutenant Colonel's voice though he could not see the man through the smoke. "Where are they?" he shouted as he came out of the tent.

"To the south. Ask for Sergeant Klinge or Corporal Falls!" The Lieutenant Colonel's voice was lost in a third explosion.

Captain Aaron von Rathenau put Major Helmut Rauch out of his mind and gave his thoughts to the grim business at hand. Before he reached the men Aufenthalt had identified, there were three more shells dropped on the Deutscher Artillery Company; by the time the barrage was over, another one hundred sixteen dead men lay broken in the trenches.

Text of a letter from Irina Andreivna Ohchenov to her uncle Pavel Ilyevich Yamohgo.

Rotterdam
September 20, 1918

My dear Uncle Pavel;

I was saddened to learn of your failing health, and of course I will not impose upon your hospitality at such a time. You have said that your nurses take excellent care of you and that you do not have space or resources to deal with a niece.

You inquired after Kiril and his family. I am sorry to have to bring you new sorrow, but Tania, Kiril's wife, died two weeks ago of the terrible influenza which is so prevalent now. Olga, their daughter, died in July. Sasha has recovered, but the physician has warned Kiril that there may still be difficulties. It has been a most trying time here. Kiril has been out of his senses with grief, and I, with so much loss behind me, do not know how to comfort him. I have prayed with him and read Scriptures, but there is no consolation for either of us. You will forgive my blasphemy when I say that if there is a God who hears our prayers, then He must be a cruel and capricious child, for there is no succor for any of us. If He is the merciful Father we have been told, then He must have become senile over the years, for we are cast down and without hope in this strange country.

Because of the great costs we have sustained, I have sold my pearl necklace and the diamond bracelets. It leaves me very little for my support when I reach Paris, as it is still my intention to come there. I am not asking you for any assistance, but the recommendation of a part of the city where I may live cheaply but not in squalor. I am still at a loss to know what to do, but in time necessity will force me to find a means for making my living.

It is everywhere rumored that the war is all but ended. I hope that this is so, since there has been so much suffering and privation. If the Kaiser is willing to accept defeat, I hope that the Allies will not insist on the utter ruin of Germany as part of their terms. There has been bitterness and bloodshed enough. After such a costly war, no one would be so callous as to insist on greater degradation. No doubt France has been the greater victim in this war, but if clemency prevails, then the wounds will heal. You told me that you believe that the honor of France will require a great deal of Germany, and you are probably correct in this assumption, but if you are, then what chance is there of any trust between nations, ever?

You also informed me that you have had no word out of Russia, and so I must conclude that those who have not escaped are trapped there, in prison or in graves. It is another blow to me to hear this, and I had come to think the blows I have already taken had numbed me. It is not entirely so.

There is a nursing order of nuns near me, and they have entreated me to aid them in caring for those struck down by the influenza. I have so far spent five hours out of every day for the last ten days working beside them in their hospital. My Uncle, it would break your heart to see what transpires there. Little lives are extinguished as easily as one might blow out a lamp. The young and the old are the greatest part of the victims. There is so little that can be done for them, but what is possible, we do. It is not uplifting work, or enriching in any way, but it must be done, and I have found that at the moment I am capable of dealing with death all around me because it seems now to be the state of my life.

When I reach Paris I will inform you of my address. I hope that this terrible influenza does not strike you, Uncle Pavel, for since you tell me your health is frail, I have no doubt but that you would be in great danger from it.

Your niece,
Irina Andreivna Ohchenov

# 9

As James Emmerson Tree turned his borrowed Rolland-Pilain in through the stone gates, he was startled to see a young woman on a long-legged, feisty sorrel mare come up beside him. He brought his gloved hand across his goggles to be certain his vision was clear.

The woman on the horse waved and pointed ahead up the curving slope of the graveled road. She shouted something that James did not hear clearly, then let the mare bound on ahead of the car. Pleasantly baffled, James double-clutched down to second gear and followed her.

The drive wound pleasantly through an avenue of Italian pines, then opened onto a crescent drive before an old stone château built on the edge of the slope. It was well-kept, unlike some of the ancient buildings James had seen in his travels. The tall, narrow windows were glazed with care, keeping the original fittings where possible. At the northern end of the château was a more recent addition, from the time of Louis XIV or XV; a curved wall of windows overlooking a stepped terrace which led to a small ornamental wood fronted by a shining artificial lake with a splendid little island in the center of it.

There was no response from the house yet, which was mildly puzzling, as all the other displaced landowners James had met had kept themselves guarded, protected, and barricaded. He had been received with suspicion and occasionally open hostility by those he had visited previously. He remembered what Madame de Montalia had told him, and thought that she might have already embarked for her archeological site, but that must be impossible. He looked around swiftly and saw the sorrel mare at the far end of the drive. At least there was someone here, he told himself, and so the long journey had not been made in vain. A glimmer of hope returned to him: the young rider might well be another displaced landowner, or part of a family that had been caught up in the chaos of the war. James made himself smile as he got out of the Rolland-Pilain.

The young equestrienne was walking toward him, the skirts of her Wedgwood-blue habit looped carelessly over her left arm. She waved as she approached, the corners of her mouth lifting as she smiled. James had been shown a portrait of the young Maria Louisa of Parma at one of the houses he had visited, and it struck him that this young woman had much the same look to her, though her coloring was different. Her hair, coming loose from a severe knot at the back of her neck, was the color of strong coffee, with yellow glints where the sun struck it. Her eyes, James saw as she came up to him, were a remarkable shade of violet.

"Bonjour, Monsieur Tree," she said as she held out her hand to him. "Welcome to Montalia." Her English was softened by her French accent but had none of the hesitancy of one inexpert in the language.

On impulse, James bowed over her hand, kissing it with more enthusiasm than elegance, saying with a kind of schoolbook precision, "Vous êtes bien aimable a un étranger."

"But you are no stranger, Mister Tree," she protested cordially. "I've expected you for the last two days. I trust you were not too much inconvenienced on the road?" Her lovely eyes danced as she pulled her hand from his.

Belatedly James remembered the expression in Phillippe Timbres's eyes when he had talked about Madelaine de Montalia. His assumption that this woman was a guest of the château changed and he felt oddly embarrassed. "You are . . ."

"Madelaine de Montalia. I thought you had guessed that. If you intend to kiss the hands of my servants, Mr. Tree, you will cause an uproar in the house." She was unflustered, poised without arrogance. "Although I know it is often dull here, I would prefer that the place be livened up in a more conventional manner. That is the phrase isn't it? Livened up?"

"It's certainly one of them," James said, making a desperate attempt not to be captivated by this woman. He had expected one of those formidable French ladies, perhaps in her thirties, with that mixture of pragmatism and sensuality that he had seen before. Nothing had prepared him for this glowing creature. Timbres, he recalled, had said he was half in love with this woman. James had assumed that Phillippe Timbres had succumbed to the practiced seductiveness that was typical of wellborn women, but now, when it was too late, he realized his error. If Timbres had been half as captivated as he was . . .

Madelaine linked her arm through James', smiling up at him quickly, mercurially. "I had expected an older man. Most of the foreign journalists are not so very young, are they? Isn't it unusual for a man your age to be on such an assignment?"

James was at once flattered and irritated by her question. "Well, this isn't a job for kids, but I'm twenty-five, Madame de Montalia, and I'd guess you're younger than that."

A faint, saddened amusement lurked at the back of her eyes. "But appearances can be deceiving. Any capable journalist knows that." She had reached the iron-ribbed oak door, and rapped on it once. "Come in, Mr. Tree. Doubtless you would like the opportunity to wash and relax after your long drive."

James suddenly became conscious of the dustiness of the long canvas coat he wore. His visored cap was gritty around the headband, and he was certain his entire face was coated with grime. "Yes, thank you. I would be most grateful . . ."

"Fine." She motioned to the middle-aged man who held the door and who James decided was the butler. "Claude, this is Monsieur Tree, the journalist from America," Madelaine explained. "Have Guillaume or Herriot see to his automobile and bring his bags to his suite of rooms."

"At once, Madame," Claude said, closing the door and bowing before going down one of the three cavernous corridors that opened onto the entry hall.

Madelaine indicated the hallway on their right. "Come. I'll show you how to get to your rooms. This place was designed to baffle invaders; I don't know if it succeeded, but if my guests are to be used as the standard, the ruse was a triumph." She walked quickly with a long, clean stride, almost boyish. She was, James saw, not very tall, probably not more than five-foot-one or -two, but with the kind of lavish body that tantalized him. He could tell that she was not tightly corseted: she moved too lightly and swiftly for that. There was none of that suffocating femininity about her, no vapid conversation or stifled expression, no exaggerated modesty, no hothouse-flower manners. She turned to the left, saying, "These are the stairs you must take," and started up them at once, pointing out as she went the two long swords on the wall. "One of those my father carried. The other is more ancient and goes back to the time of the English Henry V."

"Your father carried that sword?" It was not new-looking, and from the design, was at least one hundred fifty years old. He mentioned this to her.

"Closer to two hundred. It was his favorite." She continued on up the stairs, and when they reached the narrow gallery, she pointed to the right. "This way. As you see, there are six doors along the corridor. Your parlor is the second door on the right. I've had the place fitted out, so you will find a water closet just across the hall, that door with the glass knob instead of gold handles, and although we do not have electricity yet, there is gas-light in all the rooms, so you won't be forced to stumble around in the dark with only a candle for illumination." She had walked to the door and opened it. "I think you will find towels and soap set out for you if you wish to bathe. There are robes in the bathroom closet."

Dazed by the attractiveness of his hostess and astonished by her courtesy, James was able to mumble a few words before ducking into his room. The parlor was small but gorgeous. There were a short sofa and two chairs facing the little fireplace. All were upholstered in sculptured velvet. An Oriental carpet covered a good portion of the floor, and where it did not reach, there were small, handmade Spanish rugs. A gilt-trimmed walnut secretaire stood against the wall, the high-backed chair in front of it cushioned with brocaded pillows. James whistled slowly. He went and peered into the bedroom.

The windows were covered by full-length draperies of heavy rust satin. The bed—unusually large—was covered with a spread of Italian bargello-work. And armoire of carved ash stood against one wall, and a much more modern dressing table in the Art Nouveau style was opposite it. James stepped into the bedroom, wondering idly if there had been a mistake. The carpet underfoot had been woven in Denmark more than eighty years ago, for the state visit of the heir to the Spanish throne.

There was a knock at the parlor door, and James hastened to open it. A servant stood waiting with James' two suitcases in his hands. "We've put your automobile in the shed, next to Madame's," he said as he brought the luggage into the parlor. "Is there anything you'll require from me just now?"

"Um . . . No, I don't think so." James still was not certain whether or not he was expected to tip the servants, and so he motioned for the bags to be put down, and then said, "I'm not sure of the customs here, and I'm so afraid I might inadvertently offend one of you or Madame. If you will tell me . . ."

The servant gave him a knowing smile. "Yes, sir. It's not always easy to know what's expected. Here at Montalia, most of us are used to getting a doucement when a guest leaves, commensurate with the service we've extended, naturally. I'm

Herriot, by the way. I'll see to your automobile while you're here."

James nodded to the man. "I appreciate that. Thank you, Herriot."

"You're welcome, Monsieur Tree." He left the room quickly, and James heard his steps fade down the hall.

When he had finished unpacking, James decided on a bath. He crossed the hall and found everything to be as Madelaine had said it would be. The tub was long and deep, sitting on ball-and-claw gilded feet almost in the middle of the room. James drew himself a bath and settled back for a long soak.

He was dressed in fresh clothes an hour later, and decided to venture downstairs. He made one wrong turn, but at last found himself back in the entry hall. It was late afternoon now, and he was aware that somewhere in the château there was activity, but no one had found him. He was beginning to feel a little foolish when Madelaine emerged from one of the corridors, smiling.

She had also changed, and would have looked appropriate in the pages of *Bon Ton*. Her dress of lilac silk had a slightly raised waist and a patterned bodice not unlike some of the paintings by Klimpt. Around her shoulders she had draped a long cashmere shawl the color of bittersweet chocolate. "Ah, Monsieur Tree, I'm glad you've come down. You're quite elegant. I do like those new collars, don't you?"

James had bought his suit in London, his only real extravagance since leaving the United States. He had not worn it often, though of late it had been useful in his various dealings with the displaced landowners he had contacted. He had discovered that it was to his advantage to appear expensively groomed without being ostentatious. Until now he had not been gratified by the few compliments he had received. He looked down at his hostess and smiled. "Thank you, Madame de Montalia."

"Are all Americans so formal? I've been told that you're all too casual, but you conduct yourself as if you were at a ball." She indicated another of the halls. "This leads to the addition. I've had the salon des fenêtres set up for a buffet. I'm afraid we're in no position to offer multicourse meals here. However, my cook has done what she can and Nanette is a most ingenious woman. If you don't mind, I will keep you company and we will talk."

They had passed several small, oddly-shaped rooms, but at last the corridor widened, and then opened onto the most recently-built part of the château. The pink-and-copper light of sunset streamed in the long curve of windows. The mountains rising around the château were either fallen into darkest shadow or touched with unreal brightness. The room itself was alive with light, warm and luminous as the hearthside at home.

"Here," said Madelaine, leading James toward the early-nineteenth-century table which stood near the window. "Sit, and I will tell Herriot and Claude that we're ready."

James was at least a foot taller than she, rangy in a way she had been told was unique to the American West. Yet he felt malleable as wax to her, and did not protest as she pulled out a chair for him. He sat and waited while she went to a small door and gave her orders.

"Now then, Mr. Tree," she said, coming back to the table and taking the other chair. "You wish to talk with me. Behold me, at your disposal." She propped her elbows on the table and smiled at him. "You have a very strong chin, Mr. Tree."

This last comment threw him off guard completely. "Madame . . . I . . . That is to say . . ." Sternly he told himself that he could not let her affect him this way. "Madame de Montalia," he said with all the propriety he could muster, "you're kind to say such things to me, but I would much rather we discuss your situation here."

"Would you?" She said it too lightly for the question to be a challenge, but there was mirth in her lovely, intelligent face. "Very well, Mr. Tree, tell me what it is you wish to know."

James cleared his throat. "I told you in my letter that I'm doing a series of articles—"

She interrupted him impatiently. "Yes, I understood your letter. You were quite succinct. But as I indicated in my reply, and as you have doubtless observed for yourself, I am not much deprived here. In fact, there are advantages to being at Montalia. One of them, I must admit, is that I am not forced day after day to see the ravages inflicted on this poor country of mine." Her face had grown somber. "France has an unhappy history, Mr. Tree. Men have gone to battle in a glorious tide and returned in little more than a trickle. Think of the wretched men returning from Moscow with Napoleon. How many of them fell in those endless snows, wrapped in shrouds of ice! They followed that ridiculous Corsican in whatever direction he marched, and believed his promise of an exalted France. So the British and the Italians and the Egyptians and the Russians fed their soil with French bones." She had been staring at the far wall, an abstracted expression in her eyes, but came back to herself with a shake of the head. "It's not the best topic for conversation at a meal, is it? I had not intended . . ."

James laid one of his large hands over hers. "No, Madame. Don't apologize." His cognac-colored eyes met hers with an intensity he did not want to deny. "You may tell me whatever you want."

Madelaine gave a rueful shake to her head. "I doubt it, Mr. Tree, but I thank you for the gesture." Then she looked up as Claude came into the salon. "Very good. If you'll put the dishes out on the sideboard . . ."

"Of course, Madame," Claude said, and set the two silver-covered serving trays down as she had instructed him. "Monsieur Tree has a choice of squab and lamb. There are four vegetables to come, and a salad. Nanette regrets that she was not able to prepare the cream-of-spinach soup she had intended." As he spoke he removed the covers of the serving dishes and the room became redolent with the smell of the food. "If you will excuse me, I will fetch the vegetables."

"Do you dine like this every evening?" James asked, enjoying the luxury of the rich scents.

"Of course not. In fact, I have a . . . condition which limits my diet severely." She said it cheerfully enough, but with a finality which did not encourage him to pursue the matter. "As soon as Claude returns, take what you want of the dishes set out. Have as much or as little as you wish. My servants eat well, but we waste little here." She had sat back in her chair; one hand toyed with the fringe of her cashmere shawl.

Again James felt a moment's awkwardness. "I'm sorry," he said, wishing he had something more helpful or gallant to offer.

"I'm not. In my life I have found that most difficulties have . . . compensations." She nodded toward the little door. "Here's Claude with the vegetables. You must choose your supper, Mr. Tree." She watched him as he made his selections, and then indulged in the most trivial of dinner conversation while James had his meal.

By the time the serving dishes and plates, cups, and service had been removed, the salon des fenêtres was dark. A fire had been laid in the hearth, and Madelaine rose to set it alight. She knelt by the fireplace, and as the first fragile flames trembled on the dry wood, the gentle light showed her features to James so magically that he wished he could find the excuse to kneel next to her, to put his arm around her shoulder. He doubted he would have the audacity to do more than that, but for a moment, while she gave her attention to the fire, he imagined what it might be like to have her in his arms.

"Daydreaming, Mr. Tree?" she asked as she came back to the table.

James hoped that the room was not bright enough for her to see his face darken. "It's a little late for that."

"What an equivocal answer," she remarked. "Would you like to sit closer to the fire? Shall I light the bracket lamps?"

"As you wish," he said, rising from the table and taking a step or two toward the fire. "It might be nice to sit and talk."

"Then, please." She drew a Directoire couch nearer the hearth. "Here. It's not as substantial as the furniture in the other chambers, but you'll find it comfortable enough. The bolster is pleasant to lean upon. I fear you won't be able to stretch out on it—you'd overlap the ends."

Though he was not at all sure he wanted to, James took his seat on the couch and braced his elbow against one of the bolsters, discovering it was not as soft or as flimsy as he feared. When he was a bit more settled, he began, "You said this was home to you. Will you tell me a bit about Montalia, and yourself?"

Madelaine's smile was so vulnerable that James had to restrain his impulse to pull her into the shelter of his arms. "I was born here. This château has been in the family for a very long time. There are records in the muniment room that go back to the time this was little more than a fortified tower in the eleven hundreds. Montalia is a worn-down version of the original name: Montagne de Italia, from the days when the borders between the two countries were not as certain a thing as they are now. So, Montalia it became, and so did we. My own parents lived here a great deal of the time, although they were somewhat estranged after I went to be taught by the Sisters of Sainte Ursule. I went to Paris when I was nineteen, to be presented, you understand, by my aunt. My father came to attend my fête, and while he was in Paris, he died. My mother did not wish to come back here; she did not live much longer. So I am heir to Montalia."

James felt his heart go out to his hostess. To have such great responsibility put on her shoulders while she was still so young. "You said you were nineteen then. What are you now?"

"Older, Mr. Tree. A great deal older." She stared into the fire. "You bring back a great màny memories."

"You were at your other château when the war broke out?" He wanted a better sense of the order of events so that he could present them to his readers. At least, he tried to persuade himself that was the reason.

"Yes. Monbussy came into my hands a while ago. It's sad to hear it has been damaged. This war has blighted everything." She dropped to her knees on the ottoman cushion near the fireplace. "I am fortunate, Mr. Tree. I have this retreat of mine, but there are countless others not as lucky or as prosperous as I, and they suffer greatly. I gave a small holding of mine in Normandy over to a family who had been my neighbors, but that is nothing more than a gesture, a handful of sand taken from the beach." She leaned back and turned away from him.

"Without you the family would have been much worse off," James pointed out in a desire to mitigate her hurt.

"And without the war they would not have needed my aid at all." Madelaine brought her fist under her jaw, bracing her chin. "Do you know, Mr. Tree, I have lost count of the number of deaths I've been told of? There was a time, when I was first in Paris, when a . . . dear friend of mine pointed out to me that humankind preys upon itself far more than any other hazard of this world, except perhaps plague."

James was touched with grief. "A journalist I met, an older man named Vaughn Whitstowe, died of the influenza a few weeks ago. He had a cough, and then he grew weak, and then he was dead." He looked down at his hands. He ought not mention himself. That was not why he was here.

"A pity, but so many things are." The remark was intended to be cynical, or at least resigned, but it was neither. Madelaine stared at James, and felt his eyes on her. From her reclining posture, he appeared a great distance away. "Would you like to come nearer?"

"Madame . . ." He got off the couch and went to her as if blinded by the fire; he stood above her. "Madame . . ."

"My name," she said softly, "is Madelaine. Madelaine Roxanne Bertrane de Montalia." It had been a long time since she had given anyone her full name, but something in this American stirred her.

James' mouth was suddenly dry, his lips hot. "Madelaine." He liked the name. At that moment he almost adored her. He wanted to stretch out on the floor beside her, to hold her. The rest eluded him, for although he was not inexperienced, he had confined his adventures to women who made no demands of him but payment: he had never permitted himself to gratify any need but lust. "You're . . ."

"I'm alone, Mr. Tree. Most of those I have loved are dead. You . . . are kind, I think. Would it be so dreadful to kiss me?" She held out one arm to him.

He would have thrown himself upon her if she had not looked so full of courage. Slowly he knelt beside her, then bent over and touched his mouth to her cheek. He might have drawn back, but her hands met behind his neck. "Madelaine," he murmured, then put all his resolutions aside. Their lips met, tentatively at first, and then with esurience and a need he had not known he possessed until that moment. He bent over her, the silk of her dress, the cashmere of her shawl pressing the side of his face. All he had ever been told of women warned him that he would have his face slapped and hysterical tears to deal with in a moment, but he could not pull back from her. His arms enfolded her; he murmured, "God, sweet Jesus God," when there was space enough between their lips for him to draw breath.

Madelaine gave herself over to his kisses, accepting them as if they were rain after drought. She let her shawl drop from her shoulders, taking warmth instead from James' nearness. As his hands plucked at the square neck of her gown, she sighed, then uttered a cry of disappointment as he moved back from her.

"I don't think . . ." James said unsteadily, "that I can keep from . . . I'm going to want more of you if this goes on." He looked at her as if she were all that was left in the world, and he was breathing more deeply. "You may not know . . ."

"But I want more of you," Madelaine said, catching one of his hands in her own. "You seem to think I am unaware of what you desire. I'm not." She rolled onto her side, and was close to him again. "If you doubt it . . ." She rose suddenly and pressed her opened lips on his.

"There are servants," he began uneasily.

"I am mistress here." Madelaine looked deeply into his eyes. "I do not want to pass this night alone, Mr. Tree."

"I don't want to, either," James whispered, hoping that he had not misunderstood her. "Madelaine, if we lie together . . . Oh, hell!" He no longer wanted to use evasive terms. "I want to make love to you, to . . . to . . ."

"I know what you want," she said with sympathy. "It is what I want, as well."

James rose to his feet and reached down to help Madelaine to her feet. He pulled her tightly against him, as if she were the most ephemeral fire and he was not able to contain her with his body alone. He could not say her name, for fear it would end the closeness between them.

It was Madelaine who withdrew. "I will come to your rooms. No one will disturb us." She moved back from him, thinking that she had only once experienced an intimacy more profound than this one. Her eyes saddened, but in the dim light James did not notice. Madelaine bent to gather up her shawl. "I will not be long," she promised, then went quickly from the salon des fenêtres.

James did not know how he found his room that night. He had little recollection of climbing the stairs or counting the doors. He was more than drunk, more than exhausted. He tugged himself out of his clothes and stuffed the lot of them into the armoire, then flung himself onto his bed. What if she did not come, after all? The thought went through him like a shard of ice. What if she decided that she had been too hasty and kept to her room? He did not know where it was, so he could not go in search of her. The very thought made him dizzy, and he stumbled to his feet. He would not believe that of her. He stared down at his swollen flesh and tried to imagine what it would be like to feel her hidden warmth around him. He pulled the blankets back almost violently, and got into bed. He would give her ten minutes, and then he would fend for himself. His watch was somewhere in his luggage, and he had not seen a clock in the room. Ten minutes would be worse than eternity. He decided to count to one thousand, convinced that would be time enough.

He had reached six hundred twenty-three when the door opened and Madelaine came into his bedroom.

She was dressed in a magnificent negligee, a cloud of pale lace and threaded ribbons. She stood for a moment staring at him. "Do you want to undress me?" she asked softly.

James was barely able to nod. He got out of bed again and approached her, deeply self-conscious. Twice before in his life he had slept with a woman when entirely naked, and neither had been the least like Madelaine de Montalia. He reached out and his fingers brushed the profusion of lace. A series of nine satin bows held the peignoir together, and he loosened each of them; the little tension of that act was unendurably pleasurable. When all the bows had been untied, he slid the garment off her shoulders so that it settled like a cloud at her feet. The nightgown itself was not so challenging: he gathered the paneled skirts and lifted them over her head, letting the nightgown drop as he stared at her. For him she glistened in the dark and he touched her as if he feared she would disappear.

"James," she said, so quietly that he could hardly hear her.

He took her in his arms, letting her presence blot out the night. They sank back on the bed, bodies pressed close together. He strove to recall every nuance of excitation he had learned from the women he had hired. Then it had been a sensible matter, a way to add variety and the illusion of intimacy to a necessary act; now it was the culmination of all he had yearned for, and he reveled in her.

Madelaine's ardor ignited with an intensity she had not known for a long time, and rose steadily as James grew more insistent. When at last he opened her flesh with his own, she welcomed him, her lips moving to his neck as he reached the culmination of his passion.

Later they would learn of one another: what they had together was revelation, beyond understanding, or thoughts, or words.

James' sleep was content when it came, his dreams rapturous, but never as superbly fulfilling as that ultimate instant of lovemaking when he had known to the depths of his soul what it was to be flesh of her flesh, blood of her blood.

Text of a letter from Lieutenant Colonel Gotthard Aufenthalt to Idelle von Rathenau.

*Koln*
*November 2, 1918*

*Gnädige Frau von Rathenau:*

*By now the Ministry of War will have informed you of your son's death, and told you of the honors he is to receive posthumously, which are richly deserved. You may take pride in having raised so valiant an officer and so honorable a son.*

*As Captain von Rathenau's immediate superior officer, I had the opportunity to see him in action. Never did he falter in his duty, or turn aside from the obligations he owed his men. I wish you to know this from my own hand, as I have heard a few derogatory remarks made of him, and should these fabrications reach your ears, they would add unnecessarily to your grief. Rest assured that had Deutschland had more such as he, we would not be facing the ignominious defeat that is now ours.*

*The unit to which Captain von Rathenau was attached was, as you probably know, an artillery unit, one of those left to guard part of the retreat at Saint-Quentin. Most of these units were cobbled together out of the odd bits of companies that had been decimated by enemy fire and the hazards of the trenches. Morale was desperately low, and few of the new officers had any conception of the enormous difficulties confronted by men fighting for their lives.*

*Your son was not this sort. He had an intuitive grasp of the obstacles to be overcome and accepted his task willingly. He did not exhort his men for laxness, but fired them with his own spirit and conviction, never misrepresenting to them the tremendous danger in which they all stood. He released two men from duty because they had*

135

*families and he would not expose them to greater risks than the ones they had already survived. Sergeant Klinge and Private Lukas Jetzt were relieved of duty and sent to the rear so that they might be reunited more quickly with their wives and children.*

*With fewer than twenty men, Captain von Rathenau made a stand, holding off the advancing Allied forces for more than twelve hours. In this act of sacrifice, he saved the lives of more than two thousand men who would otherwise have been caught in the crossfire. He was entirely aware of the magnitude of the danger in which he stood, but did not flinch from his task. One man, Corporal Edmund Falls, survived his stand, in part because he was already wounded and Captain von Rathenau informed me that Corporal Falls would be called to the guns only if no other choice were possible.*

*When our surrender comes (and it cannot be far distant), you may take pride and solace in the knowledge that your son spared many from the ravages of this too-costly war. No one could wish for a better officer, in this or any army.*

*Please accept my most sincere consolations in this terrible time. You have lost a treasured son, and I have lost a Captain whom I would have wished to call my friend for the rest of my life. As it was, you were blessed by his presence for many years, and I knew him less than two days. Were it a soldier's right to envy, I would be envious of you for this long association with Captain von Rathenau. Doubtless it was the example of your family and your values that made him the admirable officer he was.*

*I thank you for reading this; I hope that in some degree I have lessened your loss.*

*Dear Madame von Rathenau, believe me to be*

*Forever in your service,*
*Lieutenant Colonel Gotthard Aufenthalt*

# PART II

## Gudrun Maria Altbrunnen Ostneige

Text of a letter from Franchot Ragoczy, Count of Saint-Germain, to his manservant, Roger.

*Schliersee*
*Near Hausham*
*Bayern*
*December 10, 1918*

*My dear Roger,*

*As you can see, I have returned at last to Schloss Saint-Germain. It is in a shambles, but from what I have been told, none of the other houses in this area have fared any better. Apparently vandals made a sweep through this district sometime last spring, and whatever caught their fancy, they wrecked. I will need to begin repairs at once, although most of the work will not be possible until the snow is gone. There is enough shelter here to make life tolerable, but not elegant. I trust that funds are available through Zurich so I may place my orders at once and do what I can to improve the place.*

*I would appreciate it if you would leave for München as soon as possible. Travel should become easier now that the Great War has ended. If you encounter significant delays, notify me so that the proper alternatives may be provided at once.*

*For the time being, it is my intention to remain here. I have discussed a few of my projects with Professor Isidore Riemen, and he is willing to make some of his findings available to me in exchange for occasional use of my facilities and notes, once I have my laboratory rebuilt. I am hopeful that living in this remote area I will be left to myself so that I may continue my studies in as much peace as possible.*

*Perhaps I should mention that I have adopted a child, a girl of about seven whom I found abandoned. If she still has living relatives, there has been no indication of it, and from what I saw when I found her, I doubt that anyone will come forward to claim her. So at my age, I have become a father, of sorts. I rely on your past experience and good advice, old friend, to guide me through this. She is suffering from partial amnesia and often has nightmares. Let me ask you to be kind to Laisha Vlassevna, for her sake if not for mine.*

*When you have your travel plans made, wire the stationmaster at Hausham and I will have an automobile sent for you when you arrive. If you are bringing extensive supplies and material, warn me of that so that transportation may be arranged in advance. It is not wise to leave goods standing about unattended at this time.*

*It has been too long: I have missed you. There is no way that I can thank you enough for the services you have rendered me in these difficult years, but if you wish anything of me, you have only to name it and it is yours.*

> Saint-Germain
> his seal, the eclipse

# 1

Outside it was snowing; inside the house smelled of mildew and drying paint. Gudrun sat in the library, an open book turned over on her lap, and stared out into the snow. Half an hour ago Walther had stepped into the room to tell her that Jürgen was at last calm again, and would probably sleep until the next morning. Gudrun sighed. It had been so delightful to be married, three years ago. Jürgen was whole and hearty, they lived in München, and despite the trying necessities of war, it had been a pleasant life. She reminded herself sternly that she was the one who had decided to come here to this remote place in the mountains. She had always liked Wolkighügel, but that had been when she was younger, when the Schloss had been filled with guests and cousins and bustling servants, so that no one ever felt alone. Now it was as isolated as a rock in mid-ocean.

Gudrun set the book aside and got up slowly. She admitted that she was cold, that she was lonely, that she was bored.

More for something to do than any other, more conscientious reason, she found the right spot in the shelves and put the book back where she had found it. She decided that she had a mild headache and therefore did not want to read anymore that afternoon. But there was little else to do. The builders were busy in the dining room and had made it apparent that her presence made them uneasy. Maximillian was at his cottage closeted with one of his strange new friends from München, and had let her know that she was not precisely welcome to join them. One hand strayed to a wisp of blonde hair, twining it around her finger absentmindedly as she watched the snow.

She was still at the window half an hour later when Otto knocked at the door. "Frau Ostneige?" the old man called out.

"Yes, Otto?" She turned away from the window reluctantly, disliking the intrusion. It was not that she was angry with Otto—far from it. The old servant had been a constant source of gruff understanding since she had returned to Wolkighügel.

"I have made a tea for you, Frau Ostneige. You had no meal at noon." He said this in a manner reminiscent of the tone he had used to admonish her when she was a child, and today she found it oddly comforting.

"That was kind of you, Otto. Come in. I didn't mean to exclude you." She was able to smile at him as he came through the door, and her blue eyes were calm. If she had to be a child to have the pleasure of Otto's presence, then it was a small enough compromise, and a relief from all the responsibilities she had been carrying.

Otto looked once at her, his brows coming together. He had a large tray in his hands and this he set down on the smaller of the two reading tables. "I have tea for you, but no coffee as yet. I have tried to buy some, but there is none to be had. The storekeepers at Rosenheim said that it would be two or three months before they would have coffee again on their shelves. The tea is good, however, from England, the sort your mother liked." He reached for the porcelain cup and lifted it as he spoke. "One cup with milk and one without. Rudi, you are not looking after yourself, and that is wrong in you. A woman with so much preying on her, she cannot afford to neglect herself as you have done. Here. Drink the tea and have one of these cakes. And do not skip supper this evening. You're getting thin as a post!"

Gudrun did not bother to deny it; it was true. She crossed the room to the table and accepted the cup and saucer he held out to her. "You are good to me, Otto."

The old man changed color slightly and made a gruff reply as he pointed to one of the high-backed leather chairs in the room. "You should sit down while you drink this, Rudi. It will do you no good if you stand and worry."

"Very well." She took the indicated chair and obediently drank the hot tea. It was stronger than she was used to, but that was an unlooked-for pleasure. The milk in the tea had been scalded, and so the liquid was very hot. She admitted that it did warm her and cheer her as well. "You're kind to me, Otto."

"Someone has to look after you, Rudi. Your husband, poor man, is less use than an infant to you, and there's no one else willing to do their duty by you." He obviously meant Maximillian, but could not bring himself to criticize the boy who had been his favorite. "Out here in the mountains, you're at the mercy of all the elements, and no one to talk to. One of these days they may string wires for those telephones and then you will be able to speak with your friends, but that's a long way off. You don't need to think of those days, but of right now." He did not sit in her presence, but the hectoring tone was more familiar than any outward behavior might have been.

Inwardly Gudrun agreed with him, but she was aware that it was not wise to take the part of servants, so she said, "You're being too pessimistic, Otto. Doubtless once the worst of winter is passed, then life here will be more lively. I could not invite my friends here while the building was in ruins, but with the spring, it will be better and then you'll see how much more pleasant life will be. There are neighbors, too, who will want to exchange visits with us."

"Don't get too friendly with Frau Bucher. She's a harpy and her reputation will not be a credit to you. And the Zweitürmes are old and terribly religious. You do not need such society. It is not fitting for you to associate overmuch with them."

Gudrun set her cup down sharply, not paying attention to any damage such an impetuous act might do to the porcelain. "But if I am not to see our neighbors, and there is no one who might be satisfactory for a woman in my position to know, what am I to do here? You say that one woman has a less-than-admirable reputation and the old couple on the other side of Hausham—and they are the ones you mean, aren't they? —are pious and old. There are not many people in this part of the mountains. I don't think it would be appropriate for me to spend my days at Bad Wiessee or Bad Tölz. What am I to do?"

Otto scowled down at his large, rough hands. "It's something that your brother should attend to. He is the man to guard you, since your husband . . ."

"Yes, but let us not discuss my husband, if you please. Maxl has his friends and his own interests. He can't be expected to spend his time worrying about me, as I do not worry about him." That was not strictly true, for Gudrun was very concerned on her brother's behalf. She did not like the company he kept, nor the hours. While it was apparent that many of his new friends were important men, few of them were wholly above reproach. One or two had shady reputations that Gudrun had heard whispered about when she was still in München. She longed to confide in someone, but knew from years of instruction that it was not a good policy for a master or mistress to confide in a servant. She had never understood the restriction because it had always seemed to her that servants knew more of what was going on than anyone else in a household. So lost was she in her thoughts that she did not hear the remark that Otto addressed to her.

"Rudi," the old man said in a disappointed tone.

She looked toward him. "Otto, forgive me. My mind was wandering. It's this endless snow and being so isolated . . ." Now she was glad to have the tea to drink because it afforded her a reason for silence. When she had drunk the last of the liquid, she held out the cup and saucer to Otto. "I've had the tea with milk; now I must have some plain, or so Mother always told me."

Otto refilled the cup with the steaming dark tea. "And remember that there are cakes here, and sandwiches."

"But if I eat those all, I won't want any supper," Gudrun protested, although she knew it was useless. Otto was determined that she should eat.

"You'll find that you do, Fräulein," he said in precisely the same voice he had used to correct her when she was first learning to ride.

"I am Frau Ostneige, Otto, not a foolish girl still in the schoolroom." She did not want to be sharp with him, but her patience was all but gone. "I will have to make some arrangements, I see, to be sure that we can entertain properly when spring comes. I'll remember what you say, but there is little choice here and it may be that we will have to make do with guests that are less than perfect. This is not München and there has been a war, so we cannot have things as they were." She set the cup and saucer aside and got up, hanging onto her elbows as she walked down the cold library toward the tall ranks of shelves which had not yet been put right.

"I don't intend criticism," Otto said, clearly hurt by what Gudrun had said to him.

"No, of course you don't," she said, smiling in spite of her irritation. "There are days that are more difficult than others, and I fear this has been one of them."

"You're not ill, are you, Rudi?" Otto asked, suddenly alarmed. "If you have caught the influenza, I will go for the physician at once. Arzt Lärm is still practicing in Gmund. He is getting along in years, but he is no doddering idiot. He will have a look at you as soon as I can bring him here . . ."

"No, no, Otto. I am well enough. I haven't got the influenza," Gudrun said, her face slightly flushed. "You have no reason to worry on my behalf. Any woman, living as I do here, would have days when she was not at her best. If it weren't for the workmen, I fear I would stay in my dressing gown all day. What else is there to do? I can't work, the roads won't allow me to have the automobile out, and with fuel in such short supply, it must be saved for important errands, not my amusement. I was wondering earlier how it was that women in isolated castles were able to pass the winters, and I thought that perhaps they all made tapestries or whatever it was they did to stave off the worst of the isolation." She flung one hand out, then brought it back against her folded arms. "You see, it is not my health that is in danger. If I were ill, this would not annoy me so. I don't mean to snap at you, Otto, or to speak deprecatingly of Maxl, but there is so little for me to *do*!"

Otto nodded sympathetically. "You always had spirit, Rudi. A fine girl, with a will of your own, that was you. I don't want you to feel poorly." He smiled as he offered her the plate with the cakes. "Here, you eat these up and I'll see what can be done about getting the sleigh out for an hour or so. How would you like that? Just the way it was when you were still in short skirts."

Gudrun was about to say that it sounded dreadful, but she saw the look in her servant's eyes, and did not insult him again. "That would be delightful, Otto. I should have thought of it myself." She wondered if she had warm enough boots for the expedition, and tried to recall where she had said to store the old moth-eaten fur rugs that had been used in the sleigh when she was a child.

"You finish up the cakes and the tea, and I'll go around to the stables and do something about getting the horses harnessed up. If we take the light sleigh, we'll only need one horse and that will leave the household better prepared in case they need to take the larger sleigh into Hausham." Otto had long since decided that he did not entirely trust the elegant Hispaño-Suiza which was parked in an empty stall.

"That's an excellent idea," Gudrun said, not concerned much either way. "I will need thirty minutes to get ready."

"Just be sure you eat those cakes and drink your tea. It's still snowing out and you'll be cold if you don't take care." With an enthused grin, Otto turned and lumbered out of the library, whistling as he closed the door behind him.

Gudrun stared at the closed door. How had she let herself get into this situation? All she wanted to do was sit in the library and watch the snowfall. But she could not offer Otto a reasonable excuse for changing her mind now. She tugged at the old-fashioned princess-cut jacket she wore, trying to smile. Who knows? she told herself. There might be someone out in this snowing afternoon who would offer her relief from her isolation and boredom. Putting her cup and saucer aside, she left the library to go to her rooms and change.

Her sleighing costume had been made before the Great War, a delicious tiered, fur-trimmed series of tunics and skirts that was both warm and flattering. A high-standing collar of Norwegian blue fox framed her face, setting off her eyes and changing the pallor of her face from exhaustion to elfin piquancy. In her ice-blue clothes, with her blue fox hat and white kid gloves and boots, she was like the Snow Princess in fairy tales. As she stepped outside, the wind kissed icy roses into her cheeks: as Otto drove the old sleigh around the end of the Schloss from the stables, he was struck with a sudden bittersweet memory of the beauty Gudrun had had as a child, which was fading steadily now.

"You bundle up well," Otto ordered her, determined to keep his feelings to himself. Had he been her father and not her servant, he could not have been fonder of her. "Make sure that you don't get chilled." He himself was engulfed in a fleece-lined coat that gave him the profile of a genial bear. When he had watched her take her place in the sleigh and draw the fur rugs around her, he turned back. "Up, Hässlich," he called to the big Holstein between the shafts. Obediently the gelding started off through the snow, the runners hissing as the sleigh moved faster.

In Hausham, Gudrun instructed Otto to pull up at the mercer's shop, and on impulse went in to look at the disappointing store of fabrics offered.

"Frau Ostneige, if I had known that you were in need of material, I would have sent to the shops in München or Wien so that you have an appropriate selection," the clerk told her, his face contorting with worry. "Here, it is not sensible to keep too many fine fabrics, and with the war and all . . ."

Gudrun smiled as she interrupted the clerk's protracted apology. "You are not to blame for the situation. I'm amazed that you've been able to keep so much stock on hand." She dared not tell him that she had come into the shop merely as a diversion, and so she pointed to some heavy muslin. "You doubtless know that Wolkighügel was broken into last spring, and we have a great many repairs to do. If you'd send up that bolt of muslin, it would be a great help. Later, when our repairs are more advanced, I'll place an order for fine fabrics, but at the moment there would be nothing we could do with them, in any case."

The clerk beamed with relief. "I will tell Herr Bisschen you called, Frau Ostneige. He will be sure that you get your muslin tomorrow morning." He could not admit that his employer was at the tavern, drunk on schnapps.

"That will be fine." By that time, she was confident she would have thought of a use for the muslin.

The clerk bowed his head. "It is an honor to have your custom, Gnädige Frau."

"Thank you." She hastened back to the sleigh, delighted to be out of the shop, away from the oppressive civility of the clerk. "Otto, I don't want to go home quite yet. Can you drive me up toward Schliersee? Is the road open?"

Otto shrugged. "Part of the way. If the road becomes too difficult, we will turn back." He was pleased to have this extra time away from the Schloss. It reminded him of the old days, and was more his idea of how the hochgebornen should live. He turned past the church and started down the narrow road that followed the rails away to the southeast. The snow had stopped and the hillsides were still, wrapped in that deep tranquility of winter. Even the wind was muted; the snow muffled the horse's hoofbeats.

Gudrun sat back in the sleigh, her hands sunk in the old muff Otto had found for her. It was dark and did not match the rest of her outfit, but it did not matter. There was no one to see her, and of late that was starting to bother her. She leaned back on the old musty squabs and let the cold air brush her face. She was sorry now that she had done nothing for the holidays. The year seemed to begin so bleakly without the celebrations she had come to love. Still, Walther had warned her that Jürgen would not be able to support any excitement. At the time a simple exchange of gifts and a tot of cognac seemed to be the most practical approach, but now Gudrun knew that she had missed the music and presents and company that had long been part of her Christmas and New Year. Now they were well into January and there was a long, empty year stretching ahead of her. "Otto," she said rather dreamily, "I think I would like to start a garden when the snow is gone. A large one."

Otto chuckled. "You've never done anything more than pick roses in all your days. Why a garden now?"

"To have something to do. Flowers would be nice. Jürgen likes them. I'd feel I was doing something rather than simply waiting while others do my work, take care of my husband. All of Wolkighügel could run on very well without me."

"Tush! That's self-pity, Rudi, and it isn't worthy of you." He pointed through the trees toward a good-sized house. "New neighbors, by the look of it. Johan at the inn said that they came here last summer and rebuilt the old Zicklein place. It looks different, doesn't it? I heard their name is Schnaubel. He's an architect, and she, they tell me, paints. They have four children, all wild as mad foxes."

Gudrun sat up in the sleigh. "Why didn't you tell me about them? You've been saying how there is no one appropriate for me to know in this place, and all the while, the Schnaubels are living here . . ."

Otto coughed. "Actually, Maximillian warned me about them. He said it would be just like you to make friends of them, and he didn't want that to happen."

"Why not?" Gudrun's voice had risen slightly. "What has Maxl to say about what little social life I have? I do not object to his friends from München, so what is there he could object to in my knowing the neighbors?"

"Well," Otto said, wishing he did not have to speak so loudly to be heard, "they're Jews. You know how Maxl feels about Jews." He gave a helpless hitch to his shoulders, knowing that he would have to disappoint one of his treasured charges.

"Of all the absurd . . ." Gudrun began in exasperation, then shook her head. "Otto, I want to stop here. Pull up, will you?"

"But Maxl would not—" Otto said at once.

Gudrun interrupted him. "Maxl has nothing to do with this. I do not make lists of his friends and I don't expect him to do that for me. Pull up. I want to meet these people."

"They might not be home," Otto suggested. "And with children, you know, it isn't always possible to receive visitors."

"Then I will leave a card. Do as I say, Otto, or I will climb out of the sleigh and walk to the house myself." There was no doubt that she was serious and after a miserable shrug, Otto tugged Hässlich around and started him up the snowy drive.

As Gudrun stepped down from the sleigh, the door opened and a boy of about fourteen or fifteen stepped out. "Who are you?" he asked her.

"I'm Frau Ostneige," she said, and smiled at the boy. "We're neighbors, and I thought it was time we met."

"Oh," said the boy. "Well, my parents are inside. Shall I tell them you're here?"

"If you would," Gudrun responded at once, and flashed a determined smile at Otto. "I won't be long," she told him, adding, "this time."

Otto lifted his hands to show the trees and the sky that he was not accountable for the quirks of his employer. "I shouldn't keep Hässlich standing more than fifteen minutes," he warned her, pleased to have this one hold over her.

"I will be out before then," Gudrun promised, and went into the house behind the boy.

The hall they entered was lined with bookshelves filled with all sorts of volumes in no order Gudrun could discern. It was a warm house, filled just now with the scent of roasting chickens. Somewhere ahead children were laughing together.

"Those are my sisters," the boy explained. "They're just children."

Gudrun made no attempt to suppress the smile that came to her lips, though part of it was painful. There had been times when she was young when her Schloss had been filled with laughter instead of the somber builders and sickness.

The boy led her into a sitting room, saying as he opened the door, "One of the neighbors, Mother. She said she wanted to meet you."

An attractive woman in her mid-thirties rose from a fashionable settee. The whole room was done in the Art Nouveau style, so that it seemed to Gudrun she had been brought into an artificial bower, and the woman's dress, with its swirling pleated skirt and loose short robe caught something of the feel of the room, for it was the sort of clothes one would expect to wear outside rather than in the house. Her face was small and her dark hair was cut daringly short. "I'm afraid . . ."

Gudrun held out her hand. "I'm Gudrun Ostneige. We're neighbors. I didn't learn until a little while ago that you had moved into this house, and I was hoping you wouldn't mind having me call."

The woman took her hand. "I'm Amalie Schnaubel. This is Bruno"—she pointed to the boy who had admitted Gudrun to the house—"and the two girls there are Olympie and Hedda. There's another boy around somewhere, and he's Emmerich. I'm delighted to meet one of the neighbors at last." There was a faint undertone of bitterness to this last statement, but her smile never faltered.

"I was hoping," Gudrun said after the most minute of pauses, "that perhaps you would want to call on me when the weather is better. I've been quite isolated here in the mountains, and it would be a great pleasure to have company again."

"That's very kind of you. We're so new here that we haven't had time to get to know the others. I no doubt feel as isolated as you do." Amalie's dark eyes flashed once as if in suspicion.

"But you have your children, and they must keep you occupied," Gudrun said, wondering why it was that Frau Schnaubel was so reserved behind her cordiality.

Amalie managed to laugh outright at that. "They do, most emphatically. I haven't finished one canvas in the last three months. That's what comes of having all of them home and no one to play with. It *is* hard being indoors day after day, but still . . ." She turned suddenly as the two girls burst out in renewed giggles. "If you're doing something I wouldn't approve of, stop it," she said mildly, then gave her attention to Gudrun again. "There's only that strange child at Schloss Saint-Germain, and we've only met her once."

"A child at Schloss Saint-Germain?" Gudrun echoed. "When did that happen?"

"Around the first of December. When the owner showed up, they told me at the train station, no one from the Schloss would come for him. He was dressed in badly torn clothing and had just the child with him. He walked from the depot to Schloss Saint-Germain, and it was snowing quite badly. When he established his identity to the satisfaction of the housekeeper, everyone went in fear of being dismissed. It has not happened so far." She smiled impishly. "In a place like this, we must look for every tidbit of news we can find. There is so little to occupy us."

"Alas," Gudrun said, nodding. "I'm surprised about Schloss Saint-Germain. All through my childhood no one ever saw the owner. All was kept in excellent condition, but never occupied."

"Yes, that's what we were told." It was apparent that Amalie Schnaubel was more comfortable discussing the stranger than talking about herself or her family.

"And the child? A girl, I think you said?"

"A Polish girl, I think, or perhaps Russian. She's the ward of the Graf. Don't remind me that we're not supposed to call them by their titles anymore. But wait until you see this man." Amalie belatedly indicated a chair. "Do sit down, Frau Ostneige. I'm afraid there isn't much to offer you, no coffee or pastries, but if you will wait a little while, then I can provide—"

"Oh, no, forgive me, but this must be a very brief call. I only wanted to introduce myself, Frau Schnaubel. My retainer is outside with the sleigh and he will be irate if I make him keep the horse standing too long. Another time, when you have an idle afternoon and are not taken up with your children. I didn't mean to inconvenience you in any way. I see you have your hands full now, and I don't want to overstay my welcome, since I have invited myself in." She looked rather wistfully toward the giggling girls.

"Do you have children, Frau Ostneige?" Amalie asked politely.

"No," Gudrun answered with a slight shake of her head. "No, my husband was hurt in the war, and so . . ."

"How unfortunate," Amalie said, warming to her visitor in spite of herself.

"I feel as if I have spent the last six months cooped up in a very small box," Gudrun said in an embarrassed rush. "It's so good to know that I am not the only young woman living up here in the mountains." Although she knew that proper social decorum called for her to leave now, she was reluctant to do so.

"I wish you could stay a bit longer," Amalie said, as if sensing Gudrun's thoughts, for she, too, was feeling the pressure of living in this remote place. "My husband, Simeon, is up at Schloss Saint-Germain at the moment, talking with the Graf. He should be back in an hour or so." She watched Gudrun a moment. "Ostneige. I don't really know the name. Where do you live?"

"At my family Schloss. As I mentioned, my husband is an invalid and so we have not been able to receive much company. My brother has occasional guests from München, but I hardly see them. We're not far from Hausham. The Schloss is called Wolkighügel." As she said the name, she saw Amalie Schnaubel's features unaccountably harden. "What . . . ?"

"And your brother. What is his name?" The words rapped out crisply as Amalie's dark eyes narrowed.

"Maximillian. Maximillian Altbrunnen. He's more often in the village. Perhaps you've met . . . ?" If they had, she could not imagine why nothing had been said to her.

"Altbrunnen. Yes, indeed, we have met." Her voice grew cold. "Is this some sort of joke, Frau Ostneige? Are you coming to see for yourself whether we live like animals or not? I gather you find it amusing to come into a Jewish household to see if we roast Christian children for supper. . . ."

"What are you saying?" Gudrun wondered aloud, appalled at the sudden turn this meeting had taken. What had begun as guarded good-will had degenerated into open hostility. "Frau Schnaubel, I'm afraid—"

"I'm not surprised. You're very brave to come here, aren't you?" She folded her arms, staring fixedly at Gudrun. "I hope you accomplished your mission, Frau Ostneige, and will have enough damning information to give Herr Altbrunnen. I'm not willing to let you remain here any longer, however, so whatever you came to do, I trust it is done."

"But . . ." Gudrun started for the door and noticed as she went that the children had grown silent. "I don't know why you're speaking to me in this way, Frau Schnaubel. I do want to be your friend. Two women, out here in the mountains, it isn't easy—"

"With the sort of company that's invited to Wolkighügel, you can't expect any of us to call there, can you?" Her rejection was absolute. "I fear I've kept you too long, Frau Ostneige. Your retainer must want to get his horse moving again."

Gudrun stopped in the door, trying to salvage what little she could of this disastrous encounter. "I truly don't know why you say these things, Frau Schnaubel. If someone from Wolkighügel has been discourteous, I wish you would tell me about it. I don't allow my staff to be insulting to my neighbors." Her face was filled with distress.

"And your brother, what of him? I take it he can speak his mind with impunity." There was less rage in Amalie's eyes now, although her guard was not in the least relaxed. "If you are actually unaware, as you claim to be, of what your brother is doing, then I think you should ask him a few questions, Frau Ostneige. You will have to forgive me if I assume that you are in his confidence."

"I will ask him. And I thank you, whether or not you believe that," Gudrun added before she bolted for the door. As she swung the front door inward, she heard the voices of the children behind her errupt in questions.

Otto was waiting, sunk deep in gloom. He looked up as Gudrun hurried out of the house, pausing to close the door behind her before hurrying toward the sleigh. "You were more than ten minutes. It isn't good for the horse to stand in . . ." He had begun irascibly, then he saw the odd expression on Gudrun's face and fell silent.

"Drive home, Otto," Gudrun said as she climbed into the sleigh. "And while you drive, tell me what you know about these associates of Maxl's who come to the house. They are my brother's friends and they enjoy my hospitality, and yet I find I know nothing about them. I have discovered that they are not merely the scholars Maxl said they are."

"Yes, Rudi," Otto said wearily as he brought up the whip. He did not know where to start or how much Maxl would want him to say. "You spoke with Herr Schnaubel, then?"

"Herr Schnaubel is at Schloss Saint-Germain. I spoke with Frau Schnaubel—that is, until she found out where I lived, and then she was most determined that I should leave her home." She pulled the furs up around her and frowned at the trees beside the road, her pretty face marred by unhappiness. "She mentioned Maxl, and assumes she knows something to his discredit and mine. She knew Wolkighügel by name and did not approve of it."

Otto supposed that this would have happened eventually, and did his best not to be too upset by it. "Well, Maxl has not been particularly discreet."

"That is not new. I did not know he had taken to involving the neighbors, however." Her tone was sharper than usual and she did not give Otto any encouragement to excuse Maximillian's behavior. "What has he been saying or doing that would cause Frau Schnaubel to order me out of her house?"

"Nothing directly I don't think," Otto said. "He's stopped at the tavern now and again. You know, the Hirsch Furt in Hausham. He meets his friends there and they talk. There's nothing wrong in that." He had driven Maximillian to just such a meeting only ten days ago. There had been a new man from München with a note of introduction. The messenger had worn an old uniform tunic, with officer's tags on the collar.

"And do they speak against the Jews in the tavern, is that it?" Gudrun's voice was flat. "Why has he said nothing to me about it? He uses my Schloss and lives out of my larder. He has told me simply that the group does certain esoteric studies and research into Teutonic history. There was no mention of Jews."

"He doesn't discuss it much," Otto agreed, hoping that this would exonerate him from any censure. "He said that he felt you did not care much for politics, and that this was not an area where women have any real talents. He wanted to spare you any demands you might feel toward his guests. He was sympathetic to your difficult situation, Rudi, with Herr Ostneige so ill." He had to check Hässlich as they rounded a sharp corner; the sleigh swayed, the runners sending up fountains of loose snow, then steadied as the Holstein began to trot down the familiar road toward Wolkighügel.

"I see," Gudrun sighed, leaning back once more, her thoughts now more desolate than they had been before she set out. It would be necessary to speak to Maxl, to ask him to apologize to the Schnaubels. And if he would not—he was often stubborn—she must attend to it herself, distasteful as it was to her. She would not allow Maxl to rob her of one of the few opportunities for friendship she had discovered since moving here.

A Benz touring car came down the road toward them, going slowly over the treacherous snow. Hässlich snorted but did not panic as Otto pulled him to the edge of the road. The driver waved in appreciation, then continued by. Gudrun turned to stare after it.

"Who was that?" she asked as Otto gave Hässlich the office again.

"I think it was the caterer from the Kristall Ufer at Bad Wiessee. He has such an automobile." He hoped that Gudrun would not wish to talk again about Maximillian. "There are quite a few automobiles there. It's the way these hotels are. They say that next year there will be a New Year Gala at the Kristall Ufer, just as there used to be."

"Do they?" Gudrun's voice was distant. "I wonder where he was going."

"You'll find out soon enough," Otto promised her, his apprehension fading as he approached the drive to Wolkighügel.

He was pleased with himself for his deft handling of Gudrun's inquiries.

If he had seen the measuring expression in her eyes, he would not have been so satisfied; Gudrun had decided that Maximillian owed her some answers.

Text of a letter from James Emmerson Tree to his cousin Audrey.

Le Faubourg Saint-Germain des Prés
Paris
France
February 15, 1919

Dear Audrey;

As you can see, I'm still in Paris, and I think they're going to okay my extension so I'll be able to stay on awhile. I like this place, and it seems to like me. Maybe you can talk Uncle Ned into letting you come for a visit. I'd love to show you around the place. With the Great War over (and it looks as if they're going to make that treaty stick, harsh as it is), there's not very much hazard, and if you're with me, there won't be any difficulties with the people here. The French are a funny lot, most of them, but not hard to deal with once they stop turning up their noses at you.

I was really sorry to hear about Mrs. Collins. The influenza has been horrible here, with a lot of deaths. The trouble is, there really aren't enough doctors and medicine yet to have ways and places to treat the disease. It spreads so fast, too. One doctor I was talking to a couple of weeks ago blames the war for it, but right now everything is the fault of the war. There was one old woman in the marketplace who told me, quite seriously, that the war had caused the shortage of eggs. She said that the chickens were not able to lay because of the sounds of the guns. Mind you, the guns have been silent for three months, but that didn't stop her at all.

Thanks for sending me that note on my articles. There are times I wonder if anyone is reading them. I'm planning on doing a follow-up little later on this year, so that everyone will see what the end of the war meant for

these displaced people. I know that the old man in Brittany
died, but I think I'll get an interview with his son, just to
wrap it up. I've asked for permission to visit the châteaux
that were wrecked, so I can give some idea of how bad the
damage has been. There are places where the owners had
fine art and antique furniture that are just burned-out
shells now. Most of these people will not be able to rebuild
because of the costs, and because much of what was destroyed is truly irreplaceable. That's a rotten thing to
have happen. Some of these wealthy families are haughty
and not easy to talk to, but most of them are willing to
say how much they miss their homes and all the good
things they had in their lives. It's hard for some Americans to understand, because the war didn't touch us all
that much. Can you imagine losing not just your father
and brothers and friends, but your house and everything
you valued, as well? It happened to a lot of people here. I
doubt they'll ever get over it.

I haven't done much more than work, but I do want to
go to the Opera and see the museums when I get the
chance. I don't know where to begin on that, but I'm going
to make time for a symphony or something soon.

I read about the airmail service between New York and
Washington. That's encouraging. Maybe one of these years
they'll have airmail service across the Atlantic, and it
won't take so long to get a letter from you. I guess they
might have something like that in fifteen years or so, and
I'll probably be back at the Post-Dispatch by then. That
airmail idea is a good one, if they can get the aeroplanes
a bit more reliable. That's going to take time, but I think
it can work. I went up in one just after the Armistice, to
look at the last of the battle lines, and I thought it was
great. There were a couple scary times, and when the rain
began we had to land, but we were up for more than two
hours, and it was quite an experience. One of these days
you'll have to try it.

The first rough figures on the Great War look pretty
grim. They figure now that more than eight million were
killed. That's eight million, Audrey. There's another seven
million or so unaccounted for—they're either prisoners or
missing. The wounded are more than the other two together. I heard the other day that they're estimating as
high as twenty million wounded. It doesn't look real, does

it? Who can imagine twenty million men, and all of them
wounded? Can you picture eight million graves? I can't.

Yesterday I talked with a reporter from Lansing,
Michigan. He said he was over here to find out how many
of the casualties were from Michigan, so he could do
stories on them for a couple of the papers. He'd only got
here at Christmas, so he didn't have any close-up experience of the war. He didn't care much about it, either. All
he wanted to know is where the red-light district was and
how much he should pay for what. It was embarrassing to
be with him, and he comes from my own country. I began
to see why it is that a lot of the French people don't like to
talk to Americans and think that our whole press is filled
with scoundrels. This guy wanted to talk about two things:
whores and baseball. It was awful. Here I am, a countryman of his, and I couldn't wait to get back to the
French and British journalists.

There was a little more news out of Russia, but nothing
confirmed. A Danish writer had been allowed into Petrograd for a week, very supervised, and he was in Paris on
a holiday, so a few of us tried to pump him. We'd heard
about the Czar and his family getting killed, but there
weren't any new details.

Did you hear that women over thirty got the vote in
Britain? A British Colonel I know predicted that it could
not turn out well. He said it was nonsense, but at the end
of a war like this one, strange things get done. The Suffragettes are just as determined as the ones at home. A
couple of them got killed during their protests, just like
that woman in the Midwest (what was her name?) who
stood in front of that Senator's train so that he could not
go to Washington to vote against votes for women. They
said the train didn't even slow down, just went over her.
One of the women here got in front of a racehorse, and it
killed her. I don't believe most of this. I know it's happening, but it's not real. Colonel Bridley said that he was
sure Parliament would revoke votes for women as soon as
they came to their senses. But when you think of the
women who came over here and did so much for the men
at the Front, and all the jobs they did at home, it doesn't
seem fair that they not be allowed to vote. They've earned
it. I hope it works out.

They tell me that Congress ratified Prohibition. It makes
me glad I'm still in France. I've learned to like wine and

*cognac, and the thought of giving them up because a
group of narrow-minded bigots prefer sarsaparilla, well,
I think the whole notion is foolish. If all the people really
wanted the country dry, they simply would stop buying
beer and wine and hard liquor. No one is forcing an
abstainer to drink. If a man would be happier with lem-
onade, all he has to do is say so. But these sanctimonious
old hypocrites, with their postures of virtue, they'll do
more harm in the long run than a man who likes his
glass of beer at the end of the day.*

*A couple nights ago I saw* Mater Dolorse. *I don't know
if many French flickers make it to Denver, but you might
like this one. I've seen a fair number of moving pictures
since the war ended, and some of them are quite good. It
isn't all just comedy over here (not that it is at home,
either, but with Chaplin and Keystone Kops all over the
place, it isn't quite the same feeling as here).*

*Thanks for sending along Tarkington's* The Magnificent
Ambersons, *which is quite a book. I'll pick up a few
things for you to read, that's assuming you're keeping up
with your French lessons. I'll get a copy of Valery's* La
Jeune Parque *if I can find one. If I can't, then I'll try to
get you a couple magazines, anyway. You'll be amused:
I'm trying to learn a little German. Crandell said he
might send me to Germany if I could learn enough of the
language to ask intelligent questions. So one of these days
I might send you a book from Berlin. I can't make much
sense of the vocabulary yet, but I've met a student from
Prussia who is willing to teach me in exchange for a few
square meals. His own family was kicked out before the
war, but he said that he was treated pretty badly during
the Great War, and I can believe it.*

*Next time you have a photograph taken, send one along
to me, will you? It's been almost two years since I've seen
you, and at your age, that makes quite a difference. I'm
pretty much the same, but a little leaner. Must be the
hard living. I was thinking just the other day that if
anyone had told me while I was in high school that ten
years later I'd be working for a big paper, living on the
Left Bank in Paris, I would probably have laughed in his
face. But here I am.*

*Give Aunt Myra and Uncle Ned my regards, and tell
them I'll write again in a few weeks. I'm glad the new car
is working out so well. I haven't driven a Packard, but*

*one of the reporters from Atlanta has, and he said he liked the way it handled.*

*I'll have to close now, since I'm due at supper with a couple of foreign journalists, but I'll keep you up on what I'm doing, never fear.*

*Your loving cousin,*
*James*

## 2

As Franchot Ragoczy entered the garden salon, his three visitors rose. "Pray, take your seats. This is apt to be a long interview and there is no reason for you to be uncomfortable." His smile, elusive and wry, touched his mouth and was gone. "Now, then, which of you is Pfahl?"

The youngest of the three, a man of no more than twenty-two, got nervously to his feet. "I am, Mein Herr."

"Educated at Tübingen, I see. Honors in Romance Languages. Most impressive." Ragoczy motioned him to be seated. "And Mauser?"

The woman nodded her head. She was older than the two men, approaching forty, with stern, intelligent features. "You have my references, I think."

"I do indeed. You've been a most busy woman." He strode across the room toward the windows. "And that means that you"—he gestured toward the third person, an awkward man of about thirty—"are Bündnis."

"Yes," was the nervous acknowledgment.

"May I ask if we'll be allowed to speak with your daughter?" Fräulein Mauser asked in her clear, precise way. "Surely we're entitled to that courtesy."

"You're a little premature, Fräulein, if you will permit me to say so. Before you meet my ward, I wish to speak to each of you privately. It might interest you to know that I had responses from more than forty qualified tutors, and you were the three with what seemed to be the most likely and useful combinations of experience and abilities. I am not going to employ all of you, but I will be more than pleased to give you statements of recommendation." His German was crisp and elegant, but slightly accented, foreign in sound without being obtrusively so. He looked at the painting hung over the hearth, and for a moment his dark eyes were distant.

The room was cozy enough, warmed by the fire that chuckled to itself on the hearth, but none of the tutors appreciated this. The chairs were comfortable, products of the early part of the last century, upholstered in striped satin, but the tutors found them unyielding as bricks. Gas-lights augmented the wan sunlight, but no one noticed the cheerful brilliance of them.

"Herr Ragoczy, it is customary to allow prospective tutors to spend some time with the child or children they will be instructing." Clearly Fräulein Mauser was not going to be put off by the Graf's good manners. "You may not understand this—"

"Fräulein Mauser," Ragoczy said with a pleasant, unnerving smile, "I do not like being pressed."

The men exchanged looks and Herr Bündnis' Adam's apple bobbed as he swallowed. Fräulein Mauser persisted. "We have not come all this way to be treated in such a cavalier fashion, Herr Ragoczy. I have had several years' experience and I must tell you that your conduct so far has been most irregular. It may not suit me to be employed here."

"And I have not yet offered you the position," Ragoczy reminded her gently. "You will have to allow me to make this interview more irregular still." He went to an antique end table and picked up a silver bell, which he rang once, then set down again. "I do not wish to be rude to you, and little though you think it, I am fully aware that each of you has made a considerable journey at my request. I've instructed my chef to prepare a meal for you, and when you have finished, I will want to speak to each of you, in turn, in my study. Roger will show you where it is when the time comes." He looked up as a middle-aged man with sandy hair and steady blue eyes came into the room. "Ah, there you are now, Roger," he said, pronouncing the name in French. "Thank you for this most opportune arrival. These are the tutors I've mentioned would be here at luncheon. I would appreciate it if you will escort them to the informal dining room."

At that, Fräulein Mauser bridled again. "The informal dining room?" she repeated, her back stiffening with each word.

"Yes. Does the arrangement displease you?" Ragoczy's features were pleasantly expressive and now showed goodwill and polite concern. "Is it that you dislike eating in the informal dining room? I gather that you think I should instruct my staff to set your places in the formal dining room. If that is what you truly desire, I will, of course, do so, but," he went on serenely, "I should point out that it has not yet been restored—as you may have heard, this Schloss was vandalized some ten months ago, and much of the damage is still apparent—and that there is no fire laid in the hearth because we have not yet been assured that the chimney is sound. But it will be as you wish."

Herr Bündnis spoke up first, his face slightly flushed. "The informal dining room would be more appropriate for us, in any case. Most tutors take their meals with the children or the servants in a big house." He did not meet Fräulein Mauser's quelling gaze. "You are good to offer us so much courtesy."

"Thank you, Herr Bündnis," Ragoczy said with a fleeting engaging smile.

Roger gave a tactful cough, then addressed the three tutors. "Your places have been laid, and I believe that the meal is ready. If you will follow me, please . . ."

Herr Pfahl was the first on his feet. "I am at your disposal. Where are we going?"

"Down the main hall and to your left. The room is a pale Wedgwood color with tall elm wainscoting; the draperies are dark peacock damask. The door is open." He waited as the three visitors came up to him. "This way, if you will."

As she left the room, Fräulein Mauser turned to give Ragoczy a long, critical stare.

Ragoczy returned her look with a degree of amusement, and once the door was closed, he shook his head, then crossed the room toward the far wall, and tapped once on a gold-and-peach-tinted panel. "Well, Laisha Vlassevna," he said as a narrow section of the wall swung inward, "what did you think of them?" He spoke in Russian now, and there was warmth in his voice.

"Must I have one of them? Can't you teach me?" As she asked these questions, Laisha scrambled out of her hiding place and made a cursory attempt to restore order to her clothing.

"Yes, I think it had best be one of them. You should have experience of someone other than myself, my child." He put one small, long-fingered hand on her shoulder. "You will not always live here with me; you have a great deal to learn before that day."

Her face grew pale. "I don't like it when you say that."

Ragoczy gave a little shake to his head. "Laisha, this isn't like you. Yesterday you said that you wanted to know new people, and now you want me to send these good tutors away."

"But I didn't mean tutors, I meant . . ." She squirmed a bit, not willing to look at him.

"You meant you wanted children your own age to play with," Ragoczy finished for her sensibly and saw her nod tentatively. "I don't intend that you should wall yourself up here. I've already asked Frau Schnaubel if she would be willing to bring her family up here one afternoon. Would you like to see Olympie and Hedda again?"

Laisha nodded, but then said quickly, "I don't want to see that Emmerich, though. He's too young."

"He's six years old, my child," Ragoczy said, chiding her gently.

"Well, you said that I'm eight." She announced this with all the conviction of youth. "He's just a baby."

Ragoczy was silent a number of seconds. "I wonder if Olympie thinks that of you? She's almost eleven." As he mentioned the ages, he felt a remote bewilderment. How could a few years matter so much? He had long been aware that such things were very important, particularly to children, but his life was so long that a decade seemed a frightfully short time. To quibble over a year . . .

"Olympie can't talk Russian," Laisha said with sudden belligerence, as if this somehow equalized the difference in their ages.

"And your German is not very good," Ragoczy reminded her as he brushed back her fair, tumbled hair.

"Well . . ." She spun on her heel and started toward the door. "I don't want to learn German. I don't like it. It sounds silly."

"But we are living in Bayern," he reminded her gently. "If you go to München, how will you manage if you cannot ask questions or read signs?"

"I won't go there," Laisha insisted. "I will stay here, and you will speak Russian."

Ragoczy reached for one of the antique chairs and pulled it over so that he could sit down. He looked at the girl steadily. "Laisha, you mustn't think that. I would not be doing you a service if I agreed to such a plan. Knowledge is the most precious thing there is in the world, my child: knowledge of things, of people. If you have knowledge then you have the only protection that endures. You must learn German. And French. And Italian. And English. Then, no matter where you go, you will be able to fend for yourself. Nothing I can give you is so valuable as that."

Laisha recognized the somber tone of his voice, and she turned back to him, looking into his dark eyes. "Can't I do that later?" she implored him.

"It only gets harder if you wait," he said with a shrug. "If you learn these things now, it will be fairly easy, but later . . ." He lifted his hands slightly to show her how futile delay was.

She was watching him carefully, her bright brown eyes wary. "What if I don't like it? What then?"

"Then you will have the right to ask for another tutor, and I will provide that for you. Not, of course"—his tone was firmer now—"for your caprice, but for real grievance. You would not be unreasonable, would you?"

Though her lower lip pouted, Laisha was able to shake her head. "I don't think so. I might." Her face turned up to his for a second, and then she looked away toward the windows. She tugged at the end of her wide sash, standing a trifle too stiffly.

Ragoczy leaned forward, his elbows propped on his knees. "Laisha, I don't want to frighten or indulge you: neither would be kind. We are both strangers in this country, Laisha. It is not wise for strangers to abuse the hospitality of the country that has given them refuge. That is what has happened here."

"But this is your house," she protested. "You own it. You are not poor."

"No, I am not poor, but nevertheless, I am as much a displaced person as you are. You cannot now return to Russia even if you decide that Germany is not to your liking. Your home is there no longer." He felt his chest tighten as he saw the wistful softening of her face. "You must learn, Laisha. That course is the only way to any sort of a happy life. Believe this."

She took a deep breath, her hands clenching to fists at her sides. "I don't like to sit in little rooms with books all afternoon and recite verbs and things."

"Nor do I. Your tutor will take you on walks while you study. You will ask questions and converse. No little rooms, no lists of verbs. That I promise you." He rose from the chair.

"I must go to my study. They will finish with their meal shortly and I have to talk with them individually."

Laisha looked down at her rumpled skirt. "I don't want to be by myself."

"You are not alone. You will not be alone." He struggled with a sudden desire to indulge her demands. He knew that she was frightened and unwilling to admit it. He was also aware that he could not afford to do this. There would be a time, and that time was near, when she would not want to be protected, and then she would resent his concession. "When you speak the language, you will find it easier to have friends."

She was staring down at her shoes and so did not see the fond smile that curved his ironic mouth. "But you'll go away, won't you? And there will be just tutors here. I remember how it was before, when there were weeks with no one but servants in the house and . . ." She faltered, and tears came into her eyes, as often occurred when one of the few fragments of memory came back to her.

Ragoczy dropped to his knees and put his arms around her. "Ah, Laisha. My girl." He felt her shaking with suppressed weeping. "You are safe here, for a time, which is the most anyone can be promised in a life. I will not abandon you, my child. You have my word on it." He had no way to assure her that his word was reliable, but hoped that she would accept it as sincere. "I travel, and my . . . work occasionally calls me to other places, but I will be certain that there is provision made for you. When you are a little older, perhaps you'd like to travel with me."

She gulped. "I *have* traveled with you."

He nodded. "But this time, we will go in a train or an automobile. We will not have to hide, or steal food. We will have a train carriage all to ourselves, if you like, and Roger will bring you chocolate in the morning." This time his smile was able to evoke one from her.

"Where will you go?" she asked, still frightened but less upset.

"Oh, Wien, Paris, Salzburg, perhaps Berlin. Certainly München fairly often. Occasionally I will have to go to Tübingen. I may go to Zurich, or Milano, or Barcelona. That's for the future. I promise I will go no farther than München until September. You will have six months of me, my child, and you will be pleased for the change." He stood up, and this time she continued to look at him. "Now, go find Roger; he's waiting to serve you luncheon."

Laisha stared hard at her guardian. "Six months," she said firmly, then turned on her heel and scampered out of the room, closing the door behind her with an energetic crash. Her running footsteps faded down the hallway.

Ragoczy went to the open wall panel, securing it with care, being certain that the latch was firmly in place. The Schloss had a number of such devices built into it, left over from less hospitable days. He felt a measure of consolation in knowing that the servants had discovered less than half of them. When he was satisfied that this one was concealed, he left the room, going quickly down the long hallway toward the back of the building.

The study was on the north side of Schloss Saint-Germain, a tall-windowed room with fine oak paneling deeply carved with an intertwining leaf pattern. There were two large glass-fronted bookcases filled with an eclectic sample of volumes, though the majority of Ragoczy's collection was in the library. A huge desk dominated the room, a lovingly-crafted monstrosity of mother-of-pearl-inlaid walnut. It had been made eighty years before in Amsterdam and at the time was a commission from the Royal Family. Now it was decidedly out of fashion, as were the three lumpish chairs in the room, all of which had been made in Ankara by a house of saddlers who had the skill to build flexible frames for their chairs so that the shape would alter subtly to accommodate whoever sat in them. They were upholstered in tooled red leather, and aside from their remarkable comfort, had nothing to recommend them. There were a number of paintings on the wall, two of them Velázquez's work, the others less identifiable. A jade lion with a broken paw occupied the center of the marble mantelpiece, flanked by alabaster birds from Niklos Aulirios. A very old chest stood empty against the far wall.

Although it seemed a complete world in itself, there was another room beyond the study, considerably larger and more utilitarian, where Ragoczy pursued his various researches. This room was reached by an inconspicuous door in the study wall, and by a concealed passage on the second floor of the Schloss.

Ragoczy took a wooden match from the box on the desk and lit two of the gas brackets. The afternoon was clouding over and the study was dark and chilly; after a brief period of consideration, he set the fire laid in the grate alight, as well, pulling the brass screen across the front of the fireplace. He drew one of the three chairs up to the desk and sank into it, staring in complete abstraction at the jade lion.

It was almost twenty minutes later when Roger gave a discreet knock on the door and announced "Fräulein Mauser," holding the door open for that formidable woman as he did.

"Fräulein," Ragoczy said, shaking off his preoccupation and indicating a chair to her. He did not rise.

As the door closed behind her, she stared at her host. "Graf, I am astonished."

"Why?" Ragoczy regarded her with utmost good humor. "Come, Fräulein Mauser, sit down so that we may have an opportunity to talk."

She shrugged. "You have not yet learned how these matters are to be handled," she said in roughly the same tone she would use to reprimand a naughty three-year-old.

"Let us put an end to this charade, Fräulein. You would like me to believe that you are to be accorded courtesy appropriate to honored guests. If I employ you," he went on more slowly, with careful emphasis on each word, "I will expect you to perform your duties without constant intrusions. I have not often had children in my charge but I have employed many persons over the years. You have been hoping to convince me that any tutor deserves more attention and distinction than is customary. That is not the most satisfactory way to begin with me." He sat back in his chair, his hands folded, his commanding dark eyes on the woman's face.

"You misunderstood me, Herr Graf," Fräulein Mauser said with a good deal less confidence than she had shown at first. She sat down heavily.

"Then you will forgive me," he responded. "You have most flattering references." His tone was brisk, his expression alert. "You must have had excellent rapport with the children you supervised."

"Surely it is more a question of authority than rapport, Herr Graf," Fräulein Mauser corrected him, unaware that she had lapsed into her old behavior. "Children must have strong authority or they will run wild. Responsible citizens are the result of authority and firmness in youth. I have had my share of success in instilling a sense of obligation and respect in my pupils." As she spoke, she unconsciously squared the ends of the scarf she wore.

"And what of the children?" Ragoczy asked her politely.

"They have done well." Her complacence was so complete

that she did not perceive the narrowing of Ragoczy's dark eyes.

"How do you mean that, Fräulein?" He had unlaced his fingers and leaned forward. "I fear, being foreign, I do not entirely comprehend what you are saying."

She brightened visibly. "I will be honored to do so. Naturally, not all foreigners are familiar with the standards of education in Deutschland. Therefore it is a great delight to tell you that those I have taught have mastered not only their own languages but also at least three others. I have recently been able to instruct a young boy in Greek and Latin as well as French. I do not generally teach Italian. Latin is preferable. Italian is a corrupt tongue, don't you think?"

Ragoczy's Italian was excellent, and he replied in that language. "No, Signorina, I don't agree with you at all." Then he resumed speaking German. "Have you Russian? My ward's first language is Russian."

Fräulein Mauser's jaw became even more square. "I know a few words, but it has not seemed to be a language for serious study. Those authors who are worth reading have been given superior translations. For the rest, there is little scholarship in that language and nothing of culture."

"And would you be willing to learn Russian?"

"Your ward will be learning Deutsch. There is no reason for me to become proficient in Russian. It would only encourage her to keep to her old ways," Fräulein Mauser said at her most tolerant. "It is not wise to encourage laxity, Herr Graf."

"Indeed it is not," he interjected, his expression set into careful neutrality.

"It may also indicate lack of proper concern on your part if you encourage her." She gave him a small, triumphant smile. "I will discuss the matter with you once I have observed the child more closely."

Ragoczy shook his head. "I am desolated to have to disappoint you, Fräulein Mauser, but I fear I will have to forgo your superior services. Doubtless someone of a more traditional bent then myself will be delighted to have you teach his children." He saw her dawning outrage, and went on most urbanely, "I have said that I will give you a proper reference as the result of this interview, and you may be certain that I will. My manservant will give it to you when he drives you to the train station in Hausham." Again he did not rise, but his dismissal was pointedly clear.

"Herr Graf, I am at a loss for words!" Fräulein Mauser began as she got to her feet.

"Then pray do not exhaust yourself with a fruitless search." He inclined his head and gave his attention to a stack of papers on his desk. He ignored everything but the violent closing of the door, which he acknowledged with a sardonic half-smile.

"Herr Pfahl," Roger announced a few minutes later, and ushered the young man into the room.

"Do please be seated," Ragoczy said to the young man, thinking that, from Herr Pfahl's manner, Fräulein Mauser must have been able to tell him quite a lot in a matter of minutes.

"I think I would rather stand," he said stiffly.

"If you prefer, by all means." Ragoczy leaned back in his chair. "You specialize in Romance Languages, and—"

"I don't know Russian!" the young man blurted out.

"I gathered that. It does present something of a problem, though not, I trust, an insurmountable one. You obviously have a talent for languages, and—" He was not allowed to continue.

"I have no feeling for Slavic tongues. I am certain I would not be of use to you, or your ward." His face had reddened and his eyes stared at the far wall.

Ragoczy sighed. "My ward is an unfortunate child, Herr Pfahl. She is very much alone in the world but for me. You must make allowances for my concern for her."

"Yes. Of course. Very understandable." He had taken one step back. "I have not worked with young students before, only those more advanced, preparing to enter the university. If I had known that your ward was not an advanced student, then I would not have sent an application for the position." He looked toward the door. "I did not mean to put you to any trouble, Herr Graf. I won't trouble you further." With that, he turned and fled from the room.

Ragoczy examined the nails of his left hand, a hand, he told himself, that he did not like to have forced. He reached into one of the pigeonholes of the desk and drew out two sheets of fine paper. These he laid side by side, then reached for two fountain pens. Holding one pen in each hand, he began to write identical recommendations.

He was just signing them when Roger opened the door again. "Herr Bündnis, my master."

"Thank you, Roger," Ragoczy said as he replaced the lids of

the pens and reached for blotters. "I will be with you in a moment, Herr Bündnis."

"Whatever you wish, Herr Ragoczy," was the prompt response.

"I trust," Ragoczy went on, pleasantly surprised by the use of his name instead of his title, "that you are not going to tell me that you do not speak Russian."

Herr Bündnis looked directly at Ragoczy. "As a matter of fact, I don't. I have some Polish, however, and a little Czech."

"Very enterprising," Ragoczy said, waiting.

"I learned both from servants at households where I have worked before." He added with sudden modest discomfort, "A few of the servants did not speak much Deutsch, and it was useful to be able to translate for them."

"As much for your employers as for you, I suspect," Ragoczy observed. He had the impression that he was being manipulated, and it was a thing he disliked. "Have you any theories on education, Herr Bündnis, or aversions to teaching one youngster?"

He hunched his shoulders and beetled his brow. "I believe in discipline, of course, and if your ward is a hoyden, we might not do well together. Still, the children I have worked with have been able to advance under my tuition. That's something. My father was a teacher in the village where we lived for a time." This admission made him even more uncomfortable.

"What village was that, Herr Bündnis?" Ragoczy asked, all attention.

"You would not know of it. He was killed in the war, in any case. My mother died of influenza last year." His features were strained. "This has little to do with my abilities as a teacher. I assure you that I have the necessary skill to work with your ward, if she is willing to do her part."

"She is an intelligent child," Ragoczy said quietly. "But not precisely like your other students. I shall expect to be informed of her progress as well as observing her for myself. Is that acceptable to you, Herr Bündnis?"

The tutor stared at him. "Acceptable?"

"There is also the matter of salary, housing, privileges, and the like, but I hope that you will give me a little time to work that out with you. When can you be ready to come here?" The questions were stern but his countenance was wryly humorous.

"Come here? Oh, by Friday. Yes. Friday," Herr Bündnis stammered, and then forced himself to speak clearly. "I will be here on Friday if that is to your liking, Herr Ragoczy. I have two trunks and quite a few books, if that is allowable."

"Natürlich. Tutors are supposed to have books." He held out his small, beautiful hand. "It is agreed then?"

"Yes. Yes. Certainly!" His grip was enthusiastic. "Vielen Dank, Herr Ragoczy."

"Gar nicht, Herr Bündnis." He released the tutor's hand and leaned back in his chair. "I will tell Laisha Vlassevna—my ward, Herr Bündnis—to expect you." For an instant he hesitated, then asked, "What is your Christian name, Herr Bündnis?"

"Ah . . . David," was the startled reply.

"David," Ragoczy repeated. "Sehr gut. I will tell my manservant to meet your train on Friday." He rose and strolled to the door. "If you care to come with me, Herr Bündnis, I will call Roger."

"Oh, yes. Of course." He followed Ragoczy hastily out of the study. As they went down the hallway, he gathered enough courage to say, "Will it be all right if I correspond with my aunt? She lives in Koln, and has no other relatives . . ."

"You may do just as you like, Herr Bündnis," Ragoczy told him as he indicated a door on the left.

It was the music room, and at the moment four workmen were restoring the plaster to its original decorative forms. Roger stood with one of the men, reading over a set of architectural drawings. He looked up as the door opened.

"Roger, this is Herr Bündnis, who is to be Laisha's tutor. If you can spare a moment to talk with him, it might be wise to arrange to meet him on Friday, when he is to come to us." Ragoczy nodded to the workmen, raising his voice to say to the room at large, "You've done very well. I am quite pleased."

One of the workmen gave a deferential wave for the rest, then returned to his labors.

Roger had already asked two quick questions of Herr Bündnis, and said, "There are trains at eleven in the morning— the one you arrived on today—and four in the afternoon. There is also another train in the summer, but that is not a consideration just now. Tell me which is convenient, and I will meet you."

"The eleven-o'clock will be fine," Herr Bündnis said nervously. "If you would prefer that I come on the later train . . ."

"It is of no concern, Herr Bündnis," Roger assured him, and left the room to settle the matter of the tutor's quarters.

Half an hour later, as the three tutors were getting into the Benz touring car to be driven to the train station, Ragoczy came upon his manservant again.

"Well, old friend, is it settled, then?" He spoke in Latin, in an accent that had not been heard for nearly two thousand years.

"It would seem so." Roger's blue eyes were curious.

"Yes. I think we had better learn a bit more about Herr Bündnis. This aunt of his in Köln—I would like to know who she is. And where his father taught. This has been a very neat maneuver, perhaps a jot too neat. You're going to Zurich and Lucerne in a month or so, aren't you?" He let the question hang.

"It might take me another four or five days to get the information you want," Roger said. His voice was carefully schooled: their conversation sounded no more important than a discussion of household supplies.

"And the others?" Ragoczy said speculatively. "I'm curious to know where they next find employment. Fräulein Mauser will not be difficult to trace, if we must, but I think that Herr Pfahl is a more difficult matter. Perhaps a word or two to Professor Riemen might be useful."

"I will be delivering your papers to him, in any case," Roger reminded him.

"My thought precisely," Ragoczy murmured. "A fine opportunity."

Roger looked thoughtfully down the road, where the Benz was taking the first of four long switchback turns. "What do you anticipate?"

"Why, nothing," Ragoczy said to him.

Roger had been with his master far too long to press him at such moments. Tactfully he turned their talk to different matters and shortly was pleased when Ragoczy excused himself to go work in the large stark room behind his cozy study.

Text of a letter from Herr August Kehr to the manservant Roger.

*SCHWEIZERBANK*
*14 NACHHALTIGSTRASSE*
*ZÜRICH*

*March 26, 1919*

*Herr Roger*
*Hôtel Françias*
*Dortmundstrasse*
*Zürich*

*My dear sir:*

*I have in hand your employer's authorization for the transfer of five hundred thousand Swiss francs to his bank in München. The situation there is, as you are doubtless aware, politically unstable. The Spartacists may have nominal control of the city, but with the Frei Korps tightening their position around the city, this cannot continue for long. As your employer has granted me certain discretionary options, I feel it would be of benefit to both this bank and your employer if we delay the transfer for a month or so until the political situation is less uncertain. For the moment, I am sending notification of the proposed transfer to the Bayerisch Kreditkörperschaft, to Herr Helmut Rauch, who will handle matters on that end of the dealings. Herr Rauch has not been with BKK for long but has been spoken of most highly by his colleagues there. I have no doubt that Herr Graf Ragoczy may repose complete confidence in this man.*

*It is my understanding that the sums your employer has deposited with Rothschild are not to be touched. May I take the liberty of saying that this is undoubtedly wise, although I could wish more of Herr Graf Ragoczy's funds were to remain with us.*

*As always, you may be sure of our continuing service
and most confidential dealings.*
*On behalf of the Schweizerbank, it is my honor to be*

> Sincerely at your service,
> August Kehr

## 3

By nine that evening, the party at Wolkighügel had divided
itself into three uneasy parts. In the library Maximillian
Altbrunnen had shut himself up with his cronies from München
in open disregard for his sister's wishes. There was a trio
playing dance music in the large dining room, and those guests
who were determined to ignore Maximillian's churlishness were
gathered there in the dogged pursuit of a pleasant evening.
The smallest group of all sat in the conservatory, doing their
best to be invisible. Gudrun set her mouth in a permanent
meaningless smile as she made her way from one group to the
other, wishing fervently that she had never decided on the
party.

She had just asked Otto to open more champagne when the
front knocker resounded through the front hall. "But who? At
this hour?" Gudrun wondered aloud.

Otto shrugged and turned away to answer the door. "Good
evening," he said with a light nod to the figure on the threshold.

"And to you," said Franchot Ragoczy as he stepped into the
room, removing his black silken evening cloak as he did. His
formal clothing was immaculate: full tails, exquisitely cut, a
white silk shirt, white brocade vest with ruby studs, a neat
black velvet tie fixed with a square-cut ruby stickpin. He
pulled black kid gloves from his hands and gave them along
with his cloak to Otto.

Gudrun stared at her guest, and for once did not quite know
what to say. She realized who the man must be, but when he
had not arrived for the dinner, she assumed that he would not
attend. She blushed slightly, unaware of how this heightened
color improved her looks.

"I fear I must apologize for my tardy arrival," Ragoczy was

saying as he started toward his hostess. "I am Saint-Germain."
He pronounced it in the French manner.

"Graf Ragoczy?" It could be no other, and the name of the
Schloss was the same, but she could not entirely believe her
good fortune. Gudrun held out her hand to him, thinking that
perhaps her party would not be a total failure after all.

He carried her hand to his lips, bowing in perfect form.
"Frau Ostneige?" His dark eyes smiled enigmatically into her
pale blue ones.

Gudrun inwardly rebuked herself for the sudden attraction
she had for this man. She reminded herself of Jürgen lying
propped in his bed upstairs, unable to take part in the festivities, his once-magnificent body withered to the thinness and
frailty of twigs. She had no right to look at this stranger so
intensely.

"Troubled, Madame?" Ragoczy asked, offering his arm to
her. Although he was not much taller than she, his bearing
provided the illusion of height. His attention was courteous
and wholly proper.

"Not exactly." Gudrun gave a brittle, short laugh. "I imagine that every first party of the season has some awkwardness
to it. And with everyone worried about München and the
Spartacists, well . . ." She gestured as if to show herself
merrily resigned to the evening. As she spoke, she went with
him toward the dining-room door. Earlier she had been worried that her peach-colored organza petal-tiered evening dress
was a bit too daring for a woman in her position, but next to
her elegant neighbor, she was relieved that she had not settled on the prim gray silk.

"The Frei Korps are closing in, and they are well-financed,"
Ragoczy said as he held the door open for her.

The strains of a popular waltz tune greeted them, and a
sporadic counterpoint of conversation. There were half a dozen
couples standing around the punch bowl and another five
couples dancing. There were twelve huge sprays of fresh
flowers on pedestals around the room, filling the air with their
perfume. The gathering looked as lively as a funeral.

A middle-aged woman in an overdone lace dress hurried
over to her hostess. "Oh, Frau Ostneige," she cried out, "Herr
Natter has been saying that the war is not over, and that we'll
see men in the trenches again before we know it. I *know* that
the Peace terms are disgraceful, and I *know* the Allies have
trampled on the honor of Deutschland, but my two brothers
were killed, and three uncles as well, and I don't want to hear

about war again!" Her voice had become quite shrill, and what little interest there had been in the music was lost as the other guests turned to look at her.

"Ah, Aloisia!" Gudrun was dismayed. In the little time it had taken her to greet this last arrival, things had become even worse. "No, no, you must not be upset. Everyone is concerned, of course. It stands to reason that those who fought would be angry at the Allies' terms, but we haven't had much time to change our thinking. To say that there must be another war, when most of us lost loved ones and . . ." She was babbling, she knew, and wished she could stop. She noticed the pressure of Ragoczy's hand on her arm, and she turned to him gratefully.

"If you would introduce me?" he prompted her kindly.

"Of course. How remiss of me." Her smile flashed gratitude at her companion. By the time she had presented all her guests to her hochgeborn visitor, perhaps the worst of this latest disruption would have passed. "Graf Ragoczy, may I present to you Frau Aloisia Inschrift; Aloisia, this is Graf Ragoczy from Schloss Saint-Germain."

Aloisia simpered and dropped a hint of a curtsy. "I'm delighted, Graf. Herr Inschrift and I have been most eager to meet you."

Ragoczy bowed to the woman. "It is a pleasure, Madame." He began to anticipate a long evening and wondered if he should have attended the party at all.

Gudrun was already drawing him away from the older woman toward the gathering at the punch bowl. Several curious glances were directed this way, and he met each one with the ironic hauteur he had mastered so long ago.

An hour later, when the musicians were playing again, Gudrun plucked at his sleeve and said to him in an undervoice, "Thank you very much, Herr Graf. I was in flat despair until you arrived."

Ragoczy looked at her, studying her face. His first impression, he knew, had underestimated her, though he doubted she knew how strong a woman she was. "It was nothing, Madame. I assure you." He looked at the couples dancing, and remarked, "I would have expected more guests at, as you say, the first party of the season."

"But there are more guests," Gudrun said softly. "My brother has retired to the library with his . . . friends, and the Schnaubels . . . Oh, I *wish* Maxl wouldn't be so difficult about Jews. The things he called—"

"Simeon Schnaubel is here?" Ragoczy interrupted her.

"He and his wife: they're in the conservatory with Gerwald and Walpurga Bohle. They're from Bad Wiessee, the Bohles, an older couple. She had the influenza, and was very ill for more than a year, but they're getting out now." Gudrun had been speaking in an undervoice.

"Simeon Schnaubel is seeing to the restoration of my home," Ragoczy said quietly. "I wish you had told me earlier he was here."

Again Gudrun flushed, thinking she had been enjoying the evening for the last twenty minutes, and in fact had been delaying the time when she must, for the sake of good manners, take her illustrious guest to meet the rest of the company. "I'm . . . sorry, Herr Graf, but . . ." She did not know what to say, and wished, senselessly, that she could walk away from the whole evening.

Ragoczy relented. "With so much on your mind, it's understandable that you would like a respite. Let me bring you some punch, Madame." He left her side and walked along the side of the dining room toward the punch bowl. As he reached for the silver ladle and a crystal cup, he heard a voice at his elbow.

"You're the one with a French title," Konrad Natter said a trifle too loudly.

"Among others," was Ragoczy's affable reply. "My family name is not unknown in Hungary." He filled the cup and turned to face the other guest.

Konrad Natter was almost drunk enough to laugh in the foreigner's face, but not quite. He had enough sense of where he was to do nothing more than sneer. "French titles. I'd be embarrassed to have one, with the war just ended and the French determined to shame us."

"But you are a Deutscher and I am not," Ragoczy pointed out mildly.

"Exactly," Natter declared, wagging one finger at the foreigner. His silver-streaked fawn-brown hair had become disordered and one strand hung over his eyes. "Exactly my thought. Ragoczy is Hungarian, but the family were Prinzes of Transylvania, weren't they, back a century or so? And where are they now?"

"Two centuries, actually, before the Hapsburgs expanded Austria. It was some time ago." Ragoczy looked at him. "You must understand better than most what it is to be deprived of your birthright, Herzog Natter." He was pleased to see Konrad

Natter blanch at the sound of his family's former title. " 'Herzog' comes as awkwardly to you as 'Prinz' does to me, but both were legitimate when we were young." With that, he inclined his head and walked away through the suddenly-loud dance music and the muted rustle of voices.

Gudrun took the crystal cup and drank eagerly. "Danke, Herr Graf," she said, her eyes very bright.

"Come, Madame, must you forever remind me of what is lost? It was unpleasant enough with Herr Natter, but with you . . ." He did not touch her or move closer to her, but Gudrun felt her life narrow down to the little space that contained the two of them. "Must we be formal?"

"Franchot Ragoczy?" she breathed, shaking her head.

He repeated what he had said when he entered her home. "I am Saint-Germain."

"Saint-Germain," she echoed, taking wicked delight in pronouncing the French. "But I must continue to introduce you as Ragoczy, and Graf, mustn't I? It is how you are known in the area. It will be expected."

"Whatever suits you, Madame." He held out his hand for the empty cup. "Perhaps you will find a moment to take me to the conservatory. I would very much like to talk with Simeon Schnaubel and his wife—I have not properly met her."

"She's a very pleasant woman," Gudrun said as she strove to check an irrational spurt of jealousy that his request fired in her. "Yes, you should meet her. It was remiss of me not to do this earlier."

The trio was playing a medley of tunes from Kalman's operetta *Die Czardasfürstin* and one of the women was attempting to sing along as she danced. The punch bowl had been refilled less than half an hour ago, and at eleven o'clock there would be a buffet supper for the guests. Gudrun looked anxiously over the room.

"They will see to themselves, Madame," Ragoczy said to her in an undervoice. "Unless you wish to remain here, in which case you have only to tell me where I might find the conservatory."

"Um Gottes Willen! If I cannot spare ten minutes for the Schnaubels, I must be a very poor hostess." She laughed a little recklessly and made a complicated gesture with her hands, consigning this portion of the party to its own devices. "Come, Herr Graf . . ."

"Saint-Germain," he corrected her quietly.

She glanced up at him as she opened the door, and did

something she had not done in several years: she giggled. Her inward shock was negated by the lightness of spirit she felt. "Saint-Germain," she agreed, and led the way down the hall toward the conservatory.

About two dozen plants had been set in tubs in the glass-ceilinged room in an attempt to show the place at its best. There was one wall that had been negligently painted so that the rude scrawlings the vandals had left on the walls could still be read. The night was cool for late April, and in the conservatory it was necessary for the four guests there to have more than their evening clothes to keep warm. Amalie Schnaubel had worn a long, sleeveless dress with a filmy patterned gauze overrobe, and was clearly the least comfortable of the four. She sat huddled in a wicker chair, her legs drawn up and her arms folded tightly across her chest. Beside her on a leather ottoman sat Simeon in a dinner jacket, looking dapper. They were deep in conversation with an older couple. The man was in proper full tails, which he wore with a great deal of ease; his wife was another matter. She was small and visibly frail. Her dress of lavender satin was new but cut in the mode of a decade earlier. In the square neck of the kimono dress she wore an impressive necklace of diamonds and sapphires.

"I'm sorry to have kept you alone so long," Gudrun said as she came into the room. "It has been a very awkward evening for you, and I sincerely apologize. You know what it was like earlier: I did not want to give further occasion for offense." She tried to smile at these four people but gave it up after two attempts.

Ragoczy had entered behind her and decided that there was no need for Gudrun to be made so miserable. He touched her lightly on the shoulder and came past her into the room. "Good evening, Simeon. It's good to see you."

"Herr Ragoczy!" Simeon Schnaubel ejaculated, rising with alacrity. He clasped the outstretched hand enthusiastically. "I never thought you would be here."

"I've wanted to meet my neighbors for some time, and this seemed as good a way as any." He turned to the woman in the wicker chair. "You are Amalie Schnaubel, are you not? I have seen your children, and since we have exchanged notes, I feel that we have met already." He held out his hand for hers.

"This is Herr Ragoczy, Liebs," Simeon explained unnecessarily.

"Yes," Amalie said, a bemused expression in her eyes as Ragoczy bent to kiss her hand. "A pleasure, Herr Ragoczy.

The children have said a great deal about your kindness to them, and your ward."

Ragoczy shook his head slightly. "It gives me a great deal of joy to see them together, and so I am indebted to you." Though his style was gallant, there was no doubting his sincerity, which Amalie found perplexing. She had expected someone more forbidding than this polished, gently sardonic man. She met his penetrating gaze and the faintest of shivers ran through her. She recognized the strength in his eyes and was strangely daunted.

"Frau Schnaubel is cold," Ragoczy said, knowing full well that the cool room had nothing to do with her light dress. "Frau Ostneige, if I may, would your servant bring my cloak?"

Gudrun murmured her assent and stepped into the hall to call for Otto. She wished now that the old bell pulls had been reinstalled in each room. At these times, it was unfair to ask two or three men to be everywhere in the Schloss. She had walked half the length of the hall before she caught sight of Otto.

"Do you want me to send another bottle of schnapps to the library? Maxl's friends have gone through three bottles of cognac so far, and they've asked for more." Otto's old features were heavy with disapproval.

"What?" For the last half-hour Gudrun had almost forgotten her feckless brother, and the question now almost dashed her newly-restored good humor. "Three bottles of cognac? And my brother says . . ." She broke off, knowing that there was no benefit in railing at him. "If they must have spirits, choose one of the lesser bottles. If they've already gone through three bottles, they probably won't notice the difference." As she turned away from her servant, she recalled the reason for her errand. "Oh, and, Otto, will you bring Herr Ragoczy's cloak to the conservatory? Frau Schnaubel is very cold and he has kindly offered it to her." As much as she admired the gesture, Gudrun could not entirely avoid the realization that she wished he had done it for her. Immediately she scolded herself for her feelings; she required a moment or two to herself before she returned to the conservatory. There was a vague sensation behind her eyes, as if she was about to have a headache. She pinched the bridge of her nose and took several deep breaths before starting down the hallway toward the conservatory.

Ragoczy was sitting on a rickety willowwork divan, discussing the premiere of *Tosca* in Rome with the Bohles. "Certainly there was a riot," he was saying, "but not because of the music itself: that came later. No, the public was outraged because Puccini insisted that the work actually start on time."

Gerwald Bohle gave a somber nod to his head. "That was not what I was given to understand. And the outrage at the impropriety of the material . . ."

"You must never have been in Roma if you think that *Tosca* offended them. There's nothing the Romans love better than scandal," Ragoczy insisted. He turned to Simeon. "Have you been to *Tosca*? Unless you hear it with Scotti, you will miss a great deal."

"I had the pleasure of hearing him in *Don Giovanni* but nothing else," Simeon said. The strained look about his eyes was gone and he was less reserved. "I don't care much for opera. Mahler—now, there's a composer worth listening to."

Walpurga interjected a comment before her husband could challenge Simeon's pronouncement. "I was hardly more than a girl when I first heard *Gräfin DuBarry* in Wien. I've often been told I have no taste at all in music, and it is probably true. I like operetta so much more than all that pounding music. Operetta is light and amusing . . ."

Gerwald smiled indulgently. "Operetta is froth, meine Freude. Well enough for an evening, but nothing—"

"But what is life without a little froth?" Walpurga asked with the ghost of an impish smile. "There is so much dreary and tragic all around us, what is the harm in wanting a bit of pastry instead of all that suffering?"

"You're probably right, Frau Bohle," Amalie said at once, before Simeon or Gerwald Bohle could speak. "After a day dealing with children, I don't want to listen to anything heavier than Lehar. When I was younger, it was different. Mozart was not deep enough for me." She paid no attention to the shock of her announcement. "My brother was a violinist, and a very serious boy. There were times he thought Wagner was on the frivolous side." The corners of her mouth turned down. "He died in Poland, four years ago." The sudden hush in the conservatory distressed her. "Please. I didn't intend to mention that. It's inexcusable. I never meant to . . ."

To Gudrun's relief, it was Ragoczy who smoothed over the awkwardness. "Hardly inexcusable, Frau Schnaubel. It is evident that you cherished your brother, and find consolation in the things he loved best. All of us have done that at one time or another," He got up from the divan and came toward his hostess. "I didn't think I was sending you on such an expedition, Frau Ostneige. I will be fortunate indeed if you ask for nothing more than a word of apology."

"You're being absurd, Graf," Gudrun objected at once. "I've asked Otto to bring the cloak. It may take a moment; he's no longer young and he has other duties to attend to." She wanted desperately to be alone with her hochgeborn guest, and the admission of this longing irritated her. It would not do! She had greater discipline than this.

"If it is an imposition, tell me where the cloak is and I'll go get it." He sensed Gudrun's inner turmoil, but did not guess its cause.

"Of course not. Otto will attend to it." She looked at the two couples with satisfaction. Yes, they were doing better, talking and enjoying themselves: their faces were attentive and their voices animated, whereas half an hour ago they had been plodding through empty formalities. It would be safe to leave them, assured that there would be no reason to worry about them. "You will think me hopelessly flighty, but I must see to my other guests." There was nothing unusual in this announcement, but Gudrun felt a stab of guilt when she realized that she was waiting for Ragoczy to come with her. She would not accept his escort, of course, but the offer would mean so much. Fearing to put the matter to the test, she left the conservatory quickly, going down the hall at a pace so brisk it was almost flight.

"Rudi," Otto admonished as he watched her approach. "A woman your age should not dash about the halls this way. What would your father say, if he could see you?"

Gudrun gave him an over-bright smile. "He would doubtless say just what you have said. But if my father were here, I should not have to be both host and hostess at this terrible party." Belatedly she noticed the long cloak of black silk Otto carried and bit her lower lip. "I must see to the guests in the dining room. The buffet will be served soon, won't it?"

"Yes. But Rudi! Wait! Maxl said he . . ." Otto shrugged as he started once again toward the conservatory, shaking his head as he thought about Gudrun's misfortunes. He was brought up short by an elegant, compact figure coming toward him. "Graf. I did not see you. May I direct you—?"

"Your mistress, where is she?" Ragoczy asked in a voice that managed to be pleasant for all its curtness.

"In the dining room, or so I think. I was trying to tell her that Maxl wants his friends to join in the buffet, but they're getting rowdy." Otto's eyes grew sorrowful. He had expected better of his favorite.

"I'll warn her," Ragoczy told him. "Where are these stalwarts now?"

"In the library. Talking politics, the way they do at the Hirsch Furt." He lifted his shoulders to indicate there was nothing a servant could do, then added, "Sometimes he goes up to Herr Ostneige's room and reads to him."

"Very kind," Ragoczy said wryly. "I'll have to find Frau Ostneige quickly, then." A wave of his hand sent Otto off down the hall, while he continued toward the dining room. He was not entirely startled to find her outside the entrance to the dining room, hands clasped tightly in front of her, her jaw rigid with suppressed emotion. "Frau Ostneige," he said quietly.

Her eyes flew open and she paled. "You!" She took a hasty step back.

Ragoczy frowned. "Frau Ostneige, I seem to have offended you. If I have done so, it was inadvertent, and I ask your pardon for whatever it was I have done."

"Offended me? Oh, no." Her slender hands came up to her face. "I wish you had not found me, though I wanted you to." She smiled miserably. "It's not fitting that I should talk to you this way. Pray put it from your mind."

"If that would satisfy you, then naturally I will." He did not step closer to her, though he had a moment when he would have taken her in his arms if she had moved toward him at all.

"Thank you, Graf." Almost unwillingly, she corrected herself. "Saint-Germain."

"For what, Frau Ostneige?" His dark eyes rested on her. "Your servant, the old man—I assume that's Otto—wished me to tell you that your brother and his guests intend to come to the buffet. Am I correct in guessing that this will be difficult?"

"What? He must not . . . ! Oh, Maxl!" Gudrun would like to have screamed at Maximillian. Just when she had got the party moving properly, Maxl and his friends would return and the evening would be in ruins.

Ragoczy saw the annoyance and disappointment in her face, and said, "Would you prefer this did not happen, Frau Ostneige?"

"Yes. Emphatically." She smoothed her dress in an effort to compose herself. "They will only want to discuss the political and military situation. It is bad enough with the Frei Korps skulking about the mountains, but when these friends of his start to talk about cultural heritage and the rest of it, it's un*bear*able. Only Natter agrees with them, and he cannot stand to listen to them too long. Earlier this evening, before they retired to the library, they had made themselves odious to everyone, particularly the Schnaubels. I never imagined that my brother would be so terribly rude to a guest in this house. He practically accused Herr Schnaubel of raping Christian women in order to pollute the race. It's all nonsense! Polluting the race, of all things, and the Schnaubels. They're our neighbors! Mein Gott!" She had kept her voice from rising, but the tension in her was like a current of electricity.

He looked at her, and some of his calm communicated itself to her. "Gnädige Frau, you must not do this to yourself. You're distraught—understandably so. But your guests ought not know it. No one will notice if you are gone for ten minutes. Those in the dining room will assume you are in the conservatory, and the others will believe that you are in the dining room. Go to your bedchamber and put lavender water on your temples and fix your hair. It will help. I'll do what I can to keep your brother and his friends from leaving the library." He was standing partially in shadow, and his face could not be read.

She gave him a short, baffled stare. "Why would you do this? It is not your concern."

"I live in this district. That is a factor. I've given a few dreadful parties myself. And you have been . . . kind to me." He did not add that he was attracted by her strength, which she did not know she possessed.

"I? Kind?" She shook her head so forcefully that more strands came loose from her carefully-knotted and pinned coiffure to tumble around her face. "Oh, no, Graf. I am not kind." Before she could reveal more of her feelings, she said, "I'll do it. If you're sure . . ."

"Yes. Go on." He said it lightly so that she would be less uneasy, but once she had gone, he grew serious once more. As he stepped into the light, the shine from a gas bracket showed that his frown had deepened. It had not been his intention to involve himself with these people at Wolkighügel, and he came to the party this evening in the hope that his appearance here would take the place of several tedious individual visits. He had not been prepared for Frau Ostneige, and that bothered him. His eyes strayed once to the way she had gone; then he turned his mind to more practical things. Long experience had taught him that it was most imprudent to press his luck with neighbors, no matter how kind or how attractive.

No one had told him where the library was, but he had seen a fair number of these large houses before and was willing to make an educated guess. The first door he tried opened onto a small room with beautiful draperies, which Ragoczy assumed was the breakfast room. He closed the door and continued along the passage. As he walked, he heard the sound of belligerent voices coming from behind the double oaken doors at the end of the hallway.

"No one in the Thule Gesellschaft should ascribe to such views!" insisted one of the contenders in a loud, slurred tone.

"You're not the one to make decisions for the Bruderschaft," reprimanded another. "When you've advanced, you will understand."

"This isn't the Middle Ages, Friedrich. Theodor is right. We must search for other solutions here. A paper is the best answer, not for news, as we have now, but to promote our views. The rituals should be saved for the more advanced Initiates." This last man was considerably less drunk than the others. His voice was powerful and clear. "It will not be done overnight, but with Dietrich here to help us, it will come to pass. In two or three months at the most we may all return to München and take up our lives again."

There were sounds of encouragement, and hearing this, Ragoczy decided it was time to interrupt. He rapped on the door. "Your pardon, gentlemen. I must ask you a question on behalf of your hostess."

The men in the library fell silent at once, except for what might have been a curse. There was a shuffling of chairs, the sound of a breaking glass, and then the door was opened by a tall young man with hair a lighter blond than his sister's. Ragoczy saw the resemblance at once, though he noticed there was a slackness around the brother's mouth that had little to do with drink. The young man glared down insolently at Ragoczy. "Who're you?"

"A guest of your sister," Ragoczy said affably. "She has deputized me to speak for her." He waited to be invited into the room.

For the better part of a minute it seemed that Maximillian would shut the door in the newcomer's face, but then he stepped back, providing just enough room for Ragoczy to enter the library.

There were nine men gathered around the fire, one or two holding open books, each with balloon snifters near at hand but for the broken glass on the floor by the feet of a thin, nervous man in his fifties. One of the men turned to Ragoczy and gave him a swift, covert scrutiny. "Who is this gentleman, Altbrunnen?" His voice identified him as the sober man who had been speaking just before Ragoczy knocked on the door.

Maximillian stared at Ragoczy. "I haven't seen him before."

"Allow me to introduce myself," Ragoczy said to the assembly. "I have recently come into this area, to my Schloss. I am Franchot Ragoczy." He pronounced the first name again, with great care. "*Fran*-zhot, not Fran-*cho*."

"Ragoczy is a noteworthy name." The speaker was a red-faced, rotund man sitting back in one of the chairs.

"Indeed," Ragoczy said.

"What does my sister want now?" Maximillian demanded. His handsome face was truculent and his dark blue eyes glittered.

"Why, only to make your evening more . . . comfortable," Ragoczy answered. "It is nearing the time for the buffet supper, and it occurred to her that since you have been busy for most of the evening, you might not want to interrupt your discussions for nothing more than half an hour of unprofitable conversation with the other guests. If it would suit you and your associates to have your buffet served here, she will have it done."

The sober man gave Ragoczy an appraising look. "Very generous of her," he said with a great deal of meaning.

"Wasn't it," Ragoczy agreed.

"That's my sister," Maximillian said, wholly unaware of the critical byplay between the two men. "Most of the time she's well enough, and my father taught her a few things. Good for her. That's sensible of her, for a change."

"Then you would like the buffet brought to you here?" Ragoczy asked to assuage Maximillian's vanity.

"Yes, yes, that's right." He was about to open the door when he turned to Ragoczy. "What's your name again?"

"Ragoczy," was the reply.

This time Maximillian essayed a friendly smile. "I recall now. The one who owns Schloss Saint-Germain. Been meaning to call on you, but haven't got round to it yet." He held out his hand. "Sehr angenehm, Herr Graf."

"Schloss Saint-Germain," the sober man said as Ragoczy shook hands with Maximillian. "You have yet another remarkable name."

"Never mind Alfred," Maximillian said. "He's always looking for significance in things. I've heard from one of the workmen that you're planning to install an electrical generator at Schloss Saint-Germain. That's damned enterprising of you." Before Ragoczy could respond or Maximillian continue, Alfred had approached them.

"Do you happen to know," he said in a forceful way, "if your Schloss is in any way associated with the eighteenth-century mystic of the same name?"

"If you're referring to le Comte de Saint-Germain, I believe there is some connection, yes." Ragoczy had assumed the blandest of expressions and spoke with an urbanity he was far from feeling. "Why do you ask?"

The other men in the room were leaning forward now, and one of them had got out of his chair and moved closer.

"Oh, curiosity," Alfred said with a wave of his hand. "This little study group of ours"—his gesture included all the men in the room—"occasionally delves into the occult, and a few of our members believe that he, that is, Saint-Germain, was one of the founders of the Bruderschaft."

"As I understand it," Ragoczy told him with the air of a man who has explained a minor misconception too often to enjoy it, "Saint-Germain has been credited with a great many things that he had little or nothing to do with."

"Then you *do* know something about him." Once again Alfred's eyes grew predatory.

Ragoczy shrugged. "In self-defense, you might say. You're not the only one to recognize the name." He turned toward the door to put an end to the conversation. "With your permission, I'll convey your answer to Frau Ostneige."

"By all means," Maximillian said. "And let them know in the kitchen that we're getting peckish."

Alfred was not inclined to let Ragoczy leave so quickly, but could do little to detain him. "I trust we may speak further, Herr Ragoczy."

"I doubt I will be staying very late tonight," Ragoczy said, deliberately choosing to misinterpret his meaning.

"There will be other times, Herr Graf," Maximillian promised blithely. "My sister will be having more of these evenings as summer comes on."

"So we will meet again, Herr Ragoczy," Alfred declared as the door closed between them. "I look forward to the day."

Ragoczy had given orders in the kitchen and spoken to Otto before Gudrun descended from her room. He approached her at once. "I have taken the liberty of arranging for a part of the buffet to be served in the library, if you do not object."

"Oh, thank you." Gudrun had brushed her hair back into the soft coronet she had made of a single long braid, and she was entirely mistress of herself again. As a gesture of confidence, she had hung two long necklaces of pearls around her throat and bosom. She seemed more formidable now. Ragoczy studied her, knowing it would not be wise to have any but the most casual of dealings with her. Yet he felt his heart go out to her for her intelligence and courage, and he doubted he could leave her to the care of her brother. As Gudrun reached the bottom step, she saw the concern in Ragoczy's eyes, and once again felt abashed. "I probably should not have let you persuade me to go upstairs, Herr Graf, but I could not resist the idea. You've been very patient with me. And to find a way to keep the men in the library from mixing with my other guests, that alone is more than I had any right to ask."

"It's nothing, Frau Ostneige." He offered his arm to her. "You'll want to go into the dining room, I think."

"I suppose it's best." She made a last-minute correction to the fall of her petal-tiered skirt. "You'll take supper with me?"

"It would be my pleasure to sit with you, but I have . . . dined recently, and I fear I am not . . . hungry again yet." He recalled the young woman from Tegernsee he had visited earlier that evening. She had been wealthy, bored, and eager for novelty, quick in her passion, but with an unadmitted need that reminded Ragoczy somewhat of Estasia so many years ago in Fiorenza, but lacking the undercurrent of madness. He had been satisfied by her gratification, but was comforted by the knowledge that neither she nor himself had any inclination to meet again. Eventually he would want a more regular arrangement, but for the time being he was reasonably content to limit himself to those women seeking relaxation and brief adventure at the various mountain lakes in the district. He did not want to admit that such encounters were ultimately disappointing.

"Herr Graf, is there something wrong?" Gudrun's question cut into his thoughts.

"No; nothing." They had reached the door to the dining room and could hear the music and muted talk beyond it. Against his better judgment, he added, "You are going to call me Saint-Germain, are you not?"

The uncertainty disappeared from her smile as she reached to push open the door. "Yes. I am."

Text of a report from the tutor David Bündnis to his employer, Franchot Ragoczy.

*July 9, 1919*

*My dear Graf Ragoczy:*

*You have asked that I prepare an evaluation of the progress of your ward, Laisha Vlassevna, and it is my privilege to do so.*

*As you yourself have indicated, this is a gifted child with a great deal of native intelligence. I have not been able to ascertain how much instruction she has had prior to my tuition, but from what I have observed of her, she has spent a fair amount of time in the schoolroom. Her grasp of languages, while she claims to dislike such study, is excellent. I suspect that she has had such instruction before, although she claims that she does not recall any lessons whatsoever.*

*We have studied a little geography, and she has very much enjoyed learning the names of the various countries around the world. She has avoided asking any questions whatever about Russia, either historically or at present, and she has a marked aversion to discussing the Great War. When I have attempted to learn more of why she feels this way, she retreats into childish petulance. I have not been able to coax her out of such moods when they are upon her and she has said that she does not wish to be cheered at those times. I would be grateful for your suggestions on the matter.*

*Recently she has said that she would like to see a moving picture, and I have given her my opinion—that such entertainments are amusing, but of no lasting merit—and told her I would inquire of you whether or not you will permit her to attend a showing of such a thing, and what you would recommend of those moving pictures available for viewing. It seems that the Schnaubel chil-*

*dren have occasionally gone into München to the motion-picture theatres there with their mother to guide and advise them. She told me that they saw an American film called* Birth of a Nation *a week ago, and are still talking about it.*

*Now that the political situation in München is more stable, it might be possible for Laisha Vlassevna to go there, properly escorted and supervised, for a day or so, and she could then have the opportunity to see more of the city and go into one or two of the shops. To finish off such an adventure with a moving picture would give her the entertainment she desires without making it the central attraction of such a jaunt. As you have told me that she is about eight years old, it is not unnatural for her to be increasingly curious. I offer my own escort, naturally, as well as informing you that Frau Schnaubel has invited Laisha Vlassevna to join her the next time she takes her children to the city. It is my belief that you would be wise to consider the offer, since your ward occasionally grows restless here, and although she does not complain, I am aware that she has a child's longing for adventure as well as an active curiosity.*

*I have recently added numbers to our studies, and she has shown herself an apt pupil in this area, as well. As long as the use of numbers is a game, she does exceedingly well, but when it is a question of learning by rote or drill, then she does poorly and her thoughts often wander. She has been most responsive to numbers in relation to music, which she says is like a puzzle. If you have not considered providing her with lessons on an instrument, then let me recommend that you do. I am no judge of musical talent, but I am quite sure that if interest and devotion are important in that art, she will prove to be a most satisfactory student.*

*From what she has told me, her hours with you are most important to her, and I would caution you that when you travel, you be certain to contact her often. No doubt there will be telephone access to private houses here before too long, and then the matter will be simpler, but letters and telegrams might do a great deal to ease her fears. A child as young as she is, with so much tragedy behind her, is more easily offset than others. It is probably unnecessary to remind you of this, for everything she tells me indicates that you have a great sensitivity to her and her plight, but because of the sort of girl she is, it is possible that she has not mentioned her fears to you, and that you have come to underestimate them.*

*She is most enthusiastic about the pony you have bought her, and so far has been willing to do her stable tasks as you have instructed her. I have learned that if I cannot find her in the library or her suite, that she is doubtless in the stables with that pony. I feel I should mention here that I do not like the attitude of the groom, Farold Kufe, who is willing to criticize the girl but not to help her. If I knew more of horsemanship I would offer to spend time with her in that capacity as well, but my experience with horses has been limited to giving a carrot to the ragman's mare. You have spent a fair amount of time with her and the pony, so you cannot be unaware of her eagerness to excel as an equestrienne. She has said that she is often afraid that the whole summer will pass and she will not have had the chance for a gallop down the hill to the lake.*

*I have enclosed with this a number of Laisha Vlassevna's essays, exercises, and examinations, so that you may review for yourself how advanced she has become. Under more usual circumstances, I would recommend that you enroll her in a good girls' school in Lucerne or Salzburg, but in this case I doubt that course would be wise. Perhaps in a year or so the matter can be approached reasonably, but for the time being, the best I can say is that she is doing well in her studies, and when the time comes that she is ready to enter a more regular schooling, she will not be unprepared for the studies, no matter how much she may dislike the method.*

*You have requested that I confer with you about her new subjects, and that is most welcome. I am, of course, entirely at your disposal, and look forward to the discussion. In anticipation of that meeting, may I suggest that perhaps the biological sciences will interest her a great deal. I must confess that I have little skill in that area, but it may be possible to arrange something with Herr Vögel in Geitau. He is retired now, but at one time he was very well-known for his work in biology, and it may be he would be glad of an intelligent student as well as a few extra marks each month.*

*I have the duty and honor to be*

*Most sincerely yours*
*David Bündnis*

# 4

Kriegskönigstrasse was a narrow lane off Türkenstrasse about halfway between the Alte Pinakothek and the Residenz; most of the buildings on it harked back to the fourteenth and fifteenth centuries, yet all were splendidly kept in spite of the recent upheavals that had beset München. The Bayerisch Kreditkörperschaft had its offices at number sixteen. The bank was small, select, and did not trouble itself with accounts of less than twenty thousand marks. It had been granted its charter by Ludwig I in the palmy days before Lola Montez, and over the years had a number of illustrious depositors listed among its accounts. It had come through the brief Spartacist government fairly unscathed and had only recently dared to open its doors once again for regular hours instead of appointments. The Bayerisch Kreditkörperschaft occupied three of the four floors of number sixteen, the last floor being the residence of three elderly sisters, rumored to be the last illegitimate offspring of Ludwig I.

On this drowsy August afternoon, activity in the bank was subdued. There had been two depositors in earlier to discuss the valuation and storing of certain valuable heirlooms, but for the last hour or so there was only the sound of the typewriting machines recently installed, and distant rush of traffic through the open windows.

Helmut Rauch had his office on the second floor, at the end of a long hallway, which was appropriate to so young a bank officer. He had spent the morning completing a report on the estate of a depositor who had been one of the victims of the May 1 atrocity. Even thinking about that wanton killing made him angry. It was bad enough that captives had been held, but that members of the Thule Gesellschaft should be shot—that was unthinkable. Now the work was done, the estate ready for the pronouncement of a judge, and in order for the heirs. He read over the last page critically and decided that it went well enough; the heirs would be satisfied and the Thule Gesellschaft would not be so obvious that those who were unfamiliar with them would recognize them. It was always better to be circumspect.

There was a diffident knock on his door, and Helmut Rauch looked up sharply. He had been so lost in reflection that he had not heard the approaching footsteps. "Yes?" he called out sharply.

"It is Schildwache, sir," said a timorous voice from the other side of the door.

Herman Schildwache was his secretary, a quiet, self-effacing young man whose family had fled during the tenure of the Communist Spartacists. The secretary was the sort of man who was all but invisible. Though Rauch had seen him not more than an hour ago, he was at a loss to recall the man's features. "Yes, Schildwache, what is it?"

"You have an appointment, sir. The gentleman has arrived." When Schildwache tried to raise his voice, it became a bleat.

"An appointment?" He pulled out his pocket watch and was startled to discover it was already two-thirty. He gathered the will up and placed it in a leather brief file. "Very good. Show him in." There was a calendar on his desk, and this he glanced at furtively, seeing only the name *Roger* on it. It was not a familiar name, and he frowned over it. He began to clear the top of his large oaken desk.

"Herr Roger, sir," Schildwache said a few minutes later as he opened the door.

"It's Roger," the man behind him corrected mildly, using the French pronunciation. "Herr Rauch?" He proffered his hand. He was sandy-haired and middle-aged, with blue eyes and a curious stillness about him. "I'm the confidential servant of Franchot Ragoczy, of Schloss Saint-Germain."

Being punctilious, Helmut gave Roger's hand one firm downward jerk, then indicated the only other chair in the office before resuming his own. "What is the Bayerisch Kreditkörperschaft to have the honor of doing for Herr Ragoczy?" At the mention of the name, he recalled the large deposit that had recently been transferred to the BKK from the Schweizerbank in Zürich; the sum, he remembered clearly, was five hundred thousand Swiss francs. He did his best to smile at Roger.

"There is nothing pressing at the moment," Roger assured him. "It is merely that my employer has been curious to learn whether or not the transfer was complete and to present the authorization of routine transfers of funds to his chequing account for the convenience of his household. He also has a

few family treasures he would like to keep in your vault."
Roger did not mention that there was a formidable vault in
the cellars of Schloss Saint-Germain that was doubtless as
secure as the one in this building: Ragoczy of late had made a
habit of placing certain valuables in the care of banks as a
precaution. The bank-held treasures were both decoys and
smokescreens for his real worth. He had investments and
partnerships in more than twenty countries, many under aliases
which afforded him a degree of protection. Roger was privy to
most of them, but rarely revealed the extent of his knowledge
to any but Franchot Ragoczy.

"You may be sure that we have excellent facilities for such
items. BKK will be honored to guard the Graf's possessions,"
Helmut declared at once. There would be a great deal of
prestige to the man who brought even a portion of Ragoczy's
fine belongings under this roof. "Please inform the Graf that
we are entirely at his disposal."

"Thank you," Roger said gravely. "My employer will be
relieved to learn this."

"Five hundred thousand Swiss francs is a good-sized sum,"
Helmut said after a moment. "Especially with the Great War
so recent and the outrageous demands on Deutschland by the
French . . ."

Roger made a dignified gesture. "During the recent war,
my employer was, for the most part, in Russia. You are
aware, I assume, that Schloss Saint-Germain has not been
occupied by its owner for more than thirty years."

"Yes, we learned that," Helmut admitted. "Russia has been
in turmoil. It is not likely that we at BKK will be able to act
on the Graf's business there for at least another two years, if
then."

"I would advise you to speak to my employer on that matter.
He is not dependent on his income from those holdings, of
course." Roger managed a faint smile that was not the least
encouraging to Helmut Rauch.

"Of course," Helmut nodded, baffled. "What are his present
intentions, do you know?"

Roger knew that Ragoczy had recently invested in the company providing electricity to parts of München, and in another
company building the cable that would carry both electricity
and telegraph to outlying parts of Bayern. "He intends to
restore the Schloss properly. His ward has an interest in
horses, and my employer had decided to add paddocks and
training rings to the cleared land near the stable. In time he

has said that he would like to install a swimming pool, for though the winters are dreadful, the summers are really quite pleasant."

"An extravagance, given the times," Helmut said severely, and with a trace of scorn. The foreigner, he thought, was as bad as the most hedonistic Münchener he had met, and that, he decided, was saying a great deal.

"You disapprove?" Roger asked, showing little emotion. He was clearly expecting an answer.

Helmut frowned and gave a stiff response. "It is not my place to approve or disapprove, of course. It would be folly for me, as an officer of BKK, to encourage your employer to deplete his resources."

"My employer has sufficient funds for occasional . . . extravagances," Roger said mildly, his faded blue eyes becoming distant. "You do not know the life he has led, or what it has cost him."

Helmut Rauch was acutely aware that if he antagonized this capricious foreigner, he might well be dismissed from his job, so he forced himself to give what he hoped was a tolerant smile. "Yes, I can understand that. The Great War was very hard on everyone."

"That is not my only concern," Roger said, then stood up. "I will assure my employer that you are proceeding on his behalf, and that you are willing to take certain of his more valuable possessions into your protection."

"Aber ja; selbstverständlich! It is only appropriate that we extend this service to those who bank with us. This is not one of those questionable institutions where we do not look after all the requirements of those who bank with us. You may assure Herr Graf . . . Herr Ragoczy," he corrected himself smoothly, "that we will be delighted to deal with him in any way that we can."

"I will tell him you said so," Roger said, and turned toward the door.

"Oh," Helmut called after him, "I have heard that Herr Ragoczy is something of a scholar."

"That is one of his interests, certainly," Roger responded, carefully noncommittal. "He has a fair reputation in certain circles, though he is an amateur."

"It is from such men that the finest discoveries often come," Helmut declared with the plainest show of enthusiasm he had shown that day. "It is always the greatest mistake to overlook the work of those who are removed from the aca-

demic world. You employer must believe this as much as I
do."

Puzzled at this new excitement on Rauch's part, Roger
paused. "I gather there is something you wish to tell him, a
thought you would like to convey?"

"Well, there is something, yes," Helmut said, faltering now
that he had begun. "There are a number of us who are . . .
concerned; yes, concerned, at what is happening to the world,
to the *people* of the world, if you understand my meaning."

Roger's eyes narrowed swiftly, then once again he was the
same self-contained man that he always appeared to be. "I am
afraid I do not. Perhaps you will explain."

Uncertain of himself now, and not knowing if it was proper
to discuss such things with a man who was only a servant,
Helmut turned and opened one of the lower drawers of his
desk, taking a book from it. This he held out to Roger. "Here,
this is for your employer. Dinster shows the problem much
better than I can; we have so little time. When your employer
has read it, I will look forward to discussing it with him."

"*Die Sünde wider das Blut*," Roger read, and could not
entirely keep from a fleeting smile. To give Ragoczy, of all
men, a book called *The Sin Against Blood*. He knew that
Helmut Rauch was watching him closely, and remarked, "I
will tell him that you sent it."

"It is an important work," Rauch insisted. "It has gained
something of a following since it was published at the end of
the war. Dinster has some quite important points to make.
Your employer ought to be aware of them."

"I'll tell him you said so," Roger promised, adding deferen-
tially, "It is not my place to say whether or not he will wish to
discuss it."

"Quite proper," Helmut Rauch said, beginning to feel approval for this man. "Not many of those in service remember
such things, these days."

Roger reached to open the door. "Is there anything else,
Herr Rauch? It will please my employer to learn that you're
willing to deal with his requirements, of course, but as he is a
foreigner, do you have anything you may want him to be
aware of?"

Helmut glanced at the window, toward the narrow building
on the opposite side of Kriegskönigstrasse, toward a high-
walled house that had been built in the fifteenth century. His
family had once owned such a house, but that was before
Bismarck's dream had shattered and the Kaiser had begun to

listen to greedy sycophants. "Your employer," he said after a moment, "is not aware of how things are with us in Deutschland. He imagines himself safe because he had fled the desolation of Russia. But this is not so. It is true that the Spartacists are gone, and that the Communist weed has been eradicated, but that is a simple matter, an obvious matter. There are dangers much more insidious here, subtle betrayals and influences that have sapped our country to its heart. Most good citizens are blind to the menace around them, and think that the only thing that dishonors them is the disgusting terms of our so-called peace. That is nothing. Who caused that war? Who profited by it, nurtured it, prolonged it? The people have not asked themselves those questions yet, but in time they will—they must. And it will mean that they are awakening from the sleep that has brought them to their knees." His voice had changed, becoming at once harsher and deeper. "Your employer might not think that there is any hazard here, but there is a great deal, and it is more degrading than he knows. Not only is our nation dishonored, it is polluted. Yes! Polluted! I myself have seen it. At the Front, I saw the face of the enemy—our inner enemy—everywhere. I could not consent to countenance this situation. But such is the power that I was denied the right to lead my soldiers in battle, to show my contempt for their aims. Your employer may fall into the error of thinking that those who appear helpless are so, and that smiles are not insinuating. Foreigners are often so eager for friends that they give their confidence where it is least deserved. The architect your employer has retained, for example, is not the kind of man that Herr Ragoczy should trust too far. You may not see the reason for this, but for those of us who have made a serious study of the matter, the difficulties are readily apparent. It is not simply that there are motives that you do not conceive of, but that the conspiracy— and you must not doubt that there is a conspiracy—has been going on for years, perhaps centuries." His eloquence suddenly deserted him and he felt unreasonably shamed that he should spend so much time talking to a servant.

As Roger opened the door, he said, "I know that you are sincere in your concern, Herr Rauch. My mas . . . employer is not much given to involving himself in the affairs of the country he lives in. He is, as you have already pointed out, a foreigner."

Helmut scowled. "This goes far beyond mere national borders. It is imperative that your employer realize this. Ragoczy is a distinguished name. Had things been otherwise, they might have been our leaders during the war, and their long traditions of service and valor might have broken the crippling hold that kept us from victory."

Inwardly Roger was very much alarmed, but his expression did not alter. Perhaps his blue eyes were darker for a moment, and perhaps his hands tightened, but there was nothing obvious in his demeanor that would show his anxiety. "I will give your book to my employer. Whatever else comes of this, my employer will initiate, if that is his wish."

"Ich verstehe," Helmut said, becoming more controlled again. "You must pardon me. I saw such things in the war that—"

Roger was curious, but did not want to have the conversation resume. "It was a great catastrophe. There can be no question of that."

"Ja; schrecklich. It haunts me to this day." He forced himself to give Roger a stern smile. "It was good of you to come. We're most pleased to have Herr Ragoczy as one of our depositors."

"He is a very wealthy man," Roger said, as if it explained everything, which, in a sense, it did.

"And it would appear, an unconcerned one." He had not intended to say that aloud, but the thought had rankled within him so that it was out before he could stop it.

"Do you think so?" Roger asked, with such an expression in his eyes that it silenced the defense Helmut had been about to make. When he knew that Rauch would not speak again, Roger gave a stiff little bow. "Thank you, Herr Rauch, on behalf of my employer. I will see that he gets this book."

"It is my pleasure," Helmut muttered, not wishing to admit how glad he was when he heard Roger's footsteps growing softer. He stared at his desk as if trying to recall what it was, then rang for Schildwache. As he waited for his secretary to appear, he began to scribble a hasty note on one of his small sheets of memo paper. By the time Schildwache stepped through the door, Helmut was sealing the note.

"This is for Herr Doktor Friedrich Krohn at Starnberg. It is essential that he receive it today. Either hire a messenger or deliver it yourself." He stood up as he held out the paper.

"Starnberg? That is twenty kilometers, at least," Schildwache said, aghast. "How am I to get there?"

"You or a messenger. Herr Kegel has a motorcycle: I am sure he would be willing to let you use it." Helmut suspected that the guard whose motorcycle he was volunteering would be in full sympathy with the errand, if only he knew its purpose.

"But I don't know how to—" Schildwache protested, and was silenced by Helmut's firm voice.

"It is not difficult. Children have learned. Ask Kegel and he will show you. This letter is very important. A great deal of money is at stake." He saw with satisfaction that Schildwache was capitulating. "Here. Take it. Talk to Kegel. I will not expect to see you until tomorrow, and at that time, you had better give me proof that the message has been delivered. No excuses. The roads to Starnberg are fairly good. You should have no trouble along the way. You may get fuel at Sauting, if necessary."

"But I—" Schildwache attempted to interrupt.

"It must be done." Helmut felt indignation burning within him. It was so difficult to deal with these simple clerks! He had given the man an understandable order, his language was concise, and yet the secretary persisted in objecting.

Schildwache sighed. "If you insist. But truly, I don't know how to ride one of those contraptions. I have never even driven an automobile. Herr Kegel may not want to release his machine to me."

"You tell Herr Kegel where you are going, and to whom you are taking a message, and I am confident that he will assist you. Come, Schildwache, it isn't so difficult. Children of fourteen can do it, so you must be able to, as well. You may like it." He had to work to conceal his contempt for this sniveling man. How could Deutschland not have been defeated, if creatures like this one were the flower of the country's manhood? It had gone too far. He folded his arms. "You must go now, Schildwache. If you are not familiar with the road, you will not want to try to drive it after dark, and that might well happen if you wait much longer." He had the satisfaction of knowing that would spur the little man on.

"Of course, Mein Herr," Schildwache said miserably, bowing again as he retreated.

"And tell Frau Aufrecht that I will want to make a telephone call, will you? I will be down in a few moments to give her the number." He waved the man away and reached to close his window. He was still apprehensive about the exchange he had had with Roger and did not entirely know why. Helmut Rauch did not spend much time in introspection, so now he did not pause to examine his feelings. Telling himself that action was called for, instead of these unrewarding rumi-

nations, he rose once more and prepared to go down to Frau
Aufrecht's telephone desk. He comforted himself with the
thought that once his note was delivered to Friedrich Krohn,
he would not have to be idle.

As Helmut Rauch was placing his call to Dietrich Eckart,
Roger had driven the Benz touring car around to Ardisstrasse,
about two blocks north of Alte Pinakothek. The building he
wanted was across the street; a barn of a place, which had
been at one time a tavern, at another a saddler's, and now was
one of the five theatres in München where moving pictures
were shown. Roger checked his watch, then reached to the
carry-compartment between himself and the passengers' seats.
Three books were there. He pulled out one in a faded leather
binding, with the title *Una delle Ultime Sere de Carnevale*.
Smiling slightly, he began to read.

Herr Kegel was not pleased with what Schildwache told
him, but when he was informed of the destination of the note,
he shrugged and took the terrified secretary out into Kriegskönigstrasse to show him how to drive a motorcycle. About
the time Schildwache began his first shaky turn on the vehicle,
the doors of the theatre opened and Roger put his book away.

Amalie Schnaubel emerged from the theatre with her own
children and Laisha in tow. She looked about, then seeing
Roger, raised her hand, and watched for a clearing in the
traffic so that she could lead them across the street.

Bruno darted ahead, narrowly avoiding an Opel omnibus.
The driver honked his horn in fury, and Bruno waved merrily,
and dashed up to the side of the Benz. "It was wonderful," he
declared, grinning up at Roger. "You should have come."

"I had other errands to do," Roger said with a smile, thinking fleetingly of his own son, who had died so very many
years ago. "Perhaps, when you have another outing like this
one, I will come with you."

"Sehr gut. We will like that." He motioned to the others,
who were crossing the street, to hurry. "I *told* you he'd be on
time," he said with haughty emphasis. "You would not be late
would you, Roger?"

"I would certainly try not to be," Roger replied. "There are
times when such things are unavoidable." There was an odd
expression in his eyes, and seeing it, Amalie felt a tremor run
through her.

"Well," she said with forced brightness, "it was a fine afternoon, and we must thank you for making it possible. Come, all

of you, into the automobile," she added, opening the doors to the passenger compartment.

"Can we keep the top down?" Emmerich asked. "It's not cold."

"That's for Roger to decide," Amalie informed him as she tried to fit both Olympie and Hedda into the same seat. "You must share, girls, because we're short of room. Laisha will ride with Roger, but there's only room for one other person up in front."

Both Olympie and Hedda objected to this, in part because they enjoyed the attention their objections got them, but they were generally well-mannered children, and settled down before too much time had gone by. Amalie got into one of the rear seats beside Bruno. "I think we're ready," she said.

Roger nodded, and fiddled with the ignition. He admitted he preferred this to using a crank, but also recognized that it was a very tricky business to get the engine to start the first time.

"Roger," Laisha began as she climbed in next to him.

"In a moment, Laisha," he answered in a low, preoccupied tone. On the second try the engine turned over and Roger leaned back, satisfied. "Now, what is it?"

In the seats behind them, the Schnaubel family was chattering enthusiastically, Hedda pleading to be driven by Mariensäule.

She spoke in Russian now. "It was an interesting moving picture. It's called *Half-Caste*, you know, and it bothered me to watch it. It was . . . not easy to think about. It bothered Frau Schnaubel, too, I could tell."

"There are times that theatre is supposed to bother you, Laisha," Roger said, also in Russian. "There are fine plays that have been bothering people for centuries."

Laisha nodded, giving a tight smile. "Yes, this was probably one of those. I don't know. I haven't been to many motion pictures." This was, in fact, the second time she had seen one, and both she and Roger knew it.

"You will see more of them, Laisha. They're making more of them every day." He had to give his attention to the road, for the traffic was growing more congested. Ahead, a small horse-drawn cart was attempting to get across the line of oncoming vehicles, and as a result, everyone had slowed to a walking pace. Behind them, a man driving the huge draft horses of a brewery wagon was cursing loudly and comprehensively. Roger turned for a quick moment to say to Amalie Schnaubel, "Don't mind him, Madame. The children will not be harmed for a few words."

Amalie smiled in uneasy agreement. "Of course. They hear as much from the workmen repairing the roads, but still . . ." She did not go on. Roger had returned his attention to the road and was not listening to her comments. With a gesture of resignation, she looked over at her daughters, thinking how many worse things she had heard as a child.

Four minutes later, the worst of the snarl had passed, and Roger was starting over the Istar on the Maximillianbrücke. There was a fair number of automobiles jostling for their place in the line, and occasionally there was an impatient bleat of a horn. It was impossible to go at any speed, but this did not cause him much annoyance. He kept up a steady progress and listened to Laisha talk to him, enjoying her conversation.

"When will my guardian go to Paris?" Laisha asked rather suddenly as they rounded the bend that would put them on the road to Miesbach and Hausham.

"Next month, Laisha. He told you that himself." He changed gears and the automobile picked up speed.

"Yes," she agreed dubiously. "And he said he would be gone no more than three weeks." Her chin was up and her brown eyes accused him.

"Then he will not be gone more than three weeks," Roger said easily. He did not want to lose patience with this child; he liked her tremendously. But it had been years since he had had to deal with any children, and he had somewhat forgotten the knack of it. Aside from Sabrina's two children, Cesily and Herbert, he had not been with youngsters on a daily basis since Niklos Aulirios had entertained Ragoczy on Crete.

"Why does he have to go?" she asked in a small, distressed voice.

"He has holdings there, Laisha. He told you that long since." The Benz tourer was rattling along at a good pace, and Roger had trouble hearing her over the sound of the motor and the noise of the tires on the road. "He looks after his property."

"But Paris is a long way," Laisha said. "He might not come back."

"He will come back," Roger promised her. "He has gone much farther than that and he has always come back. You traveled a great distance with him yourself."

The day was quite warm and the road left plumes of dust behind the automobile. Around them, the countryside was basking in the heat. Open fields bordered by deep forests spread around them, backed by the rising majesty of Bayern's great masterpieces, her mountains. Mantled in green, they were splendidly tall, their ruggedness in no way detracting from their beauty. By the time they reached Wayern, the road had grown steeper and their speed had diminished. Shadows of the peaks to the west of them had already begun to cast their twilight on the lower ground.

"I'm hungry," Laisha murmured when she had been quiet for more than ten minutes.

"We'll be home shortly. We have to take the Schnaubels home, and then we will go back to Schloss Saint-Germain." He saw that the girl was tired, and he put a hand out briefly to touch her shoulder.

In the back, Bruno and Hedda were squabbling about what church they had seen through the trees. It had had a tall conical spire which was typical of the place. Bruno had insisted that it was Saint Gregorius and Hedda was adamant that it was Saint Hyacinthe. Their voices rose until Amalie ordered them both to be quiet, when they lapsed into sullen silence. Emmerich was half-asleep and Olympie was staring dreamily down at the sash of her skirt, her eyes incalculably distant.

"Will it be much longer?" Laisha asked. She had been to München only three times and was not familiar with the landmarks.

"Fifteen minutes to Hausham, and then ten more home. Half an hour, probably," Roger answered.

"Will Professor Riemen still be there?" Her tone was slightly more nervous.

"For a few more days. He and my master have certain matters under discussion."

"I don't like him," Laisha said, and waited for the rebuke she was certain would follow this announcement.

Roger guided the Benz along a badly-rutted part of the road, thinking that it should be graded before the rains began. "He is a strange man, Laisha. He has a brilliant mind, but his life has been very hard." It was difficult to say this to the girl, for he knew that in her nine years, she had been through a great deal more than Isidore Riemen had in more than thirty.

"Well, I *still* don't like him. He looks at me . . . messily." She ran her hands down the front of her dress as if wiping something unpleasant away.

"Yes, I've noticed that," he said gently. Ragoczy, he knew, had noticed as well, and was very much on guard.

The road made a bend and they came into Hausham. The

children in the back of the automobile cheered and Laisha showed Roger a wan smile. As they went past the Hirsch Furt, four men seated at one of the benches in the front of the tavern looked up. One of them, a handsome blond man in his middle twenties, pointed at the automobile and rose, his flushed face contorted with anger.

"Jews! Traitorous Jews! Ungeziefer!" He shook his stein at them, while the other men at the bench nodded their support.

One of the four, an older man, quite stout, with a bald head and bright little eyes, studied the retreating automobile carefully, as if memorizing it.

"Mama," Olympie said plaintively once the tavern was out of sight, "why did he call us that?"

Amalie could not hide her distress. She put her arm around her daughter's shoulder. "They are foolish men, Olympie. They call many people such things." There was a line between her brows, and the smile had left her face.

"So Jews are vermin, are we?" Bruno growled. "They'll learn otherwise. They'll change their minds."

"Bruno," Amalie cautioned him, "no. It is best to ignore such things. They are just words. You know what a nice woman Frau Ostneige is, don't you?" She saw her oldest son nod reluctantly. "That ill-mannered young man is her brother. Anything you say to him will not change him and will only cause her pain. Let it alone, Bruno. If we draw too much attention to the ravings of such men, then others may start to listen to them, and that would not be wise." Ahead she saw the entrance to their home and her eyes grew wet with gratitude. That familiar house was her haven now, a place where she and her family could shut out all the vile shouts of the world.

Roger brought the Benz up to the door and set the brake, though the motor was still running. He came out of the driver's seat and opened the door for the Schnaubel family. As he held up his hand to Amalie, he said, "Don't allow yourself to be frightened by those men, Madame. They are idle and filled with senseless rage. There have been others like them before, and all they have done, for the most part, is behave in a manner to embarrass sensible men and women."

"Thank you," Amalie said as she came down out of the automobile. "We Jews have had to face such creatures before. My grandfather . . ." She did not go on.

"Yes," Roger said quietly. "If there is any difficulty, Herr Ragoczy would be pleased if you would count him your friend."

"That's kind of you to say, but . . ." Amalie was halfway to the door, motioning her children to hurry.

"It is on his authority, Madame. He has already told your husband so." His manner changed to a slightly more formal attitude. "It was good of you to allow Laisha to accompany you and your family today."

"Nonsense. Without the Benz, we could not have gone at all." She had the door open, but was able to bring the semblance of a smile to her lips. "Danke vielmals."

"Sie sind sehr liebenswürdig, Madame. It was my pleasure." He touched his hand to his peaked cap and got back into the Benz.

"What is the matter with Frau Schnaubel?" Laisha asked as she waved good-bye to the faces beyond the closing door.

"She is worried," Roger said as he put the Benz into reverse. "I can't blame her."

"But they were only rude men who were drinking," Laisha said, seeking reassurance, for there was a haunted expression in her face.

"Perhaps," Roger said as he drove back onto the dusty road and turned the Benz toward the Schliersee and Schloss Saint-Germain.

A letter from James Emmerson Tree to his cousin Audrey.

*Hotel Louis XV*
*Avignon*

*Dear Audrey;*

*Well, Crandell has given me the go-ahead for the next eighteen months, and if I show him the kind of material he says he wants, then I've got the chance to stay over as long as I want to be here. I'm just like a kid out of school, I'm so pleased. I know I'll do it right, I know I will.*

*As you might be able to tell, I'm traveling right now. I haven't had a letter from you since May, and this is September, so I guess there's something waiting back in Paris for me. I don't know if I'll be back there much before December. I'm going from here to Italy; then I'll come around through Austria and Switzerland and back into France again. I'm going to do something more than just talk about traveling. I want the readers to get a feel for the places I go, not just what kind of beds there are in the hotels, what trinkets cost, and if it's safe to drink the water. It often isn't, by the way. A lot of people over here buy bottled water if they can afford it, even though the price is going up. Some of the big estates have their own wells and filter them with a great deal of care. I might do a piece on these places, about how isolated some of them are. I know a couple of people who might let me look around their lands. That sounds "quite the snob," doesn't it? But it is true, nonetheless. Who would have thought that a kid from Denver with a Cheyenne grandmother would be palling around with European aristocrats? Not as an equal, exactly, but they don't call me a peasant, at least not where I can hear them.*

*A lot of people here are talking about the League of Nations. I know that Wilson's all for it, but it's a bit shaky because of all the hard feelings after the war.*

*There's other politicking going on too, of course. The thing that gets me is Europe isn't really all that big. Half the time, it seems to me to make as much sense as Wisconsin squabbling with Ohio about Kentucky, but they've been doing it for centuries, so they're used to it. I think I'll do something about the League of Nations, too. Nothing political, just a bit about it so that the folks back in Kansas will have a sense of what is going on over here.*

*So you've got the vote now, too. Well, at least you do when you're old enough. Looks as if the Suffragettes were right all along. You better start paying attention to everything those men in Washington are saying. You're going to need to keep up with it, or they'll keep on giving themselves carte blanche to everything they want. And I'm not making that up, Audrey.*

*The Hungarians have some hard feelings about the way the Treaty of Trianon has turned out. The whole country was chopped up and parceled out, so that there's only about a quarter of it left that's still called Hungary. So far there haven't been any serious repercussions, but that's exactly the kind of high-handed thing that will bring about a lot of bitterness.*

*That war is still going on in Russia, and we've been told that they've also got famine. What a terrible thing for those poor people. They just get out from under the Czar, thinking that there's a chance for a better deal at last, and every crackpot from the Ukraine to Siberia starts trying to swipe a bit for himself. With famine they can't afford to keep fighting. I hope they don't try.*

*Crandell tells me that there's a group of men in Pittsburgh who want to start a radio broadcasting station. That sounds really exciting. There's going to be a lot of radio used in the future, at least it looks like that to me. People like radio, or the wireless, as the British have been calling it. Give it time, and it will expand a lot. Remember, forty years ago, everyone thought automobiles were nothing more than dangerous toys and no one would ever find a real use for them.*

*When I'm back in Paris, I'll pick up some perfume to send you. There's a new one out called Chanel No. 5, and according to one woman I talked to, it's wonderful. How would you like real French perfume for Christmas? You're getting old enough for that by now. The way things are*

*going, you might not have it until Easter, but I'll try to*
*send some off to you. You can tell what you think of it.*
*The desk just buzzed me. I'll finish this later.*

de Montalia
September 19, 1920

It's been six days since I wrote to you. I did intend to
come back to the room, finish the letter, and put it into
the mail. But there was a telegram for me, in answer to
one I'd sent. It was an invitation to visit this estate, not
just to do a piece on it, but for other things.

You've got to keep this part of the letter private. Burn it
if you think you won't be able to. I know I shouldn't be
telling you anything about this, but if I don't tell someone, I'll fall apart. And who else would even want to
understand?

The woman who owns this place—there's a château and
a good-sized bit of land attached to it—had me here once
before. Had me, that's apt. She's from an old family,
obviously aristocrats. Not that she plays that up; in fact,
she says very little about it. Her name is Madelaine. I
might have mentioned her before. She looks to be about
nineteen or twenty, but she says that she's older, and
though she has that young face, I believe her. She knows
too much for a kid.

You know how we used to talk, years ago, about what it
might feel like to make love to someone? I don't think I
was more than eleven then, but I had to be, didn't I? You're
ten years younger than I am, so I had to be almost fifteen
when we talked. Neither of us knew much except from
watching the cows being serviced. I'd heard some things
from other guys, but even then I didn't believe too much
of it. And then, at the end of my junior year in high
school (I never told you about this) I finally got Becky
Hartford to let me have her. We were pretty careful, and
damned lucky. Nothing much happened from it, and
after a little while she decided she didn't like me. Don't go
spreading it around that I was first with Becky; her
husband wouldn't like to hear that about his wife; and I
don't think she'd be the kind of woman I'd want to sleep
with now. Anyhow, since then, I've been around a bit.
Don't worry. I don't make a practice of seducing virgins.
There've been a fair number of women, but none of them

*until now was what you'd call special. Most of them were
just efficient, if you follow me.*

*God, I wish there was someone other than you to tell
about this. You probably don't want to read about me and
Madelaine. But I can't talk to the journalists I know:
they wouldn't believe me, for one thing, and for another,
most of them would laugh at it, and I couldn't stand that.*

*You know, when I came here the first time, Madelaine
showed me a lot more than simple hospitality. No, that's
not right. It sounds like something that takes place in a
cheap French novel, the kind they won't let you send
through the mail, and it wasn't anything like that at all.
I've never had an experience like the one with her. It
wasn't only that she knew what to do in bed, but there was
so much more to it. You read a lot about the tricks
Frenchwomen know, and there are always rumors about
very exotic practices. Madelaine has a few maneuvers I
never heard about before. That still sounds as if she's one
of those proficient, athletic women who treat their beds as
some kind of private circus. She's not that kind at all.
Her skills are the way she makes the rest of it more
wonderful.*

*When I'm with her, she's all there is in the world.
Nothing else is real. Nothing else matters. It isn't just a
question of feeling happy, or spending so completely that
it's as if you're in heaven, or taking hours and hours to
find out how a touch truly feels, and what it does to you.
It's much more than that. Telling you the colors in it and
the subject matter doesn't show you the painting, and
that's an easy task compared to this. I can't begin to
explain it—what a terrible confession for a journalist to
make.*

*As you can see from the heading, I'm back at her estate
now, and since I've been here, she's come to my bed twice.
She refuses to spend every night with me, though I've
pleaded with her to do so. She says it would not be a good
idea, and that if I persist, she'll ask me to leave. I can't
bear the thought of not being here again, being with her.
If you knew what it was like to be loved this way. And
honestly, Audrey, I hope you do. I hope with all my heart
that someday you find someone who can banish the world
with a kiss. That looks corny, doesn't it? But that's the
way it can be. It's that way with Madelaine. Our mouths
touch, a little bit open, and she melts up against me, her*

*head not even up to my shoulder, she's such a little thing. There's nothing else but the two of us then.*

*Last night she let me carry her up to my bedroom (and you should see the place; I feel as if I'm in a royal suite). Holding her in my arms as I walked, I could have gone around the world. It was like floating, or being joyously drunk. She's not a featherweight, of course, but a real woman, one you can get ahold of and know you've got something. The way her body fitted next to mine, it was better than a chorus in harmony. She never hurries, or complains, or draws back. When we're together in bed—completely together—she does such things to me that often I'm afraid I'll faint or become so totally happy that I'll go crazy.*

*She's been away from France for almost a year. Believe it or not, she's an archeologist, and spends a lot of time digging up ruins. As you may have heard, there's been more trouble in the Middle East, and her expedition was sent home as a precaution. I know that she's planning to go again as soon as she has the opportunity, and I dread the day that happens, because it will be months, perhaps years before I can see her again. I wish I could talk Crandell into letting me go with her, and report on what it's like to go out into the middle of the desert and dig up a ruin.*

*This morning she scolded me because I was forgetting all the things I have to do, all my plans. She's right; I know that. Sooner or later (and it had better be sooner if I want to keep my job on this side of the Atlantic) I'll have to go back to interviews and stories. The Post-Dispatch doesn't want a journalist hiding out in the mountains making love all day.*

*It's so wonderful being with her, seeing the way she smiles. Her eyes are the color of violets. She's got dark brown hair, about the same shade as strong coffee, and the glints in it are yellow as topaz. I can't help writing about her this way, and I wouldn't change it if I could. She's the sort of woman who should have poetry and music written to her, and flowers named after her.*

*Her butler is going down to Digne to send off some packages, so I'd better finish this and let him mail it for me. Remember, this last part you've got to keep to yourself, Audrey. I hope it doesn't shock you too much. If it does, I'm sorry. Whatever you do, don't show it to your parents. I don't think they would understand. I wrote them a letter a couple of weeks ago, so they're pretty much caught up on me, except for this last part. They probably won't have too many questions. If they do, read them the first part, and leave it at that.*

*You take care of yourself. No more sprained ankles now that school's started, all right? And don't worry so much about your grades; you're smart. You'll do fine.*

*I wish I could stay here forever, but my next letter will probably come from Genoa. C'est la vie.*

> *Your loving cousin,*
> *James*

# 5

For the last three days it had been raining; the steady, unrelenting downpour washed the mountains, filling the brooks with mud-tinged water, finding new runnels everywhere. The forest smelled of loam and mold and wet. Only on the higher peaks was there the first dappling of snow, and it made itself felt far into the valleys in the breath of the wind that came off it. Everywhere there were fears of a severe winter, for although the rain was quite usual for November, the snow was not.

Schloss Saint-Germain, its exterior repairs and extensions completed, was snug enough and kept pleasantly warm by Ragoczy's ingenious arrangements of flues and fireplaces. When, on this Thursday morning, Simeon Schnaubel ventured to compliment him on it, Ragoczy dismissed the matter with a wave of his hand.

"You forget that I lived in Russia for a considerable time, and there the winters are markedly worse than here. You will find houses there with walls more than a meter thick and three ranks of narrow windows. I learned much from the Russians, not the least of which was how to keep a house warm in the most frigid weather." He did not add that most of what he had incorporated into his Schloss was a system that he himself had developed and had shared with his Russian friends.

"I may try something similar with my own house," Simeon remarked as he reached for his muffler, looking a trifle sheepish because his brief visit had run far longer than he had anticipated. "It would make such a difference just now. Poor Olympie has a cold—she's very susceptible to them—and Amalie . . . well, you know what women are when they're pregnant." He stopped, recalling that he was talking to an unmarried man. "That is, you might . . ."

"My dear Simeon, although I have no wife, nor children of my body, I assure you that I do indeed know what women are like when they're pregnant. How long will it be until she is delivered?" They were in Ragoczy's library, near the large fireplace so that they could take advantage of the two huge logs blazing there. A silver coffee service stood on one end table, and there was a single used cup balanced on the arm of the chair Simeon had just vacated.

"Three more months. Her physician believes it will be in the first week of February. After four children, I shouldn't be apprehensive, but . . ." He wrapped his muffler around his neck and reached for his overcoat, which was draped over the back of one of the other chairs. "I suppose no father is ever completely sanguine at these times."

"Very likely not, unless he has no feeling for the woman, or the child," Ragoczy said, rising to walk to the door with his guest. "You're really very fortunate in your family, Simeon."

"Yes," he agreed with undisguised pride.

Ragoczy opened the door and held it while Simeon stepped into the hallway. "You mentioned that you had a cancellation of work. Would you care to tell me about it?"

Simeon stared, surprised. He had told his host a bit about this most recent difficulty when he arrived but purposely had not dwelled on it. "It's a misunderstanding, Mein Herr, nothing more."

"Perhaps you will allow me to be the judge of that?" He fell into step beside Simeon.

"Oh, it's not that important . . ." Simeon began, trying to change the subject.

"Then you should not object to telling me about it." Ragoczy gave Simeon a wry smile. "Yes, I am fully aware that you would prefer not to tell me, but believe me, I do not ask merely to cause you embarrassment. Just as you are regarded as a foreigner by some because of your religion, so I am regarded, because I am. You will do me a service if you will let me know what happened."

Simeon spoke awkwardly. "You make it sound as if refusal would be churlish. Very well. I had been commissioned by the Gletscher Gipfel Gasthof to design an addition to their inn, keeping the style in the traditions of Bayern. They wanted the balconies and the turned wood balustrades, the deep-set windows . . . you've seen the mountain houses, you know what they're like. This would be more of the same, but on a larger scale. We had progressed to the stage of secondary designs, and I assumed we were in accord, but when I drove up to the inn last week, Herr Steilufer informed me that he was not convinced that I would be able to do the job that was wanted, as my family came from Hesse. He said that he had been in contact with another man from München, and they were discussing plans." He was astonished to hear how angry he sounded. "I beg your pardon, Herr Ragoczy. I had no justification to speak to you in this way."

"You had every justification," was the calm answer. "I share your indignation, since I am sure that neither of us is naive enough to assume that Herr . . . is it Steilufer? spoke the truth."

"I have no proof that he had any motive but the one he gave me. I cannot fault a man for regional pride." He said this as if to convince himself, as he had several times already. "It may be that the remarks of the men who drink at the Hirsch Furt have upset me more than I know."

"And it may be that the men who drink at the Hirsch Furt also drink at the Gletscher Gipfel Gasthof." Ragoczy studied Simeon's face, then added, "It is always tempting to look for devils instead of men, but that is a dangerous mistake, Simeon. Few men act out of real malice, just as few act out of true beneficence. Most are motivated by their desires, their fears, their greeds, their confusions. They will seize the momentary advantage if it does not demand too much and the act does not prick their conscience too deeply."

"You sound cynical," Simeon said forlornly.

"Cynical? I? No. If I were a cynic, I would see those things and be smug, but I cannot. I have seen great acts of heroism that were negated by an hour of foolishness. I have known honorable men whose honor betrayed them. I have known women of incomparable courage who were denied its expression, and so turned it inward against themselves. None of it has given me anything but sorrow, that such worth could be wantonly abused. In the face of such things, cynicism *is* somewhat tempting, since it would take the sting out of life. But it would remove the pleasure as well, so . . ." He shrugged slightly, and said in another, brisker tone, "Perhaps you and Amalie would like to join me for a performance at the Prinzregententheater. You may choose what we attend. Anything would be acceptable to me so long as it is not *Palestrine*. As much as I admire Bruno Walter, I am not part of the Pfitzner enthusiasts, and three hearings of that opera are enough. The Mascagni or Korngold should be worthwhile, if you're interested in new works."

Simeon smiled gratefully. "We would be delighted, of course. Amalie is very fond of Mozart."

"Then you have only to select the performance," Ragoczy said.

"But I don't know about the Prinzregententheater. Those unpadded wooden seats . . . I don't know if Amalie would be comfortable on them. Right now, you know, that's an important consideration." There was a reserve about him now, as if he were rid of an awkward commission.

"Then let us plan for after the child is born. We should be able to get tickets for the Gartnerplatz," he said, giving Simeon a nod of encouragement as if he had not noticed the subtle change in his expression. "If you like, I will ask one of my servants to stay with your children. Or perhaps you might bring them up here for the evening, so that Laisha might entertain them."

"That's very kind, Herr Graf, but I would not want to make things awkward for you in the neighborhood. It isn't necessary, I assure you." He looked away toward the door.

Ragoczy's quiet response caught his attention. "But it is, you know."

"I don't see what—" Simeon began, longing to escape.

"You have done excellent work for me, and there is no reason why I should not show you my appreciation," Ragoczy interrupted.

The sudden stare that Simeon gave Ragoczy showed that he was not deceived by what his host had said. He paused, then said in a low voice, "Danke vielmals, Graf. I am beholden to you." He buttoned his overcoat and looked around for his hat which he had surrendered to Roger when he arrived.

"There is no need, Simeon. This is my choice, after all," Ragoczy told him as he opened the door to the cloakroom and pulled the hat from the bentwood rack.

"I cannot change my feelings, Herr Graf," Simeon said as he took his hat. "You have lifted a great burden from my mind.

Amalie will be relieved to hear this. She was afraid that you might not want me to continue here, what with . . . recent developments. With the baby coming, her fear is not unreasonable."

"Merci bien de compliment," Ragoczy said with an ironic laugh. "I hope I am no poltroon. I have once before offered your family my friendship, and I feared then that I was not believed." He could not admit how much that had stung, for it awakened old hurt that he had thought he had put behind him. Of late he had sought to deny his essential isolation, but it was inescapable, and in the marrow of his bones, he knew it. His compelling dark eyes met Simeon's. "You have an ally in me, should you need one. I do not say this lightly."

Simeon clutched his hat, disquieted by the sincerity of Ragoczy's words. "Yes," he said at last, and opened the door to walk out into the rain to his eleven-year-old Opel Double Phaeton. He checked to make sure the top was firmly in place before climbing into the driver's seat. Only then did he turn and look back toward the door of the Schloss. "I hope that you never have to be put to the test," he said, trusting that the sound of the rain would keep Ragoczy from hearing.

But he did. "And I. It would grieve me to learn that your family was in danger." He gave Simeon a short, formal bow, then stepped back into the house.

As Simeon drove away, Ragoczy hurried down the hall, calling out, "Roger, is the Benz ready?" He did not wait for an answer but stepped into his study and opened a small wardrobe. The coat he pulled out was of magnificent black wool with four driving capes and a velvet collar. He dropped this over his arm and left the room again, once more calling for Roger.

"The Benz is ready," Roger told him as he came from the back part of the Schloss. "I understand there has been a slide on the road farther up, and they're bringing a gang of convict laborers to repair it. You may remember," Roger went on with a distant twist to his lips that was not a smile, "mountain roads can be treacherous."

"Yes, but this time I am not going far, and this is neither Armenia nor China. But I thank you for the warning, old friend." He drew on his coat and took his hat from Roger's outstretched hand. "Herr Vögel wishes to talk with me about Laisha's progress, so we will probably not be back until two or three. No doubt Laisha will be famished, and it would be best if there is some sort of light meal waiting for her." He opened the door, then turned back. "Will you replenish the earth in the soles of my winter boots? I imagine I'll be wearing them soon."

"It's already been done," Roger said, preparing to close the door.

"I need not have asked. Thank you." He waved as he went around the end of the house toward the garage and stables, his small, elegantly-shod feet raising miniature cascades as he walked through the puddles on the graveled drive.

The first crest on the road between Schliersee and Geitau was easily traversed, though it was necessary to go at a cautious twenty kilometers per hour. Here and there deep ruts awaited the unwary, and Ragoczy negotiated these parts with care. As he started up the second, longer rise, the going became more difficult. The road was not so well-maintained past the turning for Fischbachau, and Ragoczy was forced to go even more slowly. Five kilometers farther on, he came to the slide, and noticed that there was another stretch of hillside that was showing signs of sliding: he hoped that he, Laisha, and her tutor David Bündnis would be at Schloss Saint-Germain before that muddy avalanche thundered down onto the road. It was nerve-racking to drive over the slide, for only a narrow lip of road remained unblocked, and it was on the ledge side, and not too stable.

Once past the slide, Ragoczy made slightly better time, and it was not long before he entered the village of Geitau, taking the narrow lane that led to Herr Professor Vögel's house, which he had whimsically dubbed Nest.

It was a typical mountain house, the sort seen throughout these peaks in Bayern. It was lovingly maintained, brightly painted, and now, with a light powdering of snow, it looked too perfect to be real, rather like an illustration for a children's book instead of the home of a retired Professor of biology. As Ragoczy drove up, the Professor himself came out onto the porch, calling out his welcome.

"I was afraid that you might not get here, with the road in such poor condition. The postman said that he very nearly didn't make it through. But here you are. Your daughter said that you would come." He was short, rotund, and had an absent smile which masked an acute and discerning mind.

Ragoczy set the brake and got out of the Benz. "Frightful weather, Professor Vögel."

"Oh, do you think so? I like it, myself. The snow is refreshing, you see, and winter is such an invigorating season." He stood aside to allow Ragoczy to enter his house. "I might feel differently if I had to make the drive you have just made, but that's not a consideration for me." He closed the door and called out, "Laisha! Your father is here."

"Moi otyets!" she cried happily, coming out of the parlor on the side of the sheltered side of the house. "I *knew* you'd come." She flung her arms around his waist and pressed her face against his coat.

"Laisha, I'm wet, child. Let me get out of this coat." He ruffled her pale hair, smiling down at her with tender, vulnerable pride. She was young, so young, and had no real knowledge of him. It occurred to him, as it had increasingly often in the last year, that one day she would have to be told what he was, before she stumbled on the truth by accident. He had been discreet, taking no lover but those he visited in sleep, chosen mainly from those who came to the hotels at Bad Wiessee. Yet the time would come when he would have to tell her, and he shrank from that revelation as he had never shrunk from anything before. What if she feared him, or loathed him? He had often been the object of hatred and detestation, and he had learned, over the centuries, to accept this as philosophically as possible. With Laisha, his feelings were different. Her renunciation would cut to the depths of his soul. Gently he pushed her away as he unbuttoned his coat. "There," he said as he hung it on a peg near the door. "Now"—he opened his arms to her—"come here, Laisha."

She hugged him again, laughing. "You're funny, Papa."

When had she started to call him Papa? Was it last year? He knew that with strangers she always referred to him as her guardian, but she had not addressed him as such for some time. "How were your lessons?" he asked her after he had kissed the top of her head.

"Well enough, for lessons." She shrugged. "I like botany, but microscopes are silly." She broke away from him and started back toward the parlor. "Herr Bündnis says that I ought to apply myself."

As she disappeared into the parlor, Ragoczy turned to Professor Vögel. "And what do you say?"

Vögel sighed and scratched his head. "Well, Herr Graf, it is not my place to say, but no doubt the child is intelligent. She has an aptitude for science, but I have noticed of late that she is particularly interested in medicine. I'm not talking about bandaging up cut fingers; no." He hooked his thumbs into the watch-and-fob pockets of his vest. "She was examining a dis-

eased plant the other day, and was most curious. She wished
to know what it was that had caused this particular plant to
suffer from this particular disease. That, as you're probably
aware, is a very sophisticated question. When I reminded her
of our talks on genetics, she became most impatient and said
that was all trivial now. That the plant was dying was important, and although the genetic component was a factor, the
disease was the primary consideration. Her language was not
so precise, but her understanding was excellent. I've been
pleasantly surprised in her, Herr Graf."

Ragoczy did not stifle his smile. "That delights me."

"But something is troubling you," Professor Vögel said,
lowering his voice.

"Yes, but it's not what you think." Ragoczy looked away
toward the window and the falling snow. "It's so brief. The
ephemeral years are here, then gone. I treasure her growing,
though she will be gone from me so soon." He saw the sympathetic nod that Professor Vögel offered him, and did not know
how to tell him that the lifetime the Professor had lived
seemed as brief to him, who had been born four thousand
years before, as Laisha's fleeting childhood.

"I've felt that way," Professor Vögel was saying. "Often,
when I was still teaching, I would see an occasional brilliant
student who would attend my lectures and demonstrations for
one year or two, and the next thing you know, I would find
that he was presenting papers at scientific meetings as an
esteemed colleague. Well, it's the way of the world, is it not,
Herr Graf?"

"The way of the world," Ragoczy repeated, thinking of
Thebes and Babylon, or Tyre and Rome, of Lo-Yang and
Kiev, of Florence and Paris.

"And this girl of yours—oh, you need not remind me she is
not your flesh and blood; I know that well enough—she has a
great deal of promise if only it isn't stifled. It may be less
difficult for her, what with women getting the vote in England
and America, to make her way in her studies, but the academic community is progressive only in ideas. For the rest,
we are very conservative, and it may be that she will encounter more opposition than she wishes to deal with. You will
have to speak with her about that. What I am trying to tell
you, Herr Graf, is that I feel it would be wise to encourage
her to continue her studies. I know what youngsters are, and
it is possible that she may change her mind many times before
she finds her true métier. It would be a shame, however, if

she were discouraged from exploring, if you take my meaning."
He waggled his long, wispy brows once or twice in emphasis.

"It would give me great joy to see Laisha excel in work of
her choice. There has been much tragedy in her life; I wish I
could give her some happiness." He looked toward the parlor,
where he could hear Laisha in quiet conversation with David
Bündnis.

"Her memory . . . ?" the Professor asked with as much tact
as he possessed.

"No. There is no change there." Ragoczy thrust his hands
into his pockets and looked up, breathing deeply once. "Nor
have the men I have hired to make inquiries come up with any
solid information. That's not entirely surprising, when you
consider the state Russia is in. Doubtless there is someone
who knows who she is, and if any of her family is still alive,
but so far they have not been found. And I confess," he went
on more cheerfully, "that part of me would be glad if they
were not found, for then I would not have to give her up.
Eventually she will leave me, I know that, but I would prefer
to have her with me as long as possible." He shook his head in
gentle self-mockery. "Come, let us join the other two, or
Laisha will begin to fear you have given me a bad report."

Professor Vögel chuckled. "That's nonsense, but if that's
what you wish, Herr Graf, by all means . . ." He led the way
into the parlor, making an expansive gesture toward the girl
and her tutor as he approached the fireplace. "Forgive us for
lingering in the hall. We needed a moment of discussion."

"Yes, of course," David Bündnis agreed. He had half-risen,
hesitated, then taken his seat again, looking uncertainly at
Ragoczy.

"I am told you're doing well," Ragoczy said to Laisha,
dismissing her tutor with a negligent wave of his small, beautiful hand. "David, discuss botany with the Professor for a few
minutes, will you? I need a little time with my daughter."

Laisha grinned, her brown eyes dancing. "He said I'm a
good student, didn't he?"

"Yes, he did." Ragoczy took his seat on the elderly couch
before the fire, turned so that he could face her as she perched
on the hearth stool. "I didn't need him to say so, but it is
always satisfying to have one's opinions confirmed. Does it
please you to be doing well?"

"If you're happy, that's enough," she said, impulsively reaching for his hand.

He did not pull it away, but the smile he gave her was sad.

"No, Laisha, my child, it is not enough. You are not my shadow, and I will not always be with you: what you do must be for yourself, because it is what *you* wish to do. If it is, then you will have a chance to be free and happy, which is what I want for you more than anything else. Believe this."

"But you said you were glad I'm doing well with my studies," she protested, her chin quivering.

"And so I am. But if you were doing well because you thought I would like it instead of liking the studies yourself, I would be sorry. Do you want to continue your instruction with Professor Vögel, or would you prefer to do something else?" His penetrating eyes were filled with kindness and he waited without impatience for her answer.

Laisha scowled into the fire, giving his question her full consideration. Her face had a faintly Tartar cast to it, and the light from the fire revealed this plainly as it moved and shifted. Absently she pulled at a loose strand of hair. After two or three minutes she looked back at Ragoczy. "I think I would like to continue studying with Professor Vögel for a while. I am not sure I will want to learn science all the time, but right now, it's interesting to learn about the plants and other things. Later I may change my mind." This was more of a plea than a statement.

"Tell me when you wish me to make other arrangements," Ragoczy said fondly.

"All right." Now that she was sure of herself, Laisha assumed a more confident air. She straightened her woolen shirt and gave Ragoczy a beguiling smile.

"You know, Laisha, you're apt to be a handful when you're grown." He chuckled, and felt a twinge of regret that she would never be one of his blood.

"My mother was. My father said so," she declared with a saucy toss of her head. Then she realized what her words meant.

Ragoczy was already leaning forward, dark eyes intense. "Laisha, do you remember? Can you tell me any more?"

Her eyes glazed with tears. "No . . . no. I don't even know what made me . . . Oh . . . I didn't mean . . ." With a brief, anguished cry, she covered her face with her hands. She did not permit herself to sob, but her trembling was more distressing to Ragoczy than wailing would have been.

He slid off the sofa and dropped onto his knees beside her, taking her into his arms. "Laisha, Laisha," he whispered to her. "My dearest child." The sound of a step in the doorway caught his attention, and he turned with a brusque gesture to Professor Vögel so that there would be no intrusion. Satisfied that they were once again alone, Ragoczy brought Laisha's head down to his shoulder and murmured gentle, reassuring phrases to her until her tears stopped and her arms around his neck were limp. He stood slowly, carrying her with him. Without changing his hold on her, he went to the door. "Professor," he said in a forceful voice, "If you will?"

A few moments later the Professor emerged from the direction of the kitchen with David Bündnis close behind him. Professor Vögel was still wiping the remains of whipped cream from his mouth with a large linen handkerchief. "Well well well," he said as he approached Ragoczy. "Poor child. Don't be upset, little one. All of us suffer in our lives, and you have already endured the worst. Your guardian will take care of you and see that no harm comes to you."

"That is my intention," Ragoczy said quietly, hoping inwardly that he would be able to keep that vow.

Laisha turned her head so that she could see the other two men. "I didn't plan to behave this way," she said in a small, chastened voice.

"No one ever does, Laisha," David said with an uneasy smile. "We are your friends; we don't mind."

Laisha gave him a long, thoughtful look, but said nothing. She pushed away from Ragoczy's arms and dropped to her feet. After a careful adjustment of her skirt, she stared into her guardian's eyes. "I would like to go home now."

"Of course," he responded. "If you will give me her hat and coat, Professor Vögel?"

"Jawol, Herr Graf," the Professor said as he bustled about gathering up Laisha's hat and coat, which he held out to David Bündnis after he had made a halfhearted attempt to put them around Laisha's shoulders. "Perhaps you'd best . . ."

"Yes," David said quietly.

"She's not an infant, gentlemen," Ragoczy told the other two. "She is capable of dressing herself, and she hears everything you say. She is also not an invalid and does not need to be coddled." He nodded to David and watched as Laisha took her hat and coat from her tutor and put them on. "Thank you, Bündnis. You had better get ready as well: it is cold and we're likely to have slow going back to Schloss Saint-Germain. There has been a slide, as you have heard, and as far as I know, they have not brought the laborers to fix it." Looking down at Laisha, he said gently, "Are you ready?"

"Yes, Papa," she said, still obviously chagrined.

His smile widened. "Very good, my child. Bündnis?"

"In a moment, Herr Ragoczy." He was thrusting his arms into the sleeves of his overcoat.

Ragoczy took his coat and donned it, turning up the velvet collar in anticipation of the cold outside. "Herr Professor, I thank you for your hospitality and your concern. Laisha is fortunate to have your instruction, and I am in your debt for your kindness." He inclined his head, then went to the door. "Hurry to the car. There is a rug in the backseat and you may wrap it around you."

The wind was sharper than when Ragoczy had arrived, and it drove the thickening snowflakes before it, scattering them in little drifts and eddies across the Professor's porch and along the driveway. Ragoczy, Laisha, and David hurried toward the Benz, each with head bowed against the oncoming storm. The doors of the Benz were pulled open, then quickly closed. In the more open front seat, Ragoczy reached into the small leather case beside the partition to the rear seat and pulled out a black fur hat, setting it on his head so that his ears were covered.

Professor Vögel closed his door as soon as he saw that his guests were safely in the automobile; he felt a strange chill now that they were going, a chill that had little to do with the icy wind. It was not a thing he wished to examine, so he toddled back to the kitchen to get a second helping of Sachertorte and hot chocolate.

After two false starts, the Benz's motor came to life, sputtering a little with the cold. Ragoczy eased off the brake and put the automobile into gear, going cautiously, not wishing to risk a skid on the ice that was beginning to form in the deeper ruts of the poorly-kept road. Even with this care, the Benz wallowed in the gelid mud and once nearly stalled as the front wheels encountered a wooden plank hidden beneath the surface of the road. The wheels spun, grated, then caught, and the Benz moved on.

As they drove through Geitau, Ragoczy noticed the huge brewery wagon pulled up at the inn; the team of tremendous Belgian draft horses were blowing and steaming, one of them favoring his off forefoot.

"They're awfully mud-spattered," David said, speaking loudly to be heard over the motor and the wind. "Do you think the road has been repaired yet, or will we be delayed?"

"We're apt to be delayed in any case," Ragoczy responded

as he slowed, then turned and pulled into the small courtyard, keeping a fair distance from the big horses, which were showing signs of shying. He brought the Benz to a stop and called out, "Can anyone tell me if the road to Hausham has been cleared?"

The driver of the team came around the wagon and strolled over to the Benz, the large tankard of hot schnapps he carried accounting in part for his apparent disregard of the weather. "The crew of convict laborers were working on it when I came through, about an hour ago. There's twenty men on the job, and three guards to keep an eye on them. They say it will be passable before night, but I doubt it, not with the way the temperature's dropping. Still, they drive convicts harder than most workmen, so maybe it will be done." He grinned at Ragoczy, showing uneven teeth. "An automobile will have to wait, if there's any difficulty. Now me, with my team, we can forge through a slide like that. We've got over rough ground, I can tell you that. But automobiles, they're not able to pull the way a team does, and they don't understand, and so you, in your fancy Benz, will have to wait." He thought this observation so funny that he laughed wholeheartedly, spilling some of the schnapps on his sheepskin jacket.

"Danke," Ragoczy said tersely. "I trust that your team will be unhitched and given warm gruel, and the right wheeler's leg attended to, or tomorrow they will not be able to forge ahead through the snow that's coming." He gave the teamster a polite nod and set his automobile in motion again. He admitted to himself that he was somewhat concerned. A long delay on this road would mean that they would not return to Schloss Saint-Germain until quite late at night, and Laisha, who was already hungry, would be famished. He could not believe that hunger did not awaken terrifying memories in the girl, and he wished to spare her further pain.

For a little way, all went well. The snow was mixed now with sleety rain and the wind, blocked by the shoulder of the mountains, did not cut quite so deeply as it raced through the air. Three kilometers outside of Geitau, Ragoczy pulled off the road and turned on the headlamps as a precaution, for although the afternoon was not far advanced, the sky was dark and the trees around them created deep shadows that were like twilight. Getting back into the driver's seat, he turned to the two in the back and gave them an encouraging nod as he started up once more. Ten minutes farther on, they came to the slide, and Ragoczy brought the automobile to a halt as a burly guard in a long overcoat came up to them. He carried a lantern and a rifle.

"Good afternoon, Mein Herr," he said, his tone belying his respectful words of greeting. "I am afraid there will have to be a wait. As you see, we are clearing the road." He turned his lantern beam in the direction of a line of men with shovels and barrows who struggled on the muddy slope. All of them were dressed in convict clothing, with only heavy canvas jackets to protect them from the weather.

"We're at your disposal," Ragoczy said with just enough hauteur to cause the guard a touch of discomfort. "Who are these men? I see that they are prisoners, but what is their crime?"

The guard shrugged, and when he answered, his attitude was more subservient. "They are men, Mein Herr, who have come here from other countries. Most of them without money, all without friends. Some have fled the ideal society being built in Russia, some have left Poland. We have one or two Hungarians who have learned that they are not welcome in the country their towns have been allotted to. All of them came here, thinking that they could prey on the goodwill of Deutschland and the people, but they are mistaken. This is not Paris, where every cabdriver claims to be a Romanov prince, or Rome, where bankrupt Polish Counts are allowed to live on the honest toil of loyal Catholics. We are not willing to be hoodwinked by such men. So, as you see . . ."—again he directed the lantern toward the men—"we find a use for them. They may not have found the idle paradise they sought, but there will be a cleared road fairly soon, and that is important, wouldn't you say?"

Ragoczy looked at the guard. "And what will they do when they have finished their sentences?"

"Oh, that does not concern us," the guard answered rather stiffly. "They will have to make their way in the world like the rest of us."

"I see." He gazed at the men, his eyes piercing the gloom quite easily. The poor wretches, he thought, sweating and freezing at once. And what hope was there for them, if they were not welcome in Deutschland? The guard cut into his thoughts.

"You take that fellow there," he said, pointing the lantern at a tall, rain-sodden figure with military sideburns. "Claims to have been a hussar in Poland. He wanted to join one of our regiments, but they would not take him, of course. Not that there is much left of our regiments. Not allowed guns! Maneuvers only conducted with models of machines rather than the machines themselves! I know the French are spiteful, jealous hypocrites, with their searches and inspections!" He hefted his rifle. "The only reason I'm permitted to carry this is because I guard dangerous men, and may need to protect myself."

"Yes, so I see," Ragoczy remarked sardonically.

"Yes," the guard agreed, unaware of the tone Ragoczy had used. "Now, that man there is from Greece. He was a criminal there and he was one here, but we, unlike his fellow-countrymen, were not willing to tolerate his activities. He ran a brothel, you know, and bribed the officials in his homeland by offering the services of the girls—and boys—free of charge. The judge who sentenced him warned him about trying such degraded methods again. He's not popular with the other prisoners, they say, because he did not fight in the war. The man next to him, he's one of the Russians. He's something of a hard case, actually. He came here more than a year ago, and when he could not get work, he took to stealing, mostly food, but money occasionally as well. Had he had friends, the matter might have been forgotten, for they could have repaid his victims and made certain he had no opportunity to steal again. As it was, we could not let him go on. I gather that he was part of a cavalry unit at one time, but you know how things are in Russia."

"Poor man," Ragoczy said reflectively, recalling the times when he had been like the Russian; alone, friendless, having no money and with little chance of getting any honestly. Such days were far in his past, but the memory of them had not faded.

The Russian had finished filling the wheelbarrow beside him. He shoveled one last load of earth and then turned to get the wheelbarrow in hand. As he did so, he glanced in the direction of the lantern and faintly burning headlights of the Benz.

Ragoczy leaned forward at the wheel, his dark eyes suddenly intent. "*Rozoh*," he whispered.

The Russian began to trundle his load down the slope. Aching fatigue showed in the strain of his shoulders and the wavering progress of his steps. Then without warning, the wheelbarrow sloughed to the side and Rozoh went sprawling.

The guard sprinted forward at once, his lantern swinging, his rifle raised in his right hand like a club. There were confused shouts, and three of the other prisoners rushed to defend the fallen man.

"Halt! All prisoners to stay at attention!" another guard from the far end of the slide shouted. "You three! Back to your shovels. Schnell!"

The three men hesitated, then made their way back up the slope, their eyes now averted from the Russian.

Nikolai Ivanevich Rozoh lay in the mud, his blistered hands pressed to his sides, his garments soaked through. He murmured a Russian prayer and waited for the blows to fall.

"Get up, you foreign pig!" the guard with the lantern ordered, prodding Rozoh's shoulder with the butt of his rifle.

"Do not abuse him," Ragoczy said quietly. He had got out of the Benz and come up behind the guard. "Let me speak with him."

"Surely, Mein Herr, this is no concern of yours." The arrogant manner was back, and the sureness of the man irritated Ragoczy.

"You told me that he was without friends. He is not without friends now," Ragoczy told him, and as if unaware of the damage of his fine wool coat, went down on his knee beside the fallen man. "Major Rozoh," he said, speaking in Russian. "Major, you must get up."

Dazed and weary to the core of his bones, Rozoh did not respond at first. He drew his knees up and let his misery engulf him.

"Major Rozoh, if you do not get up, I will not be able to keep the guard from hurting you," Ragoczy persisted, seeing the other man's suffering. "Major, open your eyes and look at me."

How much Rozoh wanted to shut out that voice! He pressed the backs of his hands over his ears, but keeping them there was too difficult, and he let them fall again, wincing as the mud splattered on his injured palms.

"Rozoh, get up," Ragoczy repeated. "Get up at once."

Dimly, Rozoh realized that he was being addressed in Russian, and although he was too tired to be surprised, he was curious. His eyes opened a bit. There was also something about the voice, something familiar. For some reason, he thought of the monastery near Krasnoye Selo. He struggled to brace himself on his elbow as he peered through the rain at the dark figure beside him. "What?"

"That's better," Ragoczy said, rising to his feet. "I will pay your debts, Rozoh. I believe I owe you that much."

"Owe me?" Rozoh repeated, getting to his knees.

"Were it not for you, I doubt I would have been able to get out of the Monastery of the Victory, except to face a firing squad." He started away from Rozoh and said to the guard, in German, "I don't want this man to work anymore. He is hurt and ill. Inform your warden that I will make arrangements through the court to pay his debts and secure his release. I also guarantee him employment." He paused a moment. "If I should learn that any of my instructions were disregarded, it will be the worse for you."

The guard did not quite salute, but he made a sort of compromise gesture that showed he would do as he was commanded. "But, Mein Herr," he said nervously, "who shall I say . . . what name do I say?"

"Ragoczy. Franchot Ragoczy, of Schloss Saint-Germain." He had spoken loudly enough for Rozoh to hear him.

"You!" the Russian shouted as all his fragmentary impressions rushed together in recognition. "*You!*"

"Yes," Ragoczy replied with a short ironic bow before starting back to his automobile and his two baffled companions.

Text of a letter from Helmut Rauch to the schoolteacher Pasch Garbe.

19 Hautpenprinz Strasse
München
January 12, 1921

Pasch Garbe
Vorschule St. Sixtus
Landsberied Strasse
Fürsten-Feldbruck

My dear Herr Garbe:

Your name was given me by Frau Carola Hofmann, who said that you and she had discussed at length the problems confronting our poor country, particularly the lack of discipline and direction among our people as well as the scandalous depredations of the French, who every day abuse the rights of the Treaty of Versailles. Frau Hofmann has said that her late husband often discussed with you the great concerns he felt, and which still beset his widow.

I understand that you are not sympathetic to the Nationalsozialistische Deutsche Arbeiterpartei, believing them to be a rabble, composed of nothing but discontents and failures who brawl in taverns and make inflammatory speeches that do nothing more than cause alarm among the responsible citizens of München. Yet you must consider more deeply. The NSDAP is only a small part of the plan that has been developed by men who chafe at the unreasonable demands of the French and the English, who feel that each maneuver by the French and English is a calculated insult that must be avenged if Deutschland is ever to regain its rightful place as the leader of Europe.

You realize that in making their vindictive decisions, the French forgot that only we stand between them and *the expanding power of Russia. Poland is as good as lost, no matter what you may hear to the contrary. Deutschland and Österreich are the only barriers left that can successfully prevent the Communists from advancing into the cities of Europe to despoil not only our homeland, but all the other countries of the West as well. Depend upon it, in another three or four years the French will come as much to their senses as they are able to, and at that time, you will find that we will be on much different footing, and with a little skill, the NSDAP will be well-placed by that time to influence policy.*

*It is not the fault of General von Seeckt that we find ourselves in this disgraceful position, and those who point to him do not see clearly how he is as much a victim as any honorable officer in the army who fought bravely to preserve Deutschland. Rest assured that those who are in a powerful office who do not deserve it will not be able to remain there long. As I have already intimated, there are those who will be guiding the country through the men of the NSDAP, and they are influential and farsighted men. They envision a much more sweeping change than what has been outlined by the NSDAP so far, and they will strive to bring it about as soon as may be. They are not reckless, they are not impulsive, but men of great esoteric learning and patriotic devotion who have added their considerable occult skills to a keen perception of the political situation to their determined thrust to regain our trampled honor.*

*Your very objection to the NSDAP is what prompts this letter, for you and and those like you, who instruct our children, can be of great benefit to our country, helping to restore the sense of worthiness which has been so undermined. The Zeitgeist is changing, and now is the perfect time for those who would help to shape the destined future of Deutschland to gather under the banner of the NSDAP, bringing it the social position it must have in order to fulfill the aims not only of that party, but of the Thule Bruderschaft. You can aid us in transforming our beloved country from a broken one, wallowing in defeat, to a shining example to the entire world. It must begin with the young, for it is they who will carry on the dream when you and I have left the earth behind.*

*I am aware that the Thule Bruderschaft has been accused of Zauberkunst, but this is nonsense, not unlike*

*saying that the biochemists in our universities are prac-
ticing alchemy. Do not let these malicious lies influence
you in your thinking, for it is just such statements that
give succor to our enemies and keep Deutschland on its
knees. Let me invite you to join a few of us for supper
next Tuesday. We will be dining at an inn in Starnberg,
which, I must tell you, serves excellent Kalbsbeuscherl
and Leberknödelsuppe as well as fine Schwarzwälder
Kirschtorte. The wines are good, the selection is reasonable and the beer is made by the landlord himself, and
even the most demanding palate will be pleased with it. I
think you will find that Herr Eckart and Herr Doktor
Krohn will have a great deal to say to you that will
interest you very much, and in such a setting, with a
convivial atmosphere to add its benign influence, you will
become as eager as I am to aid these good men in their
work.*

*I will look forward to hearing from you in the next
three days. If you wish, you may telephone me at my
work, at the Bayerisch Kreditkörperschaft, and a message
will always reach me there. Remember that you, as a
schoolteacher, are in an enviable position to influence the
youth of our country, and it is a station you ought not to
take lightly. Consider your answer in that light, and then
let me hear that you are with us. This brings you my
cordial good wishes.*

> *Most sincerely yours,
> Helmut Rauch*

# 6

Gudrun Ostneige descended from the Hispaño-Suiza and looked
up at the shining front of the See Jewul Hotel overlooking
Starnbergersee. Thousands of electric lights glittered on the
facade and the sound of a dance band came through the door,
accompanied by the susurrus of conversation and an occasional
well-bred laugh. Gudrun hesitated, her skirt lifted for the
ascent of the eight broad stairs to the terrace.

"Go on, Rudi," Otto coaxed from the driver's seat of the

automobile. "They're waiting for you. I'll be here at one in the morning. Go on."

"But," she said uncertainly, "I don't know. I hadn't realized it would be so big a party." In her right hand she held a beaded evening bag, and this she clutched as if it were her only source of rescue. "With Jürgen so ill, for me to appear at such a gala is . . . inappropriate. I thought it would be much smaller, but this is so grand."

Otto chuckled indulgently. "You are not a flighty woman, and your devotion to your husband is well-known in the neighborhood. It's not as if your family was of minor importance, or had only been here a generation or so. The Altbrunnen house has been at Wolkighügel for more than three hundred years, and their standing is assured."

"If Maxl were here . . ." She gave a restless twitch to the lace overdress that covered her gown of silver satin.

Privately, Otto agreed with Gudrun: Maximillian ought to be here to escort his sister instead of attending yet another of those secret meetings with Eckart. He gave her a tolerant smile. "You're as bad as a girl just coming out. You're not a child anymore, Rudi, you're a respected matron of a distinguished family. You are doing nothing incorrect." He looked at her neatly-cut hair and lamented the loss of her braids for this more fashionable crop, and thought it unfortunate that her face was indeed showing signs of age. Not very long ago, she had been fresh and lithe, lovely as a birch tree, and now she was faded in spite of the modish dress and haircut, and artfully-applied makeup could not change this.

"Yes. If only the Baron were from this neighborhood, I would know what to do. Since he is a foreigner, it is more difficult. Strangers . . ." Her voice trailed off as she thought suddenly of Graf Ragoczy, who had asked that she call him Saint-Germain. His foreignness was so intriguing, and he at once so enigmatic and gallant. She started up the steps with a sigh. If there were those who disapproved, no doubt she would hear of it soon enough, but with winter beginning to fade, surely this one evening would not be too reprehensible, with spring coming on and the snows beginning to melt.

One of the hotel's staff was standing by the door in formal livery. He gave her an acknowledging half-bow and asked whose name he should announce.

Gudrun lifted her head. "Frau Ostneige," she said with the touch of arrogance that marked the hochgebornen.

"Frau Ostneige," the man announced to the room, and motioned Gudrun to enter.

As she crossed the threshold, her smile concealed her dismay. There were more than a hundred people at the hotel, all of them in evening clothing, many of them quite recognizable and much-admired figures in Bayern. Suddenly she felt a dowd, though she knew she was properly attired, that the antique blue-white lace she wore over her silver gown was as acceptable as any other woman's dress in the room, that the diamond-and-pearl necklace was elegant without being ostentatious, and her long white gloves were spotless. In confusion, she opened her beaded bag to find the little vial of scent she had tucked into it, and almost spoiled her glove by reaching for the tube of lip rouge which had lost its cap. She felt herself about to burst into tears.

"Pardon me," a man said as he pushed by her, his tucked shirt a little disarrayed. He turned and looked back once at Gudrun with a speculative expression, then blundered on through the crowd.

Gudrun looked about wildly, wishing now that she had not come. She could see none of her neighbors, although she was certain some of them must be here. Of course, the Schnaubels would not be invited, and she doubted that Ragoczy would be, as he was a foreigner. The host, however, was Hungarian, and she hoped that perhaps she would encounter him in the midst of all these impressive guests. At last she noticed Konrad Natter standing at the long bar at the far end of the ballroom. There was a balloon snifter in his hand and his profile was reflected several dozen times in the facets of the mirrors behind the bar. On most occasions, Gudrun abhorred the man and avoided him, but now she was anxious for familiar company, even if it was such a person as Natter. She started across the room toward him, threading her way through the genial clusters of chattering guests.

"Ah, Frau Ostneige," cried a voice behind her, and she glanced back to see Baron Istvan Tiborkraj bearing down on her, his old-fashioned white mustaches quivering. "How good of you to come. I was so much afraid that you would not attend because of your husband's poor health. Where is that scapegrace of a brother? Has he left you alone already?" The Baron was tall and rangy, and dressed in full diszmagyar. His dolman was of heavy red silk, thickly embroidered with a pattern of leaves, studded with peridot and tourmalines, and laced with gold. His dark green trousers were close-cut and embroided with gold. His boots were high, of red leather with a pattern of leaves stitched into them. The Order of Saint Stephen hung around his neck, dangling almost to his waist. He took Gudrun's hand and kissed it.

"My brother sends his apologies, but he was already engaged for this evening, and did not recall it until yesterday," she said in a somewhat stifled voice.

"What you mean, my dear, is that he did not want to come and found an excuse to stay away," the Baron corrected her with a wink. "He would rather spend his time building the new Deutschland than reminiscing about the old Empire. One look at these archaic clothes of mine, and he would have bolted." He tucked her hand through the crook of his arm. "You know, your father often said he was concerned for that boy, and I've only recently begun to appreciate what he meant. A capable lad, without doubt, but with very little understanding in him." He signaled a waiter, and said to Gudrun, "Champagne? Or would you prefer something less heady?"

Rather recklessly, Gudrun said, "Champagne, Baron, bitte."

"Excellent." He took two glasses from the tray which the waiter proffered, and offered one to Gudrun. "A good year, this. Whatever else you may say about the French, their wines are superb." He lifted his glass in a toast and tossed it off at once. "That's my fifth glass this evening. Don't tell my physician."

Gudrun sipped once at the sparkling wine, then looked up at the Baron. "You did not say in your invitation what this evening is supposed to celebrate."

"Why, the extinction of the House of Tiborkraj, of course. Now that my holdings are part of Czechoslovakia, there is no barony nor any other elevated state for Tiborkraj, no title, no rights of birth. We are all quite common now." He said it lightly enough, but his tired eyes glinted like old steel. "This, Gnädige Frau, is a reception for the dead, and I hope that you will enjoy yourself in tribute to that which is gone."

"But, Baron . . ." She had no idea what response her host wanted from her, and her confusion brought a becoming flush to her cheeks and throat.

"There, I have upset you, and that was not in the least my intention. Or was it the champagne?" He pulled at the waxed end of his mustache and regarded her with an arch look that once had been considered dangerous by court ladies.

"Probably the champagne. I have so little oppor . . . inclination to have it when my husband cannot enjoy it." Her color deepened and she took another sip of the wine, wanting to hide her embarrassment with this acceptable excuse.

"For all your husband can be to you, you might as well be a widow," Baron Tiborkraj muttered, then became more expansive. "It's not my place, but when I recall what it was like, when you had your first pony and I taught you to ride like the devil himself, well, then I thought you would find yourself a Graf or Herzog to woo you and be captivated by your charm and daring. But then, there are no more Grafs or Herzogs left for you." As a waiter passed with a tray of canapés the Baron reached out and grabbed two of them. "Good. Shrimp. I like shrimp." He disposed of the canapés quickly.

"I don't wish to discuss Jürgen, Baron. It is so hopeless and there is nothing to be gained by saying so." She finished the glass of champagne in a rush. Something of the underlying frenetic air of the gala was reaching her, and she felt a little wild.

"Quite right. It was an imposition to speak of it." The band had begun to play a medley of popular tunes from Berlin, and more of the guests were dancing. The Baron had to raise his voice to be heard over the noise. "Would you like me to find you a partner? I would offer myself, but I don't know any of these new steps."

"That's all right," she said gratefully. "I don't want to dance just now myself." She hated to admit that most of the new dances were unknown to her. She was confident that there would be waltzes later on, and although her skirt was not really of the best design for the fast waltzes she loved, it would be a joy to spin around the room to the light melodies of Strauss.

"In my day, it was cotillions and the czardas," the Baron said quietly. "I learned the mazurka, as well, but it hasn't been very popular for a long time."

"It's difficult, isn't it? The mazurka?" She took a second glass of champagne from one of the waiters and handed him the first glass. She was unaccustomed to wine now, and already could feel its glow touch her.

"Complicated, and took a great deal of grace and style, which was one of the reasons it was so popular at court. We—my family—were most important there, once," he went on with a bitter smile. "My grandmother was a Teleki, and they say that Janos Hunyadi himself bestowed our motto on us: 'Strength beyond death'. How appropriate that seems to-night." By this time they had reached the far side of the dance floor where a number of guests were seated at round marble-topped tables. A few had plates before them with the remnants of pastry on them.

One of the gentlemen rose as the Baron approached, showing proper courtesy to the old man. "A magnificent evening, Tiborkraj. You do your name proud."

"That was my intention," the Baron replied. "It pleases me that you appreciate my efforts."

There were fragments of conversation broken off to extend the socially correct amount of gratitude for the lavish gala.

"That's kind of you. I think that some of you do not know my charming companion," he added, looking down at Gudrun. "This is Frau Ostneige, of Wolkighügel at Hausham. Her father was Felix Altbrunnen, who was an aide to the Kaiser for several years. One or two of you may remember him."

Two women at the nearer table had been giving Gudrun's clothes and jewels careful scrutiny, and now smiled with calculating goodwill. "Tell me," one of them said, moving her brightly rouged lips with exaggerated care, "is your husband with you this evening, Frau Ostneige?"

Gudrun bridled slightly, but felt the Baron's fingers tighten on her arm in warning. "Alas, no. My husband is an invalid. He was very grievously injured in the war, and has not left his bed for three years."

"Oh," said another one of the women with a sideways glance at the gentleman to her left, "how unfortunate."

"He has borne it with great fortitude," Gudrun said with more force than she had intended. "Other men have fared as badly." She wanted to say that at least Jürgen's mind was fairly intact, unlike so many others, but she stopped the words. This was not the time or the place for such reminders.

"Well, Finster, I will leave Frau Ostneige with you and your friends. I'm sure she'd rather be with you youngsters than with me. This is Klaus Finster, Gudrun, and he will certainly tell you the names of his party. I'm afraid that between champagne and age, my memory is not what it was." He released Gudrun and strolled away, oblivious of the pleading expression in Gudrun's eyes.

"Frau Ostneige?" Klaus Finster said, being certain he had heard correctly. "Won't you sit down? Ulrich, there's a seat beside you. Frau Ostneige can sit there. Frau Ostneige, my brother Ulrich. He's been studying law, so that he can get the better of the French, but I've told him it's a waste of time. The Chancellor's office, that's where a lawyer can do some good." As he spoke, he escorted Gudrun to the chair and pulled it out for her.

Ulrich Finster was slightly flushed, and the look of his eyes indicated that he had had more to drink than was wise. The smile he directed at Gudrun was more of a smirk, and he took her hand and kissed it in such a way that she was grateful to be wearing gloves. "A great pleasure, Frau Ostneige." His fingers brushed her arm as he released her hand.

"And this is Siegfried Reiz," Klaus went on. "And our ladies, yes. The brunette with the green eyes is Hildegard, and the beauty in striped silk is Ilse." He sat down again as Gudrun sank into her chair. His eyes flicked over Gudrun once before he leaned toward Hildegard. "Do you want to dance, my sweeting?"

Hildegard turned her languid, bored countenance on Ulrich as she answered his brother. "Not yet," she said in a seductive voice. "I'm not ready yet." She looked around the room once, explaining to the others at the table, "They say that Conrad Veidt is here tonight, but I haven't seen him."

"Conrad Veidt?" Gudrun repeated, baffled at the increased excitement of the party. "I've . . . heard the name, but I don't know . . ."

"My dear Frau Ostneige, you must be living in Outer Mongolia not to have heard of Conrad Veidt," Ulrich said, resting his arm on the back of her chair. "No one would admit to not knowing him. It would be like not knowing Bismarck. Haven't you seen *Das Kabinett des Doktor Caligari*? Everyone is talking about it. A remarkable film, Frau Ostneige, full of hidden meanings."

"It's much more interesting than those Communists in Saxony and Hamburg," Ilse said, winking slowly at Siegfried. "Let me have one of your cigarettes, Sieg."

Gudrun was astonished to see Siegfried comply, offering a silver engraved cigarette case to Ilse with a smile. "They're very strong." His tone was teasing, implying more than the words indicated.

"I like them strong," she said, taking one of the cigarettes and placing it between her red, red lips, waiting for Siegfried to light it for her. When it was done, she exhaled slowly, her eyes half-closed.

"Do you smoke, Frau Ostneige?" Siegfried Reiz asked, offering her the case.

"No. No, thank you, I don't." She wanted to leave the table, feeling as if she had been transported to another, sinister world she had never known.

"They say," Ulrich was telling her, bending his head down close to hers, "that there will be talking films next year. They're already making plans to try the process out. Think what it will be like then."

Hildegard shrugged her shoulders. "It's better this way, with only the film and the music. You can ignore the titles and make up for yourself what is taking place." Her sudden laugh was low and without joy. "I went once with a . . . friend who can read lips and he said that the things the actors say to each other are . . . interesting."

The band suddenly grew louder, playing a brassy tune that Gudrun did not know. Klaus hit the table with the flat of his hand in approval. "They'll offend the old Baron, but what does it matter?"

"What song is that?" Gudrun asked, wishing she could sink through the floor.

" 'Swanee.' It's American. Very decadent." Klaus stood up. "Come, Hildegard, dance with me. We'll show them how things have changed." He grabbed her by the wrist and pulled her to her feet.

"Shall we join them?" Ulrich murmured near her ear.

"No . . . thank you. My husband . . . I shouldn't dance." She clutched her bag in her lap. "I . . . it's very hot in here. I think I must get some fresh air."

Ulrich gave her a knowing smile. "The terrace is right through that door. There's a wind off the snow. You'll be cold."

"That's all right," Gudrun said rather distractedly as she pushed in the chair. The dance band was noisy and those who danced to the music were adding to the din. At the moment there was a headache at the back of her eyes and Gudrun could only think to keep to herself for the moment.

The night was startlingly chilly after the heated atmosphere of the ballroom. As she passed through the French doors, she was shocked by the wind and the cold that went through the thin soles of her dancing shoes and up her legs. Satin and lace proved to give little protection, and gooseflesh quickly rose on her arms. For a moment she hesitated, then crossed the terrace toward the balustrade between the terrace and the garden that at the moment was bare and sere. Now that she was away from the ballroom and the door was closed, the band was only a distant sound, like music played on toy instruments.

She sighed as the frigid wind flicked past her. She was glad to have privacy, even if it meant standing in the frosty night. Gradually she became aware of another sound, more suited to her ears: in one of the other grand rooms of the hotel, someone was playing the piano. She went toward the music, trying to place it. As she had little knowledge of Italian opera, she did not at first recognize the piece, but thought that perhaps it was a transcription of something by Donizetti or Bellini. There was a pause and then another variation began, filled with long arpeggios and dizzying runs. Gudrun smiled as she listened. This was so much more to her taste than the other, and there was real delight in listening to it here alone, as if it were being played for her and no one else. She thought that if only she might have another ten minutes or so of this unsuspecting serenade, then she could face the confusion in the ballroom.

A burst of music from the band, and the sound of strained laughter came from the far side of the terrace as the door opened. "Gudrun," a voice called out.

Surprised and not entirely pleased, Gudrun turned. "Baron?"

"Baron, is it?" the voice laughed, and then she saw Ulrich Finster in the shadow of the wall. "Who would have thought the old man would still be at it?"

"What are you talking about? What are you doing here?" The questions came quickly and she tried to convince herself that it was the cold that caused her to shiver, and not the young man coming across the terrace toward her.

"Don't worry, my little dove, I was discreet. No one saw me leave, and I doubt anyone saw you, either. They were all trying to dance. Our absence won't be noticed and we can return by different doors." His smile was cynically confident as he reached her and put his hands on her shoulders.

"Herr Finster!" Gudrun said in an affronted voice. "Don't . . ."

His look grew harder. "What is this? You knew I was coming." His fingers tightened and he could feel her bare arms through the lace.

"Knew you were coming?" She stared at him. "You're mistaken, Herr Finster. It is some sort of misunderstanding. If you don't mind, I would prefer to be alone." She had never had to take such a tone with a man before and it bothered her to do so now. Always in the past she had been treated with respect, but this young man with his cold eyes and brooding mouth was not within her experience. "Please take your hands off me at once."

"You want to play that kind of game, do you?" He laughed once, his drunkenness making the outburst loud and unsteady. "I know your sort. I knew the moment the Baron brought you to the table. Poor wife. Disabled husband. I didn't need written orders to tell me what you wanted me to do."

With an effort, Gudrun suppressed an urge to laugh. To the sounds of a well-played piano and a dance band, she was having to repel an inebriated lecher. It was like something in a bad drama, she thought, and found it hard to believe it was indeed happening, that there would not come one decisive line, after which the curtain would fall and there would be applause. She gave Ulrich a steady look. "You're not yourself, Herr Finster, and I won't hold you accountable. If you will apologize and leave me alone, there will be no more said about it." She dreaded what would happen if Maximillian or Jürgen should come to hear of this episode, and it gave her the impetus to turn suddenly and break away from him. "Now you may go in, Herr Finster."

"You little tease!" he yelled at her, and she flinched, hoping that the noise from the ballroom was sufficient to cover this shout. As he came after her, he was a bit unsteady, which only made his pursuit more disturbing. "You want me to force you, do you, so you can say that it wasn't your fault, and still have your fun? Do you?" He was almost upon her again, one hand reaching out to grab her. The light blue hundred-year-old lace tore in his grasp as he lunged at her.

Gudrun let out a shocked little cry, and her illusion that this was only a poorly-written scene vanished. She turned again and tried to run in her fragile dancing shoes. The trailing lace tripped her and she twisted wildly to keep from falling.

"You wretched woman," Ulrich said between his teeth as he caught up with her, his arm going around her waist and dragging her toward him.

The piano had fallen silent, but the band was playing more loudly than ever. Gudrun pushed at her captor with her hands, but dared not cry out for fear of the scandal it would bring down on her. She must not be found in such an embarrassing situation. What she would do if anything worse happened, she could not imagine. Ulrich's hand was tugging at the neckline of the lace overdress and squeezing the flesh beneath, and he swore under his breath.

"Excuse me," said a voice from one of the side doors. "Is there some difficulty, Frau Ostneige?"

"Scheisst!" Ulrich hissed, turning abruptly toward the intruder without releasing Gudrun. "Leave us alone."

"I'm afraid I can't do that," was the mild answer as Franchot Ragoczy strolled onto the terrace. "She is my neighbor, you see, and I can't leave her in this . . . awkward situation." He was resplendent in full formal wear with a red sash across his chest adorned with the badge of the Order of Saint Stephen of Hungary as well as a heavy silver chain studded with rubies from which depended a silver device, the heraldic representation of the eclipse. "You will leave now. I will see to it that Frau Ostneige is taken home, and there will be no talk attached to this . . . incident."

Ulrich sized up the other man and laughed once more. "It would be better if you left, and did not mention what you've seen."

Ragoczy paid no attention to Ulrich, but addressed Gudrun. "I have a cloak you may wear if you wish. It is in the other room." He stepped forward, his hand extended to her.

"Leave us alone," Ulrich ordered. He was more than a head taller than the interloper and had the advantages of size and youth. "I don't want to have to hurt you."

"Do you think you could?" Ragoczy inquired with faintly contemptuous amusement. "Come, Gnädige Frau. It is time we were going."

Ulrich's face grew darker, and he turned on Ragoczy. "Let us settle this at once."

"Don't be absurd. You've caused sufficient harm as it is." He gave Gudrun a swift, understanding smile as he spoke to Ulrich.

This time the younger man said nothing. He brought one arm up and swung it rather haphazardly at Ragoczy, anticipating the blow with satisfaction.

It never landed. Without apparent effort, Ragoczy caught Ulrich's wrist as his arm descended. His small, long-fingered hand closed around it, tightening with a strength that awed Ulrich. Inexorably the pressure increased, until there was a faint grinding sound and Ulrich cried out, suddenly weak. "It is broken, Herr Finster," Ragoczy said quietly, "but the break is a clean one. If you have it set promptly and take reasonable care of it, you should have no trouble."

Ulrich staggered back, unbelieving. The pain coursed up his arm, and he cradled it against his chest. His face had gone white and he was afraid that he would be sick if he moved at all. "How . . . ?"

Ragoczy paid him no attention. "Frau Ostneige?"

She hung back a moment, dazed by what she had seen. The cold had strengthened its hold on her, and she could not keep her teeth from chattering. She kept away from Ulrich—though he no longer paid her any attention—and came somewhat hesitantly up to Ragoczy. "Thank you, Herr Graf. . . . It was not what . . . Talk would be . . ."

"It isn't necessary to explain to me, Madame." He drew her hand through the crook of his arm, as the Baron had done earlier that evening. "I have a cloak, and if you will permit me . . ." He opened the side door through which he had come and led her into an elegant little salon. At the far end was a seventy-year-old Schneider grand piano, and across the bench before it lay a black cloak lined in white silk. Ragoczy led Gudrun toward it, and before he picked up the garment, he closed the keyboard lid.

"The piano earlier; was that you?" Gudrun asked as Ragoczy draped his cloak around her shoulders.

"Yes. I've always enjoyed music." He came to face her and close the fastenings of the cloak. "That should keep you warm, and no one will notice that the lace of your dress is torn. Your hair is somewhat disarrayed, but with it cut short, no one will notice, or if they do, they will assume you have been dancing." Although he smiled, his dark eyes were enigmatic.

"Thank you. That's all I can seem to say." She trembled again, this time almost spasmodically. "I had no idea that he would—"

"No, of course not," Ragoczy cut in quickly. "We will talk about it in the automobile." He did not let her speak more, but guided her out of the salon and down the richly-carpeted hall toward the ballroom.

The dance bad was playing a *gallop*, and from the bouncing and stamping that came from the dance floor, most of the party was joining in. Gudrun stared at the figures racing through the uneven light, now in the full glare of electric brightness, now in the shadow of the ballroom balcony. Occasional shrieks and shouts marked the progress of the dancers as the pace increased.

Ragoczy located the Baron and approached him with Gudrun. "Baron Tiborkraj," he said loudly enough to be heard over the din.

"What?" The old man turned bleary-eyed toward them, and then he straightened up as he recognized them. "Oh. Prinz. It's you. What may I do for Your Highness?"

Gudrun stared at Ragoczy, uncertain that she had heard this title correctly. She knew him as Graf, not Prinz. She would have asked about this, but Ragoczy was speaking to the Baron.

"I merely wish to extend my compliments and thank you for the evening," Ragoczy said at his most urbane.

"Does that mean Your Highness is leaving?" Baron Tiborkraj inquired anxiously. "Is the gala not to your taste?"

"The gala is magnificent, and you have sent your house off with more style than any other man I can think of. A great gesture, Baron, and a heroic one. There is nothing in the entertainment that bothers me, but as you know, it is some little distance to my home, and there is likely to be snow again tonight, at least a bit farther up the mountains, and it would not be pleasant to be stranded there." With hardly a break in tone, he motioned Gudrun to approach. "Frau Ostneige has given me the honor of seeing her home, as we live not far from each other."

"Rudi, the cloak . . ." the Baron exclaimed as he saw Gudrun. "Is there anything the matter?"

"I'm . . . cold." Gudrun's voice was very small, and she felt again as if she were fifteen and had been caught playing tag with her groom.

"Frau Ostneige," Ragoczy temporized, "went out onto the terrace for some fresh air, and inadvertently locked herself out. I came upon her by accident."

"You must have cognac or schnapps, Rudi," the Baron insisted, all filled with concern. "You look quite pale."

"Oh, no, Baron," she objected. "I'll manage quite well this way."

"But you . . . Prinz, tell her. You see how she is." The Baron's concern was quite genuine and he made an urgent gesture to one of the waiters. "Cognac, at once."

"It will help keep you warm," Ragoczy whispered to her, "and it will make Tiborkraj less worried on your behalf."

Numbly Gudrun nodded, and muttered a word or two of thanks to the Baron. "I am also thinking of Jürgen," she said after a moment. "I have not been out by myself since we were married, or not to such an occasion. If Maxl were here . . ." It would have been no different, she thought with a sudden inward anger, except that perhaps Ragoczy would not have been there at all.

"Yes, it was remiss of him," Baron Tiborkraj said with a

tightening of his lips. "I think it might be wise if I were to talk
with him."

"No," Gudrun said at once. "Baron, I beg you, don't task
him about this. He would only . . . He is very much a part of
a group, and he hates to miss their meetings. If it were not so
important to him, you may be sure he would have been here."

The waiter arrived with a snifter on a tray. The Baron took
it and slipped a coin to the waiter before holding out the
cognac to Gudrun. "Here, Rudi. You take this and drink it all
before going out."

She accepted the snifter obediently, and looked over the rim
at the Baron. "I am grateful to you for your kindness."

"Not at all, my dear. It would take a callous heart to be
unkind to a woman like you." He gave Ragoczy a speculative
look. "Do you know the Finster brothers? I put Frau Ostneige
at their table. I understand they're friends of Maximillian's."

"It seems likely," Ragoczy said dryly.

"They're not always as . . . polite as I could wish," the
Baron mused, hoping for further comment from either Ragoczy
or Gudrun, and when none was offered, he said, "The music is
about to end, and then there will be a supper. You will have to
excuse me, as I have a few matters to attend to." He bowed
over Gudrun's hand, then clicked his heels and bowed formally
to Ragoczy. "Prinz, you paid me a great compliment by accepting my invitation for this evening."

"It is the least one fallen House can do for another," Ragoczy
said with a practiced inclination of his head.

"I am in your debt, Highness, and will not forget this," he
said in Hungarian, and with a salute, departed.

Gudrun drank the cognac quickly, not wishing to remain any
longer than necessary, and felt rather merrily light-headed
when she was finished. "I'm ready," she told Ragoczy, and
was glad to have his arm to steady herself.

The front terrace, unlike the one at the rear of the hotel,
was crowded, many of the guests having spilled out into the
cold night for the brisk refreshment the wind offered. There
was laughter and amusement everywhere, but for Gudrun the
whole gathering had a nightmare quality and she felt she was
watching a *danse macabre*. It was her nerves, she thought,
and the events of the last hour that had turned this festive
evening into a repulsive experience. Wrapped in Ragoczy's
cloak, she felt invisible, and was pleased to be so.

"My automobile," Ragoczy said to the doorman waiting at

the foot of the terrace steps, wrapped in a long coat of heavily-frogged blue wool. "My chauffeur is Nikolai. He is with the other drivers, I believe."

"Yes, sir, at once," the doorman said, and turned to the communication tube. "Tell Nikolai that . . ."

"Herr Ragoczy," he said.

"Herr Ragoczy is ready to leave. He and his guest are waiting for him."

Hearing this, Gudrun remembered Otto. "My automobile. Otto was supposed to come back for me at one!"

Ragoczy turned to her. "Do you know where he is?"

"At his niece's house, in Wolfratshausen. He will be very worried if I am not here when he returns." She knew she should offer to remain until her retainer came, but she could not bring herself to do so.

"If you have the address of the niece, we will send a messenger." He touched the sleeve of the doorman. "We will need a message delivered in Wolfratshausen this evening. I assume that you will arrange this?"

The doorman gave a weary answer. "Yes. We have those who will do it. How soon must it be delivered?"

"Within the next two hours, if you please." He pulled another few coins from his pocket and handed them to the doorman. "This should cover the expense of the errand."

The doorman did his best not to stare at the gold coins. "Yes, Mein Herr, this will do nicely."

"And Frau Ostneige will provide the address and note," he added, turning to Gudrun. "Do you have a pen in that beaded bag of yours?"

She shook her head. "No, I don't."

"I have paper, if the Gnädige Frau wishes it," the doorman said, and offered her a small lined notebook and a leaky pen.

"My gloves . . ." she moaned as she saw the ink stain the fingers, but her shrug was resigned. More than her gloves had been ruined this evening. She scribbled the note quickly, and wrote the address with care as she handed the notebook and pen back to the doorman.

"Danke," the doorman said. "It will be delivered within the hour."

As he spoke, a Benz touring car drove up to them and waited. "Herr Ragoczy," called out the Russian voice.

"Yes, Nikolai. Thank you." He escorted Gudrun into the passenger compartment of the automobile, and pulled the door closed. Then he leaned forward and opened the glass separating the passengers from the driver. "Nikolai, Frau Ostneige lives at Wolkighügel. We will go there before returning to Schloss Saint-Germain.

"Very good, sir," Rozoh said, and set the Benz in motion.

As Ragoczy settled back in the seat, Gudrun stared at him. "You will freeze," she said with chagrin even as she pulled his cloak more tightly around her.

"Oh, I doubt it. And there is a fur rug in the chest under this seat. If you would like to have it." He did not add that there was also a layer of his native earth there, as well as under the driver's seat.

"Fur? Oh, yes." She said it impulsively, like a child, and when Ragoczy rose enough to remove the fur rug from the compartment beneath the seat, she laughed and almost clapped her hands.

"There," Ragoczy said as he wrapped the rug around her and slipped his cloak around his shoulders. "You'll be warm enough, I think."

"Yes, oh, it's lovely." She snuggled down into the warmth. "What will I tell them about the dress? I'm coming home early. Walther isn't expecting me. There will be questions."

"That's handled simply," Ragoczy said with a dismissing gesture. "You tripped on the ice and the fall tore your gown. Which is why you came home early. The Baron already knows that you were out on the terrace, and so far as anyone but Finster, you, and I know, you were alone. I will say nothing, and Finster is likely to be quiet, as well. Make light of it and no one will think anything about it."

"That will do, I guess," she said, the warmth and the aftermath of fear making her suddenly very tired. She felt her eyes begin to close. "Pardon me, Graf."

"Please, rest if you wish, Frau Ostneige." He was looking out the window at the lights along the lake. Fifty years ago there would have been darkness at this hour, and the earlier illumination would have been the faint amber glow of candles and lanterns. But now the lights were brighter, sharper, like diamonds flung on the darkness.

The Benz turned toward Beuerburg and Königsdorf, and Starnbergersee was lost in the night behind them.

"Baron Tiborkraj called you Prinz," Gudrun said suddenly.

"It was my title once, and the Baron keeps to the old ways." He hesitated a moment. "It is true that I am the son of a king, but the kingdom is gone now." This was accurate enough, as far as it went. He did not mention that the kingdom had ceased to exist roughly four thousand years before.

"How sad," she murmured, no longer resisting the drowsiness. After a moment, her head fell against his shoulder as she slept in the swaying automobile.

Ragoczy did not move her: he continued to stare out the window, an equivocal smile on his lips.

Text of a letter from Colonel Phillippe Timbres to the adjutant in charge of restoration supervision.

*Chalons-sur-Marne*
*April 9, 1921*

*Restoration Office*
*Reims District, Marne*

*Dear Adjutant Couteau:*

*In response to your orders, I and my staff have completed the survey of all major damage done to buildings from Epernay and Givry on the north to Auxerre and Belfort on the south. Each building is cataloged, and the owner or owners, when known, are indicated and their present address included. In many instances there are no current locations for owners, and a diligent search will be required if these good citizens are to reclaim their property. There are several landowners who have already requested that they be allowed to sell off their holdings. With the ruin of fields and homes, the owners are without sufficient funds to restore their holdings, and it is my recommendation that priority be given to these distressed people, for they are the ones who are in the greatest need. Many of them have been bankrupted, and the sale of existing lands, no matter their condition, would mean the difference between a genteel life and the burdens of poverty. As soon as it is possible, this matter must be decided, and the parties notified.*

*A few farmlands will be useless for some time to come, and there are those who refuse to return to fields so lavishly sown with corpses. To these citizens I would suggest that immediate reparation of some sort be made. The trenches may be filled, but what they contain will never be forgotten.*

*I will present myself in your offices on April 20, as*

*requested, and at that time will answer the questions you
and your staff might have. As exhibits of what we have
found, I will provide photographs, so that a full and
accurate assessment of damage may be determined. Should
you require more than that, you have only to tell me and
I will set my staff on it at once.*
*I have the honor to be*

> *Most sincerely,*
> *Phillippe Timbres, Colonel*

# 7

Across the Seine, the Louvre stood magnificent in the moon-
light, the streetlamps around it like a necklace. Franchot
Ragoczy looked at it, his dark eyes remote, lost in the past.
Behind him, at Number 9, Quai Malaquais, the neglected facade of Hôtel Transylvania frowned over the street. It had
been well over a hundred years since he had walked here, and
Ragoczy felt the now familiar sadness that overcame him at
such moments. The Faubourg Saint-Germain-des-Prés was not
as he remembered it. New wide boulevards, straightened to
allow for cannon fire, cut through the ancient, twisted streets.
There were buildings he had not seen, and those he knew of
old were not as he saw them in his memory.

He was almost sorry that he had come this way, and seen
this building as it was now. In the days when it had been his,
it had glittered with richness and care. Even after it had been
gutted by fire, he had seen it repaired and made more
magnificent than ever. He had not wanted to part with it, but
with the shadow of revolution over him, he had taken what
had seemed the wisest course, and sold the splendid place.
Looking at the uncurtained windows and damaged steps, he
wished that he had not. He might, he told himself, have transferred it to one of his many aliases and kept it. That would
have done little good, he realized, and only staved off the
inevitable for a few years, until the Corsican Corporal had
taken hold of France. He approached it, recalling the years he
had owned it. Was his private chamber still intact, that golden
room with the silken draperies of Chinese brocade? Vividly

he recalled that night in October 1743 when he had first embraced Madelaine de Montalia. Madelaine. The thought of her possessed him, as it always did, and for an instant he closed his eyes, hearing her say, "With all those centuries, you still have concern for me?" as she looked at him with wonder. Madelaine, who had known him from the first for what he was, who had loved him without reservation. How much he had longed for her in the years since she had changed, and come into his life. It had been at Hôtel Transylvania that her father had been killed and she nearly made a sacrifice to Saint Sebastien, whose calcined bones lay somewhere in the cellars of the building. It was useless to think of her, to miss her, for the change had separated them in a way nothing else could. Those of his blood must seek the living, not one another. He had done so, and so had she, and neither had dared to be overmuch in each other's company.

His love, where he bestowed it, was genuine, for his nature was not capable of that deception. Yet among those who had known his passion, Madelaine was most cherished. All were unique and treasured, but Madelaine had come to him for himself alone, and he never, before or since, found such acceptance in any other person.

Ragoczy deliberately turned away from Hôtel Transylvania, and took a paper from his coat pocket. He had a scrawled address on the cheap, lined sheet, one that had been given to him by a servant in the house of Pavel Ilyevich Yamohgo, where he had called earlier. He read it again, renewing his shock that Duchess Irina Andreivna Ohchenov should be reduced to living in the squalor he remembered the Rue des les Minces Chèvres to be. For some little time he stood, wondering if it would be wise to visit Irina with Madelaine so much on his mind. That question had perturbed him on other occasions, but at no time as much as it did now. He glanced back over his shoulder at Hôtel Transylvania, thinking that perhaps he should not have come this way. But it was done now, and could not be altered. He knew himself well enough to realize that he wanted to see the building, had, in fact, been avoiding this moment during his other recent journeys to Paris. He gave one short, resigned chuckle. His homeland had disappeared millennia ago and was almost lost to the memory of man. The temple where he had served so long lay under the sands. His villa outside Rome was a ruin. His palace in Seville was rubble. His house in Shiraz had been destroyed. His compound in Lo-Yang had been burned to the ground. His palazzo in Florence had been taken down to provide stones for the expanded city walls. Now Hôtel Transylvania was touched by decay. One day his Schloss would crumble, his manors in Russia would mingle with the earth. He ought to be used to the continuing loss, but he was not. He wrenched his gaze away from the Hôtel and forced himself to walk away from it, into the maze of streets that had not been part of the transformation wrought by Napoleon Bonaparte.

Half an hour later he finally came upon the Rue des les Minces Chèvres, and he looked in appalled sorrow at the narrow lane, the cobbles in poor repair, the buildings sagging and fetid with the weight of centuries of poverty. He had seen such streets before, in many cities, had occasionally lived in the stench and despair they spawned, but as always, his soul was sickened by the hopelessness and degradation that were manifested in slums.

There were few people about, it being past midnight. One man in a greasy jersey and tight trousers gave Ragoczy a calculating look as he went past, and from one of the windows above a woman in a torn blouse leaned out and whistled unmelodically.

At number 14, Ragoczy stopped. A small light above the door staved off a little of the darkness and showed a door that had been painted red many years ago. Ragoczy knocked twice and then tried the latch. He stepped into a room the size of a closet which might, in charity, be called a lobby. There was a warped desk for the concierge to one side of the narrow staircase, and a set of letterboxes on the opposite wall. The place smelled of stale vegetables and bacon grease.

"Concierge?" Ragoczy called out, not too loudly, and waited a moment before repeating this.

There was a grumble from the door behind the desk, and eventually a woman of indeterminate shape and age peeked out. "Who are you? What are you doing here?"

"I am come to see Irina Ohchenov. I understand that she lives here. Will you be good enough to tell me which is her room?" Ragoczy adopted the aristocratic manner in the hope that the woman would cooperate with him.

"She's not the sort who sees the likes of you," the concierge answered with a nasty smirk. "Holds herself very high up, does she, and never passes the time of day with any of us."

"That's not surprising," Ragoczy said quietly. "Is it worth twenty francs to you to tell me which is her room?" He reached into his pocket for the money as he spoke.

"Twenty francs? Why should you pay me that if you don't want to work some mischief with her? I want no trouble here, mauvais oiseau. So far the police have left me alone. You aren't going to change that." She folded her arms and glowered up at him with hostility.

"What *would* it cost to make you willing to allow me to visit Madame Ohchenov?" he asked wearily. "Thirty francs? Forty? Or shall I simply shout her name until she hears me?"

"Fifty francs," the concierge said at once. "Fifty. And for that, I expect no noise, and no notoriety, whatever it is you want with her. If you plan murder, I will describe you to the police. They take a dim view of people killing Russians."

"If I were going to do Madame Ohchenov harm, I would scarcely announce myself and offer you a bribe—if I bothered with you at all, it would be to silence you. Now, which door is Madame Ohchenov's?" He saw the woman's eyes widen for an instant, and then she spat once, near his feet.

"The money first. Give me the fifty francs." She leaned across the worn desk, her eyes eager.

Ragoczy counted out the fifty francs with care and handed them to the concierge. "Count them for yourself, as well, ma petite. I would not want to cheat you." His expression was ironic and disappointed at once.

"I warn you, Monsieur, I will not forget you." She tucked the fifty francs away in a pocket of her shapeless dress. "Assez! Her door is the third on the left at the head of the stairs. She has a bedroom and a parlor, so you will have to knock loudly. If my other tenants are disturbed and complain, you will have to leave." With a satisfied nod, she went back through the narrow door and closed it with great finality.

"Quel plaisir," Ragoczy remarked to the darkness, and went up the stairs. He heard an argument in the first room he passed, conducted in Neapolitan Italian in low but vehement voices. There was a scuffle, the sound of a piece of furniture overturning, and then silence. The next door was quiet, as was the third door. He hesitated, then lifted his hand and rapped softly. "Irina Andreivna," he called out softly, continuing in Russian, "please, open the door. Duchess. This is Count Ragoczy. Wake up, my dear." He listened, and there was no response, so he knocked again, more forcefully. "Duchess, wake up."

He heard the sound of movement behind the door and a sleepy few words. Steps approached, and from the room beyond, he heard Irina say, "You're speaking Russian."

"Da, mayah sestra," he answered. "Let me in."

The bolt was drawn back, and the door opened so that a yellow sliver of candlelight cut into the dark hallway. Irina's wan face looked out at him. "It is you."

"Yes, it is I," he agreed. "May I come in?"

She put a hand to her brow to push away the strands of hair disordered by sleep. "Of course. Please." She pulled the door wide and let him enter. "What time is it?"

"Quite late. Forgive me for coming at this hour." He closed the door behind him and looked quickly around the parlor. The light, he saw, came from a vigil candle placed before an icon of Saint Veronika. Nothing else in the room, save Irina herself, was Russian. There were two shabby chairs with poorly-mended cane seats, a settee that might have been new fifty years before, a plank-topped table with two flowerpots on it, and an old chest with simple iron fittings.

Irina watched his eyes, and sighed. "It isn't much, Count, but I have very little left, and must guard what there is carefully." She wore a cotton kimono robe over her nightgown and her feet were bare. As she drew up one of the chairs, she indicated the other. "Do sit down, Count."

Ragoczy stood quite still, his elegant suit of fine black wool, white silk shirt, and black silk tie contrasting uncomfortably with his surroundings. He approached Irina's chair and looked down at her, concern in his penetrating dark eyes. "How has this happened, Irina? Tell me."

"This? Why, it is the best I can do for myself, Count." She rubbed her eyes. "When morning comes, this will be a dream."

"I am no dream, Irina Andreivna; not now." He laid one hand on her shoulder. "You have an uncle in Paris, a wealthy man who lives quite well and is without heirs. How is it that I find you here?"

"He does not want me, or any of us, if there are any left," she said simply. A year ago she would have railed at Pavel Yamohgo, but she no longer believed that this mattered. Her Uncle had denied her, and that was the end of it. She looked toward the torn curtains that hung in the window. "My cousin and his family . . . there was the influenza. Olga and Tania died, and Sasha had never properly recovered. Kiril took the boy with him."

"Where?"

"Canada, I think. He said that was where he wished to go. I gave him a pearl bracelet to sell for their passage." Yes, she thought, this is most certainly a dream. She had had just such another only the week before, when she had dreamed—oh, so vividly, so convincingly!—that she had been walking along the Seine with Leonid and the children, all of them alive and well and happy, comfortable and pampered, as they had been. At one point in her dream the Seine looked more like the Neva to her, and Notre Dame had become the Fortress and Cathedral of Saints Peter and Paul. It had been real to her, as real as the Count was now, but when the morning had come, all was as it had been the day before, and her heart was desolate.

"Irina!" Ragoczy said again, more sharply.

"It is good of you to come," she said vaguely, still staring abstractedly at the curtains, her thoughts drifting.

"Irina, listen to me," he insisted kindly, taking her face in his hands and turning her toward him. She was worn, tired, he saw. There was white in her hair now, and the creases around her eyes had deepened, delineated by grief. "Irina, my dear. I want to help you. Let me help you."

She laughed a little sadly. "How? In the morning you will be gone."

Ragoczy was taken aback as he realized that she did not believe this was happening to her. "In the morning I will be here, and for two or three days more."

"Ah." How clever it was of her dream to tell her this. She hoped she would not waken for some time yet. It was pleasant to think that Count Ragoczy had cared enough about her to seek her out and offer his assistance, and she wanted to keep the illusion as long as she could.

He read her doubt in her eyes. "This is no illusion, Irina. Touch my arm. It is as solid as your own. Feel my hands on your face. You have not dreamed me, or conjured me up from your memories."

"I thought the same before," she sighed, but reached up obediently and put her hands on his arms, as he had told her to do. "There now. I have touched you. For the present I am persuaded. You are real."

"And I will be so tomorrow, I promise you." His hands dropped to his sides. "Why have you borne this, Irina? If not your uncle, then surely you must know others who could assist you, keep you from this."

"Most of the Russians I have met here are living for vengeance or with dreams of their glory. I want no vengeance. There has been too much suffering already. If my former life were given back to me, I would not be the same, and the innocence or ignorance I had then could not be restored to me.

There are those who assume that if Russia could change by magic back to the old ways, they would return to their lives as if nothing had happened, but that isn't possible, is it?" She pressed little pleats into her robe, and then smoothed them out. "Is it?"

"No, it isn't possible," he said, looking away from her and filled suddenly with memories of loss—of land, of position, of friends, of treasures, of love.

"Count," she said, looking down into her lap, "you do not know how often I have wanted to die, so that this would end at last. I have lacked the determination to leap into the river, or drink poison, or step in front of a speeding taxi. I lack courage, I suppose." Her tone was very matter-of-fact, and for that reason, if no other, Ragoczy believed her completely.

"You must not do that," he told her, his dark eyes on hers once again. "Your life is brief enough without that." He bent and kissed her forehead. "Let me help you, ma Duchesse. About your mourning I can do nothing, but I can alleviate your material situation." He knew, and the knowledge was quietly anguished, how very trivial his gesture was. Those things which Irina most deeply desired—her family—were beyond any power of his. All he could provide was a more pleasant setting for her grief, yet that much he was determined to do.

"But how?" She had stopped resisting his presence, telling herself that she would accept him, and if he turned out to be a dream, she would deal with that when morning came, as she had done with other dreams.

"I have money," he said somewhat grimly, feeling the inadequacy of it, "and there are better places to live."

"But I cannot afford them," she said at once. "And I dare not come to rely on you, Count, for who knows when it will all come to an end again, and I will be left with . . . nothing. Oh," she went on with a hint of a smile, "you mean what you tell me, I'm certain. You're not like so many of the others. But Leonid did not intend that our family should perish, and yet it happened. It may be that there will be another war, or the influenza will return, or another disaster will come upon us, and you would be unable to continue as you had begun, for excellent reason. And I, having grown used to depending on your kindness, would be worse off than before."

Ragoczy touched her shoulder. "You are a remarkable woman, Irina. Tell me, then, what you will accept from me."

She caught his hand in hers. "If you truly wish to help me,

then tell me how I may make my own way in the world. There must be work that I can do that will provide enough money to let me live comfortably. I find I need very little. Two or three rooms to myself and decent food would do. I feel useless now. If you know of someone who would employ me. Not yourself, of course. It would be too great a reminder to have you always near at hand."

"As you wish," he said, thinking that she was very sensible, though the truth stung him. "In what capacity would you want to work?"

She knew that his curiosity was genuine, and that pleased her. "Well, I do know something of housekeeping, but only in a supervisory capacity. I do fine needlework, but in Paris this is not rare. I am competent with children, but I don't know if I could stand to work with them yet." As she spoke of these discouraging prospects, the sense of unreality finally left her. She was actually awake, she realized, talking to Count Ragoczy, who somehow had sought her out and was offering her his help. Her mouth trembled and she began to weep. "Dearest Christ, you found me!" Impulsively she kissed his hand, holding it against her cheek as she felt a tenuous, painful joy.

"I have said so all along," he reminded her wryly, then added, "Ah, ma Duchesse, ma Duchesse."

She wiped her eyes with the hem of her sleeve. "The last time I saw you, I was crying, too." She tried to make light of this, but the very statement brought another surge of tears.

Silently Ragoczy offered her his white silk handkerchief, waiting while she exhausted her overwhelming emotions.

When she had again mastered herself, Irina handed back the silken square. "You looked for me. You took the time to do that."

"Why, yes. You told me you would be at your uncle's, and when I discovered this was not so, and that no provision had been made for you, I wanted to see that you were well. One of your uncle's servants told me of this place." He looked around the room, his expression carefully neutral.

"Don't say anything," she requested, "please. I wouldn't be able to stand it. I know what this building is like, what the street is like. I must scrub every day to keep the vermin out of my bed. My food is never quite fresh and what I have is nibbled by rats if I leave it unfinished. There are murders here which the police ignore, and things are bought and sold that horrify me."

Ragoczy nodded. In his previous stay in Paris, more than a

hundred years ago, he had seen such districts. The Inn of the Red Wolf had been in just such a blighted lane, and the alchemists who gathered there had seen as much as Irina. "It would be better if you did not continue to live here," he said to her, his face strangely gentle.

"But where can I go? I have told you how it is with me—I have a little money, which I must husband. No one will give me more, I think. If I had work, real work, I would walk out of this place at once."

"You will have work," Ragoczy promised her. "And I will see you out of here."

Though she doubted this, she thanked him and touched his hand again. This time she felt it not as a dream, but as his substance: the hand was smaller than her own, beautifully shaped, with a firm palm and long fingers. It was well-cared-for, as was everything about Ragoczy. "You searched for me. I can't believe that."

"Believe it." He lifted her hand to his lips and kissed it once.

"Yes, you are here," she went on, faintly bemused. "Why did you bother? Why do this for me?"

"You helped me, Irina, when I was desperate. I owed you this much, surely." He turned as a sudden crash sounded in the hallway. "What!"

"It is the Algerian, I think. He has fights with the woman he lives with." She was accustomed to these outbursts, and paid no heed to the sudden argument that flared in the hallway. "They have a daughter who is ten and the woman wants to sell her. So far he has not consented, but the price keeps going up, and they are very poor."

A loud exchange of gutter French came through the door; then there was a shout and a door slammed.

"They will be quiet now," Irina said after a moment. "Once the door closes they are through for another day."

Ragoczy said nothing, not wanting to offend Irina. He had heard and seen far worse in his wanderings, but he still had the capacity to be distressed for those trapped in poverty.

"The woman says that the girl will be treated well by the brothel owner, and it would be better to have her protected under the madame's roof than prey to the rabble of the streets." She let out a long sigh. "The child is a pert waif, and already there are those who watch her. I was thinking that at least I never had to make such a decision for Ludmilla. If my children had lived, and were with me, it would be their lot, as well as that girl's. Evgeny would have worked, but the others were so young . . ." She ran her tongue over her lips, nervous at her thoughts.

Abruptly Ragoczy said, "The employment isn't important. Tomorrow I will find you more suitable quarters. There is little I can do, but at least this . . ."

"It's not necessary," she assured him. "They leave me alone."

Ragoczy looked down at her, his expression quite remote. "Ma Duchesse, there is not a great deal I can do for you, or for any of the poor wretches out there, but I must do something. You do not believe, do you? that I could leave you here, after seeing this place." He almost added *and seeing you*, but he stopped the words in time.

"Finding me work is more than enough. No one has been willing to do that for me." She got up out of the chair and went over to the icon. "I have learned, in the last two years, to be inconspicuous. That way, I believe I can get on without being too much hurt. If you want to aid me, I am grateful, but it must be done with prudence, so that there will be no cause to notice me." She looked blindly at the old saint's face, shivering from something other than cold.

"As you wish," Ragoczy said after a moment. He should have looked for her sooner, he told himself. He should not have assumed that she was in the care of her uncle. "I will take you tonight to my apartment. Oh," he added quickly, seeing her stiffen, "you need not fear that. I have a small staff and they will understand that you are my guest and nothing more."

She touched the neckline of her robe in some confusion. "Your guest . . . But I thought . . . was there . . . do you want . . . How do I thank you?" She turned suddenly crimson, seeing the hurt in his dark eyes at the sharpness of her insult.

"Do you think I insist on payment for this minor assistance? Spasibah, Irina Andreivna, vi ochen lioubyesni. A fine compliment. How opportunistic I must seem to you, if you think I was prepared to use your difficulties for . . . You have believed that I could trade on your misery. Am I so vile to you?" His indignation was colored with old despair, and the intensity of his outburst disturbed him. "What do you take me for?"

"You misunderstood . . ." she began in a small voice, shrinking back from him. "No," she capitulated after a moment of hesitation. "You didn't misunderstand. That was what I meant, but the reason . . . I have seen too much on those streets, and with my cousin. I have grown unused to honor." Here she faltered, her words becoming still more quiet. "I have been lonely, and frightened, and I thought that if you were willing to help me, it was because you also wanted me."

Ragoczy's anger was gone. "My dear—" he began compassionately.

She did not let him continue. "I wanted . . . you were so kind before, at the dacha. And it has been so long. I've thought that if one of the men who spoke to me in the street had the least trace of . . . humanity, I would have gone with him if only for the comfort of it."

"Irina, I don't know what to say to you." He had come up behind her and with one hand smoothed back her hair. "I don't wish to trade favors with you. That was not my intention at all. My bed is not a marketplace."

"I know," she said, leaning near the icon so that the little flame from the vigil candle threw her face into shadow. She had done it badly, and now she would be left here.

"My dear," Ragoczy said, standing very close to her, not touching her. "Listen to me, Irina."

"I'm listening," she murmured. There would be the polite phrases, the promises that meant nothing.

"Find your valise and whatever you wish to take with you. We'll leave now, if that is satisfactory to you." He waited until she turned to look at him. "What have you that you wish to take with you?"

"Nothing," she said. "A little money, three dresses. That's all I have, Count."

"Then pack those. Put on the dress you prefer. I will wait for you." Again he kissed her hand, his features hidden by shadow.

"And the icon," she said after a moment. "It was in my bedroom when I was a child. I used to think . . ."—she tried to laugh and failed—"that she was a relative of some sort, one I had never met . . ." The words trailed off. "I will pack."

As she went into the cramped room where her bed was, she had to resist the urge to look back at her visitor, to convince herself that he had offered her this escape from what had become the most intolerable prison. She threw open the door of the little wardrobe and stared in dismay at the rumpled, patched dresses that hung there. She pulled the least threadbare one from its hook and began to draw off her robe. In ten minutes she had tugged herself into the dress and gathered the others in a heap. There was a carpetbag on the floor of the wardrobe, and she pulled this out and stuffed the garments into it without pausing to fold them. They were disgraceful, she knew, and hoped for an instant that the Count's generosity would extend to allowing her to purchase something appropriate to wear to work. No employer would hire her if she presented herself in any of the three dresses. Her shoes were cracked and the soles nearly worn through, but she pulled them on and buttoned them, then opened the commode by her bed and from under the chamber pot took a small stack of bills, which she tucked into her skirt pocket.

"Your icon," Ragoczy said, handing her the sacred portrait as she came out of the room. "You will want to take this with you."

She pressed the icon to her breast as she came toward him. "Thank you, Count. Even if it should happen that you can do nothing more, thank you for this much."

Ragoczy had looked over her dress and shabby bag and resolved to be sure that she did not have to live this way again. If he could not find someone to employ her directly, he would authorize one of the companies he owned under various aliases to hire her. He pulled open the hall door and stepped out. "Come with me, ma Duchesse."

She followed him down the stairs and out of the building. The street was quite empty and the one lamp at the far end flickered and sputtered. The electric streetlights that made Paris glitter had not penetrated this portion of the city, and it was as dark as it had been a hundred years ago.

At the corner, Ragoczy directed them toward the nearest boulevard. It was now almost three in the morning, but he thought it would be possible to find a taxi there. In fifteen minutes they were seated in an old Renault and across the Seine.

"I feel I am the girl in the folktale, riding in a magic coach that will turn back into a stone in the morning," Irina said as she watched the lights go by.

"You're more likely to be too busy to be concerned about coaches," he remarked. "I have been thinking about your situation. You're skilled with languages, aren't you?"

"Fairly, but I haven't the credentials for tutoring or teaching. I made inquiries when I first came here." She directed her attention from the street back to the man beside her. "It will have to be something else, Count."

"Do you think so? I have a few friends who need translators, not for their children, but for scholarly work. Have you skill enough for that?" He saw her hesitation, and added, "Ma

Duchesse, an old friend of mine has often lamented that she has not had the opportunity to learn Russian, and her Greek is sketchy. She has often required a translator to work for her, and she is not the only person I know who needs such services performed."

"Yes, I thought of that, but had no one who could introduce me, or tell me whom to contact." She sighed, and some of her newly-found hope dimmed.

"That may be, but I do know those who would use your skills and pay you well for them. Tomorrow morning, I will call Professor Louis-Onfroi Servie and speak to him on your behalf. He is learned in Slavic languages, and he often is asked to recommend a translator. Would you be willing to see him in a few days? He is a brusque man, but appreciates real knowledge. Well?" He knew he was pressing her, but it seemed to him that she could easily sink back into the apathetic despair which had held her so long.

"I suppose it is possible, but he will not wish to deal with me. I am so . . . This dress is shameful, and the rest are worse." She folded her arms defensively.

"Then we will see that you have proper clothes. It is a minor matter. And when you have secured your post, then you will be able to select the place you wish to live. Until then you may stay at my apartment, and my staff will care for you. We're almost there."

The cab had turned down a pleasant tree-lined street flanked by tall, elegant buildings that were quite new. It slowed and pulled up at the third from the corner.

"Thank you," Ragoczy said to the driver as he leaned forward to pay the fare.

The driver touched the brim of his cap as Ragoczy and Irina got out, then started away down the street, a moving point of noise in the stately silence.

Ragoczy's apartment was on the top floor overlooking a court with a garden three stories below. It had nine large rooms, beautifully furnished and well-maintained. Ragoczy pointed out the various doors to her, finally opening one. "This is for my guests. There is a bathroom adjoining, if you wish a hot bath. My study is across the hall if you need anything." He placed her carpetbag on a low Empire stool and turned on three of the lights, revealing gray-and-gold walls with bronze-green draperies. He studiously avoided the mirror over the dressing table.

"Count, this is magnificent," she whispered. It had been so

long since she had touched fine fabrics or known the pleasure of simple comforts.

"Then enjoy it, ma Duchesse. I will instruct my house-keeper to see to your needs in the morning." He was about to close the door when she detained him.

"What will your housekeeper think, Count, when she discovers me here?" The question had been nagging her, and she was wary of the answer.

"She will be pleased. Madame Jardin has been with me for more than a decade and during most of that time she has seen little of me. She would like to have me in Paris more often, and if you are here . . . I can't control her thoughts, my dear, and would not wish to. But I will explain who you are, which will impress her, I think." He had almost completely closed the door when he heard Irina come toward him. "What is it now?"

"What will I do? I am ashamed to sleep in my nightgown in this bed." She felt heat in her cheeks.

"If you must have a robe, there is one in the bathroom. It will be large, but adequate. Use that until you have something to replace it."

"Thank you," she said softly.

"My study is across the hall." He closed the door to the guest room and opened the door opposite. The wood-paneled room was of pleasing proportions, so that its size was not immediately apparent. Two sofas stood facing each other in front of the little fireplace, and near them a large desk fronted on three tall windows. In the day, it was light, but now it had the privacy of darkness. Ragoczy pulled off his jacket and opened the door to a small closet. He took down a lounging robe of black brocade shot with silver thread, and this he donned, loosening his tie after he knotted the sash of the robe. He sat on one of the sofas and propped his heels on the brass stand by the hearth. He permitted himself to feel a touch of satisfaction. He had failed many times in his life, but at the moment he was beginning to hope that he might salvage a few things of worth from the wreckage of war and revolution. Too many times in the past he had seen the destruction carry all with it, leaving only ruin behind. He sensed that there would not be a great deal of time to prepare for the next onslaught, for the world was moving faster than when he had been young. A year ago he had doubted he could succeed, but recently his confidence had grown. "If it's not a fool's paradise," he said to the walls. Belatedly he turned on the lamp beside the sofa and smiled at the warm glow it provided. How many times he had wished for such a light to be had for no greater effort than the pulling of a string or the turning of a socket! Studies which had been called heresy and had been practiced in fear and danger were now the province of chemistry and physics and were hailed as the foremost progress of mankind.

He was still relishing this ironic amusement when he heard a timid knock at the door. "Irina?" he called out as he went to open it.

She was still damp from the bath, her hair wrapped in a towel, the oversized robe engulfing her. "Oh, it was so lovely," she said as she came into the room. "All that hot water, and the soap soft, smelling of violets."

"I'm pleased that you enjoyed it," he said, motioning her to the other sofa.

"I don't feel so contaminated any longer. My hair hasn't been this clean in years. I lay in hot water for almost fifteen minutes, and I don't think I've ever done that." She dropped onto the sofa and laughed cautiously as Ragoczy took his seat opposite her. "I . . . I loved it, Count, every moment of it."

"Excellent." He indicated the towel around her hair. "If you need a comb, I think there is one on the dressing table."

"I'll find it." She braced her elbows on her knees and leaned forward. "Will you come with me? All the time I was in the bath, I was thinking of you. Before, you gave me so much comfort, and . . ." She stopped abruptly.

"And?" he prompted gently.

"And I realized that . . . It has been a long time, Count. Leonid is gone, and the children are gone, but I am alive, and if I am to live a new life, it must be without those dear ghosts haunting me. You . . . What you gave me before was more than the pleasure we had." She swallowed but did not turn away from the power of his eyes.

He regarded her steadily, not moving. He could not deny his own need, and the disappointment that occasionally accompanied the ephemeral gratification that he obtained from the women at the resorts and inns of Bad Wiessee and Bad Tölz. Irina was known to him, and he recalled his time with her with longing. He rose, holding out his hand to her. "I'll comb your hair for you."

Irina was wise enough not to question this. She took his hand and together they crossed the hall to the gold-and-gray room. She sat in silence while he worked out the tangles in her damp hair and made one long plait down her back. The stray wisps around her face dried in fluffy close curls, and in spite of the white streaks through her hair, she felt more youthful than she had since Leonid died.

When he was finished with her hair, Ragoczy reached down to the tie that held Irina's robe around her. He felt her shiver of response as he touched her bared shoulder, and his own desire intensified. It had been too long since he shared this particular love with a knowing woman. He drew her to her feet and into his arms, her discarded robe falling to her feet. Yet he held her off briefly. "Are you certain this isn't misplaced gratitude?"

"Gratitude is a part of it," she answered, pulling him close to her again. "What is wrong with that? You've cared for me, and I am grateful. It also pleases me that you did so. You've survived the worst that could happen, and you are not entirely crippled by it. You give me hope." She kissed him, her need igniting as their lips met.

"Ah, Irina, ma Duchesse," he said, his face against her cheek.

She did not speak; a series of quiet, joyous whimpers was all the sound she made as he brought her passion to a pitch to match his own. Her body trembled with fulfillment, and the emotions she had so long denied flooded her. She clung to him in his ecstasy, carried by the strength of his fervor to the greater exaltation than she had ever known, that began to fade only with the night. She pursued it in sleep and so did not know when Ragoczy left her bed, and did not hear his gentle words as he touched her smiling lips with his own.

"I, too, am grateful, ma Duchesse."

Text of a letter from Herr August Kehr to Franchot Ragoczy.

*SCHWEIZERBANK*
*14 NACHHALTIG STRASSE*
*ZÜRICH*

*June 17, 1921*

*Graf Franchot Ragoczy*
*Schloss Saint-Germain*
*Schliersee*
*Bayern, Deutschland*

*My dear Graf:*

*This is to confirm your telegram of June 15 which requests that the sum of twenty thousand Swiss francs be transferred out of the Ziegeldich Gesellschaft, with the assurance that this will be attended to at once. However, I feel it my duty to point out that your fears that this company is planning to manufacture arms is not well-founded, for the terms of the Versailles Treaty and the mandates of the League of Nations most specifically forbid such activities, and Deutschland, having not yet recovered from the severity of her defeat in the Great War, could hardly be anticipating another major offensive in the foreseeable future. I do applaud your caution, of course, and will indeed pay more attention to the emerging industries in Deutschland.*

*You will find enclosed an accounting for the total cost of restoration of Schloss Saint-Germain. The major items, as you see, are the steel reinforcements of the fifteenth-century portions of the Schloss, and the installation of generator and electricity. Interior work on moldings and other hand-finished items are also significant factors in cost. The rebuilding of the stables will bring the total to approximately three hundred seventy thousand francs.*

*While having no intention of imposing upon you, I feel that I must mention that this is a very costly enterprise. Your funds, as I am sure you know, are more than sufficient to pay for such extravagance several times over, but as you yourself have observed, the current financial outlook is most disturbing, and a little care now may save you much unpleasantness in the future.*

*I have made the inquiries you have requested, and I am pleased to report that I have found two Velázquez paintings and a folio of sketches by Botticelli. The larger of the two Velázquez works is a portrait of the author Calderón at work on* La Vida es Sueño, *and the smaller depicts peasants at Mass. I have taken the liberty of enclosing the prices requested by the present owners, and will proceed upon receipt of your instructions, should you desire to purchase either of these paintings. The Botticelli has not yet been appraised, but when that has been done, I will inform you of it immediately. Your deposit of gold has been received and assessed; the report is enclosed for your records. If you anticipate another such sizable deposit in the future, may I suggest that it be delivered in person rather than consigned to the care of servants? You have told me that Herr Roger has your complete confidence, but there is hazard in carrying so great an amount, and in this case it is not the matter of temptation, but the possibility of robbery which concerns me.*

*I look forward to our continuing transactions, Mein Herr Graf.*

> *Most sincerely,*
> *August Kehr*

## 8

When the pony cart made the turn toward the stables of Schloss Saint-Germain, Amalie Schnaubel was laughing with her children and Laisha. It was a hot summer day, encouraging lethargy: the air was soft and warm, the roads were dusty under the trees, and the lakes glimmered, their cold depths inviting swimmers to enjoy their placid waters.

"I haven't been swimming in years," Amalie said to Ragoczy as he strolled forward to meet the party in the pony cart. "I'd forgotten how much I like it." Her hair was wet, and for a moment she reminded Ragoczy of his night in Paris with Irina Ohchenov.

"I'm delighted you thought of it, then," he said, smiling now at his ward. "And you, Laisha, did you like it?"

Laisha answered earnestly, with the careful concentration that was characteristic of her. "Yes. I swim well, and that is part of the pleasure."

Olympie and Bruno grinned. "She beat us all," Olympie said proudly. "I could not catch her, or Bruno either."

"That's because you did not mind being caught, and I did," Laisha said with a toss of her fair hair. She was growing rapidly, developing a coltishness as her arms and legs lengthened. She had more energy than grace at the moment, and a stubborn determination to excel at all she did.

"Why should it matter?" Bruno teased her. "It's only an hour spent in a lake. It's not important."

Laisha turned to him with sudden tension. "*Everything* is important. That's where people make their mistakes; they think that only certain things deserve attention, but that's wrong. Isn't it, Papa?"

"What a ferocious, fey child you are," Ragoczy said fondly. "Of course everything is important, but time, Laisha, there is so little time."

Amalie sighed in agreement. "And time has made my departure necessary," she said as Ragoczy handed her out of the pony cart. "Hedda is watching Dietbold, but it is time I was with him again." This announcement was met with protests from her three children with her.

"I will have Nikolai drive them down later, if that would be satisfactory with you, Frau Schnaubel," Ragoczy suggested. "There is no pressing reason for them to leave, is there?"

"Well," Amalie said, considering the offer, "I don't suppose they can get into any more mischief up here than they can at home. If it is no imposition, then of course I accept for them."

"Hardly an imposition," Ragoczy told her as the three children voiced their approval. "Emmerich and Bruno can take turns trying to beat Laisha. I don't know if Olympie finds that idea very attractive, but they're all more than welcome. I have certain projects that need my attention, and this will give me a little more time to myself. There. Once again time is the crucial factor, isn't it?"

"As always," she agreed. "Anything I add would be ungracious."

"Then it's settled. Nikolai will bring Bruno, Olympie, and Emmerich back after supper. Your husband should be home by then." He walked beside her toward her automobile, squinting in the brightness.

"Is there something the matter?" Amalie inquired as she noticed his discomfort.

"I am . . . somewhat sensitive to sunlight. An inconvenience at this time of year." He held the door open to her. "Thank you for allowing your children to stay."

"I'm delighted you want them." She fiddled with the ignition, and when it caught, she waved to her children, who were just getting out of the pony cart. "If they become troublesome, just send them home."

"I'm not anticipating any difficulties," Ragoczy told her, and stepped back to allow her to drive away. He started toward the shade of the entranceway and relief from the relentless brightness, shading his eyes with his raised hand. He was stopped by Laisha, who ran impetuously up to him and threw her arms around his waist. "What's this?" he asked, looking down at her. "Is something wrong, my child?"

"No," she said after a moment. "I was afraid that you wouldn't watch me play."

"I will. But not right now." Even with his native earth in the soles of his shoes, the sun was beginning to distress him. "I have a few things to attend to in my library, and then I'll come out to watch you. Where are you going to play?"

"On the court." She had improvised a kind of volleyball court not far from the stables. The net was made from old kitchen towels sewn together and hung between two pine trees, and the space was irregular, but she had said she preferred it to more formal arrangements.

"All right." He did not add he was pleased that there would be shade under the trees, affording him some protection. "Take Bruno and Olympie and Emmerich into the kitchen for some refreshment, and then let me know you're ready. Will that do, Laisha?"

"That's fine," she said, releasing him. "I want to put on my riding breeches, anyway."

"Very good," Ragoczy approved, going into the open door at last.

"Graf Ragoczy," Bruno called out as he saw him start to

close the door, "is it all right if we pick some of the flowers? I'd like to take some to Mother."

"Of course," Ragoczy answered from the darkness of the doorway. "Leave me a few, Bruno."

The young man—for he was clearly no longer quite a boy— laughed merrily and sprinted off toward the back of the Schloss.

Roger was waiting in the hallway, his lined and tranquil face amused. "She's a fine girl, my master," he said as he closed the door.

"She is," Ragoczy agreed at once. He went toward the library, then paused. "Have you had any word from Petrograd?"

"No. I fear that's a lost cause." He gestured his helplessness. "The way things are there, I doubt it would be possible to investigate further."

"That's what I've been worried about. Well, I suppose that we have to be let go. A pity. There is much I've learned here that could be of use. . . . An inexpensive synthetic fuel would be a great deal of help, and not just there. We can't depend on the Americans forever, no matter how much petroleum they have." He opened the door to his library. "In half an hour I'm expected to watch Laisha best the Schnaubel children at volleyball. Remind me, if I become too engrossed."

"You won't need it, but very well." Roger turned away and went off toward the stairs that led to his master's private quarters.

Amalie Schnaubel turned off just before Hausham, glad to be getting home at last. It had been a wonderful afternoon and for the first time in many weeks she felt both relaxed and optimistic. With any luck, Simeon would return with good news and the apprehension that had sapped her strength and her good humor would be gone. She was glad that Simeon had taught her to drive, for with him working at some distance from home and their house so isolated, she felt less vulnerable with an automobile at her disposal. She pulled into her driveway, bringing the Opel to a halt not far from the door. As always, she checked the brake carefully and left the gear set in reverse. She brought her purse and the traveling case containing her wet bathing costume out of the automobile and went into the house.

Hedda met her at the door, her homely features set in worried lines. As she had so many times before, Amalie sighed for this child, hoping that she would reveal some acceptable talent or intellectual gift that might compensate for her good-hearted but disastrously plain face. She kissed Hedda on the forehead. "How did it go today?"

"Fine," Hedda answered. "There were some men here earlier who wanted to talk to Papa about something, but they went away. They said to tell him that they'd be back."

"You didn't let them in the house, did you?" She tried to keep her tone from being critical, but saw from the way the child pulled back from her that she had not been able to do so. "Hedda, Hedda, don't be so worried," she said, putting her arm around the girl. "I'm not angry with you, little one. There are precautions we learn to take with those we love. I wouldn't want anything to happen to you, or to Dietbold. I didn't mean to be sharp with you."

"They were hard men," Hedda said, as if in explanation of her reaction.

Amalie thought of the many cruel remarks she had heard from those living in the area, and made a moue of distress. "Yes, many of them are. They're very . . . clannish here," she said lamely, wishing she could shield all her family from the rancor of the landowners.

"It's because we're Jews, isn't it?" Hedda asked blandly. "They don't like Jews."

"That's part of it," Amalie admitted. She had come to the nursery and stood over the high bed where Dietbold lay. The boy was sleeping, his hands clenched on either side of his head, his mouth pursed.

"Why don't they like Jews? Why don't they like *us*?" Hedda demanded, her voice raising a little in her hurt and confusion.

"Because of . . . oh, there are many things, but it starts with religion. We've told you about the Christian beliefs, Hedda. Now, hush, or you'll wake your brother." She thought of her own ambivalence when she had realized the hatred in which Jews were held. She had been not quite nine, younger than Hedda, and her parents had reminded her that it was the fate of God's Chosen People to suffer in this world. At the time she had felt inward nobility that had helped her to disregard the slights of children at school and their parents, but more recently, when she saw her own children made victims of intolerance, she found it more difficult to recall that inward purpose that had sustained her through her own youth.

"Why do we have to be Jews, if people don't like them?" Hedda's tone was sharper, and it was apparent now that she had been frightened.

"Because we are, Hedda. And I don't want to hear any

more of this right now." She watched Dietbold stir in his sleep, making little grunts. "I'll have to change his diapers when he wakes up," she said inconsequently.

"I won't be Jewish," Hedda announced, and before she could be rebuked for this, she ran out of the room and up the stairs, seeking that corner of the attic where she often sat with her daydreams for company.

Amalie's throat was suddenly tight with unshed tears. Automatically she reached to pick up her infant son as he started to squawl. It was so much easier with babies, she thought as she opened her blouse for him. There was a rocking chair in the corner, and she sat there while Dietbold nursed, trying to shut out the uncertainties of her life and concentrate only on the satisfaction of that little mouth on her breast. Later she would find Hedda and do her best to explain. For the time being, she wanted to be content with her life, if only for the ten minutes of peace here in the nursery.

She had changed the boy and straightened her clothes when the knock came at the door. Frowning slightly at the interruption, she was about to leave Dietbold on his bed but he cried when she put him down, so she dandled him on her hip as she went to the front door.

There were five men, one of them somewhat familiar to her: Konrad Natter, that was the name. He had been at a party somewhere—was it that dreadful evening at Wolkighügel?—and had shunned her and Simeon. She stood quite straight. "Yes, gentlemen? Is there something I can do for you?"

The best-dressed of the men gave her an angry smile. "Yes, Jewess, there is."

Amalie went faintly pale at the fury in his eyes. "If this is all you want, then I must ask you to leave."

"It is we who ask you to leave, Jewess," Natter said, bracing one hand against the doorframe. "We had assumed that your husband made arrangements already."

"My husband is not here. He should return soon." She tried to close the door. "If you will excuse me, I have duties to attend to."

"She's got another one of them," one of the men muttered, nodding toward Dietbold. "They're determined. Give them that."

Amalie was now genuinely frightened, and she pushed at the door again. "Get out of my house!"

One of the men shoved the door open so that Amalie staggered back. Dietbold began to wail.

"Her house! What right have you to this house, you whore!" Natter yelled at her as he followed her into the entryway. "These houses are for Deutschlisch, not the likes of you. You're draining our country, polluting our blood."

With an inward sickness, Amalie realized that all five men were half-drunk and filled with alcoholic bravado. "Leave now, and I will not complain to the police. If you do any harm here, then you will be prosecuted." She wanted to sound reasonable, but the shrill edge of fear robbed her words of conviction.

"You think you're clever, you Jews, but there are those of us who are not deceived." This time the speaker was a tall, middle-aged man with military bearing. "You were the ones who brought us to ruin in the Great War."

"That's a lie," Amalie whispered, fighting the panic that threatened to overwhelm her. "A lie."

"Do you say that an officer would lie?" Natter demanded, reaching out toward her. "You filth! You human offal!"

*"Get out!"* Amalie shrieked as the last of the men forced his way into her home. Dietbold was yelling now, his tiny fists pulling at her blouse, his whole body turning plum color from his infant hysteria.

"Listen to her!" the well-dressed man shouted. "Leave here!"

"No, scum," the middle-aged man declared. "We will not get out. Our duty lies here. You were warned."

"Warned?" Amalie repeated to herself. What had Simeon not told her? She looked about her, seeking safety in a house that suddenly seemed inhospitable to her.

"We have our task to perform!" Natter cried out.

This was supported by boisterous approval. "Deutschland will be protected!" the middle-aged man said in ringing tones.

With a stifled scream, Amalie broke away from the man and ran down the hall toward the kitchen. There was a back door, if she could reach it, and perhaps she could get away. If not, the stout wooden door would discourage them, and then they would only vandalize the house. . . . Then she thought of Hedda, and cold dread seized her. What might these drunken, brawling, hate-riddled men do to her child? She sobbed and clutched Dietbold more tightly to her side, wasting precious seconds as she fought the confusion. If she screamed out, she would alert the men that Hedda was in the house, but if she did not, the girl might come down the stairs to investigate . . . Oh God, God, God, she thought as the sound of feet behind her spurred her to action again and she raced toward the kitchen.

She dragged the door open and rushed through it, trying to swing it closed in the face of her pursuers.

Konrad Natter reached the door before it was shut and with a bellow jerked it out of her hand and thrust it sharply back against her.

The thick wood caught her with terrible force across the chest and forehead, stunning her and jolting her nearly off her feet. She swayed, her hands out to keep from falling, and Dietbold dropped from her protective hold onto the brick floor, where he twitched once before blood began to seep out of his nose.

Nausea churned in Amalie and she tried to focus her eyes. Holy God, what had happened to her life? Five minutes—was it only five minutes?—and all was in chaos. "Dietbold?" Her breath was ragged and her vision shot with streaks of color. Looking down, she could not think how her baby came to be on the kitchen floor with a halo of blood around him. Uncomprehendingly she reached out for her son, and was restrained by a brutal grip on her arms.

"Did you see what she tried to do to Konrad?" the middle-aged man inquired of the others. He was out of breath but not entirely from running.

"Friedrich, you hold her," Natter said, thrusting Amalie at the middle-aged man. "Careful. She'll bite you if she can."

Amalie was crying breathlessly, her thoughts in disorder. She tried to speak. "My baby," she panted. "He's . . . He needs me. Let me go . . . Let me go!"

Friedrich held her from behind, taking savage delight in holding her in a painfully twisted way. "What about the infant?"

Helmut Rauch pushed through the press of men, taking care that his fine suit not touch anything in the kitchen. He bent over the pitiful limp figure and poked at it three times with his finger, noticing with distaste the blood welling from mouth and ears as he pressed. He drew back, wiping his hand fastidiously on his pocket handkerchief, as if he feared contamination. "He's dead, all right."

"They kill their own children, the monsters," one of the men shouted to the others. He was by far the most drunken, his face and neck florid from beer-and-schnapps.

"Dietbold!" Amalie howled as she saw Friedrich lift her child by his leg and hold him as if he were some obscene trophy. Sounds rumbled in her mind, shutting out the cheers of the men in the kitchen. She gathered all her strength and wrenched herself out of the grasp of the two men who restrained her now. Vaguely she was aware of sudden, debilitating pain, and the uselessness of her right arm, but it was not important. As if moving underwater, she reached for Friedrich to save her baby. The hand that she could move had already curved into claws which jabbed for his eyes before grasping her child. There were sounds in her throat that caused Helmut Rauch to gag.

The others shouted in the confusion, two careening into each other as they strove to hold back the raving woman.

"The shoulder!" Natter shouted as he caught her arm and was rewarded with an agonized screech.

"Dislocated," one of the men said, awed in spite of himself. "Stop her!"

It took three of them to bring her down, and by then she had gouged three deep runnels in Friedrich's face. Her mouth was open and her hair was matted on the side of her face with Dietbold's blood. She felt herself tumbling through an enormous gulf, growing smaller and smaller. The pain from her dislocated shoulder went through her in volcanic waves.

"Hold her, can't you," Helmut demanded, stepping back from the pile of men.

"She's insane! A devil!" the youngest man shouted as he tried to pin her thrashing legs to the floor.

Amalie flailed in the men's holds, past thought. There was a sharp, searing pain, as light exploded in her head, and then darkness.

"That stopped her," Natter said, rubbing his hands on the front of his jacket.

Helmut frowned. "Kicking her in the head . . ."

"It stopped her," Natter repeated, his voice rising. "You saw what she did to Friedrich."

The men on the floor got up slowly. The youngest of them cleared his throat as he looked back at Amalie. For a moment the kitchen was very quiet.

"Where's the baby?" the most drunken man asked.

"I have it," Friedrich said, staring down at the dead infant. There were a few halfhearted cheers.

"We'd better leave here," Helmut said after a moment. "She did say that her husband would be back."

"We'll do the same for him," one of the others boasted.

"Don't be foolish, Erich," Natter snapped. "What if we were recognized? The Jews have bought off half the judiciary in the country. They'd do for us at once."

"Then what now?" the youngest asked.

"We must not be seen here," Friedrich said slowly, and as he spoke, he put Dietbold on the floor beside his mother. "This . . . got out of hand. It's too soon."

"Where is the rest of the family? Here?" Erich had changed color and his throat began to work convulsively.

"They would have done something." Helmut sounded more confident than he felt, for the reminder that they might have been seen disquieted him.

"They're cowards," Natter dismissed the question.

Friedrich looked down at his blood-spattered clothes. "I can't be seen like this."

"There are scratches on your face," Erich pointed out with distaste.

"That's easily explained," Friedrich said impatiently. "The clothes are another matter. This was done badly, gentlemen." He walked around the two bodies on the floor. "We must not act foolishly now. This was rash, but we can salvage it, I think."

"How?" Helmut asked, going to the far corner of the room.

"We must make it seem that it was the work of . . . oh, one of the dissident leftist groups will serve. A few slogans scribbled on the walls, and ripped upholstery, and it will remind the police of the vandals who wrecked so much in this area three years ago." He looked around the kitchen as if seeking inspiration. "Heisel, Erich, you two take one of the butcher knives and cut up the chairs in the front rooms. Pull books off the shelves and slash a few paintings. Make it look wild."

"Friedrich, how long . . ." Heisel began, his drunkenness fading as he spoke.

"Thirty minutes at the most. Twenty would be better." He dismissed them with a wave. "Konrad, find some paint and put slogans on the wall. Don't be too particular about your spelling."

"Thirty minutes?" Natter asked.

"Fifteen, I think." Friedrich was already directing his attention to Helmut. "The Bruderschaft is not going to be pleased with us, I fear."

Helmut nodded. "Nor the Gesellschaft."

"Oh, they mean little. They're useful for many things, but there is no power in them, and very little philosophy. It is the Bruderschaft that is the heart of Thule, and its real strength. For Erich and the rest it is enough that they can give financial aid and social acceptability to all of us. In time, thought will change and the people will see that we have been right all along." He stared down at the bodies again, then made a click with his tongue. "There's blood on my shoes. Yours, too."

Helmut reacted with greater disgust. "Be damned to her."

The remaining man, who had been silent, chuckled now. "Most certainly she is. Christianity and the Bruderschaft agree on that." His clothes were rumpled from his part in the battle with Amalie, and his hard Nordic features were marred by a bruise over his left eye. "You must do something about those marks on your face, Friedrich."

"I suppose you're right," Friedrich said. "Gott im Himmel, it stinks in here. It's as bad as the trenches were." He held the edge of his sleeve to his face. "Let's get out of here."

"Yes; at once," Helmut said with relief. He was afraid if he remained in the kitchen much longer he would become physically ill. It was bad enough having to be near Jews, but sharing the room with a Jewish corpse was intolerable.

Friedrich looked at the third man. "What will you tell the Bruderschaft, Martin?"

"About today, do you mean?" The man considered. "For one thing, this was ill-conceived. I've already said so. You should not have allowed the others to drink so much. It probably wasn't wise to kill the woman, or if it had to be done, it should have been more methodical. But you have made a good recovery, Friedrich, and your initiate standing should not be endangered in any way. In your case, Rauch, I haven't yet made up my mind. When I have given the matter some thought, I will tell you my conclusions." He glanced down the hall. "From the sound of it, Heisel and Erich are enjoying themselves."

As if to confirm this, there was a second splintering of glass followed by an enthusiastic whoop.

"That's the sort of behavior we should not encourage in one another. It is well enough for the people to comport themselves so recklessly, but those aspiring to the Bruderschaft need more discipline." Martin gestured to the two men. "Come. We'll have to see what's been done."

In the hallway they found Konrad Natter with a jar of children's paints. He was tracing words and designs on the walls. There was an unpleasant gleam in his eyes and he wielded the brush as if it were a weapon.

Martin and Friedrich stared at his work, and then Martin turned to him, controlled fury making his voice shake. "I told you, *leftist* slogans! This is NSDAP. Paint it out, you idiot!"

Natter glared at Martin. "What right have you to—?"

"If you do not know that, you have no business in the Thule

Gesellschaft," Martin cut him off sharply. "Do you want to bring the police around, asking questions, interfering? If these words are read, that is what will happen. And it will be the worse for you, Herr Natter."

Natter's bluster faded under this scathing attack. "Communists, then. I'll make a hammer and sickle. That should be satisfactory." He turned back to his work, red creeping up his neck by his collar.

Five minutes later the six men were out of the house and on their way back to the Hirsch Furt in Hausham. They were boisterous at first, then grew sullen and quiet as Martin gave them his first evaluation of their activities. By the time they drew up at the tavern, most of the men wanted drink badly, and two of them were cold with fear.

An hour after the men had departed, the pony cart from Schloss Saint-Germain rattled up the drive toward the Schnaubels' house. The three children in the back were singing one of the Russian songs Laisha had taught them, with Nikolai joining them on the chorus and occasionally correcting their pronunciation. Bruno held a large bouquet of hybrid poppies and peonies in his hand, and Emmerich carried half a dozen roses. Olympie's hands were empty but there was a small basket at her feet.

"There now, we're here," Nikolai said as he looped the pony's reins around the brake as he had done as a boy in Russia. He got down from the driver's box and let down the steps for the three children. "Be careful with your flowers, Emmerich."

The boy wiggled impatiently. "It was silly to bring the flowers. We have flowers here," he told his older brother.

"They're nothing like the Graf's," Bruno said wistfully and truthfully. "Mother likes them. I heard her say so."

"It's silly," Emmerich persisted, but held the roses with care as he descended to the pebbled drive.

"Your mother won't think so," Nikolai said to the younger boy.

Olympie extended her hand to be supported. "If you'll bring in the basket," she said grandly to Nikolai.

"Oho, quite the little Czarina, aren't you?" But he lifted the basket out of the cart and followed them to the door, where the two boys waited.

"What's keeping her?" Bruno wondered aloud when he had knocked a third time.

"She's probably in the nursery with Dietbold. She might not

hear us." Emmerich reached out and gave the door a hearty blow.

Olympie was looking about absently, her mind on the supper she and her brothers had shared with Laisha. She liked the Swedish tarts the cook always made for her, and wished she had been able to eat another. Her glance strayed across the windows of the drawing room, and she stared, puzzled. "See. The window's broken."

Both of her brothers scoffed at this, but Nikolai, standing a little behind them, looked where Olympie pointed. "They *are* broken," he said, a coldness settling into his spine. In a quiet voice he said, "Bruno, try the door. Slowly."

Bruno scowled at the Russian driver but obeyed, and was worried when the door opened for him. "Mother always keeps it locked."

"Bruno . . ." Emmerich whispered. "I don't want to go in."

"That's stupid," Bruno said, but with little conviction.

Olympie had stepped into the hall, and as her eyes adjusted to the afternoon dusk of the hall, she gasped. "The walls!"

Nikolai stepped through the door, moving the children aside. His pulse was suddenly heavy in his head as he looked at the scrawled letters and symbols on the wall. Images of the bloodiest days of the Revolution pressed in on him.

"The chairs are all cut up!" Emmerich called indignantly from the living room. "And the pictures are broken."

"Where's Mother?" Bruno asked quietly, looking to Nikolai for help.

"The nursery?" Olympie suggested.

"Mama!" Emmerich yelled. "It's us! Come out!"

"I'll look in the nursery," Bruno said, and went cautiously off in the direction of that room.

"Rozoh," Olympie said uncertainly, "where are they?"

"I don't know. We'll find them." He tried to smile, but his mouth only grimaced.

"Mut-ter!" Emmerich cried out, standing at the foot of the stairs. He still held the bouquet of roses in his hand, but the blooms had been forgotten and were battered now, dropping petals in a fragrant wake behind the frightened boy.

"She's not in the nursery," Bruno announced solemnly from the end of the hallway.

"Where's Hedda?" Olympie said.

Emmerich pushed past Nikolai and his sister, starting to run toward the kitchen, calling for his mother. He had dashed halfway into the room before he saw what was on the floor, and the smell struck him.

Nikolai had started after the boy, and was almost to the kitchen door when he heard Emmerich's shrill scream. Nikolai did not pause; he was in the kitchen before the sound had ceased to reverberate through the house. His years of soldiering steeled him, so that he was able to lift Emmerich into his arms and close the door on the terrible sight, but his mouth tasted of bile.

"Was that my mother?" Bruno asked, trying to get into the kitchen.

"Yes," Nikolai answered, attempting to hold the kicking, screeching Emmerich in his arms. "Don't go in, Bruno."

Olympie's teeth were chattering. "Shouldn't we help her? Rozoh?"

The Russian's eyes filled with tears. "I'm sorry," was all he could say.

Emmerich's renewed shrieks were answered by a wail from the floor above them.

There was the sound of an automobile in the driveway, and a cheerful greeting called out. "I'm home in good time!"

Then, as Hedda started down the stairs and Olympie began to cry, Simeon Schnaubel opened the door of his home and stared in bewilderment at the abandoned roses at his feet.

Text of a letter from James Emmerson Tree to Madelaine de Montalia.

*Amsterdam*
*September 4, 1921*

*Madelaine de Montalia*
*Hotel Anglais*
*Bucharest, Romania*

*Dearest Madelaine:*

*Try to keep me away. I'll meet you in Lausanne in three weeks or go to Australia for the shame of it. But what on earth are you doing in Bucharest? Take my advice and stay out of that area. There's too much going on in that part of the world, what with Charles trying to get the throne of Hungary back for himself, and with the King of Yugoslavia just dead, there's no telling what will happen next. That area could be another Persia, and I don't want to see you caught in it. You told me yourself that one of the reasons you decided to come back to France was that with the new King of Syria just in power, you didn't want to endanger your team. What makes you think Romania is much different from Syria?*

*They say that the Avus Autobahn will open in Berlin next week. There are half a dozen journalists who are going over to have a look at it. Everyone is saying that it's the way of the future. It would make things a lot easier to have auto roads with a decent surface and more than two lanes. I'll take you driving on it, if you like. I've got a new automobile, a Mors. It's two years old and there's a dent in it, but it's still the greatest thing I've ever owned. Maybe after Lausanne we can drive up to Berlin and try out the Avus Autobahn.*

*I've been trying to get some reactions to General Mitchell's contention about aeroplanes and navies. The*

Dutch are great seafarers, and no one has paid them much attention, so I've been asking shipbuilders if they could make a ship safe from aerial bombs. Since General Mitchell sank the Ostfriesland, there's been quite an argument about it. The generals can't make up their minds, but the shipbuilders tell me that they are pretty much worried. I'd like to get the opinion of some of the shipbuilders in Germany, but I don't know if they'd talk to me. After all, the Ostfriesland was one of theirs, and General Mitchell sank it.

Now that the Civil War is over in Russia, I'm going to see if I can get in there to do a story on the famine, which is supposed to be terrible. I'm not holding out much hope for being permitted in, but I want to try. If I go, it'll be a fairly quick trip: Crandell doesn't want me that far away for very long. I understand there's going to be a relief act passed back home so that the U.S. can send food over to them. That would be a story to file.

I've missed you so much, Madelaine. I dream about you at night, and that Dr. Freud wouldn't have to guess about these dreams, believe me. I can't wait to see you. I've arranged to have ten days for you. When I thought you wouldn't be back for a time, I considered going back to the States for a little time, but now that you'll be in France, I'd rather have my vacation time with you than in Denver or St. Louis or New York, for that matter. I'll be at the Reine Marie on the twenty-sixth, that's a promise.

I've got to get two more interviews into the mail tonight, so I'll close now. Besides, there are things I can't tell you in words, and if I try much longer, this letter is going to have to be written on asbestos.

> All my love, and I mean that,
> James

# 9

There was a stand of birches around Wolkighügel, and behind them the pines offered their eternal shadow. The first touch of autumn had already spangled the leaves and a few lay on the ground like coins. This afternoon there was still enough warmth left in the air to permit Jürgen's servant to carry him out onto the narrow terrace at the back of the Schloss, where the sun could reach his parchmentlike skin and impassive face. Walther sat nearby, a book open and unread in his lap.

"May I come out?" Gudrun asked, and saw Walther start as she spoke to him.

"Of course, Frau Ostneige," Walther said, but there was that ill-concealed resentment that had become familiar to Gudrun over the last two years.

"I didn't mean to disturb you, but I have so few chances to see Jürgen these days." She had put on a new dress, a modest and becoming afternoon frock in lavender wool. The skirt hem was only four inches above her ankles, but the condemning glance that Walther gave her made her feel a hussy, and she darted a challenging look at him.

"He's not up to visitors," Walther said grudgingly. "But you, being his wife . . . Come ahead." He half-rose, then sank back in the chair.

"Yes, wives are different, aren't they?" Gudrun said sweetly before she turned to look at Jürgen. She had never got used to the shock of seeing him so changed. He was little more than a husk, and everything she had ever loved in him, ever known, was gone. She forced herself to smile affectionately while telling herself the whole thing was a travesty. "I'm glad to see you outside, Jürgen," she said in a bright, loud voice. It had been more than a year since she was able to address him as husband.

"He doesn't respond much," Walther said. "I've asked the doctor about it, but there's nothing they can do. There's nothing anyone can do but care for him and trust that God will restore him."

"Yes," Gudrun said, wanting to shout that it was a lie.

"Jürgen, I'm having our neighbors over to tea. We're being very English today, with little cakes and sandwiches. I wish you could join us. Walpurga is very frail now, but she does like good conversation. Gerwald hates to deny her the opportunity to get out. You might remember them." She searched Jürgen's faded eyes for some sign that he had heard her, but there was nothing. She stepped back, almost sighing.

"He is growing tired, Frau Ostneige," Walther informed her. "When he is tired, he does not show much interest."

"No," she said sadly, thinking that Jürgen must be tired all the time. Poor man, if he was, to have to be locked away from the world, wanting nothing more than rest. She looked up, shocked, a flush tingeing her cheeks. There were those who would condemn her for such sentiments, and quite rightly. It was not her husband's fault that he had become something so . . . alien to her. She leaned forward a bit. Yes, that was it. He was like a creature from another country, another planet, with nothing in common with her.

"Perhaps I should take him in, Frau Ostneige?" Walther's tone was always polite, but the contempt he felt for her was apparent.

"Why is it necessary? The air is pleasant, isn't it?" She took petty satisfaction in opposing him. "You've said so many times that he has few pleasures, why deny him another ten minutes here?"

Walther glared at her. "Gnädige Frau," he said, becoming more subservient as his annoyance increased, "I'm sure you mean kindly by your husband. I must point out that a man who is not often in the sun must limit his exposure to it, or risk burning. Your husband is in no condition to stand a burn at the moment."

"Then move him so that he is in shadow. Or will that make him cold, which we must also not risk?" She let her voice become sharp for the last of her question, and did not wait for Walther to answer. "Oh, do as you think best. Doubtless you believe that I am too feckless to keep him alive if he were left in my care. But remember that this is my home, Walther Stoff. It is not Jürgen who pays you for your attentive care, but I. Without my inheritance and caution, we would not have Wolkighügel, or fuel to burn, or food on the table. Before you rebuke me, reflect on this."

"I am aware of the financial arrangements here, Gnädige Frau," Walther said through tightened teeth as he recalled those days, not so very long ago, when it would have been unthinkable that a woman should address him, or any man, in such a tone. "But let me say that your husband was my commander in battle, and for that reason, if no other, I would not desert him if it meant that I begged bread for him on the meanest street in München."

"Luckily, that isn't necessary," Gudrun countered, thinking that it was infuriating to be lectured in this way. "I will leave you, Walther, since I am clearly not wanted here." She looked once at Jürgen as she turned to leave. She wondered if he heard the argument, if he understood it, if he cared it was happening. There was no change in his face, and his eyes had the same vacant expression she had seen so many times when she had tried to speak with him. She sighed, thinking it hopeless.

"I will inform you when Herr Ostneige retires," Walther announced with great formality, his badger-gray head lowered with derisive courtesy.

"How kind," Gudrun murmured, and stepped back into the rose sitting room, which faced the stable and an area which a century ago had been a rose garden and was now being cleared for a tennis court.

"There you are!"

Gudrun turned as her brother came through the door. "Maxl, you're back." In spite of herself, she was glad to see him. "I'm surprised you're—"

"Well, there was no reason to stay two weeks, after all," he said with a merry wave of his hand. "There were a great many people—the von Grünstrasse clan is as enormous as ever, it seems—and it was really rather boring, so I came home. It wasn't as if I was that far away." He reached up to loosen his tie, grinning at her. "I stopped in München and brought a friend with me. You remember Helmut Rauch, don't you? The banker? Now, there's a man you should know better, sister mine. He has been making predictions about the sad state of the economy ever since we crossed the Istar."

"But . . ." She chose her words carefully, knowing how easily Maximillian could take offense. "I am having company at tea. They . . . It's Gerwald and Walpurga, and I don't think you'll find them very entertaining. . . ."

"Those old fossils? I should think not! Whatever possessed you to invite them?" His outrage was faintly mocking.

"Well, you were not here, Maxl, and they are neighbors. It's difficult enough with Jürgen ill as he is, but this way I don't feel completely walled up in this place!" She was astonished at her own indignation. "Oh, Maxl, pay no attention. I . . . I've had a quarrel with Walther and I think I'm still upset." She saw some of the thunder fade from his brow. "I'm sure your friend is welcome here, my dear, and if you think he would enjoy having tea with us, then, by all means, come to the main drawing room. With a straightened tie, however." She was pleased and relieved to see the smile come back into his eyes.

"What a minx you are. I'll speak to Helmut, but don't expect us. I think we may take the horses out for some exercise. Maybe stop at the Hirsch Furt for a little refreshment. What time do you expect the orgy to be over?" He reached out and gave an affectionate pat to her cheek.

"I doubt they'll stay later than five-thirty, and I've asked dinner to be served at eight." She had done no such thing, but she knew her cook would require time to prepare for two more guests, particularly if Helmut Rauch had as hearty an appetite as Maxl did.

"Well, no doubt we'll be back by then. Don't eat it all by yourself, will you?" He glanced out the window toward the terrace. "Poor old Jürgen. I don't suppose there's been any change?"

"I haven't been aware of any," she answered carefully.

"Terrible thing. Let's not dwell on it." He ambled toward the door and turned to smile at her. "I know you've been worried about me, but I assure you, Gudrun, I'm not quite the wastrel some of our friends think I am. When things change, you'll see that . . ." He stopped and shrugged. "We'll talk later."

"Very good." She sighed as the door closed behind him. For the better part of a minute she stood quite still, her gaze fixed on nothing more than the pattern in the carpet. What if she simply ran away? she asked herself. What if she packed a bag, took the Hispaño-Suiza, and drove to . . . anywhere? Leave Wolkighügel to Maxl and Otto and Jürgen, forget everything that had been her past and become someone else, someone quite new. . . .

The little clock on the end table chimed the half-hour and Gudrun scowled at it. No, it was not possible. She was an Albrunnen and an Ostneige, Wolkighügel was her home, and it was comtemptible to think of abandoning her responsibilities like one of those reckless American heiresses she occasionally read about in the magazines. She was part of a tradition, an honor. She smoothed the front of her dress and went into the hall, deciding that she must first placate the cook, and then ask Otto to run a few errands for her.

Maximillian was not aware of these troubled thoughts that plagued his sister. He sauntered out into the L-shaped courtyard and waved to Helmut, who was pulling a suitcase from the trunk of his new Mercedes. "We've arrived at the wrong moment," he called out. "Seems my sister is having a couple of ancient neighbors in to tea. If you can imagine that!" He laughed, and if the sound of it was a trifle wild, neither man noticed it enough to remark on it.

"Then we're imposing," Helmut said heavily.

"Nothing of the sort. You and I can take a couple of horses and go for a ride. Gudrun keeps the stable—not the way it was when our father was alive, but there should be five or six passable animals to choose from. It's a pleasant day for it, don't you think?" He was eager to show Helmut his most charming manner, as he had the uneasy feeling that the young banker did not think well of him.

"I haven't brought riding clothes." He had set the suitcase down and fastidiously wiped his hands with a large linen handkerchief.

"Who needs them? It's not as if we'll be making a social event of it." He tried to make light of the objection without seeming a complete boor.

Helmut responded sharply, with something of the manner he had used to his subordinates in the army. "My dear Altbrunnen, I haven't brought my boots, and it would hardly do to greet your sister at dinner with shoes that stink of horses. If we're to have an outing, let it be in the automobile."

"Oh, very well," Maximillian said, realizing that Helmut was right in his objections. "There'll only be the three of us at table, and I don't know how much of a stickler my sister will be under the circumstances. You could probably wear your slippers and leave the shoes out for Otto to clean."

"That might be an imposition on the staff," Helmut said, and got the information he wanted.

"That's no trouble. There are seven servants here at Wolkighügel. In the old days there were a lot more, but there isn't much of the family left, and no one entertains on the grand scale these days." A petulant droop to his mouth altered his features subtly, so that they were no longer quite so fresh and appealing; there was a taint to him.

"Seven servants. With times the way they are, that is

impressive," Helmut remarked, encouraging Maximillian to talk.

"One of them's her husband's nurse, Walther. Then there's Otto, who's been here since I was a child. There's a grounds-keeper, very old now and most autocratic. He's Hungarian and he lives next to St. Leonhard's, at the south end of Schliersee. He would live on the island in the lake, if he could manage it. Then there's Frau Bürste, she's new, a cook-and-housekeeper sort. Gudrun used to have both a cook and a housekeeper, but there was no reason to have them when she couldn't keep them employed most of the time. Lilli comes in twice a week to do cleaning and washing, and gives a hand in the kitchen when there's to be a party. Dieter takes care of the gardens, what there are of them, and minds the horses—he had a bad wound in the war and keeps to himself. He has a daughter living in the village Schliersee, and sleeps there most nights, though there's a groom's room in the stable. Walther, Otto, Géza, Frau Bürste, Lilli, Dieter . . . who've I forgotten? The Czech. Miroslav, that's the one. He does the repairs and such things. Last year he replaced most of the slates on the stable roof, and he's painted the gamekeeper's cottage, where I live. Most of them don't stay here all the time, you'll notice. Just Walther, Otto, and Frau Bürste. It used to be that there were a dozen servants, all living in, but well . . ." He gestured fatalistically and grinned. "Those were other times, weren't they?"

"They were," Helmut said as he lifted the suitcase and started toward the door. He had been far more interested in what Maximillian had told him than he had allowed himself to reveal. At first he had not understood why it was that Eckart and Rosenberg, after two meetings of the Bruderschaft here, had decided that they must find a better location. Helmut had thought that Wolkighügel was ideal, but he was aware now that it was not as isolated as he had first thought. Still, he reflected as Maximillian opened the door for him, if the eco-nomic state became much worse—and he was certain that it would—Frau Ostneige might well have to reduce her staff, and then she might be willing, for a few considerations, to give the Thule Bruderschaft the use of three rooms in the Schloss.

"Maxl, what are you doing?" demanded a cross voice behind them as Otto surged through the door. "That's not your task, my boy."

Maximillian set the suitcase down in the entry hall and

turned toward the old man. "I thought I'd spare you the trouble. It isn't much."

"It may be," Otto said condemningly, "that there are those houses where they have forgotten how guests are to be treated, but this is not one of them. I will take the Herr's bag to his room." He stepped up and took the case. "His is the room across the hall from yours."

"Yes," Maximillian agreed. "I assumed it was."

"Then you see to introductions here and I will tend to this." He turned toward the stairs without another word.

"There's no use arguing with him," Maximillian sighed. "He'll simply remind me he dandled me on his knee, and that will end it."

There was a light step in the hall, and a moment later Gudrun came into the entry. "Maxl! I thought you weren't . . ." She cut herself short as she saw his guest.

"We're just bringing Helmut's bag in, Rudi. We won't linger. You remember Herr Rauch, don't you?"

"Yes, I believe we've met before," Gudrun said rather coolly as she offered her hand to the banker.

"A pleasure, Frau Ostneige, and a kindness to permit me to stay here with your husband so ill." He considered kissing her hand, but thought better of it and contented himself with a single squeeze of her fingers.

"My husband has been an invalid since 1917, Herr Rauch. It is nothing new to me, and I do what I can to carry on life here in spite of his condition." She looked at her brother and smiled warmly. "You'd best hurry on your way, Maxl. It might be awkward if you leave after Gerwald and Walpurga arrive."

"We're halfway out the door already," he promised her, and cocked his head to Helmut. "Come, my friend. We must be going or we'll be trapped here, back in the 1880's. We'll be back in time for dinner."

"Fine," Gudrun said absently. "There's no need to change, either of you. We don't dress en famille." She gave Helmut a vague nod and went off toward the kitchen, wishing she knew what it was about the man that made her shiver. She chided herself for letting her imagination run wild, and decided that it was all part of her despondent state of mind. She opened the door to the kitchen and fixed her face with an expression of goodwill.

"Otto said that your brother has come early, with a guest," said Frau Bürste as she pressed her flour-covered fist into a large bowl of rising dough.

"Yes, I'm afraid that's so," Gudrun said. "They will not take tea with my guests, but will want dinner this evening. I haven't a notion how long they intend to stay—you know what Maxl is—and I know this is an inconvenience, but if you will give Otto a list of the things you will need, I will send him to get them for you."

The older woman did not speak at once; she was occupied with turning the dough and spreading the new top with butter before once again covering it with damp cheesecloth. "I'll do that, Frau Ostneige, and I thank you for the consideration. However, I doubt it will be that easy. Food is becoming quite expensive and some of the better items are scarce." She frowned, making her wide, blocky face pucker around her nose.

"Perhaps you'd be willing to include a few alternatives, then, and that way Otto will be able to select the best he can find." She tried to conceal her inward shrinking. The cost of everything was becoming outrageous, and she feared what might happen to her carefully-monitored funds if this continued. Another year of such high prices and her personal reserve would be depleted.

"I'll do that," Frau Bürste said again as she went to the sink to wash her hands. Over the sound of the water, she said, "I don't like to mention it, Frau Ostneige, but I've caught Dieter taking food again. This time it was eggs and cheese."

Gudrun sighed. "How much?"

"Ten eggs and two rounds of cheese. That's a fair amount. He said it was for his daughter, but I've heard that she sells the food he brings her to the Blau Pferd and does very well for herself. If it was just the two of them going hungry, I wouldn't mention it, but . . ." She wiped her hands on her apron and turned around. "I don't know what to suggest."

"I'll have to give him a warning, of course," Gudrun said slowly. "If it happens after that, I must let him go. I don't know if Geza would take over his duties or not. Miroslav is hopeless with the horses . . ." She bit her lower lip. "Tell Dieter that I wish to speak to him before he leaves, would you, Frau Bürste?"

"That I will. More's the pity." She went to the icebox and pulled out a plate of little sandwiches, showing them to Gudrun. "One of cold, and the hot ones are in the warming oven. I'll make the tea when your guests have arrived."

"Thank you, Frau Bürste." Gudrun nodded to the stout woman, then left the kitchen, trying to think what she could say to Dieter that would convince him to stop taking food. She paused in the doorway to the main drawing room and stared out across the room, through the lacy curtains to the drive where the Mercedes was just turning away from the Schloss. The sun made Maximillian's hair a golden halo, then they were gone. Gudrun shrugged away the worries that beset her and went across the room to the phonograph to select a few of the operetta arias that Walpurga liked so much. Otto would come in to keep the machine cranked for them. Her afternoon began to fall back into a familiar pattern.

"We got away in time," Maximillian said with delight as the Mercedes sped down the dusty road. "I can't imagine why anyone would want to spend the afternoon with those two creatures."

"Your sister might have liked us to stay, if they're as bad as all that," Helmut said sternly.

"Not she. This is the kind of entertaining she's been doing for years. She probably enjoys it. We'd only be in the way." He leaned back in the seat and stared up at the sun glancing through the trees.

"Still, at times she must wish for more excitement than this. She's a young woman, after all, and this was not the sort of life she used to lead." Helmut slowed the Mercedes as they rounded a curve and came within sight of Schliersee.

"That was years ago." Maximillian shrugged, and the movement was much the same as his sister's had been.

"And what about these neighbors? What are they like?" The automobile jolted over a pothole and Helmut cursed quietly.

"Very old. Always talking about the Kaiser and Austro-Hungary, the old days in Wien and Berlin. To hear them, everything then was Paradise and since the Great War we have lived in Hell." He gave a discontented shake to his head.

"Not Paradise and Hell," Helmut said as his brows flicked together. "But this Republic of ours is intolerable, Max, and you know it." He tapped his fingers on the steering wheel. "These old people; are they sympathetic to our aims, do you think?"

"I haven't any idea," Maximillian answered, startled by the question. "Oh, they complain about how badly things have been handled and they are apprehensive about the Communists and the French, and they damn the Treaty of Versailles more regularly than they piss, but for the rest? Gerwald likes to think of himself as cosmopolitan, which is the greatest nonsense."

"Cosmopolitan?" Helmut inquired.

"You know the sort—well-traveled, or so he claims, with friends, he says, everywhere and of all types—who makes a virtue of diversity. I gather he was something of a rake when he was young and used to dash off to Paris when he had the chance. Insists he knew Wagner and met Lizst; talked to Dumas. Not that he approves of the French, but men of his generation didn't let that stop them from a good time."

Helmut listened to the description with increasing annoyance. "I've met a few of them," he muttered. "They say 'be tolerant' when they want to be lazy. If it weren't for those, there would not be problems now. They were the ones who sat back and let the Jews insinuate themselves into all the positions of power, who indulged in wine, women, and song while their birthright was filched from them." His knuckles were white on the steering wheel and his voice was pitched much higher than usual, although no louder.

"They're not quite that bad," Maximillian protested. "For one thing, they were never highly placed."

"It makes no difference," Helmut insisted. "Every one of them is guilty of treason against our race. Look about you, Max, and keep your eyes open when you do. You've heard the Bruderschaft's truth, and you have accepted it. Why do you make allowance for these old people simply because they take tea with your sister?" He was so intent on what Maximillian would say that he skidded as he entered the next curve and had to struggle to hold the Mercedes on the road.

Maximillian quickly recognized his error and hastened to correct it. "Oh, I don't suppose Gerwald likes Jews any better than the next person. He's civil to everyone, but that's the way they were taught forty years ago. And there's the matter of the Schnaubels. You heard about that, didn't you? The mother and infant were murdered and one of the other children has screaming fits now. No one wanted them living here, of course, but the killings, that struck most of us as going too far. A mother and her youngest child! It's one thing to get rid of the Jews, which we must do, naturally, but killing is something else again."

"They are killing us," Helmut said very quietly. "Every hour of every day, they are destroying us. What does it matter that a woman died, or an infant, when our whole race is being consumed and subverted by them?" A muscle in his cheek started to jump as he went on. "How can you speak in this way, Max? You're one of those Initiated, and you have seen the danger in which we all stand, and yet you say that the death of two Jews is going too far. Our Vaterland is in ruins, and the jackals of France and Britain tear at it while the Jews urge them on, but you quail at the death of two Jews!" He pulled to the side of the road. "Do you understand what is at stake here? Have you forgotten all you have learned? Well?"

"But . . ." Maximillian faltered, turning pale. "Yes, I know what they have done to us. Mein Gott, Helmut, I have seen for myself the destruction of most of my family fortunes"—he had long since convinced himself that his own profligacy had little to do with it—"and I know how dire our predicament is. I wholly sympathize with the plans to remove all Jews from Deutschland. Obviously this must be done, and quickly. But we are not barbarians, Helmut. We are people of honor, and when a woman and a child are butchered by those who invade their home, that is not the conduct that is appropriate for one of us. We must set an example for the world to follow, and do all with purpose and order. By all means," he said, gaining confidence as he saw Helmut's expression change from condemning rage to something less formidable, "let us be rid of the Jews, but not by slaughter, which only shows how much they have corrupted us by their wiles and cunning. We must not succumb to that degradation. To applaud the death of the Schnaubel woman and her child contradicts all that we strive for as members of the Thule Bruderschaft. If we are to master the world, then it must be made plain that we are deserving of that state, or there will be nothing but disorder around us. Eckart has said the same thing. You have heard him. We condemn the Jews as worse than scum, but we mimic their behavior, which is more abhorrent in us than in them, for they were never bred to be masters." He stopped quite suddenly, his face showing two hectic spots in the cheeks, as if he burned with fever.

Helmut studied his companion a moment, then said slowly, "I hope you will forgive me, Max. For some time I have thought that your devotion to Deutschland and the Thule Bruderschaft and Gesellschaft was superficial, that you were amusing yourself with matters beyond your comprehension. I see now that I was wrong."

Maximillian blinked and sat a little straighter in the leather-covered seat. "I had not intended to give that impression," he said a little tightly. "But there are so many dour old men muttering about divining rods and the Sacred Chalice and the rest of it that I want to . . ."—he lifted his shoulders and his easy smile returned—"There are so many people who would be put off by the sobriety of some of the Bruderschaft. They would see them as men not in touch with the world. If we are to achieve our ends, it must be because all Deutschland flocks to our banner, not because there have been the proper incantations spoken at the dark of the moon. The incantations should be saved for more serious work, not the conversion of the masses."

"I am not the only one who has underestimated you," Helmut went on, almost to himself. "You must not be angry with them, Max. In these degrading times it is so tempting to forget our destiny and surrender to the debauchery." Again Helmut regarded Maximillian without speaking. "The Frei Korps does not appeal to you?"

Maximillian pursed his lips with distaste. "A rabble, full of bullies and braggarts with nothing better to do than harass their betters. It was probably the Frei Korps who killed the Schnaubel woman and the child."

Helmut winced at that accusation, and he had a sudden vivid recollection of that blood-washed kitchen and the still, broken figures on the floor. "Frei Korps?"

"Well, who else would have done such a thing? Consider, Helmut, how it must appear to those who hear of it. When Frei Korps troops murder, that is their way; there is no . . . art to it."

Friedrich had said very much the same thing, Helmut recalled, and Konrad had dismissed the idea as unimportant. Yet clearly this was not the case. Cautiously he said, "I thought I had heard that there were slogans on the wall that pointed to the Sparacists or Communists . . ."

"A clumsy device," Maximillian said at once, tremendously pleased that Helmut was paying him so much attention. "Anyone could have done such a thing. Besides, there are few Communists in this part of Bayern, and a good number of Frei Korps. The innkeeper at the Schneeglöckchen in Gmund said last night when he heard of it that it had to be Frei Korps because they would not tolerate anyone killing Jews but themselves. Remember what they did to the Russians. It's all the same."

"Yes," Helmut said slowly. He knew he would have to talk to Friedrich as soon as possible. There were a few telephones at Bad Wiessee, and he might be able to call München before . . .

"Helmut!" Maximillian repeated, alarmed.

"I . . ." He passed his hand over his brow and began again. "It's the banker in me," he improvised. "I have just thought of a document I should have given to the investment manager. It's for a considerable sum . . ." He pretended to be discouraged. "I'll have to drive back and hope that I can reach there before the safe is closed."

Maximillian was taken aback, and then smiled. "Must you do it yourself, Helmut?"

"I . . . no, I don't believe so . . ." He paused and looked down the road with irritation.

"Then let us go into Hausham. The stationmaster there has a telephone, and I know that your bank has one as well. You can give your instructions to one of the officers." He was delighted to see the relief on his friend's stern features. "One of these days, we'll have telephones in the private houses here, and that will make it all much easier."

"Yes, it will," Helmut conceded as he put the Mercedes in gear and started toward Hausham.

Basking in the approval of Helmut, Maximillian allowed his fancy free rein. "You know, that would be something for the Gesellschaft to work on, improving the lot of these isolated villages. You know what people are like away from the cities— or perhaps you don't, it doesn't matter—they have very set ideas and are not impressed with promises or the grandeur of the bright streets. But give them something that is of real benefit, that they know will make their lives better without changing them, then they will uphold you through anything."

Ahead on the road a herdsman held up his hand to halt the car while he drove a dozen spotted dairy cattle from one field to another. He made a rude gesture as the Mercedes at last drove past.

"What about that man?" Helmut asked sarcastically. "Would a telephone benefit him? Would he be able to use it?"

"Of course he would use it," Maximillian insisted. "He's an isolated man. Now, if there is an emergency, for example, one of his children is injured, he must return to his house, find proper transportation and then get his child to the physician, assuming the man is available, and not out treating someone else. With a telephone, he would call to find out if the physician was available and arrange, perhaps, for the man to come to him rather than move the child himself. Be sure he would recognize the worth of such a thing." He sat for a moment, then added, "Why, if the Schnaubels had had a telephone, they might have been saved; the barbarians that killed the woman and child would, in all possibility, have been apprehended, as well. That's the benefit I mean. Don't you agree that there would be support from these people then?"

There was cold sweat on Helmut's brow as he listened to Maximillian. The man was right! In future they would have to be much more careful. To quell the debilitating fear that shook him, he sped up and forced himself to concentrate on the road.

Text of a letter from Duchess Irina Andreivna Ohchenov to Franchot Ragoczy.

7, Rue de Belle Isle
Paris, France
December 7, 1921

Franchot Ragoczy
Schloss Saint-Germain
Bavaire, Allemagne

My dear Count:

I have at last met Professor de Montalia, and I must thank you for introducing us. She is all you promised, and more. What a charming woman, and with such an air of youth for all her scholarship. I am beginning to believe that my life is not wholly lost.

She has already requested that I provide her with translations from the Greek which she says she knows indifferently. She has also requested that I add more languages to my knowledge, for she is certain that I will be very much in demand. It is her contention that most translators are excellent at moving one set of words from one language to another, but rarely do they manage to convey the sense of the words as well. In this, I am flattered to say, she says I excel. With such encouragement it would be terrible of me to refuse.

My work with Louis-Onfroi Servie continues, but on a less demanding level than that with Professor de Montalia. I fear that Professor Servie thinks of himself as a great romantic where women are concerned, and it is difficult both to keep him at arm's length and suppress my laughter when he begins his various maneuvers to seduce me. It is a bit tiresome, although part of myself is pleased that a man would still bother with me.

That is not intended as a reflection on you, Count, for I cannot regard your embraces as mere seduction. It is not

294

entirely wise for me to say this, but nonetheless I must
tell you that I am unable to forget the time I have spent in
your arms. Should you ever wish another such night with
me, you have only to send me word. I know you will not
be offended when I say that my love for Leonid is not in
the least diminished by what you have given me; if anything, I have discovered in myself a greater capacity for
affection and pleasure than I knew I had, so that my life
is enhanced. I would like to go on, but there is no way I
can express to you here the depths of my feelings. Emotion, unlike words, does not seem to translate at all, not
even onto paper.

I have, as you may have noticed, found a new home. I
have five rooms, sunny and light, on the third floor of a
building not quite fifty years old. There are electric lights
in the rooms and brand-new plumbing. Professor de
Montalia located this place for me and was kind enough
to vouch for me to the landlord, who lives in far more
lavish quarters than this. Two of my rooms are as yet
largely unfurnished, but I have an office where I have my
desk and a fair number of books. In general I am most
frugal, but books have become my greatest weakness. For
six weeks it was food, but now that I have begun to believe
that I will not quite starve; my passion for books has
grown almost to a mania. With Professor de Montalia
urging me to study more, I am forever inventing excuses
why I must buy this book, or that one. How strange it is
to be discovering this in myself at this age.

My Uncle has continued to refuse to see me, and so I
have decided that I have no uncle. It is easier than
tormenting myself with vain hopes that he will come to
his senses and welcome me. I told Professor de Montalia
of my decision and she asked if I would not wish her to
contact my Uncle on my behalf. Her generosity humbles
me when I think of it. For a time I considered letting her
do this, and then I accepted at last that the reason that he
had not asked me to visit him, that he has consistently
refused to see me, is that he does not want to see me. I felt
quite devastated when this first occurred to me, but now I
no longer worry when it crosses my mind. But then, I am
no longer living in squalor, with nothing to sustain me
but memories and the absurd hope that my uncle would
relent.

I have stopped feeling quite so much the exile and have

*something of the sense of, perhaps, a colonist. You must
understand that to some degree. I hope you do. It would
sadden me greatly to think that you, of all men, felt
exiled. It is apparent to me, however, that I will never be
anything but Russian. Of course I enjoy the French and
Paris is a beautiful city: this is something of a new
discovery for me, part of my new quarters and the delight
of working. In my heart, however, I hold the memory of
St. Petersburg, my dasha, Moscow in autumn, all those
things. Nothing will supplant them, nor would I wish it.*

*Recently, by the way, I have found an Orthodox Church
where they sing the Masses with proper choirs, and it
restored me more than I can express to hear those chants
and the liturgy once again. I have a link at last to the life
I left, and it does not pain me to think of it.*

*I do not know when you plan next to be in Paris, but
let me request now that you will visit me, whenever you
are here. I look forward to your company, and the opportunity to thank you again for all you have done for me.
No, pray don't object to my gratitude again, for I assure
you that it is far from my only desire.*

*Most fondly,*
*Irina*

*P.S. Christmas is nearly here, and for the first time since
I came here, I can face it without dread. Perhaps it will
be some time before I can anticipate it with joy, but for
now, it is enough that it does not sink me into despair. I
will go to Holy Archangel and listen to the choir, have a
meal in a restaurant, and see a film. Be glad for me.*

## 10

On the other side of the double-glassed window, icicles pressed
their ghostly fingers toward the shifting drifts of snow. A high
wind had sent overburdened branches hurtling into the air to
crash against walls, roofs, and other branches; it was hooting
its victory down the chimneys, making the well-laid fires dance
and crackle.

"Will Papa be safe?" Laisha asked Roger for the fifth time that hour. "He was supposed to be back at two and it's after four now."

Roger looked up again from his record book. "Laisha, this is the worst storm of the winter. It's hardly surprising that he has not arrived. Nikolai said that the road is blocked with snow, and it will take time for him to get here from the train station." He said it patiently enough and with his usual calm. "I have known him longer than you have, and have seen him come through much worse than a snowstorm."

She sighed and opened her book again, staring down at the page, which could not be made sensible. She held out for as long as possible, then closed the book and ventured to ask, "Isn't there something we ought to do?"

"Everything that's required has been done," Roger assured her, thinking again of the second pair of earth-lined boots he had persuaded Ragoczy to take with him on his trip. He was glad now he had insisted on the precaution.

Laisha folded her hands and walked slowly and deliberately around the library. "Is Papa . . . if he were delayed, how would we know?"

"He would send a telegram," Roger said, and added with a twinkle in his faded blue eyes, "which would not be delivered until after he was home, if the stationmaster is following his usual pattern."

"But if something had happened to him . . ." Laisha's brown eyes were suddenly enormous. "He could be hurt, or freezing, or killed, or . . ."

"It is unlikely," Roger said with a firm gentleness that was intended to close the matter.

"But think of what happened to Bruno's mother. Olympie said that no one should have to die in his own house." She looked around her, with some apprehension. "They could come here, couldn't they?"

Roger totaled a column of figures before answering. "Laisha, my master has traveled through Tibet in the winter, and the Gobi Desert in the summer." He had accompanied Ragoczy on both those journeys and recalled one day, when in the full glare of the sun, they had faced a band of robbers. It had been many months before the agony of that encounter was over. "Of the two of them, the winter was kinder. Don't fear for him, Laisha."

"But what if he doesn't come back?" Her voice was little more than a whisper and there was something in her face that was an echo of the catastrophe that had overtaken her at that burned-out manor in Latvia.

"He will. That I promise you." He closed his book and got up from the writing table. "Come. We'll get you a cup of chocolate and a slice of kirschkranz. By the time you finish that, my master will probably be home."

"Will you have some with me?" Laisha asked, brightening in spite of herself.

"Not this time," he responded, adding inwardly, *or any time*.

"What about dinner? Enzo is sure to say I shouldn't have sweets now." She fell into step beside Roger, looking up at him with the quiet intensity that was so much a part of her.

"Enzo is not master in this house. And he loves to make desserts. I'll deal with him if he objects." There was a short flight of steps leading down to the kitchen, an oddity of the building left over from the days when it had been more of a fortified stronghouse than a Schloss, when a bake house had stood where the gardener's shed was now and a high stone wall had enclosed most of the stableyard and back garden, and cabbages, onions, and potatoes grew there instead of peonies and roses. The only feature that had not changed was Ragoczy's extensive herb garden, and it, with the other plants, was lost under the snow.

The kitchen was large and warm. A commercial refrigerator hummed in one corner and a modern stove with six burners squatted in the center of the floor, a polished copper hood over it. Enzo DiGottardi stood by the chopping block, trimming the fat off a leg of lamb. His long white apron was nearly spotless, and he whistled through his teeth as he worked.

"Good afternoon," Roger said as he held the door for Laisha to enter.

"To you as well, Signor Roger," he answered before beaming at Laisha. "My Principessa has come to see me."

"There aren't any Princesses anymore," Laisha declared impatiently.

"But of course there are," Enzo said as he set the leg of lamb aside. "There is a Queen in the Netherlands. There is a Princess or two in England." He crossed his arms and looked down at her. "What do you want of me, fanciulla?"

Roger answered the question, sensing that Laisha would not be willing to banter with the cook this afternoon. "A cup of your excellent chocolate and a slice of the kirshkranz."

"But dinner—" Enzo began, as predicted.

"We still don't know when it will be served. If there is any difficulty, I will answer for it." Roger drew up one of the high stools to the long counter where Enzo prepared the occasional formal meal that was served to guests at Schloss Saint-Germain. "There you are, Laisha."

Laisha climbed onto the stool while Enzo wrapped the leg of lamb in waxed paper and put it into the refrigerator. Then he set about assembling the ingredients for his chocolate. As he warmed the cream-rich milk, he talked, apparently expecting no comments from either Roger or Laisha. "You must warn the Conte," he began, "that the price of food is still rising. That leg of lamb was three hundred twenty marks, half again as much as it was a year ago. It doesn't seem like much, you know, a few extra marks here and there, but in very little time . . . I have heard that steps are being taken to control this, but how is it possible? Every man wishes to have his bit of profit, and if he must pay fifty marks more for a bottle of wine, then when he serves it to his diners, he will charge seventy more for it, or he will close his doors." The milk was near simmering and he took it off the burner and dropped into it shavings of dark, bittersweet chocolate. After a moment he began to stir this with a wooden spoon. "You probably heard that Frau Ostneige dismissed one of her staff for stealing? He was taking food, naturally, and selling it again. We'll be seeing more of that. I told that heathen Nikolai that we're fortunate to have an employer who is well enough off that he can accommodate these prices. You may be certain that Frau Ostneige cannot. Most of the nobilità here have the same trouble. You wait, a year from now, when the costs of things may have risen by half again, there will be fewer servants in the Schlosses and not as many guests at the resorts at Tergensee and Starnbergersee. And it is possible that the prices may go that high. There are those who say it isn't going to happen, but I am not as sanguine as they. You may think that I have become alarmed over nothing." He added a few drops of vanilla to the chocolate. "Every night I thank my blessed guardian angel for bringing me here, to Schloss Saint-Germain. When I see the peril of others in my profession, and then I look about me, at these marvelous electric lights and the refrigerator, at the stove which runs on gas instead of wood, and I recall that the Conte has been willing to guarantee my employment, then I know I have had the most remarkable fortune. Here I had been afraid that no one would wish to employ a Swiss like me. Italian-speaking Swiss are not well-loved here. But luckily the Conte is a foreigner as well. Where I feared there would be nothing but drudgery, I have all this." He had taken down a large, delicate cup from one of the shelves, put a doily in the saucer, and begun to pour the chocolate. "My duties are, for the most part, light, and what I do is appreciated. My kitchen is heaven, my employer is rich. What man can ask for more?" He brought the chocolate to Laisha and placed it in front of her. "You must not drink it yet. You will burn your mouth and not taste the goodness of it."

"Thank you," Laisha said quietly, interrupting his monologue.

"A great pleasure. I will find a slice of the kirschkranz for you. If you want whipped cream on it, I will provide it, but that may be a bit too rich." He had gone back to the refrigerator and taken out a covered platter which contained the kirschkranz, a ring-molded pastry of sweet, heavy cake laced with kirsch liqueur, crowned with cherries and strewn with powdered sugar. He regarded it judiciously and then cut off a small section and put it on a fine porcelain dish. "This is too much, of course, but you will enjoy it, and if you do not eat all your dinner tonight, well, one evening should not harm you. There's a bit more chocolate in the pan if you want it. If not, I will put a little brandy in it and drink it myself."

"I don't think I'll want it," Laisha said as she took a first cautious sip of the hot, dark liquid.

"Tanto bene," Enzo said with a satisfied sigh. "It will be difficult tomorrow night, having that sad Signor Schnaubel and his children here. It is good of the Conte to ask them, but I cannot believe that it will be a happy evening. I have planned a good meal, not too fancy, so that the children will enjoy it, and it will be served properly, but I must tell you that it distresses me to think that I can do no more for them. What matter if they are Jews? It is one of the British writers— Milton, I think—who asks if Jews are not as other people. Haven't they hands? Don't they bleed? It is with the most profound sorrow that we know they bleed."

"It was Shakespeare," Roger remarked quietly.

"Ha! Whenever anyone wishes to credit a British writer with wise thoughts, they say it is Shakespeare. Ridiculous! It is as bad as the Italians, who think all their poetry was written by Dante."

The rear door to the kitchen banged open and Nikolai Rozoh, bundled in a sheepskin greatcoat, came into the room. His boots were crusted with snow and his fur cap, pulled down low on his forehead, looked as sugared as the kirschkranz. "Mother of a rabid wolf," he said in Russian as he thrust the door closed against the howling cold. He pulled off his cap and wiped his brow, going on in his awkward German, "I've seen to the horses, and the automobiles are properly covered. It's as bad as the winters back home, out there."

"Get your great carcass out of my kitchen!" Enzo ordered, staring aghast at the Russian. "Look what you're doing!"

"I'm getting out of these clothes," Nikolai said calmly, and pretended not to hear Laisha's giggle. "I could use something to drink. Schnapps will do." He tugged off his gloves and dropped them to the floor. "And if there's any of that wonderful soup left, I'll have a bowl."

"If you were a civilized man, I would be offended," Enzo announced with great dignity, "but as you are a Russian, with no culture at all . . ."

"I'm a Russian," Laisha pointed out as she finished her chocolate. "And you call me Princess."

"That is a matter entirely different," Enzo told her, but the color that flamed in his face said otherwise.

"I've looked over the generator. There's fuel enough and it seems to be running well," Nikolai went on as he came into the kitchen and pulled up another of the high stools. "Unless a branch falls on the housing, I can't imagine what would go wrong with it. I heard that the lights at Bad Wiessee have all gone out. The drifts are bringing down the wires." He sat down, ignoring the pile of garments he had abandoned just inside the rear door. "The postman said that it would be several days before the power is restored there."

"The postman?" Laisha asked, the intent look back in her brown eyes again.

"He was on his way to Spitzingsee in a light sleigh. He wanted to borrow a lantern, in case he should be delayed and have to search for shelter in the dark. I gave him one from the stable." He glanced once at Roger.

Enzo, who had opened the wine closet and taken out a bottle of cognac, paused in the act of pouring a generous tot for Nikolai. "A lantern, of all things. You would think he had been provided one."

"They're low on kerosene at the station. That's what he told me." He accepted the glass Enzo handed him and drank deeply.

"Did the postman say anything about the trains?" Laisha asked after a moment. Her fork was stuck into the kirschkranz but she had not tasted the pastry.

"Not much. Oh, you're wondering about Ragoczy's are you? He said that there was a delay at Sauerlach. I wouldn't expect him for another hour or more." He finished off the cognac. "That stirs the blood in my veins again. I felt like a block of wood out there. What about the soup?"

"In good time," Enzo informed him, but had already taken a covered enamel pot from the refrigerator.

"It's amazing the way cold perks up the appetite," Nikolai said, and looked up as the inner door opened again. "The brainy one," he sighed as David Bündnis came into the kitchen.

"I wondered where you were," he said to the four gathered there. "I looked in the library . . ."

"Is it time for my lesson?" Laisha had at last begun to eat the pastry, and there were flakes of powdered sugar at the corners of her mouth.

"Yes. We can delay until you're finished with the treat," he said with a resigned sigh. "Have you prepared today?"

"Naturally," she said through a forkful of kirschkranz.

"I want to give your guardian a favorable report when he returns," the tutor went on with a critical edge to his voice.

Laisha looked across the room at Bündnis and chewed the last of her pastry thoughtfully. "Herr Bündnis, I am prepared for my lesson. You admit yourself that most of the time I am." She got off the stool. "I will want to wash my hands, and then I will come to the library." No one spoke until she had left the kitchen and Bündnis had followed her, closing the door.

"Must be a strange life for her," Nikolai mused a few minutes later. "Orphaned, living in a foreign country in a houseful of men. A pity that the Count isn't married. It might be easier going for her."

Roger shrugged. "We tried a housekeeper for a year, shortly after we came here, but there was too much talk. She did not want to stay and Laisha wanted the woman gone." He went and picked up Nikolai's coat and hung it on a peg next to the door. "I have a few tasks to attend to." He started toward the hall door when Enzo called.

"What time is dinner? No one has told me." With one exasperated gesture he indicated his predicament.

"Shall we say eight-thirty? If that is reasonable. I will provide my own meat and the Graf—"

"Will fend for himself. Why does he keep a cook when he does not eat? He must eat. What is this privacy he insists on." He shook his head. "No, don't bother to tell me again. I don't know why his studies require this of him, but so be it." He gave his attention to Nikolai, who was eagerly waiting for a generous bowl of the soup that was heating on the stove.

Roger left the kitchen and went toward Ragoczy's private quarters. He was aware of the oncoming dark and the relentless storm, but this did not worry him unduly. He was more concerned with the tempers of the household. This afternoon was not the first time David Bündnis had snapped at Laisha, nor the first time Enzo and Nikolai had exchanged sharp words. So far nothing had come of it, but it could not continue without difficulties arising between the two men. Ragoczy had warned him of the eventuality, and at the time Roger had shrugged it off. Now he saw that his master was right, and would have to decide what was to be done.

In Ragoczy's study, he busied himself with filing, pausing once or twice to read through the reports he handled. He frowned at the ranting pages of the *Völkischer Beobachter*, which were kept with less radical papers. Two years ago the paper had been nearly bankrupt and the leadership was confined to the smallest and most discontented minorities in Bayern. Now it was fairly prosperous, with an expanding appeal. There were a few copies of the old *Berliner Morgenblatt*, and he glanced through them, remembering the years spent there just after the Zollverein began. So engrossed was he that he did not hear the door to the laboratory open and the soft, firm footfall behind him.

"Interesting?" Ragoczy asked, so close to him that Roger nearly jumped.

"It must be," he said as he closed the old newspapers. "I didn't know you were here."

"Neither does anyone else. I came in through my private quarters." He sat down in the Turkish leather chair. His dark, loose curls were damp but otherwise his appearance was entirely correct, from his black woolen suit to the fine white silk of his shirt and properly knotted tie. His collar was soft, held by a silver stay, and the points were slightly rounded. "I have had a most intriguing six days, old friend, and I do not say 'intrigue' lightly."

"At Berlin?" He finished putting the newspapers away and closed the large file drawer. "Or Essen."

"Both, but Berlin was particularly . . . provoking." He rested his elbows on the arms of the chair and tapped his fingertips together. "I wish now I had not agreed to the six-year project with Professor Riemen, or that we were not so involved with it. How inconvenient our success is."

Roger had known Ragoczy long enough that he said nothing.

"My departure now would cause comment, and the work would be compromised. If we remain, there are risks. I thought as the train sat on the tracks at Sauerlach that it might be best to send you and Laisha to Paris, away from this place." He spoke easily enough and his beautiful voice was light, but there was pain in his dark eyes.

"Laisha would not want that," Roger said. "She was distressed because you were late this afternoon. For that matter, she does not know you are back. It would not be a kindness, my master, to send her away from you."

Ragoczy managed a brief, wry smile. "I believe you, because I want to. Where is she? Perhaps I had better inform her of my return." He had started to rise, but Roger's words stopped him.

"She's in the library with Bündnis, doing geography lessons."

"With Bündnis?" Ragoczy repeated. He settled back in the chair. "That is somewhat awkward." There was a steely quality in his tone as he went on. "That was one of the interesting things I discovered while I was in Berlin. Those Prussians are so jealous of Bavaire that they occasionally speak out of turn." Without any comment, Ragoczy switched from French, which he had been using, to Latin. "At one of those endless formal receptions, I happened to . . . shall we say overhear? a conversation that disturbed me, and a bit later, when there had been a good deal more champagne served, one of the men who had been in on the earlier conversation began to talk, rather belligerently, with me. His name, as I recall, was Emil Gansser. Very properly dressed, connected with the Junkers as well as most of the commercial concerns in the north, I gather. He gave me something of a harangue on the perils of the modern world. German nationalism was one of his themes. He has little good to say for Communists, the French, the Jews, or any foreigner. Not unlike what has been coming from most of the radical groups in München, of course, but this man is not a street-corner agitator, or an ex-soldier playing at war. He is powerful, and a great many men in authority listen to him."

"But as long as Bavaria and Prussia are at odds . . ." Roger began.

"They are all worried about the inflation. Everyone was talking about it, making brittle jokes." He paused. "Herr Doktor Gansser let something slip. He warned me that I had better be very careful, because they were watching me. Later he told me that I should not take his remarks seriously. He was so insistent that he had meant nothing by them that I became concerned." He got out of his chair and strode the length of the room. "I have done a little investigating these last two days, and what I learned has . . . displeased me." He stopped by the tall, narrow window and stared out into the dusk and the snow. "It seems that Gansser's lapse was no more than the truth. There have been reports sent quite regularly from this Schloss to certain political gentlemen. It will not continue."

"If you dismiss the . . . tutor?" Roger inquired.

"Doubtless I will have a reason, one which they cannot dispute and which will make sense to them." He came away from the window. "Will that bother Laisha very much, do you think?"

"She does not have any marked affection for Bündnis," Roger said after giving the question his consideration. "If someone more . . . encouraging were to take his place, she would not object too much."

"I had hoped that would be your opinion." He thrust his small, beautiful hands into his pockets. "I have had spies enough around me that by now I should be used to it and think of them as no greater pests than ants or flies. But I've never learned to do this. And that a spy should teach my child . . . !" This last was in a language that was ancient when Rome was a village on the Tiber. It revealed more than anything else about him how great was his distress.

"My master—" Roger exclaimed.

"A moment, old friend," Ragoczy said quietly, and after the better part of a minute, said in French, "It has haunted me, that thought. Of the three of them, Bündnis seemed the safest. What was wrong with me then, that I erred so?"

"And if the others were also sent?" Roger asked. "You might have had no choice that would have been better."

Ragoczy gave this his consideration. "It may be. If this group is as pervasive as the hints indicate, that may have been their intention all along. And Vögel. What of him, I wonder?" He shook his head. "Laisha must not know about this. I will not have her made a pawn. Bündnis and those men behind him may think her that, but they are wrong." Once more he paused. "The time is so short. It was yesterday I found her in that chicken coop. Now look at her. She will be grown and gone in the course of an afternoon, I think. To have something so petty, so foolish as *this* come near her—by all the forgotten gods, Roger—sickens me. There is suffering enough in this world without this cynical exploitation."

"Yet she will have to discover it sometime, my master. Otherwise she will be unarmed in a dangerous world. You say that she will be grown soon. It's true enough, and in that little time, she must learn a great deal." Roger watched Ragoczy and saw the tired nod he gave.

"Do all fathers feel this way? Or is it that I have come to it . . . shall we say late in . . . life?" He touched his forehead, then let his hand drop. "I doubt she could be more my child if my seed had started her."

Roger was taken aback, but his expression changed swiftly. He had never heard Ragoczy, in all the time they had been man and manservant, say such a thing.

"Don't be alarmed," Ragoczy told him, self-mockery twisting his mouth. "I'm not becoming dissatisfied with my lot at this late date. There was one time in Thebes, long before you knew me, when I think I was mad because nothing I tried enabled me to take a woman as other men. That was before I discovered what it was to love a woman, love instead of take." He raised his head. "That's not important; it's long past. Though I do wonder now, what kind of father I might have been."

"You are the best father for Laisha Vlassevna," Roger said. "I have been thinking of my own children, my son who died of tetanus and my daughters who were alive when I was sent to Rome. I was a good father for my boy and one of my daughters, I think. But the other girl, Mila, I could not fathom her at all, and I know I did many things that were unwise, and yet I could find nothing else to do. She drew away from me and I have never known why." He cleared his throat. "It was so long ago, but I still remember."

"Listen to us," Ragoczy said with an effort to take off the melancholy that threatened to possess him. "We're like gray-beards sitting in the sun, reminiscing about our youth. I must go deal with Bündnis, which will make me a far better father than standing here debating with you, old friend. I recall when I first engaged Bündnis that I was concerned, but months went by, and there were other matters to occupy my attention, and I did not *look*; I did not *see*. My blindness . . . You are good to bear with me, Roger." He touched his tie once, as if assuring himself that he was at his most impressive, and started toward the door. He paused on the way. "I must go to Bad Wiessee before too much time passes. When the storm is over, there will be one or two women who will enjoy a holiday interlude, and I . . ." He looked down. "I wish that Madelaine . . . But that's useless." He opened the door and strode off down the hall.

Laisha was sketching the out line of the old Austro-Hungarian Empire when she looked up sharply, the point of her pencil poking through the paper in the region of Bohemia. "He's here!" she cried out over David Bündnis' reprimand, and ran toward the library door. "Papa!" she called happily before the door opened.

"Yes," Ragoczy said as he stepped into the room. "I've finally returned. I spent a good portion of the afternoon sitting in a train going nowhere." He hugged her as she hurtled into his arms, thinking inconsequently that at the rate she was growing, she might well turn out to be as tall as he. "How have you been, my child?"

"Bored!" she declared roundly. "It's been snowing, I can't take my horse out, it's too deep for the automobiles to drive in and Nikolai says that the sleigh needs repairs. So I have been sitting indoors and reading until nothing makes sense. I practiced the viola, but it's no fun when you don't play with me. I've learned another Satie piece on the piano, which no one here wants to listen to anymore. Herr Bündnis keeps saying that I am wasting a great opportunity."

"No doubt," Ragoczy said rather dryly as he glanced toward the tutor. What a shy, unassuming man he was! What a superb disguise it was! "Guten Abend, Herr Bündnis, I hope I see you well?"

"Quite well, Herr Graf." Bündnis, as always, managed to convey disapproval of any display of affection.

"I am aware that you're at lessons just now, but perhaps you would be willing to interrupt your instruction long enough to have a word or two with me?" His manner was as politely urbane as ever; only the glitter at the back of his dark eyes mirrored his true emotions.

Bündnis hesitated for an instant, then smiled. "Of course, Herr Graf. It would be my pleasure."

"Indeed." He stood back from Laisha. "Will you give me ten minutes with your tutor, my child? And when you are finished with your lessons, we'll play duets for an hour, if you would like."

She gave a kind of skip and grinned at him. "Lots of Mozart and Ravel," she said promptly. "I get to choose them."

"Of course," he promised her. "You may return in ten minutes." His eyes followed her as she left the library.

"May I be permitted to know if I have offended you in some way, Herr Graf?" the tutor asked in his most decorous tone.

"Offended me?" Ragoczy inquired as he turned toward Bündnis, and for an instant there was something in his face that frightened the tutor. It was gone at once and Bündnis wondered if he should credit it to nerves. "What would make you think that, Herr Bündnis?"

"Why . . . nothing. That is why I asked." His recovery from his blunder left him edgy. His Adam's apple bobbed against his old-fashioned stiff collar.

"I see." Ragoczy came across the library and took a seat at the end of the table. It was the only chair with arms and a high, upholstered back, other than the two lounging chairs by the fire. "I have been thinking, Herr Bündnis. I am somewhat concerned about my . . . ward. She is, as you doubtless have noticed, growing up. I would estimate her age to be about eleven now, and that is something of a difficult time for girls, is it not?" His slight but commanding hauteur kept David Bündnis from speaking. "This concerns me a great deal, as well it might. She is in a household of males, and while I do not fear for her in that regard, I know that she would benefit from the presence of women. She will want to learn from them, not simply the academic subjects that are necessary, but social matters, the courtesies and graces that will make her young womanhood more enjoyable to her."

"Herr Graf, I don't . . ." As quickly as his objection came to his lips, it faded under Ragoczy's penetrating gaze.

"At first I considered bringing in a woman tutor to work with you," Ragoczy went on as if he had not heard Bündnis. "But that has been tried once, and as you recall, it did not answer. I have decided, therefore, to engage two female tutors for Laisha. They will give her the instruction she requires and aid her in learning all those things a young woman must know. They will also act as each other's chaperons, and that will quiet all but the most egregious gossip." He leaned a little forward in the chair. "I will, of course, provide you with references and a reasonable bonus for your diligence. Shall we say about thirty days from today your employment here will be ended?"

"Herr Graf, this is absurd," Bündnis declared when he found his voice.

"How is it absurd, Herr Bündnis?" Ragoczy inquired, his fine brows raising.

"Well, she is doing so well just now . . ." Bündnis said, and it sounded weak, even to himself. "It might set her back to have new teachers who demand so many new things of her. She is a very intelligent child, as you are aware, but because of her unique problems, she could find a change disorienting, and it would have a bad effect on her work." His voice was slightly shrill. "If I were to remain here for a time, the transfer would be more easily made, I think. Laisha would be prepared for her new tutors and—"

"Yes, I did think of that myself," Ragoczy said, cutting off Bündnis' babbling. "And there is something in what you say. Nevertheless, I believe that this way is the more reasonable. Laisha will have a short holiday. We may travel a bit if the weather is improved. That will provide her the transition without having to deal with tutors who may, because of their habits, be at cross-purposes. That would be far more disruptive to Laisha than a complete change of teachers."

David Bündnis sat quite still for a moment, then said, "You are foreign, Herr Graf, and for that reason you may find yourself imposed upon. If you are determined on this course, I trust you will let me recommend a proper agency to contact for qualified tutors?"

Ragoczy's smile was not at all cordial. "How kind of you, Herr Bündnis, but I will decline your offer. I believe that it will be best if I select the tutors for Laisha. I have associates in Switzerland and Denmark who will begin to investigate for me."

"Switzerland and Denmark?" Bündnis said, appalled. "How will such teaching help her? This is Deutschland—"

"Ah, but as you have pointed out, I am a foreigner, as is my . . . ward. I have found it necessary to be familiar with other peoples and other societies in my life, and it is likely that Laisha will face the same requirements. It is time that she develop a little broader view, don't you think?" His lip turned sardonically.

Once again Bündnis floundered, attempting to keep some little influence with this disturbing man. "No doubt you're right. But as Schloss Saint-Germain is her home, it is appropriate for her first instruction to be Auf Deutsch. The rest will come later."

"Herr Bündnis, Schloss Saint-Germain is not my only holding. I have dwellings in other countries, and it may become necessary for us to live elsewhere—it is a risk that all foreigners encounter, is it not?" He spoke coolly, logically, and his eyes never left Bündnis'. "I am not an unreasonable man, Herr Bündnis, and I am aware that money is becoming difficult to come by, with inflation eating up what little gain there is. You will not be asked to put yourself at a serious disadvantage. I have said I will provide you a bonus, and I assure you now that it will not be paltry. A man of your ability should have no difficulty, even in these uncertain times, in finding some employment that is to your satisfaction." He rose, looking down at David Bündnis. "You would be wise to accept this. I will not change my mind."

"It's not my place to argue with an employer," the tutor said through closed teeth.

"I see it's not," Ragoczy responded with infuriating affability. "I will be pleased to be kept abreast of your plans, Herr Bündnis, so that you need not be overly inconvenienced by this change." He went to the door and was about to leave the library when David Bündnis said, "I don't think this decision is very wise, Herr Graf."

"Don't you." Ragoczy closed the door firmly and went off toward the music room.

Text of a letter from Franchot Ragoczy to Simeon Schnaubel.

*Schloss Saint-Germain*
*Schliersee, Bavaria*
*April 22, 1922*

*Dear Simeon;*

*Your letter arrived yesterday, a very welcome and un-
expected pleasure. I am sure that your business with
your cousin will prosper, what with your experience here
and his American training.*

*It is good to know that your children like Chicago, and
that you have been able to begin to establish yourself there
already. I have never seen that city, but from your description of the lake and the surrounding countryside, it
must be a pleasant place.*

*How unfortunate that Hedda has not recovered from
her shock. I fully sympathize with you, and wish that I
could disagree with your decision, but I cannot. A child
with episodes such as you describe must receive more care
than you can provide. You say that a home nurse has not
been the answer; you would not wish to harm her or be
separated from her, but if she has attacked Emmerich
twice, then you are wise to follow the suggestions of the
physicians and the alienist you mention. After such tragedy, this must add to your sorrow, and doubtless your
grief will not fade quickly. To say that I share your
feelings would be presumptuous of me, but I do assure
you that I understand your anguish, perhaps more than
you know.*

*The sale of your house has been completed, but with the
current rate of inflation you will realize less than you
ought from the transaction. I have taken the liberty of
sending the money through Switzerland rather than Germany so that as much of the value as possible may be
preserved. I had hoped to do better for you, but it was not*

possible. So far the inflation has been held a bit in check, but there are signs that these devices will not work long. I would suggest if it is within your ability to do so, that you remove all monies you still have invested here in Germany and either purchase items of value, such as antiques or jewels or gold, or convert the sums into dollars or pounds. It is quite likely that you will lose your funds entirely if you do not do so.

Laisha is doing quite well, and I thank you for remembering her. She is determined to master the viola and has begun to make a fairly acceptable sound on the instrument. She tells me that I learned to play so long ago that I have forgotten how difficult it is to begin, and she is undoubtedly right. Her new tutors appear to be doing well with her and she tells me that she likes them, but that may change as time goes by. Naturally, I am pleased with her progress; the quickness of her mind is a constant source of delight and pride to me.

Do keep me informed of your wishes regarding your investments, and more, of how you go on in the New World. I confess that I miss the nearness of you and your family, and I deplore more than I can say the reason for your leaving.

Remember me to your family, and be assured that I will do all that I can to guard your interests here.

Most sincerely,
Franchot Ragoczy
*his seal, the eclipse*

# PART III

Graf Franchot
Ragoczy

von Schloss
Saint-Germain

Text of a letter from Elsebin Arrild to Franchot Ragoczy.

*March 3, 1924*

*My dear Gráf Ragoczy:*

*I am sure that my colleague Rosel Speits will be in accordance with me in most of my comments regarding our pupil, Laisha Vlassevna, but I urge you to consult with her as well as myself so that you will be perfectly satisfied with our evaluation.*

*First, the progress Laisha has made in the past year in languages is most encouraging. Her French is quite good, her Italian a little less so, but adequate, her English is weaker, due to difficulties with pronunciation rather than any basic misunderstanding of the tongue. Her Latin is progressing, but she is not much interested in that language except in its relation to her interests in botany and history. It is my recommendation that we should not place too much emphasis on Latin until her desire to know it is somewhat stronger. If you disagree, I will, of course, stress that study, but I see very little purpose being served by such a method.*

*Mathematics, at which she has long excelled, now seems not to interest her with the same degree that she was at this time last year. In the two years she has been my pupil, I have noticed that her mathematical concepts have been more active in the study of music than in the matter of abstract mathematics. Perhaps you would not object to my adapting our studies to a more musical structure, for that way I know that her interest will continue to be piqued.*

*In the area of music she has made a good deal of effort, and this is shown in her continually-developing abilities with piano and strings. She has recently improved on the violin so that she plays it almost as well as she plays viola. It may be that she will want to study one of the woodwinds as well, or at least she says that now. If she is still so inclined in six months, I would advise you to provide her with instruction on the instrument of her choice.*

*I believe I have remarked to you before on the need for a more active social life for Laisha. She is well-behaved and has a pleasant manner about her which is sure to make her liked, but she has had little opportunity to try her wings and I fear that in time this will become a disadvantage, and she will become one of those quiet young women, who, although they have a great deal to offer, remain eclipsed by the more vivacious damsels who have had more opportunity to be with others. You have discussed the various circumstances that have led to her withdrawn life, and to a great degree I am sympathetic, and for the first year I was with her, I agreed with you completely. It is most awkward that she should have so little memory of her past, for it must lead to uneasy moments in company. Of late I have encouraged her to say that she is Russian and that she would prefer not to discuss her earlier life. The failing in that is that it may be assumed that she is moving in a higher social rank than the one she was born to, but her bearing, her appearance and the introspective charm she has achieved will serve her in good stead there. Her intensity is another matter, and one that might be less well-understood than her reticence. You have said before that those who love her will admire and encourage her intensity, and in a sense you are entirely correct. However, it has been my experience that young women with such disconcerting airs do not do well. You have told me that it is not necessary for her to worry about the wealth of the husband she will eventually have, but it would be most unfortunate for her to be deprived of an advantageous match because a man was put off by her forthrightness and somewhat fierce demeanor. I am aware that many young German men are enthused over Vikings and Valkyries, but that does not mean that they would be happy with one in the drawing room. You have said that it is many years until Laisha must concern herself with a husband, but you forget that she has already reached the age, according to your estimate, of thirteen. In a year or two she may well be going to dancing parties, for girls do that earlier now than when I was young. At sixteen, if she is like her contemporaries, she will be entering an active social life, and unless there are some changes, she will not be prepared for it.*

*I am aware that now Laisha says she would prefer a more academic life than the majority of girls have, but it is easy for her to say this now. In a year or two, she may well change her mind, and it will not be easy for her to acquire in a year the skills other girls have been learning for a decade. Of course it is laudable that she wishes to continue her studies, and her devotion to music is remarkable, but you must be aware that with girls of this age, such things often become secondary or tertiary once they have discovered the male of the species. In one sense, she already has, through living in this household, but a guardian and servants are not quite the same thing as a handsome boy not much older than she is.*

*Rosel Speits and I disagree over this point, incidentally. It is her contention that Laisha should be allowed to choose for herself, and to a point I concur, but I know that there are demands that will be made of this child before much longer and it is best if she is prepared to meet them. A girl who can discuss only music and botany is not much use at a party. Miss Speits has said that there are many young men who would be delighted for such conversation, but you will agree that if Laisha is excluded from various occasions, she will not have the chance to discover that sort of young man for herself.*

*I had not intended this to be so much devoted to Laisha's social developments. That I have done so indicates how much the matter is on my mind. It also shows, I think, how well Laisha has done with her studies, for if these were faltering, I would not be so concerned with these other matters.*

*Of course, I am at your disposal to discuss these or any other aspects of your ward's education.*

*Respectfully,*
*Elsebin Arrild*

## 1

When the final salute was fired, French soldiers held the rifles, but it was the only sour note in Jürgen Baldemar Ostneige's funeral. The churchyard of St. Sixtus at Schliersee was satisfactorily full, many of the men attending defiantly in uniforms from the Great War. It was a sunny May afternoon, warm enough for topcoats to be left at home and bright enough to make the dark clothes of those gathered around the grave seem incongruous.

The minister intoned the familiar graveside words in a monotonous drone when the guns had been fired. Few of the mourners paid him much attention.

"It's a damned insult, I say," Konrad Natter whispered to Maximillian Altbrunnen as the ritual handful of earth was tossed on Jürgen's coffin. "French soldiers here, when it was the French who made an invalid of him."

"It was the French or nothing," Maximillian hissed back. "My sister thought this would be better."

"Women!" Natter said quietly. "She should have come to me. I could have arranged something. There are ways to deal with these situations. Why didn't you suggest it?"

"Because she didn't ask me," Maximillian muttered, and moved a step or two away from Natter.

Gudrun, flanked by Walther Stoff and Klaus Ostneige, Jürgen's imposing older brother, watched the coffin from the shadow of her black hat and veil. Her blue eyes were dry, as they had been since Walther had come in tears to her room in the first flush of morning to tell her that her husband was dead. Of course Jürgen was dead, she thought. He had been dead for years, and this was the first time the rest of them had noticed it. She went through the motions of grief with no more feeling than she might have had for a lost piece of jewelry.

Then most of it was over and the gathering around the grave broke up, bits of darkness moving into the blooming sunlight. Gudrun let Maximillian guide her back to the waiting Lancia Lambda with black crepe streamers obscuring its light fawn color. Behind her, Klaus was speaking to one or two of the officers attending the funeral, his voice rough with impatience.

"This is not the time, Natter, nor the place. I will call on you before I go back to Hamburg. This latest French ploy is an outrage, but this is not the place or setting to discuss it." Klaus regarded Natter closely for a moment, his cold eyes flickering with some remote recognition.

"I will look forward to it. A pity about your brother. A great loss." Natter said the words automatically, with little feeling in them. "I understand you are a friend of Rudolph von Sebottendorff."

"Yes. It is a great honor." Klaus gave him a curt nod and hastened after Gudrun as he saw Maximillian hold the door of the Lancia for her.

"Are you all right?" Maximillian asked in an undervoice.

"I am very well, thank you," she said, as she had been saying since she left Wolkighügel earlier that day. "I'm . . . tired."

"Do you still want to be alone, or should I come back with you?" He looked uneasy as he asked this, and his glance strayed to Konrad Natter and Helmut Rauch, who waited by the Mercedes.

"You needn't come back. I will put myself in Otto's care and Frau Bürste will look after me once I get home." She looked over the people filing past her automobile and felt empty. She had nothing to say to any of them, and had no interest in their company or their sympathy. "I need time to myself, Maxl."

"Selbstverständlich. I won't come along then. Don't worry about me—I'll take care of myself." He closed the door to the passenger compartment and waited until Otto climbed into the driver's seat. "Take care of her, Otto."

Otto mumbled a few words as he started the automobile. He did not know what to say to Maxl, his favorite, for this behavior. It was most improper for Gudrun to be left alone, and for her own brother to go off . . . ! He shook his head as he put the Lancia into gear with a jerk. As they drove out of the churchyard, he turned briefly to Gudrun to say, "Do not be concerned, Rudi, I will look after you."

"Thank you, Otto. I know you will." Her voice lacked inflection and her eyes were staring without seeing.

Behind them, Walther's old Opel sputtered into movement, following them.

It was a short, familiar drive to Wolkighügel, accomplished

in silence. As Otto drove through the gates, he saw that there was another automobile parked, waiting. He leaned backward and gave Gudrun a warning. "I'm afraid there will be visitors, Rudi, no matter what was said earlier."

"Yes, I see," she responded listlessly. Her eyes ached and she felt half-drowned, but it was not appropriate for her to receive guests, no matter how unwelcome, in that manner, so she touched her hat to be certain it was in place and pulled on her black gloves. "Do you recognize the automobile?"

"No. It looks new." He frowned at the unknown vehicle and added as he noticed the emblem, "It's French."

Gudrun was mildly surprised. She got out of the Lancia before Otto could come and hold the door for her. She held her purse in her left hand, thinking that she would have to be prepared to greet whoever had arrived. At the door of her own home she paused and thought that perhaps she should knock, but after a moment she found the courage to open the door.

"A French Citroën," Otto whispered as he came up behind her. "It's one of those new ones, the B2. What do the French want with us?"

"I will ask," Gudrun said, trying to think where her visitors might be. She was standing undecided when Frau Bürste hurried out of the smaller drawing room, a look of consternation on her wide face. "Frau Bürste? What is it?"

"French inspectors," she said in an undervoice. "Two of them."

"French inspectors? What do they want here, and today?" Her puzzlement was oddly welcome to her, giving her something to deal with other than her husband's death. "They're in the little drawing room?"

"Yes. I've offered them wine, which they've refused. I don't know . . ." The worried sound of her words was most unlike her and she made a visible effort to control herself. "I will provide whatever refreshment you wish, Frau Ostneige. Cold meats, pickles, and three kinds of bread would be the easiest to prepare."

"Do that then, and I will expect you to serve it in . . . fifteen minutes?" She heard another automobile drive up as she spoke and recognized the rattle of Walther's Opel. Quickly she added, "Walther is here. It might be best if he does not deal with the French. His sentiments are extreme where they are concerned."

"I'll take care of that, Frau Ostneige," Frau Bürste assured her as she went toward the side door Walther habitually used.

There was no reason to procrastinate further, Gudrun told herself firmly. She breathed deeply and licked her lips once; it was a nervous habit she had had since childhood. With measured steps she went to the smaller drawing room.

The two men rose as she entered the room, and the older of them bowed slightly. "Frau Ostneige?" he inquired in his French-softened German. "I am sorry we must disturb you at this terrible time. We would not do it if it were not of the utmost importance."

"I am afraid you have the advantage of me, Captain," she said, glancing at his uniform. "May I have the pleasure of knowing your name?"

"I am Blaisot Juenecouer. My companion is Lieutenant Odon Simault. You cannot know how sad it makes us to have to come to you at this tragic time, but sadly, it is not our place to defy our orders." He gave her a curious stare, as if attempting to see her face through her veil. "You understand this, I hope."

"You are both officers," she responded, "and in Deutschland, this would indicate that you are gentlemen as well. My husband was a military man, as you undoubtedly know, and he was an honorable man." She crossed the room to one of the three small settees in the room and sank down upon it. "It has been quite a difficult day for me, gentlemen, and I would appreciate knowing what brings you here. From what you imply it is urgent."

"Yes," Lieutenant Simault said in a voice startlingly deep. "We would have called later if it were not the case."

"That's kind," Gudrun said automatically, finding the words meaningless. She watched the two men shuffle their feet slightly and avoid looking at her. Finally she asked, "Will you tell me why this was so urgent?"

"Naturally. It is difficult to know just where to begin," Juenecouer declared, and steeled himself for his explanation. "You are aware that by the terms of the Treaty of Versailles the possession of arms is forbidden here? We have right of inspection, so that there can be no abuses of this provision."

"Yes, I know of the terms of the Treaty of Versailles," she said quietly. "The insane inflation of last year was in part the result of that Treaty. With reparation payments what they were, and the economy exhausted . . . But you are not here to discuss the monetary situation. You're worried about arms."

"With good cause," Simault muttered, but Juenecouer shook his head.

"We have tried to be diligent, and for that we have made ourselves odious. But the Treaty must be upheld, Madame. You know that it must. And for that reason, we are investigating reports that there are those with a cache of weapons here, men who practice military maneuvers with their hoarded weapons, men who, while not in the army itself, nevertheless are aided by men in the army, who have the support of Bavarian regiments." His words came breathlessly as he spoke, as if he anticipated these armed men to swarm down out of the mountains while he talked.

"And you think to find the weapons here?" Gudrun stifled a quick explosion of laughter. "My good officers, you may feel free to search anywhere you like at Wolkighügel if it will relieve your minds. I will admit that there is an illegal rifle in the stable. We have kept it for dealing with animal pests, and last year, when bushel baskets of currency were needed to buy a pound of butter, one of my servants shot two deer so that there would be meat in the larder. That was illegal, as well as having the rifle. If that proves me to be dangerous, well . . ." She lifted her hands and dropped them into her lap.

Simault glared at her suspiciously, but Juenecouer sighed expressively. "Madame Ostneige, your candor is much appreciated, and lamentably rare. It is not our intention to deprive you of the rifle you have, although we must report its existence for a determination if it is permissible for you to keep it. That is out of our hands. The rest . . ." He began to pace the room now, and a little of his sympathetic manner deserted him. "We will not tolerate abuses of the Treaty. There are those who wish to make war again, and we know that they train here in these mountains. Our aeroplanes have occasionally seen squads of men in fields being trained for war, men not in the uniform of your army, in places where there has been no authorization for such activities. Many of those locations are near you. It may be that in the last year you have seen such activity?"

So that was the actual thrust of the inquiry, Gudrun realized. She responded at once. "You may have heard that my husband was an invalid. I did not get about much while he was bedridden. If there are such groups, I have not seen them."

"Or heard of them?" Simault put in quickly.

This time Gudrun paused, trying to remember a fleeting comment she had heard Maximillian make several months ago.

"I am not certain, but I think I heard mention of troops of some sort, but I recall nothing definite."

"Have you ever heard mention of Kurt Lüdecke? Or the Sturmalteilung?" Now the question was rapped out, without the pretense of courtesy.

"I don't think so. The Sturmalteilung are the troops you mentioned?" The name was not one she knew, but there was an association in her mind. "I recall that one of my neighbors discussed the SA with my brother last year. I paid very little attention, and my brother did not mention it to me. If these are the same troops, that is the extent of my knowledge of them." She felt uneasy answering the question and volunteering this information, but she was too worn to question or resist them. If she told them what she knew, they would go away and she would have time to herself at last.

"Have you ever met General von Lossow?" Simault demanded of her.

"My husband was not of his rank," Gudrun replied softly. "I am afraid that the Commander-in-Chief of the Army in Bayern is a more exalted person than those he knew. My father knew von Lossow slightly, but that was years ago, before the Great War."

"And what of your brother?" Juenecouer asked. He did not press her as Simault did, but both men were implacable in their insistence.

"I don't know all my brother's friends, but he has never been much taken up with soldiers of any rank. Military life does not appeal to him." Her voice faded to little more than a whisper.

"That's a rarity in a German," Juenecouer said to Simault in French, and neither man noticed that Gudrun understood them.

At that moment there was a rap on the door and then Frau Bürste entered carrying a large tray of cold meats and pickles. "I will bring the bread and butter in a moment, Frau Ostneige," she said as she bustled over to the side table and set down her burden. "Also, if the gentlemen will tell me what they prefer to drink. We haven't got coffee, with the price still as high as it is, but there is wine and beer, and I have some English tea."

Both Frenchmen stared at Frau Bürste, and then Juenecouer spoke to Gudrun. "This is not necessary, Madame."

"It certainly is. I was taught as a child that any visitor was entitled to proper hospitality. If you will tell Frau Bürste what you prefer to drink, she will bring it to you at once."

The men exchanged glances. "The beer would be best," Juenecouer said for both of them. "It is not entirely correct of us to accept this, but if it is as you say, and you believe that you must . . ." He stared at the thin-sliced meats on the tray. There was smoked ham and chicken breast, two kinds of cold würst, roast beef, and pickled fish, as well as four small cold chops of venison. Sour cherries and vegetable pickles were set in small dishes around the meats, and a pot of mustard completed the spread.

Frau Bürste bustled out of the room, trying to smile at Gudrun as she went.

"You do not appear to have done badly for yourself of late, Frau Ostneige," Simault said with a meaningful smile.

"I have recently reduced my household yet again," Gudrun said tightly, "and for that reason, I have been able to practice a degree of economy. It means that those who work here must be more devoted and industrious, and so far they have been willing to accommodate me." This was not strictly true; with the best will in the world, Otto was feeling his age and could no longer keep up the tasks he had willingly undertaken. She caught her lower lip with her teeth. "If there is inflation again, then I may well have to give up my home." To her amazement, her voice caught and she had to breathe deeply to keep from crying.

"But you survived the inflation of last year. You have just said so." Simault folded his arms, regarding her closely.

"I sold most of my jewels to do so," she said quietly, "and three of my household were willing to stay and work merely for the roof over their heads and meals. We dug up half of the flowers and grew vegetables, and we sold all but one of the horses to the butcher." She had not considered how horrifying it had been: at the time, her concern was to get through it with as much of her world intact as possible. Now, speaking to the officious Frenchmen, she was aghast that she had been willing to part with her jewels and horses, had dug in the ground like a peasant to find the new potatoes.

"In France, during the war, women ground the limbs of trees to make bread for their families. They didn't have jewels or horses to sell because the Boche took them away. And often there was no roof over their heads." Simault lashed out at her and his face dared her to attempt to justify herself.

"I am sorry for that. I am sorry for all those who suffered in the war. I have been reminded of its brutality every day since they brought my husband back to me, his body wasted and his

mind unreachable. His torment ended the day before yesterday, gentlemen, and I have not yet accustomed myself to his
absence." She remembered that Walther had come into the
house shortly after she did, and tried to put him out of her
mind. What would she do with that man, now that Jürgen was
no longer alive? She did not want him here at Wolkighügel any
longer, but she could not bring herself to dismiss the man who
cared so vigilantly for her husband. She gave the Frenchmen a distracted look and said, "I'm sorry. I didn't hear your
last comment. My mind was wandering."

"A convenient excuse," Simault said. "I was telling you that
I was not in the Great War, being too young then to serve,
but I stayed at home and watched my mother starve to death
to keep three children alive."

Gudrun shook her head, unable to comment. She was grateful to Frau Bürste for returning then with a basket of assorted
breads and rolls and a dish of butter curls in one hand, and
two large steins foaming with beer clasped in the other. As
she put these down beside the tray, she looked from one man
to the other. "Will there be anything else?"

"I'm sure this is sufficient," Juenecouer said eagerly as he
reached for one of the plump rolls and pulled it open with his
large square hands.

Simault picked up one of the steins and tasted the contents.
"You have no sense of wines here, but I will allow that your
beer is quite good." He drank once, then set the stein down so
that he could help himself to the cold meats.

"Frau Ostneige," her housekeeper-and-cook said with all the
authority she possessed, "when you have a moment, I must
speak to you in the kitchen." With this announcement, she
bobbed a little curtsy to the men and left the room.

Juenecouer had taken a large mouthful of the sandwich he
had made for himself, and so could not speak at once. "Madame
Ostneige, when do you expect your brother to return?"

"I'm afraid I don't know. I told him I wanted some time to
myself, and so he is apt to stay away for most of the evening,
or the entire night, if he finds himself in congenial company.
I'm afraid he did not tell me where he was going." She was
fairly certain he would be with Helmut Rauch and Konrad
Natter, but she chose not to mention this; she felt she must
hold something back from these men.

"And I suppose you wish we had not come today," Simault
suggested.

"Yes. I wish you had not come at all." She rose from the

settee and went to the door. "I will be back shortly. I have not washed my hands or been to the toilet since the funeral, and I should do these things."

"Of course," Juenecouer said emphatically. "We will not be long with this meal, and then we'll continue our conversation. You haven't a telephone here, have you?"

"No, I haven't. Is there someone you wish to call?" She would take delight in sending them into Hausham to the stationmaster for such a chore.

"No, it is only that if you have one, we would have to ask that you do not use it quite yet." Simault favored her with a nasty grin and went back to slicing the roast beef.

In the hallway, Gudrun found she was trembling. Her temples rang and her neck was stiff from being held erect all day. She glanced toward the hall to the kitchen, wondering if she should consult with Frau Bürste now, or wait until she had relieved herself and taken three aspirin. She had not yet made up her mind when she heard the sound of horse's hooves coming up the drive. It was all she could do to keep from screaming.

Otto came in from the rear of the house. "I'll take care of it, Rudi. Don't you bother with it now." As the horse neared the front entrance, Otto pulled the door wide and placed himself in the middle of it, doing his best to be imposing.

Gudrun had not moved, and now she stared beyond Otto into the full radiance of the sunlight, where a well-conformed gray horse stood as his rider dismounted. A moment later Franchot Ragoczy handed the reins to Otto.

"I won't be long," he promised the servant as he stepped into the entry hall. He was dressed for riding in a claret-colored hacking coat, with buff-colored riding breeches and roll-top pullover. His high boots were fine black leather. In his hand he carried a small wreath of cypress, rue, and white roses.

"You," Gudrun said, taking a step toward him.

"I am sorry I did not come earlier, but yesterday we had French officers inspecting every nook and cranny of Schloss Saint-Germain." He bowed over her hand, brushing it with his lips. "You have my sympathy, Madame. You have come to the end of a long, fruitless ordeal and no doubt having it finished is as difficult to accept as the death of your husband itself." He straightened up. "I've brought this for you."

She took the wreath from him. "How thoughtful. Most of the tributes were at the funeral."

His dark eyes were sad. "My dear, flowers mean nothing to the dead. The tributes should be for the living. Whatever grief your husband knew is over now. You are the one who must live." He added kindly, "It is a little thing."

No one had said that the flowers brought to the church were for her, and for that reason what he told her seemed strangely improper, but she could not find it in herself to reprimand him. "I am grateful, Graf." Impulsively she lifted her veil so that she could see him more clearly. "I thought that since you were not at the funeral, you did not intend to—"

"I never attend funerals, not anymore," he said rather sharply. "I haven't been to one since a much-loved friend of mine died in Florence. That was many years ago." How that city had mourned, he remembered, all draped in red and black for Laurenzo.

"I understand," she said, because she did not.

He seemed to know this. "I have seen too many of those I love die, Madame, and I mark their passage in my heart, not the earth." He bowed again, but did not take her hand. "If there is anything I may do for you, you have only to send word."

"That's very kind." It was her unthinking response, and when she had said it, she was dissatisfied. "I will let you know. At the moment I can't think of anything, but probably I will discover any number of things that I would appreciate your help on."

He stepped back and was about to leave when she called out after him.

"Graf Ragoczy, I don't think I've ever seen you in colors before." It struck her as odd that this, of all times, would be the occasion when he would not dress in black.

"Oh, I have a few things that are not black. In this instance, I chose these garments so that I would not be stopped by the other French inspectors. One of the groups they are looking for apparently wears all black or all brown. It becomes tedious to answer the same questions five or six times in eight kilometers." He shrugged slightly. "This is more convenient, at least for the moment."

She smiled at his explanation, but under the smile there was dread. "You said that there were French inspectors at your Schloss."

"Yes. Why?"

"They are here now. They may not be the same ones, but

two French officers . . ." She gestured vaguely toward the door to the smaller drawing room.

"I see. That is their Citroën in the drive?" He did not expect an answer from her. "It is . . . unfortunate that they could not wait to speak with you."

"They are worried," she said, not quite meeting his dark eyes.

"It doesn't excuse them," he said in a tightened tone. "Would you like me to speak to them? As I am a foreigner, I have a few advantages in dealing with them."

"Danke. No." She would so much rather have said yes.

"If you are certain . . ." He hesitated, offering her the chance to change her mind. "It would please me to do this for you, Madame."

She shook her head more quickly, fearing that if she spoke at all she would weep. What was it about this man that disarmed her so? She ducked her head to him. "I must wash my hands and return to . . ." One hand turned in the direction of the smaller drawing room. "Excuse me."

"Of course. I did not want to intrude." He gave her a slight, curiously majestic bow and turned away from her. He motioned to Otto as he went toward the open front door. As he passed the old servant, he said in an undervoice to him, "Will you let me know if Madame Ostneige requires anything? She may not ask for it, and I would wish to aid her, if she needs aid."

Otto straightened himself. "That is a kindness of you, Herr Graf. I will keep it in mind." He thought as he spoke that it should be Maximillian speaking such words, not this stranger from up the mountain.

"I appreciate that, Otto," Ragoczy said courteously, handing him a Swiss ten-franc coin as a doucement. Then he took the reins and mounted.

"Herr Graf," Otto called out as Ragoczy was about to ride away down the drive. "I have not seen that breed before. What is he?" It had been years since he had had the opportunity, no matter how brief, to discuss horseflesh.

"He's a cross; half Orlov, half Lippizaner. I've been breeding them for a while. They have excellent stamina, good manners, and beautiful gaits. It was good of you to notice him." He kept his seat with the ease of long expert horsemanship. He shifted his weight and the gray bounded forward. As Ragoczy glanced back over his shoulder, he saw Gudrun's pale face watching him from a second-story window.

She did not know why it made her so sad to see him leave, but as she stared out the window, she wanted to fling it wide and shout to him, asking him to come back. But that would not do. She was a respectable widow and there were French officers waiting to speak to her. She had certain obligations to her family and to Jürgen's memory. She drew off her gloves and set them on her dressing table. When she had been young, there had been a chambermaid to tend all her clothes, but now she looked after them herself. Carefully she removed her hat and set it beside the gloves. Her short-cut hair was somewhat disarranged, and she found a comb and set about neatening her coiffure. Her black dress was correct, and she still had a mourning necklace among her few jewels. She had found it yesterday, and she took it now from its velvet-lined case, admiring for a moment the fine matched pearls and carved onyx beads which hung in three long strands from an ornate silver clasp. As she stared into the mirror, she dropped the necklace over her head, regarding the effect critically. It struck the right note, she thought, severe enough but elegant. Unbidden, an image of Graf Ragoczy came to her mind, in his usual garments of black and white. His appearance was always correct, always concinnous. So she would borrow a page from his book, she thought as she made a minor adjustment in the necklace so that the clasp sat on her left shoulder. The small pearl drops she wore at her ears went well enough with the necklace that she did not bother to change them. From one of the drawers she took a silk shawl and draped it around her shoulders, liking the shimmer of the steel gray against the black wool. Her only concern was that it might seem to the Frenchmen that she was a bit too well-turned-out for a woman who had been hard-pressed by the recent monetary debacle. It would not be correct to apply cosmetics to her face now, but she could not resist wishing that she might rouge her cheeks and lips and put a hint of blue on her eyelids. That would be for later, she promised herself, and went out of her room toward the bathroom at the end of the hall.

When she came back downstairs ten minutes later, she found Otto waiting for her in the entry hall. "Is something the matter?"

"Not precisely. I was worried about you, Rudi." His old eyes were not as alert as they had been, and she could see that there was a tremor in his hands. "You need looking after, and there is no one to do it."

"There's Ragoczy," she pointed out, laughing a bit.

Otto let out a long, exasperated breath. "A foreigner, Rudi. He isn't one of us. You should not need to seek among foreigners for assistance."

"But since no one else is willing, let's be satisfied with him." She felt a moment of unexplained excitement possess her; then she exerted herself and put such nonsense out of her mind. "The Frenchmen?"

"Still in the smaller drawing room. They asked for a second stein of beer." He planted his hands on his hips. "They say that there is nothing to compare with French wines, but they drink our beer willingly enough."

"Which Frau Bürste provided?" she asked a bit anxiously. It would be difficult if they had been refused this privilege.

"Natürlich. I was attending to guests at Wolkighügel before you were in long skirts, my girl, and I'll thank you to remember it." Otto's bluster was meant in play, and for that reason, he made a great show of his indignation in the hope that Gudrun would laugh.

"Don't hector me, Otto," Gudrun said, cutting the old man's performance short. "I am not in any state of mind to enjoy it."

"It was said in jest," he explained helplessly even as he walked beside her to the door to the smaller drawing room. "I did not intend . . ."

"It's all right, Otto," she said, her voice soft with fatigue. "I will deal with these men as best I can, and then perhaps I will have a little time to myself." She realized that she had left the wreath Ragoczy had given her hanging on the door handle to her room. "Would you find the wreath for me? It's upstairs. Put it over the mantel in the dining room. It is appropriate for there, don't you think?"

"Maxl will ask about it," Otto warned.

"Then tell him. It was a generous gift from a neighbor. What can my brother have to say against that?" Without waiting for an answer to her question, she went to deal with Simault and Juenecouer.

She found out that evening, when Maximillian returned, not quite sober, and in a rare mood of belligerence. Upon learning of the French visit, he railed at his sister while she sat self-contained and silent.

"You actually let them roam through this building, looking into closets and drawers, as if we were irresponsible children? You let them do that? Rudi, what was *wrong* with you? Don't you understand anything at all? The French are our sworn enemies. They will use any method they can think of to humiliate us and shame us. You aided them in that when you let them inspect the Schloss. Inspect! You don't know what filth there is in their minds." He roamed about the little salon adjoining the dining room where coffee was served after dinner. As yet the meal had not been eaten, although Frau Bürste had informed Gudrun that it was ready.

"I had no choice in the matter, Maxl," Gudrun said patiently, as she had done three times already. "I am not about to stand in armor at the door and repel them. It would make a great deal more trouble for us than their inspection has done."

"How could it? You let yourself succumb to your fear and permitted them to violate this place and every rule of decency men honor. I suppose that if they had demanded it you would have opened your legs to them, too." As soon as he saw her expression, he knew he had gone too far. "Rudi—"

"That is enough!" she said, getting to her feet. "I have endured my husband's funeral today, and having French officers rummaging through my home, but I will not stand for this treatment from you!" She was astonished at the strength of her anger. "When I returned from the funeral, the Frenchmen were already here. What was I to do—throw them out? Who was to help me? You were gone off with your friends—"

"You said you wanted to be alone," he reminded her petulantly.

"Otto is not one to grapple with visitors, and neither Frau Bürste nor I have any skills in battle. Herr Ragoczy offered to speak to them for me, but I refused. They had already been given my hospitality. I could not alter my position without causing a great deal of awkwardness and suspicion—"

"Ragoczy? When was that impudent foreigner here?" Maximillian's face was flushed and his blond hair hung lankly across his forehead. He brushed it away with his fingers.

"That impudent foreigner came to give me a tribute wreath, which was very kind of him. He offered to help me, if I needed it." She started toward the dining-room door. "Come. Dinner will be cold if we don't sit down soon."

"I'm not finished discussing this with you, Gudrun . . ." Maximillian told her, blocking her way. "I don't like that man coming here."

"And I do," she responded tersely, pushing past him.

He lounged in the door as she took her seat at the head of the table. "Like that, is it? A little soon after Jürgen's demise, don't you think?"

"If accepting the offer of help from a neighbor makes me a

trollop in your eyes, then I suggest that you provide the aid he has offered." Gudrun was holding her emotions in check as she spoke. She took her napkin and spread it meticulously in her lap, then rang the bell beside her carved crystal wineglass. "Sit down, Maxl. We will talk more after dinner if you insist, but I haven't the heart for it now."

Maximillian took the place at the far end of the table, so that his back was to Ragoczy's wreath. His blue eyes burned at her. "If you think I will let you make a fool of yourself over that man, Rudi—"

"You have nothing to say about it, my dear," she cut in, motioning him to hold his tongue as Frau Bürste brought in a tureen of Leberknödelsuppe.

They spoke of pleasantries and trivialities over their seemingly interminable meal, and all the while Maximillian's eyes bored into his sister with fury and contempt.

Text of a letter from Helmut Rauch to Wilhelm Ludwig Unzeitgemäss of the Bayerisch Kreditkörperschaft.

*Rahm Hotel*
*Wotanstrasse, Nymphenburg*
*June 3, 1924*

*Herr Wilhelm Ludwig Unzeitgemäss*
*Bayerisch Kreditkörperschaft*
*9 Kriegskönigstrasse*
*München, Bayern*

*Herr Unzeitgemäss:*

*I have in hand your notice of my termination of employment at BKK. You state that this is not an easily-made decision, and that you fully appreciate all that I did for the BKK during the monetary crisis of last year. You further inform me that your reservations about my various political activities must be included in any and all comments given to other prospective employers I approach. In other words, Herr Unzeitgemäss, you are prohibiting me from finding work anywhere in this or any other city in Deutschland at the present time. You state that you believe that my political involvements, while nominally a matter of personal choice, in this case are potentially embarrassing to the BKK and its depositors.*

*Fine words for one who last year asked that those who stayed on at the BKK work for nothing until the mark was stabilized. You seem to have forgotten that I was one of six who agreed to this, and spent many hours of my own time attempting to salvage as much as was possible in that terrible time. I was not one of those who left the BKK instead of keeping at my work. It is my political philosophy which you now find so repugnant that prompted me to support you and the BKK through that time because I have a fervent faith in Deutschland and the future which we must act now to make ours. From what your unspeakably offensive letter says, you do not share my convictions. Yet you defend your colleague Harnisch for voicing his opinions, which I find disgusting.*

*The time will come, I warn you now, when those of you in high positions will be exposed for the swine you are, when your treason will be clear to the most innocent of our people, and at that time you will bitterly regret your action this day. You despise the NSDAP, and say that those who belong to it are lunatics and rabble. There are thousands of lunatics and rabble in this country, then, for the membership of the NSDAP is growing daily, and we will be the path to the future of our Vaterland. When this happens, you will suffer for what you do now. This is not an idle threat, Mein Herr Unzeitgemäss; it is a sacred vow.*

*Wholly sincerely,*
*Helmut Rauch*

# 2

Paris was stifling: summer held it in a hot, moist grip that reduced everyone in it to stillness at midday. Under the trees of the great boulevards those few hardy souls who cared to venture out would pause to stand and wipe their glistening faces, looking like melting wax sculptures.

On the quiet Rue Jelentaire most of the fashionable, small houses were quiet. Only Number 16, near the corner, showed some signs of activity inside. It was a narrow house, two stories tall with a trellis over the walkway to the door. Wisteria grew up and over the wooden posts that supported it, and in the spring the scent filled the air. Today all the plants were limp, and even the small fountain beside the entrance ran flaccidly into the lotus-shaped bowl that supported it.

"What ghastly weather," Madelaine de Montalia remarked to Irina Ohchenov as she dropped down on the sofa in the living room. Most of the furniture, which was the best Louis XV and XVI, clashed oddly with the Art Nouveau decor of the building, but Madelaine did not seem to mind. She opened the neck of her blouse another two buttons and lifted her coffee-brown hair in her hands. "Why did I come back from Greece, if the weather is to continue this way?"

"Perhaps because you thought the politics would get hotter," Irina said with sad laughter. "You're wise to stay away."

"Probably," Madelaine agreed. "Saint-Germain would agree with you," she added after a moment.

"Saint-Germain?" She considered. "Oh, you mean Count Franchot Ragoczy."

"And Balletti and Weldon and all the others." Madelaine chuckled. "I'm glad he sent you to me, although," she went on after a moment in a more serious tone, "I have yet to think of what more to do with you."

"Do with me? Are you planning to dismiss me?" In spite of herself, there was fear in her voice. She had finally achieved some little of what she wanted in her life, and now it was again in danger.

"Of course not. You may translate for me until you are old and gray, and I will be delighted. But is that all you want in your life, Irina? Don't you miss what you had before? I know I do, and I have not lost a husband and children." She turned on the sofa and opened one of the windows. "It makes no difference, but I wish to believe it does. If there were a breeze—"

"What have you lost?" Irina interrupted her, and then stared at Madelaine, shocked to have spoken to her in such a way.

"It's rather complicated," Madelaine said without any resentment. "Saint-Germain might be able to explain it to you better than I can." She touched her brow where no moisture lingered, and sighed. "We ought to do some work today, oughtn't we?"

"If you like," Irina said quietly. "I did not mean to upset you, Madelaine. I should not have—"

"Don't be silly, Irina," Madelaine interrupted her with fond laughter. "You're entitled to your questions. As I'm entitled not to answer them. In this case, it is only because I don't know what to tell you."

"You needn't tell me anything," Irina said at once in an effort to be rid of her own embarrassment.

"That's not the point." She closed her eyes, one hand to her brow. "I can't express it. No matter." With a sudden graceful movement she sat up. "Lolling about doesn't finish projects, does it? I have those photographs of tablets I mentioned to you, and we should go over each of them. I've made rough translations, but there's much that I can't make any sense of, and I haven't any idea how the tablets relate, or *if* they relate."

Irina rose from where she had reclined on a small chaise. "We'll see what we can piece together by the end of the day. One or two connections might make all the difference. It worked that way before." She followed Madelaine out of the room toward the back of the house, where a sizable lumber room had been converted into Madelaine's study.

"You know, I do like this house. I'm glad I bought it." She had also lined the cellar floor with earth from Montalia; it made the place quite restful. "I will ask Sophie to stay on and look after the place next time I'm gone on a dig."

"She'll probably be more than willing." Irina had noticed the admiration Sophie had for her employer on more than one occasion.

"I hope so. Where did I put those photographs?" This last was addressed to the air, and she began to pull open file drawers almost at random. "When I returned I was so exhausted, I put them away until I could catalog and file them properly, and you see what's come of that."

"Shall I help you?" Irina offered, going to the second file cabinet.

"No, no, just give me a little time . . ." She pulled out two more file folders, gave their contents a quick glance, and cast them aside. "It's better this way, actually. Before, everything had to be sketched carefully, and all texts copied, and that led to chaos. Quite often it was impossible to tell if a mark was meant to be part of the inscription, or a crack in the tablet, or simply a place where the pencil slipped. Not that photographs are infallible, but they're clearer, most of the time." She had examined another seven file folders, each of which she dropped onto her desk. Finally she pulled one from the drawer, opened it, and held it up victoriously. "Here it is, Irina. I *knew* it was in this drawer. Now," she said as she opened the folder. "There are thirty-six of these, as you can see. The writing is Greek, but a fairly early version of it. Some of these tablets look like lists, but I can't be sure. There are numbers that make it seem more like a list than not, and I may be allowing myself to be persuaded." She went to a long worktable and began to set the photographs out on it. "I want to see first if there is any overall pattern or development to the tablets, and then I want to review my notes on translation. I made most of my studies on the boat and then on the train, and both those modes of transportation, as you know, are distracting. Particularly boats," she added with feeling.

Irina looked down at the photographs, studying them closely. At first this aspect of her work had not been more than superficially interesting to her, but now that she had spent some time with Madelaine, she was beginning to understand the young woman's fascination with these relics of the ancient past. She picked up one of the photographs and stared at it. The Greek was indeed quite archaic, which added to the challenge. "I make out the word 'bird' here," she remarked.

"Where? Oh, yes. And there's something about sheep or wool, but I don't quite know how to make sense of it." Madelaine lifted one of the photographs. "There's something on this one about young women and boys. I think they must have been slaves because it is said that they're being traded or purchased. I can't get over the feeling that these, instead of philosophical dialogues or mathematical comments, are merchants' receipts." She shrugged her shoulders eloquently. "Well, in future, the archeologists who dig up Paris may find as many guides to the city for tourists as great works of literature. And the merchants were as important to the development of Greece as her philosophers."

"Shall I keep notes, or would you rather we organize this first?" Irina had not been paying a great deal of attention to what Madelaine was saying.

"Yes, please do. It's a bit awkward at first, but it does make the task easier." She lifted four of the photographs and handed them to Irina. "These all seem to be of a similar sort. What do you think?"

Irina took the photographs and perused them. "Yes, there is a strong similarity. I think I'll see if there are others like them." She went to the desk and picked up one of the notebooks lying on it. "May I use this one for notes?"

"Certainly," Madelaine said without turning, and then glanced around. "Wait a moment. Is anything written in it?"

"I don't . . . no, wait. There are some . . . gracious!" she exclaimed as she read one or two lines of the poetry at the back of the notebook. The hand was not one she recognized, and most of the poems were in English, but one or two were in French, and more than adequate to indicate the tenor of the collection. "A suitor?"

"Not precisely," Madelaine said elusively. "We meet now and again."

"And he writes these poems to you?" Irina had closed the

notebook at once, but a few of the phrases she had glanced at remained fixed in her thoughts. The man, whoever he was, loved Madelaine with a physical passion that bordered on idolatry. Irina was both slightly scandalized and envious. She thought of the nights she had spent in Ragoczy's embrace, amazed at the immediacy of her recollections.

"Yes. He writes them, and late at night, when we're alone, he reads them to me." She looked at Irina. "I don't mean to distress you. I've assumed that you're aware I am not a nun."

"That did not cross my mind," Irina said, not entirely truthfully.

"And my . . . tastes are diverse," Madelaine added with a twinkling smile. "This young man . . . I don't know what there is about him. It's not his poetry, if that's what you're wondering. There's more to it. Such deep currents do not always run between lovers, but when they do . . ." She broke off a little ruefully. "I shouldn't be saying these things to you. It must be the heat that has loosened my tongue."

Irina did not say anything for a moment, and then she put the notebook back on the desk before asking, "What about those, on that shelf?"

"They're all new. Go ahead and use one. There are pencils on the top-right drawer of the desk."

A few minutes later Irina had gathered her supplies and had set about the task of attempting to classify the sorts of tablets shown in the photographs. Madelaine stood on the other side of the table, a pen in her hand, scribbling recognizable phrases and copying the measurements of the individual tablets from her field notebook.

More than an hour had gone by in this way when there was the sound of a knocking at the front door. Madelaine looked up. "Who? What time is it?"

Irina blinked with her interrupted concentration. "Is there . . ."

The knocking came again, louder this time.

"There certainly is," Madelaine said. "Were you expecting anyone? I don't think I was."

"Of course not. I would not arrange to meet my few associates here," Irina said with dignity.

"Why not? I would not mind it. You are a superior worker and you always show fine results. I don't mind if you reward yourself for this with a guest or two for afternoon coffee." She had put her notebooks aside and begun to button her open blouse. "I hope whoever it is doesn't leave just as I come to the door," she said as she hurried out of the room.

The sound was more determined as Madelaine went down the hall. She ran her fingers through her tousled hair, which did not improve it a great deal. It occurred to her again, as it had occurred to her once or twice in the past, that she would do well to cut her long, heavy hair. She thought, as she reached for the doorknob, that she looked like one of those pre-Raphaelite women, with hair floating around their faces in a cloud.

The man was standing in shadow with light behind him, and Madelaine did not recognize him immediately. "Your pardon, Monsieur . . . ?"

"Madelaine," said a voice she knew, reproachfully.

"Colonel Timbres!" She pulled the door wide and beamed at him. "What an unexpected pleasure to see you."

"Not Colonel any longer, my dear. I am Monsieur Timbres now." Her enthusiasm now offset his first impression of their meeting. He stepped into the house and took her hand, carrying it to his lips. "I heard from one of my army associates that you were in Paris, and I could not resist the thought of seeing you again."

"How delightful," Madelaine responded, putting her hand through his arm. She could see, now that he was in her house, that the last few years had aged him. His dark hair was shot with gray and his facial lines were cut deeply into his flesh. He moved vigorously, which was reassuring. "It has been some time, Phillippe."

"Since Monbussy," he agreed. "Whatever became of that château?"

Madelaine's face darkened a moment. "It did not come through the war very well, I fear. The whole of the south front was blasted off, and a good portion of the roof was ruined. I have not yet made up my mind what to do about it. The farmers in the area look after it, so there is no vandalism, but I'm not sure I wish to live there at the present." She remembered the excellent advice Saint-Germain had given her on such matters. "In time, I may change my mind," she said thoughtfully. In ten or twenty more years she would need a place where she could disappear for a while, and Monbussy might answer very well. She could occupy herself in repairing and restoring the château.

"I hope you will, Madame. It would be a great pity to see such a fine place left to decay." He had been walking beside her toward the rear of the house without being aware of it. Now he paused and looked around him. "Where are we going?"

"To my study. You have caught me at my work, and with my translator here, I do not wish to lose time. Will it bore you to sit with us for half an hour while we attempt to finish putting these photographs in order? If we interrupt the work now, I fear that it will be quite a while before we can complete the task."

Timbres was slightly disarmed by her questions. "Of course not, Madame. It might be more convenient if I left and returned at another time." He looked around the study, at the stacks of books and papers and the three tall file cabinets. There was an old-fashioned feel to the room, although the furniture was modern enough save for the tall secretaire in the corner.

"Don't be a goose, Colonel. You are more than welcome here and it is my pleasure to have company now." She smiled at Irina for the first time. "This is my translator, Colo . . . Monsieur Phillippe Timbres. Monsieur Timbers, Madame Irina Ohchenov. She prefers not to use her title now, although it was Duchess."

Phillippe Timbres took Irina's hand and kissed it perfunctorily. His attention was on Madelaine, and he stared at her. "You have not aged a day," he said in a low voice as he took his seat in the chair before the secretaire.

"Isn't it absurd?" she said lightly. "I have the most lowering fear that one day I will . . . look in the mirror"—she gave a short, sad laugh at the words—"and discover that I am one of those crones whose faces are so filled with wrinkles and lines that they seem to be made of lace."

"Impossible," Phillippe said, aghast.

Irina gave Madelaine a curious glance. "You have known Monsieur Timbres for some time, then?"

"We met in . . . was it 1917, Col . . . Monsieur?" She did not wait for his confirmation. "I was at my château Monbussy, and the war required that I leave it. You were a Major then, or was it Captain?"

"A Captain, Madame." He cleared his throat as he stared at her. It was almost seven years since he had seen her, although they had exchanged a few letters since then. She must, he knew, be close to thirty, and yet she did not appear to be more than twenty. Her youthfulness, which had so attracted him when he was thirty-eight, at forty-five perplexed him. "You have let your hair grow."

"Yes," she said, touching it. "When I am on a dig, it is impossible to have it properly cut, and so I leave it alone.

This weather has persuaded me that it may be time to have it trimmed again." She turned back to Irina. "This good man was sent to tell me that we were required to evacuate the building for the army. He was kindly and most sympathetic. I cannot tell you how much I appreciated his concern." She held out a photograph she had been studying. "Does this belong with that second stack you are working on?"

Irina took the picture and stared at it. "I believe you're right. There is that strange word again." She pointed it out with her pencil, and Madelaine bent over the photograph with her. "I cannot make sense of it, but perhaps in time . . ."

"In time," Madelaine repeated. "When I was young I was so afraid that there would not be enough time." Musingly she picked up another photograph and scribbled a few notes on the paper beside her. Then she stopped and looked at her notes again. As always, she was using her abbreviations for more obvious features of the tables, abbreviations that would later be returned to their proper forms by Madelaine's typist. She blinked as she perused the page. "Irina," she said in an odd tone, "what do you make of this?" She handed her the sheet of notes.

"Your usual remarks," Irina said after she had given the words a quick scan.

"And in the photographs?" Her violet eyes grew brighter. "What do you make of those peculiar words?"

"I have told you," Irina said disinterestedly. "In time I will determine what archaic form is being used."

"But it isn't archaic," Madelaine said, allowing her excitement to show. "It is the same as the rest of the tablet, but it is like *this*"—she held up the sheet—"like the notes I keep. It's not a strange word, it is an abbreviation of some other sort of simplified notation." Her smile was triumphant.

Irina gave a startled, happy shriek. "Of *course!*" She seized the nearest photograph and began to scribble down the phrases she had questioned. Where there were repetitions, she made a note of the words before and after them, and as she worked, Madelaine bent over her, pointing out other curious combinations of letters. Irina perused them, leaning back in her chair, then offered the photograph to Madelaine. "I'm not entirely sure, but it appears that this combination of letters is part of a name. Perhaps two names."

"Yes." Madelaine nodded as she looked at it. "How does it read, assuming that this is the company or person making the transaction. What is the name of your company, Monsieur Timbres?" she demanded.

"Joseph et Dognac," Phillippe said, surprised by the question.

"Let us try that. Here. As I make it out, it says 'by' or perhaps 'to the seabird a,' well, some quantity or other 'of red wine in containers with bread grain and' another quantity, apparently 'of oil. On the mandate' or 'order of,' let us say, 'Joseph et Dognac.' I don't understand the 'seabird,' but it might be slang."

"Or a ship, or an inn," Phillippe suggested, caught up in her excitement.

"A ship or an inn?" Madelaine grinned at him. "Oil, wine, bread grain . . . Irina, we have come upon a cache of sales receipts!" She laughed aloud. "We may even be able to determine where the orders came from and where they were going."

Irina smiled now, as well, and began to enjoy a feeling of success. They had achieved a great deal, she thought. And if she had been hoping for a more exalted revelation, she did not let that minor disappointment show. "We've done well, Madelaine," she said in her low, pleasing voice.

"We've done splendidly," Madelaine retorted. "Irina, you do not know what this represents. You have not been on digs, as I have, and striven for years to complete just one set of documents on a small area. This may seem trivial to you, but I know from my own experience that this is a major accomplishment, and when it is known, your part in it will assure you as much work as long as you wish it."

"That is, if we can complete this work," Irina said carefully.

"We can. We will," Madelaine told her as she thumbed through one of the piles of photographs. "I have the place of discovery for these, of course, and there are good photographic records of the tablets in situ but now the trick will be to determine the points of origin, and whether these were items of import or export." She had lapsed back into the slightly abstracted manner that indicated great concentration.

Seeing this new activity, Phillippe Timbres stood, saying with awkward courtesy, "I must be de trop, Madame. With your kind permission, I will return another time when it is more convenient. I know you wish to be left to . . ."

Madelaine's eyes met his and she set the photographs aside. "You must not leave, Monsieur Timbres. You have been part of our discovery, and it is proper that you stay with us. This is a most important accomplishment and it deserves some celebration. I have been digging up ancient history for quite a few years, and this is one of the best bodies of information I have found yet. It's true that the work is only beginning, and it will be some time before we have prepared enough translations to make useful deductions from them; it may require another visit to the site to photograph more of the tablets, although these are the best of them. When that is done, we'll be too exhausted to celebrate. We must do it now. I will find the champagne and you, Irina, see what Sophie has left in the refrigerator."

"But, Madame . . ." Phillippe protested with an amused and helpless gesture toward Irina for support. "I have done nothing. I have merely appeared, after several years, and I can have no real claim on—"

"Captain Timbres," Madelaine said quite seriously. "You know better than that."

Phillippe had the oddest sensation as he nodded. "Very well; I will stay."

"C'est bien," Madelaine murmured, and bounded out of the room.

Irina regarded Phillippe with humor. "She is a fine archeologist, but there are times she reminds me of my . . ." She stopped suddenly, her expression becoming somber.

"Of your . . ." Phillippe repeated, aware of the pain in Irina's eyes.

"It was nothing, Monsieur," she said in a stifled tone.

"Your daughter?" he asked with a great deal of sympathy.

Irina was unable to speak, but her mute nod confirmed his guess. She turned toward the door, hoping that Madelaine would make as impetuous a return as her departure. The clock on the wall seemed now to have slowed to half its usual beat.

"Pardon me, Madame. I did not mean to intrude. I was afraid that inadvertently I contributed to unpleasant memories. Will you forgive me?" He had taken two steps toward her, concern on his deeply-marked features.

"Let us say no more about it, Monsieur Timbres. With the way things have been, all of us have such memories, I am sure." She made an unnecessary adjustment in her blouse and could think of nothing else to do with her hands. "Madame de Montalia is most fortunate to have this study, for it is always cool in the summer."

"Yes, I had noticed that," Phillippe remarked, taking the lead from her. "I have not seen this house before. I obtained her address from her banker. Since I was the one who ordered her out of her château, he was willing to tell me where to find her now. It took some persuading at first, but when I mentioned how she and I had met, he was willing to part with the information." He once again took his seat and did not permit himself to look too long at Irina Ohchenov.

"She has mentioned Monbussy to me," Irina said, bringing herself back under control. She had not felt that keenness of loss for more than a year, and the strength of her emotions alarmed her. The clock once again began to keep normal time.

"I can see that it would have been best to send her a note asking when I might call, but it was so simple to come here that I did not think, and when Monsieur Saufin told me that Madame de Montalia was at home, and not off in a foreign country, I'm afraid I did not think as I should." He ventured a quick glance at Irina and saw that her color was better, the lines around her eyes less marked.

The door opened and Madelaine came in with a silver tray with two glasses balanced on one hand and a bottle of champagne clasped by the neck in the other. She knew at once that there had been a difficult exchange between Irina and Phillippe but nothing in her outward manner revealed this. She put the tray down quite expertly and lifted the bottle of champagne. "It isn't very old—1920, in fact—but I haven't anything better here."

"I haven't had champagne since . . ." Irina broke off again, remembering that Ragoczy had given her champagne after he had brought her to his apartment. It had been the second night she stayed there, and he had seen that she was given an elegant meal served in the old way, with heavy silver and linen napery and crockery so fine it was translucent. "For quite some time," she finished lamely.

"Nor I," Phillippe said at once.

Madelaine was twisting the wire guard holding the cork, a determined smile in her eyes. "It will be just an instant more . . ." The wire came free and the cork moved very slightly in the neck of the bottle. Madelaine set her thumbs against it and began to ease it out. She was faintly aware that both Irina and Phillippe were watching her intently, and her attention faltered.

At that moment the cork flew out of the bottle with a loud retort and champagne frothed out over her hands.

"One of you, get the glasses!" she said loudly, holding the bottle away from her skirt. "We'll lose half of it."

Phillippe reached the desk first and took both the glasses, thrusting them under the cascade. He could feel his mouth smile. As the first glass filled with bubbles, he slipped the second into its place.

"It's fine now. Hold the glasses steady and I'll pour." Madelaine nodded to Phillippe as he lifted the glasses for her.

"But where is the third glass?" Irina asked as she belatedly noticed the number.

"Oh," Madelaine said with a blithe gesture as she set the bottle down, "I should not have any of it. It doesn't agree with me."

Phillippe, who had held out one of the glasses to Madelaine, now brought it back and looked chagrined. "But then, it isn't . . ."

"My dear, this wasn't necessary," Irina said at the same time.

"Well, we can't put it back in the bottle. Do drink it. I would not like it to go to waste even if it is only 1920. Four-year-old champagne. You may not thank me for it." She went to her chair behind the desk and dropped into it. "Let us toast the good ship *Seabird* and her crew."

"We don't know it was a ship," Irina reminded her, taking the glass Phillippe gave her. The scent of the wine was delicious, too tempting to be denied.

"We will hope that it was, because that will mean that these records are more important than they would be if it is merely an inn or a counting house." She lifted her heavy hair off her neck.

"Then, to the good ship *Seabird*," Phillippe said, and raised his glass to Irina.

"To the *Seabird*," she echoed dutifully, and sipped with guilty delight. It was, as Madelaine had warned them, not very good champagne, but the sharp taste was welcome in the warm afternoon. The bubbles skittered in her nose, making her fear she might sneeze.

"Thank you, Madame," Phillippe said to Madelaine as he lowered the glass. He had barely touched the wine, not wanting to offend his hostess. She was so young to be serving them, he decided. If she were his age, like Madame Ohchenov, then it would be easy to accept the hospitality that Madelaine was offering. "I'm not used to wine in the afternoon."

"And you a Frenchman," Madelaine teased him. "All the more reason to enjoy it. If you don't, Sophie will probably get tipsy on it."

"That's true," Irina said unexpectedly. "Sophie is a fine maid-of-all-work, but she does like her wine." She stared down into the glass and then hastily lifted it to her lips and let the champagne fill her mouth.

"I wonder if what the *Seabird* carried in her hold was half as refreshing as this," Phillippe said in what he hoped was a playful tone.

"Probably not," Madelaine said. "From what I understand, the Greeks and the rest of them used resins in their wine then as they do now, and I doubt there was much aging done. Saint-Germain would probably know," she added.

Irina stared at her. "Why should he know that?"

Madelaine realized her error at once, and let herself be flustered. "He knows so much," she said with some confusion. "I've rarely seen him at a loss."

"Who is this?" Phillippe inquired as he downed the last of his glass and considered asking for more.

"By all means, Monsieur Timbres," Madelaine said with a nod toward the wine bottle. "It won't keep." Then she answered his question. "Saint-Germain is . . . a blood relation."

"An all-knowing uncle?" he suggested as he poured out another glass and refilled Irina's. He feared he was being unwise, but could not bring himself to leave the house. How had Madelaine contrived to remain so youthful? She had suffered great privations during the Great War, he knew that better than many. At the very least she was approaching thirty, and still she had the look of a schoolgirl. The questions continued to nag him, and he wished that he knew Madame Ohchenov better and was able to discuss the matter with her.

"Not precisely," Madelaine said. It was possible to envy Irina. It had been so long since she had gone to that room in Hôtel Transylvania!

"Are you troubled?" Irina asked, as Madelaine got up impatiently from her chair.

At once she remembered herself. "No, of course not. I am anxious to get to work on the tablets. No, not yet. You are tired, and so am I. In the morning our heads will be clearer and we will start fresh. It is not wise to rush these things."

"My head will certainly be clearer," Irina declared recklessly. "And possibly it will be sore as well. I've got out of the habit of drinking." Her tone was now oddly chastened. "The champagne is lovely." There was very little left in her glass, and she doubted it would be wise to have more.

Phillippe was almost as cautious as Irina. "The bottle is almost empty. Would you mind if we did not drink. . . ."

Madelaine shrugged. "Do as you wish. I hardly intended the

wine as a penance. It is for you to enjoy." There was a touch of sadness in her face as she spoke, and then she got to her feet. From the faint color in Irina's face, the champagne was affecting her. Madelaine went to the door and opened it. "It's growing cooler. The sun is going down."

"So soon?" Irina said, her Russian accent blurring with her French.

"It is getting on," Phillippe agreed as he consulted his pocket watch. "In half an hour at the most, I must be gone."

"I hope you will come again another time," Madelaine said as she looked at him steadily. "And it may be you will bring us good luck again."

"If that is what you want of me," Phillippe murmured as he set down his wineglass and bowed over Madelaine's hand.

She did not answer him and her smile was enigmatic. When Phillippe released her hand, she went to Irina. "Let me take the glass."

"It may be best. I fear it's gone to my head." The heightened rosiness of Irina's complexion gave witness to this as well as dispelling the pallor that had become so much a part of her. Her eyes sparkled and there was a lightness about her that had been missing for a very long time.

"Would you like me to walk to the corner with you?" Madelaine asked, unable to subdue the impish smile that plucked the corners of her mouth and nudged two small impressions that were not quite dimples into being.

"I'm able to manage," Irina said grandly.

Phillippe caught the quick request in Madelaine's eyes and intervened. "I will be happy to walk to the corner with you, Madame Ohchenov. I am going that way in any case." He was rewarded by the increasing warmth in Madelaine's eyes.

When Irina and Phillippe were gone, Madelaine sat in her darkening living room, her head resting on her arm, which lay on the back of the sofa. She told herself that she was waiting for Phillippe, although she doubted he would return that night. Was it kindness that had led her to force the other two into each other's company, or was it caprice? Saint-Germain had warned her of how disastrously easy it was to think of humanity as toys, things to amuse you with their clever antics. She did not think that was why she had served the champagne and watched Irina and Phillippe fall under its spell. Yet her motives, she admitted, were not entirely noble. It had been entertaining to see how those two rudderless lives had responded to the opportunity she provided; that was true enough, but her feelings were not derisive. That lightness of spirit Irina and Phillippe had experienced was not entirely due to the wine, and, recognizing that, Madelaine felt her alienness acutely. She could, if she tried, still remember what the warm glow of champagne felt like, but it was far in her past and it was beginning to fade.

She leaned back and stared out through the window at the dusk-blue sky. She could feel the giddy pulse of Paris begin to race, filled with a thousand kinds of drunkenness. Madelaine longed for the company of Saint-Germain, as ultimately unsatisfying as it was. His hard-won compassion would give her comfort she had from no other, and her profound sense of separateness would be forgotten for a while.

There was soft laughter from one of the buildings across the street: Madelaine turned to listen to it, to the abandon of it, and wished, briefly and searingly, that she could share the intoxication of the lives around her.

There was, she reminded herself as she got up from the sofa, one rapture, one delirium left to her. She hoped it would sustain her.

Text of a letter from James Emmerson Tree to his cousin
Audrey.

*La Caccia, near Pisa*
*Italy*
*July 4, 1924*

*Dear Audrey;*

*I'm staying at a very pleasant inn today, and tomorrow I am supposed to leave for Rome, that is assuming that I have permission to travel and the proper credentials. I had to ask Crandell for special letters in order to convince these people that I'm not going to do anything to their precious Bennie. The Facisti take this all very seriously and I don't have much choice but to go along with it. There's just been some sort of law passed that imposes strict censorship on the Italian press and I suppose they're trying to make it stick for foreigners as well. If that's the case, this could turn out to be a wasted trip. What Crandell is hoping for is a new slant on the murder of Giacomo Matteotti, and since the chances are pretty good that the Facisti did it, they probably won't be very helpful. Matteotti wrote a book about the Facisti, exposing their various illegal and violent acts, and they're the ones who have the most reason to shut him up. Now that they're in power, they're not going to let bad news out. That Mussolini is an odd one. Half the time he struts around like a turkey cock that no one would ever take seriously, and the rest of the time he maneuvers like Machiavelli.*

*After I leave Italy, which could be in a couple days, the way things are going, I'm going to try to get into Austria and Germany. Everyone's holding their breath about the new German currency. This Dawes Plan, if it works, could make the difference there, but I don't know that simply renaming the money will make that much of a change. The plan will go into operation in September, I think, and so far things appear to be fairly stable, but it's really too soon to tell. They've boosted the taxes outrageously, and I don't know if the German people will be prepared to keep paying so much, especially after what they've been through the last few years. I understand that last year it cost 400,000 marks for a streetcar ticket. The Rentenmarks have been accepted so far, and once the Reichmarks come in, they might be able to make it stick. I know that some of the government is all for investing in the synthetic-petroleum program that the Farben cartel is sponsoring, among others. There's a man named Bosch at Farben who is all for it, but investments right now are very dicey, as my British colleagues say. Still, there's no doubt that they're at the top of the chemical heap, and they'll probably stay there unless they run out of money.*

*Thayer was over last month, and we had dinner in Paris. I've mentioned him before—he's the guy who acts as Crandell's courier. He bought one of those new Oakland automobiles and says it's fine. He's been offered a job with that new paper in New York, the* Herald Tribune, *and he'll probably take it. After a bottle of good young Beaujolais, all he wanted to do is sing "Yes, We Have No Bananas" at the top of his lungs, so I'm not much up on what's been happening back at home. Those magazines you've been sending me help a lot, and if I haven't thanked you for them, I ought to. I'm glad you're sending me fiction magazines, too. If you can pick up a few more copies of* Weird Tales, *I'd really like those.*

*Speaking of newspapers,* Le Figaro *is being bought by François Coty, a Corsican. You know the kind of luck France has had with Corsicans. I don't know about that guy. He sounds a lot like Mussolini and those right-wing Germans.*

*You might not have been following what's happening in Russia since Lenin's death. They've got a triumvirate going on, in the old Roman fashion. Stalin, Kamenev, and Zinoviev are the three. It's too soon to tell how that will turn out, but as I recall, the triumvirate didn't fare too well in Rome. Russia may look like it's settling down, but I wouldn't bet on it, not until Trotsky is either in power or out of the picture completely. This latest ploy with China will bear some watching. Much as I want to*

*be first with a big story, Russia is one place I'm in no
hurry to go to get it.*

*I don't know if you'll get a chance to see* Greed, *but if
you can, do. Renoir knows what he's doing, and I liked
this a great deal. It's better than Munrau's* Nosferatu *I
told you about last year. I haven't seen Leni's* Waxworks
*yet. I'll let you know about it when I do. You said that
you don't get too many European flicks in Denver. That's
a pity. Griffith is okay and Ford looks pretty good, but
they do things differently over here. There's a wider range.
That means when they're awful, they're hideous, but when
they're good, they're amazing. Some of these directors
pull off a triumph one year and fall on their faces the
next, and it doesn't seem to change things. Can you
picture Walsh doing* Doktor Mabuse? *It's possible that
one of the reasons is that filmmaking isn't centralized in
Europe and it looks as if it's turning out to be in America. And when you think of how little Europe is, the
diversity is impressive.*

*How are things going toward rounding up the Ashley
gang? We keep hearing rumors that they're almost caught,
and the next thing you know, they're playing hell with
Florida again. I was told—Thayer told me before he got
onto the Beaujolais—that this time they really are going
to be put out of business.*

*Who is this Jerry you've been seeing? He sounds to me
a bit too slick. If he's all that attentive, what does he
expect? And if he doesn't expect the usual thing, why is he
doing it? I know this looks as if I don't want you to enjoy
yourself, and after what I've told you about Madelaine
and me, you probably think I'm a spoilsport. But it's
because of Madelaine and me that I'm warning you.
Look, Audrey, there are a lot of men in the world who
don't know that they can have more than one kind of
relationship with a woman. Most of the men I know take
something offered. Or they buy it. And they don't always
go to the professionals to buy it. You tell me that Jerry
always brings you presents, and they're expensive presents sometimes. What does Jerry want in return for his
presents? Does he want to marry you, and he thinks you
have a purchase price, or he has to impress you that he's
well enough off to afford a wife? Does he want to make
love to you, never mind marriage? Those aren't easy*

questions to ask you, and you probably don't want to answer them, but better now than later. Does he think that if he gives you enough, you won't be able to ask anything but presents of him? You say he won't allow you to do anything for him: well, Audrey, honey, that isn't as flattering as you seem to think it is. Does this Jerry really think you're helpless, or does he want to make you that way? You say that Bella Jennings is jealous. Why?

You're probably ready to tear this letter up, and I guess I wouldn't blame you if you did. I make a fine example, don't I? I'm almost thirty-one and still single, running around Europe for a living. And, of course, having an occasional mistress who's part of the old French nobility. That makes me a fine one to give you advice, doesn't it? But believe it or not, I might be the best person to talk to. Don't let this guy bribe you or railroad you into something you don't want. You can tell him no, Audrey. Let me ask you one last, very crude question: do you want to lie down and let this Jerry inside you? Because if you don't, it might be better to look around for someone else. And if you tell me that sex isn't on his mind, then you ought to find out what is.

If Aunt Myra hasn't seen the doctor yet about that stitch in her side, you make her go. Uncle Ned might be mad at her for it, but better than having her in the hospital. If she says she can't spare the time, you drive her both ways. None of us is indestructible, and a woman of Aunt Myra's age should keep an eye on herself. Sixty-two is getting up there.

I liked the picture you sent. The new porch looks very nice. You didn't tell me anything about the dog on the steps. Is he new, or have you not mentioned him?

Let me know how your trip to Seattle turns out. I've never been there, but they tell me it's a beautiful setting and a pleasant city. I don't think I ever met the Wagoners, but give them my greetings in any case; if they're sensible enough to like you, then they're fine people.

Have a good summer. I'm glad you're getting a chance to travel, but I wish you were coming over here, so I could show you around Europe. I know some of the things I've told you about it make it out to be a dangerous place, but don't let that worry you. Most of it is beautiful, the people aren't ogres, the food is great, and there's no place at home that feels the way it does here.

*Promise me you'll think about what I said before you're in too deep with Jerry.*

*I'll try to write again when I'm back in Paris. In the meantime,*

*Much love,*
*James*

## 3

Maximillian slammed the parlor door and glared at his sister. "Otto told me you're entertaining tonight," he said furiously.

"That's correct." Gudrun had not risen when he stormed in on her, and now she stared out the window, smiling slightly, determined to remain composed.

"You've asked that foreigner to visit!" Maximillian's face was flushed and his mouth was set in a mulish line.

"Yes, I have." She smoothed her skirt methodically. It was a deep blue, like darkened Wedgwood, of loose, unpressed pleats in heavy linen. A long, demure tunic jacket with a wide, low belt was worn with it. There was nothing provocative about her clothes, except their quality and cut.

"Just a little tête-à-tête supper, that's all." He strode toward her, snapping his fingers angrily. "Jürgen hasn't been in the grave even six months, and already you're flaunting yourself!"

"Flaunting myself?" she repeated, looking at him at last. "I have made every effort to conduct myself with propriety. Graf Ragoczy is not going to dine with me. He has accepted my invitation to play cards. The servants are here. *You* are here. You don't suppose that I'm going to lock myself in my bedchamber with him for two hours, do you? We will play cards or chess and for a while we will converse. It is entirely acceptable behavior, Maxl. No one would find it shocking or . . . questionable. The Graf has been a guest here before and his standing is good."

"He's a foreigner. He had that man Schnaubel work for him. His chauffeur is a Russian!" Maximillian rounded on her, his hands becoming fists and his voice rising. "Don't you know how that will appear?"

"To whom?" Gudrun asked with defiance in her blue eyes. "To your bigoted friends? To those sots at the Hirsch Furt? To Konrad Natter? Are they the ones you're thinking of, Maxl?" She stared at him until he turned away from her. "You worry about me now, when I have at last got the courage to enter the world again. When I was immured here, with a dying husband and my servants, it didn't matter to you, did it? Your friends approved of that, and you believed what they told you about what I have done. You were delighted that you did not have to concern yourself with me. Now that I have a chance to have life again, you come here, with your noise and your blustering, and you tell me that you will not tolerate what I do. You haven't the right to talk so to me, Maxl. It is not up to you to speak to me this way." Her eyes met his and although she did not speak above her usual quiet level, there was strength in her that her brother had never seen before. "The years you left me alone here I found self-reliance because there was nothing else I could do. You were not here to see this. You chose to escape, and that is your privilege, but you have forfeited any say in my life."

Maximillian stared at her, aghast. "You're hysterical."

"No. A year ago, two years ago, I might have been, but no more." She sighed as she looked away from her brother. "I cannot let you do these things to me, Maxl. I know you believe that you want to protect me, but I don't need or want your protection. I want to play cards with Graf Ragoczy. I want to visit my friends in München, or have them visit me, whether you approve of them or not. I want to live in the world again, and not in Jürgen's tomb. You may dislike this, Maxl, but you cannot deny me."

"We'll see about that." He started toward the door, but her voice stopped him.

"If you interfere in any way, Maximillian, I will not want you here any longer. I will not pay your debts. I will not entertain your friends. Volkighügel belongs to me, not to you." She had been afraid to speak to him in this way, but now that the words were out, she was oddly exhilarated. Nothing Maximillian could say or do now would alter the truth of what she said.

"I am your brother," he reminded her as the color drained from his face.

"Yes." She did not answer his tentative smile with one of her own.

"I am thinking of your welfare."

His charm, which had so long delighted her, now seemed pathetic. "You may believe that you are, but it is not so, mein bruder. You are interested in preserving your position here, and that is fine with me, upon certain conditions."

"The debts?" He spoke quickly, and his tongue darted over his lips.

"In part. We are no longer wealthy, Maximillian. We have very little left, and you have not been willing to remember that. You wish to have your automobile, and I am willing to provide you with fuel for it, as I need the same for my automobile. You have the cottage to live in, and Frau Bürste will prepare your meals for you as she has done in the past. I expect that she would be disappointed not to have the pleasure of serving you. I am not able to pay for the entertaining of your guests, not on the scale you have said you wish to provide them. If you want to serve ham, it must come from our own pigs, and that means that you must take it into account. I have worked out an agreement with Hansi the butcher: I will provide him pigs on a regular basis if he will share the meat with us and occasionally trade for other cuts. I have sold all but one of the horses, and Miroslav has agreed to look after the pigs in return for the use of the groom's quarters in the stable. I am amenable to such an arrangement, and he has said he is pleased. I will still pay him a small stipend, but it will not make the same demands on my purse that his work has required in the past. I have also arranged to purchase three cows, and from that we will have milk. Miroslav will attend to that, as well, and we will have butter and cheese not just for ourselves, but to trade with others."

Maximillian had been regarding her in horror. "Trade? Cattle? Pigs? What has come over you?"

"The world, Maximillian." She got up slowly and approached him. "You have not paid much attention to our situation, even when the money was so worthless that a bale of hay had more value than a stack of bills. You have been blind to that—"

"Blind? Why, it was the Thule Gesellschaft that revealed the truth behind the inflation. It was no accident, but a determined effort on the part of our enemies to destroy us completely. You complain about stacks of banknotes, but *we* were the ones who saw the deception that lay behind this—"

Gudrun cut in just as he had done. "And what did you do about it? Did you sell anything you valued to provide for this household? Did you?"

"The Gesellschaft required my assistance," he said with petulant dignity.

"Did it? And this household, where you have lived and provided food and lodging to those members of your Gesellschaft, did you ever pause to think how it was that they were fed, or where their blankets came from?" She was angry now, and she glared at him without shame. "I have almost no jewels left, Maximillian, and much of our best furniture is gone. You didn't notice, I suppose, because there were other chairs in the lumber room which replaced those I sold. It was not my choice to give up grandmother's harp or the two French highboys in the master bedroom. And if you knew how pitifully little those treasures brought us! Most of it went to pay Walther for his nursing, and I have always *hated* Walther. Then you brought those six men here, and you drank and ate for five days as if there were money in the world and you did not have to think where the Froschschnekel in Rahm or Krautwickerl came from. Otto went poaching on Ragoczy's land for birds and fish to feed you. He made himself a criminal to keep you and those men in food!" Her indignation grew as she thought of the wary expression in the old man's eyes when he had returned with three ducks tucked under his coat because he did not dare to carry a bag.

"But that's just the *point*," Maximillian tried to interrupt. "Don't you see, our *enemies* did that to us. Otto was only a victim of their schemes."

"And that makes it *right*? Then why didn't you go after the pheasants and the sheep with him? Did you assume that we were immune to the inflation here?" She had screamed this last, and it was with an effort that she controlled her ire. "You say that you were aware of what was being done, but you took no action."

"The Bruderschaft was—"

She did not let him say any more. "What? Murmuring incantations? Painting symbols on the sides of houses? Very important work, I am sure." As she moved away from him, she had to press her hands to the sides of her nose to keep from weeping.

"You don't know how important it is if you mock it. You are permitting the lies of our enemies to deceive you." He folded his arms, thinking himself at last on secure ground. "This is not a matter of money or poaching, but a question of survival of the German people. You do not know how deep the hatred of our race runs in those who seek to bring us down. We have kept our purity, and it is more than they can bear, because with our purity comes our power."

Gudrun stared at him. "And for that, you let Otto, who has cared for you since you were an infant, risk capture and imprisonment? You say this was not a question of money, and it must be so, if you can dismiss it in that way."

"You're overwrought, Rudi," Maximillian began, and got no further.

"That is the least of it," she declared, facing him again. "I wonder why I put up with you. If I were wise, I would insist that you abandon this nonsense. But then you would act covertly, I suppose, and I would have no idea what madness you were embarked upon. This way, I have some notion." It was amazing to her that she could be calm after what had been said. "Maximillian, listen to me for a moment. You say that you are doing important work, and I suppose that justifies all your actions to you. Don't interrupt me, bitte," she said more sharply as he came toward her. "My conditions are reasonable, given our current circumstances."

"And we will turn swineherds," he said with contempt.

"Better that than thieves," she countered. "You may continue to live here, but if you must entertain, you will have to pay for it or make whatever arrangements are suitable."

"The crisis is over, Rudi," he told her with extreme patience. "You need not make all these sacrifices to frugality."

"That's not certain," she responded. "And much of what we had is gone. We will not recover it. You are not a man to seek regular employment and I have nothing to sell but my heritage. We must become accustomed to this."

"I forbid it!" Maximillian burst out.

"You have nothing to say in the matter," Gudrun reminded him. "You abdicated that privilege. You have no right to question how I live, or what I do. I will not embarrass you, be—"

"Not embarrass me? What has this entire discussion been but an embarrassment?" He flung his hands into the air and strode toward the door.

"I am not quite finished, Maximillian. You had best hear me out so that we will understand each other." There was such finality in her tone that her brother once again turned toward her. "If you are willing to occupy yourself with tasks here at Volkighügel, you will be paid for your efforts, as the others are. But beyond that, I cannot give you any more money because I have not got it myself. I will pay for three new sets

358 *Chelsea Quinn Yarbro*

of clothes a year for you, and any reasonable travel expenses on your automobile, but that is all I can do. I simply can't afford anything more: understand that, if you can. You still have a trust fund that will give you a little money for your activities, but for the rest, you must manage as best you can." She regarded him. "You aren't a child, Maximillian. You haven't been a child for years."

"I should say not!" he expostulated. "But from your tone, I gather you think that I have been. You're the one who should consider what you say. It is so easy for you, isn't it, to blame me for the money you have lost and the desperate straits of all Germany. If that is how you regard me, I am surprised that you allow me to remain here."

"Were things less precarious, I would not." Her temper was wearing thin again, but she strove to control it. There was no point in yelling at her brother now, when he had so clearly decided that he was an injured party at the mercy of feminine caprice. "I know that I have obligations to the family, and there are too few of us left for me to ignore that association entirely."

"And, naturally, you want to keep an eye on me," he added for her with bitterness. His handsome features were marred by the cynicism of his words. "An irresponsible child is what you think I am. How generous of you to permit me to remain here. And how very cautious of you. Do you think that I cannot be trusted to manage my own life? Do you think that I will squander your hoarded resources—"

"There are no hoarded resources. I wish there were," Gudrun told him sadly.

"That is what you want me to believe, I am certain. Well, no doubt you believe that you're the one who has been abused in this, but you must realize that I have spent years trying to find a way to restore the honor of all Deutschland while you have been occupying your time worrying about how much pork you can trade to the butcher. It's useless to try to explain to you how gross your error is!" He strode across the room, passing her as if she were no more than a servant. "You have become a tool of our enemies. I should have seen it long ago, but I did not permit myself to subject you to that close scrutiny that is required of me. I was sure you, of all the women in the world, would not succumb to the blandishments of the—"

A soft tap at the door interrupted his tirade, and a moment

later Otto stepped into the room. "Graf Ragoczy is here," he said woodenly to Gudrun.

"We are talking!" Maximillian yelled at the old servant.

Otto stared at the angry face and belligerent hands of the man who had been the one child he had loved best in the world. "You are not to speak to your sister in this way, Maxl," he said softly. "It isn't right."

"You don't know what *she* has said to *me*," Maximillian objected.

"It doesn't matter. There is a guest in the house and you are loud enough to be overheard in the stables. Gnädige Frau," he said to Gudrun with a slight bow, "I have asked Graf Ragoczy to wait for you in the smaller drawing room. I will set up the card table there."

"Thank you, Otto," Gudrun murmured, filled with relief at this opportunity to slip away. "Don't bother about Maximillian."

There were tears in Otto's eyes as he answered, "If that is what you wish."

Gudrun gave the old man a reassuring pat on the hand and then left the salon. She walked rather slowly, hoping to bring her emotions back under control. By the time she opened the door to the smaller drawing room, she was breathing more regularly and her hands did not shake.

Ragoczy was on the far side of the room near the one tall case containing three old fiddles, the last survivors of her grandfather's collection of folk instruments. As always, Ragoczy was immaculately groomed: his black three-piece suit had been cut by a master tailor in Paris, his white silk shirt was the best to be found in Rome, the black silk tie had been made for him in London from the finest heavy material woven in India. The stickpin holding the tie was a magnificent ruby in a silver setting.

"Good afternoon, Graf," Gudrun said rather timidly from the door.

"And to you, Madame Ostneige," Ragoczy said as he turned toward her.

She read in his dark eyes that he had heard the argument, and she felt her cheeks darken. "I'm pleased you could come."

"It is gracious of you to say so," he said as he crossed the room and bent to kiss her hand.

She felt her blush deepen at this courtesy and chided herself for permitting her mind to make so much of such a minor gesture. "There will be a table for play in a moment, and, if you like, refreshments."

Ragoczy favored her with an enigmatic smile. "Have what you wish, but you need not think about me." He motioned toward one of the sofas. "Do you mind if I sit down?"

Gudrun admired his deft manner and smiled as she chose one of the two high-backed chairs. "On an afternoon like this one, neither of us need stand on ceremony, I think."

He nodded once as he took his place on the sofa. "Are we the extent of the card party?"

"Yes. I asked Gerwald but he refused, as I feared he might." She saw her hands join and twist in her lap as if they were quite independent of her will and not part of her self at all.

"Then I am doubly honored that you extended the invitation. Not all women in your position would wish to spend the afternoon with one guest."

Damn the man! she thought. Would he now persist in the sort of condemnation she had already withstood from her brother. "But we're neighbors," she said in a small voice. "I have hoped you would come here more often . . ."

Ragoczy's eyes met hers. "That would not be entirely wise. I am a foreigner, Madame, and for that reason I am circumspect." His expression lightened. "But I am pleased you want to play cards. It is often quite boring to be so isolated."

"I would not think you were bored, Graf," she said politely, grateful for the courtesies he so willingly extended to her.

"I'm not." He nodded toward the cabinet where the fiddles lay behind glass. "A commendable display."

"It is kind of you to say so," Gudrun sighed, "but I fear that the best pieces are gone now. There were two hammered dulcimers and those Hungarian instruments . . . I can't recall their names. They're not unlike zithers, but they are hammered, too."

"A cimbalom?" Ragoczy asked, making no attempt to disguise his interest. "How recent an instrument?"

"I don't recall, but apparently my grandfather bought it from Gypsies. That might have been as early as 1840, since he began his collection when he was quite young." She was almost calm now, and her hands were steady in her lap.

"That was before the Schunda improvements. I wish I had seen it." He did not quite smile, but there was a softening to his wry mouth.

"I did not know you were interested in folk instruments, Graf," Gudrun remarked. "Had I known, I would have . . ." She hesitated, not wanting to admit that she had parted with much of her grandfather's collection.

"Offered them to me?" Ragoczy suggested gently. "I wish you had. Perhaps, if there are other instruments in the collection, you would care to let me examine them one day." He noticed her reluctance and added, "You need not fear that I want to take advantage of our being neighbors. If you have instruments that you are willing to part with, I give you my word I would pay a good price and provide you the option to repurchase them at the original price whenever you wished to do so."

"That's very generous," she said after a slight pause.

"Oh, hardly that. I merely have a . . . liking for music." He turned toward the door as Otto came through it with a baize-topped round table clutched awkwardly to his chest. He tried to speak, but was puffing too much from the exertions to get any words out. Finally he brought the table to the center of the room and set it down with an explosive sigh.

Ragoczy had half-risen and asked Otto if he required help.

"No, no, Herr Graf. It wouldn't be right for you to do tasks like this," he panted as he slapped at the baize with an old handkerchief. "It is most kind of you to ask, but it would not be appropriate." He brushed his fingertips across the green cloth and was apparently satisfied with the results. "I have both a chessboard and cards, whichever you wish, Frau Ostneige."

"Graf?" she inquired politely.

"Either will do, but I know more chess than I know card games for two." That was somewhat correct, for most of the card games he knew were learned at gambling tables and would not be those Gudrun would play.

Her smile did not slip much, but she said, "I will have to resign myself to losing, then. My chess, I have been told, is dreadful." That had been back when she was first married, when Jürgen had tried for the better part of a year to teach her to think ahead for more than two moves. She had objected at the time that she did not want to second-guess what her opponent would do, preferring to respond to the moves as each arose.

"Surely not," Ragoczy said as he rose and held out his hand to her. "I know you are an intelligent woman and with your background you must find the game amusing."

"But who plays it for amusement?" she inquired with mock horror. "A game of chess is a serious matter, Graf."

"Perhaps," he allowed as he led her toward the table where Otto was just setting the chairs in place. "We will see how it goes. If you like, I will handicap myself. Would you like me to give up a castle or a bishop?" He waited while she seated herself, and then took the chair opposite her.

"That would not be a sensible thing to do, I think," she said, and turned to Otto. "The larger board, I think, with the Italian pieces."

"As you wish, Frau Ostneige." The old servant achieved half a bow before bustling out of the room.

"He will not take long," she said to Ragoczy, and then dropped her eyes, not wanting to look too deeply into his. She had the most disquieting sensation as those penetrating dark eyes touched hers, as if he could see into her very soul, and understood all that was there. She had dreamed so often of real compassion, but now, confronted by it, she wished only to escape.

"You're troubled, Madame," Ragoczy said. It was not a question.

"Somewhat," was her evasive reply.

"There was some unpleasantness when I arrived." His small hand covered hers.

"A private matter, Graf." She did not look at where their hands touched. In desperation she let her attention be drawn toward the windows covered now with shirred curtains. It was impossible to see what lay beyond them, for even the sunlight was muted.

"I didn't mean to intrude, Madame; I intend to offer you my service in whatever capacity you might require it." His voice was still light, but there was no mistaking his sincerity. "You have merely to ask me."

"It would be inexcusable of me to foist such confidences on you," she said rather stiffly as she tried to pull her hand away.

"Oh, come, Madame," Ragoczy said, an affectionately derisive note in his tone. "You have not had such reservations before. Are you afraid that I will assume that your invitation was for more than an afternoon's amusement? It would give me the most profound joy to believe that, but I am aware you do not wish a lover, not even for the afternoon."

Her short, trembling sigh betrayed her and she felt the shameful stain color her cheeks again. "No, no, Graf. Chess or cards . . ."

"Of course," was his urbane comment as the door opened again and Otto returned to the room bearing a heavy marble chessboard and a large rosewood box tucked under one arm.

"I have it, Frau Ostneige," he said as he set the board

down, heavily askew, on one side of the table, where the balance was precarious. Quickly he placed the box before Gudrun, and then reached for the board to improve its placement on the table.

"Thank you, Otto," she said in an uneasy way. "I know it was difficult for you to carry the board."

"No such thing," Otto said with determination. "The only trick was bringing it up the stairs, and I did not allow that to hamper me. The whole question is one of the right distribution of weight." With this pronouncement, he left the room again, closing the door firmly behind him.

Gudrun opened the box in front of her and pulled out the chessmen. The white men were made of alabaster and the black of onyx. The pieces had been carved in the early part of the seventeenth century by a master craftsman. No two were alike: all the pawns held their pikes and muskets in different postures; all four castles were dissimilarly shaped and armed; the knights were mounted on destriers of diverse action and temperaments; the bishops prayed, blessed, and admonished; the queens were alternately energetic and regal; the kings theatrically splendid and determined.

"Magnificent," Ragoczy said as Gudrun set the men out on the board.

"Yes," she agreed. "I . . . I have not been able to bring myself to part with them, though they are very valuable and I do not play often. My father, I have been told, turned down two excellent offers because he did not wish to sell them. Doubtless they should be turned over to a museum, but I cannot bring myself to do that." She picked up the haughty white queen. "I used to take them when I was a child and set them out in my room where I could play games with them. I made up stories about them. This woman, I decided, was a Swedish princess who had been given to a Hungarian king as a bride, and discovered that she could not love her husband. When my father taught me to play chess, which he did in order to keep this set safely in its box, I could not bring myself to play the white side because I was convinced I was making it more difficult for the white queen." She tried to laugh at these fancies of her youth, but found her throat was too tight.

"What an unfortunate queen," Ragoczy said. "Would you rather I play white, then?"

She held the piece more tightly. "No. I think it is time I tried white."

"As you wish." He began to set up the black pieces on his side of the board, pausing occasionally to admire them.

When she had set up her men, Gudrun sat for some little time, staring down at the neat squares. Her mouth was firm but her eyes were distant. At last, recalling herself, she rather perfunctorily moved her queen's bishop's pawn out two squares. She paid little attention to her guest's move—king's rook's pawn to the fourth square—and brought out her queen's knight. "I haven't played in some time," she said on her third move. "I'm not very good at it."

Ragoczy withheld his judgment. He knew that she was paying very little attention to the game, and for that reason he did not spend much time thinking out his moves. He did not enjoy chess very much: it had lost its attraction more than a thousand years before when he had played a game for lives. Even a match as trivial as this one brought back memories that pained him, of the five men and two women who had died because of the pieces he lost. That nine others had lived because he won gave him scant comfort.

On her seventh move, Gudrun left her queen exposed to one of Ragoczy's knights. She started when he called her attention to it, looking guiltily at the board. "I wasn't thinking," she said.

"Would you prefer not to play?" he asked lightly, sensing that she was troubled.

"Well . . . I was taught that it was rude to interrupt a game." She tried to laugh at this absurdity but did not do more than catch her breath in her throat. This was turning out to be a more difficult afternoon than she had anticipated, and she did not know why.

Ragoczy regarded her a moment. "Madame, what is it? Would you prefer I leave?"

Maximillian's humiliating diatribe sounded in her mind, and her face colored with shame and defiance. "No. Of course not." The words were louder than she had intended, and sharper.

"More questions of rudeness?" Ragoczy inquired kindly. "You may send me away, you know, and I will not be angry."

Gudrun avoided his eyes. "You would say that, wouldn't you? no matter what you thought." The afternoon had promised so much and was turning out so badly. She did not have enough determination to send him away now. If only she had not spoken to her brother, let him fill her with doubts and questions. She realized that Ragoczy was speaking to her, and forced herself to pay attention.

". . . then perhaps a walk? We need not go far, and neither of us is dressed for strenuous climbing, but an hour away from here would refresh you." He had risen and was holding out his hand to her.

"A walk?" She did not wish to admit she had not heard him at first.

"More of a stroll, then." His smile was fleeting, and he did not press her.

"Yes," she said after a brief consideration. No one would blame her for walking with her neighbor. It was done often, and even a recent widow could not be censured for such an activity. She returned the smile and put her hand in his. "A walk would be very nice."

Once out of the drive for Volkighügel, they took the path that led to Freudenreich and Eck, past Louisenthal and into Dürnbach. It was a pleasant way, skirting the edge of the fields, and their pace was leisurely. In very little time the discomfort Gudrun felt was dispelled by the ease of Ragoczy's manner. She began to enjoy herself. The air was heady with the smells of the end of summer, and it was warm enough to give a touch of laziness to the day.

"That is better," Ragoczy said as they crossed a little bridge over a brook that was nearly dry.

"Better?" She was startled to hear him speak.

"You are more relaxed, Madame." He resumed his walking, close enough to be companionable, far enough away from her that she did not feel put upon or improper.

"I would like it if you would call me Gudrun," she said, feeling more daring now that they were out on this country lane. Somehow she was less hemmed in here, and no longer subject to the restrictions that dictated the conduct of her every hour within the walls of Volkighügel.

"And not so very long ago, you agreed to call me Saint-Germain," he countered. His expression was amused, without any of the harshness she often perceived in men's eyes. "In public, you are Madame Ostneige, which is as it should be. Here, you are Gudrun."

"Here," she corrected him, "I am Rudi." She laughed at her nickname as she said it. How long it had been since she had experienced the buoyancy of spirit that filled her now.

"Do you wish me to call you that?" he asked as he pointed out a pheasant cock just bursting from cover. "Beautiful, isn't he?"

"Yes," she agreed.

"Yes, he is beautiful, or yes, I may call you Rudi?" He had stopped walking and now regarded her with steady, serious eyes.

Recklessly she put her hand through the crook of his arm. "Yes to both of them, Saint-Germain." Her French accent was dreadful, and she repeated it, trying to soften the syllables.

They had come to a bend in the path that wound through a copse of birches, where light winked down through the leaves and the white branches whispered and beckoned in the gentle wind. There was shadow here, and a sense of privacy that closed out much more than the fields around them. Wild rosemary grew beside the trail, and the scent of it was like a summer perfume.

Gudrun's hair was slightly disarranged now, and wisps of it feathered around her face, giving her an elfin halo. Her dress, though demure, was flattering to her overly-thin body, and she sensed the admiration her companion did not voice. "Listen to the leaves; they're telling secrets."

"Are they?" He moved so that he faced her yet kept her hand in the bend of his arm. "What secrets?"

"Oh, tragic ones about hopeless lovers, murmuring unkeepable promises," she said with just enough mockery to let him know she thought it was silly. "Werther, Faust, all of them."

" 'Werd' ich zur Augenblicke sagen, 'Verweile doch, du bist so schön—' " Ragoczy quoted, his dark eyes on her. "What more unkeepable promise is there? Poor Faust. What man could win such a bargain as that one?"

"Is that what the leaves are saying? Do they want the wind to linger?" Gudrun felt suddenly, wonderfully breathless.

His answer was ironic, his eyes tender. "Every lovely moment must fly, and every dreadful one."

"Oh," she said, gazing at him. She had not noticed until now how much sorrow there was in his face, how much compassion. Timidly she lifted her free hand to touch the firm line of his jaw, half-fearing that he would rebuke her, half-fearing that he would not. She did not know what she wanted of him, but he had sounded a chord within her that she had not heard before. "Even this? Must this fly?"

Gently he took her in his arms, letting her head lean against his shoulder. "Especially this." His lips were erotic, warm on her. It was a strangely peaceful kiss, one that she could accept without feeling herself a traitor to Jürgen or her life. Then her pulse quickened, and she moved her head. She was secretly disappointed when he did not urge her to further intimacies:

he kept her within the circle of his embrace, the stillness holding them together.

"Graf . . ." she said when she could trust herself to speak again.

"Saint-Germain," he reminded her, his voice little more than a whisper, hardly louder than the sough of the leaves.

"I didn't mean . . . anything . . ." Reluctantly she stepped away from him, wishing she knew why she felt pressed to do so. Her fingers ran along the piping of her tunic with the same automatic gesture of a nun telling her rosary. It was absurd to place such importance on a single kiss, she told herself as her heartbeat grew louder. She turned to look at the white-bodied trees. "I wish you had not kissed me."

"Truly?" He was neither contrite nor accusing.

"No."

"Ah, Gudrun, you see?" he asked quietly but with such feeling that she was suddenly overwhelmed with the poignance of their touching. "The moment is gone, and it cannot be recalled or recaptured, splendid as it was." He brushed her cheek with the back of his hand. "No, don't be distressed, Rudi."

"I'm not," she said as she continued to finger the piping of her tunic.

"You have no reason to fear me." He waited until she looked at him. "You are afraid that this will change everything, aren't you? That I will not offer my arm to you, or receive an invitation without assuming I have been given certain . . . liberties." He did not need to see her guilty nod to know he was right. "This changes nothing, my dear. I am still your neighbor, and, I hope, your friend."

Konrad Natter had said something very like that to her shortly after Jürgen died, and then had attempted to seduce her six weeks later. She had been willing to pretend that it was the result of a misunderstanding, but she did not deceive herself with believing that Natter wanted anything more than access to her body. It was tempting, so tempting to listen to Ragoczy and imbue his words with a truth she doubted they possessed. "You will expect concessions, won't you?" Her chin had lifted and she could not forget her brother's warnings.

"Why should I?" His expression was at once sad and amused. "What would either of us gain from it? Suspicion? Dislike? Yes, I am aware of how you would feel. Why should I want to sully the delight I take in your company? And yet you are worried that I will force my attentions on you, aren't you?"

"I . . . I don't know." It was not entirely the truth, but she could not bring herself to say more than that.

"You will never have more from me than what you want," he said in a low voice, his dark eyes glowing. "I wish you could believe this."

She gave a wistful smile. "I wish it, too." As the birch trees trembled around them, she quivered, more with a sudden tumult of longing than with chill.

Ragoczy stepped back from her. "Come; it is getting late."

"Yes," she agreed, falling into step beside him, steeling herself to deal with the coaxing or blandishments she had encountered from others.

They never occurred. Ragoczy spoke easily of crops and horses, of the telephone he had just installed at Schloss Saint-Germain, and eventually she put her arm through his again, and drew closer to him as they walked through the long bars of yellow light of this September afternoon.

Text of a letter to Franchot Ragoczy from Simeon Schnaubel.

*Chicago, Illinois*
*November 4, 1924*

*Graf Ragoczy*
*Schloss Saint-Germain*
*Schliersee*
*Bavaria, Germany*

*Dear Graf:*

*I never thought to salvage anything from the financial disaster that struck Germany, and so I am doubly grateful to you for your closing of my affairs there. It was a kindness to do so much, as I am still unable to think of our home there without grief and pain. The children, too, are filled with anguish when Bavaria is mentioned.*

*I have decided that it would be senseless to return to Germany, and so I have made application, through my uncle, to become a citizen of the United States of America. There are strict new laws limiting the numbers of new citizens, but we have been assured that since I am established in a profession and have been able to provide employment to a number of Americans as a result of the expansion of my uncle's business, many of the difficulties that make the way hard for others will not be there for me. The callousness of this no longer has the capacity to upset me as it would have once. Life, I have learned, is not fair, and there is nothing that can be done to make it so. That being the case, I will seize what it offered me and use it to protect and advance my family, what there is left of it.*

*You inquired about the children. Bruno is finishing his first year at Northwestern, where he is studying psychology. He has become fiercely intellectual and is determined to discover and label all the secrets of the mind. Olympie* has entered a private school for girls—costly but apparently worthwhile, as she is doing well. Emmerich has been a bit of a problem: he is enchanted with the gangsters here, and thinks that they are like the old freebooters of the past instead of the bloodthirsty creatures they are. I have tried once or twice to draw a parallel between the behavior of these gangsters and the monsters who killed my wife and son. He does not think there are similarities, but that is, in part, because he believes that the murderers were working with official sanction in Bavaria, whereas here the gangsters are clearly outside the law. Hedda is another matter, and quite a sad one. She has been hospitalized for some time and there has been no improvement. Her physicians say that they have exhausted their skills and the psychiatrist can do nothing more than observe her. Most of the time she sits alone in her room staring out the window at nothing. I have been told that she often does not move for hours at a time. Nothing I have said or done has made a difference, and I despair of her. The Rabbi of our synagogue, Beth Israel, has been to see her and has no word of encouragement to give, except to remind us that God visited much suffering on His People. I find that is little consolation. Bruno chides me for this, but admits that he has not much faith himself.

My uncle is urging me to marry again. He has introduced me to a widow, pleasing, attractive, well-off, and sensible. She is a year older than I am, of good Austrian family. I know that this would be a wise thing for me to do, and I am seriously considering it, although I know that I cannot offer Sarah much of myself—I no longer have much to give. She has told me that she is aware of this and it does not mean too much to her, for she has fond memories of her husband, who died six years ago in a tragic fire. We have decided to give the matter six months' consideration and then discuss it again, to find whether we are still both of a mind to conclude the match. I am aware that my children like her, which is a most important thing. She is fond of them, as well, and has said that she wants the chance to have a family of her own before she is too old, a time that is fast approaching. I'm not certain I can face fathering another child, but that is not yet a decision to be made. Time enough in six months to settle that between us, should we agree to marry.

*You asked about Coolidge, and I gather that you believe he is not handling the economics of this country well. His second term will tell the story, or so my uncle thinks. I have not seen enough of American politics to understand the workings of them. It may well be as you say, and there will be monetary stresses in the next few years, but I doubt they will be as severe as what we saw in Germany.*

*Thank you for sending Mann's* Der Zauberberg. *I have not been able to read it, although I understand that it is excellent. There are too many memories holding me for me to be able to look at it. One day I will read it, but not now.*

*I don't know if the Leopold-Loeb case is being discussed in Bavaria, but it is very much at the center of attention here. An attorney named Darrow has defended them, on psychiatric grounds. It is not a question of guilt but of punishment. You would probably applaud his humanity, but having seen my own son butchered, I have little sympathy for two rich youths who murder for the thrill of it. Darrow's humanity does not extend to the League of Nations, incidentally, which he opposes. From what I gather, he has made himself a reputation defending those criminals no one else would touch. Honorable in its way, I suppose, at least by American standards, but my heart demands sterner justice than what I find here.*

*I will pass along Laisha's note to my children, who will be pleased to hear from her. You say that she is growing up rapidly, which is the way with all children. She is a strange child, but one I was fond of.*

*About the furniture you mention: you have got reasonable and more than reasonable prices for other items, and whatever you should wish to pay will be more than acceptable to me. I had entirely forgotten about that storage room in the old carriage house. If you had not checked it, the pieces would have gone unnoticed indefinitely. As you say the current owners are not going to ask for them, it pleases me that you would want them.*

*Should you come to this country, I hope you will find the time to visit here. I do not think I will return to Germany again. This is a very large country—I had no idea how large until I got here, and even now I must remind myself of its size—and the distances are not al-*

*ways easily traveled, but let me promise you a sincere
welcome here, if you desire to come to the Midwest.*
*Many thanks, and my very good wishes to you.*

*Sincerely,*
*Simeon Schnaubel*

## 4

In the last year, Laisha's hair had darkened to a caramel
blonde that made her very brown eyes seem even more like
chocolate than they had before. Her body had begun to change
as well, growing quickly to a gawky height that confused her
almost as much as her emerging womanhood. She had been
told quite sensibly what was taking place within her, and what
she could expect now and in the future, but nothing prepared
her for the sensations that pricked her, the inexplicable longings,
the discomforts that were not entirely unwelcome, the turmoil
that could make her giddy one moment and despairing the
next, the unsettling redefinition of her body. For the first
time since she had come to Schloss Saint-Germain, she had not
enjoyed the Christmas holidays, and this afternoon, with the
New Year not quite four days old, she found herself fighting
an all-consuming boredom that she had never experienced
before, and did not know how to define.

"Laisha," Ragoczy said as he stopped playing the Haydn
sonata she had asked to hear earlier that day, "what is the
matter?" He fingered the keys lightly, ripples of music cascading from the ormolu-decorated Erard grand piano.

She shrugged, her face sullen. She did not often complain to
her guardian, but she was determined to do so. "Nothing ever
happens here," she said when she had thought about it sufficiently to be deeply aggrieved.

"How unfortunate," Ragoczy remarked, showing an infuriating lack of fighting spirit. He played a few bars of the
opening section of Mussorgsky's *Pictures at an Exhibition*, his
small hands stretching to accommodate the extended chords.
It was a difficult piece for him, one he played more for the
challenge of it than because he did it well.

"Yes, it is." She folded her arms, her face closed and unrevealing.

"What would you rather do?" He repeated the ninth and tenth measures, then went on. "The snow makes it difficult to travel, but it is not impossible. With the telephone out of order because of the broken wires, it will take a little time to make arrangements, if you have something you wish to do instead of stay here."

She answered him immediately this time. "I've never been anywhere. You're always going off to France and Italy and Sweden, and you leave me here like a sack of old groceries." Her chin was squared, determined and grudging.

"Not a sack of old groceries," he protested gently. "At the very least, overly-formal clothes." His smile softened his eyes, and it was all he could do to keep from chuckling. After so many years, he had become a doting father.

"It doesn't matter," she insisted. "I am left here, with my tutors and horses, and Roger and Nikolai to guard me."

"Would you prefer to be sent away to school?" He had considered it before, but she had always wanted to remain with him, and it had been recommended that with her background, boarding school might not be best for her. Ragoczy had been secretly pleased with that decision that kept her with him, where he could watch her grow, learning, maturing. He saw her now as the overgrown, bony girl she was, but he had encountered her sort many times before. His Laisha was the sort of girl who would be lanky and graceless until she was twenty or so and then, she would suddenly develop dignity and elegance and grace which would last her through all her life. He tried to picture her as a grown woman, tried to imagine her suitors, her husband, her children. Did all fathers feel as he did, that only the most understanding, the most gifted and sensitive of men would be worthy of her?

"No, of course not. School would be too . . . strange. If I am able to pass the examinations for the university, and Rosel says that I will be able to, and so does Professor Vögel, then why should I bother? I remember what that cousin of Olympie's said of her school, how they had to sleep in drafty dormatories and never argued with the teachers. I *always* argue," she said, as if it were a point of honor.

"So I understand," Ragoczy said gently. "I think that is part of learning, don't you?" He was playing an air by Handel now, paying little attention to the embellishments of the familiar melody.

"Yes." Again the touch of defiance lifted her chin and brightened her eyes. "That's why I want to travel."

"To Paris or Stockholm?" he inquired. "My next trip will be to Wien, and then, in April, I will go to Venezia. Would you like to spend your birthday on the Grand Canal?" They had arbitrarily assigned the day of their meeting, April 17, as her birthday, and she had been pleased with this.

"The Grand Canal? In a gondola?" Her dissatisfaction had faded and she grinned at him. "Would you let me?"

He nodded, and began to play a song he had not sung for more than three hundred years. " 'Colla febre di gioia mi manca./ Ma piu bramo la pace per il mio cor,/ Or' senza speranza e senza rancor.' " Quite suddenly he stopped playing.

"Papa? What is it?" She had seen that flash of pain that occasionally crossed Ragoczy's features.

"I was remembering a friend. He's dead now. He sang that song one autumn morning, not long before he died." He got up from the piano, knowing that he would not be able to play for a while.

"What was his name?" Neither she nor Ragoczy spoke much of the past: she recalled so little of it, and he found it too difficult, or so she feared.

"His name was Lauro." He said it quietly, with so little emotion that Laisha knew he had not yet ceased to miss his friend.

"Italian?"

"Florentine." He turned back toward her. "I have a house in Venezia. You might like to stay there for a few months. I will arrange for tutors there, or you may take Miss Speits and Miss Arrild with you."

"Would you be there?" She was anxious to go, but dreaded the thought of being left alone in an unknown, foreign city.

"Part of the time. I have business in Milano and Roma, and I would go there, and to Lausanne. Would two months be enough for you?" He saw her enthusiasm and her caution. "You needn't make up your mind at once. With the snow so deep, I will not be going far at the moment. By March I will have to make plans."

"Oh, by March I should be able to be ready." The regal disdain with which she spoke was so unexpected and so inappropriate that Ragoczy, in spite of himself, laughed.

"My child," he assured her a bit later, "you must not be angry with me. I have known Princesses who would have given their jewels to be able to behave as you just did." With an affectionate smile, he came across the room to her. "You're my treasure, Laisha."

"No matter who I am?" There it was, in that trembling question, all her fear, her doubts that would probably never have answers.

"No matter who you are," he said, making a vow of it. "You are my daughter—"

"Your ward," she corrected him sadly.

"My daughter. If the man and woman who gave you birth came through that door at this instant"—he gestured toward the music-room door—"you would still be my daughter in everything but . . . blood." He hesitated. "And that well, that you will never be, and so we will not be concerned with it."

She sighed. "I sometimes wonder if I have brothers or sisters? What if I am the child of a servant who was dressing up in the noble children's clothes? What if one of those who burned the manor found the dress and put it on his own child?" She had heard many times the tale of how Ragoczy came to find her, and each time she was filled with such questions.

"You're tormenting yourself needlessly, Laisha," he said. "It doesn't matter."

"It would matter to Nikolai," she said with certainty. "He . . . he reminded me that I was a noble and he a peasant." For the previous five months, Laisha had had an intense crush on Nikolai Rozoh which had been as short-lived as it was ardent.

"It was kind of him to say that," Ragoczy told her. He had had two interviews with Nikolai, who had feared that he would be dismissed because of Laisha's obvious attachment to him. At the time he had assured Ragoczy that he had done nothing to bring this on himself, and that fond as he was of the child, he was much too old for the girl, had done his best to convince her of this, but she had known him for enough time to think . . .

"Yes. I see that it was," she said in a stifled tone. "I didn't know he minded that much. I just thought that he wanted to show me what I felt wasn't enough for him, since he's older and has lived through so much." Her head lowered and her cheeks darkened to red.

"Laisha, my dear, you will feel this again—" Ragoczy began, but she interrupted him.

"I know better than that now."

"But it's not your mind, your intellect, that does this. You're a bright student, with real gifts and an active curiosity. But you are also becoming a woman, and your body does things to you. Your mind is not isolated from your body. With the greatest determination in the world, you can't escape the consequences of maturing." He was aware that she did not entirely believe him, that she thought this was a reassuring and polite lie invented for her.

"Did you feel that way, when you were my age?" This time she was more forlorn than defiant.

"Well, I am male," he said, evading the question. "And it was . . . a long time ago." Would he ever tell her of those nearly four thousand years? When she was older, he might, or so he promised himself when faced with her inquiries.

"And you don't remember?" Her voice caught.

"Very little," he admitted. "Enough to know that for two or three years I baffled myself. In my homeland, there were customs and rituals to modify the transition, and there was war, so that when I could stand it no longer, it was possible to take up arms rather than battle myself." He had ridden with his father's warriors five times before they had been overcome by the stronger, better-armed southerners. The god, in whose service he was promised at birth, led them, his speed and strength setting an enviable example to those who fought with him. Ragoczy had gained that speed and endurance but had also learned caution. As a youth, he had been reckless to the point of folly.

"Why is it that I'm always being told I'll understand when I'm older, or I'll be ready, or tolerant, or all the rest of it?" She was not complaining now, but asking a weary question with as little emotion as possible. "I *do* want to know, Papa."

"Yes, Laisha." Ragoczy went to her side, brushing the soft wool of her jacket as he gave her a fleeting hug. "Part of it is that it is true. Many things are not understood until age gives them a perspective. Eventually that difference becomes . . . less important. The rest of it . . . there are many things adults have no more comprehension of than an infant. There are things that frighten us. Miss Speits cannot talk about anything having to do with dissection because of her fear of such things. Her uncle was a butcher, did you know? They used to bring the children to watch the slaughter so that they would know where their food came from. Miss Speits becomes ill if asked to eat lamb." He breathed deeply. "No one is immune from such fears, and it is strange to see how ashamed people are of them. You saw what this can do when you asked Miss Arrild to tell you why she would not step into the new telephone box at the station in Hausham, if she wished privacy. At the time, she gave you an unconvincing response and later would not discuss it with you, claiming she would explain it to you when you were old enough to understand, which means that she does not intend to discuss it at all, and is depending on you to forget the incident and her promise. There are many people who cannot endure small, closed places, and she is one. If you were forty instead of fourteen, Miss Arrild could not tell you why she fears this, but it makes it less painful for her to postpone the entire matter."

Laisha had been watching him with a guarded expression. "Do I not remember because of fear?" The question was flung out defiantly, impetuously.

Ragoczy turned toward her, compassion in his dark eyes that contrasted with the carefully flippant tone of his answer. "Are you certain you don't want to wait until you're older to examine that?"

She set her hands on her hips, determined to be angry, but she could not stop the spurt of laughter that shook her. "You can't stop me."

"I don't wish to stop you," he said gravely. "But you must forgive me, my child, for not wanting to see you hurt."

"Do you think I would be?" she demanded.

"Do you think you wouldn't?" He went back to the piano. "Laisha, if you wish to be aided to regain your memory, I will do whatever I can for you. There are alienists and other physicians who work with such cases, and I will put you in their care. If it were safe to do so, I would take you back to Latvia so that you might see what has happened there. At the moment that is a great risk, but in time conditions will alter, and then, should you wish it, I will see that you have the chance to go there." His face was somber now and he did not make any attempt to conceal the depth of his concern. "The reason I hesitate is that once that path is chosen, it is difficult and often impossible to leave it. You must be quite certain that you wish to learn these things."

"I think I am," she said, with emphasis on "think."

His left hand picked out a few notes at random. "As you wish. If you tell me the same thing in one week, I will make whatever arrangements are necessary." Before she could object, he explained. "You've said that you are bored this afternoon, and you have just been through a . . . trying few days. A week isn't long to wait, Laisha. There is no dishonor in changing your mind. What you want is a hard-won thing, and for that reason, all I ask is that you be certain. Will you do that much for me?"

Laisha wanted to find out why Ragoczy had suggested such circumspection, but did not quite have the determination to ask him. She pulled at her untidy hair and moved closer to the piano. "A week of this snow . . . In a week, let us talk again."

"We may talk before then, if you wish it," he said quietly. "I am . . . a trifle old to be a father for the first time, Laisha, and so I must ask you to bear with me."

"But you *will* do it, if I say I want it?" She was not able to hide how deeply she wanted his consent.

"Yes, provided you understand what you're doing. This isn't something you should attempt on a whim." He was silent for a little time while Laisha bit her lower lip. "If there were a way I could simply wave a magic wand and restore your memory to you, intact, painless, I would do it in an instant. But I think it might take much time and great anguish to bring back what you have lost. You did not forget from caprice, but from some emotion or event so . . . overwhelming"—he could not say "hurtful" or "terrible," for that would bring more concern to her—"that you shut it away. You must face that now, and be prepared to learn the reason for it. I'm not saying this to threaten you, Laisha, please believe this. Your suffering hurts me as well; to cause you more without reason . . ."

Laisha could not express herself now, as he turned toward her. Her confusion was too complete. How wonderful it was to know that he did have so much love for her, and how baffling. She had done nothing to deserve it, or so her tutors had insisted on many occasions. She had been instructed in the right manner she should display toward her guardian, whose generosity was remarkable. Her behavior was not in the approved style, and yet it had gained her more than she had known was there for her. "Miss Arrild says I shouldn't . . ." she blurted out, and swallowed hard against the knot in her throat.

"What?" Ragoczy studied her, searching for the cause of her sudden reserve.

"It isn't right that I should talk to you this way." She said it so quietly that she was almost inaudible.

"Isn't right? How? What makes you believe that?" He was perplexed but asked his questions lightly, with a touch of amusement in his dark eyes.

"You are my guardian," she recited. "I have an obligation to you for your kindness and care, and—"

"What nonsense is this? You make me sound like an ogre." He laughed gently.

"You're fine," she said in a soft voice, and then grinned. "You'll take me to Venice, though, won't you?"

"You have my word on it." He offered his hand to her and she took it gravely, her young features settled into as adult an expression as possible.

"In April." She stared at him, determined to fix the date.

"In April." He had come to admire her intensity, and was pleased when she fixed him with her deep brown eyes. This girl would not be bullied, he told himself proudly. She would not become one of those passive, flowery women he had seen often in the past sixty years. Nor would she take the giddy, decadent course, striving for that frenetic gaiety that marked the bright places in Paris and Berlin. She would keep to her own path.

"What are you thinking, Papa?" she asked, folding her arms.

"I am thinking that you are intelligent and independent, and that I am fortunate to know you." He sat down on the bench and began to play a Chopin étude that he knew Laisha liked. As he played, he remarked, "You know, a hundred years ago, pianos didn't sound this way. They were softer. Not as wide, with lower bodies, very thin, and they didn't always hold their tuning very well. There've been a great many changes made in the last century."

"Did you like those other pianos better?" she asked, more of her attention on the notes than on what he said.

"No. At my age you either learn to enjoy progress and change or you begin to retreat. I've played those pianos, and these, and the newer ones being made. Each has its virtues, and each its disadvantages." He finished the étude and turned to Haydn's *Gypsy Rondo*, playing it lightly.

"How long have you had this piano?" She rubbed her hand over the extravagant ormolu ornamentation.

He almost told her, but caught himself. "It was brought here immediately after it was made. That was about 1890, I believe." He had purchased the piano in 1887, but decided not to be too specific: Roger had told him that Laisha occasionally of late asked very pointed questions about her guardian.

"Thirty-five years ago." She ran her finger around one of the more elaborate decorations at the top of the treble front leg.

"Roughly," Ragoczy said, missing one of the octave bounces and striking a jarringly wrong note.

"You were younger than I am?" She could not think of him as a child, no matter how she tried. Yet she wanted to piece together his life, as if it might be a substitute for what she could not remember of her own.

Ragoczy stopped playing. "You're fishing for something, Laisha. What is it?"

She flushed but did not deny it. "I've been trying to learn about you. Roger says that I should talk to you. He doesn't answer my questions."

"That is very wise of Roger," Ragoczy observed with a smile. "He is much in my confidence, and has been with me . . . half my adult life." It had been almost two thousand years since Roger had become his manservant, since he had found Roger being abused in the rain near the incomplete Flavian Circus, yet he had not lied to the girl.

"He comes from Cádiz?" Laisha persisted.

"Yes." It had been Gades when Roger lived there.

"He doesn't look very Spanish," she said. Now that Ragoczy was willing to talk with her, she wanted to make the most of her opportunity.

"I suppose he doesn't. But think of all the peoples who have come to Spain. Visigoths, Moors, Franks, Romans—there's no end to it. You've seen blonde Italians, haven't you? There are also fair Spaniards." He played a few inexpert bars of a Cimarosa sonatina, then broke off and began one of the Beethoven "Bagatelles."

"I suppose so," she said uncertainly. "I haven't traveled very much—"

Ragoczy laughed unhappily. "You've traveled a great deal, child, but not for pleasure."

"And I haven't *seen* much," she went on, admitting to herself that what he said was correct. "I've only been to Zurich and Turin, and that was over a year ago."

"And this spring you will see Venice. It is a beautiful place, filled with splendor and illusion. The Venetians are handsome people, very much like their city. La Serenissima; Venezia, whose mists are bright." He began to play Offenbach's *Barcarole*.

"You've traveled a great deal, haven't you?" she asked a few moments later.

"Yes. Not always by choice."

"Where have you traveled?" She pounced on the question, her brown eyes wide and eager.

His answer was guarded, calculatedly flippant. "Oh, a great many places."

She raised her voice. "Where?"

He considered another evasive answer, then changed his mind. "Most of Europe, of course. Russia. China. India. Persia. Africa. Egypt. I've been to Mexico once." He looked up at her, a self-deprecatory smile on his features. "I much prefer to travel by land: being on the water always makes me ill."

"But you swim," she said, startled. There was a small pool at Schloss Saint-Germain, and Ragoczy often enjoyed an evening's exercise there. Because of the severe winters, the pool was indoors, or at least, that was the explanation he gave.

"True, but that's different." The pool was sunk into an excavation lined with his native earth, which made the water quite pleasant.

"You mean you get seasick?" she asked incredulously. She took such pride in her guardian's elegance and confidence that she could not imagine him in the throes of such an affliction.

"Unfortunately, yes. Most abominably." Once again he changed the work he was playing, choosing this time the refined, didactic music of Padre Soler.

"Seasick. You." In spite of her good intentions, she giggled.

"It's not very amusing when it happens," he said with mock severity. His symptoms were not the usual ones, but his discomfort was just as intense. "Be grateful I don't take you to London. The Channel crossing inevitably upsets me."

"I would like to go to London," she said at once, hoping to take advantage of his willingness to include her in his plans.

"One day you will, doubtlessly. And perhaps, if I can bear the thought of the Channel, I will come with you." He looked down at the keyboard. "Do you like Soler?"

Laisha sighed, recognizing in that deft change of subject that Ragoczy was not going to let her interrogate him further. "A bit. I like Handel better."

"As you wish." He stopped in mid-phrase and began to play Jupiter's Song from *Semele*. He had reached the second part of the melody when there was a deferential knock on the door. "Come," he called without interrupting the music.

Roger came into the room. "I'm sorry to interrupt, my master. There is a . . . gentleman here to see you. He insists that it is urgent."

Ragoczy continued to play. "Who is this visitor?"

"He used to work for BKK, and now is employed by the *Völkischer Beobachter* in some capacity. Doubtless it has to do with finance. He claims to have met you, and he does not remember speaking to me." Roger said this quite calmly, but there was enough indignation in his words to reveal his emotions.

"Rauch? What does he want, did he say?" Ragoczy frowned as he played, his divided attention making the simple piece more difficult than it should have been.

"No." Roger snapped the word.

"Very well. Show him into the morning room and tell him I will be with him shortly. Have Enzo make up a tray of biscuits and cheese for him." He glanced up at Laisha. "Will you mind, my child?"

"If you must speak to him . . ." She left the rest hanging, but did not truly object.

"Apparently it's necessary," he muttered as he brought the music to a close. "I don't know how long this will take. If you would like to meet me in my study later, we might continue talking."

"Papa," she said impulsively as Ragoczy rose, "why did you look so sad when you were playing that last piece?"

"Did I look sad?" Ragoczy asked, genuinely startled. He thought a moment. "I had a friend, many years ago, who liked the story of Jupiter and Semele. I suppose I was missing her."

This was an unexpected opportunity, and Laisha seized it anxiously. "Who was the friend?"

"Her name was Olivia. She lived in Rome." He was not able to smile, but there was a gentling of his expression. "You would have liked her, and she you."

Laisha experienced an instant of consuming jealousy that was gone almost before she felt the heat of it. Her father was a man, and she was not so naive that she did not know he had a man's needs, but he had never before said a woman's name with quite that inflection. Her father had never mentioned his women at all. Her father . . . she pressed her lips together, gazing seriously at Ragoczy as he crossed the room. He was her father, and she accepted it at last. Her parents were less than ghosts to her. She had no life that did not include him, or none that she could remember. She gathered her courage and called out as he stepped into the hall, "What became of her? You said 'was.' "

Ragoczy turned back, and answered with old grief. "She died, my child."

"Did you love her?" She had not intended to ask the question, but having said it, she held her breath for his answer.

"Very much. But if you are worried that this detracts from you, do not be. Until I found you, I never knew what it is to be a father, and for that I am grateful. That's the least of it. My daughter, my child, you are so precious to me that—"

"There you are," said a stern voice from down the hall. "I have been waiting."

Ragoczy met Laisha's eyes before he closed the door, saying to his visitor, "I have been occupied with my . . . ward. It is my habit to see to her music instruction myself."

"Isn't that a bit indulgent?" Rauch suggested as he matched Ragoczy's brisk stride. "It often spoils a child to have too much attention."

"Does it. I will have to take your word for it, Herr Rauch," Ragoczy said in a tone that did not encourage further discussion on that topic. He reached the door to the morning room and held it politely. "Pray, come in and tell me what it is you require of me so urgently."

Rauch found Ragoczy's manner a trifle disquieting, and he hesitated before crossing the threshold into the gold-and-rose-colored room. "I don't suppose you've heard from one of us before now?"

"One of us?" Ragoczy repeated as he pulled the door shut behind him. "No, I don't believe so. You are employed by the *Völkischer Beobachter*, as I understand it. No one from that paper has talked to me." He did not add that he found the rantings of that publication repugnant.

"Not the *Völkischer Beobachter*, no, the NSDAP. A representative of the SA has been talking to various landowners in this part of the country." He glanced around at the French furniture and Italian paintings and could not mask his distaste.

"The NSDAP? What do they want?" Ragoczy kept up a pleasant expression, but he was wary of this man and the air of determination that clung to him like an odor.

"It's the SA, really. You have heard of them? The Sturmalteilung? Herr Gansser mentioned it to a few of your neighbors, and we have assumed that you were aware of our requirements." Helmut Rauch stood very still. Even in his business suit he gave the impression of wearing a uniform.

"No one has talked to me. On the other hand, I have indeed heard of the SA. From what I have learned, I doubt I would be in a position to help you." He kept his manner polite, but there was not the least hint of cordiality.

Apparently Helmut Rauch did not notice this. "Oh, you're wrong there, Graf. You are in a most excellent . . . location.

Yes. This estate, with the mountain behind it and the lake so near, it's ideal. You must realize that. There's no better situated land around Schliersee." He favored Ragoczy with a rapid movement of his lips that might be mistaken for a smile.

"I fail to see how that concerns the SA, Herr Rauch." He was lying: already he was certain he knew the purpose of the man's intrusion, and he grew increasingly apprehensive.

"That is because you have not been made aware of the great forces being marshaled in the cause of Deutschland. Too long have we been made to cringe under foreign tyranny and international disgrace." He remembered Maximillian Altbrunnen saying something of the same sort and wished he had the same oratorical gifts of that young man.

"But I am not Deutsch," Ragoczy reminded him quietly.

"Your name is a distinguished one. All of Hungary knows it." He glowered at the other man. "You are of an age that you can still recall the glory of the Empire. Austro-Hungary and Deutschland together can change the face of Europe."

"That has already occurred," Ragoczy said, keeping his voice steady. "I am not one to wish for war, Herr Rauch."

"Not war, Graf, *preparedness*. Our army is mocked by the cruel despots in Paris and the incompetents in London. We are not allowed weapons or armor to practice our drills in the field. What use is it to disguise a bicycle as a tank and pedal around an open field? That is where the SA comes in, and why I've come to speak to you." He placed one hand on his hip and watched his host, waiting for the moment of realization to sweep over him.

That realization had come to Ragoczy already, but he had not welcomed the information it offered him. "I can see that an army should have weapons for target practice as well as armored vehicles to take on maneuvers for training purposes, but how does the SA propose to alter this? The French and the English are not going to stand aside and allow the terms of the Versailles Treaty to be flaunted by the NSDAP or anyone else."

"And you approve?" There was a controlled fury in his voice, and his hands clenched at his side.

"It is not for me to feel one way or another. My position here, being that I am a foreigner, does not provide for an opinion." He regarded his visitor urbanely. "You were employed by Bayerisch Kreditkorperschaft and know fairly well how my affairs stand, including my alien status. There are

those who would not look favorably on my interference, in any
way, in your politics."

"This is a different matter." Helmut kept from grinding his
teeth with an effort of will.

"Because you are involved in it?" Ragoczy inquired sardonically. "I am afraid that I don't wish to put my entire household
in jeopardy because of a local political squabble. You will
probably find that reprehensible, but—"

"You don't understand!" Helmut burst out. "You don't understand at all. You've been watched because of your friendship with that Jew Schnaubel. I am trying to give you the
chance to make yourself less endangered. There are those who
are not pleased to learn that you were the one who aided the
man to sell his house, and took care of the transaction. There
is a man in Berlin who expressed to me his great displeasure
at what he had learned of you."

Although Ragoczy felt himself go cold, he kept his appearance of faintly condescending politeness. "What business is it
of anyone in Berlin?"

Helmut began to pace around the room. "You're being stubborn, Herr Graf. You are refusing to look at the situation in
an unbiased manner. You are letting yourself be led by persons who are without honor. You behave as if none of this can
touch you, but I warn you now that you will find it is otherwise. We are not simply a group of discontented radicals given
to street-corner oratory and beer-hall brawls. Our men do not
all come from the army, or from the unemployed, but from
very high places, to those you would not believe. In defying
me, you anger them, something a man in your position cannot
afford to do. You had best heed my warning, because—"

The door opened unexpectedly and Roger came into the
room bearing a tray. "The food you requested. I am sorry it
took so long." He carried the tray to the brass-topped table by
the window. "Excuse me, Mein Herr, but would you prefer
wine or beer? We have an excellent Mosel from Burg Landshut."

Helmut glared at the manservant, but at last he barked out
a response. "It makes no difference to me. Bring me either."
He had wanted to turn down the offer, but with the food
already in the room, such a refusal would be ultimately boorish, and any opportunity he might have to talk sense to this
obdurate foreigner would be lost.

"I think the Mosel would please you more," Roger said
calmly before he left the room.

"Now, Herr Ragoczy . . ." Helmut recommenced once the door was safely shut.

"Do have something to eat, Herr Rauch. You may harangue me later, if you wish, but if you do not taste the food, I will have to sustain two lectures today; one from you and one from my chef." He gestured to the table, and stood aside so that Helmut would have easy access to it.

"I am not particularly hungry . . ." he said stiffly.

Ragoczy shook his head. "You must make some effort. My chef is Italian, and for him, cuisine is a matter of honor."

There was no gainsaying that affable, charming, determined man. Helmut was in his house without proper invitation and was being received with full hospitality. If he failed with this man, he would earn a great deal of displeasure from the Bruderschaft. That thought settled in his guts like a lump of hot coal. The Bruderschaft was not forgiving. So he muttered a few words of thanks and sat down at the table, studying the fare on the tray. At least, he thought with ponderous humor, if he had to be condemned, he would indeed have a hearty last meal. As he reached for a long, thin roll, he looked at his host in surprise. "You are not going to join me, Graf?"

"Alas, I fear it isn't possible for me to eat all the fine food Enzo prepares. I hope you will excuse me." He bowed slightly and took his seat in one of the chairs nearby, close enough to the table to allow conversation, far enough away that it would not embarrass Helmut to eat. He was about to say something more when Roger returned with the bottle of wine, which he opened with a flourish.

"Will there be anything else, my master?" Roger asked when he had poured out the first glass for Helmut.

"No, that is all: thank you, Roger." His manner was unruffled, but there was concern and anger at the back of his dark, penetrating eyes. He sat back and waited for Helmut to speak again, all the while wondering how much he dared say to this zealous, inflexible guest.

Text of a letter from Professor Isidore Riemen to Dag von Freigrundstück of I. G. Farben.

*Breitnau*
*March 10, 1925*

*Dag von Freigrundstück*
*Hotel Hartenburg*
*Mainz*

My dear Dag:

Your office told me this note would reach you at this address, and so I have written at once, assuming that if for some reason this does miss you, it will find you at the end of your holiday. I, too, have taken some time to myself, as you can see from my heading. Of late, things have begun to go well, so that I have decided that a little time to myself is not going to force me to return to a complete disaster.

The work, as I told you in November, is going far better than I had expected. Without Graf Ragoczy we would not be nearly so far advanced. It is a pity that the man will not consent to working with you directly, but he has told me many times that over the years he has preferred to work alone, in his own unorthodox ways. You know what the old hochgebornen are, and he is one of the worst of them; not at all like you, Dag, and your sensible ways.

The formulae you have requested have been sent to Farben by messenger, and as soon as you are back at work, you will have the chance to examine our results. As I have warned you in the past, there is nothing so concrete here that you can at once begin to issue new shares in the division, but I believe that we are moving much closer to a workable synthetic fuel. It is Ragoczy's belief that we should also devote time to making a more efficient fuel for aeroplanes. Apparently he agrees with the

American General Mitchell, that aeroplanes are the wave
of the future. I have been cautious about this, but I take
this opportunity to mention it to you now, in case you
wish to give the matter your consideration. Certainly
there are more aeroplanes about that need fuel, but compared to automobiles and trucks, it is the merest dot on
the graphs. I do agree with Ragoczy, however, that improved fuels for aeroplanes mean improved range and
load capabilities, and so I do not dismiss the matter out
of hand.

A sad matter about President Ebert. So young—only
fifty-three. But I imagine that the last few years have
each been a decade to him, what with all he has had to
bear with. The dissatisfaction in this country is most
discouraging. I see it every day in my students, and I
wonder what will become of them when they are my age,
and faced with the responsibilities of maturity.

I realize you are concerned about the possibility of
charges being brought in regard to Antonia von Fritsch. I
have discussed the matter at length with her uncle, and he
now realizes that it was all a misunderstanding. It is true
that I enjoy the attentions of little girls, but what man of
our years does not? Let me assure you that it appeared
much worse than it was. The child is to be sent away to
school next year, by the way, and so the gossip, if any,
should end with that. You need not be concerned that
there will be any unpleasant repercussions regarding this
event.

Ragoczy and I have recently discussed the insecticides
being manufactured in the United States. He believes that
circumspection is advisable because of the hazard that is
present in any poison. While his caution is laudable, I
think that it would not be unwise to experiment. Crop
losses to insects are staggering, and if there is a way to
preserve more foodstuffs, then it must be considered as
much a priority as political stability.

Speaking of political stability, Ragoczy mentioned in
passing that one of the more radical political groups in
Bayern, the NSDAP, has been giving him some trouble.
Nothing serious, of course, but a man of that sort does
not wish to be troubled by malcontents. There is apparently a man associated with the Völikischer Beobachter
who has made importunities of Graf Ragoczy, who has
pointed out that he cannot align himself one way or the

*other, as he is not Deutscher. You have friends who can mention this unfortunate situation, haven't you? I would hate to see this man move to France or Italy because he has found our countrymen less than hospitable to him. We cannot afford to be deprived of his abilities, or turn them over to our enemies. He believes that at the moment we lead the world in biochemistry, and if this is so, it would be wise to keep so excellent a scientist with us. For all his peculiar methods, he has more skill and understanding than most men achieve in a lifetime.*

*Let me know what you think of the formulae and I will devote myself to expanding the applications as soon as I return to my laboratory.*

*I hope that your holiday is as pleasant as my own. You know, there is nothing so stimulating as a long walk in the country, seeing the mountains in their first color. It is cold, but that is simply more stimulation. In the summer one is lethargic, but with spring making its first appearance, I am met each day with some new miracle, and I find life coming back into my soul.*

*Most cordial regards,*
*Isidore Riemen*

## 5

Laisha ran down the steps of the palazzo, shouting with delight. "Oh, Papa, it's *beautiful!*"

Ragoczy got out of his new silver-blue Isotta-Fraschini Tipo 8A and held the door open for her. "I thought you'd like it."

"I do!" She reached him and fell laughing into his arms. "You said you would have a surprise, but I didn't think it would be *anything* like this."

"Well, you insisted that you wanted to ride home in style." He ruffled her hair, which had recently been cut into one of the newer modes, so that two wings of hair framed her face and stopped just below her earlobes. She was wearing new clothes as well, very stylish in the *garçonne* cut introduced to fashion the year before by a young modiste called Coco Chanel. Her jacket had a boyish collar, and her skirt, falling only ten inches below her knees, was pleated and embroidered at the hem. In another few years, Ragoczy thought with a little sadness, she would be ready for her social debut.

She put her hand in his and beamed at him. "Papa, Papa, you are simply magnificent!"

"Mille grazie," he said. "Now, tell me what you have been doing all morning."

"I have been to il teatro municipale, which is quite beautiful. I like Verona, but I didn't think I would at first. When you decided to come here, I was not very happy about it." She said this in a rush, as if he might not have been aware of her sulks and pouting when they left Venezia.

"So it's all for the best?" he asked with some amusement as they started up the steps.

"Probably. Only now, I don't want to leave for Paris, so I'll probably pout all over again." They entered the palazzo side by side and she nodded toward a large bouquet of flowers. "Those are from the Cabrinis. Aren't they pretty?"

"They certainly are," Ragoczy said wryly, thinking of the family's oldest son, who was clearly smitten with Laisha and found a constant variety of excuses to send her presents. "I suppose Gaetano brought them."

"Naturally," Laisha said pertly. "He always brings them."

Ragoczy was silent for a bit as they walked through to the central, flower-filled courtyard. "You know, Laisha," he said quietly, "you find his attentions flattering and amusing, and there's nothing wrong with that. But I think you don't realize how deeply he feels about you. Don't laugh at him, no matter how foolish he may seem to you. There is nothing foolish about love."

She sighed theatrically. "But when he comes here, telling me that the night has been a thousand years because he has not seen me, well, what can I do? It's *ridiculous!*"

"I knew a woman once, a very brilliant and capable woman, who was not pretty, although she was made of beauty, if you cared to look for it. No one ever said to her those things that you dismiss, and her soul was parched with need for them." He frowned distantly, remembering Ranegonda in her stark, cold keep.

"Did you say things like that to her?" Laisha asked shrewdly.

"Only twice. The first time, she was gruff with me, and it took me a while to understand that she wanted such words so much that she could not admit her longing even to herself."

He stopped and looked at an orange tree which stood in a tub near the small fountain in the courtyard. "The Romans had an arrangement not unlike this, with the atrium in the center of the house. At first they were closed rooms with a good-sized hole in the ceiling to let in light, but later, they became more Greek, turning into peristyles, courtyards like this one." His villa in Rome had had two atria, which was most unusual.

"About the woman," Laisha said. "What became of her?"

Ragoczy looked away. "I was hoping to turn the subject."

"You initiated it," was her rejoinder.

"Yes; I did." He moved a few steps away from her, disquieted by the strength of feeling her memory could evoke in him after more than a thousand years. "There was famine, and because of it, there were riots. She was killed in one of them."

"Oh," Laisha said, suddenly very serious. "I see why you did not want to tell me." At that moment she looked very young, like a lost child instead of a grown girl on the edge of womanhood.

"My own emotions had something to do with it," Ragoczy admitted. "You don't need to think . . ." He gave a turn of his hand. "My child, what I wanted to tell you is that love, welcome or unwelcome, is still love."

"All right," was her guarded response.

"Tell me, do you like Gaetano?" He started toward one of the side doors, motioning her to come with him.

"I don't know," she said. "Sometimes I do. Occasionally he treats me as if I were a ten-year-old, and completely ignorant of the world, which I am *not*." Her indignation sharpened her tone and lent fire to her eyes. "Besides, he's only seventeen and hasn't been anywhere. He likes Mussolini, too. I don't understand how anyone can do that."

"You aren't Italian, Laisha." It was not an explanation, but it diverted her a moment.

"Yes, and sometimes Gaetano acts as if that were a crime. I've told him I'm Russian, which I probably am. He doesn't approve of Russians." She folded her arms as they went toward the conservatory.

"It's fashionable to disapprove of Russians. You mustn't blame him. He doesn't disapprove of you." He held the door for her so that she could step into the plant-filled room. The air here was pungently green, very rich, as if a seed tossed into the air could sprout from it. Laisha wrinkled her nose. "Why does Principessa Antonino let you stay here?"

"She and I are old friends," Ragoczy explained, motioning her to a marble bench.

"She must be sixty." Laisha sat down, taking care with her new clothes.

"Seventy-two, in fact." Ragoczy did not sit, but picked up a long smock from its hook by the potting bench. He donned this, continuing to speak with Laisha. "I have known various members of her family for a good portion of my life."

Laisha puzzled over this, then took her courage in her hands. "She said something to me when she was here, something about you."

Ragoczy stopped in the act of adding potting soil to a small wooden tub. "Oh? What was it?"

"She said that you hadn't changed, in all the years she has known you." It was frightening to say such things. She could feel a tension she did not understand gather in Ragoczy's mind.

After a bit, Ragoczy resumed his task and said with a lack of concern he was far from feeling, "Those of my blood generally age very slowly. The Principessa, like many old people, is kindly in her memories."

"Is that all?" Her fingers were gripping the unyielding marble.

To his sorrow, Ragoczy discovered that he could not lie to his child. "No. It is not all. But it is enough."

Laisha jumped to her feet, her face pink and her deep brown eyes swimming with tears. "Why won't you tell me? Why do you always pretend you don't know what I'm talking about? I don't care what you've done. Everyone kills people in war, or they are killed. You don't trust me. You think I'm as much of a child as Gaetano does, and it isn't fair!" She pounded her fists against her legs as her voice rose.

"No, no, Laisha," Ragoczy protested, distressed. He had always known she was an observant child, and living so close to him, as she had done, he ought to have anticipated this moment. He had known there would be a time when he must offer her some explanation, but he had hoped that it would be later, when he was more prepared to face her disgust. And when would that be? he asked himself sardonically. Would there ever be a time when he could face her revulsion, her loathing?

"What is it?" she demanded, the tears coming at last.

He put his trowel aside and came to her, taking her into his arms. "Laisha, my girl, my child, my daughter, no, no."

"Why won't you tell me?" she asked again, pressing her face into his shoulder.

"Because," he said quietly, stroking her hair as he spoke, "I am afraid."

Her tears ended in a hiccup. "That can't be—"

"It is."

"—the reason." She brought one hand up and wiped her eyes. "I cry all the time here. Gaetano said that I'm worse than the Italians."

"Russians have that reputation," Ragoczy said with a trace of amusement.

"Papa, I keep *asking* and *asking* and *asking*, and all you do is put me off with another tale, or information about the Romans. What *is* it?" She sniffed, uncertain of what to do next.

"Laisha Vlassevna, can you trust me?" he asked her, and felt her nod. "Then will you believe me when I say that I am no criminal, at least not in the accepted sense. I have done things that have been against the law, but such things cannot affect you. You tell me that you have heard the Principessa speak of me. You told me a few months ago that Roger would not answer your questions. I have not done this to harm you, my child, but because I feared then, and I fear now, what you would feel . . ." He stopped, and went on in a gentler tone. "I admit that I am older than you think me. Much older." He met her eyes as she looked at him.

"How much older?" she asked in a whisper.

"A great deal older." He stepped back from her, taking her hands in his. "My friend Olivia, whom I mentioned to you? Do you recall her?"

"Yes. You said she died in Rome."

"So she did. In 1658." He watched her face as she considered what he had said.

"But if you knew her . . ." She was breathless, and her hands tightened on his without warning. "If you knew her, you were . . . alive then."

"Yes." His face was somber now, his dark eyes intent.

Her face blanched. "Oh." It was hardly audible, and for that reason more devastating to Ragoczy.

"Do you begin to see why I am afraid?" He released her hands. "I should not have told you, not now. In a few years, I might have found a way to prepare you for this, but . . ." He could not ask her what she felt toward him now. As often as he had faced the abomination of others, there had never been as much pain for him as there was now, as he looked at the girl who had become his child. What would she do, he thought, if he had told her the whole truth—that it had been nearly four thousand years since he rose from his grave, that he was not quite what she thought him—in the plainest language? With this minuscule piece of information, Laisha was staring at him, eyes enormous in her face, mouth half-open. He could offer her no consolation, no lying promises that he was a sort of conjurer's trick.

"Papa?" she whispered.

He clung to that word with all the strength of his despair. "Yes?"

"I . . . I won't tell anybody." It was the only thing she could say to him. Her feet, she thought, were turned to marble, and her body was somehow not her own. She could not move, either to flee or to seek the protection of Rogoczy's arms.

"Thank you." He was able to keep the irony from his voice, but not his sadness.

"I won't."

"Yes: you have told me so." He saw how ambivalent she felt, how deep in conflict she was. Against his better judgment, he stretched out his hand to her, justifyng the action to himself by deciding that an adult might have the right to choose whether or not to reject him, but someone as young as Laisha would need the reassurance to gain confidence. He knew it for the rationalization it was, but he did not withdraw his hand.

For Laisha, that simple, pleading motion broke the spell that held her. She dashed forward, flinging herself against Ragoczy's chest, her arms tightly around him. "Papa, Papa, Papa, Papa," she repeated, as if in prayer.

With nameless gratitude, Ragoczy put his arms around his daughter. Often, when consumed with grief, he had wished that he had not lost the ability to weep; now he had no tears for joy. If Laisha could accept so much, she might one day be willing to know him for what he was, and not shrink from him. But what would he say to her? My daughter, I drink blood *but not your blood*. "My child."

"Is that why you don't want to live in Zurich?" she asked a bit later.

Ragoczy had gone back to his potting, but he paused in his work. "It is one reason, yes. There are two eminent professors there, men of great learning. I worked with them more than forty years ago, and should I live there, they would call on me, out of courtesy, unless I chose to be a recluse. Which I prefer not to do. Recluses attract too much attention to themselves."

"But they never see anyone. How can they?" She had passed her initial shock and was caught in the first tremors of excitement. Her guardian, her father, was not just an exiled nobleman, which she had long assumed; he was uniquely old, a man of great experience and mystery. And he had taken her in. Her youthful vanity began to assert itself once more.

"For the very reason that no one sees them. What more fertile ground for speculation? I have tried to be isolated, but it does not suit me or my . . . nature. A foreigner like me must be visible, or he becomes an object of suspicion. That still may occur, of course, but when one has friends, well, there are certain options available." He took a small jar from a rack by the potting table and opened it.

"What options?" She had braced her elbows on her knees and her chin in her hands.

He began to mix a bit of the fluid from the jar with water. "First, there is being abreast of the news. Someone living away from society does not hear those first whispers that may mean survival to him. Then, there will be those who take the time to warn him when there is danger. That is most essential. And a man with friends has a degree of power—it can easily disappear, but it is better than nothing." That had happened to him in the past, too often. "A man who has friends is less easily made a scapegoat."

"But then . . ." She faltered. "The nobles of Russia had friends."

"True enough, but most of them were other nobles. They needed friends among the peasants." He poured the liquid mixture over the seedling in the tub.

She considered this. "Because it was the peasants who revolted?"

"In part. The peasants and those who aligned themselves with their cause. You may see echoes of the same thing here, with the Duce. He offers an alternative to the aristocracy, though what he proposes is simply a different set of nobles." He picked up the tub and set it on one of the platforms. Most men would have had to struggle with such a burden, but he lifted it easily.

Laisha waited until he had finished arranging the tub to his satisfaction. "Papa, would the professors in Zurich recognize you?"

"Very probably. We were colleagues, and one of them worked with me on a daily basis for more than eight years." He had selected another tub. "We have been asked to call on the Cabrinis around sunset. Do you mind seeing Gaetano twice in one day?"

"Oh, no," she said, her humor improving. "If he says anything too silly, I will try not to laugh."

"You're a woman of the world today, are you?" He was once again mixing potting soil.

"Not yet," she admitted. "One day I will be. I'll be tall and very elegant, like Ariana Scintelese. I'll wear lace stockings that cost hundreds of marks a pair and dress only in silk. I think one of those long ivory cigarette holders would be right, don't you?" Her voice deepened in an attempt to achieve the rich, husky sound of the sensual, sophisticated women she had seen and longed to emulate.

"You'll probably be tall," Ragoczy allowed. "For the rest of it, if that is what you want to be, then by all means indulge yourself. But if you don't truly feel inclined to being a social siren, don't waste your time with it." He had taken another seedling and was setting it in the large tub.

"I wouldn't do it capriciously," she protested, shamming insult. "Only stupid women do such things for mere amusement."

"Mere amusement," he repeated, chuckling once, a little bitterly, as he thought of the women at the resorts of Tegernsee and Bad Wiessee. Their interest in him was, as he knew too well, mere amusement.

"I think I would like to be passionate. My heart would be broken many times, but my soul would shine as bright as diamonds." She opened her arms, exclaiming as she did, "I want to be enthralling!"

Ragoczy poured more of his mixture over the seedling. "What poets has Gaetano been reading to you? And don't tell me that he has not been reading you poetry."

Laisha dropped her arms and gave an embarrassed titter. "Leopardi, Guerazzi, di Giacoma, and some of D'Annunzio. He's the one who's in trouble. And sometimes he reads me Byron. His English is very bad."

"Is yours good?" he asked in an affectionate tone.

"It's better than his." She got up from the bench and came over to the potting table. "What are you doing?"

"Transplanting. The Principessa has a desire to line her

drive with pine trees, and so I have offered to grow them for her." He indicated another four seedlings. "These are the last of them. I've prepared most of the others already."

"How strange. Pine trees." She gave him a wistful smile. "I miss the pines at Schloss Saint-Germain. I didn't think they would matter at all, but while we were in Venezia, I began to ache for the sight of a grove of trees, *any* trees."

"It isn't practical to have a large grove of trees in Venezia," he chided her as he set the next tub in place.

"No. I liked Venezia. I think I like Verona, too. Italy is a golden country, Papa, but I'm starting to want to see Schliersee again." She clasped her hands together, a bit self-consciously.

"Do you want to go back?" There was no criticism in his voice, nor any hint of it in his expression.

She nodded. "I would like that. I miss Roger and . . . and Nikolai. I am quite sensible about Nikolai now."

"Yes, I realize that. And so does Nikolai. He has said so to me. We all realize that you needed time to have that infatuation run its course." He was quite certain that she did not wish to be reminded of how devotedly she had followed Nikolai.

"I've thought that perhaps one of the reasons you agreed to bring me with you to Italy was that you were afraid that if I remained at Schloss Saint-Germain I would pursue Nikolai again." She unclasped her hands. "I wouldn't do that, Papa. I wouldn't . . . not anymore."

"Yes, girl, I know," Ragoczy said, continuing his work on a third tub. "I told you that none of us blamed you for your feelings. They were intense, but that's to be expected."

"If you remind me again that I am young, I will scream," she warned him, her eyes brightening.

"Then I won't, but that will not change the facts. Ma si muove." He set another seedling pine in place.

"What does that mean?" she asked, recognizing her father's deft way of changing the subject, but unable to resist it.

"It means, 'but it still moves.' Galileo said it or something like it, when he was forced to recant. He had published a paper that said the earth moves around the sun, and—"

"But it does!" Laisha exclaimed.

"Yes. But the Church did not agree. Your reaction just now was his. He recanted but remarked that it changed nothing. Ma si muove." He reached for his special liquid and dribbled it onto the little pine sprout.

"Papa, what's that?" She was pointing to the fluid he had mixed.

"It's for plant growth. My special secret, Laisha." He lifted the jar. "I make it up in large batches, very concentrated, then I dilute it and use it to help new plants grow. I've got a good supply of it at Schloss Saint-Germain. I use it on the roses and my herbs."

"But what is it?" She knew that his garden was much-admired and had often been surprised to see how much finer his flowers were than others in the neighborhood.

"A secret; I told you." He stepped back. "Now, go along and take your bath. We'll have to leave for the Cabrinis before too long. And perhaps you might want to dress a bit more à la jeune fille? I don't mind your clothes, but unless you wish Gaetano's mother to be even more worried about him than she is, it might be wise to take the time to be a bit less . . . adult."

"I'm not a child," she said, not quite hotly.

"Laisha, I am quite aware of that, but neither are you quite a lady of the world. Your moiré dress with the lace trim would be ideal—not too young, but not as worldly as that outfit you're wearing." He smiled his encouragement at her.

"I don't intend to be dowdy, or a fairy-tale miss!" Her hands were on her hips and she had that familiar combative stance that he had seen several times in the last few years.

"Of course not," Ragoczy said at once. "You will look completely charming, which you are, and at the same time you will not have to deal with Madame Cabrini's sharp tongue. You remember that the last time we visited them, Signorina Voltatempo had a most uncomfortable time of it."

Laisha swallowed once and relaxed. "I remember. But she wouldn't do that to me, would she? Since I'll be there with you?"

"You must recall that her son has been coming here making calf's eyes at you for some little time. If you arrive in your grandest clothes, she will think that you are attempting to snare him, and she will defend him. Yes, I know," he went on without giving her a chance to interrupt him. "You wish to present the best appearance you can, and that is unobjectionable; but in this instance, you will find it better to consider the wider ramifications of your actions. This woman is not the sort who will be capable of accepting you on face value, or dress value."

"But there's no reason for her to be that way," Laisha said, trying to sound as sensible and grown-up as possible. "I'm not going to . . . to *seduce* Gaetano."

"That may be, but she will not believe it, particularly if you wear that dress." He took a rag from the pocket of his smock and wiped his hands fastidiously. Earth, he thought, might be necessary to him, but slovenliness was not. "Go on, my child. And do not look daggers at me, please: when you are an old, old lady, you will still be my child and I will call you that."

"Will you be . . . alive when I am an old, old lady?" Some of the awe she had known earlier returned, and she held her breath for his answer.

"As alive as I am now," he promised her.

"And will you be an old, old man?" She could not imagine him wizened and bent, walking with a cane. He would always be straight and impressive, graceful in his movement, compelling in his manner, she was certain of it. He wore an invisible mantle, she thought, for he was the most regal man she had ever seen. To see him reduced in any way—he would not be Ragoczy.

"I'm an old, old man already." He touched her shoulder lightly, to turn her toward the conservatory door. "Go on. If you don't dawdle over your flowers, you will have time for a good, long soak. Lisa will help you dress, should you wish it."

"Oh, all right," she said, obeying him at last. When she reached the door, she turned in the hope of having the last word. "I'm not going to be compliant about my clothes forever, Papa."

He laughed outright, one of his rare, free laughs. "Heaven forfend. I didn't think you would be."

She raised her chin, to let him know she was miffed, but there was a smile on her lips that gave the lie to the tilt of her head. She made a crisp turn on her heel and left the conservatory, followed by Ragoczy's mirth.

On her way to her room she determined to avoid the hall where Gaetano's flowers were, but as if of their own accord, her feet guided her there. She stopped before the luxurious display, smelling the perfume they exuded, entranced by their prettiness. That Gaetano would want to give these to her! Her mirror told her that she was too tall and gangling to be worthy of such a gift, but Gaetano had insisted that she was wholly perfect, and that it was the flowers that were honored, not she. At the time she had very nearly laughed, and now she was glad that she had controlled herself. She picked one of the half-opened roses and cupped it in her hands. It might be, she conceded, that Ragoczy was right. If she flaunted herself, it would not be her, but Gaetano who would bear the brunt of

Madame Cabrini's wrath. He would be the one who would have to listen to those scornful words. She turned toward the stairs slowly, and mounted them in thoughtful silence.

Ragoczy lingered at his tasks for almost half an hour, and finished putting all the seedling pines into the tubs where they would grow for the next five years. He liked gardening, although he rarely took the time to indulge in it. Most of the time he devoted to his research, his reading, and his music. He had acquired the skill in those tranquil years when he had presided over the Temple of Imhotep. Those days, the temple itself, were long vanished, but the interest remained with him, a tenuous link to those distant times. The chiming of a clock in the hall warned him that it was time to dress, and he left the conservatory for his rooms reluctantly, the smell of the plants still in his nostrils.

By the time she came down from her room, Laisha had taken Ragoczy's advice to heart. Her dress was of a subdued copper, and cut to compliment her lanky frame. It was wholly appropriate to her age. Her shoes had little heels, but only the severest critic would find fault with them. She carried a beaded bag in one hand, and ecru gloves.

Ragoczy was waiting for her, suavely elegant in a magnificently-tailored tuxedo of heavy silk. His shirt was pin-tucked in the front, his silver-and-ruby studs were discreetly impressive, his silken bow tie was properly and splendidly black. If there was anything in his ensemble that could be criticized, it was the thickened soles of his evening shoes. He took his daughter's hand, saying with an approving nod, "An excellent compromise. I give you full credit. That's a beautiful frock, and you look lovely, but there is nothing precocious about it. Madame Cabrini may gnash her teeth, but she cannot snipe at you."

"Would she try?" Laisha asked so sweetly that Ragoczy felt uneasy for a moment.

"My child, she is your hostess. Don't press her too far." He started toward the door. "Have you a scarf for your hair, or should I put the top up?"

It was a beautiful dusk, with the sunset just starting to fade, going from gold to a bronze-green, to sterling silver. The air smelled of myrtle and thyme. Laisha looked up at the powdering of stars overhead and said, "I've brought a scarf. Leave the top down. I want to let the whole night rush over me."

Ragoczy held the door of the new Isotta-Fraschini for Laisha, and when she was seated on the blonde leather upholstery, he closed the door with a flourish, and went around to the driver's side. "We may have to have the top up coming back, but for the moment, Laisha, it will be as you like." He started the automobile and drove off down the long, sloping drive toward the newly-paved road.

Laisha was leaning back, her butterscotch hair brushing the polished rosewood that trimmed both the front and rear passenger compartments. Her scarf was a fine tissue of amber silk which did little more than contain her hair. She searched for the constellations that Ragoczy had taught her the year before, and felt faintly smug that she could recognize so many of them. As the Isotta-Fraschini rolled past the tower of an old church, she turned to Ragoczy. "Papa? Do you know what I'd like?"

"Not at this instance, no," he replied.

"I would like to learn to fly an aeroplane." When he said nothing to this, she went on. "Wouldn't you like to soar through the air, chasing the birds? I think it would be the most wonderful thing in the world, to be up there. Cities would be like toys, wouldn't they? And people like ants."

"It is a long way to the ground," he remarked enigmatically.

"Of course. That's the thrill of it," she told him, then went back to staring at the sky.

By the time they arrived at the Cabrini villa, Laisha was almost dozing, an enchanting half-smile on her lips. She looked up with a start as Ragoczy brought the Isotta-Fraschini to a halt in the courtyard of the Cabrini home. Dusk had closed in around them, and the afterglow in the west was darkening steadily.

Arcibaldo Cabrini himself came ambling out of the high, carved door to welcome his guests. "Che fortuna!" he called out, raising his hand in a negligent greeting. "We were wondering when you'd get here."

"Are we late?" Ragoczy asked as he closed the door to his automobile and went to open the door for Laisha.

"Not really, but you know how impatient my wife becomes when someone is expected." He was tall and saturnine, with a deceptively lazy manner. "Come in. We're having dessert in the loggia."

"I'm sure Laisha will be delighted to join you. I must decline, but I'm sure you understand that no discourtesy is intended." His Italian was excellent, as were most of his languages, but there was a faintly archaic sound to his phrases, unlike his German, which was rigorously contemporary. In all his various tongues he had a slight, unidentifiable accent that had baffled more than one expert, and Cabrini was no exception.

"You've explained your customs to me before, yes, yes. But I have yet to detect the source of this. I have heard Italian spoken by men from all over the world, including, once, a Japanese, and you sound like none of them."

Ragoczy approached his host, Laisha at his side. "You must enjoy your puzzle, Signor Cabrini, to take such pains with it."

"Naturalmente," he said with relish. "And your so-charming ward. A great pleasure to have you visit us, Signorina Laisha. Doubly so, for now Gaetano may spend an evening at home, for a change."

Laisha did not know how to react to these words, but she felt Ragoczy's warning touch on her arm, so she smiled politely. "I am sorry to have deprived you of him, Signor Cabrini." Her Italian was oddly pronounced, but passable. "He has been a pleasant companion during our stay in Verona." She was rewarded by a quick, admiring smile from Ragoczy.

"My wife tells me that he haunts your villa. Don't let him take advantage of your hospitality," Arcibaldo Cabrini warned her with a teasing wag of his finger.

"Your boy is always welcome," Ragoczy said as they went through the doors of the villa. He had chosen his words carefully, so that Arcibaldo would not construe the relationship between Laisha and Gaetano as more serious than it was.

"He is growing up," Arcibaldo sighed. "You will discover that as well, Conte. One year they're bouncing balls in the nursery, and the next they are driving automobiles and taking university examinations."

"I have some intimations of that already," Ragoczy agreed, and looked around to see Giacinta approaching. "Buona sera, Madama Cabrini," he said, and bowed over her proffered hand.

"And to you, Conte. We were very pleased to hear you would visit us." She was an imposing woman, one given to plum-colored dresses and massive necklaces. Tonight she was formidably arrayed, in an astonishing gown of dark rose peau de soie with gold spangles and a number of heavy gold bracelets as well as impressive earrings of amethyst and gold. "Good evening, Laisha. My son tells me that he spoke with you earlier today."

"He did," Laisha said at once. "He brought me some beautiful flowers." She thought that she sounded absolutely vapid and inane, but she saw a faint, frosty smile form on Madame Cabrini's wide mouth.

"Gaetano is a thoughtful boy," she murmured as she started away down the hall. She had not gone far when she added, as if it were an afterthought, "Oh, Conte, by the way, we've had the piano tuned just yesterday, and I am anxious to hear it played properly. I've been told you're an expert on the instrument, and no doubt you would enjoy the opportunity to play. When one is traveling, it is not often that such a treat is possible."

"You don't have to, if it is an imposition," Arcibaldo put in with an apologetic lifting of his hands.

"How could it be that, my dear?" Giacinta challenged him, her voice colored by a shrill obstinacy.

"I cannot thank you enough for thinking of me," Ragoczy said to Madame Cabrini, turning slightly to give a philosophical wink to Laisha, who had to stifle the giggle that threatened to burst out of her.

With a smile of triumph, Giacinta led her guests into the loggia, where the family was gathered, confident that while her guardian was playing, Laisha would have no time for her oldest son.

Text of a note from Gudrun Ostneige to Graf Franchot Ragoczy.

*Wolkighügel*
*June 2, 1925*

*Schloss Saint-Germain*

*My dear Graf:*

*I have just been told of your return yesterday, and wanted to welcome you back at my first opportunity. You have been gone six weeks, I know, but it has seemed much longer, for every day I had thoughts of your many kindnesses to me.*

*This morning I recalled our pleasant walk, and the consideration you showed me. At that time I was not in a position to appreciate how much your suggestions meant to me. Since then, I have reexamined my attitudes, and I have discovered that I would very much like to learn more of you.*

*If you find that you have some time free of an evening, perhaps you will be kind enough to share it with me? I am aware that with the passing of time, you, too, may have reconsidered the matters we discussed, and if that is the case, I will not trouble you with any request greater than an hour of your delightful conversation. However, if there is more you would want, I believe it might be attainable. As I see it, nothing you might wish is beyond reason.*

*You are doubtless aware that my brother lives here, in the gamekeeper's cottage, and for that reason I would recommend that you not pass that way when you come. It is presumptuous of me to say this, but matters might be somewhat easier to arrange if you would come on foot, so that Maximillian will have nothing to complain of.*

*I will risk your ire and say that I have missed you, Saint-Germain, and sign this with anticipation,*

*Rudi*

## 6

For once James arrived at the hotel ahead of Madelaine. The concierge had recognized him and showed him a calculated deference which James knew had more to do with Madelaine than himself. He tipped the man the proper amount and carried his own bags up to the room.

It was a large chamber at the southwest corner of the third floor, and one he and Madelaine had shared before. The walls were a sea-green, the upholstery and carpets predominantly champagne, with touches of Chinese red here and there. As the day was quite warm, the windows were open and the curtains billowed in the breeze off the lake. James set his bag down and took off his jacket. Two years before, he would also have loosened his tie, but he had observed that European men did not often do this, and in the last few months he had picked up the habit; instead, he began to roll up his sleeves.

He opened the closet door and found two fine, well-used leather bags—Madelaine's—which surprised him. Usually she was waiting for him when he arrived, either in the lobby or in this room. A coldness rippled over him that had nothing to do with the balmy weather. Madelaine was here, in Lausanne, but she had not waited for him, had not met him. His first assumption was that something had gone wrong, that she had been asked to return to Paris, or Athens, or Cairo, wherever it was she had been. His second one was more mundane: she had gone shopping or for a walk. She had never done it before, but he had never arrived so early in the afternoon. Perhaps she always spent an hour in the shops or with friends. She had not mentioned she knew anyone in Lausanne, but he had never asked her if she did.

There was a small balcony outside the tall French windows, and often they sat there of an evening, looking off toward Lac Leman. It was a perfect name for it, he thought, at least in English, for a leman was a lover. Now he stepped out onto it, the heat of the afternoon hard on his arms. He looked up and down the street, hoping to see her coming toward the hotel, but although there was a fair number of people about, not one of them was Madelaine. After ten fruitless minutes, James went back into the room and tugged at the bell pull impatiently.

Thinking belatedly that she might have left him a note, James went to the dresser, which was untouched, and then to the walnut desk in the corner. As he approached, he saw a scrap of paper on it, and realized it was a visiting card. So she did have friends in Lausanne, at least on a visit.

Just then there was a knock at the door and James turned toward it. He crossed the room quickly and opened the door to the bellboy who stood respectfully outside.

"Is there anything wrong, sir?" the bellboy asked with that careful combination of deference and superiority James had learned to admire.

"What time did Professor de Montalia arrive, do you know?" he demanded rudely.

"I was not required to bring her bags up to the room, but as I recall, she arrived shortly after ten this morning." The propriety of this reply made his boorishness all the more unacceptable.

"Do you know where she is now?" James was able to be more polite in tone, but he wanted to shake the man for the information.

"Madame left at noon," the bellboy informed him stiffly.

"Was she alone?" He felt like a fool asking these questions, but he could not stop now that he had begun.

"I believe a gentleman called for her," the bellboy said, stressing "gentleman."

"I see. Thank you." He remembered to tip the man before closing the door firmly. Then he stood by himself in the center of the room. It was ridiculous, he told himself, to be jealous. Her visitor, whoever he was, should not concern him. Madelaine knew other men. She had colleagues over most of Europe. There was nothing suspicious in her caller. It might be a treat for her, or professionally advantageous to see this man, this gentleman. It could be that he was a friend of hers or her family. Certainly it made more sense for her to attend to these courtesies now than to do so once she was with him. He gave her precious little time for anything but himself. There was no reason for her to sit around the hotel waiting for him, when she had the chance to meet with friends and associates. For all he knew, she did this every time they came to Lausanne. The explanations tumbled through his mind, each one possible, each one rational, and they only made him more distraught.

On impulse he strode to the desk and picked up the calling card.

It was the old-fashioned kind, fairly large, with an heraldic device embossed in one corner. He studied it, not recognizing it. There was a black disk in the lower center part of the shield, with curved wings spread above it. Above it, in the center of the card, was a signature: the card had been signed, not printed. He turned the card toward the window in order to read that small, slightly archaic hand.

*Saint-Germain*

"Saint-Germain. Saint-Germain," James repeated, tapping the card against the base of his thumb. Saint-Germain. Saint-Germain des Prés. Faubourg Saint-Germain. Those early days in Paris, with the Great War clamoring and battering at all of Europe. That was where he knew the name. That was what made it familiar, he insisted to himself. And all the while, he was trying to recall when Madelaine might have mentioned that name, and what she had said. He consoled himself as best he could with the thought that he could not know everyone she did. Saint-Germain sounded noble. The gentleman might be living in exile. Or he might be Swiss, the French-speaking variety. What was he afraid of? He could give no easy answer to that terrible question, but it haunted him as he crossed the room once, twice, the card still in his hand.

An hour later, his mood had fluctuated violently twice and he was considering leaving, with a note for Madelaine that would let her know that he was not to be trifled with. It was more than he could bring himself to do. He could not cut himself off from her. In frustration, he paced the room for what seemed the hundredth time, and then stepped out onto the balcony again.

There was a bit of a breeze now, and the first long shadows were sliding across the lake, fingering their way along the streets of Lausanne. Below on the street, a group of school children in severe uniforms chatted together, turning as one as an elegant silver-blue Isotta-Fraschini pulled up in front of the hotel.

James leaned forward on the balcony, staring down at the automobile, his breathing almost stilled.

The driver brought the automobile to a halt and stepped out of the door. He was dressed in a fine black suit. From what little James could see, situated as he was almost directly above them, the man was not old, or at least his dark, loosely-curling and beautifully-groomed hair showed only auburn highlights and not a trace of gray. He walked around the Isotta-Fraschini, to hold the door for his passenger, whom James recognized at once as Madelaine. As she got out of the automobile, the driver bent and kissed her hand. James would have cheerfully throttled him. Madelaine detained him a minute or so, her hand still resting in his. James knew from the way she stood, from the movement of her head as she spoke, that what passed between them was serious. The man nodded once, then relinquished her hand with a reluctance that made James grind his teeth. As Madelaine waited, the man got into his Isotta-Fraschini and drove away. Only then did Madelaine start up the four low steps to the hotel's entrance.

In the five minutes it took Madelaine to reach their room, James felt the Reine Marie become a prison, a torture chamber. Everything he had feared was true, and to a greater extent than he had imagined. Madelaine had another lover, a man who wore fine clothes and drove one of the most luxurious automobiles made. What defense did he have against such a rival? His youth was the only thing that might be in his favor, and that was quickly becoming a thing of the past.

The door opened and Madelaine stepped into the room. She was wearing a low-belted afternoon ensemble of cotton twill that exactly matched her violet eyes, and carried a light fox wrap over her arm. As she saw him, she opened her arms to him, smiling with delight. "James! You're here already."

At any other time, he would have rushed to embrace her, but this time he held back. "I've been here a couple hours," he said evasively. "I thought the concierge would tell you that."

She gave a puzzled frown, but did not chide him. She tossed her wrap and handbag onto the bed. "He didn't mention it. There was a party of Spaniards taking his attention."

James had seen the Spaniards arrive earlier and was almost prepared to believe her. "I thought you'd be waiting," he said lamely.

"Is that what has you in the sulks?" she inquired with a smile. "I was afraid that you had a hangover or some other similar affliction."

"Thanks for your high opinion," he snapped, wishing he could stop himself from saying these hurtful things.

"But I assumed that it was almost required of American writers living in Europe. It has to do with your absurd Prohibition." She seated herself on the edge of the bed and turned to look at him. "If it is not a hangover or influenza, something is bothering you. What is it?"

He was about to deny this, but before he could stop himself, he said, "I saw you drive up just now."

"Oh? Were you on the balcony?" If she resented his watching for her, there was no hint of it in her voice or her demeanor.

"I was watching the lake," he lied. "An auto like that one attracts a lot of attention."

"So it seems," she said, regarding him speculatively. "Are you angry because you think people stared at me in that automobile?"

"I'm not angry!" he shouted.

She checked whatever rejoinder she was about to give, sitting very still while James began once more to pace the room. "Something has put you out of humor. You have never behaved this way before."

"That man kissed your hand!" James declared, knowing that had little to do with his feelings. His suspicions had been building from the moment he had found her bags in the room.

"Of course he did. He's very courteous." She was determined to calm him.

"And you went to him before you thought I had arrived. You wanted to be alone with him, didn't you?" He was saying all the wrong things, and was horrified that he could be so irrational.

"Yes, I did want to be alone with him," Madelaine admitted evenly. "I needed his advice." She sat quite still on the bed, making no extraneous moves that would indicate nervousness or guilt.

"You talked to *him*? About what?" He stood still, leaning a bit forward, his cheeks showing higher color than usual.

"About you."

Slowly James approached her, not certain what he intended to do. In a strained voice he asked her, "What did you say to him?"

Madelaine's violet eyes met his cognac-colored ones. "I told him everything about you."

"And about us, I suppose?" He wanted to shake her, to kiss her.

"Yes, that as well." She reached out to touch his hand, then drew back.

He stared down at her in confusion. "Why?"

"Because I had to," she said simply, and for the first time sounded less confident and calm.

"Had to? Why? What business is it of his?" The worst of his fury was over, and in its wake he felt a hollowness.

"I had to speak to someone I could trust." This time when she reached for his hand she felt his fingers close around hers. The grip was rough, but she did not draw back from it.

"And you couldn't trust me?" There was more pain in his face now, and a hopelessness.

"That was what I had to determine," she answered quietly.

"So you went to that man." He was trying to make sense out of what he was hearing. "Who is he?"

"A friend. A very old friend." Something in her voice warned him, and he tried to pull away from her. "James."

"An old friend, is it? I saw the way he kissed your hand. That was no old friend!" His eyes felt hot, as if he had a fever, and he pressed his free hand to them.

"All right," she said wearily, "say what you must."

James would have given anything to have kept silent, but he had gone too far to stop now. "I saw the way he touched you! God damn it!" He struck his open palm with his closed fist. "Am I boring you?"

"No. That was why I had to speak with him." She had the look of a woman about to weep, although her eyes were dry.

"About us!" Outrage made him quiver, and his voice was not quite steady.

"Yes. I've told you that." She laced her fingers together over her knees and stared down into her lap.

He saw her misery in the slump of her shoulders, the aversion of her face, but his own wretchedness arrested any sympathy he felt. He put his hands on his hips and stood back from her, not trusting himself to remain so near. "Am I supposed to be grateful?"

"You ought to be," she whispered. "I've never spoken to him about anyone before."

"Anyone before?" he mocked as the hurt went through him. "The rest of the parade has gone by on its merry way?"

Her eyes were defiant as she looked at him. "Yes! Oh, bon Dieu, why are you doing this to me, James? You have never been this way with me before."

"Well, how would you feel? If you were in my place. I arrived here, set for being with you for six days, and then I find out that you have someone else on your schedule as well." His words grew unsteady toward the end, and he looked away from her.

"There was a time when I would have felt as you do; when I

was very young." Her admission startled him, and he swung back to stare at her. "It is the truth, mon cher." She covered her face with her hands.

"So you're going to cry for me, are you?" The challenge was sharp, sarcastic, and anguished.

"No."

"Why? You never know: it might work." He folded his arms as if to brace himself against her.

"Because I can't," she burst out, dropping her hands.

"Oh, come on, Madelaine," he sneered, but even as he said the words, he recalled all the times he had been with her. Never once had she shed tears. He scowled down at her. "You're not kidding, are you?"

She shook her head, and after taking a long, shuddering breath, she said, "That was one of the things I had to talk to him about."

"About not crying?" He had a perplexed look in his eyes.

"Indirectly." She got up from the bed and walked toward the windows. "I've never had to face a situation like this before."

"None of your other lovers has ever been jealous?" This was intended to cut and sting.

"It has never mattered," she murmured, unaware of his shock, for she looked out across Lac Leman toward the west-ward mountains that were taking on a bluish tinge as the afternoon advanced.

"Then he's not the only one, this Saint-Germain?" he demanded of her.

She turned abruptly at the name. "How did you know?" There was a fierceness in her that he had seen in rare flashes.

"I found his card. That was the man, wasn't it? In the Isotta-Fraschini." His manner was brazen to mask the complex emotions that rose in him. Madelaine had thrown him off-guard with her acceptance of his anger, and now her attitude unnerved him.

"Yes," she said as she mastered herself. "That was Saint-Germain."

He had never seen such an expression on her face before, and it told him more than any words could how profound her feelings for the man were. "Then he *is* your lover." This was a statement without heat as he verged again on despondency.

"He *was* my lover," she corrected him quietly. "He was my first lover."

"And you've never got over him." He was defeated, he

knew it. That elegant stranger he had glimpsed just once, whose face he would not know, who might be tall or short, and for all he knew, famous, distinguished, or notorious.

She made a dejected and valiant attempt at smiling. "No, I never have."

For James the ground seemed to open under his feet. All the time he had made love with Madelaine, she had been longing for the unknown Saint-Germain. "Are you going back to him?"

"I can't," she said, shrugging. "It isn't possible."

"He's married?" he asked eagerly.

"No."

It was inconceivable to James that this could happen, but he suggested it anyway. "Has he ceased to love you?"

"Oh, no." Her answer was quick and confident. "It is not a question of loving each other. But we are of the same blood now, you see."

That "now" nagged at him, but he ignored its promptings. "He's not your father, is he?" He recalled that Madelaine had told him her father was dead. "Or your uncle or brother?"

"No, none of those things," she said with care.

"But surely being in-laws does not stand in the way." He was increasingly baffled, and although each question brought its own pang, he could not avoid asking them.

"Neither of us is married," she reminded him. "That is not what I meant. It was what I had to discuss with him. This is more difficult than I thought it would be."

"Because I'm mad at you?" he said uncertainly.

"No. Saint-Germain warned me . . ." Her eyes were tragic when she looked at him, and pleading.

"Warned you? Of what?" He came toward her, wishing now to solve the mystery and to save her from whatever torment she was suffering.

"You must understand that when he finally told me, I knew. I had known from the first, and even then; it was not easy for him. I've never told anyone before; I never wanted to, or had to." This oblique explanation was given with great care. She spoke deliberately, without excitement. She would not look at him.

The breeze off the lake, now that the western slope cast a long shadow across it, was suddenly chill. The curtains billowed and the draperies swung heavily.

"But you have to tell me." He took her by the shoulders as he came up to her. "What is it? What?"

She broke away from him, raising her hands and then dropping them, as she had before. "This is futile," she said in an undervoice.

But James heard her. "Futile, is it?" He pursued her across the room, determined now to discover what it was that so distressed her. "Then tell me what it is. Have you got a disease or—"

"Not exactly," she answered.

He paled. "You're ill? Is that why you don't eat with me?" He caught her arm and pulled her around toward him. "Whatever it is, however long you've got, it doesn't matter. I'll stay with you. I don't care what happens to my job, if you need me." He was silent as she began to laugh without any humor. "Tell me, Madelaine."

"All right," she said heavily, and then, without preamble, announced, "I'm a vampire."

James froze, the start of an incredulous smile fading as he looked at her. "You're joking." He waited. "It's got to be a joke. Right?"

"No."

"Aw, hell, Madelaine, you don't expect me to believe . . ." he protested, the words trailing off. "There aren't any vampires. There are legends, and the Stoker book—you know the one."

"*Dracula*," she supplied.

"That's it. And the Murnau moving picture, but none of it's *real*." He tried for a chuckle and almost made it. "If you're a vampire, where's your fangs? I thought all vampires had big, long teeth."

"Oh, James," she moaned, "don't. It's hard enough without you treating me as if I were fooling you, or slightly mad." As she spoke, she went to close the window and shut out the cool wind.

He followed her. "What is it, really? Why can't you tell me?" All the things he had imagined were nothing compared to this revelation—if revelation it was—she had given him. A vampire? In 1925? "Why do you want to scare me away?"

"I *don't* want to scare you away," she insisted. She was leaning back against the frame of the French windows. "That is what I want least to do. But I had to tell you. It's necessary."

"Necessary? What nonsense are you handing me?" His derision was obvious, but he assumed an air of exaggerated patience as he listened to her.

"It isn't nonsense. Truly, James, it isn't." She crossed her arms, hands tight on her elbows, the knuckles showing white. "You're probably going to laugh at me and walk out of here, but that can't be helped. I must *tell* you, even if you give me no credence whatever. Later . . ." She gave him a long, piercing stare. "James, let me speak, and don't interrupt me a moment, for your own sake."

He nodded and stood back from her. "Go on."

"James," she said in a low, calm voice, "when you first met me, and we slept together, you told me that you never knew French lovemaking was so different and exciting. It isn't. What happened that night, and every other night we have made love, comes not from my being French, but my being a vampire. No, don't distract me. There's more." She walked away from the window. "You know I never eat, or that you have never seen me eat. You must take my word for it that I don't. Since . . . since my death I have got my nourishment from things other than food."

"You're not serious," he muttered, all the while thinking of the many times he had urged her to dine with him, and the graceful, inconclusive excuses she had given him. At first he had been worried about it, but then, when she continued to be healthy and wholly desirable, he had ceased to be troubled, deciding that like some modern women, she preferred to eat alone so that she would not be tempted to indulge her appetite.

"Completely. That's part of the change—"

"Wait a minute here. You said since your death—your *death*?" He knew, rationally, that he should not ask her anything, for it would tend to make her think he believed her. "That's a delusion, Madelaine."

She gave him a quick, measuring look. "How old would you say I am, James?"

"Wh . . . what?" This sudden switch in subject nonplussed him.

"Answer my question. How old do you think I am?" Her hands had moved to her hips, and she faced him almost belligerently.

James cleared his throat. "Christ, Madelaine, I don't talk age with women." He rubbed his jaw. "All right, all right. Just looking at you, I'd figure you were around twenty, twenty-one, maybe. I know you've got to be older. You've said so yourself. But if I didn't know better, yeah, twenty, maybe twenty-three at the most."

"And how old did I look when you first met me? That was

some time ago, remember." She waited for him to answer, a fixed, unhappy smile on her face.

"About the same," he conceded quietly, then asserted himself again. "But that doesn't mean anything. Some women have those kinds of faces."

"Good bones, you mean? That's not it." She walked slowly toward the dresser. "There is a mirror in the second drawer. Will you get it out for me?"

"Why?" He started to do as she requested, then drew back. "You mean that old saw about vampires not reflecting? Everybody has a reflection."

"Then there's no reason you shouldn't get the mirror out, is there? She waited for him to go to the dresser and take out the mirror, but refused it when he held it out to her. "No. If I take it, you'll think it's sleight-of-hand. Bring the mirror here, and stand beside me, with the mirror in front of us." She stood very still while James took his place beside and slightly behind her. "Now, hold up the mirror."

James did as he was told, amazement dawning on his face as he stared into the glass. His face was clearly reflected, and his shirt with the collar slightly askew, his tie chain at just the right place on his chest. That was what most drew his attention, because there was no way he should have been able to see it. Madelaine was standing where the chain was: he could feel the pressure of her back against it. As he gazed into the mirror, she leaned her head back on his shoulder, turning her face toward his neck. He brought his free hand up and tangled it in her hair, holding her more tightly against him.

"What do you see?" she asked. After one look at the mirror, she had not bothered to check again. Empty mirrors still bothered her, and she had taken Saint-Germain's warning to heart and kept very few of them in the places where she lived. Yet mirrors were not as bad as running water when she was unprotected by her native earth, and once in a while she liked to sit and gaze at the place her reflection should be, and tell herself that there was a hint of her presence.

"I see . . . myself." He was barely audible.

"Yes." She sounded so resigned that James glanced at her in alarm.

"How did you do this?" He held the mirror closer, almost touching her, as if that might reveal the illusion.

"I'm not *doing* anything. It's the way I am. None of us have reflections." She turned slowly and put her arms around his waist. More than a century ago, Saint-Germain had told her of his fear of being loathed, and for the first time she knew in her soul what he meant. "James?"

"You're not here," he told her in the oddest tone. "I can't see you at all. I can see my hand in your hair, but it looks like it's dangling in the air. I can see the wrinkles in my shirt where you're close against me, but nothing of you."

Her arms tightened. "Do you begin to believe me?"

"I don't know." His response was distant, and he reached out for the dresser to put the mirror down. "I don't understand it."

Softly, diffidently, she said, "Can you still love me?"

"This is crazy," he protested, but his arms went around her and he kissed her hungrily. "I don't know how you do it, or why you're going to such lengths to convince me of such an absurd thing, but it doesn't matter." Again he sought her mouth with his, enjoying the recklessness that came over him. "You aren't going to get rid of me with a cock-and-bull story like this one."

"I don't want to get rid of you, James. That's the problem." She held off from him when he attempted to kiss her again. "I should have told you this two years ago, when you would still have had a choice, but I could not bring myself to do it. I didn't want to see you turn away from me with hatred." Her body trembled and she held him more closely.

The familiar, intoxicating desire for Madelaine was starting to claim all of James' senses, but he could not resist asking, "Why should you have told me, when you knew I wouldn't believe you?"

She gave a long sigh. "Two years ago there was still a chance that you had not been with me enough to be changed, but that's no longer the case. When you die, my dearest, dearest James, you will not remain in your grave: you will be as I am, as Saint-Germain is. Too much has passed between us." It was as much of an apology as she would ever make to him.

"I'll worry about that then," he told her roughly as his need for her became more intense. No woman he had ever had evoked passion in him as she did. She was a drug, a frenzy, an elation within him, a tempest that rocked him to the limits of his soul. The urgency of his body's hunger was enhanced by a greater fervor that permeated every aspect of his life with inextinguishable joy. Whatever was wrong with her—and for the moment he was prepared to withhold judgment—it made no difference to him, or his ineffable longing for her.

Madelaine answered his desire with her own, sinking into his embrace with evanescent rapture. She had learned to fire the senses in others, but never since Saint-Germain had her own been so overwhelming. They tumbled together onto the bed, legs tangled, arms enfolding each other. Their clothes were discarded in hasty, untidy heaps and the covers kicked back. It was delicious to feel the force of his love, to exult in their prolonged and shared fulfillment, to be carried on the flood of his rapture so completely that she hardly needed to put her lips to his throat to be entirely gratified.

The room was almost dark when they were able to speak again. Madelaine lay close against James' side, her hand on his chest, her head pillowed on his shoulder. As his mouth brushed her forehead, she smiled.

"Madelaine," he murmured to her hair, "nothing about you matters to me but what we have together. That's why I was jealous this afternoon."

She traced the outline of his lips with one finger. "You have no reason to be."

"If you say so." He stroked her side slowly, languorously. Then he jumped: she had tweaked one of his nipples playfully. "Hey!"

"Well, you do it to me," she pointed out, and began to rub his chest lightly. A bit later she said, "I was serious about the change, James. It will happen to you unless . . . unless your nervous system is destroyed when you die. If it is not, then you will live as I do, as Saint-Germain does."

"Don't start that again," he pleaded.

"But I must. Otherwise I would not be able to continue sharing your love, and more than anything else, I want to be with you." That was not quite correct, she thought, for she had never lost her yearning for Saint-Germain. But those who had changed could not seek love from one another, and of the lovers she had had since she left her grave, none had brought her what James had.

"Don't talk like that," he reprimanded her softly.

"Two more things, James, and then I won't say anything more unless you ask questions of me." She touched the place on his neck where the two little marks were, no worse than shaving nicks.

"Fair enough, so long as you get it out of your system." He rolled toward her onto his side so that they were touching the length of their bodies.

She gave a breathless little giggle. "You're distracting me."

"Good." He kissed her closed eyes.

"James, please. It won't take long." Her fingers pressed his chest.

"Go ahead, then." His hold on her did not lessen, but he made no more attempt to kiss or caress her until she had finished speaking.

"I want you to understand that I've never lied to you, though I haven't always told you the complete truth. I've never wanted to mislead you because I have valued your trust, and returned it. That is a rare thing with us. If I did not love you, your desire and its satisfaction would be enough; it would suffice me. Saint-Germain has said to me before that I would find such love, and I did not believe him until you came. That's the first thing. The second thing is more difficult to say." She hesitated, then plunged into it. "I was born at Montalia. The year was 1724, the date was November 22. I went to my grave in Paris on August 4, 1744. But, as you can see, I did not die."

Hating himself for his cynicism, James said, "I can research those dates, you realize."

Her smile amazed him. "I hope you will. That's why I told them to you."

James did not know how to respond to that, but with the movement of Madelaine's hands on his back, his buttocks, his thighs, words and dates became unimportant. There was only the softness of the sheets and their sweetly ravished senses in the gentle summer night.

Text of a letter from Carlo Pietragnelli to Roger.

*Geyserville, California, USA*
*September 5, 1925*

*Mr. Roger*
*c/o LaTour Bank*
*Brussels, Belgium*

*Dear Mr. Roger:*

*I don't know how to thank you, but my hat's off to you for everything you've done. This afternoon a man from the Bank of Italy in San Francisco stopped by and showed me the papers, so everything is done up properly. You and that silent partner of yours have been real lifesavers. I don't say that idly. Since Prohibition was introduced, those of us raising wine grapes have had a rough time, with no end in sight. My nearest neighbors were forced to sell out because they couldn't keep going, with no place to market their wine but the illegal ones. I pray that you won't regret your investment.*

*You mention that your silent partner has had dealings with European wineries, which interests me a great deal, as you probably guessed. If he has the grafts you mentioned, I am most heartily anxious to try them out. The hock wines haven't been all that popular over here, but when and if the ban on liquor is lifted, there's no reason I can't try it on the public. As for the Rhine grafts, yes, by all means, ship them. Our results have been uneven with Tokay, but I'd like to see if I can develop a hybrid.*

*The Zinfandel you asked about, I'm afraid I can't give you a lot of information because there isn't much known about it. There were some vines being shipped here and the label on the box looked like Zinfandel, and no one could figure out what it was supposed to be, so they planted it, and that's the wine they got.*

*You tell your silent partner for me that my whole*

*family will remember you and him in our prayers. I was beginning to think that I'd have to move down to San Jose and take up citrus growing. Now, I'm not saying anything against oranges, but once you've got wine in your blood, if you take my meaning, it's near impossible to be happy with anything else. My grandfather, when he was living back in Italy, started the family in the business, and we've been at it ever since.*

*The way this Prohibition's going, we'll have some fine, fine Pinot Noir when it's over, with plenty of age on it. I'll ship you some just as soon as the government okays my export permit. I don't want to do anything that might give them the least excuse to change their minds. They're being very fussy these days, what with all the booze coming in from Canada, and the bathtub gin.*

*I've got to be frank and tell you what I told the man from the Bank of Italy; I don't think there's much chance of Europe learning to like California wines. Why should they, when they've got some of the best wine in the world on their doorstep? I hope that I'm wrong, but I want you to think this over if you run into trouble with it. If that silent partner of yours is as smart as I hear he is, then it's necessary to let him know I appreciate the risk he's taking on me and my vines.*

*One of the things I plan to do with that money is to buy my neighbor's acres. They're lying there, going to waste, and I think I can do right by them. It will mean a couple new vats, but there's more than enough in your investment to allow for that. Besides, between Prohibition and the cost of living being what it is, there are plenty of men about who are willing to work for a reasonable wage and three squares a day.*

*The priests on the other side of the valley aren't doing too badly now, though they've admitted they're in a bit of a pickle. They can always make sacramental wine, which is about all they've done recently. The trouble is that the cellarmaster comes from another one of the vintner families around here, and he's been itching to experiment. Since he hasn't been allowed to do it with his own vines, I thought I might ask him to take a look at what I've got here, just to give me his opinion, you understand, not as any kind of partner. He knows wines and I think he'll be willing to give me a hand on the sly if I let him experiment on the new acres.*

*You have my word that I'll keep you posted on how the
vines are going, and what the wines are like. Anytime
you have any questions, you write to me here, and I'll get
a letter off to you fast as I can. If a man has investors
like you and your silent partner, he doesn't need a guardian angel.*

> *With gratitude,*
> *Carlo Pietragnelli*

# 7

Earlier in the day there had been a threat of rain, but now fat
white clouds buffed the sky to a deep, shining blue. It was still
quite cool, so that the participants and judges at the equestrian competition were pleased to wear crew-necked jerseys
over their shirts and under their hacking jackets. The spectators were not so formally restricted in their dress and most
were wrapped in sensible coats, and a few had knitted rugs
thrown around their shoulders or over their laps as they sat in
the stands.

Ragoczy stood by the ermine-dun mare he had given Laisha
the previous spring. The girl herself was properly dressed,
her field boots glossy but not so shiny that they looked brand
new, for that was considered ostentatious and the mark of a
novice. Her heavy twill jodhpurs were an unorthodox shade of
taffy which matched her shirt and stock. She was wearing the
permitted jersey, of a heathery green, and her jacket was the
same dark brown as her eyes. She was drawing on her light-
colored pigskin gloves, her nervousness revealed only in her
quiet manner and the studious frown she often revealed when
tense. She fixed the wrist button and adjusted her cuffs, then
gave Ragoczy a quick smile.

"Zhelahyu udachi," he said quietly to Laisha. "You don't
need it, from what I can see of the others, but I'd probably
wish you good luck if all the other horses were spavined and
their riders were novices."

Laisha gave a reluctant smile and reached for the stirrup.

"Do you want a leg up?" he offered.

"No," she replied as she mounted. She gathered up the

reins in good form and rose once to be quite certain that the stirrup leathers were at the proper length. Ragoczy held the crop up to her. "Thank you, Papa," she said in a rather abstracted tone.

"This is a small gathering, Laisha. You know almost everyone here. It will be easy for you. Just use a little caution on the water jump: the ground is soggy." He patted the mare's neck and glanced once at the girths. It was not necessary to do so, but he had got into the habit when she was first learning to ride and had not yet made the effort to change it.

"They're fine, Papa," she said with a smile.

"Yes. I know that." He stood back. "The assembly area is open now. You can ride over anytime you like."

She frowned again. "I think I'll let Babieca walk a bit, to warm up."

Ragoczy knew from her tone that she was avoiding the moment when she entered the contestants' assembly ring. "You are not a stranger here, Laisha."

"But I'm a foreigner. This is Bayern. I am Russian." She brought her head up with the pride that she wore as armor. "The Federkiels never let me forget that." Her heels nudged Babieca's flanks and the mare started off at a brisk walk. Laisha rode well, with no extraneous movement to confuse the mare or endanger herself. Ragoczy watched her with troubled pride, then went briskly toward the spectators' stand. His own riding clothes were black except for the white shirt and stock, but this was almost completely obscured by the black jersey he had pulled on against the afternoon chill.

There were about two hundred people in the stands, most of them coming from the immediate area, from Schliersee, Hausham, Freudenreich, and Schufss. More than half the spectators made up the community of landed hochgebornen and their families. Forty years ago, such an event would have been the occasion for balls and great display, but those days were gone, and now the Society of Huntsmen did not expect the enormous banquets and elaborate parties. A few of the older people lamented the change, but none of those complaining were in a position to sponsor more elaborate festivities, and the younger household heads were relieved not to have to face such an ordeal. Among the more socially elite, there were others, occasional men in worn riding clothes, with weathered faces and keen eyes. These were the horse breeders, more interested in the animals than their riders, always searching for new stock.

As Ragoczy approached the stands, he heard Roger call out to him, and he turned toward the familiar voice. "Yes?"

"I'm sorry to disturb you," Roger said as he came up to Ragoczy. "A telegram has just been delivered to Schloss Saint-Germain, and you may want to take action on it while you are at the depot in Hausham."

Ragoczy's fine brows raised in some surprise. "What is it?"

"The government in Italy has declared—" Roger began.

Ragoczy interrupted him. "You mean that Mussolini has grown covetous again. Well, what does he want?"

"He has taken over all foreign-controlled stock in the various electrical companies. The investment you have in Milano alone is substantial enough—"

Ragoczy laughed unpleasantly. "Let us inform Signor Mussolini that I am willing to sell all my shares to my Italian agent. Surely he cannot object to Balletti owning my shares."

"He may investigate Balletti," Roger warned.

"Let him. Balletti has been known as a recluse for some time. He is indulged because he is a Conte, and the world he knew is gone." He folded his arms a moment. "I will have to arrange for Balletti's death soon, I fear. I don't think I can keep up that particular identity much longer. I was short-sighted when I did not invent more family for him, because it will be difficult to keep that connection active." He stared off toward the trees. "For the moment, send the telegram to Italy and make the offer. We should have a response in two or three days, and in that time I will make the proper authorizations. Then I think that it might be best to withdraw the investments from Italy altogether, except for that experimental arm of Fiat in Modena. Assign them to Giovannini—I haven't used that in a while. I doubt Mussolini will want to force the foreigners completely out of that market, for he needs more production there, not less."

"Just the electrical companies, then, assigned to Conte Balletti. What is his first name?"

"Cesare," Ragoczy answered promptly. "He is understood to be Germano's grandson and Francesco's nephew. I thought it might be wise to avoid repeating those names quite so often, what with all the records that have been kept in the last century." He began to walk toward the spectators' stand again. "That may become something of a problem in future. You remember what it was like in Rome for a time. I had to move very carefully and stay at the edges of the Empire until Hadrian was in power, and after that, it was when Heliogabalus wore the purple that it was safe to return. These confoundedly accurate records!"

"Do you contemplate moving from here?" Roger did not appear the least ruffled by his own question, although he knew from long experience that such changes were often harrowing.

"Not at once. My work here isn't finished, and the way things stand in the rest of Europe, there is little point. Should the political situation shift again, it may be necessary. But at the moment, I would rather live here than in Italy, for instance. Eastern Europe is in chaos, still. Greece would not be wise, since there is little work progressing there that is in line with my own studies, and Greece is not a place where Laisha would thrive. It might be sensible to transfer more of Balletti's funds to America and Mexico. There is less chance of war there than here." He had been speaking Latin, but as he got within hearing distance of the stands, he switched back to German. "If you will send that first telegram for me, I will be most grateful. Tomorrow or the next day will be time enough to review the predicament."

"Very good, sir," Roger said with the proper deference.

Konrad Natter, who was sitting on the nearest end of the stands, looked up as Ragoczy approached. "Your ward is riding, I hear."

"Yes, Herr Natter. I've only just left her to prepare." He did not like the man, but knew enough to mask this with excellent manners.

"The Society of Huntsmen qualified her?" Natter asked with no attempt to conceal his sneer. "It was not always so: this is an event for Deutsche."

"But I have seen in the records that Lajos Marosar was the Grand Master of the Society for more than ten years. Surely a society that tolerates a Hungarian to lead it can bear to have a Russian girl compete at one of its events." His face was bland and his words were wholly respectful, but his back was very straight and the light in his dark, dark eyes quelled Natter's next objection.

"It's a lax state of affairs," was all Natter decided to say, and that was more of a mumble than a challenge.

"All Europe is in a lax state of affairs," Ragoczy pointed out before moving on to the steps to his place in the stands. As he walked, he thought a moment about the endless tiers of seats at the Circus Maximus, extended to hold sixty, then seventy, then eighty thousand people, and still the crowding was ferocious, and there were constant plans to increase its seating capacity. Here there were no marble seats, no hawkers of wine, fruit juices, nuts, or meat-filled breads. One fresh-faced boy of fifteen or so stood by a barrel and filled the proffered steins to the spectators if they approached him. Such a child would not have lasted five minutes with the Roman crowd.

His seat was toward the top of the stand. Earlier in the day he had taken the precaution of putting a pillow down, which was a fairly common practice. That the center of the pillow was filled with his native earth was his private concern, and one he was in no hurry to mention.

The fourth of six young men was finishing up his display of his five-gaited mount. He was not an expert rider, but his instincts were right, and he carried himself better than most of the others had. At the conclusion of his ride, he dismounted in the elaborate tradition of the Austrian hussars fifty years ago. Ragoczy, watching him, suspected that the young man's grandfather probably taught him to ride.

"Herr Ragoczy?" a voice on the ground behind the stands called out quietly.

Ragoczy turned, and smiled as he recognized Gudrun. "Good afternoon, Frau Ostneige," he said, half-rising as he spoke. "I did not think to see you here, or I would have suggested you permit me to take you up in my automobile."

"That's hardly necessary," she said quickly. "My brother has brought me, and . . . He prefers to escort me himself to such neighborhood events." The last was said with an apologetic smile that served to point up the sorrow in her eyes.

"I hope you will have time to talk after this next competition. I would come down now, but Laisha is riding in the next set, and I want to watch her." He made no excuse for his partiality, nor did he feel he had to.

Gudrun looked around anxiously, then called up to him, "I hope she wins."

Ragoczy was mildly surprised by this sudden kindness and he responded at once. "I will tell her you said so."

"Danke, Herr Graf." The reason for her reserve was quickly apparent. Maximillian came around the end of the stands with a brimming stein in one hand and a notebook in the other. "Maxl," she said, going to him and putting her hand through the crook in his arm. "I think we'll have to ask Otto to bring the rug. Herr Ragoczy has just told me that the stands are even colder than it is here on the ground."

Maximillian showed Ragoczy one disapproving glance, then

gave his attention to Gudrun. "You're probably right. Whatever possesses the Society of Huntsmen to have these gather-
ings in October, I will never know."

What Gudrun said to her brother was lost in the sound of
the megaphone, as it was announced, to a flurry of applause,
that the last set had been won by Rudolf Maler. The junior
competition in hunt riding was called, and the names of eleven
contestants were read off. Laisha, Ragoczy noted, was placed
in the tenth position, which was not entirely to her advantage.
The last rider was a good five years younger than she was,
and had never finished the course before.

The first two riders, a boy of about twelve and a girl a bit
older, did acceptably but without distinction. However, they
were part of a large hochgebornen family in Bayrischzell who
had lost almost everything they possessed in terrible inflation.
At that time they had traded most of their luxuries—paintings,
silver service, fine furniture and carpets, automobiles, jewels—
to keep from starving. Now they had their Schloss and land
and very little else. The horses the two children rode had been
borrowed from more fortunate friends. The spectators accorded
them more applause than their performance warranted, but
this was to be expected.

The fifth horse stumbled on the watery jump and the result-
ing swath of exposed mud quickly became a hazard, growing
wider and more uneven with every hoof that touched it. By
the time it was Laisha's turn to compete, there was a boggy
marsh on the far side of the little pond that constituted the
water jump. The committee of judges had almost decided to
stop the competition, but now, with the set so nearly over,
they allowed the rides to continue.

Laisha had watched the other young riders take the course
with a critical eye. The first half of the course did not trouble
her; she had often had more demanding rides around Schloss
Saint-Germain. Babieca would not have any difficulty with the
various obstacles she would have to clear. There were a few
other hazards which bothered Laisha, not the least of which
was the water jump. She was fairly certain that if she attempted to take Babieca over it as it was laid out, there was
no way to keep them from falling in the treacherous mud.
That meant, she reminded herself, that she would have to
avoid the mud. She heard her name called over the megaphone
and came out of the waiting ring. She pulled her cap onto her
head and looked once at where her crop looped over her wrist,
then rode to the foot of the judges' stand. After the required

salute, she clapped her heels to Babieca's side and started into the course at an easy canter.

Ragoczy watched with pride as Laisha cleared the first two jumps with room to spare and in such good form that one of the more enthusiastic spectators in the lower part of the stand clapped appreciatively. Like Laisha, Ragoczy was concerned about the water jump, and wished he had talked it over with his daughter before she set out on the ride. Yet he knew that Laisha would not have welcomed such interference; it was her ride, not his, and she must do it as she thought best. Had she been younger, then he might have insisted that they review her strategy before she began, but she was past the age when it was advisable to treat her so. She was, he reminded himself, an intelligent and capable girl who would soon be a young woman. His eyes followed her over the third jump with real approval. She had a good sense of pacing, and Babieca was not yet using her full strength on the course. But the fourth jump, the water jump, loomed ahead, the size of Schliersee itself in his mind.

Laisha gathered the reins more firmly, her hands lying close to Babieca's neck. She adjusted her weight as she had been taught to do, then swung her mare off the course so that she was coming at the water jump at an angle. The jump would be longer but would not end in a sea of mud. Her crop slapped against the mare, just enough to urge her to a greater effort. She rode as close to the low hedge before the pond as she dared, then felt Babieca gather under her. The mare soared into the air, recognizing her rider's signals for a long reach. She obeyed, coming down lightly on the very edge of the pond, made an easy recovery, and was back on the set trail.

One of the judges was standing up, his face a deep plum color. He was shouting something even as the other two reached up to restrain him. As Laisha rode the rest of the course, the argument became more heated, and finally the enraged judge insisted that the secretary of the event, who was announcing with the megaphone, come to their stand.

By that time Laisha had drawn rein in front of the stand and was waiting for the usual dismissal, which she did not receive.

"You!" the angry judge bellowed at her. "You're that foreign girl, aren't you? There," he insisted to his colleagues. "I told you what would happen if we relaxed our standards. You saw what she did, how she behaved. No child of mine would be permitted to ride in such a way! You!" He directed his baleful gaze at Laisha again, this time with such malevolence that one of the other judges grabbed his elbow as if to restrain him. "Do you realize what you've done? It is not permitted! You deviated from the course. You are disqualified, and if I ever see your name entered on an event sponsored by the Society of Huntsmen again, I will have it stricken from it, I warn you. We are here to promote sport, and there can be no sport without discipline." His color was less alarming, but he was definitely not appeased. It was only at the urging of the other two that he resumed his seat. He took a sheet of pink paper and scrawled on it, and with a defiant stare at the other two, handed it to the secretary. "Read it precisely as I have written it."

Laisha was very straight in the saddle now, and she met the judge's eye. "Would you rather I took that jump, landed in the mud, killed myself, and crippled my horse? And if I were Deutsche rather than Russian, would you still condemn me for my actions?" She did not wait for a response, but kicked Babieca's sides sharply, so that the mare was jolted into a gallop. The assembly ring was near at hand, and she knew she was supposed to pull up there, but by now her temper was taking hold of her and she wanted to vent it, if necessary by exhausting her mare and herself.

"The judges have made a decision," the secretary brayed through the megaphone, his discomfort making his voice strident. "The ride by Laisha Vlassevna Ragoczy is being disallowed because of willful alteration of the prescribed course. The judges censure the rider for her deliberate actions which are insulting both to this gathering and to the Society of Huntsmen. Laisha Vlassevna Ragoczy is hereby banned from further participation in activities of the Society of Huntsmen."

Before the secretary was through, Ragoczy had risen from his place in the stands and tucked his pillow under his arm. He made his way down the narrow stairs to the ground, and started toward the cleared area where most of the automobiles were parked. As he walked, he saw Laisha ride away from the judges' stand, her face set with infuriated humiliation. He called out to Roger as he neared the parking area. "Laisha's ridden off toward the main road. We'll have to follow her."

"Ridden off? But what made . . ." Roger said as he pressed the ignition pedal, then fell silent as he moved aside to let Ragoczy enter the Isotta-Fraschini.

"The judges disqualified her ride because she took the water jump at an angle. It was an excuse, of course." He was backing the automobile out of the parking area as he spoke, and the concentration he gave to driving did not distract from his indignation on Laisha's behalf. As he reached the verge of the way, he turned the Isotta-Fraschini and then set out at a fast rate for the main road.

"How did she ride?" Roger asked as they rocked onto the newly-graded way.

"Beautifully." Ragoczy smiled briefly. "She covered the course better than any of the others, and the judges knew it. They had to discount her, or give her the award, and that would not be a popular decision." He held the steering wheel in an unwavering grip as the automobile took a tight curve on two tires.

"You warned her of that possibility, didn't you?" Roger said, showing no concern for his master's incautious driving.

"Yes. She's not unaware of the difficulties we both face here. With Röhm's SA about, some of the others are starting to feel brave again, and they say things they would not have dared to say a year ago." The main road was visible now through the trees, and Ragoczy, showing a moment of prudence, reduced his speed before turning onto the crudely-paved surface. "She is on the Flusslauf Schweif. That's about two kilometers farther along."

"She might already have crossed," Roger pointed out.

"She might. But I am counting on Babieca being tired after the ride. Laisha might not care what she does to herself, but she will have a care for her horse." He reduced his speed still more and at last drew the automobile up on the shoulder of the road and set the brake. He got out and went to the place where the well-kept equestrian path emerged from the trees. A close, swift study of the ground showed that many horses had come that way recently, but all were going toward the competition area rather than away from it. He had reached the place ahead of her. With a greater sense of confidence, he went back to the automobile. "We're in time. I'll keep watch for her." Roger gave a turn to his hand to show that he understood, while Ragoczy went back to the Flusslauf Schweif to wait.

It was not quite five minutes later that he heard the sound of an approaching horse. The animal was trotting without much enthusiasm, and as the mare rounded the bend and came into sight, Ragoczy heard her slow to a walk. As he watched, he saw Laisha slump in the saddle. She was capless now, and her hair flew in disordered strands around her face, and there was a scratch along her cheek where a branch had lashed her during her mad plunge away from the competition area.

Ragoczy stepped into the middle of the path and waited as horse and rider approached.

When Laisha saw a figure emerge from the shadows, she gathered up her reins, prepared to ride over the stranger. She had no intention of being caught alone here. Then she recognized Ragoczy and for an instant her courage almost failed her. She wanted to turn and run, but that would complete her humiliation, and so she held Babieca firmly and let the mare walk up to the man in black.

"Laisha," he said as he raced up to catch the reins. He patted the mare's neck where it was dark with sweat, and heard her heavy breathing.

"I'm sorry," she forced herself to say.

"Sorry?" Ragoczy was so startled that he said the word sharply.

She flinched. "Don't chide me, Papa."

"I'm not chiding you, Laisha," he said at once, conscience-stricken. "Why would I do such a thing?"

"Because I ran away." She sounded so full of self-loathing that it was all he could do not to insist she dismount so he could hold her as he had when she was a child.

"I thought that was anger and discretion. Murdering the judges would not have been approved of, and I feared it was that or flight." He was able to imbue his voice with enough sympathetic amusement that she looked down at him and did not avoid his eyes.

"I did want to choke him," she said carefully, not investigating her feelings any more than necessary.

"Quite understandable. He richly deserves it," Ragoczy remarked at once, making no concession to good manners. "He is a disgrace to the Society of Huntsmen and you have my word that I will speak to each of their officers about this."

"You will?" She had started to cry but was not yet aware of the tears on her face; her anger prompted them, not her shame. "I want you to tell them exactly what he said, and how he said it. I want them to treat him like a . . . a . . ."

"An un-house-broken cur?" Ragoczy suggested. He could not bring himself to call her attention to her weeping, though his heart ached for her.

"At least. He looked at me as if I were a Hun in church!" She sobbed, once, twice, then bent over Babieca's neck and let her grief rip through her. "He had no right! No right! To do that to me!"

Ragoczy held the mare steady until Laisha mastered herself. "Let me hold your stirrup for you," he said, one hand closing on the metal.

Laisha kicked her feet out of the stirrups and slid off her mare. With unsteady hands she removed her gloves and rubbed at her face, which only served to make the grime more noticeable. "I don't need help getting off my horse," she said stiffly.

"I know that. I want to do something for you, and that was the best I could think of at the moment," he said, trying to still the curt retort that could come so easily to his tongue. What he thought of as insignificant had a world of importance to his child, and he would not belittle her sensitivity.

"I rode the best of any of them!" Her head came up and she waited for him to offer those phrases of cold comfort she had heard other parents give their children that afternoon.

They did not come. "Yes, you did. It was a fine ride, and you showed excellent judgment at the water jump, which is undoubtedly what upset the Huntsmen so much—none of the others had thought of it." He put one hand on her shoulder. "If there were any way I could shield you from this, Laisha, I would. You must believe me. But one day you will be grown, with a life of your own to live, and then you would not be pleased that you had been protected, because you would not be able to find your strength. This was not a test, and I did not think you would be treated so boorishly, and had I known what would come of this, I might have tried to dissuade you from entering the competition, but you have not been too badly harmed by it. You've only had to face ignorance in action sooner than I thought you would have to. Eventually you would have seen it."

"They disqualified me because I am Russian." She sniffed.

Ragoczy slipped his arm around her shoulder completely. "No, my child: they disqualified you because you are not Deutsche. There's a difference."

"And you?" She looked at him. She was less than half a head shorter than he, but her slender, awkward height, next to his deep-chested, trim stockiness, made her appear to be slighter than she was.

"They must tolerate me, for the Society of Huntsmen have had Ragoczys in their number since the end of the Seventeenth Century. However, in the last sixty years, no Ragoczy has been awarded a greater recognition than the recording of their names on the honor rolls. The ribbons and pheasant cockades have, strangely, all gone to the Society's countrymen." With his arm still around her shoulder, Ragoczy began to walk toward the road. He led the mare with his other hand.

"Doesn't it make you furious?" Laisha asked. "It would make me."

"It . . . disappoints me. But it is such a common failing, Laisha." He thought of those ridiculous chariot races in Rome when only the Greens were allowed to win because the Emperor belonged to the Greens; of the contests in Spain when the King's Champion won every list, unhorsed or not; of the riding feats in Russia, where noble members of the Imperial Guard never lost. He stopped just before they reached the road. "You rode best today, and you know it. That matters, not what the judges did. If you had not ridden best and knew that as well, you would still have won more than anything they might have given you."

She sagged against him. "I know, Papa. But I wanted something to show, so they'd all know it."

He kissed her forehead. "It is very pleasant to get that recognition. When I was younger, I looked for that mark of approval, and I was . . . seduced? addicted? by achieving constant recognition." He wondered then, as he had so many times in the past, if his status as Prince had been a consideration in his awards; he had the disquieting feeling that it was. "It came to an end when my country was overrun by our enemies. After that, I learned what it was to stay alive." Had he been that reprehensible, or had he merely been very young, as Laisha was young? Those days were too far in the past for him to assess them now.

"My country was overrun by its enemies, too," she said, with a touch of pride, as if this gave them another bond.

"So it was." They resumed walking toward the road, and a moment later stepped out into sunlight. A truck laden with produce rattled by, and Babieca lifted her head sharply in protest. Ragoczy kept hold of the rein in his firm hand so that she would not balk.

Roger got out of the automobile as he saw Ragoczy and Laisha approaching. He held the door open as he gave the girl a quick, sympathetic smile.

"What about Babieca?" Laisha asked as Ragoczy motioned her toward the automobile.

"Roger will ride her back to the Schloss in easy stages. You

need a bath, and those scrapes ought to be attended to."
Ragoczy had already got into the driver's seat and was waiting for Laisha to take her place beside him.

"Babieca's my horse. I'll take care of her," Laisha declared
with a stubborn set to her jaw.

"Ordinarily I would expect that of you," Ragoczy told her.
"But in this instance you will be kinder to your mare letting
Roger ride her than you would be if you were in the saddle.
Your head is probably aching, and if those scratches are at all
deep—which I doubt, but I don't know for sure—a long, slow
ride would not help either of you. If Babieca needs a bit more
rest, Roger can arrange to put her up on the way home and
stay over with her. Does that relieve you, or are you going to
insist on this mortification of the flesh to salve your own
conscience?" He spoke in a level tone, as if he were addressing
exhausted troops rather than one determined girl.

"I didn't . . ." she protested, then opened the door of the
automobile. "I do have a headache. I almost mistimed a very
little jump going over the stream."

Ragoczy gave her a rare, delighted smile. "One of the hard-
est lessons to learn is to save your strength for the struggles
that are necessary. You're doing well." He signaled Roger.

"My master?" Roger had mounted Babieca.

"Bring her along, and if there's any trouble, go to the old
posting inn at Hausham. They have good facilities for horses
still." He started the Isotta-Fraschini.

"As you wish, my master." He steadied the mare as the
automobile rolled out onto the road.

When they had been driving for almost ten minutes in silence, Ragoczy said to Laisha, "Tell me, do you feel you would
want to move from here?"

Her eyes were startled as she turned to him. "You mean
send me to school?"

"No, not that." Ragoczy's dark eyes were narrowed. "I have
at most another year of work on my current project, and then
I will be at liberty to travel again. Italy wouldn't be wise, but
there are other places . . . I have a house in London. When
Professor Riemen and I finish our tasks, do you think you
would like to leave Bayern?"

"Leave?" She weighed the word as if it were unfamiliar to
her. "What is London like?"

"Very English, very civilized. They're insular, both geo-
graphically and metaphorically, but you might like the place."

He turned onto the road that led up toward Schloss Saint-Germain and on around Schliersee.

Laisha considered it. "Do you want to leave here?"

"It might be wise," he answered carefully. "You've learned about what has happened in Italy. It could happen here as well. This afternoon . . . I didn't like what I saw. It was not simply the judges' bigotry—many people in the stands approved of the decision. There was no argument from the Society of Huntsmen members who attended." He tapped lightly on the horn, warning a shepherd near the road to watch his flock.

"I don't know very much English," she said after a short silence.

"I can teach you. So can your tutors. In a year you should be fairly fluent." He left the road and started up the drive to the looming bulk of Schloss Saint-Germain.

"Will you want me to make up my mind quickly?" She sounded worried now, and Ragoczy was swift to reassure her.

"No. Nothing has to be decided immediately. Give it your consideration, and if you wish, we can discuss it again in a few days. I should have your response by, oh, next May. It will take a little time to arrange for travel and moving, and you may want to come with me to London once or twice before you make up your mind either way." He brought the Isotta-Fraschini to a halt in the courtyard of the Schloss, near the door.

"I *will* think about it," Laisha promised as he came around to open the door for her. "But not tonight." Her smile was tremulous as she made her forlorn way into the Schloss. She had wanted very much to travel, she reminded herself as she went up to her room. Why did Ragoczy's suggestion distress her so much? Then she put the matter out of her mind, giving her attention instead to dealing with her tutors, who always fussed over her: she hated being fussed over.

Text of a letter from Irina Ohchenov to Franchot Ragoczy.

Paris, France
December 18, 1925

Schloss Saint-Germain
Schliersee
Bavaire

My dear Count;
   In case Professor de Montalia has not already written
to you, I wanted you to know that our translating from
those tablets I mentioned to you a while ago has gone very
well and the excitement about them is still increasing in
the academic community. Not that this means a great
deal in the general order of things, and if you stopped a
man at random on the street and asked him about the
work, he would know nothing of it and might well think
you were mad. However, since the presentation of the
work, I have had more requests for translations than
I would have imagined possible a year ago. I've actually
had to select those projects I will undertake and those I
will not. This is something of a change from my first
work. I am gaining confidence, not only in my work, but
at last I feel that I can live the life I have wanted to make
for myself. If you had not found me in that terrible place,
no doubt I would be dead by now, surrounded by the
ghosts not only of my family but of myself.
   As you may know, I have discarded my title. It has no
meaning to me any longer. Duchess. But of what? Where
is my country? I am not simply an exile—my position no
longer exists, and so I have decided that Irina Andreivna
Ohchenov will bow to history and set aside those glorious
prefixes to her name. I do this with mixed emotions, but I
know it is best. What brought it home to me was the other
evening. I was riding in a taxi—I can afford to ride in

taxis now, and I indulge myself with them—and recognized the Russian accent of the driver. He, realizing that I was also Russian, began to lament the loss of the old days, and to decry the current state of affairs, while he made predictions about the triumphant return of the nobility to Russia as soon as the Communist dogs had killed each other off. This man was driving a taxi in Paris, and ranting about balls and jewels. I felt embarrassed by the whole conversation, although I could not at the time determine why. I should have been in sympathy with the man, who, I believe, was a distant relation of Leonid's. Instead I was compelled to pity him, to regard him as a wounded, crippled creature. He boasted that for many Frenchmen, riding in a taxi driven by old nobility was something of a cachet. He seemed to me then to be like the dancing bears I saw as a child. He had a store of tricks, but that was not what made him loved—it was that a formidable creature had been reduced to the state of a clown.

From what I have seen of events in Germany, all is not well. Perhaps Hindenburg will prove the proper leader for them. Reporting here is highly biased, of course, but it appears that there is more unrest in that country than assumed at first. What is this National Socialist German Workers Party? There are numerous mentions of them in the press and it is claimed that they have over 25,000 members. They appear to be similar to the Italian Fascisti, which is alarming in itself. I have recently read that the NSDAP is derisively known as Nazi. There are fascist organizations in France, of course, but they are not so large or as influential as this organization appears to be. In reading over what I have written, I feel I am being strangely cautious. How many times I say "appear," as if I am hoping that things are not so bad as they seem. It may be that the radical right wing is simply more vocal in Germany, but I doubt this is the case. Allowing for the alarmist tone of much French reporting, it still appears—I have said it again—that they are a most powerful faction. You, living where you do, will have a better idea of the strength of that movement. I hope you will be able to reassure me, but I fear that there is danger from these Nazis. My own experience with radical politics will doubtless tend to make me more apprehensive than most, and

*for that reason you may convince me that I am running
from shadows. I hope that is the case.*

*You may be pleased to know that I have actually re-
ceived an invitation for the holidays. Phillippe Timbres,
who was introduced to me by Professor de Montalia, has
asked me to spend the Christmas season with his brother
and their family near Orleans. I have never seen that
city—I have hardly been outside of Paris—and Monsieur
Timbres tells me that I will enjoy it. He was an officer in
the Great War, which is how Professor de Montalia came
to meet him. He left the Army over a year ago and now is
working for Joseph et Dognac. You may have heard of the
company. They are builders, and although their major
work is offices, there is a division that specializes in
restorations of older homes and châteaux, and that is the
part of the business he works in. You will doubtless
wonder why I have accepted the invitation. At first, I
wondered myself. But I have seen a fair amount of
Phillippe Timbres, and I admit that I like what I see. We
are neither of us young, and our lives have been touched
with tragedy. I could not feel for this man as I did for
Leonid, but that is no matter. Should he decide that he
does want to marry me—and he has suggested the possibility more than once—I will know that my life will be
pleasant with him. He has two orphaned nephews who are
at the moment living with his surviving brother, and has
said that should we eventually decide to marry, he would
like to raise these two children. One is thirteen and the
other nine. It would be delightful to have children again.
At my age I am hardly in a position to take on an infant,
but two youngsters are another matter.*

*All that is for the future, however, and I assure you
with all my heart that I look forward to seeing you again
in March, as you mentioned in your last letter that you
would be in Paris then, on your way to London. You are
not as much a part of my life as Monsieur Timbres is,
but what you give I have had from no other, and I do not
wish to be deprived of that unique love you share with me.
Should I decide to marry Phillippe Timbres, I will not shut
you entirely out of my life. Should you wish to stay away
from me, that is another matter, but as long as you are
willing to seek me out, be certain that I will welcome you.
I doubt I will mention that to Monsieur Timbres, though
he is not one to be ruled by his jealousies. I am aware*

*that there have been other women in his life. It would be ridiculous if there had not been. He knows that I have been married and that there has been one lover beyond my husband. I have not told him who, but he does know that it was my lover who found me in a slum and brought me out of it, and for that he is grateful. In many ways, he is very French, which I suppose should not astonish me.*

*Professor de Montalia, as you probably already know, is in the Middle East on another dig. She left at the end of September and does not intend to return until October next year. She has said that her work there is promising, and she wishes to take advantage of the comparative peace while it lasts. We have decided to exchange letters at two-week intervals so that neither of us need ever be far from news of the other. She is of the opinion that isolation is dangerous in these times, and doubtless she is correct. I have agreed to forward letters to her, and should you wish it, I will provide you with her address and the means by which to reach her. The expedition has a small aeroplane at its disposal and with this to fly from the dig to Damascus, mail should not be too long in transit.*

*Your ward sounds wonderful. How fortunate for both of you. Not every child would be comfortable with you, Count, no matter how circumspect you are. A girl like Laisha, however, will thrive in your company. When she is ready to enter society, I hope you will bring her to Paris so I may meet her. If I have decided to be Madame Timbres, then I will ask for the pleasure of chaperoning her one evening, either to a concert or one of those dreadful women's salons. Don't be troubled that she has not reached her true beauty yet. Give her another ten years and you will be astonished. Those women who emerge from the chrysalis of youth in their twenties and thirties have their beauty for the rest of their lives, and are not like those fragile blossoms that are faded before they reach twenty-five. Slender girls are popular at the moment, so that should present no difficulty, as it might have not long ago. For the rest, you have only to wait a little time, which, as you remarked to me, will pass all too quickly.*

*I must close now, but not before I wish you the joys of this year's end. Until now, I have found it hard to think of the holidays, but with Monsieur Timbres's family offering their hospitality, it does not depress me as it has before. I am not so blind as to assume that the stay will*

*be totally without sadness, yet I believe that there will be
more joy than grief, which, I have learned, is better than
most of us can wish for.*

  *With my love and my prayers,*

                                                    *Devotedly,
                                                        Irina*


# 8


Gudrun looked up with a puzzled frown as Otto held out the
calling card. "Helmut Rauch? Are you certain he wishes to see
me? Maximillian is not here."

Otto nodded slowly, as he did everything slowly these days.
His body had sagged, his steps were dragging, and his face
had slipped into drooping folds as if it were made of wax and
had been left in the sun too long. "He was most insistent."

"I can't imagine why he should wish to see me," Gudrun
said, thinking aloud. She got up from her desk. "Has Miroslav
finished with cleaning out the gutters?"

"All but two, Rudi." Otto gave a sigh. "He is not as quick
about it as he used to be. He says that heights dizzy him.
They never used to," he ended querulously.

"He's older, Otto," Gudrun said sensibly. We're all older,
she thought. Except, perhaps, Franchot Ragoczy: she was
still uncertain about him.

"Herr Rauch seemed impatient," Otto observed by way of a
hint.

"In a moment, Otto. I have a letter to finish." The letter
was to her second cousin in Berlin, asking if he would be
interested in purchasing some of the older furniture at
Wolkighügel.

"He told me it is urgent," Otto complained.

"And I will be with him directly," Gudrun said with asperity. "I am not at that man's beck and call." She did not want to
see Helmut Rauch; the man frightened her with his sudden
demands and darting eyes that would not hold hers for more
than a few seconds at a time.

"Very well." Otto drew himself up so that Gudrun would
know he was offended. He turned and went out of the room.

Gudrun sat for another five minutes, her hand to her head, staring at the fireplace on the far side of the room. She had had a fire burning there an hour ago, but it was little but embers now and she did not know if there was wood enough to spare from the kitchen to rekindle the flames here. Frau Bürste would never complain, but Gudrun knew that the woman often skimped in a manner that distressed her. Tomorrow, she promised herself, she would have Miroslav chop down three or more of the old trees near Maximillian's cabin. That way, her brother would have fuel and the main house could also be kept warm. She thought of Schloss Saint-Germain, with its new gas-fueled stove, its generator that kept the electricity working all year long, and sighed. It would be a long time before such luxuries could come to Wolkighügel. She had got one of the huge water heaters that attached to the kitchen stove, and so there was always hot water now, but the rest of it—the electricity was out now, as it often was in the winter, and kerosene lamps stood on the tables in the hall, lit even in the afternoon because of the darkness of this winter day. There was so much to do with this huge house! If Miroslav had not been willing to climb to the snowy roof and chop the ice and debris out of the gutters, then the eaves might have been damaged or broken by the time the thaw came. If her cousin in Berlin did not wish to buy anything from her, she would have to think of another way to pay for the various repairs that the whole estate needed so badly. This last thought turned her back to her half-finished letter, and she devoted the next few minutes to the careful wording of her request. When she was satisfied with what she had written, she addressed the envelope set aside for it, sealed it, and affixed the stamp. Each gesture was treasured because it was a delay. She should have had the courage to deny herself to Helmut Rauch, she thought. The trouble was that the man was so much in Maximillian's company that he had come to assume that he must naturally be entirely welcome at Wolkighügel. She turned up the watch on her brooch and saw that she had been here alone for more than a quarter-hour—Rauch had probably decided that she was being deliberately rude. She took the letter and went into the hall.

Rauch was in the library, his expression stiff with disapproval. He rose in grudging courtesy, favoring Gudrun with a minuscule inclination of his head which she was free to regard as a bow if she wished. "I hope I do not disturb you, Frau Ostneige," he said icily.

"As to that, Herr Rauch, you did come at an awkward moment, and I could not leave what I was doing just at once. It was good of you to wait." That, she decided, would make what few amends were possible.

"You realize that a day like this, it is not easy to call on anyone. The snow is deep, and mild as it is at the present, there could well be more snow by nightfall. I had not intended to linger here." He folded his arms and remained standing.

"Gracious," Gudrun said with a nervous titter, "you sound most serious, Herr Rauch." She took a chair near the fire, grateful for the warmth it gave. She had not realized how cold she was.

"It is necessary that we have a brief discussion, Frau Ostneige. From what your brother tells me, you have not yet expressed a great deal of interest in his activities." He stared at her an instant; then his eyes flicked away, going now to the portraits over the door, the books in the glass-fronted case, the bound manuscripts in the far shelves. Looking at Gudrun disturbed him. "Has he told you of our mission?"

"No, Herr Rauch, he has not. Nor have I encouraged him," she added pointedly.

"That was not completely wise," he said in an admonitory tone.

"Wasn't it?" Her chair was old, leather-upholstered. Frau Bürste had recently rubbed it with an oiled rag so that it glowed. If it were not for her distressing guest, she would think herself lucky to spend a few hours here in the library curled up in this fine old chair with a book to amuse her.

"You should be concerned. Everyone should be concerned." He frowned, annoyed at Gudrun's lack of response. "You do not seem to be aware that we are now at a crucial moment in our history, Frau Ostneige, and those who vacillate will be judged by future generations as laggards and worse."

"I doubt I will have future generations, Herr Rauch," she said softly. "I have no children and am not likely to have them."

"There! You see! You are speaking as if your life is done, and there is no more need for you to fulfill your woman's role. It is precisely this ignorance that must be combated now before we can achieve our dreams. It is more than just the NSDAP or the Thule Gesellschaft. Together these forces will once again weld Deutschland into a formidable unity." He slammed the flat of his hand onto the table and leaned forward.

"It sounds far-reaching and ambitious," Gudrun said quietly, attempting to determine how long she would have to listen to his ranting before she could excuse herself.

"It is far more than that. It is the future of the world we are discussing, Meine Frau. You must see beyond the limitations that have blinded most of this country to its strengths and obligations. The Vaterland has been shamed and humiliated long enough by those decadent popinjays of France and Britain. It is the destiny of Deutschland to lead the world, not slink in the shadow of others. Now is the time for decisive action. There are over twenty-seven thousand men in the NSDAP. All of them burn with the light of their mission. *Our* mission. We of the Thule Gesellschaft and Bruderschaft have given our powers into the service of the great ideal. It isn't enough." He strode down the room, growing more enthusiastic. "You cannot imagine what we can accomplish, given the opportunity."

"I look forward to learning more about it in time," Gudrun said as if she were speaking to one of her old and wayward uncles.

"I dislike that condescending tone, Frau Ostneige!" Helmut declared emphatically. "This is not some idle fancy I am telling you of, but a plan that will alter the face of the world and bring Deutschland back into the position of prominence that is rightfully his. The Vaterland is not so called for amusement. It is the father of the world, and for that reason must guide the other nations in their growth. You do not know how many look to us for discipline and strength. You find it difficult to believe, do you?" His accusation was very sharp.

"Herr Rauch—" Gudrun began, but he cut her short.

"There have been funds sent to us. From those who are the rightful masters of Russia, from the financial giants of the United States of America, from titled men in Britain . . . the list is a long and impressive one. Every encouragement is given us, both in money and in advice. We are not asking for the power to lead again only to satisfy our besmirched honor, but in response to the pleadings of the entire civilized world." His face was flushed now, as if he were slightly drunk.

"That may be the case, Herr Rauch. There is very little I can do one way or the other." She felt stifled in this warm, restful room. Rauch was filling it up, pressing the air out of it and out of her.

"This is the very belief that must be obliterated from our thoughts. We must remember how much we have done in the

past. You think now of your widowhood and you devote yourself to your husband's memory—"

"I don't think this is any—" Gudrun began, as if she had
been insulted.

"Which is the great strength of our women, who submit
themselves to the will of their husbands and the Vaterland.
You do not go in search of the tawdry excitements that have
been foisted off upon us by the decaying cultures of other
countries. You have maintained yourself as a proper Deutschen
must. It is well-done of you. It is from women like yourself
that our new country must take the example. No one will be
shocked by the sight of a Deutsche in indecent French clothes,
smoking cigarettes and dancing to lewd music. Our women
shall be an example to every woman in the world. You conduct
yourself with modesty. You have a bit too much of the air of
command, but doubtless that is the result of the unnatural
burdens you have had to carry because of your husband's long
years of ill health. With the proper husband to care for you
and guard you, this unbecoming behavior will be gone and all
your native sweetness and submission will flower again."

"This is most—" Gudrun started to object, and again Helmut interrupted her.

"It is not entirely correct of me to be so blunt in my speech,
but I wish to convey to you the importance of what is taking
place here, to show you how much a part you can play. It is
not simply your femininity that marks you—your husband was
a man of great respect and your family has long been looked
up to as foremost of the hochgebornen. You do not stand
alone, Frau Ostneige, but you represent all that is finest in
our beloved country." He stopped in front of the fireplace and
smiled down at her. "You can make quite a unique contribution, for your support, not only financial, but social, would
open doors to us that could change our position. It is true that
we have many who sympathize with us in both the army and
the old nobility. Many of them are members of the Gesellschaft and Bruderschaft. But there are others who have been
reserved with us and—"

Gudrun stood up. "Herr Rauch, is all this an attempt to coax
me into giving your NSDAP money and provide invitations to
a few parties?" The air of command of which Helmut had so
recently complained was quite visible.

"Naturally, that is a part of—"

"Because, Herr Rauch, I think you should know a few
things. From what you say, I gather you have been speaking

to my brother. Maximillian is under the impression that I have a great deal of money left in my inheritance and am keeping it from him because I fear he will squander it. There is some justification in that fear. Maximillian went through his share of the money some time ago and lives here now at my sufferance. But that is not because I am a wealthy woman, Herr Rauch. Quite the contrary. Between the losses to my family during the Great War, my husband's long illness, and the depredations of the inflation of two years ago, there is very little left here. We used to have horses, but those have been sold. We had a coach and a sleigh, but they are gone too. I did not part with them on a whim, Mein Herr, but out of direst necessity. My staff now consists of my housekeeper, who is also my cook, the handyman, and Otto. Ideally there should be ten servants to run this house, another two for the grounds, and three for the stable, assuming there were horses to care for and coaches to be maintained. Maximillian does not concern himself with this part of my life. I'm sorry if he has given you a . . . romantic picture of our situation, but he does it to keep from being distressed. You must forgive him." She started toward the door. "I have work I must attend to, Herr Rauch. You will excuse me?"

"Frau Ostneige," Helmut said sharply, detaining her. "I confess that what you have said is not entirely in agreement with what your brother has told me. I have been a banker, and it is not difficult for me to verify what you have said—"

"Please do. And then, if you will be good enough to explain it all to Maximillian, I would be most appreciative." Her hand was on the door latch and she had to resist the urge to bolt from the room.

"Don't leave quite yet, Meine Frau. I must ask you a few more questions." He had taken up his stance before the fire, the flames appearing to crackle at his feet and climb his legs.

Gudrun took a deep breath. "Herr Rauch, you force me to remind you that none of these things are your concern. What my monetary situation is has no bearing whatsoever on you. I doubt you have anything more to say to me."

"Let me have a few more minutes of your time. It will be worth your while." He lowered his voice with the intention of calming her; it had the reverse effect.

"What is it, Herr Rauch?" Gudrun leaned against the door, her hands behind her back clutching the latch.

"I may have underestimated you. I tried to appeal to your love of country, but there is more to patriotism than mere slogans. You are wise to be prudent with your resources, for we are still at the mercy of the foreign powers who trespass on our homeland. You have seen what their meddling can do to us. But you are not aware of the insidious traitors who infest every part of our lives, who are working relentlessly to destroy us and the whole of Western civilization."

"Oh, come, Herr Rauch. Are you trying to convince me that there is a conspiracy directed at Europe?" She thought that Rauch might be mad, and decided that she had best humor him a bit longer.

"But there is! You have become so used to the situation that you are no longer aware of the danger. You are like a farmer who grows his crops on the side of a volcano, forgetting that one day it will erupt again and bury him and his crops in burning lava. That is what our enemies depend upon, that we will be lulled into assuming that our antagonists are those we have met on the battlefield. It is not so!" He took several impulsive steps toward her. "I saw for myself how these devils work, when I was at the Front. I was expected to hold a position with an officer who was a Jew, one of the very people who brought us to such ruin. The man was killed, Gott sei Dank! He was not able to work his malice with me. We lost good men on that day. The officer was one of the pernicious von Rathenau—"

"Walther von Rathenau was a fine man, my father told me, and never has any man, gentile or Jew, served Deutschland better. His death was a disgrace to all of us," Gudrun said firmly. The whiteness around Helmut's eyes and mouth grew more marked, but she went on. "If you were one of those who consented in his killing, you are the foe of this country, not the Jews you vilify."

Rauch blinked twice. "They have bewitched you, Frau Ostneige."

"If that is the case, they also bewitched my father and his father as well." Her tone was politely dry, but Rauch did not notice her sarcasm.

"Jawol," he said heavily. "It is an old, old plot they have. They are patient, Frau Ostneige. That is what no one understands. It means nothing to them if generations pass so long as their ends are served." He went back to the fireplace. "You are probably not aware that you have been surrounded by Jews all your life, and they have manipulated your thoughts so that you are no longer able to see what is so clearly apparent to us. Your music teacher, for example, was a Jew, and filled your hours with such men as Mendelssohn. There are better composers to study."

"Herr Rauch, you grow absurd." She had the door half-open behind her now. "I am sure you believe what you are saying. Doubtless there are many who agree with you."

"Without your help, Frau Ostneige, your brother will not be able to advance any further in the Thule Gesellschaft. He seeks to belong to the Bruderschaft and all that it implies. He has been given provisional Initiation, but without your encouragement, he will not be allowed to learn the innermost secrets, which is what he most deeply wants to do. If you have feeling for him, you will reconsider your attitudes." He smiled, intending to be ingratiating, but to Gudrun he appeared sinister. "It is characteristic of the Teutonic people that they demonstrate great loyalty in the face of the perfidy of other races, and your willingness to defend the Jews who seduced you with their nonsense about international liberalism shows more clearly than anything else how much you have retained of the true nature of our people."

"Herr Rauch . . ." She pulled the door completely open.

"Say you will think about this. I will leave a book for you, which will clarify more than anything I say the nature of the struggle at hand. Read it, Frau Ostneige, and see what has become of us all, so you will know at last that I have not been talking to no purpose. You will find a great deal of wisdom in these pages." He pointed to a volume that lay on one of the small reading tables. "One of our number wrote it while in prison, Frau Ostneige. He was not afraid to defend his beliefs, you see. The officials know that he is right, for his sentence was lessened. There is more in *Mein Kampf* than in any other ten books written in the last fifty years."

"I . . . I will look at it, Herr Rauch. Now I must go. I have my household tasks to attend to . . ." She was into the hall and walking away from the obsessed man in her library. Her hands were shaking and she pressed them together as she walked, trying to quell the fear she could not conceal from herself. If these were the sorts of men who were the Thule Gesellschaft, she could do Maximillian no greater harm than assisting him to become more entangled in their affairs. What sorts of men had such hate-filled thoughts guiding them? She had not realized that she had gone to the kitchen, but as she opened the door, she saw Frau Bürste look up from the pastry dough she was rolling.

"Frau Ostneige," she said, startled. "Is there something wrong?"

Gudrun tried to laugh but her voice shook and she ended on a sob. "Oh, that dreadful man Rauch has been here. I . . . I don't know what it is about him. The more I see of him, the more I feel I have been . . . contaminated."

Frau Bürste snorted. "That one. I've seen them before. They're the kind who come as guests and end up terrorizing the chambermaids. They justify their actions by claiming it is their right to do so. Oh, yes. I know the sort." She applied herself to rolling the dough again, and the muscles in her large arms stood out with the force of what she did.

"I'm so glad to hear that," Gudrun sighed as she came into the room. "Not that I approve of such men," she added hastily. "I didn't mean that. I thought no one else disliked him as much as I do. Maximillian approves of him wholeheartedly."

"If you will permit me to say it, Frau Ostneige, your brother has convinced himself that he is one of a group of superior men. They're using him. That Herr Rauch does not admire your brother, and has little use for him."

"Oh, he has a use, all right, that was made very clear to me," Gudrun corrected her with undisguised bitterness. "Maximillian told Herr Rauch, and heaven knows who else, that we have money. Rauch wanted a donation of some sort from me. I doubt he believed my denial. What am I to do about him?" Gudrun burst out.

"If you took my advice," Frau Bürste said as she paused in her labors, "you would tell that ingrate that you will no longer support him. If he had any gainful employment, it might be different. But who is it who brings unexpected guests here and eats up our food and drinks our beer and wine without so much as a little consideration, or asking if it might be inconvenient? There's less of it than it was, and your brother always declares himself contrite when you remind him of what difficulties you have, but he's a wastrel, Frau Ostneige, and there's no getting around it, or excusing it. Those men, Rauch and that lot, they know it too." She had gone far beyond what was usually permitted of a servant to say, and stood waiting for the reprimand she deserved.

Gudrun put her hands to her face. "He is my brother. I have no one else near to me."

Frau Bürste blinked in surprise, then came across the kitchen, her heavy, waddling tread as stolid and dependable as the woman herself. "Frau Ostneige, Frau Ostneige, you're overwrought." She put her hand awkwardly on Gudrun's shoulder, leaving a faintly floury print on her shoulder. "There, my lady. What did I say? There's no reason to pay any attention to me. You tell me to keep my place next time."

Gudrun looked up at her housekeeper. "It's ridiculous for you to say that, Frau Bürste. Who has a better right to speak to me? We would not run Wolkighügel without you. No one here has done more. You have every right to say what you think about how this household goes on."

"If your grandfather or your father heard you speak this way, Frau Ostneige," Frau Bürste said severely, "you would have a sore rump for days. It isn't at all fitting that I should tell you these things."

Frau Bürste was right about her father and grandfather, Gudrun thought. Neither of those stiff-spined men would have admitted to any servant that they had a voice in the conduct of household affairs. But neither her father nor her grandfather had been through the privations that she had undergone. "I am grateful for your advice, Frau Bürste," she said, feeling strangely saddened. "I'll consider everything you've told me. You must not hesitate to discuss such matters with me in the future. Otherwise, it will be impossible for us to keep our spending within our means." And, she added to herself, it would not be necessary for this demeaning letter. If her uncle did not aid her, she would have to approach others with the same request, and they would not be as understanding or as discreet as her uncle would be, no matter what his answer.

"That's an excellent thought, Frau Ostneige," Frau Bürste declared. "Now, you go back to your work and leave me alone until I get this meal to cooking. You don't need to be worried about how I go on here. For this month we're saving a little money."

"Because Maximillian's friends don't care to try driving out in the snow," Gudrun said shrewdly.

"That's part of it. Off you go," Frau Bürste said as she bustled Gudrun out of the kitchen.

Gudrun remained in the hallway, undecided. She dared not return to the library for fear Herr Rauch had not yet left. The thought of another encounter with the man chilled her more than the cold of her home. There were servants' stairs to the upper floors, and although she called herself craven for using them, she made her way to her rooms that way, thinking that she needed a bath.

When at last she came down to dinner, she had changed to a

fine black dress, more suitable for an evening at the theatre
than a meal at home without guests. She took a glass of sherry
by herself, and had already finished half a bowl of Westfälische
Bohnensuppe when Maximillian came into the dining room.
His face was flushed, and from the unsteadiness of his walk,
this was not entirely due to the weather.

"I've talked to Rauch," he said without preamble.

"Would you like some soup?" Gudrun offered him, reaching
for the ladle.

"I said, I've talked to Rauch." He was sulking and he
refused to look directly at her; he directed his gaze toward the
curtained windows.

"Yes. I heard you." Without waiting for him to say anything
more, she began to measure out soup into the second bowl
beside the tureen.

"Is that all you have to say?" He pounded a closed fist on
the table for emphasis.

"That's all." She handed the bowl to him.

With a sweep of his arm, he knocked the bowl away from
her, sending stock, beans, and smoked-sausage slices spraying
over the table, the carpet, and his sister. "I won't have it!"

Gudrun was on her feet at once. "That is quite enough!" She
reached automatically for her napkin, but it, too, was soaked.
She gave a quiet scream and dropped it on the floor. "Maximillian!"

He sat hunched over his plate, his face set. "You angered
me."

As she pulled the bell rope, Gudrun brought her rage under
control. "Go to the kitchen, Maximillian. Frau Bürste will feed
you there." She wiped her face, ready now to attack her
brother with knives and whips.

"While you, lady of the house, dine here in solitary state?"
He had not risen, and now he reached calmly for the tureen.

"No," she said through clenched teeth, "while I try to salvage this dress you have so wantonly ruined."

"Don't bother about that," he said, then gave her a sheepish
smile. "I was vexed with you, Rudi—"

"Don't call me that!"

"It was silly to throw the soup, I admit it," he continued as
if he had not heard her. "But there isn't much harm done. A
little hot broth is easily cleaned up."

"This dress is silk," she informed him as her fury renewed
itself. "It is ruined."

"Well, then get another one. That's three years out of fashion, anyway. It's time you got yourself something a little better." He lifted the ladle and tasted the soup, giving an appreciative nod. "She's a good cook for all that she's an old busybody."

For well over a minute Gudrun could not speak, so consumed was she with anger and helplessness. She did not recognize herself when she brought herself to address her brother. "I cannot get another dress, Maximillian. I don't have enough money to buy one. Why won't you accept it? This isn't 1912 anymore. Our money is *gone*!" She had not moved, but Maximillian shrank back from her, dropping the ladle into the soup and staring at her with the guilty smile of a six-year-old.

"But Rudi . . . Gudrun . . . you're not . . ." He picked up his napkin and began to mop at the spilled soup, wanting to make amends.

"Get out of this house, Maximillian. I don't want you here anymore. You can stay at the gamekeeper's cottage and I'll see that you are fed. But you're not to enter this house again until I invite you." She turned abruptly and hurried out of the dining room. She was aghast at her fuming temper. For the first time she had wanted to attack her brother, pounding him, wounding him, making him recognize in his flesh, in his bones, that he had abused her, and this was her repayment. As she climbed the main stairs, she looked down at the greasy dampness that spread over the black silk. She wanted to cry. One thoughtless, spoiled act and her best dinner dress was ruined, and she was supposed to be appeased by the thought of buying another because the dress she wore was no longer in fashion. She put her hand to her eyes, reaching to steady herself on the banister as a short, passionate tempest of weeping swept over her. Then she made herself stand up and walk the rest of the way to her room with the dignity she had been taught to demonstrate.

Like a sleepwalker she got out of her dress, thinking that her life had come apart again this day. First it was Rauch, and now Maximillian. Her dress lay at her feet in an untidy pile: she could not bring herself to touch it again. She patted her hair and discovered that it had soup in it, as well. She would have to bathe again, and choose something else to wear at table. Gudrun sat on the side of her bed, fingering her now stained chiffon slip, thinking that she would not return to the dining room now. Without being quite aware of it, she drifted into a half-sleep, her thoughts fading so that pleasant, long-ago images could take their place, soothing her so that she did not have to grapple with all the problems confronting her. In an hour, she told herself, in an hour I will bathe and dress. In an hour.

Frau Bürste, unaware of what had taken place in the dining room, gave a last check to the tray she was preparing to take to the dining room. Otto had told her not more than five minutes ago that Maximillian was home at last, so she had hastily added two more Schneebällen to the dish with the Kalbsvögerl. There was also a plate of Geschmälzte Maultaschen. The hearty food gave off richly fragrant steam, and Frau Bürste smiled to herself. Despite the necessary economies she practiced, she flattered herself that she served a better meal than was to be had in many places where there was more than enough money for elaborate cooking. Carrying the tray with the ease of long practice, she left the kitchen and crossed the hall toward the dining room, her mind already thinking ahead to her own dinner, which she could begin as soon as she served Frau Ostneige and her brother.

Maximillian looked up as the door opened. He had a full bowl of soup before him and was seated at the far end of the table, away from the spills that spread over more than half the table. "If what you've got there is half as good as your Bohnensuppe, I'm delighted I got back in time to enjoy it."

"What . . . ?" Frau Bürste muttered, baffled at what she saw. "How did the soup get spilled? Look at it!" she went on, dismayed, as she put the tray on the table. "Why, it's all over. Look at the carpet!"

"There was a bit of an accident," Maximillian said blithely. "My sister dropped the bowl she was filling and . . . well, you can probably tell what happened. She's gone upstairs to change." He resumed his meal, smiling widely at Frau Bürste.

"Spilled? This does not appear . . . What has happened here?" she demanded, her hands planted on her hips. "What have you done to your sister?"

Maximillian's features darkened. He was a little less handsome now than he had been two years ago, or three. His pale hair was thinning and there were heavy lines under his eyes, which were emphasized by the first few broken capillaries in his cheeks. "What's wrong with you, Frau Bürste? Why must I have done something to my sister because the soup is spilled?"

She did not give him an answer. "I must get water," she muttered, starting from the dining room.

"Oh, Frau Bürste, before you go," Maximillian called after her, "I'm having some friends here next week, for a day or so.

They'll stay with me at my cabin, but I want to have one good dinner here, with your fine cooking. There should be about six of them, so you'll have to buy another barrel of beer; we get dry and thirsty on these winter days."

She had closed the door on him while he was still talking. She had to do something about the carpet at once, clean it with soap and water before the soup soaked in too deeply. Yet she could not bring herself to do this chore until she had talked to her employer. As she climbed the stairs, her head swam with worries, so vague and faceless that she could think of no way to express them, even to herself. As she reached Gudrun's door, she heard a groan and then a prolonged crack as the eaves on the one side of the roof that had not been cleaned by Miroslav at last gave way under their burden of ice and snow.

Text of a letter from David Bündnis to Hermann Göring.

> *Baiersbronn*
> *April 14, 1926*

*Braunkaserne, SA*
*München*

*My dear Herr Göring:*

It is indeed an honor to answer your questions regarding the man calling himself Franchot Ragoczy of Schloss Saint-Germain. As you mentioned in your letter of the second of this month, he claims the title Graf, and this is upheld by those of the old order. I have no reason to doubt his right to call himself Graf, or to question his lineage. The Ragoczys may no longer be Princes of Transylvania, but they are still a most powerful and respected family. I doubt that any man would take that name on himself unless he was legitimately entitled to it.

It has been some time since I was employed by him. How he found out my association with the Army I do not know, or my dealings with Röhm, but find them out he most certainly did. On the day I left, he laid out to me precisely what my activities had been and to whom I had been reporting since I first undertook to serve as his ward's tutor. He was generous in his severance monies, and did provide me with a fair recommendation, but he made it abundantly apparent that if I made any effort to continue my activities concerning him, he would do everything he could to have me exposed and disgraced, and I most sincerely believed him. To this day, I would be reluctant to act contrary to his instructions. This letter, should he ever learn of it, is enough to bring his ire down upon me. While I doubt you would endanger me through thoughtlessness, there are those who are not as reliable, and I hope that you will regard with utmost confidence the information I provide you now.

453

*From what you have said, you are aware that Ragoczy has been working with Professor Isidore Riemen on a project of some importance. From what I learned of their work at the beginning, it is involved in the manufacture of synthetic fuels. How far this has advanced, I have no way of guessing, but if it is true and Ragoczy is planning to leave Deutschland for England, then they have either succeeded or they have met with enough difficulty or failure to convince both men that it is not worthwhile to pursue the matter further. From what I learned of the man, it was apparent to me that he does not leave a task incomplete. If you have not already discussed the matter with Professor Riemen, then it might be best if you inquire of him where their research stands at present. I have heard that the Professor is not averse to our cause and might be willing to give you more data than I have. I surmise that it is possible that their discoveries, if any, will be offered to those who support us before they are presented to those belonging to the opposition.*

*I am afraid that I have no more information than you do about the identity of Ragoczy's ward. In the years I was her tutor, I learned very little about her. The accent she has in Russian suggests that she was part of a noble household, but at what level and in what capacity, I do not know. I made several attempts to speak with the child, but there I must admit that I failed. It was not a question of lack of trust, but a genuine loss of memory. I am convinced that the girl does not know who her family are, and that she has not deliberately deceived anyone about her birth. She is an intelligent child with a quick mind. She has also learned a few of her guardian's haughty airs, and this makes for a self-possession that is alarming in such a young person. If Ragoczy has decided to go to London, it is natural to assume that his ward will go with him. You say in your letter that they have already traveled to Italy and France. More traveling should not be all that strange for the girl. She has a lively curiosity and might enjoy the experience of living in another country for a time. If you wish to dissuade Ragoczy, I doubt it would be possible to enlist his ward in your cause. Also, as she is privately tutored by a Swiss and a Danish woman, it is not easy to approach her in any case.*

*The chauffeur, Nikolai Rozoh, I do not know well. He*

came into the household after I was part of it. From what
I could piece together, he was in the Army at the time of
the Revolution and was either a bodyguard or fulfilled
some other similar function for Ragoczy, which is why
when the Revolution became more disruptive, he was
forced to leave the country or face death for aiding one of
the "oppressors." Rozoh keeps very much to himself, tend-
ing to the automobiles and horses as well as doing many
of the odd tasks around the estate. He works very hard
and is said to be a pious man. I doubt very much he
would be willing to involve himself in politics again.

The servant Roger is something of an enigma, and very
loyal to his employer. He has been known to joke that he
has been with Ragoczy since the Flavians ruled Rome, by
which I gather that his family has long been servants to
the Ragoczys. He claims to be Spanish, but I see little of
Spain in his countenance. I doubt Roger would be any
use to you.

Enzo, the chef, may be another matter. He is expert at
his job, but I believe he is chronically in need of money.
That may not be the best footing for the work you require,
but there may be no other cause open to you. I would
suggest that he be approached away from Schloss Saint-
Germain, and handled with great tact.

It may be wisest to allow him to leave the country
without interference. From what I learned of him, he is
not working with anyone opposed to us. He is not a
politically motivated man. While I agree that his wealth
might be put to excellent use by the NSDAP and the SA,
it might be more trouble than anyone would like to get the
funds into our hands. I do not speak out of any thought
for the man himself, for foreigners are as much a problem to us as our inner enemies, but it might not serve our
purposes to have the people learn where our funds are
gained. I believe that Ragoczy would not hesitate for a
moment to tell the newspapers about any harassment he
might experience. If he departs for London, it is always
possible to confiscate his estate for our own uses, which
would benefit us all in the end.

As you have Herr Rauch's evaluation of Ragoczy's
dealings with his various neighbors, you will not need my
response, but I give it nonetheless. To say that he was
generally respected would appear to me to be the best way

*of stating it. Rauch is correct in his judgment that most of the hochgebornen in the Schliersee area are willing to receive him as a guest but not as an intimate friend. Apparently this suits all parties quite well, for I never saw any indication of rancor on anyone's part.*

*With Rauch, I agree that Ragoczy is not Jewish, although he has been known to have Jewish friends, such as the Schnaubels. I assume that his primary interest there was the children, who provided playmates for his ward. I was not encouraged to discuss the matter with him, and on those occasions when I attempted to sound him out, he turned the conversation to other subjects. It is known that the Ragoczy family has, in the past, made use of Jewish traders to move messages and funds for them, and for that reason he may not be wholly aware of the danger in which all the world stands, but it would be better to provide him an example of these manipulations we recognize so readily rather than to try to convince him by argument alone.*

*In the years I worked in his household, I saw no evidence that Ragoczy was part of any group of persons plotting to overthrow the state. He did not attempt to hide any of his activities from me, not even his occasional visits to the resorts at Bad Wiessee, where he met women. None of the women were ever brought to Schloss Saint-Germain and there was never any indication that he had more than a man's passing need for female flesh. I was not aware of any prolonged intimate contact with a woman. He did occasionally receive letters from women, but I doubt there was a clandestine significance to them. He most emphatically did not behave as a rake does, but neither did he exhibit the usual behavior of a lover.*

*Let me reiterate my conviction that this man poses no threat to us, either here or abroad. He is something of an eccentric, but that is the way of foreigners. I have said that he is not active in political causes—let us not give him any reason to change his mind. A man of his wealth and business connections might bring unwelcome and undue attention to our party in a way that would lose us much of what we have gained. Placed as you are, you must certainly appreciate this danger more than I do.*

*It has been my great pleasure and honor to answer*

*your questions, Herr Göring, and believe that this letter*
*brings you my unending commitment to the ideals that*
*you exemplify so admirably.*

> With profound respect,
> David Bündnis
> Secretary to
> Max Erwin von Scheubner-Richter

# 9

Brienner Strasse and Schleissheim Strasse were filled with
traffic, and the circle where they came together with three
other streets was a maelstrom of automobiles, buses, trucks,
and horse-drawn vehicles. The only compensation for this irritating and so far mysterious delay was the magnificent spring
weather. Overhead the sky was stunningly blue, as if painted
by an optimistic artist. A solitary aeroplane was the one flaw
in that splendid vault, but it was not at all intrusive, for it was
to the east of the city, perhaps destined for Wien or Linz or
Salzburg. A great many Müncheners surged along the sidewalks, most of them moving at a brisker pace than the vehicles in the street.

"I don't want to come up to see Professor Riemen," Laisha
said to Ragoczy as Nikolai cursed a battered Delahaye, its
wooden body gouged and weathered, as it nosed in ahead of
the Isotta-Fraschini.

Ragoczy sat beside her in the backseat. "You don't have to,
of course."

"I don't like the way he looks at me. He's always trying to
touch me." She gave an uncomfortable hitch to her shoulders.

"What would you rather do?" Ragoczy knew the various
rumors that had been circulated over the years about Professor Riemen's liking for young females; he did not want to
alarm Laisha, but he was also relieved that she was willing to
occupy herself in other ways while Ragoczy concluded his
business with the old chemist.

"There are bookstalls, and a few shops. How long will you
be?" She reached for her purse, which lay beside her on the

seat. "I have a little money, so if I find something I want to buy . . ."

She was giving herself an excuse to dawdle and thus be assured that she would not have to see Professor Riemen at all; Ragoczy sensed it, and accepted it. "Would you like a little extra, in case you want to get something special?" He was already reaching for his billfold, pulling out two ten Reichsmarks.

"Thank you," Laisha said shyly as she took the bills. Of late she had recognized that her father's generosity was not what most young women experienced. It was not simply a question of money, but of time. She knew now that very few fathers set aside two hours every day to spend with their children. Ragoczy always spent time with her playing duets, reading, or simply talking.

"Spend it frivolously, if you like, but not foolishly." He patted her shoulder and leaned forward to talk to Nikolai in Russian. "Go by Professor Riemen's office first, and leave me there. Laisha is going to do a little shopping, and may need you."

Nikolai nodded, not taking his eyes from the traffic. "It will be faster once we pass the obstruction up ahead, whatever it is."

"Do as you think best, Nikolai. I have every faith in your good sense." He sat back again and looked rather abstractedly at the crowding. "You know, in Imperial Rome, only single-passenger chariots and sedan chairs were allowed in the city between dawn and sunset. Early in the morning, the farmers would arrive with produce and livestock, unload in the Swine Market, then drive their carts back outside the gates and hurry back to deal with sales. Then in the evening they would go back out of the city to get their carts and bring them in to load up again. The only exceptions were carts and wagons bringing animals to the Games. Cities may have to resort to such laws again, if this sort of thing continues."

They had come in sight of the reason for the traffic backup now. An old truck, painted brown and lavished with swastikas, had been turned on its side. A number of angry men in brown shirts stood around it, shouting at another group of men who wore no uniform other than matching smug smiles. Two policemen on BMW motorcycles kept off to one side, elaborately refusing to restore order between the two groups of men.

"A shameful business," Nikolai muttered, then repeated this loudly enough so that Ragoczy could hear.

"Yes, it is," Ragoczy agreed.

"Those Nazis, they're getting too high-handed." Nikolai honked once at a Citroën that was pressing too close to him.

"Those what?" Ragoczy had not heard this derogatory nickname but once before.

"You know, the NSDAP." He was almost past the overturned truck, and he made a quick, obscene gesture at one of the men in a brown shirt as he maneuvered the narrowest part of the bottleneck created by the truck.

"I didn't know they were called Nazis," Ragoczy said, a bit startled, for he generally made a point of learning such things.

"Well, they don't call themselves that, and those who do aren't the sort of company you keep, Count," Nikolai told him as he changed gears and picked up speed.

"I see," Ragoczy murmured, then fell silent while the last few blocks were covered.

As Nikolai drew the Isotta-Fraschini up to the curb, Ragoczy reached down for his large briefcase of fine-grained black leather. He reached the door handle and turned to Laisha. "I should not be much more than an hour. These are the last results on our tests, and I want to be sure Riemen understands them. Once we're in London, it will be more difficult for him to ask questions about the procedures done."

Laisha shrugged. "I'll keep busy. I haven't been book-buying in more than a month." She went on confidentially, "It's not that there aren't enough books at the Schloss already, but those are your books, not mine."

"I understand that," Ragoczy assured her as he started to step out of the automobile. On impulse he leaned across the seat and kissed her cheek. "Enjoy yourself, Laisha."

She grinned covertly and waved to him as he slammed the door. She very much liked these moments when she was on her own: she felt quite adult now, as she was driven through the streets in this elegant automobile with a chauffeur. If only Nikolai had a proper uniform instead of the woolen hunting jacket he wore in good weather. She decided not to let that minor consideration mar the day for her. "Nikolai, I want to browse through bookstalls. The old-fashioned kind, with horses drawing them."

"Very good, Miss Ragoczy." Nikolai had very recently taken to addressing her in this formal way and she had not yet made up her mind about it. On the one hand it was marvelous to be treated as a grown person by someone who knew her as a child, but on the other, she missed that camaraderie that had marked her relationship with Nikolai for so many years. And being called Miss Ragoczy, though she supposed that was the proper name now, was disconcerting. Her father never called her that—he would simply introduce her as "my daughter, Irina Vlassevna," and give no explanations. Yet she supposed that she would grow accustomed to it in England, where everything would be different anyway.

They were forced to pass the truck again, and this time there were more brown-shirted men striving to right the cumbersome vehicle. There was a short, portly man supervising the work with military precision. The smiling men were no longer in sight.

Less than ten minutes later Nikolai pulled into a parking place across the street from eight horse-drawn bookstalls. "There you are, Miss Ragoczy," he said as he turned off the motor. "I'll be waiting for you unless you need me to come and carry bags for you."

Laisha tossed her head. "I won't buy that much. But if I should need your help, I will call you." She did not wait for him to open the door for her, but got out of the automobile on her own and made her way carefully across the street. Her purse was tightly clasped in her right hand and her curve-heeled shoes with double straps made a sharp rap on the cobbles as she went. She felt so marvelously mature. If only she had worn a hat and gloves, no one, she told herself, would think her anything but a well-established young lady. Reaching the bookstalls, she regarded them with a practiced eye, noticing which had the widest selection of books to offer. The sixth and seventh stalls seemed the most promising, and she made her way toward them, going through the crowded street with less practiced skill than she would have liked. At the sixth stall, she found four men blocking her way, each with his nose in a book, so she went on to the seventh stall. Here she fared better, finding a variety of biographies, one or two of them quite extensive. She selected one on the life of Paracelsus because her father had mentioned him occasionally. That book was under her arm as an intended purchase and she was immersed in von Jofmannsthal's *Der Schwierige* when she heard the sounds in the street grow louder. Puzzled and irritated at the interruption, she looked up briefly and noticed that there were a great many people gathering at the far end of the block.

"Fräulein," the owner of the bookstall said to her a few minutes later, "it might be wise if you left now. I am going . . ."

Laisha reached for her purse. "I will buy these, then. Danke."

The owner made hasty change and offered it to her without courtesy. He said as he climbed onto the driving board of the wagon, "You'd best get off the street, young lady. It looks damned unpleasant down there."

"I'll be careful," she said, smiling her appreciation. She turned toward the end of the street where Nikolai was waiting and was astonished to see that the crowd had grown to alarming size. There were many men in brown shirts pushing their way along the sidewalks on both sides of the street. She looked for Nikolai and could not find him. For the first time that day she was frightened. Slowly at first, then with gathering speed, she began to move away from that brown-shirted wall, away from the place where Nikolai had parked the Isotta-Fraschini, back toward that part of the city where Ragoczy had been left.

Professor Riemen read through the last of the sheets Ragoczy had given him and shook his head. "You're quite right, the project is not feasible at this time, not with prices what they are. It is a relief to know that it is possible to manufacture fuel if it ever becomes necessary. The equipment for making this synthetic petroleum is another matter. That steel-reinforced ceramic shell is quite innovative . . ."

"Do you think so?" Ragoczy said with half a smile. It was his most recent modification on the athanor, the alchemical oven that had been in use in one form or another for over three thousand years. The huge egg-shaped ceramic form supported by a net of steel stood in the laboratory at Schloss Saint-Germain, reminding him every time he looked at it that one of the great achievements of alchemy was the Egg.

"I have never seen anything like it," Riemen declared emphatically. "It is this originality of thought that makes your contribution so very valuable." He looked down at the neat series of structural drawings that accompanied the report. "With these, I suppose it will be possible to construct the equipment. It would suit me better if you were here, but, well . . . It is enough, I suppose, that we have the plans."

"They are complete, Professor. You have my word on that." Ragoczy's tone was sharp.

"My dear man, I never thought anything else," Professor Riemen said at once with an unconvincing chuckle. "It's been the Great War, that's the problem. Everyone is suspicious. I have thought that most of the scientists in this poor beleaguered country of ours would abandon us for less demanding lands. It has not happened yet, though I understand that a few of the Jewish professors have discussed leaving. It would be a great pity, but one can understand why they wish to do it. Puft! A few radicals paint slogans on one or two buildings, and the academicians tremble. This nonsense will pass, Herr Graf. It must."

"I had neighbors who had more than a few radical slogans painted on their walls. A woman and her infant were killed, Isidore, and almost nothing has been done about it because they are Jews. I do not blame my neighbors for going to America." He got up from his chair and took a turn about the elegantly-worn room. There were three floor-to-ceiling bookcases separated by tall, narrow windows. The carpet was large and old, from Turkestan. Professor Riemen's desk was made of deep-grained mahogany and gave off a faintly pinkish shine where the sun struck it. What did Isidore Riemen have to fear in such a place as this, where he was protected and catered to?

"I have heard from Berlin that there will be interest in this process from Farben, as they have indicated all along. They will not find the cost encouraging, but their men may know a way to reduce the outlay." There was a congratulatory ring in his voice, and it was apparent now that he was relieved that Ragoczy would not be here to share his honor.

"You will do well with it, I know," Ragoczy said automatically, thinking that it was now time to conclude their discussion.

"I confess that I hope so," the Professor admitted. "We have come through difficult times, and I am not anxious to experience another such problem again."

Ragoczy made a short, polite comment as he looked out the window. In the street, two stories below, he saw four uniformed policemen go by on horseback.

"Our work is singularly complete, thanks to your thoroughness. I'm sure it will be received with enthusiasm even if it is not commercially promising." He, too, wanted to bring their hour to a close. "I won't deny that I will miss our association, Graf Ragoczy. If more men in our line of study took your degree of interest in the future, there would be little to worry about."

Ragoczy came back from the window and shook hands with Isidore Riemen. "It is kind of you to say so, Professor. It is a great compliment coming from someone of your experience."

His attention was distracted by the sound of an alarm bell. His brows rose. "What is it? Fire, perhaps?"

Professor Riemen shrugged hugely and sighed. "No, for that there is a siren now. I would imagine it is another riot. They're becoming monthly affairs. If it isn't the Right, then it's the Left. Sometimes they fight among themselves, sometimes they rush through the streets to no purpose. The police contain them in a small area, if they can, so that the damage is kept to a minimum. When everyone is exhausted, the leaders are arrested and the rest go home."

"Riots?" Ragoczy asked. "How . . . unpleasant."

"A nuisance, nothing more. A few cracked heads, broken windows, smeared paint. The police have learned the pattern and they know who most of the leaders are." He picked up the report one last time. "Don't be apprehensive about the riot. Most of the time they don't get out of hand. This is what you should concern yourself with, this fine research. Leave the hooting to the madmen."

Ragoczy hesitated. "It would be wise to be cautious, dealing with madmen."

"Ach, ja." Professor Riemen laughed, as if what Ragoczy had said was witty. "How amusing you are, Graf." When Ragoczy said nothing more, Riemen was once again serious. "I wish you would change your mind about remaining here long enough to present this paper for academic meetings. There is a major gathering in Frankfurt in September, and that would be the ideal time—"

"That won't be necessary, Professor. My work on the project is over and I find little interest in spending endless hours debating its use with others." He also was reluctant to bring so much attention on himself, for he had a number of associates in the academic world who might recognize him from fifty or sixty years ago, which would, he told himself with little expression, be awkward.

"I will make every effort to have it clearly understood that this is as much your work as mine. You deserve the credit for developing the equipment and designing the actual process." He said this last with less enthusiasm, already begrudging Ragoczy his share in the work.

There was a second alarm bell ringing now, and the two insistent sounds impinged on the cozy office and intellectual calm of the building.

"Do as you think best, Riemen." Ragoczy was plainly preoccupied now. He thought of Laisha on her book-buying expedition as the alarm bells grew more demanding.

"Is something the matter, Graf?" Professor Riemen inquired, his tone becoming gruff.

"The bells. They concern me. . . ."

"But why? The police will shortly have matters in hand." He leaned back in his chair with a complacent smile on his face.

"Doubtless," Ragoczy responded. "But I am concerned about my daugh . . . ward. She was planning to shop while we concluded our business."

"Laisha Vlassevna? A delightful girl. Delightful. You must be very proud of her." The Professor had a ruddy mouth and his tongue ran over it, making it redder still.

"I am," Ragoczy said automatically. The bells were now three, and he felt impelled to leave. "Thank you for the time, Professor Riemen, but I fear I must excuse myself. If there is to be a riot, I would just as soon be out of München before it gets under way. And I would prefer that my . . . ward not be exposed to it." He was already reaching for his empty briefcase and his light topcoat, both of which lay on the arm of an overstuffed chair.

"No doubt a sensible course, Herr Graf. If our political friends would only share your attitudes, and conduct their upheavals elsewhere, it might make matters easier for all of us." He got up and came around his desk in an unhurried way, his light-gray eyes glittering as if made of ice. "Have a good journey, Herr Graf. I hope you will find London to your liking. I have never admired the British, but it may be different for you: the British are not overly-fond of Teutons."

"They are somewhat insular," Ragoczy agreed.

"Another witticism. How funny." He made a snorting sound that was probably laughter.

Ragoczy knew that good manners called upon him now to say something very flattering of München and the whole of Deutschland, but with the alarm bells ringing, nothing came to mind. He twitched the corners of his mouth once in what might pass for a smile. "But I have been in London before, Herr Professor. I have a house there." It had been more than twenty years since his last visit, but he did not add this.

"Then you know what to expect. The food is bad, all of it. The beer is tolerable." These pronouncements were given as if they were absolute laws.

"I doubt that will bother me," Ragoczy said sardonically.

"So!" Professor Riemen glowered at him, feeling insulted.

"Let me wish you every success with the presentation of the papers and with selling the process. The terms of our sharing of profits, if any, are in the contract, are they not?" He said this quickly as he hurried toward the door. "Do keep me informed of your progress, Riemen. It has been . . . instructive, working with you." He wondered if he had imagined it, or if there was more noise filtering in from the streets. His bow was a swift ducking of his head as he slipped out the door, leaving Professor Riemen standing alone in his office, his face darkening as the enormity of Ragoczy's boorishness enveloped him in fury.

The elevator was in use, so Ragoczy ran down the two double flights of stairs to the entrance and the street. He glanced about once in the hope that he would see the silver-blue Isotta-Fraschini waiting for him, Laisha in the backseat reading. It was a vain wish, and he knew it before his eyes told him that Nikolai had not yet returned for him. He knew that his chauffeur was a realistic man and would not expose himself or Laisha to unnecessary hazard. If the riot were anywhere near them, Nikolai would find Laisha and remove her from danger. It was entirely likely that they were caught in the traffic snarls that were building up in the area as the police closed off streets in an effort to contain the riot. He pictured his automobile inching along with the others on Sendlinger Strasse or Sonnen Strasse, and tried to comfort himself with the thought. As he hastened down the street, four more policemen on motorcycles roared by. At the corner they turned left, toward the south. Ragoczy watched them, then began to follow them, moving as fast as he dared. As he threaded his way through the crowded streets, he attempted to convince himself that Laisha must be safe and that it was quixotic to go into a riot area. The police had doubtless got those who were bystanders out of the rioters' path if Nikolai had not. Oppression settled on him darkly and he increased his pace again. He was capable of much greater speed and had stamina no unchanged human could match, but for centuries he had schooled himself to reserve his swiftest run for the night and hidden places, where it would not be noticed; as it was, though he was still walking, he was moving faster than many men could run.

The sound of angry voices raised in one howling chorus that was punctuated by the breaking of glass marked the fringes of the riot area, where a dozen policemen had formed a human barrier against the milling mass of men behind them. A brute-faced Sergeant was shouting to the others to hold firm.

"Excuse me, Sergeant," Ragoczy said as he came to a halt at the line of policemen. "Sergeant?"

The man turned, and his little eyes took in the stranger who had addressed him: obviously foreign, obviously wealthy. "What is it, Mein Herr?"

"I have reason to believe that my automobile and my chauffeur and my daughter are in the area you're cordoning. May I pass, please?" He took his most commanding attitude without making himself appear threatening. The Sergeant was nearly a head taller than Ragoczy and had the look of a bully.

"I can't allow that, Mein Herr." From the expression he wore, he enjoyed the exercise of power.

"But you can, you know," Ragoczy said in his most reasonable tone while his impatience seethed through him. "I am able to fend for myself."

The stare the Sergeant gave him indicated that the man doubted it. "Sorry, Mein Herr. These are my orders: no one is to pass. Otherwise we'd have to let more of the rioters in, as well."

Ragoczy took a step back. "Very well. Thank you." He took a few steps back and dropped his coat and briefcase; then he sprinted away at half his possible speed, toward a restaurant down the street, the kitchen of which, he knew, opened onto an alley that gave access to the blocked streets.

"Herr Graf!" the headwaiter said as Ragoczy burst into the restaurant. "We have been ordered to close." He did not attempt to stop Ragoczy, however, for he knew this was the owner's patron and accorded special privileges.

The chef, an enormous man with a starched cap atop his bald head, looked about in astonishment as Ragoczy ran through the kitchen and out the back door. He had not thought that the Graf had any interest in politics, but there he was, and there was a riot half a street away. He reluctantly put his freshly-cut vegetables into a huge crockery bowl and covered them. If he could not serve them tonight, he decided, he would add them to the soup tomorrow.

At the opening of the alley, Ragoczy could see a large number of men in brown shirts with swastika armbands shoving and shouting. Several of them were smiling in their excitement, and there were at least two with rifles. As Ragoczy watched, a group of five men approached the mob. They were also dressed in the SA uniform, but these were obviously men of some importance. When the oldest of these men—a lean, tall fellow of about fifty—began to speak, those around him grew quiet and gave him their attention.

"It is senseless to oppose the police," this man said in a penetrating tone that was doubtless learned on the battlefield. He was silent while the others roared out their disappointment. "There are cattle enough within the cordon. The Spartacists have their meeting place two blocks away, you will recall. It is time they learned who speaks for the Vaterland. Not they!" he bellowed to be heard over the sudden wave of noise that burst from his followers. "They are wed to Russia, to those causes and destructive doctrines that have once already threatened to ruin this city!"

This time there was no quieting them. The officers stood aside as the men swept back from the police barrier toward the narrow streets where others waited.

Ragoczy saw the five officers draw apart for a murmured conversation, and while they were so occupied, he raced out of the alley and away toward the street where the booksellers brought their stalls. He went rapidly now, not running yet, but at a pace that could easily outdistance most athletes. His speed was deceptive, for he moved with singular ease and grace, fluid as a shadow. Once he almost caught up with the body of brown-shirted men, some of whom had paused to smash the windows of a grocery and to throw the produce into the street. He had to get ahead of the men, he knew that, but so far he had been given no opportunity. Finally he ducked into a narrow side street which lead to the Steuerplaz where the bookstalls were often drawn up. There was a small church near the end of the street, an ancient building with high, oval windows of colored glass. As he rounded the end of the church, he could see that he was ahead of the mob at last.

Large numbers of men were milling here, and there were occasional tussles between the brown-shirted group and others not in the same color. One bookseller was trapped, his heavily-laden wagon unwieldy and his old horse sidling nervously as more and more men pressed around him.

Ragoczy made his way through the crowd to this unfortunate. He reached the side of the bookstall and started to climb.

"Nein!" the driver shouted, and while his horse made an attempt to bolt, the driver lashed out at Ragoczy with his whip.

"Stop! I won't hurt you!" Ragoczy shouted as he caught the whip and pulled it from the driver's hands.

The driver belatedly realized that his horse was plunging and snorting, his flanks dark with sweat. He strove to gain control of the animal, and as he did, Ragoczy moved closer to him.

"Where were you selling today, my friend?" he shouted in the driver's ear in order to be heard.

At first the driver did not respond: he was busy with his horse, and terror had stopped his throat.

"I need your help!" Ragoczy shouted at him. By now the crowd around the bookstall was so dense that the horse was unable to move and the high-balanced wagon was beginning to rock as the little square filled with struggling men.

"What?" The driver was white-faced and shaken, unable to move and unutterably frightened by his own inactivity.

"My daughter is here somewhere!" Ragoczy yelled at the driver, and cursed as the man shrank back from him. "Where were your stalls today?" he demanded, the full force of his dark eyes commanding attention.

The driver pointed off to the right and he wagged his hand helplessly. "There. A block up, maybe two." He turned, shocked, as he saw his horse fall, the harness shafts splintering as he went down.

Ragoczy did not stay to see the rest of the old driver's plight: at the far end of the plaz he could see the brownshirts from the barricade coming. They were in orderly form now, marching in neat ranks, shouting as they marched that Spartacists were Jewish swine and traitors to Deutschland.

Many of those in the plaz took up the shouting, while others threw themselves on those who offered such insults. On the far side of the square the first of the battles were joined. As the first blows fell, a small number of the brownshirts broke away and started down the adjoining streets. Not long after, another group did the same.

Trapped in the middle of the roiling conflict, Ragoczy thrust his way through the closely-pressed men to the far sidewalk, where the fragments of broken glass made the footing less certain. There were fewer men here, although it was still crowded, and Ragoczy could make better progress. He went toward the street the driver had indicated, shrugging off those who tried to stop him. When he was almost to the street, he saw a silver-blue Isotta-Fraschini on its side, tires cut, front window shattered. A crumpled figure was still in the driver's seat, one arm draped over the steering wheel as if protecting it. Ragoczy rushed up to it, and knelt down beside the automobile.

Blood matted Nikolai's grizzled hair, and there was a long gash down his cheek that oozed blood. His color was pasty and his breath labored.

With gentle hands Ragoczy made a superficial assessment of the injuries. There were broken ribs and one of his hands had been crushed by the studded heel of a boot. When men pressed close to him, he shoved them away with formidable strength. At last he moved Nikolai enough so that the body of the automobile would protect him. Then he spoke sharply. "Nikolai! Where is Laisha!"

There was no response at first. Ragoczy was not certain that Nikolai could hear, and if he could, if the noise in the plaz, which increased constantly, blocked out his own demands. He leaned down so that his head was less than a handbreadth from Nikolai's. "Rozoh!" he ordered with all the authority in his voice. "Rozoh! Where is Laisha Vlassevna!"

It seemed useless; then Nikolai's eyelids fluttered and a few words in Russian came from his bruised mouth. "Not here. Looked for her. Drove . . ."

"Drove where?" Ragoczy shouted, dread coming over him with cold talons.

"Next street. Next street." His eyes rolled up and he once again lost consciousness.

Ragoczy rose, looking about in desperation. What next street? There were four streets that came together here. He spun around as he heard a shot, and saw that a number of the brownshirts were armed. Nothing would protect Nikolai, or himself, or Laisha, from bullets. Reaching down into the back of the automobile, he tugged once, stepping back as he did. The Isotta-Fraschini groaned and crumbled as he pulled it over onto its back. The automobile was now completely ruined, but Nikolai lay safe in the pocket between the seats and the paving. It was all he could do now.

As he pushed his way through the plaz, Ragoczy reminded himself over and over again that Laisha was a sensible young woman who would recognize danger for what it was, and not seek adventure for the excitement of it. There were houses and restaurants and shops along the street. Surely she would take refuge in one of them and stay there until the fighting was over. He quickened his pace as he started down the first street, his eyes scanning the crowd, the shuttered windows, the ruined shopfronts, in the hope of seeing Laisha. Ahead the road dipped and veered to the left, opening into a sort of court before diving back between the narrow walls of the old buildings. He paused at the highest point of the road and looked down. The court was half in shadow, but he made out a flash of dark-blonde hair and a bit of pumpkin-colored fabric. There were brownshirts all around her, one of them reaching for her arm even as Ragoczy caught sight of them.

Laisha stared in shock at the hand closed around her wrist, unable to believe that such a person would so much as approach her. "Release me!" she ordered, too offended to be frightened.

The man and his companions laughed, and one of them recognized her accent. "A Russian. Probably one of the Spartacists," he suggested, touching her shoulder with ungentle hands.

Heedless of the attention he might gain, Ragoczy ran now, down through the narrow street to the court where Laisha struggled. Those foolish enough to be in his way were thrust aside. But in those seconds he ran toward her, shouting out her name, he saw one of the brownshirts lift a rifle, and holding it by the barrel, swing the butt full force into the side of her face, splintering bone, sending blood and other matter spraying over the hands that held her.

"*No!*" he screamed as he saw Laisha start to fall. He did not say it in German or Russian, but in a tongue that had not been spoken for more than thirty-five hundred years.

The men around Laisha exchanged looks and were still not yet aware that she was crumpling, was dead. Then one of them saw Ragoczy racing toward them and said a few terse words to his companions. They faded into the crowd, each going in a different direction.

Ragoczy hardly saw them. Every atom of his being was concentrated on the blood-spattered pumpkin-colored dress. As he ran, the men on the street gave way to him now, and a few of them hurried away. The sounds, the figures around him, were nothing to him, less substantial than shadows or ghosts. He stopped beside her and fell to his knees.

Blood was still pumping from her broken face, and bits of bone stuck to her skin. Three teeth were caught in the tangled mat of her hair, a bit of her jaw attached to them. Her nose was ripped so that the nostril was only a tattered bit of flesh. Her eye was crushed in its socket.

Gently, so gently, Ragoczy took her up in his arms, cradling her shattered head against his chest, grief burning through him like vitriol. He repeated her name softly over and over, rocking her as he did when she was a child. "My daughter, my daughter, my daughter," he murmured to her, unmindful of the blood and fragments of brain that befouled his fine clothing. Now there would be no social debut. She would never be courted, or married. He would never have the rare delight of holding her child in his arms as he had held her. The elegant woman that was promised by her lankiness would never emerge. These things flitted through his mind, and none of them made any sense to him. He felt her blood seep through his jacket, his vest, and his shirt, hot against his skin. He would never laugh with her again, never play duets with her, or correct her accent in French. Gaetano Cabrini would wait in vain for her return to Verona. She would not pester him with her endless, treasured questions. He knew death, had tasted that bitter cup once, but he denied it now while all his senses recognized it.

The police found him, still on his knees, Laisha in his embrace like a broken doll, some forty minutes later.

"The foreigner," one of the men said, looking about for the Sergeant.

Another of the men bent down to speak to him, but when he tried to touch Ragoczy's shoulder, his hand was shrugged off.

"There's a coroner's wagon coming, sir," the first one informed him.

"Get back," Ragoczy said, so quietly and fiercely that the policemen stood away from him.

There was an awkward pause; then the youngest of the policemen said, "She's dead, Mein Herr."

Ragoczy's dark eyes burned down on him. "And what is that to you?" He knew that had he been capable of weeping, he would drown in his tears. No loss he had suffered, not the sun-ravaged Hesentaton, not the brave, pitiful T'en Chih-Yü, not Jenfra eaten up with plague, not his three killed in the Circus Maximus, had torn at his heart as the death of Laisha did now. Holding her, feeling her so still, was racking torment to his soul, and yet he could not bear to put her down.

In the silence, Ragoczy got to his feet, and with Laisha close, secure against him, he walked from the court toward the wreckage of his automobile.

A letter from Helmut Rauch to Maximillan Altbrunnen.

*Rahm Hotel*
*Wotanstrasse, Nymphenburg*
*May 31, 1926*

*Wolkighügel*
*Hausham*

*My dear Maximillian:*

*This is a most distressing letter for me to write to you, for you know the esteem and respect we have held in the past requires that I address you with honor, although I believe that your actions do not warrant it.*

*In the time you have been with the Thule Gesellschaft, you have repeatedly expressed your willingness to enter into the Initiates of the Bruderschaft, declaring that you are one with us in heart and spirit, devoting to us your every thought. This is required of those entering the Bruderschaft, for there the true work of Thule is done. There should be no deception, no lies among members of the Bruderschaft. You have known this for a considerable time, and yet you have, as I discovered recently, been misrepresenting yourself to us in a most shameful way.*

*I have recently talked to your widowed sister, who has told me that the fortune you have insisted is at your disposal, does not, in fact, exist. I have been at pains to investigate this claim of hers, for you have been so ada-mant in the past concerning the availability of funds that I believed it was her opposition to us that spoke, and not her penury. In my years with BKK, I established a great many useful associations, and I made use of them recently. Had there been any monies of the sort you have mentioned, I assure you I would have discovered them. In all my inquiries, I have found nothing to support your claim that you have considerable wealth, and a great deal to give credibility to your sister's insistence that there are not*

*enough funds left to keep your family estate functioning
beyond the most minimal level.*

For this reason, I have been forced to recommend that
your name be dropped from consideration for Initiation,
and that certain punitive measures be set for you. Your
squandering of your sister's little funds is most improper,
and that you made us party to this is even more unacceptable. You speak of Deutschland being an example to
the world, and I have always agreed with you. Is it
proper that such an example be of a young man who
drives his widowed sister into the poorhouse? You are
hochgeborn, and for that reason, there are privileges that
go with such birth, but you will not find such things here.
At the meetings of the Bruderschaft, there is no question
of birth, for the Initiation is a birth in itself, and such
distinctions are no longer applicable to those who wish to
number among us. You will submit to whatever chas-
tisement is given you. In this way alone can you reestab-
lish yourself with the Bruderschaft. In time, should you
prove to be truly reformed and penitent, then your application for Initiation may be reconsidered. This is by no
means a sure thing, I must warn you. You may also elect
to leave our numbers, but if this is done, you will at no
time be allowed to deal with any of us, in any way again.
You will have to resign from the NSDAP and attend no
more meetings of this or any other Pan-Teutonic group,
for it is our intention to notify all such lodges of your
conduct and inform them, in detail, of the action we have
taken and the reasons for it.

I will call upon you in person to inform you of the
action to be taken against you, and to offer my apology to
your sister. The Bruderschaft will require a week to consider what is best to be done. At the end of that time, hold
yourself in readiness to receive me. If you should attempt
to avoid this meeting, we will be forced to be more mili-
tant in our treatment of you. Discipline is the mark of an
Initiate of the Thule Bruderschaft and it is my intention
to instill that sense of discipline in you by whatever
means necessary. There is no place in Deutschland that
we cannot reach you, and very few foreign locations where
our arm cannot stretch. It is best if you acquiese in our
demands at once, and show yourself amenable to our
strictures. Otherwise, I will not be responsible for what
will become of you.

*It is my most sincere hope that you will accept your penalties with humility and devotion. There is no other means for you to redeem yourself in our eyes. It would restore our faith in you if you will comply in every particular with our demands and show yourself to be ashamed of what you have done. Should this not be the case, then be certain that the wrath of the Bruderschaft will follow you, not only in the flesh but the spirit as well, and there will not be one day, one hour, when you will be free of our vengeance.*

*For the Thule Gesellschaft and Bruderschaft, I cannot sign myself your friend.*

*Helmut Rauch*

# 10

Although her boudoir clock had chimed two, Gudrun was still awake. She sat propped up by pillows, her bedside lamp casting its soft light over the page of the novel she had chosen quite at random nearly five hours ago. So far, she had read roughly fifty pages, for her mind often wandered back to the graveside ceremony that afternoon when Laisha Vlassevna was buried. Until that service, she had not seen Ragoczy since his daughter's death three days before. She had been appalled by the pain she had seen in his face, and had spoken the first words that came into her head: "I wish I could console you." He had nodded in a remote way, and turned to listen to the other empty phrases that were offered him by those dozen or so people who had attended the funeral.

Would he come? She alternately hoped that he would and that he would not. Her heart ached for him, but the helplessness she felt in the face of Laisha's death reminded her again of the long years Jürgen had taken to die, and the memory twisted within her afresh.

On impulse, she rose from her bed, and pulling on a lace-trimmed bed jacket, made her way into the dark hall, and from there to the broad staircase to the lower floor. The carpets were soft under her bare feet, even those that were worn—as she knew most of them were—or of such age that they no longer kept their shape or color. At the foot of the stairs she turned toward the kitchen, feeling her way along the wall. She chided herself for this precaution: she had lived at Wolkighügel for almost half of her life and she should have known these passages as she knew her face. Tonight, however, she felt a stranger here, and nothing she touched seemed familiar.

In the kitchen she turned on the light, grateful for the new electric lines that had been strung early in spring. Why, she asked herself, had she not turned on the lights in the hallway, and could think of no satisfactory answer. She was not actually hungry, but she thought that a bit of food might make her sleepy; she felt giddy with fatigue, but not the least inclined to sleep. There were some berry-filled pastries in the cooler, and after a brief debate with herself, Gudrun took one and bit into it. Sweetness flooded her mouth and she nearly gagged. Very slowly she finished it, finding each bite more cloying than the last. When she was through, she poured a generous glass of wine and drank it much too quickly. Then she went out into the hall again, leaving the kitchen light on and the door half-open.

She was almost to the stairs when she heard a low voice speak out of the darkness. "Gudrun!"

She might have screamed had she not been so scared. As it was, a little yelp escaped her and she pressed back against the wall. Yet she had recognized the voice, and after a few seconds she brought her hand up to the closing of her robe and whispered, "Saint-Germain, you . . . startled me."

"So I perceive." He came toward her through the darkness, his eyes not needing the light.

Between the wine and the aftermath of her fright, Gudrun was strangely pliant as Ragoczy drew her toward him. She let her raised arm drop and brushed a stray crumb off the lace as she felt his hands on her shoulders. "Ah-h-h," she breathed as he gathered her close to him. In the year since he had become her lover, she had never felt his ardor so burning as she did then. This was not the pleasant, languorous prelude to a night of satisfying dalliance, but something much stronger, born more from his grief than from his desire for her. His hands were laced together behind her neck now, and he opened her mouth with the pressure of his lips. Her temples pulsed as her need for him grew sharp in her.

"Gudrun," he murmured against her ear, tracing kisses over her cheek, the arch of her brow. He had not expected to find such passion in her, and he stepped back from her, holding her shoulders once again.

She swayed once toward him, as though caught by the tug of a magnet. Her pale skin was delicately flushed, her blue eyes were huge, and she sighed her protest. "Saint-Germain."

Ragoczy shook his head slowly. "If you would prefer I left, I will not blame you. I am . . . not myself tonight." He had, as their lips touched, quenched the scorifying pain within him. The kiss was ephemeral, the mourning omnipresent.

"No. No." She brought her hand to her mouth, as if to seal the touch of his lips there. "Don't go."

"I don't want . . ." His words trailed off. To disgust her? To hurt her? To use her? He was quietly appalled at the force of his craving for her, which bordered on insensibility. "Perhaps I should leave."

"Stay!" she whispered with urgency. He could not do this to her, call her unacknowledged yearning from where it was hidden in her soul, and then abandon her, dizzy with anticipation and unfulfilled.

His breathing was unsteady. "I may not . . . be gentle."

"Then do not be," she responded more boldly than she had before. "Do what gives you solace. You won't neglect me." His doubt made her more certain. "When Jürgen died, I spent many nights plagued by desire, and nothing could release me; it was not my body alone that hungered, but my heart, my whole being." She took one of his hands in hers, her fingers wrapped tightly around his.

"Oh, God," he whispered, wrung by his esurience. He lusted for forgetfulness, if only for an hour, for the anodyne twining of flesh with flesh. He did not withdraw his hand.

"Come. To my bed." She led him down the hall, this time walking with complete confidence, unfaltering. They went up the stairs quickly, silently, and she let herself smile now, pleased with her strange serenity.

At the door to her room, she turned to him and leaned against him. How much she liked his strength, she thought. Then she was through the door, drawing him after her.

In the dim light of her bedside lamp, she saw that he was in his black riding clothes, a roll-top pullover taking the place of a proper shirt. Tonight his features were uncommonly pale and there were hollows in his face that were not usually apparent. His dark eyes were hot as burning coals. She did not know what to say to him, now that she realized the depths of his anguish, so, wisely, she said nothing. Slowly she let her bed jacket fall to the floor, her eyes never leaving his face.

He came to her then, sliding her nightgown from her shoulders, letting it join the bed jacket crumpled by the fringe of the spread where it brushed the baseboard leg. Ragoczy's hacking jacket was also discarded as he reached for her.

The times when he had come to her before, Gudrun had always felt that much of him was held back from her, not out of any lack of affection, but as a result of habit. Now she sought him with her hands, her eyes, with the softness of her lips, the accommodating curve of her body against his. His desolation stirred her more than his fondness had done, and she sought his love with all her will.

Ragoczy gave her numberless kisses, on her face, her breast, the curve of her hips, her inner thighs. He touched her, felt her tremble, tighten, and give a sobbing laugh as her spasm shook her. He was glad for her, pleased that she could find such pleasure in so bleak a world.

"Let me see you," she whispered when the delicious pulsations had subsided.

"No." He liked the feeling of her skin under his hands, and the sight of her, pale and slender on the soft blue spread.

"But why not?" As long as she did not see him naked, she believed that he was remote from her, that there was a part of him she would never touch.

"I am badly scarred, Gudrun. Most people find the sight distressing. Surely this is enough . . ." His lips grazed the curve of her breast, teasing the nipple, closing around it with a gentle pressure that radiated through her with prickling desire.

Her head rolled back as she took a long, shuddering breath. Her questions scattered from her thoughts as she succumbed to the resurgence of her passion. Now she was unwilling to think, for it detracted from the warmth that washed through her, setting all her skin afire, sensitive to the least brush or lightest caress. She was weak with the fervor he offered her. Never had she been so roused, so deeply responsive to the least nuance of lovemaking. She trembled like the strings of a violin, and like a violin, her excitation instilled its shivering thrill in him. Her face and neck were flushed, deepening to a rosy shade as he brought her again to that ecstatic pitch of complete gratification, requiring nothing of her but that she find the furthest reaches of her desires.

It took longer for her to come to herself this time, and when she did, the glorious lassitude that engulfed her did not encourage her to question him again. She traced the deep grooves in his face with her finger, smiling faintly. "You've done nothing for yourself."

"Not yet," he allowed, not wishing to tell her that he did not yet trust himself to take what he required of her. His despair was too close to him, and should he indulge himself while the emptiness haunted him, he feared he would search for oblivion with Gudrun, taking more from her than she was able to give.

"Don't worry," she whispered, aware of his hesitancy, if not the reason for it. "I don't want to keep you from . . ."

He kissed her lightly, chastely. "In a little while, my own. Not yet."

Although it was June, the mountain air was brisk at night, and Gudrun began to feel chill. She slipped free of Ragoczy's encircling arm and tugged back the covers.

"I will warm you, Gudrun," he said to her, pulling the blanket free and wrapping it around her as he used it to hold her close to him. He kept his arm around her but stared past her toward the windows and the night beyond.

"Saint-Germain?" she said when he had been silent for more than ten minutes.

Immediately he gave her his attention. "Forgive me. My mind was wandering." He began to stroke her with long, light touches that were sensuous but without the force of his earlier precipitancy. He took strange comfort from the texture of her skin, from the motion her breath gave her body, from the shiver that traced the same path that his hands did.

"Oh, ja, dort," she moaned softly as Ragoczy began a featherlight caress of the petal-soft rosy folds between her legs. Even as she felt her apolaustic sensitivity renew itself, she also admitted a private disappointment, a melancholy so faint that she scarcely knew it for what it was: Ragoczy would not share his heartbroken sorrow with her. She could alleviate his loneliness for a little time, but the greater suffering he would carry within him, alone. This faded from her mind as she soared with increasing rapture. Never had she been awed by tenderness, but now, with those small, beautiful hands working their enchantments on her and his lips awakening and soothing, evoking her most tempestuous exaltation, Gudrun shed the quiet dejection that had colored her life for so long. Now she rejoiced, her body, her soul a glorious paean. So wholly possessed was she by the ineffable splendor of her gratification that she was hardly aware of Ragoczy's mouth on the curve of her neck. In the next instant the culmination of his desire joined with hers and together they blazed in the night, radiant as a comet.

Gudrun did not know if she had slept or if her passion had so consumed her that she had been magnificently mute and blind. She blinked, her eyes opening rapidly, then more leisurely. Ragoczy lay beside her, one arm around her, his dark eyes open and sad. "Saint-Germain," she said to him, and he looked toward her.

"Gudrun," he murmured, with such abiding kindness that she burst into tears. He turned on his side and embraced her while she wept.

"I . . . I don't . . . know why I did that," she said when she had brought her overwrought emotions under some control.

"Never mind, my dear," he said to her, one hand ruffling her tousled hair.

"I haven't done that . . . before." Suddenly she blushed, as if the other nights passed in each other's arms were somehow inappropriate to mention.

"No, you haven't," he whispered, wishing there were a way he could tell her what her passion had given him. His grief was undiminished, but now it was bearable, and for a time he would not give way to despair.

"Do you mind?" She had found an edge of the sheet and was wiping her eyes with it, for, absurdly, she could not speak without crying.

"No. I don't mind." He continued to stroke her hair, and after a while he felt her breathing become more regular as she faded into sleep. For the better part of an hour he stayed beside her. Once or twice he kissed her, though he said nothing. When the first faint tremblings of the approaching dawn came to him in the rustle of the leaves, the flutter of birds, and the subtle, distant restlessness of animals, he moved away from her, rising with care so that she would not be disturbed. Gently he drew her bedding over her, then bent to get his jacket. He stood looking down at her, grateful now that she showed her years, her maturity, for he doubted he could have touched her if she had seemed too youthful.

He went swiftly and silently through the Schloss, letting himself out by the door in the pantry, then passed through the empty stableyard. The path to Schloss Saint-Germain went off through the woods, and he kept a rapid pace over most of it. He was mildly surprised to see a light in the gamekeeper's cottage where Maximillian lived, but he did not pause to investigate.

The sky was starting to face toward morning when he reached his Schloss. He stood at the side gate looking up at the stone front. Once the place had been more of a fort than a home, but that was in the Fourteenth Century. Now, with additions and improvements over the centuries, it was something of a showpiece, and as he regarded it, he despised it. He went in the heavy wooden door as if entering a prison. Just six weeks, he thought as he crossed the courtyard, whose paving stones were laid over a generous portion of his native earth. Six weeks from now, they would have been in London. It had been all arranged; he had been at pains to make sure there were no difficulties, either here in Bayern or in Britain. Six more weeks, so that she could finish her studies with Professor Vögel and so that he could accommodate all the new paperwork that was required of him. Six weeks, and they would have been gone from this wretched country, from brown-shirted men who killed young women in the streets. There was a thickness in his chest, and his throat tightened convulsively. Six weeks, only six weeks! The sound he made was terrifying and pitiable to hear, anguish without the solace of tears. He stood before the entrance to his quarters and could not bring himself to move. The Schloss was too full of her. The library rang with her questions, the music room echoed with her song. He would listen for her step in the hall, wait for her impulsive laughter. He leaned his back on the door, forcing himself to be silent. He would not go into the Schloss. There were Nikolai's quarters in the stable, and with Nikolai still in the hospital, he could lie down there. Without his native earth beneath him, he would get little rest, but at the moment he preferred oblivion. He was almost out of the courtyard when the main door opened and Roger stepped out.

"My master," he said quietly, in Latin.

Ragoczy did not turn, but he halted. "Roger."

"Come in, my master." The middle-aged manservant said this easily enough.

"I . . ."

"You must, my master." There was a catch in his voice, the only indication of the sorrow he felt, both for Laisha and for Ragoczy.

"When it's light." He started to walk again, but Roger's voice followed him.

"And then you will say in the afternoon, and in the afternoon, you will say in the evening. Simeon Schnaubel went back to his house, to get it in order. So must you." He waited, holding the door open.

Ragoczy sighed, knowing that Roger was right. Eventually it would have to be borne. There had been so many other losses, how was it he could not accept this one? With laden steps he came toward the door.

"I have packed most of her things in trunks, my master. You will have to tell me which you wish to keep; the rest must be—"

"Disposed of," Ragoczy said harshly as he entered the Schloss. Luckily there were a number of crates standing in the main hall so that it was less like a place that was lived in. It already had the faint musty smell of empty buildings.

"Tell me what you wish done, and I will attend to it," Roger said quietly as he closed the door.

Ragoczy pressed his hands to his face, then said with more resolution, "There are schools for girls, aren't there, that need clothing? Send the clothes there. Choose a school in France or Italy. I want nothing of Laisha left in Deutschland. It has her bones already; it can have no more of her."

"As you wish." Roger strove to keep a neutral tone, but the effort was telling on him. He required a little time before he spoke again. "Her other things?"

"Do as you think best," Ragoczy capitulated. "I want to keep her viola. Her books . . . I will look at them later. Eventually, I suppose, I will come back here. Enzo will take care of it for me."

"He has asked if you would object to his bringing a wife here." Roger felt on more secure ground now.

"He may do whatever he wishes. There is more than enough in the caretaking fund to permit him to have half a dozen children about the place . . ." He stopped, his eyes closing against the torment of what he had said so carelessly.

"I will tell him," Roger said in a level voice.

"Thank you." He stared around the entry hall. "Six weeks."
Roger said nothing.

"For the rest . . . I will decide later." He looked at Roger, a knowing, ironic grimace on his lips. "I *will* decide. But not quite yet. I need . . . rest."

"Yes." Roger waited, watching Ragoczy start up the stairs to his bedchamber, which was over the library.

"Roger," he said over his shoulder, "don't wake me. I need . . . time."

Roger could not bring himself to make any answer.

"And I will want the names of the men who killed her, and where I can find them." This last was said coldly, with such complete and inexorable condemnation that Roger felt some of the sorrow he shared with Ragoczy answered by this request.

His bedchamber was actually two rooms. The first was more of a sitting room, with a long sofa upholstered in brocaded cloth and an elegant wardrobe opposite a good-sized closet. There were a number of paintings on the walls, one or two obviously the works of masters. Ordinarily the sight of these would provide a moment of pleasure for Ragoczy, but not this morning. He hardly saw the paintings, the little Tibetean statue, or the antique clock that clicked on the far wall.

The second room was smaller, and as austere as the first room was luxurious. Here there was a narrow, hard bed made atop a long chest. One utilitarian chest under the single, small window. Ragoczy pulled off his jacket and folded it, then got out of his trousers. When he was naked, he took a simple black robe from the chest and wrapped it around himself. The thin mattress did not alleviate the hardness of the earth-filled chest beneath it, but Ragoczy did not object: he had slept this way for nearly four thousand years. The force of his native earth was claiming him, and for once he surrendered himself to the stupor that in those of his blood passed for sleep. In less than a minute after he had stretched out and closed his eyes, the suspension had come over him. His breathing was slowed and almost imperceptible, his senses damped and remote.

When his eyes opened again, the room was dark. He lay still for several minutes as he recovered his full awareness. His memory of the last few days rushed back to him, bringing desolation with it. As he rose, he forced himself to a detached calm. He had things he must do. He went down the hall to the bath and spent the next half-hour in a curiously ritualistic washing. When that was done, he returned to his room and dressed in a black vested wool suit with a white silk shirt under it and a tie of dark red Italian silk. His shoes were thick-soled, to accommodate the lining of native earth. When he was satisfied with his appearance, he left his room and went down the long hall toward the part of the house that had been Laisha's.

At the door to her chamber, he faltered. Then his calm reexerted itself and he was able to enter, to look around without being filled with agony. That was not gone from him, he knew, and in time it would return with all its miserable strength, but for the time being, he was able to act, to decide.

Roger had been busy during the day, Ragoczy realized as he looked about. Most of Laisha's things were packed in carefully labeled boxes. Her bed had been stripped and the sheets and blankets were among those items ready to be sent to whatever place Ragoczy designated. He was tempted to open the boxes, to examine the contents, but that would accomplish nothing. He went from box to box, reading what Roger had written and marking each with his instructions. It took him well over two hours to accomplish the entire task, and for that time he did not allow himself to think. Here was a box of jerseys, let the girls' school have them. Here was a box of riding gear, send it to his housekeeper in Paris, who had a horse-mad niece. Here was a box of lace handkerchiefs and gloves, send them to Irina Ohchenov, who might to able to use them herself, and if she did not, would know of those who would want them.

When at last he left the room, his hands shook and his eyes were sore, but at least it was over. He repeated that to himself as he descended to the main floor and went along to his study.

Most of his possessions were packed away, some to be stored, some ready to be shipped to London. He looked around him as if the room belonged to someone else. He hardly recognized his desk, and the bookcases looked like toothless gums now that they were empty. He did not linger there, but went through the door into his laboratory. The athanor dominated the room, a huge white egg of steel-reinforced ceramic, just as he had described it in his report to Professor Riemen. It was cold, but the gauges that flanked it showed that it was capable of containing great pressure and heat. There was a large number of glass retorts, some of fantastic design. These were all cleaned and set on shelves. Since this room would be doubly-locked when Ragoczy left, he made a last careful check of it, noting the careful arrangement of equipment. He had hoped that he would make a more complete laboratory in London, but that no longer seemed real to him. As he left the room, he set the locks.

He found Roger in the library, putting the more valuable editions into a wall safe. "I don't want the vandals to find so much, next time," he remarked as Ragoczy watched him work.

"A wise precaution," he agreed, staring around the room.

"Do you want any of these shipped to England?" Roger asked, not liking the disturbing tranquility Ragoczy displayed.

"No, I don't think so." He walked the length of the room slowly, as if testing it.

"Should we leave the packing to Enzo?" Roger kept a covert eye on Ragoczy.

"If you wish." He paused in front of the hearth. "I don't think we'll go to London just at once. A bit later, perhaps."

It was no more than Roger had expected, but he still could not help asking, "Why? Your house is waiting for you."

"No. It was waiting for me and Laisha. In time that will not trouble me as it does now, and then I will go there." He turned toward Roger. "You don't approve, do you?"

"Not entirely," Roger answered carefully.

"Because you fear I will turn morbid? As I did after T'en Chih-Yü was killed?" The careful phrases and perfectly controlled tone said more about his pain than anything else.

"Yes." He put down the stack of books he had been holding.

"Then we must go somewhere vivacious. I thought perhaps Wien. Waltzes, old friend, and whipped cream with everything." He knew he could not force himself to laugh, but he made a jeeringly lighthearted gesture.

Roger straightened up and regarded Ragoczy with sadness. "I think it is a mistake."

Suddenly Ragoczy burst out angrily, "A mistake! Her death was, no doubt, a mistake! Had I left Riemen's room ten minutes earlier, had I been faster, I might well have found her in time. Fifteen years old, and they killed her as they might have killed a rat or a dog!" He was quiet as swiftly as he had been shouting.

"And Wien will not change that, my master."

"Very likely not," Ragoczy agreed urbanely.

"You have already completed arrangements for London." This was not truly an argument, and both of them knew it. Ragoczy had long since established homes and financial resources in every country in Europe and a fair portion of Asia.

"They will not go to ruin because I take my time getting there," Ragoczy observed, not permitting himself to bicker with Roger.

"One thing then, my master," Roger said.

"What is it?"

He busied himself with another pile of books while he phrased his request in his mind. "Do not insist on leaving at once."

Ragoczy's smile was singularly unpleasant. "No: I have a few matters to attend to first."

Again that icy breath touched Roger. "The names?"

"And where I may find them." He stared at the cold hearth. "It may take a few days."

"I am not a patient man." Ragoczy shook his head. "A hundred years ago, I would have been confident that a month could go by, or two, or a year, and still those I sought would be within my reach. But now, with trains and automobiles and aeroplanes constantly in motion, I am afraid that they will escape me."

"They will not," Roger promised him. "You may rely on that."

"I do, old friend." There was a slight softening in his expression, and with it came the shadow of grief. "I had such hope for her."

Roger could not look at Ragoczy at that moment—it was too private, that anguish—and when he looked up again, Ragoczy had left the room and Roger was again alone with the books.

Text of a letter from Maximillian Altbrunnen to his sister, Gudrun Ostneige.

*Wolkighügel*
*June 17, 1926*

*My dear sister;*

*I had not realized until this last month what I have imposed upon you and the intolerable burden I have been to you. It has been brought home to me that I have done you a grave injustice and that my actions have come near to compromising you as any that could be done short of selling you into bondage, which would be a shame so enduring that nothing could ever efface that from the records of our family. In compelling you to pay for my extravagances, I see now that I have done that which is without honor and lacking in the pride that is the mark of the Teutonic peoples. It is all well and good for the reprehensible Latins to impose on their relatives and be supported by the only wealth in the family, but among our race, self-sufficiency and family honor must come foremost. We are, after all, descended from those knights who rode to Russia, and when defeated by the barbarian Nevsky, accepted their excommunication with a grateful heart and with understanding. That is what it is to be Deutscher and hochgeborn. Were these times the same as those early days, I would bow my head to the demands of family honor and go into exile. Family honor requires no less of me now, and I acknowledge that with humility. I cannot exile myself, of course, but the honor of the family and the race demand a sacrifice of me, and I will make it gladly.*

*Let me advise you, my sister, although I have not been much in the way of doing so. Put your trust in Helmut Rauch. He has nothing but the greatest respect for you, and with his background and knowledge, he has the means* to guide you, as all women must be guided by a man. I did not see that much of what has been troubling you is the lack of a firm hand that a man would provide, keeping you from the natural waywardness of women. Your appalling dependence on the foreigner Ragoczy would not have occurred if I had known how much you needed my assistance in your work and my greater wisdom in your life. Doubtless you sensed this, but had no way to tell me of it. I see that your modesty held you back, and I, in my blindness, thought that you were merely nagging me because of my way of life: no, I did not comprehend your need to submit to a man's strong will.

There is little I can leave to you except my regrets. I have bequeathed what little is left of my inheritance to the Thule Bruderschaft. I know you will applaud this decision, for the work of the Thule Bruderschaft overshadows all else in importance. And you need not fear that the Bruderschaft will let you be cast adrift in the world. They will guard you and guide you, even as I should have done. They will keep you from harm and will warn you when there is danger. Their learning is superior and their cause is the most sacred—the preservation of the Teutonic race.

I have left a note for Otto, as well, and he will be charged with the duty of disposing of my body. I would prefer that you not deal with such things, for not only will you be completely overset by my death, it is not a woman's place to arrange such matters. Otto will do the job properly, and the Thule Bruderschaft will provide the funds for my interment. You are not to concern yourself with it at all. I know that Helmut Rauch will be present to give you comfort and the benefit of his strength. It would please me if you would be willing to marry him. Widowhood is not natural for you, and a man such as Helmut Rauch would care for you as a woman ought to be cared for, with firmness and affection. I have little right to require anything of you, so reprehensible has my conduct been, but if a brother's dying wish holds any power with you, my dear Gudrun, you will not reject Helmut Rauch if he should so distinguish you by asking your hand.

This is little enough to apologize for the abuse I have heaped upon you, but you must believe that it is sincere.

Your loving brother,
Maximillian

# PART IV

# Madelaine Roxanne Bertrande de Montalia

Text of a letter from Professor Isidore Riemen to Hermann Göring.

München
July 10, 1926

*My Dear Herr Göring:*

*I confess I was surprised to receive your letter of last week, and more baffled by your questions. I had not known there was so much interest in Graf Ragoczy, or I would have observed him much more closely in the years we have worked together.*

*Yes, I fully realize that the process he and I have developed could be of great value to our rival nations of Europe, and I am conscious that his lack of alliance does, in some degree, make him a dangerous person to have roaming Europe. However, as I have assured the Board of Directors at Farben, there is little either of us can do at this point. It is true that the process we have developed is successful, but the cost of it is prohibitive. I cannot imagine that a serious application of the methods will be used for some time, due to the expense involved. This has nothing to do with nationalities, Mein Herr, but with finance. Ragoczy himself is quite wealthy, and it was his personal funds that made much of our research possible. I doubt he will wish to invest such sums on a regular basis, since there is not any great chance of a return on them.*

*It was my understanding that Ragoczy would live in London, but since the lamentable accident that resulted in the death of his ward, I understand that he has not made any firm commitments on actual departure date. It would seem that he still intends to leave, however, since his Schloss is all but closed, his chauffeur has been released from the hospital and sent to Paris, and his cook has been given the caretaker title at Schloss Saint-Germain.*

*Your suggestion that the progress Graf Ragoczy and I made was the result of occult or alchemical studies is laughable were it not such an insult. Herr Ragoczy is a man of science, not the mumbo jumbo of the past. He has told me that he has read the works of the alchemists, but that is not the same thing as giving them credence. That his invention in some way resembles the laboratory (if this is not too scientific a word for it) equipment of the alchemists, then it is because he has seen that behind the absurdities of their methods there were a few useful inventions that it would be wise to pursue.*

*You may be surprised to know that it was Ragoczy himself who mentioned the coincidence of his estate's name with that of the charlatan Count de Saint-Germain who made such a fool of so many highly placed men in the Eighteenth Century. He remarked that there has been a consistent rumor that the man was part of the Ragoczy family, and doubtless it amused the previous Graf to name his estate in this way, particularly since there is apparently a rather tenuous tie to that name. He also remarked that one or two others have noticed the similarities and been curious. This man is no charlatan, let me assure you of that at once. He is a serious man of science who has the good fortune to be rich enough to afford to follow his fancy in his studies. It is a pity there are not more like him in the world. My work would be made significantly easier were I to have his continued patronage.*

*I hope you will forgive my candor, but I cannot agree that this man is likely to offer his services elsewhere, or to demand huge sums not to do so. I agree that there are those who might take such reprehensible steps, but this Ragoczy is not one of them. From what I have heard, he is more anxious to leave so that he might be free of the memory of his ward's untimely death. Such things can be a great shock to a man, and I gather that this was the case with him. For that reason, I doubt he will be much involved with his researches for a time. In half a year, I may well write to him and suggest that we continue with our project, which, by that time, may again take his interest.*

*Let me say that it reassures me to know that the NSDAP is interested in such realistic matters as the acquisition of adequate fuel supplies. Most political groups, if you will forgive me for saying so, have a tendency to describe all* the materials necessary for a better life for the country, but are silent on how their goals are to be accomplished. Your letter, with its cogent observations, reveals to me that my friends who have spoken highly of the NSDAP have not been misled by occasional promises of a glorious future with no link to our present times.

Of course you may show this letter to whomever you like. I am honored that you would think of such a thing. I agree that the scientific community is notoriously uninterested in the politics of the Vaterland, and doubtless their contributions would be much more valuable if they appreciated all that was at stake. If, as you suggested, my interest might in turn interest others, then by all means pursue the matter.

No, I have not met Herr Hitler, but I have read Mein Kampf and found it to be a most intriguing work. I would certainly appreciate it if you could arrange to introduce me to the man, for I have a number of questions I would like to ask him. There is such a proliferation of political parties that it is often quite bewildering, but it seems that the NSDAP is on the right track, striving for unity and purpose instead of division.

If there is anything more I might do that would assist you and the NSDAP, you have only to let me know of it.

> With most cordial respect,
> Professor Isidore Riemen

P.S. Should I learn where Ragoczy is at present, I will most certainly inform you of it, but I cannot believe that it is necessary to go to all this trouble over the man. To reiterate what I have already said, he has never shown himself to be an enemy of Deutschland, and I cannot attribute hidden significance to his disinclination to become active in our political activities. You must remember that he is not Deutscher himself, and with Transylvania, which was the principality of the Ragoczy family, given to Romania, and the Austro-Hungarian Empire a thing of the past, there is little to induce him to act. He oftentimes remarked that his country no longer existed. Another man might choose to adopt another country as his own, but as Ragoczy is of the nobility, he told me once that he was tied forever to his native earth. A touching comment, don't you think?

# 1

Irina Ohchenov stared at the man whose knock she had answered. He was unknown to her; a tall, grizzled figure with a fresh scar seaming the right side of his face. He leaned heavily on a cane, and although it was a sultry afternoon in Paris, he wore a proper coat over his obviously-new suit.

"Madame Ohchenov?" he repeated, continuing in Russian, "my employer, Count Ragoczy, gave me this address and told me to call here as soon as possible after I arrived in Paris."

"Ragoczy?" she said, but held the door open, and stepped aside for the man to enter.

"Yes. I have been his chauffeur." He waited for Irina to close the door, and then followed her into the sitting room.

"Have a seat, Mr. . . ." She motioned to a low sofa she had recently bought. It was not the first order of fashion, but it was well-made and comfortable, and she was certain that her visitor would prefer the comfort to appearance in any case.

"Rozoh, Nikolai Rozoh." He gave the hint of a bow before sitting down. He sighed as he eased his legs out in front of him, then gave her an apologetic look. "Your pardon, Madame Ohchenov. I haven't been out much, and I'm somewhat stiff."

"Yes, I can see that." She chose a high-backed chair and settled into it. "What happened, Mr. Rozoh? Or don't you care to discuss it?"

Nikolai sighed heavily. "It isn't pleasant. And that is not why the Count asked me to call on you." He hesitated, and then launched into a well-rehearsed speech. "I have brought some boxes with me to Paris. They contain girls' clothes. Most are in good condition and would doubtless be of use to some-one. Without doubt there are charity schools you know of, or the children of friends, who could use these garments. Count Ragoczy would like you to see that these are sensibly distri-buted, and he thanks you for helping him at this unhappy time. You have only to tell me where I am to bring the boxes and when you wish them, and I will have it done."

"Gracious," Irina said with an uneasy laugh. She began to fiddle with the tortoiseshell bracelet on her arm.

"He said you'd know best what to do with them." He was not quite able to look at her. As a young man he had ducked too many times when the lord rode by.

"But why? Is Laisha growing so fast that . . ." The change of expression on Nikolai's face alarmed her. "What is it?"

"You haven't been told?" he asked, appalled. "But I thought . . . He said a letter was sent . . ."

"I was away, in Orleans, for about a month. I haven't yet gone through my mail." She went cold all over. "What haven't I been told?"

"There was . . ." He stopped, blinking quickly. "It was the last day in May."

"*What* was the last day in May?" Her voice was not pleasant now, and her face was pale. "What are you talking about?"

The sound of her voice must have carried throughout the apartment, for someone called from another room, "Irina, is anything wrong?"

Nikolai gave his hostess a quick, accusing look. "I thought we were alone."

"My friend Phillippe is here," Irina explained, flushing, and furious with herself. "I was visiting his family in Orleans. When he has an afternoon or an evening free, he comes here." She was not entirely sure why she felt the necessity to tell this to her visitor. It might have been because he came from Ragoczy, and for that reason, was owed more than ordinary courtesy.

There were footsteps in the hall, and a tall man in his late forties strode in. There was something protective in his attitude, and his face showed a degree of concern that pleased Irina to see. "What's going on here?"

Irina gestured toward Nikolai. "This is Monsieur Rozoh," she said in French, ignoring Nikolai's grimace of worry. "He has brought a message from Comte Ragoczy. Monsieur Rozoh is his chauffeur."

"Then where is the Comte?" Phillippe asked, resting one hand on Irina's shoulder.

"I don't know." She turned to Nikolai and spoke again in Russian. "The Count is not with you, I gather?"

"No. I'm not sure where he is. I believe he is still in Bavaria, but . . ." He shrugged.

"Is he all right?" This question came quickly, and with a note of agitation that neither man missed.

"I don't know," he said, unconsciously echoing her words.

"What has happened to him?" She leaned forward, arms folded and resting on her knees. "What took place?"

Phillippe interrupted before Nikolai could speak. "What has he told you?"

"Not a great deal yet, my love. I have discovered that Comte Ragoczy is not here, but nothing else of significance." She looked up at Phillippe with an unspoken plea in her eyes.

"Would you rather I left you alone?" He could ask without feeling the doubts he had known when he had first become interested in Irina. She was a comfortable woman, he knew, one who would not resort to subterfuge or deception with him.

"For the moment," she said, grateful for his sympathy. "Otherwise I will have to spend the entire time translating for both of you, and it will take too much time as well as being awkward."

"Very well. But call me if you think I should be here." He touched her hair affectionately, nodded once to Nikolai, and left the room.

"Now," Irina said, returning to Russian, "please tell me what has happened. We won't be interrupted again."

Nikolai coughed once. "It will be difficult for me."

"Then do not force yourself to speak," Irina said at once, thinking back on all that she had witnessed and later could not bring herself to mention without renewed horror.

"But you must know," Nikolai objected gravely. "I wish you had read Roger's letter."

Irina started to rise. "If you like, I will find it, and then you may tell me whatever the Count asked you to say . . ."

"No, no. It would take too much time." He passed one hand across his forehead and gave a nervous hitch to his shoulders. "I'll tell you. I'll tell you." He leaned back against the heavy cushions at the back of the sofa. "Did I mention already that it was May 31? I think I did."

"Yes." She settled again, her face somber.

"We went into Munich. The Count had business to attend to, and Laisha wanted an outing. She liked being driven in the Isotta-Fraschini; she was very aristocratic in her tastes."

Irina noticed the use of the past tense in reference to Laisha. What had happened to the girl? Was that what was in Roger's letter? To cover her apprehension, she said, "So is Count Ragoczy."

"It's in his blood," Nikolai agreed. "There was a lot of traffic. Do you know Munich? The main streets are quite good, but most of them are too narrow for all the automobiles and trucks that use them. It becomes quite difficult to get around. There had been a truck overturned, one owned by the NSDAP, the National Socialist German Workers Party. They are a Right-wing political faction, very powerful in Bavaria and with some influence in Berlin. They often fight with the Spartacists and other Leftist groups. Someone had turned over one of their trucks at a traffic circle, and it took some time clearing it up. The police did nothing, and so the NSDAP men sent for more of their members, and put the truck back on its wheels again. It was all very efficient, once it was done. But by then the Nazis were in a bad mood, every one of them."

"Nazis?" Irina interrupted, recalling the word with surprise.

"It's a not-very flattering nickname for the NSDAP." He rubbed one large hand over his hair. "We'd gone past the truck when I was driving the Count to his appointment with Professor Riemen. There were a number of men standing around it. When we came back past the circle, there were more men, all striving to right the truck. The others who had been watching earlier were gone, for the Nazis were in a vicious frame of mind, spoiling for a fight with someone. I hadn't noticed that there were more of them in the streets, but there must have been . . . there must have been." He shook his head, seeing again that pleasant afternoon, the snarled traffic, wondering, as he had every day since then, how he could have failed to notice those groups of sinister brownshirted figures.

"Did you fight with them?" Irina was concerned, thinking that this man might have left Germany illegally. She wanted to urge him to come to the point, but held her tongue.

"No, not then. That came later. It was just an inconvenience, you understand, one of those minor delays that are forever happening. We had been told that the Count would be busy for about an hour, and as Laisha did not want to accompany him to his conference, she planned to go shopping, to buy some books, and then we were to return for the Count, and he had promised to take Laisha to a motion picture—I forget which one, though it may have been *The Thief of Baghdad*. She was very excited, but tried not to act as if she were. You know what girls are like at that age, don't you?"

The image of Ludmilla dressed for a party rose unbidden in Irina's mind, and she bit the insides of her cheeks to keep from crying. Ludmilla had been such a pretty child, and dressed in white with tucks and ruffles and lace, she had been festive as a wedding cake. "Yes," she said a moment later. "I do know."

Nikolai cleared his throat. He read Irina's expression and knew that he had trespassed on a painful memory. "I did not mean . . ." He shook his head. "There are times, Madame Ohchenov, that I am an ass. I was a soldier, and we were not taught manners, only fighting. If I offended you, I did not intend to."

"Yes, Mr. Rozoh. I'm aware of that." She had seen his sort before; solid, reasonable, dependable men who had followed Leonid and been cut to pieces by insurgents. Oh, dear, she thought, this will never do. I will spend the afternoon thinking of Russia, and I must put it behind me, for my Russia is gone. Her hands were shaking. "Please, go on. I must know what had happened."

"Of course," Nikolai said miserably. "Have you ever seen Munich?"

"No." She plucked at the little frill of lace on her cuff.

"It is like most cities: there is an inner, old city, and then there are rings around it, and extensions. The Frauenkirche is pretty much the heart of the old city. It dates from the Fifteenth Century, the Count told me. Many of the streets are narrow and mean and the buildings are packed tightly together. There have been plans to tear them all down and start afresh, but nothing has been done. It is near there that the book-sellers draw up their stalls. You have seen the sort in Petrograd, Madame, the wagons fitted with shelves so that the books may be displayed. Laisha liked these particularly, and so we went looking for them. We had done this before, several times. Of late, Laisha preferred to do her shopping on her own, rather than have me tag along. So I parked the automobile and read the newspaper. My German is not good, and I have made a point of reading the newspaper to improve it." He shifted his weight on the sofa. "Pardon, Madame. I . . . cannot remain still all the time or—"

"Do as you must, Mr. Rozoh. Would you like anything? I have both cognac and aspirin, and you are welcome to either or both." She rose, noticing the line of sweat on his upper lip. "Are you in pain?"

"A little," he admitted as the color drained from his face.

"Excuse me a moment, Mr. Rozoh," she said, and went down the hall toward the kitchen.

"Is everything all right?" Phillippe asked as Irina passed his door.

"I don't know. He has not yet told me everything. But he is hurt, poor man. I was going to get him a bit of cognac and an aspirin or two."

"Both are in the kitchen," Phillippe reminded her. He had come to the door, and now he reached out and touched her hair. "Do not let him distress you, or take advantage of your kindness."

"Of course not, but as he comes from Comte Ragoczy, I must hear him out, Phillippe."

"Yes," Phillippe agreed, but with the shadow of a frown between his brows. "A strange man, Comte Ragoczy."

"He is," she said as she went on into the kitchen, opening the cabinet over the sink as she listened to Phillippe.

"Is he a good man? A nice man?" Phillippe had followed her into the kitchen, and he busied himself with taking the cognac from the shelf and pouring a generous amount into a wineglass.

"Comte Ragoczy? A good man?" She had lifted down the aspirin bottle and paused in the act of taking a few of the white tablets from it. "I don't know that I would call him good, or nice. But, oh, Phillippe, he is so very, very *kind.*" She flushed at her own outburst, and covered her confusion by pouring three tablets onto her palm.

Phillippe had recorked the cognac and had a second or two to arrange his features into a smile. "Kindness is a rare quality," he said as he turned to Irina, holding out the glass to her. "It is much rarer than goodness and niceness, certainly."

Irina took the glass and her eyes met Phillippe's. "It is not just for Comte Ragoczy that I want to speak to this man. He is Russian, Phillippe."

"Yes, my love, I realized that," he said with some amusement. "There. Go tend to him and find out what it is that distresses him so much. Otherwise we will have no peace today."

She was still as he leaned forward and brushed her lips with his. "Thank you, Phillippe," she whispered, and neither of them thought it was for the kiss.

Nikolai had pushed one of the sofa cushions under his knees and was struggling to brace himself against the arm of it when Irina returned. He looked up sheepishly. "I hope you will not object, Madame Ohchenov. If I can ease the strain . . ."

"Do as you think wisest," she said at once, holding out the glass and the aspirin tablets.

"Spasibah," he said as he took the glass and drank. When the glass was half-empty, he took the aspirin. "I am grateful,

Madame Ohchenov," he went on when the cognac was gone. "I will be better now."

"I hope so, Mr. Rozoh," she said, sitting down in one of the chairs instead of on the ottoman.

"I've been thinking about it all again," he admitted. The glass dangled by its stem from his fingers. "I try to accept what happened, but I can't, any more than the Count can."

"But what *did* happen, Mr. Rozoh?" Irina demanded, her patience almost deserting her now that she had come back to her guest.

"A terrible thing, Madame." His voice darkened as he spoke. "I told you that we went down to the bookstalls in the old part of Munich, Laisha and I, didn't I? And that I parked the Isotta-Fraschini near the stalls?"

"And read the paper to improve your German," Irina supplied for him.

"Good. That part of the city is always crowded, with all sorts on the street. Every now and then, I would look up, just to be certain that all was well with Laisha. She was such a pretty girl, with her dark-blonde hair and deep brown eyes."

There was the past tense again. Irina's throat grew tight as she listened.

"She was in a pretty dress, too, a kind of pinky-gold color, with a silk scarf around her neck, the same color." His voice drifted off, and then, without prompting, he resumed his story. "I was not paying a great deal of attention. I couldn't, because she resented it when I did. I saw her go to the last but one of the bookstalls and look over a few of the volumes in that serious way of hers. I saw her take one of the books down and read a few pages. When I looked up again—it wasn't more than five minutes later, truly—there were a great many men in the street, Nazis in their brown shirts with the swastika armband. Then I heard the sound of breaking glass, where one of them had hurled something through a shop window. The others with him cheered him on, and a few of them kicked what was left of the glass out of the window. This gave the rest of them courage, and they began to smash windows all along the street. I looked to find Laisha and could not see her, and so I started the automobile and determined to drive down the street and take her up with me so that we could get away swiftly. Riots . . . you've seen them, Madame, and you know how quickly the violence spreads."

Irina nodded. "Yes, I have seen riots before."

"Then you share my fear of them." There was not the least

doubt in his statement. "And this was a riot beginning, a large one, with well-organized men. In that quarter of the city there were many of the Nazis and the Spartacists, who regularly got into brawls, and there were also businesses owned by Jews. The Nazis are against the Jews in all things, for they have said that the German loss of power and money is due entirely to Jews. They make a point of beating up Jews and wrecking their shops."

"Jews are not well-loved in Russia, either," Irina reminded him sadly.

"No, but it is not like this." He hesitated, swallowing hard. "I should not have started the automobile. I think that was my greatest tactical mistake. Had I gone on foot, there is a chance I might have reached her, or found her, at least. As it was, there I was in a poor street in an Isotta-Fraschini Tipo 8A; not the sort of transportation seen very often in that area. As the automobile started to move, a few of the brownshirts, the SA men, saw it, and one of their leaders shouted that it must be stopped. More than a dozen men ran at me. I should have driven through them, but I didn't. I didn't think they would . . ." He lifted his hands to show his helplessness, and the wineglass dropped to the floor, shattering. "Oh, God," he burst out. "I am sorry, Madame Ohchenov. I am a clumsy oaf!" He tried to get up, but Irina stopped him.

"I will tend to it later. Tell me the rest of it now." Her self-possession was a facade, but a successful one, and communicated itself to Nikolai.

"But the glass . . ." he protested.

"It will be there when you are done. Go on." She made herself lean back in her chair and wait for him to continue.

"All right. Yes." He wiped his hand over his sweating upper lip. "The men that followed me, they climbed all over the automobile, and one of them grabbed my arms while another covered my eyes with his hands. I had tried to keep my hands on the steering wheel, but I could not. They dragged me out of the driver's seat and . . . beat me. When I had fallen, one of them stood on my shoulders so that his comrades could kick my ribs. The others turned the automobile on its side and threw loose cobblestones at it. The windscreen was in pieces. I tried to get to it. I suppose I wanted to stop them. I may have thought I could still drive away. I was not thinking at all, Madame. Not at all." He looked up suddenly, and saw Phillippe in the doorway.

"Is there trouble?" Phillippe asked Irina.

She was startled to hear him: Nikolai had claimed her attention so completely that she had not heard him come into the room. "Ah, ah, no. That is, there *is* trouble, but nothing to concern you, my dearest. Monsieur Rozoh's story is . . . appalling. Please, let him continue."

"What happened to the glass?" Phillippe gave a pointed look to the broken bits.

"He dropped it," Irina explained with some asperity. "Phillippe, *please*. I would not ask this of you if it were not important."

He stood a little straighter. "Very well. Call me if you require my assistance," he said, and with a curt nod to Nikolai, he left the room.

"I do not mean to anger him," Nikolai said in a low voice.

"He is not really angry; he is worried. There have been men of the OGPU asking questions about Russians living in Paris, and he is afraid I will be one of those to enter the House of Special Destinations. He regards all Russians with suspicion because of this." She hated taking the time to clarify this, but feared that Nikolai would not tell her all that she must hear. "Finish your story, Mr. Rozoh."

But Nikolai stared at her. "The OGPU is in Paris? They are *allowed* to be here?"

Irina sighed. "Not openly, no, but they are here nonetheless, and as long as those they deal with are Russians, the French are in no hurry to interfere." She gestured in the direction of the door. "One of the reasons Phillippe is urging me to marry him is that there can be no attempt to remove me to Russia, for as the wife of a Frenchman, I would have protections that I lack now."

"Why do you hesitate?" Nikolai asked, then held up his hand. "I will ask you later. You wish to know the rest. And it is so difficult to tell you."

"Thank you," Irina murmured.

"I told you that I crawled toward the automobile, didn't I? And that it was lying on its side?" He nodded with her. "Yes. There was chaos all around me. There were men running and fighting, and there was such noise, though some of it was only the roaring in my ears from what had been done. I got as far as the automobile when I must have fainted. When I opened my eyes, the Count was bending over me, asking me where Laisha was. I tried to tell him, or show him, but I doubt I said much that made sense. My mind was fogged, and I must have been more . . . It was the oddest thing. I thought that the

Count put me under the automobile, and then pulled it over on top of me. Nothing else saved me, and the Isotta-Fraschini was indeed over me when the police found me, but . . . It was a large automobile, and quite heavy. One man could not turn it over. It's impossible." He frowned deeply. "I wish I knew what *did* happen."

"And Laisha?" Irina prodded him.

"The Count went to find her. But they killed her, just the same. I saw him with her body in his arms. He would not let them take her from him. He kept saying, 'She's my child, my child,' and holding her."

"Oh!" Irina exclaimed, feeling her grief in sympathy with his. "Oh, the poor man."

"I didn't see much more of it. I heard later from Roger that he carried her all the way back to Schloss Saint-Germain, on foot. How could he? He must have been given a ride by someone, but still . . ." He drew a deep breath. "I saw him two days later. I was in the hospital still, because of the broken ribs and concussion. The Count was arranging to have me sent back to his Schloss as soon as the physicians were willing to let me go. He came to my ward and spoke with me. He told me that he did not hold me in any way responsible, and wanted to assure me that he would not dismiss me because of the incident. His face . . . his face was terrible. His eyes were like hot iron. He was so . . . distant." He stopped, thinking back to that day, and once again knew that touch of absolute fear that had run through him then. "He said he would find the men who killed her and would kill them. It was as if he were telling me what time he would want the automobile to be ready. He was . . . I don't know." His voice had become very quiet, and when he looked at Irina, he saw she had caught her lower lip between her teeth. "What is it?"

She turned away from him. "I was thinking that he will do what he has promised. Those men, whoever they are, are . . . doomed." She tried to laugh, to end the icy desolation of spirits that had come over her, but the sound was more of a sob, and she choked it back. So Laisha was dead, she thought, and crossed herself, not noticing that Nikolai had done the same. "The Count told me about her, when I saw him. Had she been his own flesh and . . . blood, he could not have loved her more."

Nikolai pinched the bridge of his nose between thumb and forefinger, and said in a thickened tone, "I don't . . . I can't

. . ." He brought up his head. "I was told it was a very small funeral, and that he sat through it without shedding one tear."

"Then his heart must be weeping within him," Irina said quietly.

"Roger said . . . he has been with the Count for a very long time. I understand, and he said that he had never seen him so overset. He kept talking about China, saying that had not been as bad as now."

"What did he mean, did he tell you?" Irina was puzzled.

"He said that a warlord who was a friend of the Count's had been killed in a similar way, but would not elaborate. With an effort he got to his feet and reached for his cane. "Count Ragoczy said that I was to wait for him here, that he would come to Paris eventually, and that until then, he wanted to be sure that I was safe. He told me to come to you, because you would be willing to teach me French. . . ." He looked down at her. "It is not necessary, Madame Ohchenov. You are a Duchess and I am a soldier."

Irina laughed strangely. "We are both exiles, Mr. Rozoh. Of course I will teach you French." She thought for a moment. "Where is the Count, do you know?" Before he could answer, she went on, "No, you said you did not, didn't you?"

"He is still in Germany, I think." Nikolai knew without doubt that the Count would not leave until those who had killed Laisha were dead. He would leave Germany only to follow them.

"And when he has revenged her, what then?" Irina asked, but expected no answer. She rose from her chair. "Mr. Rozoh, I am grateful to you for bringing me this news, but it saddens me more than I can express to hear of it. I would much rather have heard it thus, from you, than read Roger's letter." She walked the length of the room. "Had he improved at all when you left?"

Nikolai shook his head. "He was no different from that day he came to the hospital. He was always very polite, and he behaved with complete propriety, but his eyes did not change and I heard him at night, twice, walking through the Schloss. Once he spent the greater part of the night in the music room, playing all the things they had played together, all the music she liked. It was worse than weeping, that music." He had not mentioned this to anyone before, and he studied Irina to see what her reaction might be.

"Dear God," she said quietly. "The clothes you have brought, they're hers, aren't they?"

"Yes. They're hers." He went carefully to the bookcases. "He could not bear to look at her things. Roger packed it all. He purchased a Minerva and had the boxes put into it, and then told me to come here. He said . . . he would be here later." There was little conviction in this last statement, and the exchange of glances he had with Irina revealed her own doubt to him.

"Yes." She bent to pick up the largest of the pieces of broken glass. "He will come, of course, eventually. But what will happen to him?" She held the shards carefully, so as not to cut herself on them.

"Roger was worried about him. He did not say so; he's not that sort, but he had a look about him . . ." Nikolai gave an embarrassed shrug. "I wish there were something I could do, but the Count would not permit it, not from me, or anyone."

Irina had not been paying a great deal of attention to what Nikolai had said, but this last caught her attention. "How do you mean, not permit it?" She deposited the glass in a ceramic ashtray.

"He . . . there is something about him, I don't know how to describe it, but I have seen it. If you offered him your help, he would be polite and most appreciative, but he would not accept it. He will not let Roger give him comfort or help. If he will not take it from Roger, he most certainly will not let *me* assist him," Nikolai said with quiet hopelessness.

"Do you believe he needs help? Yes, I can see you do. And from what you have told me," she went on with more strength of purpose, "I would agree. The pain of losing a child is . . . very great. For him, given his nature"—she glanced away from Nikolai as her memories of her nights in Ragoczy's arms surged through her—"it would be more painful, I think."

Nikolai found it difficult to speak, but forced himself to say, "I owe him . . . everything. He could have refused to aid me. I expected that of him, but . . ."

"Expected it? Why?" Irina was faintly distracted: there was an elusive idea at the back of her mind, and she could not get a grip on it.

"I had met him in Russia, under . . . awkward conditions." That cold monastery kitchen, with Dmitri and Yuri drunk, and almost no food left, those little monks' cells with their noble prisoners. Nikolai flinched as he recalled how Ragoczy had tricked and overpowered him.

"What conditions?" Irina asked a second time.

With a strange laugh, Nikolai said, "I was his jailer. He

escaped. I should have had sense enough to fly with him, but . . ."

"Jailer?" Irina stared at him. So this was the man Ragoczy had told her about in her frigid dasha? This was the man he had left in his cell? And he was now his chauffeur? "How like him!"

"I suppose so," Nikolai said, and shook his head over it, as he had so many times in the past. "Do you see why I believe I must try, somehow, to help him? He found me working with a crew of criminals repairing a road. He paid my debts and gave me employment, when I had been his jailer. If I do nothing for him now, then . . ."

Irina came up to Nikolai and put her hand on his arm. "Mr. Rozoh, you're quite right. Something must be done. But you admit you cannot do it, nor can I. And if Roger is stymied, then . . ." She stopped and put her hand to her cheek.

"You've thought of something?" Nikolai said, feeling hope for the first time. He looked down at Irina's face. "What is it?"

"I'm not certain it is possible," she cautioned in a soft, tense tone. "But there is a chance . . . I've never been precisely sure how things stood between them, but each has spoken of the other with such endearment . . ."

"Who are you talking about?" Nikolai asked, beginning to feel impatient with Irina, and chagrined that she might have found the thing that he had missed.

Irina started out of the room. "I must write a letter at once, Mr. Rozoh. If you will excuse me? Phillippe will show you out."

"But, Madame Ohchenov . . ." he began, starting toward her.

"The French lessons? Is that it? Come on Tuesday in the afternoon. We will begin then. Forgive me, now . . ." Irina favored him with a distracted wave.

"Who are you writing to?" Nikolai shouted after her.

She came back to the door and gave Nikolai a long, thoughtful look. "If I tell you, you must not say anything. I don't know that it will work, or that it will do any good at all."

"You have my word that I will not mention the name," Nikolai said with great formality. He thought of the officers he had had in the army and of the integrity one or two of them had possessed. This middle-aged woman reminded him of those officers, and he took his oath with great seriousness.

"I trust your word, Mr. Rozoh. If anything comes of this, I will notify you of it at once. It might require time." She tried to remember how long her last letter had taken to reach that desolate part of Syria, and was annoyed that she could not.

"I will be coming to you to learn French. You may tell me then if there are developments." He studied her a little, wondering what she had looked like when she had been a Duchess, with servants around her and the grandeur of the Imperial Court as her setting.

"Excellent. That way, you may also tell me what news there is of Count Ragoczy. It may work; it may work."

"Fine," Nikolai said, waiting. "Roger told me he would send me notice of their plans, so that I can be ready to receive them when they come to Paris. By that, I imagine he means that I will know when to drive the Minerva to the rail station to meet them."

"That will be a wonderful day," Irina said quickly. "Perhaps we will be able to speed it a little. Pray that I have not guessed incorrectly, Mr. Rozoh." She banished her frown and her doubt at once, and said with a determined little nod, "I am going to write to Madelaine de Montalia and tell her what you have told me."

This announcement was clearly supposed to evoke some sort of response from Nikolai, but he said nothing, for unlike Irina Ohchenov, he had never heard of Madelaine de Montalia. He watched Irina turn and hurry away down the hall, and a few minutes later Phillippe Timbres came to escort him to the door, saying nothing but the few words courtesy required, so that Nikolai decided not to ask the man what he knew of Madelaine de Montalia, if, indeed, he knew anything at all. He would have been amazed had he lingered for half an hour to hear what Phillippe Timbres said when he saw the letter that Irina had written.

"You can't send this, my love."

"What?" She looked around at him. "Why ever not?"

"It isn't appropriate. You presume too much. It would be most unwise to post it."

"But I must," Irina said, at her most reasonable as she began to write delivery instructions on the envelope.

"It is no concern of hers, Irina." For some reason he did not entirely understand, Phillippe felt distress on Madelaine's behalf. "They hardly know each other. This is far too personal to be shared with a mere acquaintance."

"Do you think that is all they are?" Irina asked him with an odd, unreadable expression. "I didn't get that impression from either of them."

"Oh? What impression did you get then?" He was as close to being angry with her as he ever came.

"I think that they have been very close at one time. There is something that happens to their eyes when they hear the other's name." She hunted in her desk drawer for stamps as she spoke, and at last found what she was looking for.

"They are lovers?" Phillippe asked incredulously. "Are you suggesting that?"

"Not now, of course, but I think they were, when Madelaine was young." There was a little brass postal scale on the desk, and she placed the envelope on it, adjusting the counterweight on the beam.

"Madelaine *is* young," Phillippe protested with a growing lack of ease.

"Do you think so?" Irina asked quietly. "I did once, but not anymore." She put four stamps on the envelope, then regarded Phillippe seriously. "My dearest, I do not want to alarm you, or to do anything that displeases you, but it is necessary, I promise you, that I do this. Without Comte Ragoczy's help . . ."—she exhaled shakily—"well, it is a debt I can never repay, but this will reduce it in part. I cannot stand by idly and leave him in pain. He did not leave me."

"Comte Ragoczy!" Phillippe scoffed. "He sounds like one of those characters in romantic novels. The tall, mysterious foreigner—"

"He isn't tall," Irina said patiently.

"And noble, too," Phillippe went on, paying no attention to her interruption. "The savior of those in distress!"

"He was that, for me," Irina said.

"Why?" Phillippe inquired.

She regarded him with dignity. "You would laugh if I told you, Phillippe, and then I would be angry with you. I do not wish to be."

Phillippe's face fell, but he could not resist adding, "There is a character in a novel with his name, now that I think of it. In *Manon Lescaut*, there is a Prince Ragoczy who owns Hôtel Transylvania, the old gambling establishment."

"The Ragoczy name is famous in Hungary, Phillippe. They were a most illustrious house." She got up from the desk, the letter in her hand. "Were there only the Comte, the name would be honored enough."

Phillippe pushed his hands into his pockets, saying somberly, "You know him well."

Irina met his eyes levelly. "Very well. Without him, I would be dead by now. And you see, Phillippe, I know what it is to lose a treasured child, and I sympathize with him."

For a short time Phillippe said nothing, then he took her hand that held the letter and kissed it. "You say he saved your life, ma amie, and for that I must be grateful to him, whoever and whatever he is. Do what you must, but try not to be disappointed if your plan does not work." The smile that Irina bestowed on him almost banished the jealousy that he felt, both because of Madelaine de Montalia and this Comte Ragoczy he did not know.

Text of a letter from James Emmerson Tree to his cousin Audrey.

*Liege, Belgium*
*August 3, 1926*

*Dear Audrey;*

*I was very sorry to hear about Aunt Myra's death in June. She was a very good woman and I will miss her. From what Uncle Ned told me, you were the one who made the difference for her in the last few weeks, and I gather he was not much help for you. He kept telling me in his letter that women are good at sickroom things and men aren't. What he meant was that he didn't want to deal with Aunt Myra's illness and so he left the whole thing in your lap. He might not ever tell you that you did a good thing and did it well, but I will. You did a selfless and courageous thing, Audrey, and you deserve more credit than you'll probably ever get, but if my opinion means anything to you, then rest assured that it is the highest possible.*

*You may wonder what I'm doing in Belgium; the answer is, I just got kicked out of Germany. I was touring the country, doing a number of articles, most of them for Crandell but a few for magazine sales, as well, and in Berlin I covered some meetings and rallies of the National Socialists, the ones they call the Nazis, when they aren't being nice. Whatever it was I did (and I still can't find out what it was), I stepped on somebody's toes, because the next thing you know, I was being asked to leave, and none too gently. I've been looking over my articles, and for the life of me, I don't know what it was I said that offended them. The National Socialists were very strong in Bavaria for a time, but they're really spread out in the last couple years. They sound a little like the Ku Klux Klan, only about Jews instead of Ne-*

*groes. They keep talking about economics and race as if they were the same thing, and the need to preserve the Pan-Germanic culture. There are those in Germany who believe that the National Socialists will be the next major power in politics, but I'm not so certain. They're well-organized and they have a neat, military look to them, but it seems to me that most of their membership is working-class, and the Germans are awful snobs. If they're going to get anywhere, they're going to need a little more blue blood in their ranks, or they aren't going to be taken too seriously. If they could convince one of the old Kaiser's kids to come out in their favor, then I think they'd be a real threat. I don't know what Hindenburg thinks of them—that was one of the things I was hoping to find out while I was in Germany—but he's got a fair amount of power now that he's President and it could be that his favor or lack of it will tip the scales for them. One thing that the National Socialists have done is started an organization for kids, kind of like the Scouts but more political, called the Hitlerjugend, named for one of their leaders. It's something like the Ballilla in Italy. Both of them seem pretty strange to me; it's like their kids are all turning into political watchdogs, and that is a move they might learn to regret.*

*I did get to the Krupp works at Essen. They're really impressive. There's a new merger going on in steel in Germany, by the way: Rhine-Elbe and Thyssen's company are now Vereinigte Stahlwerke, or United Steel Works. I will say this for the Germans: when it comes to technology, they're right on the mark.*

*I haven't heard much out of the Middle East, but with the French bombarding Damascus last May, things could get tricky there again. Not that I mind all that much, except my Madelaine is in Syria, and I worry about her.*

*They tell me that airlines are springing up all over America, particularly in the West, where the distances are greater between cities, and the roads pretty rugged. When are you going to get into an aeroplane and hop over to Chicago? I understand that Congress is about to create an Air Corps for the army. Billy Mitchell must be having a laugh over that, after all the grief he's been given.*

*I saw Metropolis while I was still in Germany. Now, there's a disturbing flicker, let me tell you. I also saw that Czech play RUR, and that, on top of the other, was a lot to handle. Now, I like gadgets as well as the next guy, but both of those pieces had me worried. I kept wondering, while I watched them, what the workingmen thought of them, because it strikes a lot closer to them than to me. If I worked in a factory, I think I'd want to go as far into the country as I could and live on a farm until the end of my days. I wish my German were better. I know I missed a lot. I've picked up a copy of Kafka's Das Schloss, to try to improve.*

*I hear there's another novel by Willa Cather due out next year. I used to like her work a lot, but I must be getting out of touch, because it doesn't appeal to me as much as it used to. Maugham interests me a bit. And I still like Mark Twain. I wonder what it is about Cather? Or what it is about me. I haven't had time to read the magazines you've sent me, but I'll catch up, so you keep on sending them. I loved that story about wizards in Central America in* Thrilling Wonder Stories. *By the way, do you know anything about the guy who calls himself E. Hoffman Price? I've read three or four of his stories so far in the magazines and I wonder what he's been up to to be able to write like that. Most of those writers sound like they're hiding out in a room somewhere in Cleveland, making it all up, but this Price fellow might actually have been somewhere.*

*I'm going to try to get an interview with Gertrude Ederle before she tries to swim the Channel. If she does it, then the interview will be twice as valuable, and if she doesn't make it, then it will be interesting because I got it before she got into the water. She didn't make it last year, but I think she's showing a lot of courage to try again. Some of the British journalists don't like the idea of an American swimming their Channel, and don't much care that she's an Olympic champion. I told one of them that if he felt that way, he could swim the Channel, to show her how it's done.*

*So you're really going to move to Seattle after all. I hope that things work out for you there. It sounds as if the job offer is a good one, and I think you will like being away from Denver for a time. Travel does make a difference, Audrey. I still wish you could find a way to get over here and let me show you a little bit of Europe. You'd enjoy it, and there's a lot to do. It may seem odd of me to suggest this, especially after being tossed out of Germany*

*and saying I have doubts about Italy, but that doesn't
change things: you can see things here that can't be found
anywhere in the good old USA. Sure, I know there are
things the U.S. has that don't crop up over here, but it's
not quite the same thing. I'll probably be in Europe for
another year at least, and if you find out that you can
afford it, make the try, will you?*

*Reading over that last paragraph, I just realized that
it's more than nine years since I was in the U.S. I know
it must have changed a lot, with new roads and buildings
everywhere. Uncle Ned mentioned that there were more
than a dozen big new buildings going up in Denver, and
the main roads were getting paving. It's hard to picture,
but when I get back, I'll have to take a few weeks to be a
tourist and see what's being done.*

*The Mors is running just fine, thank you. I had some
work done on it before I went to Germany, and it hasn't
given me a bit f trouble. I had it up to around eighty
miles per hour on one stretch of road, and I loved it.
That's not to say that your Oakland doesn't sound fine—
it does. I know you'll find it useful in Seattle, with all
those hills.*

*I'm going to be back in Paris for a while, so you can
reach me there. Crandell wants some pieces on the Americans living here, you know, the artists and writers that
flock around Gertrude Stein. I've met her a couple of
times, so it shouldn't be too difficult to get introductions
to most of them. The nice thing is that I'll have a little
more time to myself, and a chance to do a couple of the
things I've wanted to do but haven't had any real time for,
such as go to the museums. Do you realize I've only been
to the Pomme de Terre once? I've never seen the Ballet
Russe. I'll have a chance to do those things, and who
knows? I might get a few pieces out of doing those things.
Sometime next year Crandell wants me to go to Scandinavia and write about what's going on in those countries,
especially with the changing political scene in Germany.
So Copenhagen and Stockholm, here I come. I'll see if I
can find someone to teach me a little Swedish before I go.
I doubt I'll be able to get by on French and a little
German.*

*Now, listen, Audrey, you take care of yourself. If Uncle
Ned tries to talk you out of leaving because he wants to
keep you around, you tell him no, and get in your Oak-*

*land and head for the West Coast. You've done everything that you can for your parents, and don't you let him tell you any differently. Just make sure you send me your address when you get to Seattle, so that I can stay in touch with you.*

*When they finally decide to do away with Prohibition, I'll send you a case of good French wines to enjoy. Now, that's something to look forward to. And a little Rhine wine, too. I don't understand why the government persists with Prohibition: all it does is give rise to more crime and another excuse for interference. I've probably been living in Europe too long, or haven't gone to church enough, or something of the sort. The whole thing strikes me as absurd. I see Americans over here, and they spend enormous amounts of time and money simply getting drunk, because they don't get to drink at home. They're convinced they're doing something very naughty. You'd think they were ten-year-olds sneaking a taste of Papa's beer, instead of well-to-do adults off in a foreign country. I've been embarrassed by the way they behave.*

*Enough of this. I want to tell you once more that you did more for Aunt Myra than anyone could have asked you to do, and that you did it well. Remember that, will you, Audrey? There's nothing wrong in taking all the money she left you—six thousand dollars may sound like a lot of money right now, but you'll see that it isn't as much as you think it is. You're going to need it in Seattle. Don't let Uncle Ned hector you out of one red cent.*

*Take care of yourself, and enjoy yourself. You can do both at once.*

*Your loving cousin,*
*James*

## 2

A weathered sign hung over the door of the old tavern, showing a clumsily-executed bird and a vaguely canine head: "WOLF UND RABE" it said below. The entrance was narrow, for the tavern was sandwiched in between two large buildings, and the few rooms that the landlord had to hire were stacked up above the taproom and were reached by a rickety staircase.

Ragoczy took this all in as he stood in the low, dark entryway. The sour odor of stale beer did not offend him, but he viewed the establishment with distaste. He made a fastidious brush at his lapels, as if to rid himself of any contamination the tavern might pass to him.

The landlord appeared from the taproom, his round cheeks flushed under day-old stubble. His belligerent manner changed abruptly when he caught sight of the elegant stranger waiting in the entry hall. "Mein Herr. I heard someone enter."

"Yes." Ragoczy gave him a crisp nod.

Somewhat nonplussed at having such a person in his establishment, the landlord looked around once and began again. "Is there something you wanted, Mein Herr?"

"You are expecting Herr Vortag, Herr Abscheu, Herr Recht, Herr Krümmer, and Herr Grube, are you not?" Ragoczy's voice was coolly polite, but there was a look in his eyes that made the landlord quail.

"Ja. Ja, I am expecting them, but not until later, you see." The words came out in a rush and he made nervous chopping gestures with his large, thick hands.

"How much later?" Ragoczy asked, saying the names to himself in his mind, the names that Roger had brought to him the day before.

"An hour, two at the most. They are attending a meeting, Mein Herr. They are part of the SA, and it is—"

"I am aware of their activities," Ragoczy cut him off.

The landlord bobbed from the waist, thinking desperately of ways to deal with the stranger. "Of course, of course. They will return at eight, perhaps nine. Not before then, Mein Herr." He wagged one hand toward the taproom. "As you see, it is early yet. I serve no beer until the half-hour."

"I am not interested in beer. I wish to see those five men." He stared at the landlord, and the big man could not meet his eyes.

"Selbstverständlich. I understand," he babbled, moving his arms again in the same hacking emphasis he had used before.

"Where are their rooms, bitte." He clearly expected a prompt and sensible answer.

Almost wholly terrified, the landlord forced himself to speak in measured and thoughtful terms. "Two of them live here, the other three have rooms elsewhere. But, Mein Herr, there is a room, out on the rear courtyard, and they often spend their evenings together, over a few steins, and an occasional pipe. They have put up a few photographs and other mementos of their SA activities—"

"Have they." Ragoczy's jaw tightened. "How charming."

The landlord coughed, and said, "If Mein Herr would like to wait for them there, it is more likely that they will come to that room before they enter here. They do not spend much time in the taproom because of the Spartacists, you understand." He rubbed his jowls, and the beard growth made a scratching sound that aggravated him. With one quick glance he made sure that the hochgeborn intruder had not been too disgusted with his slovenliness.

"Where is this courtyard?" he asked softly.

"It is through the taproom and then . . . there is a small kitchen, just space enough to keep würst and a bit of bread, you understand. Next to the kitchen there is a door, with a brace . . ." In his nervousness he began to twist the sash of his discolored apron.

"Show me, please."

"Yes, naturally. At once." He was pathetically grateful to be moving, and he led the way with ponderous haste through the taproom to the door he had tried to describe. "The courtyard is immediately outside, and the room is attached to the old stables, on the left. There are four or five steps down when you open the door, and two good-sized lanterns for light. I can give you matches . . ."

"It will not be necessary," Ragoczy told him as he reached to open the door.

"Ja. Excellent." The landlord pulled himself to the side, away from the man in black. "They will be back before nine, Mein Herr. Rest assured."

Those distant, smoldering dark eyes rested on his. "You've already said so."

"Indeed. I have, ja." He had nearly untied his apron by now, and was anxious to return to the taproom and the familiar noise and bustle that would soon fill the place. He had long accustomed himself to the unruly customers his tavern attracted, and now, seeing this refined, distinguished, sinister stranger, he appreciated his rabble as he never had before.

"I trust you will not mention that I am waiting for them," Ragoczy said, with the hint of an ironic smile.

"If you prefer not. Though they will probably come directly to the extra room, you understand, so as not to get into any brawls." He grinned ingratiatingly, and motioned for Ragoczy to go through the door.

"Thank you," Ragoczy told him, holding out a twenty-mark note.

The landlord's eyes widened greedily, but he forced himself to refuse it. "Nein, nein. It is not necessary, Mein Herr. Not in the least."

"Nevertheless, you will do me the honor of taking it," Ragoczy said, tucking the bill into the landlord's apron pocket.

"But . . . it is too much," the landlord protested.

"Occasionally, one is entitled to too much," Ragoczy said as he opened the door. "If you cannot bear the thought of such good fortune, buy a round of drinks for your regular customers. That should take the edge off it for you." Before he heard the landlord's response, he closed the door and looked around him.

Courtyard, he decided at once, was a euphemism. This was nothing more than a rectangle of old, uneven flagging, many of the stones prized up or broken. Piles of refuse lay against the far wall, and from the sound of it, offered rich scavengings for rats and other vermin. He could hear the whine of a cat in the passage that connected this pocket of squalor with the narrow, rutted alley beyond. The day had been warm, and the approach of evening provided little relief, and the fetid stink of half-rotten vegetables hung on the air like a mist. From one of the old, dilapidated buildings that backed onto the courtyard there came the sound of crying children and a female voice raised in weary anger. Ragoczy's hands closed at his sides as he listened, and his resurgent grief hurried him toward the room the landlord had indicated.

The door moaned and the hinges sagged as he pressed it inward. There were scuttlings in the far corner, and a hollow rattle as something fell. Ragoczy paused on the top step, his remarkable eyes taking in the drab little room. As the landlord had told him, there were a few curling photographs stuck to the wall with pins, and a number of runes painted on the broad, simple molding that ran around the room about a hand-breadth from the ceiling. Ragoczy recognized the symbol for Thor and the sign of the Fennris Wolf, but the rest were not familiar to him. He came down the stairs and crossed the room to the one table, and half-seated himself upon it; one foot on the floor, the other dangling as far as his knee, that leg being hitched up onto the planks. With folded arms, he waited in the dark for the five men to return.

As much as he wanted to be quiet, his attention stilled but for this one purpose, thousands of memories flitted through his mind. The Armenian spy dying under the pressure of his hands; the Coptic monks pursuing him with most unmonklike spears; the burning town on the road east of Damascus; the rush of water through Kali's temple; the stone-visaged Czar with his lancers waiting at the gates of his castle in Lithuania; Laurenzo's agonized voice asking, "If you were God, Francesco, what would you do with me?"; Le Grace tied to a singletree in Saint Sebastien's stable; the spider in the mirror; his servants fleeing the mansion in St. Petersburg before the soldiers came to arrest him; Laisha lying under the straw in a chicken-coop, wearing an elaborate dress that did not fit. He closed his eyes in a useless attempt to shut out her face.

There was a soft thud in the courtyard, and Ragoczy guessed that one of the tenants had dropped some more refuse from an open window. Someone shouted unintelligible curses at someone else, who returned them with vigor. Two cats began to yowl and were silenced by the crash of a bottle hurled in their direction. From the tavern came the sound of loud greetings and an outburst of ribald laughter. The evening had begun on this warm August night no differently from most other evenings.

Ragoczy paid little attention to these sounds, for he had heard their like for nearly four thousand years. He supposed that soon someone would start to sing, and a little later there would be a quarrel and perhaps a fight. Most of the time he regarded these things with indifference, but tonight he was glad of them. Let them bray out their songs, scream their insults, he would welcome them all. He lifted his head as another altercation broke out in one of the dwellings behind the courtyard: a predatory smile curled his lips.

Half an hour later there was a great deal of friendly rumpus in the taproom so that Ragoczy did not at first hear the approach of the five men he was waiting for. There were sounds of quick military strides on the courtyard flaggings, and a deep voice shouted an order.

"Heinz, this is still a drill. Stand properly."

"Don't be such a martinet, Friedel," one of those outside the door complained.

"Shut up, down there!" bellowed someone from a window above, the words echoing ominously in the narrow passageway.

"Keep to yourself, you old fart!" the one who had been called Friedel shouted back.

"I'll have the police on you!" the upper voice announced.

"Go ahead!" one of the others taunted. "We've got three hundred policemen in the NSDAP already. Do you think they would act against their own party members?"

There was a resounding crash as a window was indignantly slammed down. The men in the courtyard chuckled.

"Very well, very well, you men," Friedel said with gruff humor. It was not easy to hear him over the enthusiastic voices in the taproom. "Keep in formation."

"But the meeting is over, Friedel. Röhm isn't here to tell you if you're doing it right," a voice that Ragoczy had not heard before said in an injured tone.

"We've got to maintain discipline at all times," Friedel insisted, plainly loath to give up the power he had, if only over four men. "That is the essential component of the SA. Every unit should be able to function independently, but have skill and discipline enough to be part of the larger groups."

One of the men said something that Ragoczy could not hear because of the sudden increase in noise from the tavern.

"Do you hear that?" Friedel said loudly, remonstrating with his men. "That is what we must overcome. It will not happen if we relax our discipline and our purpose every time we are out of sight or hearing of an officer. Remember that. You, Romuald, see how you are standing. That does not become a member of the SA. It is more fitting for those lax bastards in the taproom. Your belt is not tight, and the tail of your shirt is out. If I were as demanding as Röhm is, you would face disciplinary action for it."

"For the sake of our feet, Friedel, let us stop this. I want a beer and a pipe." The complainer was given support by the others.

"Then get into formation so I can dismiss you," Friedel ordered them.

There was a loud crash as a bottle shattered in the passageway.

"Damned Spartacists," one of the men in the courtyard shouted, and was immediately yelled at by a man in one of the buildings above them.

"Better Spartacists than Nazis!"

Ragoczy listened to the exchange of insults with a set, ferocious smile. He would not have to wait too much longer. His eyes were on the door, waiting for the moment when the five men would walk through and close it behind them.

"That's better," Friedel barked, and Ragoczy pictured him

strutting around the four men he commanded. "Straighter there, Heinz."

"Friedel!" one of the men shouted at him. "Finish up!"

"All right! You are dismissed!" He had to yell this to be heard over the song that resounded in the taproom.

"Well, that's over, Gott sie Dank," one of the men said as he opened the door to the added room.

"Did you notice that there's to be a meeting about preparing for the elections? We want to get as many of our men working on that as we can." This was Heinz, and he followed the first man down the stairs. "Get the lantern, why don't you?"

"I don't have any matches. Hey, Vincenz, did you bring matches?"

"And tobacco. You fellows always forget yours." He had a rich, plumy chuckle, and Ragoczy watched him make his way cautiously to the center of the room, where one old brass-plated lantern hung from a hook.

Friedel was the last one in, and he slammed the door with vigor. "There, that shuts up those infernal radicals!" He made a contemptuous gesture in the general direction of the tavern.

Now that the men were in the room, Ragoczy recognized three of them. Heinz was the one who had grabbed hold of Laisha's arm. Friedel had called her a Spartacist because of her accent. One of the others whose name he did not know had been the one to swing the rifle that killed her.

The match scraped and flame spurted at the tip. There was the hollow sound of the glass chimney being lifted, and then a low, cozy light spilled through the room.

"Good evening, gentlemen," said Franchot Ragoczy, Graf von Saint-Germain. He did not stand, but this did not detract from his authority.

The five men stared at him, most in astonishment, but Friedel was outraged.

"Who the devil are you? This is a private meeting room!" He came stumping down the stairs, his face slightly flushed.

"So the landlord informed me," Ragoczy said urbanely, choosing not to answer the first question. "But then, I wished to speak to you, so . . ."

"You have no business coming here!" Friedel blustered, but Vincenz laid a hand on his arm.

"Don't be so hasty, Friedel. Look at the man. You know that we have instructions to be deferential to the hochgebornen, and he is one such." He had reached into a pouch he carried on his belt, and extracted a bit of dried-out tobacco, and now he stuffed it into his pipe with the air of a man eager to be hospitable.

"What did you want to speak to us about?" Friedel inquired suspiciously with a truculent gesture to the others.

"The thirty-first of May." His affability was unfailing but icy. "I hope you recall it. With all your various activities, it may not be foremost in your memories, but I encourage you to give it your consideration." His lambent eyes went from one man to the other, and none of them could return his stare.

"There was a riot that day," Vincenz said a bit uncertainly.

"Bravo." Ragoczy folded his arms, determined to contain his rage until the men here knew what they had done, what they would pay for.

"It wasn't much of an affair. Those Spartacists overturned our truck." Heinz glared at Ragoczy as if he were responsible for this insult.

"Very good."

"I didn't know there was anything of note that came out of it," one of the others said in a surly tone. "The police stopped the whole thing in less than two hours."

"A mere two hours. What luck," Ragoczy said with a sarcastic nod to the five men. "Do you recall any of the glories of that short . . . occurrence?"

"Nothing much happened," Vincenz growled.

"Nothing much happened?" Ragoczy repeated, as fury coursed through him. His dark eyes glowed now, but the men did not notice this.

"A few broken windows," Heinz said with a shrug.

Ragoczy got off the table and took a few steps forward. "How strange. I understood that there were five businesses ruined—"

"Jewish Spartacists," one of them said, as if that negated the complaint.

"—and more than twenty men badly beaten—"

Friedel made a snorting sound. "It was a riot. What do you expect?"

"—more than thirty automobiles were wrecked or damaged—"

Romuald, who was the youngest man there, snickered. "Only a fool would leave an automobile in those streets. They're fair game."

"—and sixteen men were killed."

The five SA Brownshirts were quiet.

"Oh, yes; and one fifteen-year-old girl."

"What—?" Friedel began, but Ragoczy did not let him finish.

"She was my daughter." Ragoczy looked at the men now with detestation in his face. "Perhaps you can remember, if you make the effort." He waited. "No? I will describe her to you. She was tall, very nearly my height, with dark blonde hair and brown eyes. She was wearing a pumpkin-colored dress. You"—he pointed to Heinz—"held her by the arms while that . . . that *animal!*"—he swung around on the man whose name he did not know—"held his rifle by the barrel and bludgeoned her with the butt."

"Now, now, now," Friedel said with an indulgent smile, starting toward Ragoczy with a confident air. "I can see why you're upset, Mein Herr, but there must surely be a misunderstanding here. It's always easy to blame the NSDAP. If your daughter was . . . killed, you can be sure that no member of the NSDAP did it. The Spartacists, they're different. You know how cheaply all Communists hold human life. If the girl was killed on the thirty-first, you should be looking for a Spartacist bully. They were the ones who started the riot, when they overturned our truck. The police will support us, I know."

"I have no doubt of it," Ragoczy agreed, letting the man go on, wanting to give him every opportunity to damn himself.

"You were wise to come to us, of course, because we can probably help you. We know where those men spend their evenings. It is in the interest of public safety that we know such things. Let us lead you to them, and we'll help you to teach them a lesson they won't soon forget." His men made sounds of halfhearted encouragement, and one of them hooked his thumb into his belt. "The trouble is, those Spartacists are suspicious of their own kind. It's not surprising, when you consider their background. It must have been that they realized your daughter was Russian, and they—"

"I did not tell you she was Russian," Ragoczy cut in, his soft voice acidic.

"Of course you did," Friedel insisted, looking to the others. "I remember."

"No."

Two of the men came closer to their leader, and one of them muttered a few words under his breath. Friedel glared at him, then looked back at Ragoczy, determined to brazen it out. "If you did not mention it—Romuald thinks you didn't, but he is the youngest of us—then we saw it in the reports of the riot. That's always the sort of thing you read about in the newspapers."

"Her name was not mentioned; the only comment was that a young woman had been one of the victims that day. I know this is true, gentlemen. I paid enough to keep her name and nationality a secret." He came a few steps closer to the men. There was now less than four paces between him and Friedel.

"Word of such things always gets out," Vincenz informed him in grand tones, with a pugnacious set of his jaw.

Friedel took up the argument gratefully. "Yes, of course. The police may keep such things out of the paper, as you claim, but they gossip among themselves, and there are many of them in the NSDAP. Young Russian women are not that common in München that the police would not take some notice of her." He was feeling his way with more confidence, less impressed with the man in black. He had been jarred by the stranger's catching him in the matter of the girl's nationality, but he was sure he could convince the man that he had learned of her being Russian from some believable source. "We of the NSDAP know and trust the family and hold it sacred; the most sacred institution in all Deutschland, and the foundation of all Teutonic culture. No one here would willingly harm a young person—Gott im Himmel! for that we would have to be monsters."

Ragoczy's smile was that of a condemned heretic to his Inquisitors. "You have chosen the word, not I."

"A figure of speech," Friedel insisted, and glanced uneasily toward the steps leading up to the door. The landlord would not like it if such a hochgeborn gentleman as this one was hurt in this room, but if he were to leave here, there was the narrow passage and no one could fix the blame on them if this man were found there, perhaps unconscious, around midnight. The police would not pursue the matter too pointedly, for the stranger was not Deutscher, and being elegant, he could only expect to meet with difficulty in this part of the city. Little would be made of it.

"As you say," Ragoczy murmured.

Sensing his opportunity, Friedel reached out as if to take Ragoczy by the arm. "Come, then. We'll see to your aid—"

Two swift steps closed the distance between Ragoczy and Friedel. He could no longer contain his rage: it was just such a gesture that he had seen when these men surrounded Laisha. He reached out for the leader, his small hands closing, inexorably closing around the base of the man's jaw.

Friedel gasped in shock, and then his voice grated a sound that was intended for a yell, but was cut off as Ragoczy pressed through jaw, throat, and neck. A little blood dribbled from the corner of his mouth before Ragoczy let him drop to the floor. The whole attack had taken less than six seconds from the time Ragoczy first touched him until his head wobbled back as he lay, the lower part of his face sagging unnaturally inward.

"What the Devil . . . ?" Heinz cried out, startled by the swiftness of Ragoczy's movements. It was impossible that Friedel, big, hale Friedel, who was a head taller than the foreigner, should be lying at the man's feet.

From the taproom came a lusty, stomping chorus, words and melody alike blurred by beer and distance. One of the voices was particularly loud, a steam-whistle sort of tenor that blasted away at the song as if trying to get the best of it.

"Friedel!" the one whose name Ragoczy did not know shouted, coming near the fallen figure. He stared in disbelief, then turned toward the intruder. "You had no reason to do this."

"You killed my daughter," Ragoczy said with utmost certainty.

"No man does this to us!" Heinz declared, glowering at the lone figure in black, nodding to his three comrades. He did not realize that Friedel was dead. "You don't attack *us* with impunity." He squared his shoulders and motioned to his companions. "That's no way to treat those willing to help you battle those murdering Spartacists." As he spoke, he saw with satisfaction that the other three were positioned to block the foreigner's escape. "He never did anything to you. Spartacists killed your daughter."

Ragoczy responded with deceptive calm. "You lie."

"Never!" Romuald said, a jeering note underlying his denial.

"*I saw you!*" Ragoczy said softly, venomously. "I saw you all."

Heinz gave a short, unconvincing laugh. "And where were you then? You've been confused."

"I was trying to reach her," Ragoczy answered, and his body tingled with the memory of that futile run he had made.

"Very touching. And for that you knock Friedel out." His bluster was more emphatic as he gained ground. The foreigner was small, though from the look of him he had some strength. It would not be difficult to subdue him.

"No, not knocked out," Ragoczy told them with terrible satisfaction. "He's dead. As you will all be."

Romuald was the only one of the four who faltered at this announcement, and he did not hesitate for long. He was closest to the body, and smelled the odor of relaxing sphincters. For an instant he thought it could be possible that Friedel was dead, but the idea was dismissed as quickly as it arose. Friedel had shit himself, that was all, and once they had beaten the foreigner, they would tease Friedel for this mishap.

The crowd in the taproom had launched into yet another song, this one accompanied by great thumpings and bangings as the men drummed their steins on the tables to emphasize the powerful three-quarter beat of the verse.

"Is he armed?" Romuald asked as his sole note of caution. "If he's got a knife or a pistol . . ."

"I? Use weapons on the likes of you?" Ragoczy inquired, one brow raised. "I leave that to your sort of scum." It was deliberately provoking, the taunting attitude he took. Grief vied with fury within him, robbing him of his incisive judgment. He had the measure of these men now, and it was the final curb on his rage, for they had to *know* what was happening to them, and why. His full might gathered strength in his sinews and blood.

Heinz and Vincenz had stiffened at his contemptuous tone, but the man whose name was unknown to Ragoczy said to the others, "If he's unarmed, we can take him—easy!"

"Don't let him out of here," Romuald added, his voice unnaturally high with excitement.

There was a general motion of agreement, and the four men ranged a bit wider; Ragoczy maneuvered into the center of the half-circle they formed. One of the men chuckled, and the others hushed him.

"You had no right to kill her," Ragoczy said to the men, and saw nothing in their faces but joyous hatred and lust for aggression. Recognizing this, remembering it from other faces in Babylon, in Rome, in China, he had no compunction about revenging Laisha, for he had gone beyond that now, as he faced the four men. There was, in an isolated, sane part of his mind, the forlorn hope that one of them might show remorse or contrition for her death and the part he had played in it. Nothing of that was apparent as the four began to close in on him, ready for the fight, eager for it. Ragoczy reached out one hand, to prepare himself.

"He's having second thoughts, and we haven't touched him yet," Romuald gloated as he closed in on Ragoczy's left side.

Ragoczy did not deny it, knowing that they would believe their own lie. He let Heinz come within arm's length, then seized him, lifting him over his head as Heinz kicked and squawked in surprise. There was the beginning of a protest on his lips as Ragoczy swung him with deceptive lazy ease into the wall behind him.

"What's going . . . ?" Vincenz shouted, taking one involuntary step aside, ducking the determined swipe of Heinz's foot.

Now Heinz was screaming, and the other three men, incited by the sound, rushed forward to restrain Ragoczy. He paid them little heed, even when one of them clambered onto his back and tried to reach around his head to gouge out his eyes with his thumbs. Ragoczy continued to turn, careless of his own safety now that his wrath was consuming him. He carried Heinz with the momentum his weight gave him, slamming the howling man into Vincenz with such force that Vincenz swore and staggered back, narrowly avoiding colliding with Romuald. The man holding him from behind broke his grip.

"Stop him!" the man whose name Ragoczy did not know cried out, watching for an opening that he could use to advantage. He did not join Vincenz and Romuald in their impulsive rush at the foreigner, but held back, waiting.

Heinz shrieked as Ragoczy released him, to send him hurtling through the air, one of his flailing arms crashing into the kerosene lantern, which swung wildly, then went out, extinguished by its own fuel. Heinz slammed into the banister by the stairs, accompanied by the sound of breakage that was not entirely from the wood. He coughed once, then was still.

With the room dark, Ragoczy had an immeasurable advantage. He looked at Heinz and was satisfied to see blood spreading around him; in the close heat of the little room, there was not much difference between the hot blood and the hot air. Ragoczy let his senses expand, searching out those others in the room by their breathing, their pulse, their terror. The intensity of their fear lent him force, and he welcomed it as he had not done in more than three thousand years. The nearest man was Romuald, who was tugging off his belt, preparing to use it as a whip. Ragoczy leaped at him.

"What?" Romuald began as two small, astonishingly powerful hands fixed themselves in his shoulder, one above and one below the joint.

"Romuald?" Vincenz shouted, groping in the dark toward the sound of the scuffle.

A horrible yell filled the room as Romuald's arm was drawn back, farther back, back and up, until, with a tearing, sucking sound, the shoulder shattered and bone pressed out through skin and cloth. Ragoczy strained one last time and pulled the

arm from Romuald's body, then stood back as blood foun-
tained from the destruction of his side. Romuald's skin was
clammy with shock, and he shuddered, twitched, and vomited
before losing consciousness.

Vincenz had listened to the rending of flesh with awe, and
had been unable to move for several seconds. Then he had
reached for one of the chairs and slammed it on the floor,
getting himself a serviceable club with a splintered end. He
rushed forward, in the direction he thought Ragoczy must be,
all the while shouting to the other man, "A chair leg! Use a
chair leg!" He brandished the club before him, and was almost
upon Ragoczy when he tripped over Romuald's outflung foot.
With a cry he threw himself forward, bringing his weapon
down as he tried to regain his balance.

An instant too late Ragoczy saw his danger, and twisted to
avoid the chair leg, but the club smashed into Ragoczy's forehead, over his right eye, with such force that if he had been a
man like those he fought, he would have been severely
concussed. As it was, his vision blurred and pain rolled through
his head and down his limbs as he strove to reach Vincenz
before the man could bludgeon him again.

"Hold him, Vincenz!" the other man shouted, busy with his
own task.

There was no response from Vincenz, who dodged Ragoczy's
arm once, escaping the backhanded blow before grappling
with him, as much for balance as to gain a fighting advantage.
They swayed together, shoes slipping in blood; then, without
warning, Ragoczy fell back, as his own blood ran into his eye.
He wiped it away impatiently as he spun around toward Vincenz
just as the club descended on his back. He lurched with the
blow and bent under it even as he ran at Vincenz, his shoulder
low enough to catch him at the waist.

It was not as easy to lift Vincenz as it had been to lift Heinz.
The man was heavier, and Ragoczy was still fighting dizziness
from the cudgeling to his head and back. His wrath grew, and
he bent the man as he raised him, pressing his neck to the side
with such force that there was a snapping sound, as if a tree
limb had broken, and Vincenz sighed once as his head drooped.
He was dead before Ragoczy dropped him.

The last man had been a bit more cautious, and he had
unwound the wires holding the back slats of the broken chair
together. When he had a good-sized length of it, he started
toward Ragoczy. He heard Vincenz fall, and was on the alert,
bringing the wire up and reaching out to find the foreigner.

He brushed past him, and pivoted toward him, dropping the loop of wire in the area he thought Ragoczy's head should be, and jerked.

Before the wire drew taut, Ragoczy knew his danger. If his neck was broken, as Vincenz's had been, he would die the true death, as surely as anyone. It was a seductive possibility, and as the wire bit into his skin, he almost abandoned himself to it. The rest were dead and his vow was nearly fulfilled. To be rid of the anguish of life tempted him. But the man who held him now was the man who had killed Laisha, and he, of all of them, would have to pay the price. He felt his blood soaking the roll-top collar, and there was a ringing in his head that banished thought.

In the taproom, someone was making a speech, his emphatic phrases being greeted with cheers and hoots whenever he paused for breath and drink.

Ragoczy let himself sag against his assailant, then, bracing himself, he kicked back sharply, catching the man in the shin with a clean, hard impact that snapped bone. The man gasped, but did not release his hold on the wire, which was biting deeply into Ragoczy's flesh. Ragoczy brought his heel down on the man's foot, this time on the other side, and smashed through shoe and foot, all the while trying to get his hands on those of the other man, knowing that if he could, he could pry them open and break free. He kicked out one more time, and the tension of the wire lessened. There was a rush of pain through him as blood welled around the wire, but Ragoczy forced himself to ignore it. In ten minutes he would have to rest, but there was enough time left to deal with the last man. He seized the man's hands, bent from the waist, and sent the man tumbling over him to land near Vincenz. The man was moaning, thrashing feebly, his venom-filled eyes searching the darkness for Ragoczy.

"I almost had you," the man said, his voice ragged.

"Yes."

"You shit-faced dog!" the man burst out, reaching for Ragoczy one last time.

With the end of his rage, Ragoczy kicked at the man, catching him at the sternum, watching the life go out of the man's eyes as he saw again the butt of his rifle smash Laisha's face.

They were singing a wailing, sentimental song in the taproom when Ragoczy stumbled into the courtyard behind the tavern. He was weak, now that his fury was gone and there was only agony left. He staggered toward the passageway, overwhelmed with the reek of death that clung to him. His fingers told him that the bruise over his eye was a bad one, and his neck burned where the wire had been. Without warning, his legs buckled, and he collapsed against the wall, sliding down to the flagging in a near-faint.

The courtyard was quiet when he came to himself again. There was no noise in the tavern, and all the lights in the surrounding buildings were out. Ragoczy got to his hands and knees and began to crawl toward the street, his mind full of Laisha when it was full of anything at all.

Text of a telegram from Madelaine de Montalia to Irina Ohchenov.

*Peshawar*
*September 28, 1926*

*Madame Ohchenov:*

*Have message stop grateful for news stop will depart within the week and should be in Paris by Nov 1 stop will advise time and place of arrival stop rely on Roger for additional information stop am very concerned stop*

*de Montalia*

## 3

Gudrun Ostneige folded her hands in her lap and let Konrad Natter continue his tirade uninterrupted. She put her mind on other things, such as the birds she had seen whisk past the windows a few minutes before.

"It is shameful enough that a woman of your standing should prefer the company of her social inferiors, but when you seek out foreigners instead of your own countrymen for your favors, it goes beyond anything tolerable. If I had not been told of this, I would not have believed it." His face was flushed and he paced the length of the dining room with a great deal of energy.

"*Who* told you these things?" Gudrun asked, knowing someone in her household had to have gossiped about her.

"Someone who cares for your reputation more than you do, Frau Ostneige. You can be sure of that. You said that you have not taken a lover, but that Hungarian from up the hill has been seen here late at night, and you have always been up on those nights he was on your grounds." Natter stopped and folded his arms. "Do you deny that?"

"He's not Hungarian," was all she could think to say.

"The point is, he is not Deutscher, and that is all that matters. Bastard Russian or Slav, it means nothing. Your tastes are appalling, if you seek out men such as this Ragoczy fellow." He gave this last pronouncement with a great deal of satisfaction.

"You cannot blame me for that," Gudrun said as she got to her feet. "No, it is my turn now, Herr Natter. You have assumed you have a right to dictate to me how I must live, which is not the case."

"It is only my concern for you," Natter protested unctuously. "You have no one to guide you now, and someone must be willing to protect you from yourself."

Gudrun felt tears in her eyes, not from sorrow but from anger. "And you have decided that you—*you*—have an obligation to watch over me? I am an adult, Herr Natter. I have taken care of my life for almost a decade, and during that time all you offered me was insults!" She wiped her eyes with the back of her hand. "Now, you presume an authority that I would never allow you!"

Natter's face became solicitous. "I did not mean to distress you, my dear. You are overset because of my severity—"

"No! I am not overset! I am *furious!*" she shouted at him. "Listen to you! You pompous, lecherous fool!"

"Gudrun!" Natter exclaimed harshly. "You forget yourself."

"Not I, Mein Herr. You have had your chance to bully me, and I have listened to you with more patience than you deserve, but now I am telling you that I wish you to leave Wolkighügel. I will tell you when you are welcome here again." She trembled with rage, and wondered at her reckless nerve that sustained her against this man.

"I see." Natter bowed to her with cold formality. "You have made a great error, my dear. I was prepared to give you my advice and protection, but you will have none of it. You tell me that I am not welcome here. Very well. But there will come a time when you will beg me to return to you, and I doubt I will answer your summons, not after what I have heard from you today." He clicked his heels together and nodded in her direction. "I will let myself out."

She followed him to the door. "You will forgive me, but I

wish to assure myself that you have left," she said coldly as he went down the hall.

"You're a foolish woman, Gudrun," Natter said to her as he pulled the door open. "You have let that foreigner blind you to your birthright, and you will have to pay for that stupidity."

"Good day, Herr Natter," Gudrun told him, staring at him as if he were a stranger.

Natter made an impatient gesture, then stepped out into the sunlight. He slammed the door closed behind him.

Gudrun wandered back to the dining room, thinking that her lunch was quite ruined. She could not stand to eat another bite now, and she was quite fatigued. Twenty minutes with Konrad Natter and she felt as if she had been up for thirty-six hours in the middle of a storm. She sat down, putting her head in her hands. He had the gall to speak to her as if she were a recalcitrant child and not a woman nearing middle age. No one had the right to upbraid her as he had done. She tore off her thumbnail with her teeth, glad at the hurt of it. With a sigh she rubbed at her eyes, pleased that she had stopped crying. How dared he think that he had reduced her to tears! Certainly she had wept, but he could not believe she was angry. She got up from the table and walked the length of the dining room. Someone in her household had been talking about her, and because of that she had endured the last half-hour. She hated the idea that her servants gossiped, and could not imagine any of them saying things about her that would bring forth Natter's righteous indignation. She smoothed the front of her blue dress automatically, unconsciously preparing herself to deal with the three members of her household. Obviously the one who had been speaking about her would have to be dismissed, but she dreaded that. How could she manage without Frau Bürste or Miroslav or Otto? She thought again that it might be as well to give up Wolkighügel and find herself a small house nearer to München, where she could fend for herself, with only a housekeeper. Her father would be ashamed of her cowardly thoughts, and her mother, if she were alive to see what had become of the magnificent Schloss, would have nothing but scorn for her. All her life she had been taught to uphold her family traditions, and now she could not break with her past. This was where she had been a child, the one place she regarded as safe. She and Maximillian had grown up here, and it was all that remained of her early life, now that her brother was dead.

She paused, remembering how he had looked when Otto had

brought her to the gamekeeper's cottage, his old face drawn with emotion. Maximillian was dangling from one of the beams, his once-handsome face dark, as blue as plums, his blackened tongue protruding and huge, his eyes, the whites suffused with blood and bursting from their sockets. What had he stood on, she wondered again, to do this to himself? The police had decided that he had crawled out on the beam and dropped over it, but at the same time they admitted to her that it was strange that Maximillian had died of strangulation and not a broken neck. Such a drop, they explained very carefully to her, usually broke the neck. And no man would prefer slow death to a quick one. Gudrun trembled, rigorously suppressing a notion that had been with her since she had read Maximillian's farewell note to her: that he had not committed suicide, but had been murdered. When she had asked the police, they had dismissed the idea, but Gudrun could not rid herself of the suspicion.

With a curt gesture she banished this speculation, knowing she was using it as a way to avoid dealing with the unpleasantness that confronted her now. She would have to question her staff, and how much she disliked doing it! She sighed as she went through the door and started toward the kitchen, where she knew she would find Frau Bürste.

The housekeeper was stouter than she had been a year ago, becoming a bit more massive every year. She was sitting at the kitchen table, the household accounts spread around her, a deep frown on her pleasant features. As Gudrun came through the door, she looked up. "Oh." Rising properly, she colored a little. "I did not realize, Frau Ostneige, that it was you. I expected Otto to—"

"It isn't important," Gudrun said quickly. "You need not keep to ceremony for my sake. If we had a complete household and there were scullery boys in the kitchen, that would be another matter, but with only the two of us, it's not sensible to have so much formality." She thought, as she smiled at Frau Bürste, that she had let too much distance develop between the two of them. A servant's loyalty and discretion were not automatically bestowed, and if this woman had spoken to others about Ragoczy's visits, it might well be that she did not have the same sense of household that Gudrun had. She resolved to be more concerned in future.

"It *is* a hard thing, getting up every time," Frau Bürste allowed, relaxing back into the chair.

"And there are so many more important things than that," Gudrun said, rather clumsily trying to introduce her inquiries.

"Such as the price of poultry. We'll do well to buy more chickens, Frau Ostneige, and get our eggs and meat from them. Butter isn't up to four billion marks, as it was before, but prices are creeping up again, and that's a fact. If we brought in another dozen hens and half a dozen ducks, we'd be well-provisioned. The price of grain to feed them isn't nearly as high as the cost of eggs." All the while she tapped her pencil on a sheet of paper before her. "Miroslav said he will purchase two cows for us, which will take care of the milk problem, and if we have one of them bred, we'll have veal—"

Gudrun's burst of laughter was more alarmed than amused. "You'll have me a farmwife, Frau Bürste!"

"And why not? There are those who would want to be farmwives in these times." The housekeeper folded her meaty arms. "Meine Frau, I have seen you consumed with worry, and I have watched your resources dwindle and disappear. I know that you have only one pearl necklace left, and that your last diamond went to pay for your unfortunate brother's funeral. You say that you sold his automobile because you had no use for it, but I know it was to get the money from it. It's shameful that you should be in such a state. I've urged you before to farm here, and you have not done so."

"But this is a hunting lodge," Gudrun protested. "I thought I'd made that plain." Her family would be horrified if she converted it, becoming little better than the farmers around her. Her concessions so far were half-hearted.

"There," Frau Bürste soothed as she put the paper aside. "It will wait for another day. It's waited a long time already."

"But we have a cow," Gudrun protested as she tried to sort out what her housekeeper had told her.

"Only one, Frau Ostneige, and she does not provide adequately. Sheep could be grazed here, but there really isn't enough open field for them. A few more pigs, on the other hand, should do very well." She said this cautiously but with real enthusiasm, as if pleased for this first sign of real attention on Gudrun's part.

Gudrun shook her head. "I . . . I can't talk about this just now, Frau Bürste." She took a turn about the kitchen under the housekeeper's puzzled eye. "I have learned something. It troubles me."

"Not more debts from your brother?" Frau Bürste made no effort to hide her disgust. "It was bad enough that he never aided you, but to see you placing yourself in worse circumstances because of that wastrel . . . I won't alter my opinion of him, Meine Frau, so don't give me a reprimand."

How could such sympathy be criticized? Gudrun asked herself. A few words at her sister's house, and rumors might easily spread. She had to be delicate in what she said, knowing that Frau Bürste might not understand that her words had been repeated. "I did not know you felt such loyalty to me."

"Someone must, Meine Frau, and I don't see others doing so." She was at once protective and belligerent, her round face turning rosy.

Gudrun gave her a wan smile. "I'm afraid your championing me has led to some . . . awkwardness."

Frau Bürste blinked. "How?"

"From what Herr Natter has just said to me—"

"Him!" Frau Bürste said with scorn.

"It's all very well to be dissatisfied with him, Frau Bürste," Gudrun said stiffly, "but when it is your own talk that gives rise to his complaints—"

"Complaints? About what?" The housekeeper was on her feet now, her voice turned gruff. "If there is anything said against you, I will know how to deal with it."

"I'm afraid you already have." Gudrun sighed. She had not intended to be so direct, but now the accusation was out, she thought it might be easier.

"I already have? What nonsense is this?" She went on without giving Gudrun the opportunity to reply. "If he has come here bearing tales and said that he had them from me, then he is more despicable than I believed. You find out who he's been talking to, and I will deal with the person."

"But . . . Oh, this is more difficult than I thought!" Gudrun put a hand to her forehead. "Frau Bürste, I know it is not always possible to keep your feelings to yourself, and it is only natural that you should discuss your life here when you visit your sister, but . . ." She faltered, reluctant to go on. "Whatever you say to your sister, you must realize, may be repeated. And this is a small world here, where there are few true secrets. Not that I would wish you to condone immorality or lend your support to a liaison you thought was clandestine" —which would be the opinion of most of the people around her, Gudrun thought—"but remarks may be misinterpreted and—"

"Do you tell me that there has been talk about you, Meine

Frau?" the housekeeper demanded. "Is *that* what has happened to distress you?"

"In part," she hedged. "I gather from what Herr Natter said that he had heard rumors and they disturbed him . . ."

"And he came here to talk about them with you? How dare he?" Frau Bürste came across the kitchen quite swiftly, considering her bulk.

"I asked him that myself," Gudrun confessed shakily.

"I shouldn't wonder," Frau Bürste agreed. "What did he accuse you of?"

Gudrun shrugged. "For the most part he was objecting to my . . . friendship with Franchot Ragoczy. He believes I should . . ."

"Take a countryman for a lover?" Frau Bürste asked, so gently that Gudrun hardly recognized her voice. "Oh, I know he has been here, late at night. And I have seen the way you smile the next morning, as if you were made of light, and joy. You are so beautiful then, Meine Frau, like the world made new."

As a flush stole up her cheeks, Gudrun did not know what caused her the greater embarrassment—knowing that Frau Bürste was aware of her meetings with Ragoczy or the emotion she revealed. "Frau Bürste . . ."

"He was here two nights ago," the housekeeper went on. "His Schloss is closed, but he came back to see you. He left a little before dawn."

Gudrun found she could not speak. She jumped a little when Frau Bürste put her hand on her shoulder.

"You were radiant that morning, and sad."

"Yes," Gudrun said, feeling breathless. "He did come. So that we could say good-bye to each other."

"Did you want him to go?" Frau Bürste asked tenderly.

"Yes. Yes, I did. He is so full of mourning for his daughter, and there is nothing I can do . . ." She lifted her hands helplessly.

"Meine Frau," the housekeeper said, "I have never discussed you with anyone. Not my sister, not the pastor, no one. I've been afraid that if I did, they would sense something and would . . ." Her plain round face creased with consternation. "I have said a little about your brother. My sister believes that I stay on here because I want to marry Miroslav." Her laughter was more painful than any tears would have been. "I let her think that, because . . ." She broke off and with a visible effort moved away from Gudrun. "I should not have said anything. I never intended to. You must forgive me, Frau Ostneige."

For several seconds Gudrun did not trust herself to speak, fearful that she would giggle, and bring more hurt to her housekeeper. How absurd it was for her to address her so formally and yet make such a declaration. "Mein Gott." She closed her eyes.

"I did not intend . . . anything. I have been married, and I was content with my husband. Do not think otherwise. I am not one of those women who turn away from all men. He was kind to me, and we did well together. When he died, I mourned for him. But he was not the sunshine of my life, and there were no children, only those he had by his first wife." She spoke urgently, in a low voice, as if she were afraid to stop.

"Frau Bürste . . ."

"I promise you I will not say anything of this again, but once, Meine Frau, just this once, let me tell you. I will not remind you of this later, and I will not change. But those years I watched you suffer and could do nothing but run the household so that it did not interfere with your life. I saw what became of your husband, and the marriage you did not have. I saw your brother lie and cheat and steal, as charming as a French actor in Berlin. You bore it all, and tried to live as if all was well with you, and it broke my heart. When Ragoczy came, for the first time you were happy. I wish it had been me that made you so, but how could I begrudge you your delights when you had endured as much as you had?"

Gudrun shook her head, wishing she could think of something to say. Was it proper to thank her, and pretend that she misunderstood what Frau Bürste was telling her? Her thoughts flitted like frightened minnows, and she did not know what to do.

"You are lovely as lilies and birch trees," Frau Bürste said, "and because you are slender and pretty, they all think you are weak; they do not know how much strength you have, and what burdens you have carried. I have not been deceived, and I have been astonished by what you have done to save your brother, this house, your life."

"No. Don't," Gudrun protested halfheartedly, too much relieved by what Frau Bürste said to want her to stop. She had not been wholly misunderstood. Someone other than Ragoczy had known how difficult her life was. She smiled at her housekeeper.

"If I were as strong as you are," Frau Bürste went on less

hectically, "I would have enough courage to leave you, but . . . it isn't possible, unless you send me away. I pray you will not. It would be agony to wonder every day how you are and what has become of you, with only Miroslav and Otto to look after you. Miroslav does not care for you, but for the estate, and Otto is . . . old. And old-fashioned." She frowned, and did not continue.

"Old-fashioned. Yes, he certainly is that," Gudrun said in the silence.

"He doted on Maximillian," Frau Bürste added with a touch of resentment.

"Maxl was his favorite. He never recognized how much . . ." Gudrun stopped, belatedly reminding herself that she must not be so open with her staff, not even with Frau Bürste—especially with Frau Bürste—where those of her family and social class were concerned. Yet she had to talk with someone, and Ragoczy was gone, to Wien or Praha or Berlin, and there was no one else she felt she could trust.

Suddenly Frau Bürste mastered herself. "What is the matter with me?" she asked the air. "You must want a cup of coffee and a little tart. I've made some up with apples, and you'll like them, I think." She began to bustle about the kitchen, taking a plate from the cupboard and hurrying into the pantry.

Gudrun had been unable to finish her lunch and doubted that she could face food now, but years of training could not be denied, and she remembered her father telling her about appreciating willing servants. Frau Bürste was not quite that, but Gudrun knew that it would be unkind to refuse what the housekeeper offered her, and so she drew a second chair up to the kitchen table and called out, "You must have some with me, Frau Bürste."

The housekeeper reappeared, her expression startled. "You should not eat here, Meine Frau."

"I'm not interested in sitting alone in the dining room with so much on my mind, and the salons are not set up for serving meals. It's less trouble for all of us if I have my coffee here with you." She was able to explain this pleasantly, and wondered if it might be unkind to create this familiarity with her housekeeper. "This way, we will not be disturbed."

The housekeeper smiled, and there was such pathetic gratefulness in her eyes that Gudrun had to look away from her. Frau Bürste came up to the table with two plates, each with a tart on it, and set them down. "I'll make the coffee, and you can tell me what Herr Natter said. There must be some way to determine how he got his information."

"Yes, I hope there is," Gudrun said politely.

It was more than an hour later that Gudrun left the kitchen, and her brow was furrowed in thought. She made her way through the halls toward the part of Wolkighügel that had once been designated the servants' wing. It was largely unused now, for only Otto kept quarters there. For once, Gudrun did not look forward to seeing the old man, and try as she would, she could think of no kind way to question him. She hoped that he might be busy somewhere in the house, and provide her an excuse to delay her conversation for a day or an afternoon or half an hour. But advancing age had taken its toll on the old servant, and it had become his custom to spend two hours resting in the afternoon, and he opened the door to his rooms on Gudrun's second knock.

He has so little hair, she thought as she stepped through the door. When had it gone? He was always a little bald, but now his pate was shiny, without even a trace of down to remind him of the hair he had once possessed in such abundance. "Otto? May I speak with you for a moment, please?"

Otto beamed at her and motioned her to a chair. "Ach, ja," he said, his slippered feet making scuffing sounds on the threadbare carpet. "Of course, Rudi. At any time."

Gudrun tried to respond to this fondness and discovered that she could not. Her hands were knotted at her sides and she could not look at Otto without dreading what he would tell her. "You are feeling well?" she inquired, buying herself a little time.

"Of course, of course. The knees are a bit stiff in the morning, and my hands, sometimes, but that is expected at my age, eh?" His manner was jocular but his watery eyes were wary. "I'm doing quite well, Rudi."

"I'm pleased to hear it," she said inanely as she sat down.

"But that isn't why you're here, is it?" he said as he sat down opposite her. He gave her an anxious smile. "You haven't been back here in . . . well, it is more than a year, of course."

"That long?" Gudrun asked, as much of herself as of Otto.

"At least. You brought me my supper when I had that bad cold, but for the most part, you leave me to myself. Maxl used to come and talk to me," he added with a sense of injury. "He'd come here of an evening and tell me of his activities, and what was in store for Deutschland. He had real faith in the Vaterland, not like some of the others who've forgotten how much the world owes to us." He had found his pipe and was stuffing tobacco into it in an absentminded fashion.

"I didn't know that Maximillian talked with you," Gudrun said quietly.

"Of course he did. He could not talk to you, he told me that many times. But he knew that I respect the old ways." He nodded repeatedly and lit a match, holding it out before bringing it up to his pipe.

"And you both thought I do not?" Gudrun felt hurt, and wished she could find words to defend herself. "I have tried to live as my father and husband wished me to."

"Your father and husband never wanted you to befriend Jews or foreigners," was the crusty retort that Otto gave without apology.

"You mean the Schnaubels and Graf Ragoczy?" Gudrun demanded, angry with herself for feeling such a child in Otto's presence.

"Among others," Otto answered as he drew on his pipe. "You're a woman, and you've lacked guidance, so it's understandable that you would not . . ."

This was precisely the same sort of infuriating nonsense that Gudrun had heard from Konrad Natter, and she had no patience with it. "It is not for you to advise me, Otto. I am responsible for myself. If you believe this of me, you should have asked to be released from your duties here and given notice."

"But someone had to look after you," Otto protested, his weak old eyes unexpectedly moist. "And I promised Maxl—"

"Promised Maxl?" Gudrun asked, a coldness coming over her. "When? What did you promise my brother?"

Otto avoided her eyes. "He wanted to be sure you were safe. He was worried about you. I know you think he did not know what you were going through, but he had more important things on his mind. He had to attend to them, for your sake as well as his. Your family honor required it." As he became more defensive, his voice got louder, so that he was nearly shouting when he finished speaking.

"My family honor required that Maximillian kill himself? That he waste our money until there was nothing left? How does that benefit the family, Otto? Tell me." She stared at him, thinking that he was a stranger to her, a man who had come from the past when she was a child, indulged and careless. He had never seen her as anything else, she recognized that now, and had loved her brother because he was the son of the family, endowed with all virtues by that fact.

"That was something else. The Bruderschaft has its rules, Rudi, and Maxl was not one to take his vows lightly." His tone was becoming surly: Gudrun had cast doubt on his beloved Maxl.

"The Bruderschaft required that he kill himself." She wondered if Otto had become senile and had lost himself in imagined memories and dreams. One of her uncles had done that, always thinking that it was time to lead a battalion against the Poles. Everyone had politely ignored him, allowing him his fancies when they were not too inconvenient. She decided she must do the same with Otto. "Did he tell you why?"

"It was the nature of his vow. Those of the Bruderschaft serve high purpose, and their goals are the most exalted. Any man who does not believe that he has lived up to the demands of the Bruderschaft has an obligation to erase his failure from their company. Maxl always demanded such perfection of himself . . ." He wiped his nose with an old gray handkerchief.

"This is the Thule Bruderschaft? The one that Eckart leads?" She had always assumed that the organization was typical of so many men's brotherhoods, an excuse for privacy and casual debauchery.

"They are great men, those of the Bruderschaft. Maxl was worthy of them, but could not see the greatness in himself." Otto huddled back in his chair, his shoulder toward Gudrun. "He told me that you did not understand, Rudi. He explained it all to me."

"Perhaps if he had explained it to me as well, I might have been more lenient with him," she suggested shortly. What was it that her brother would confide to a servant but not to his sister? She sighed, and Otto, hearing it, was more kindly disposed to her.

"There, Rudi. I know it's been hard without him, but you will learn. I will help you. . . ." He drew deeply on his pipe. "The Bruderschaft will watch over you."

Gudrun narrowed her eyes. "Herr Natter and Herr Rauch are in the Bruderschaft, aren't they?"

"Both of them," Otto answered with pride. "And both of them respect Maxl. They were the ones the Bruderschaft sent to discuss his vow with him. They were with him that last day, trying to dissuade him from his disastrous act." He fingered his loosely knotted tie and nodded two or three times.

"How do you know?" Gudrun managed to keep her voice

level as she asked, but her thoughts screamed in her mind. Those two men had been with Maximillian before he killed himself. What had they said to him? What had made him write to her as he had done? She knew better than to ask Otto, but the malaise that had been growing within her became a deep-rooted anguish.

"Maxl told me. I saw them." Otto responded gruffly. "I went to the gamekeeper's cottage to speak with Maxl, and he said they had left."

But had they? The question rose unbidden in Gudrun's mind, shutting out the confusion. "Did he say anything else?"

This time Otto hesitated before he spoke. "He told me that I should . . . look after you, because you were . . . easily misguided."

"Unlike himself?" Gudrun could not restrain herself from asking.

"You don't understand," Otto declared once more. "You did not pay attention to anything he told you, and you would not let him show you how you were compromising yourself and your family and your country."

"Which he was not." She wanted to scream at Otto, to tell him that it was Maximillian's profligacy that had brought them to the edge of ruin. Yet everything she had been taught since childhood weighed against this. Her hands trembled as she asked, "What have you done that he asked you to do, Otto?"

"The Bruderschaft . . ." He broke off. "Someone has to be responsible for you, and Maxl had the promise of the Bruderschaft that they would keep you from harm." He sat straighter in his chair. "He entrusted me with the task of informing the Bruderschaft of your activities."

"What!" Gudrun had expected this, but now that the words were spoken, her indignation and resentment flared within her. "You dared to discuss me with those men?"

"Rudi—" Otto began in his most conciliating manner.

But Gudrun gave him no opportunity to continue. "You spoke to Herr Natter and Herr Rauch about me? Did you? And you live here, accepting my wages which I have sacrificed so much to give you? You have eaten the food on my table, and then have told others about my life?"

"You're not thinking, Rudi . . ." Otto said uncertainly.

"I believe you are right. I have assumed that you were loyal to me, and all the while you have been—"

"Rudi . . . this isn't like you . . ." He reached out to pat her arm as he had done since she was four.

She moved back from him. "No! You do not know what I am like. You don't admit what Maximillian was like. You were seduced by him, doting fool that you are, and you have been taken in by vile men!" She got out of the chair. "Konrad Natter was here today, presuming to tell me that I must give up my friends because he did not approve of them. That happened because of you, Otto. You were the one who carried tales to them."

"Maxl instructed me—" he began, then quailed as she rounded on him.

"Maxl! *Maxl!* MAXL!" she screamed; then her voice became tense and low. "Maxl had no right to do that, and you had no right to act as you have done. I tell you, Otto, I will not tolerate it. When Herr Natter informs me that I have been indiscreet with a man he does not approve of, I will not have it!"

"But Ragoczy came here at night, Rudi—"

"I am Frau Ostneige to you, Otto. I am not Rudi. Rudi was a child, and I have not been a child for a quarter of a century. You never saw this, and I, stupid creature that I am, found it charming that you still remembered me as I had been." She went to the door. "Since you have chosen to give your respect and fealty to Natter and Rauch and the rest of the Thule Bruderschaft, you may get your keep from them as well."

"What?" The old man was astonished; his faded blue eyes were huge with it.

"Tonight, Otto, I want you gone." Why, she asked herself, was it so much worse that Otto had betrayed her instead of Frau Bürste or Miroslav? Was it that she had known him all her life and readily believed all she had been told of a servant's fidelity?

"But . . ." He stared at her, one hand reaching out.

"Tonight. No later." As she pulled the door open, she heard Otto cry out, "But I have always been at Wolkighügel. I have always served Altbrunnen."

"No. You stopped serving me and my family when you spoke to Konrad Natter." There was no satisfaction in closing the door on him, only a desolation that bit into her with remote fury as she made her way out of the servants' wing.

Text of a letter from Helmut Rauch to Hermann Göring.

*Nymphenburg*
*October 29, 1926*

*My dear Herr Göring:*

*I was honored to have your letter of the 24th, and have made all haste to answer once I had assembled the material on hand and added what I could learn from others, so that you could have as complete an assessment as possible. I quite agree that it is a most shocking thing and it is most wise of you to insist on this investigation. If there is any way in which I may be of further assistance to you, I hope that you will call on me at once so that I will be able to give whatever aid you require.*

*I have been to the Wolf und Rabe, which, as I am sure you know, is a workingmen's tavern in Geltbeutel Strasse. I spoke with the landlord there, and he provided me with a description of the hochgeborn visitor which matches that of Graf Franchot Ragoczy. He tells me that the man came to his tavern and asked about our SA men who met in his back room off the courtyard. He indicated that he wished to speak with them privately, and bribed the landlord handsomely.*

*You are as aware as I am what became of Vortag, Abscheu, Recht, Krümmer, and Grube. Heinz Vortag left the SA meeting when they were dismissed, and his men came back to their tavern with him, as they had done so many times before. Vincenz Grube was planning to go to his sister's house when he had finished having a drink or two with his friends. His sister said that he often stayed out drinking quite late and thought nothing when he did not arrive by eleven at night. Romuald Abscheu was supposed to stay with Krümmer, and neither of them were missed until long after they had been killed. Recht worked as a railroad dispatcher, and when he did not arrive for*

*work, his supervisor informed SA headquarters, since the
man is also a member of our party. It was shortly after
ten in the morning when the police asked the landlord to
open his back room.*

*It is the opinion of the investigating officers that Ragoczy
hired men to kill the five men because he believed that
they were responsible for the accidental death of his daughter last May 31, during the riot. He had told the police
that he had witnessed the killing himself and that it was
deliberate murder. The officers, allowing for his overwrought state, listened to his complaint then, and later
questioned the SA officers who had been in charge of riot
maneuvers. They assured the police that the girl's death
could not possibly have been the result of SA or other
NSDAP activity, and so they quietly dropped the matter.
It has been assumed that Ragoczy did not believe that the
police had done a proper investigation, and stated formally that he believed the police to be biased.*

*From what I have been able to discover, Ragoczy sent his
manservant to various workingmen's taverns to listen to
what was being said, and in two or three weeks had
happened upon the Wolf und Rabe, where he was told
about Vortag's group meeting in the back room. Being a
cautious man, he verified this for himself, along with the
evenings Vortag's men were to be found there, and then he
placed this information in the hands of his employer, who
hired thugs to attack our men.*

*We have not yet been able to find out which group of
bullies did the work, but the police have determined that
there were at least six men involved, and they have said
that they assume the crime occurred in the following way:
Ragoczy arrived at the tavern, ostensibly alone, but actually accompanied by his hired men, who waited in the
street while Ragoczy convinced the landlord to give him
access to the back room. The landlord, seeing one unarmed man, somewhat undersized, did not anticipate trouble and agreed, after the bribe I have mentioned, to let the
man have entrance. Ragoczy proceeded into the courtyard, where he summoned his men, and they went into
the back room to wait for Vortag and his four SA members.
There was a great deal of noise from the tavern, and for
that reason the battle between Ragoczy's toughs and the
SA fighters was not readily apparent. The landlord informed the police and myself that the taproom is often*

*quite rowdy, and it has been assumed that the noise was covered by the singing and talking that occupy most of the patrons of the tavern, some of whom are Spartacists and might well have agreed to aid Ragoczy in concealing this atrocity, for Ragoczy has admitted that he spent a great deal of time in Russia before and during the Great War. It would not amaze me if I should learn that many of them had been bribed, as the landlord was, to be more than usually active that night in order to give him the chance to conduct his attack uninterrupted.*

*I will not dwell on the hideous state of the bodies; the police report does that concisely enough, and there is nothing I can add to their photographs and records that would provide information of any particular use. The policemen who saw the back room have told me that they are convinced that the attack was well-planned and executed—what an ironic word, under the circumstances— by men of unusual ferocity. One of them must have been quite large, because it would not be possible for a small man, or men, to inflict such massive wounds.*

*You ask my opinion of Graf Ragoczy: I must admit that I have not met him many times, and foreigners are not always easily understood by our more logical, direct race; still, I have formed a number of impressions of the man, which, in confidence, of course, I will be pleased to eluci- date. Ragoczy, as you probably know, has a title of Graf from the old Austro-Hungarian Empire, although he apparently is not part of the family by that name who were directly removed from power in the Eighteenth Century. He has explained that he is a member of the older branch of that family, the first Prinzes of Transylvania. He himself does not use the title Prinz, but could do so with propriety, should he choose to do so. He appears to be in his middle forties, about one and two-thirds meters tall or a shade more, of trim form but built on robust lines. He has pronounced cheekbones, very unnerving dark eyes, dark curling hair that shows an auburn highlight, and a certain wryness to his countenance that is not always pleasant. He gives himself the air of a man who knows a great many secrets. I have been told that his strength is fairly formidable, but have seen no demonstration of this for myself. He is reputed to be something of a violinist and pianist, but again, I have not heard him play, and so have no judgment to offer in that regard. His manners have been called good, but he is much too haughty and sardonic for my taste. It is the old way, I suppose, and when I see it so clearly, I can fully understand why it was the old alliances were doomed to failure.*

*Yes, I do believe that Ragoczy could be a dangerous man, but whether he is or not has not been determined. A man as wealthy as he is must always be reckoned with, for he will have the capacity to purchase many things, such as misguided loyalties and the gratitude of others. I have no definite proof that he has done so, but I believe it possible that he may have aided several of the Jewish families in the area, for what reason, I cannot say. He is often capricious.*

*He has, I believe, formed a romantic alliance with a neighbor woman, but I doubt it has progressed too far. I do not agree with the lady's late brother that the two are actually lovers, because it often seemed to me that he— the brother—would take the most extreme position as a matter of course. I do believe that this lady is greatly interested in Ragoczy, but in large part because she has many pressing problems and he has the capacity to relieve the most pressing. I cannot believe that this woman would prefer a Jew-loving foreigner to a proper Deutscher, yet it was the thing her brother feared. In time I hope to demonstrate that her brother was incorrect, but that is not your immediate concern, and does not materially affect Ragoczy.*

*At the time I was employed at BKK, I was somewhat familiar with Ragoczy's investments and sources of wealth, which were fairly extensive. While there are many investments in this country, he has also other sources of revenue in other countries. I am aware that he maintains an apartment in Paris and fairly lavish quarters in Venice. He has paid for telephone lines to his Schloss, and the building is electrically wired and powered by his own generator, which reveals his extravagance as well as anything could.*

*You suggest that his family may have connections with the Bruderschaft, and I am aware that there have been Ragoczys in our Lodges before, but Dietrich's assumption that this man is in some mysterious way connected with the great fraud of the Eighteenth Century, to Comte de Saint-Germain, I can only say that I find such an idea absurd. Ragoczy may have the address of a courtier, but I doubt he has the intellect or the interest in occult teachings. He has never shown the least curiosity about the Thule Bruderschaft, and in fact has been faintly condemning of the Gesellschaft. He is clearly a product of Nineteenth-Century materialism and rationality.*

*I will be happy and honored to discuss any aspect of this further with you at the march on the twelfth of next month. But let me take the liberty of saying that I very much doubt that Ragoczy merits so much attention. I believe that my life and mind are being put to finer use in the cause of National Socialism than in the investigation of an exiled Hungarian nobleman whose time has long since passed. Should you decide that you require me to investigate further, of course I will do so, and with all the attention I can bring to such a task. However, I doubt that there will be much gained from such activity. It would be one thing to find his hired thugs and let the police deal with them, but the man himself, that is another matter. It is my understanding that he wishes to leave Deutschland, and I believe we should allow him to do that, without hindrance. It is always possible to seize his funds invested here for our own uses, which is doubtless part of your plan. Beyond that, I believe we may count ourselves lucky to be rid of him, as he might prove to be a thorn in our side, criticizing and in general casting doubts on our high purpose. You must not think that I would consider him a serious threat to us, but he might be an embarrassment, particularly since he is still convinced that Heinz Vortag and his unfortunate men were responsible for his daughter's death. By the way, I am sure you know that the child was his ward, not his daughter, and I doubt that he will carry the matter too far, as she was not his actual flesh and blood. Those of noble background often find excuses to harry those they imagine to be their social inferiors. This does not reflect on you, Herr Göring, of course, for you have shown yourself doubly worthy of the respect due the hochgeborn, for you have achieved that state of mind where your thoughts are educated and elevated, at the same time demonstrating a genuine appreciation of all that makes the Teutons the master race of the world. Such perceptions cannot be expected of a man with Ragoczy's back-*

*ground. All those Eastern Europeans are such bastard
races that they are quite hopeless.*

*With my full regard and esteem, and in fellowship for the
Thule Gesellschaft and Bruderschaft, I remain*

> *Most sincerely at your service,*
> *Helmut Rauch*

## 4

Scrofulous patches of dirty snow littered the street, and
above the darkened baroque roofs, the sun was rising, a reddened bruise in livid clouds. Off to the right a boat whistle
hooted at the dawn, a forlorn sound in the cold new day.

Ragoczy paused in front of the elaborate and old-fashioned
front of his house on the east side of Salzgries, looking up at
the pillars, in need of paint. He started up the steps, then
turned around. To his left was the tower of Ruprechskirche,
and beyond it, magnificent in the distance, the tall, narrow
spire of Stephanskirche. On his right, the less imposing roof
and spire of Santa Maria am Gestade. He went to his door and
rapped sharply twice.

Almost three minutes later a sleepy servant came to the
door. He stared at his employer, for Ragoczy was still in full
evening clothes, with the Order of Saint Stephen of Hungary
fastened to a wide scarlet sash. His long silk-lined cloak was
opened and he had lost his top hat. "I'm back," he said as he
came through the door.

"Ja, Mein Herr," the servant agreed dully. "I see that you
are."

"Where is Roger? Tell him that I wish to see him at once, in
my room." He turned away toward the stairs, but paused
when he realized that the servant was still in the entry hall, a
frown deepening on his brow. "Well? What is it, man?"

The servant flushed. "Nothing, Mein Herr. We were told
that you might be out quite late, but . . ."

"I don't usually give servants an account of my actions,"
Ragoczy snapped, then added flippantly, "I have been at the
opera."

Both Ragoczy and the footman knew that the opera had been over several hours before, but neither pointed this out.

"I did not mean . . ." the footman began, stammering as he tried to meet Ragoczy's ironic gaze.

"Of course not," Ragoczy relented urbanely before continuing on up the stairs to his quarters. As he walked, he removed his cufflinks, holding them in one hand as he went into his private chamber. His head ached and fatigue hung on him like a sodden garment. Slowly he removed the scarlet sash that crossed his shoulder and chest, thinking it marked the path of the proper katana test cut. He had had such a sword once, but had lost it on that miserable voyage out from Spain. With care he unfastened the elaborate gold-and-red centered sunburst of a badge, taking care not to snag the jewel-tipped silver rays on his brocaded cummerbund. When, he wondered, was the last time he had worn the full regalia of the Order? It had been the middle of the last century, certainly no later than 1860. There had been a gala at the Schönbrunn Palast and the Empress Elizabeth had attended, her glorious dark hair cascading in loose curls down her back, her jeweled bodice emphasizing her tiny waist. He had seen her once after her son's tragic suicide at Mayerling. All the fire had gone out of her then, but she had been curious about Ragoczy, and had spoken to him for an hour or so before departing again for Greece. Ragoczy set the large badge and scarlet sash aside and dropped his cufflinks onto his dressing table.

He had drawn on a black silk dressing gown when Roger knocked once and entered the room. "Yes?" said Ragoczy without turning.

"You wish to bathe?" His voice was wholly neutral, but his blue eyes surveyed Ragoczy with care.

"It would be a good idea," Ragoczy said in a remote way. "I probably stink of perfume. One of the women kept dousing the room with it."

Roger was wise enough to inquire no further; he picked up the clothes Ragoczy had laid across the chaise.

"It was a gambling establishment, not a whorehouse," Ragoczy said sardonically. "Not that there weren't women available, but they were not the primary interest. I saw one man," he went on dreamily, "with three women accompanying him. All of them were gorgeous creatures—very lean and glossy—and he paid them no more mind than he did the furniture until he had lost most of his money. Then he fell on them: he had his shirt off before they were quite out of the room. What, I wonder, would Doktor Freud make of that?"

Pausing in the act of hanging up the suit in the armoire, Roger said, "Were you lucky?"

"I didn't play much. There's no excitement in it for me anymore, and without the excitement"—he set aside his nail file—"what reason is there to risk money on the falling of a card or a ball?"

"You were out quite late," Roger observed.

"Yes. Yes I was," Ragoczy said, looking at his manservant. "Do you worry about me, old friend? It isn't necessary."

"Isn't it?" Roger asked, without expecting an answer.

"I could visit every gambling hall in Wien and it would not matter, even if I lost every night. I won't do it: losing bores me as much as winning does." He wore a gold aviator's watch on his left wrist, and now he removed it. "Do you remember Paris? The way Claudia's husband strove to ruin himself at the tables? I never understood how he could keep at it as he did. That was devotion of no mean order. He truly worked at his ruin. Poor Gervaise."

"Your bath will be ready in ten minutes," Roger said from the door, not quite able to keep his tone even.

"Thank you, Roger," Ragoczy told him. "But for the sake of all the forgotten gods, don't treat me as if I were an invalid or slightly mad."

"Of course not, my master," Roger said quietly. Both men were speaking Latin now, and Roger added in that language, "It would do no good, in any case."

"You know me too well."

"And that is no advantage on occasions such as this," Roger responded as he pulled the door closed. He had not intended to speak bitterly, for he felt no anger, only sorrow. Long ago he had realized that Ragoczy would never accustom himself to the pain of loss, that no matter how often he saw death, he would never grow used to it, would never surrender to stoic indifference. Roger himself had learned a philosophic acceptance but had never been able to give it to Ragoczy: he had instead to watch while mourning ate its way through his master like slow poison. Roger hurried along the hall, not wishing to give himself the excuse to speak to Ragoczy again for a little while, until he was composed once more, and able to speak to him without increasing his master's pain.

Before entering the bathroom, he stopped to collect two

large, thick towels from the linen closet, then began the task of setting up the new electric heater Ragoczy had bought the week after he arrived in Wien. The little wire coils were soon glowing red and gave off the odor of burning dust. Roger disliked the thin, acrid smell, but Ragoczy ignored it, reminding Roger once that the streets of Rome had smelled far worse most of the time. As the bath filled with hot water, Roger set out brushes and soap and a razor, planning to shave Ragoczy as he bathed.

"Almost ready, I see," Ragoczy said a few minutes later as he came through the door. He caught sight of the shaving gear. "You're undoubtedly right." His hand moved over his chin, feeling the stubble. "It grows slowly, but it does grow."

Roger turned off the taps and stepped aside as Ragoczy got out of his dressing gown. "You will find soap, a sponge, and—"

"Yes, as always," Ragoczy interrupted him, the affection he felt for his manservant robbing the words of any sting. The hot water rose around him as he stepped into the tub. "They haven't really got the knack of this sort of thing yet. Rome was the best time for baths. My private bath at Villa Ragoczy was almost five meters on a side and over a meter deep, not like this cockleshell." He leaned back in the hot water, self-consciously holding the sponge across the wide swath of white scars that crossed his abdomen. "Well, it is relaxing, just the same."

Roger filled the sink with water and put the bar of soap into it. While he busied himself with working up a thick lather, he said, "There were two callers last night, while you were out."

"Oh?" Ragoczy sank lower in the tub so that just his face protruded from the water. Distorted by the water and the confines of the tub, Roger's voice, as he went on, sounded alien and sinister.

"Yes. They came about seven-thirty, in an automobile with Bavarian tags. Balas admitted them and explained that you were out for the evening. They then asked to see me. I spoke with them briefly."

"What did they want, these men in a Bavarian auto?"

"Not what they said they wanted," Roger replied with asperity. "They told me that they represented a firm that wished to purchase Schloss Saint-Germain. I explained that they would have to speak with you, but that I doubted it was possible you would sell." He had enough lather now, and he worked the stiff-bristled brush into it. "If you would, my master, a little higher?"

"Of course," Ragoczy said, accommodating him, chin tilted back. "There are a few times I truly miss being able to see my reflection. Whenever I'm forced to shave myself, I long for a glimpse of my jaw, to be certain I've done the job properly. What peculiar forms vanity takes."

"You might grow a beard again," Roger suggested as he lathered Ragoczy's face.

"And worry about the trim of it? When beards are in fashion again, I might." He fell silent as Roger's finger touched his face.

"These men," Roger went on as he took the first swipe with the razor, "did not believe me when I said you were out attending the opera. They waited in their automobile for nearly an hour after they left the house. They were clearly keeping watch on the place."

"Interesting," Ragoczy murmured.

"They promised to return today to speak with you. I did not tell them when they might expect to find you at home. One of them was reading the *Völkischer Beobachter*, and the other had an interesting lapel pin, with a swastika on it." He wiped the foam from the razor's edge aganst a hand towel draped over his knee.

"The Sturmalteilung, do you think, or the Thule Bruderschaft?"

"The Thule Bruderschaft, I suspect," Roger said, resuming his expert shaving. "The SA would not be so subtle."

"You're undoubtedly right," Ragoczy sighed when he could move his chin again. "So it isn't just the men at the back of the tavern, then, but something more."

"They might not have linked you to those deaths," Roger said, but without much conviction.

"You don't believe that any more than I do," Ragoczy said, closing his eyes.

"They probably are not aware that you were the one who killed the men," Roger said with some force. He concentrated on Ragoczy's firm chin, taking care to pull the skin taut before grazing it with the razor.

"But they have associated me with the killing by now. The landlord could describe me, and it's likely that the police have helped them." His voice hardened. "You may be sure the SA will have help from the police; they're all cut from the same cloth."

Roger, sadly, could not and did not deny this. "If these men are Thule, they will be dangerous to you."

"So they will. And I to them." He turned his head so that Roger could work more easily, and the hot water swirled around his neck and chest.

"What precautions will you wish to take?" Roger inquired when he had finished shaving Ragoczy and was gathering up his equipment.

"I don't know yet. Ask me in an hour." He had reached for the soap and had begun to lather the sponge.

"They may have returned in an hour," Roger reminded him.

"They may be watching us right now," Ragoczy countered. "Whatever the situation, we have the advantage. We know that we are their target. They don't see that as advantageous, but that's all to the good." He began to scrub himself vigorously.

"What clothes do you want me to lay out?" Roger asked from the door.

"I think I will rest for a while," he answered, splashing the soap off his arms. "This afternoon, I will need a dinner jacket, but not the tails. I am attending an informal concert at Madame Ilse's. Silk shirt, with the pin tucks, and the onyx cufflinks and studs, I think; the rubies are too flamboyant." His smile was mocking. "I will want to be wakened at four."

"At four," Roger repeated, striving to conceal his despair.

"I will go out at six, and I'm not sure when I'll be back." He slid back in the tub again, immersing himself once more.

"What about protection?" Roger asked, hoping that Ragoczy would not be so reckless as to leave the house unaccompanied.

"If these men are circumspect, they will not come after me at once," Ragoczy said with unconcern. "And if they do, they will discover their folly."

"My master—" Roger tried to protest.

"You, on the other hand," Ragoczy continued over him, "will have to be fairly cautious. I want you to go to the rail station around noon."

"For any particular purpose?" Roger inquired resignedly.

"You will purchase tickets: we are leaving for Praha tomorrow. I want to be on the first train out." He gave Roger an ironic smile. "No matter how I feel, old friend, I will not endanger you—you should know that after so many years."

"I am not thinking of my safety, my master," Roger said quietly just before he closed the door.

Ragoczy let his breath out slowly as he lay back in the hot

water. The worst of it, he told himself, was that Roger was right; he was being careless, taking chances that were foolish. Did he believe he could continue to do so with impunity? His nearly four thousand years taught him that he could not. He exposed himself for no reason other than he might be discovered. What was he doing but tempting fate, pushing his luck to the extreme? He shook his head. Was it only that he could not surrender his pride long enough to die the true death, and so he sought it at the hands of others? Or was it more complicated than that? Did he want someone to pull him back from the brink? "I don't know," he said aloud, and the tiled bathroom echoed his perplexity. The night before, he had gone to the bed of a drunken woman in the vain hope that he would imbibe her inebriation as they made love. He had known it was not possible, and the encounter had gone badly, for there had been neither the ephemeral satisfaction of desire nor the oblivion of alcohol. Ragoczy put his hand to his head, astonished afresh at his own absurdity. Why, after so long, did he think that he would be able to share that woman's—or anyone else's—stupor? It was another example of his enchantment with risk. At least he had sense enough to know that he must leave Wien, though he doubted that Praha would be much of an improvement. And from there, where would he go? He laughed silently, jeeringly. Perhaps he would go to Berlin, try the ultimate hazard. Then he would be too caught up in his own danger to think any more of Laisha.

Once out of the tub, he wrapped himself in the larger towel, then bent over the sink to shampoo his hair. As he rubbed most of the moisture from the loose, dark curls that would be groomed into neat waves as current fashion demanded, he stared at the empty mirror, thinking that the movement of the towel would startle anyone who saw it hanging in vacant air, buffing at nothing. It had taken many centuries for him to be able to look into reflecting surfaces, and considerable time after that not to suffer from vertigo when he did. Now he regarded the whole thing as unimportant—a phenomenon that offered a private amusement, though there were no mirrors in his private chambers.

His bed, in its austere alcove, was high and hard; a thin mattress laid over a chest containing his native earth. Ragoczy did not remove his dressing gown, but pulled it more tightly around him before leaning back, drawing up the thin black coverlet, and releasing himself to sleep.

"My master," Roger said again as he touched Ragoczy's shoulder.

"What time is it?" Ragoczy asked as he came abruptly awake. The curious, almost frightening dream shattered and fled, leaving Ragoczy with nothing more than an underlying disquiet he could not account for.

"Ten minutes after four. The two men were here at one and have promised to be back by five." He did not emphasize anything he said, but the warning was clear.

"Then I will have to be away before then. What did you tell them?" He was already rising, running one hand through his hair, his thoughts turning gratefully to the two hostile men from Bavaria.

"That you needed time to recover from last night's adventures, and that you were not civil when disturbed." Roger took the dressing gown Ragoczy held out to him.

"Very wise. And the tickets?" He began to dress in the clothes Roger had set out for him.

"To Praha? The train leaves at six in the morning." He thought for a moment, then added, "I don't know if I completely succeeded in eluding them. I think I did, but if they ask any questions at the rail station, they will discover where we are bound."

"That would be a risk in any case," Ragoczy said unconcernedly as he set the studs in his shirt.

"I have made no reservations in Praha . . ." he went on, hoping Ragoczy would tell him what he wished.

"Good, for we are not going there." He smiled at Roger's hastily-concealed confusion. "We are continuing on to Berlin."

"Berlin?" Roger looked at Ragoczy in disbelief. "There are two men from Germany who are attempting to find you, and they do not mean you good. Do you understand that?"

"Yes," Ragoczy said, his fine brows raising. "I would rather settle the matter."

"Then why not go back to München?" But even as he asked the question, he realized Ragoczy's reason, and wished he had not spoken.

"That is not possible," Ragoczy said somewhat dryly as he began to knot the velvet bow around his neck.

"I did not . . ." Roger faltered.

"I know." Ragoczy's vulnerable compassion filled his countenance, and he met Roger's blue eyes with his dark ones. "If you wish to leave, you may. But do not try to protect me from this."

"And if you should die?" Roger asked sharply.

"You know what to do," was Ragoczy's laconic answer. He bent to pick up his dress shoes of shining patent leather. "Have our luggage ready by midnight, if you decide to travel with me."

"By midnight, very well." Roger's expression was impassive, and he resolved not to betray his concern again.

"Put the cases in the dustbin in the pantry, then dress in workman's clothes and take the dustbin away. If those SA or Thule men are the snobs I think they are, they will pay no attention to you. A plumber's case should be sufficient disguise. I will join you at the rail station half an hour before the train leaves. I'll need a change of clothes." He indicated his finery. "This will hardly do for the train."

"Hardly," Roger agreed, attempting now to match Ragoczy's urbanity.

"Excellent," Ragoczy approved.

"And what will I tell the staff?" Roger asked a bit later as Ragoczy reached for his fur-collared black evening coat.

"Undoubtedly they have heard about the two men. A few dire hints should be sufficient." He picked up a brush and began to set his hair in order. "Blind men do this so well, but I am always left with the dread that I haven't got it right. Perhaps it's because I can see everything but myself."

Roger, who had discussed this with Ragoczy on various occasions for nearly two thousand years, said nothing. His glance wandered over the room, selecting those items he would pack and those he would leave behind. Ragoczy had not kept a house in Berlin since the time of Frederick the Great, and that meant that he would have to provide certain of Ragoczy's particular necessities, including enough of his native earth to render him comfortable.

"If there is any difficulty, send Balas to Madame Ilse's before eleven, with the message that there is trouble with the drains. It might be wise to spill some water in the cellar, so that the staff will not be surprised at such a message. If I have not heard from you by eleven, I will go to the rail station at five." He adjusted his cuffs and brushed his sleeves. He was very elegant now in his long coat. All that was lacking was a hat, and he took a fur cap from the armoire, placing it carefully on his head.

"There may be snow tonight," Roger mentioned as Ragoczy started toward the door.

"I'll keep that in mind." He inclined his head very slightly. "Until tomorrow, old friend."

Roger answered absently, already gathering up clothes and preparing them for the trunk he had so recently unpacked.

Ragoczy left his house by the back door and made his way down a narrow alley to an even narrower passage that led to Franz-Josefs-Kai fronting the Donau Kanal. It would take him a bit out of his way, but he was fairly confident that his departure would then be unnoticed by the two men whose automobile had Bavarian tags. He walked quickly, finding the icy air to his liking. He passed a group of Czech women, probably residents of the Zinskasernen from their look and manner, hastening toward the Marienbrücke and chattering among themselves. One of the women curtsied to him, and another crossed herself. Ragoczy favored them with a negligent bow before striding away from them.

Madame Ilse's establishment was not in the most elegant part of the city, but it was near enough to the Theater an der Wien, the Musikverein, and the Ringstrasse that it was readily accessible to those who found its fervid appeal more compelling than the refined pleasures of concerts and operas. There were certain concessions, however, and the concert this evening was one of them. Those who needed to salve their consciences with a nod to culture could spend an hour or so listening to chamber music before taking a place at the gaming tables or retiring to one of the very private rooms with a compliant young lady for company.

"Herr Graf," said the butler as he took Ragoczy's coat and gave it into the care of a lesser servant. "A pleasure to see you again, if I may say so, Mein Herr."

"You may say whatever you like," Ragoczy responded good-naturedly as he handed over his fur cap, not with some regret, for it was warm and he would be leaving it behind. He strolled into the grand salon, where Madame Ilse herself rose from the bargelike sofa where she usually held court, and came toward Ragoczy with open arms. "Herr Ragoczy! How kind of you, Graf." She spoke Wienerisch, as everyone in the city did, but with an underlying trace of her Silesian origins. She was an ample woman somewhere between thirty and forty, with an enviable complexion, pale blonde hair, and avaricious eyes. As she linked her arm through Ragoczy's, she favored him with an enthusiastic smile. "You will enjoy our entertainment tonight, I think: it is something uncommon."

"I am all anticipation, Madame," he assured her with unfelt gallantry.

"And later, perhaps, you will wish to avail yourself of something more . . . exclusive in the way of amusement."

"As you say, perhaps," Ragoczy murmured as he returned her to her sofa and bowed over her ringed hand. He made an unhurried circuit of the grand salon, then entered the largest of the gaming rooms, remembering the nights he had walked through his own establishment in Paris. The styles were different, but the underlying frenzy was not. He had encountered it before, from Nineveh to Wu-An to Namur to Tlaxcala to Paris. Only the stakes changed: the lust remained the same. He purchased a reasonable number of chips from the cashier then went to the rouge-et-noir table.

"So you are back," said a fair-haired young woman about half an hour later.

Ragoczy looked up. "I am waiting for the music to start."

"I've heard that before, but they always stay at the tables," she said, taking the empty chair beside him. "The concert begins in ten minutes, and you're winning." The ancient cynicism was at variance with her fresh features and lithe body, but was clearly the most genuine thing about her.

"In bon punto," he said, rising and tossing a chip across the green baize to the dealer.

"But you're winning," the woman protested even as she took his arm firmly.

"And another time I will lose. Why does that bother you?" He tweaked her fair curls, sighing. "My dear, would you be terribly offended if I asked you to bring me one of your associates who has dark hair?" Those light curls reminded him too much of Gudrun, and her youth was an uncomfortable echo of Laisha.

The young woman shrugged, but her back stiffened. "As you wish."

Ragoczy held out three embossed chips to her. "In recompense, for any disappointment I have given you."

The three chips represented twice what it would cost the Graf to take her to bed, and the young woman made no attempt to suppress her smile. "Naturally, at Madame Ilse's we are eager that the patrons should have the best entertainment." She pulled away from him and said, "Dark hair? Tall? Short? Buxom?"

"Dark hair, over twenty-five, if you please. Hungarian or

Polish or Slav, it doesn't matter to me." He would not be with her long in any case, and he wanted as few memories stirred as possible.

"Russian?" the fair-haired woman asked.

"I think not," Ragoczy said sardonically.

"We have a Hungarian woman on the staff, but she's playing the flute tonight. I could send her a note for afterward . . ." The three chips seemed to require that much effort, at least.

"Fine." Ragoczy was about to go into the concert chamber but was stopped by the fair-haired woman's low laugh.

"I understand," she told him with a salacious wink, "that Beatret plays flute very well."

"I'll keep that in mind," Ragoczy said, and entered the concert room.

An hour later, when the fourteen-piece ensemble had made its way through three Vivaldi concerti, Ragoczy began to wonder if he should continue to wait for Beatret, for he had the uneasy feeling that he was under observation. In an establishment like Madame Ilse's, it was possible that men with enough money would be able to follow him, or, if they were desperate, pay for his capture. It was nothing to look forward to, he thought, knowing that any extraordinary display of strength here would bring about the sort of notice he was anxious to avoid.

"Herr Graf," said a voice beside him, and he looked up to see the Hungarian flautist who a few minutes ago had been playing reverse turns and runs with the little orchestra. "Lisi said you wanted to spend some time with me."

Ragoczy rose and kissed her hand. "Enchanté, Madame."

"Merci," she responded awkwardly, but determined to show him courtesy.

"How much time have you free?" he asked as the other listeners made their way from the concert chamber to the supper room and gaming tables, or to more intimate assignations.

"All evening, Herr Graf. The next music on the program tonight is string quartets, and then Beethoven piano sonatas. My flute will not be required again until Wednesday night." She proffered the case as if it were proof.

"Then you might not be averse to spending a few hours with me." He offered her his arm as he said this.

"It would be my pleasure," she said in her reserved way, and indicated which direction they should take when they entered the wide hallway.

Beatret's room, like most of the women's rooms, was on the third floor, a small, well-decorated place with an unusually large bed and four large paintings dominating the walls, done in a style reminiscent of Rubens. There was also a settee, a dressing table, a washstand, and a beautiful antique chair with heavily-padded arms. The carpet was thick, decorated with a border of badly-executed cabbage roses, and the draperies were heavy enough to put the room in twilight on the brightest day.

"Madame Ilse requires that we settle the price first," Beatret said.

"I would like to engage you for the entire night," Ragoczy responded at once.

"That is more expensive," she said, then added, "but I like it better. It's less demanding. I should warn you that if you want to do anything out-of-the-way, I will have to get Madame Ilse's permission. She's very strict about that."

"Nothing out-of-the-way, I promise you." He did not add that he intended to do little more than discuss music until it was time to leave. He held out the rest of his chips. "I believe this will cover it and leave something extra for you."

Beatret stared at the chips. "Very generous." Her voice was flat, as if she feared what might come next.

"I have two favors to ask of you," Ragoczy explained gently.

"Go on," she said, a careful look in her eyes.

"First, I would like you to drink two or three glasses of wine."

"Why?" She had not put down her instrument case, and she raised it slightly, as if requiring its protection.

"Because I want you to be sleepy."

"Do you like your women asleep?" she asked, unsurprised. She had been at Madame Ilse's for three years, and there was little that could faze her.

"No. I want you to rest. That's all." He indicated the bell pull. "Two tugs means wine, doesn't it?"

"Yes. Do you bring yourself off while watching me sleep?" She was beginning to be amused by him. "I can close my eyes and work you, if you like. I have strong hands."

"That won't be necessary," he said, giving the bell pull two firm shakes.

She lifted her shoulders. "As you like. What is the other favor?"

"If anyone should ask, do not tell them how we passed the night." He pulled up the chair and sat down.

Beatret laughed once, harshly. "No need to fear that. A woman like me doesn't want it spread around that she's most interesting asleep."

"I'm sure you do not have to deal with those like me very often." His dark eyes were ironic, although his manner was unfailingly polite.

"Not very often," she agreed with a giggle, and turned at the knock at the door. She went to open it, and a liveried servant brought a chilled bottle of champagne and two glasses into the room, opened the bottle with a flourish, and left as soon as the two glasses were filled.

"Have your wine, Beatret," Ragoczy said, and watched while she took the glass.

"You're not joining me?" she asked.

"No." He watched her as she drank, and said, when she put the empty glass down, "In a few minutes I will want you to have another glass. In the meantime, you might care to tell me where you got your training on the flute. You play quite well, and from what I heard downstairs, you have some background in music."

"My father taught me," she said shortly. "When I was younger."

Ragoczy reached over and refilled her glass. "You do Vivaldi well."

"I like it," she said. "But Herr Graf, I hope you are not one of those tiresome men who always want a woman like me to tell him the details of her life."

"Only if you wish to. Otherwise, you can tell me what you think of Bach and Mozart."

Beatret drank her second glass of champagne more quickly than the first. "I like Mozart. Bach not so much. Haydn is enjoyable." She refilled her glass for herself. "My father wanted to transcribe Paganini for flute, but never did much with it." She finished the glass and gave him an inquiring look. "Should I have another?"

"If you wish. It will go flat, in any case."

In the end, Beatret drank five glasses of champagne before her eyes became heavy and her slurred words disjointed. She was glad to get into bed, to have Ragoczy tuck the covers in around her as she murmured a few senseless phrases of thanks.

Ragoczy sat in the antique chair, listening to the sounds from the lower part of Madame Ilse's. He heard the string quartet play at midnight, and the piano at two. Shortly thereafter, the house became quieter. Finally a distant clock struck four. Ragoczy rose and went to the window.

It was a long way down to the pavement, but there was a narrow ornamental balustrade that ran around the house just below the fourth-floor windows. He opened the window and climbed out.

Earlier that evening it had snowed, and there was now a thin film of ice on the balustrade, and a frigid wind that whipped over the city. Ragoczy eased Beatret's window closed and then steadied himself on the narrow, slippery surface. He wished he had worn something more substantial than his patent-leather evening shoes, but anything else would have attracted attention, which he did not want. The balustrade was slick underfoot, and the house was dark.

It took him the better part of twenty nervous minutes to make it to the corner of the house, and there he teetered while trying to decide if he should jump to the street there or at the next corner. The cold had its hooks in him, and he knew that he had best jump while he had the strength for it, although there was no way to get a running start on the three-meter gap between houses, and the wind buffeted him eagerly. He touched the side of the house to steady himself, and pushed away from the wall like a racing swimmer as he launched himself across the space.

His shoes slithered as he landed and he reeled, grabbing for support. Finally he wrapped one arm around an old chimney pot, hoping desperately that the crumbling masonry would hold him. His hands were scraped, but the bricks were firm. This roof was steeper than the first, but there was a wide gutter that afforded him a safer purchase than the balustrade had. He went more quickly, and crossed to the next roof without mishap.

On the third jump, his hands slipped on the ice slicking the ornamental tiles. He clung with one hand, scrabbling with his feet, his other arm windmilling in the freezing air. At last he swung near enough to an attic gable to grapple a hold, and he hauled himself onto it, tearing his dinner jacket as it caught on the rough surface of the tiles. He huddled in the lee of the gable, reminding himself that he had sought excitement and had been rewarded in full measure. He decided that he must soon get down to the street and find something to cover him. A man in a dinner jacket on a night as cold as this would cause attention, but now that the back of the garment was in tatters, he would have to find a way to conceal the damage, or face the necessity of answering unwelcome questions. He was not confident that he had gone far enough to be out of range of the two men sent to watch him, but he decided that it would be wiser to get down to street level, where he might find a workman up early or a party-goer up late, who, for a price, would provide a coat or jacket for him.

At the far edge of the roof, he found a thick drainpipe, and, hand over hand, let himself down to the street.

Text of a wedding announcement sent on December 10, 1926.

*Lieutenant Colonel Jerome Jaubert Timbres (Army of France, Ret.)*
*announces with pleasure*
*the marriage of his nephew*
*Phillippe Olivier Salaun Timbres*
*to*
*Irina Julija Olga Andreivna Ohchenov*
*formerly Duchess of Russia*
*in a private ceremony*
*on November 16, 1926*
*at Saint Sulpice, Paris*

*At home at*
*29 Avenue Rapp*

# 5

Nikolai pulled the Minerva to the curb beside the Gare de l'Est, directly under the *stationnement interdit* sign, trusting that the French police would not penalize such an elegant and expensive automobile. He was ten minutes early for the train from Trieste, and had been assured that it would arrive on time. He reached into his small carrying case and pulled out a garish magazine that promised to reveal untold depravity on the part of highly-placed government officials. Although Nikolai did not expect anything very shocking, he did find this the most painless way to improve his understanding of French, and was pleased to spend time reading the lurid tales.

Inside the rail station, there was the usual high level of

bustle and chaos, and the continual rumble and hiss of trains. As Madelaine left her first-class compartment, she found herself in the middle of a party of chattering Sisters of Mercy, their huge coifs making them look like gigantic tulips in a fast-moving garden of weeds. She raised her hand to signal for a porter and was not particularly surprised when she was not able to summon one. With a sigh she stepped back into the carriage and retrieved her two large suitcases and a smaller valise. She did not regard these as a burden, but as an inconvenience. She began to thread her way through the confusion, occasionally looking about for Irina, whom she half-expected to meet her here, in spite of the telegram she had sent saying that she would manage for herself. There were no familiar faces, she realized as she looked around again. This did not bother her as it might have a century ago. She had begun to accept the transitory qualities of the world around her, as Saint-Germain had told her she would. As his name came to her, she felt his familiar image grow within her, and she frowned with worry as she recalled the disturbing letter Irina had sent her.

She was on the sidewalk now, out of the cavernous building and caught in the throngs hurrying to and from the enormous station. She was uncertain whether she should take a motor-bus or the Métro to her house, and she set down her cases while she debated the matter with herself.

"Madame," said a voice at her elbow, and she turned to see a large, craggy man of scarred visage looking down at her. He wore a chauffeur's long coat and a beaked cap. "Are you Professor de Montalia?"

Madelaine studied the man without revealing her surprise. "Yes."

"I am Nikolai Rozoh. I'm Rogoczy's driver." He touched his forehead in salute.

"Is he here?" Madelaine asked, startled.

"No, but he sent me here to Paris when he left Bavaria." Unconsciously Nikolai had come to attention, and Madelaine recognized him for the soldier he had been.

"I see." She waited for some explanation.

"Madame . . . Timbres said I should meet you." He noticed that two or three poorly-dressed men had stopped to stare at them, and he flushed, the scar standing out on his face as his color deepened.

"Madame Timbres?" Madelaine was more curious than confused.

"Duchess Irina," Nikolai clarified with a cough.

Madelaine laughed. "How like her. I tell her not to meet me, and so she sends me a chauffeur. I was trying to make up my mind about taking a motorbus or the Métro, or risk everything in a taxi." She smiled at him more openly. "You said your name is Nikolai Roz . . ."

"Rozoh," he said. "Madame Timbres asked me to bring you to her new apartment so that she can explain her fears."

As she picked up her cases once more, Madelaine said, "You're the man she told me about, aren't you? The one Saint-Germain or Ragoczy or Balletti or whatever he's calling himself at the moment had with him that day."

"Yes," Nikolai admitted unhappily. "That was the other reason Madame Timbres sent me; so that I could tell you what I know." He indicated the Minerva and started to take her bags.

"Thank you. I've grown heartily weary of dragging those things all over the world." She relinquished the two suitcases, but kept the valise. "My notes are in here, and they're all that matters." That was not entirely correct, for one of the suitcases contained a good portion of earth from her estate at Montalia, but in Paris, where she had more than five caches of earth already waiting for her, it did not seem dangerous to hand so little of it to the chauffeur. As he held the passenger door open for her, she said, "So Irina and Phillippe are married. I hope they are very happy."

"It would appear so," Nikolai said, and closed the door before walking around to his own door.

Madelaine rolled down the window separating passenger and driver. "How long will it take to reach wherever we're going?"

"Avenue Rapp," Nikolai told her. "That will depend on traffic, Madame. And weather. It was raining at breakfast, and, as you see, may do so again."

"Yes; it was raining east of here." She thought of that first December she spent in Paris, with her Aunt Claudia. Her father and uncle were newly-dead and she had begun a decline that had killed her the following summer. She had learned to hate the low gray clouds that hung over the city. She could expect little else but storms at this time of year, but that knowledge did nothing to ease the apprehension that had coalesced within her, like a cold stone behind her ribs.

Nikolai pulled out into traffic, driving the big, luxurious automobile in a dignified manner, scorning the antics of the little Renaults and Fiats dashing about the street. As he drove, he told her in a quiet, passionless way what had happened in Munich on the last day of May.

By the time Avenue Rapp was reached, Madelaine was somberly thoughtful. She had supposed from Irina's letter that Laisha's death had been accidental, yet Nikolai was convinced that it was deliberate, and Saint-Germain shared that conviction. She had fallen into an introspective silence, and was somewhat startled when Nikolai drew the Minerva up to the front of a large apartment house in the Art Nouveau style by the architect Jules Lavirotte, whose work was no longer as fashionable as it had been twenty years before.

"We are here, Madame," Nikolai said. "I will have to find a place to park the automobile, and will join you directly."

"Fine," Madelaine said somewhat absently. "No need to bring my suitcases in; I'll want to have them with me when I go to my house."

"Very good," Nikolai said, and got out of the automobile to hold the door for her.

"I wish I'd brought an umbrella," Madelaine remarked as she started toward the elaborate door. "It will be raining in half an hour."

"I have an umbrella, Madame," Nikolai assured her, and got back into the idling Minerva.

Madelaine nodded, thinking that Saint-Germain had trained his chauffeur well. She entered the elaborate lower lobby and rang the bell marked with the name Timbres, and heard a tinny version of Irina's voice tell her to take the lift to the third floor, and that theirs was the second door on the right.

"How wonderful to see you again!" Irina said with genuine delight as she opened the door.

"And you, Madame Timbres," Madelaine responded with a smile as she stepped into the small entryway. "Nikolai told me, and I am very happy for you both."

"You must come in. Phillippe has taken the day off work, just to be able to see you and thank you for introducing us. Absurd, isn't it?" Her face was more joyful than Madelaine had ever seen it, and she moved as if she had become a girl again.

"Enchanting," Madelaine said wistfully. She had followed Irina into the front parlor, a large room with beamed ceilings over which wonderfully symmetrical vines twined in ordered ranks. She extended her hand to Phillippe as he rose from the sofa under the largest window. "My congratulations, Phillippe."

"Thank you, Madelaine," he said, adding uneasily, "You haven't changed."

"No. I don't." Her tone was flippant, but Phillippe sensed that she would not welcome any more comments on her perpetual youthfulness. She regarded Irina and Phillippe, thinking that they would do well together, would grow old together and die together while she kept on, no different in a century than she was now. Shaking off this disturbing thought, she looked about for a chair, and selecting one, she said to Phillippe and Irina, "I had not intended to take so long to arrive. My plans were to be here more than two weeks ago, but there was a government inspector at the dig and he was forever demanding forms be filled out and questions answered, and that meant that I was needed. The real problem was that he had no idea what was going on, and dared not admit his ignorance, and we were all forced to pretend he was well-informed, which simply prolonged the whole farce." She adjusted her skirt, draping its pleats becomingly. "On digs, I wear trousers. The official was scandalized."

Irina had taken her place on the sofa next to Phillippe, and she said, "We were becoming concerned. When your telegram arrived, Phillippe chided me, but—"

"You were apprehensive," Madelaine finished for her. "So was I, once or twice. But I am here now, and I must find out everything I can from you." She leaned forward, her head slightly to one side. Phillippe, studying her, remembered that she had held herself just that way the first time he met her, nearly a decade ago.

"Nikolai told you what happened?" Irina asked.

"Yes, as you did in your letter. Is there anything more? Has Saint-Germain, perhaps, come to Paris?" It was a tenuous hope, and she could tell from the haste with which both Irina and Phillippe expressed their confidence that they would have word soon that there had been no additional news.

"Do you know where he has houses?" Phillippe asked. "We had no addresses other than the château in Bavaire, and so have not been able to—"

"I know where a few are," Madelaine said, cutting him short. "Do you mean that you have heard nothing from Roger?"

"Nothing," Irina admitted. "I called his banker, but, well, he could not tell me anything, even if he knew."

"I see." Madelaine tapped her fingers on the arm of her chair. "Rozoh said that Saint-Germain saw the girl killed. Did he?"

"I don't know," Irina answered. "I have two boxes of her clothes, to give to charity, but I haven't been able to bring myself to do it. I don't know why."

Madelaine had seen such reluctance before, the last denial of absolute loss, but she said nothing. Instead she rose and paced about the room, paying little attention to the middle-aged couple on the sofa.

"If there is anything you wish us to do, Madelaine . . ." Phillippe prompted her. "It was not entirely fair to bring you back from . . . was it India? . . . and then leave you without any assistance. I haven't a great deal of spare time, but I am willing to put what there is of it at your disposal."

"Very good of you, Phillippe," Madelaine said, giving him a steady look. "I have had the impression recently that you would be more comfortable if you did not have to deal with me at all. Was I wrong?"

Phillippe looked away from her. "Not entirely. But your friend came to my wife's aid when she needed it, and I can do no less for him." He cleared his throat. "I will hold my peace about . . . other things."

His candor saddened Madelaine, and she looked toward the far wall. "It is very good of you. Irina is not the only one in his debt: I owe him . . . everything."

Irina was startled to feel her eyes fill with tears. She had never heard Madelaine speak of Saint-Germain with anything other than fondness, but this ardent, hushed passion was new to her, and she guessed for the first time the depth of love Madelaine had for Saint-Germain. "There must be a way to get information about him," she said, her voice not quite steady.

"There must," Madelaine said with impatience. "After all, this is almost 1927, not the Dark Ages. We have telephones and telegraphs and . . ." She broke off. "James."

"James?" Phillippe repeated, baffled.

"You should know him," Madelaine said sharply. "You sent him to me—an American journalist. He came here to cover the end of the Great War."

"Tree?" Phillippe exclaimed. "Is he still in France?"

"I don't know," Madelaine replied truthfully. "But it should be simple enough to find out." She glanced up as the doorbell rang.

"That is Rozoh," Irina said, getting up from the sofa and going to answer the door.

In the few moments they had for private conversation,

Phillippe looked narrowly at Madelaine. "You've known Tree well?"

"Very well," Madelaine said, and there was no way Phillippe could misconstrue her meaning. "We have met off and on for what? eight years? I was hoping to see him sometime before summer. It never dawned on me until now that . . ."

"That he might help you find his rival?" Phillippe suggested. "Are you so certain he will?"

Madelaine could hear Irina and Nikolai exchange greetings in Russian, and she made a cautioning gesture at Phillippe. "It's not quite what you think, Phillippe. And it is just possible that James will understand."

Instead of disputing this, Phillippe said, "You truly do not look an hour older than the day I met you."

Madelaine chuckled desolately. "You should see Saint-Germain."

Phillippe would have liked to pursue that comment, but he gave his attention to Nikolai, who had been trying to think of ways to reach his employer.

"I have thought that Madame Jardin might have a way to contact him, in case of emergencies—and this is an emergency. She told me before that she did not, but if I were to tell her why we are troubled, she might be able to give us information we could use to find him." He gave Madelaine an apologetic look. "I've seen your portrait, Madame, in costume."

"Oh?" Madelaine inquired.

"In Ragoczy's apartment, in his bedroom antechamber. You were wearing an Eighteenth-Century ball gown. I've often wanted to know why he had you painted in such clothes."

Madelaine had sat for hours in that stifling room where the artist had his studio. The spring had been unseasonably warm in 1744, and she had dreaded the long, boring hours in full grande toilette. "I imagine he liked the dress," she said nonchalantly, concealing the marvelous, irrational pride she took in knowing he kept her portrait near him.

Irina exclaimed over the quality of the portrait, which she had seen when Ragoczy had first brought her to his apartment, but Phillippe said nothing, regarding Madelaine with greater uncertainty than he had known before.

It was dark and raining by the time Nikolai drove Madelaine to her narrow, dark house, and inquired if she needed his assistance.

"Thank you, I will manage," she said as she fumbled with her suitcases. She was stronger and less tired than Nikolai, and was not eager to have him waste his energy and goodwill on so trivial a matter as the moving of her suitcases. "There is something I would appreciate, however, if you would be willing to do it," she added as she gave up struggling with the umbrella and resigned herself to getting wet.

"If it will aid Ragoczy, you have only to ask it," he said at once. "Would you like me to hold the umbrella for you?"

"It isn't necessary," she told him, then said more emphatically, "Tomorrow morning, there is something you can do for me, Rozoh."

"What is it, Madame?" he asked quickly, secretly aghast at Madelaine standing there in the rain, her suitcases and valise held clumsily. He had seen many displaced persons, and it seemed to him that they had the same look to them. He could not get out of the Minerva and order her to accept his assistance, but was sad that he did not.

"I want you to call the various American journals in Paris and find out if they have an address for a James Emmerson Tree. He works for a paper in St. Louis, I think, or he did last year. Tell them that it is imperative that I reach him, and be sure to leave my name. James would be in town for me and not for others, perhaps. I will want to know where he is, in any case. Will you do that?" She felt her grip on one of the cases slipping, and swore quietly but thoroughly.

"James Emmerson Tree?" Nikolai repeated, stumbling over the unfamiliar syllables. "I will do as you ask."

"Let me know as soon as you have information, and I will give you my instructions then." She stepped back from the automobile and hurried toward the dark porch of her house. At the door she fumbled for her keys and required a moment to work the lock. A thin trail of water seeped down her collar and around her neck.

The house smelled musty, and there were three neat boxes of mail on the table by the front sitting room. Madelaine let her suitcases fall and closed the door, hoping that Irina had remembered to have the lights turned on, for although she did not need them to see in the dark, reading was difficult, and she had a great deal of studying to do in the next few days. When she had got to her bedroom, she discovered to her relief that the electricity was connected and the light bulbs replaced so that they worked properly. She got out of her wet clothes, leaving them in an untidy heap by the closet. Her nightgown was a long robe of black silk, a gift from Saint-Germain six or seven years ago. As she pulled it on she was consumed with worry for him, wondering what would happen to him now. In the past, Roger had always found a way to inform her of Saint-Germain's movements, but a quick glance through the accumulated mail had shown that this time no such missive had arrived. Now, as she settled herself in bed to sleep away the fatigue of travel, she was puzzled by the silence, and wondered again if James or anyone would be able to assist her. Saint-Germain knew from millennia of practice how to vanish, and she feared that this was such an occasion. If that were the case, nothing she, nor the police, nor James could do would bring him to light until he chose to be found. It may be, she thought, that all I wish from James is his love, and the rest is an excuse to ask for it. If Saint-Germain had disappeared . . . She could not believe it. Saint-Germain would not let her be so worried, so *alone*. He had promised he would not desert her, and she believed it. No matter what became of him, he would find a way to get word to her. The realization was scant comfort, but she had no other to sustain her. James would be overjoyed to see her, and would know which newsmen to speak to. Or there would be a letter from Roger in the morning, informing her that Saint-Germain was coming to Paris. These and other welcome notions vied for her attention, and after a short while turned into dreams.

Two days later, as snow drifted over Paris, Nikolai drove Madelaine to an address on a short street off the Rue de Rennes. The Minerva was large enough for Nikolai to have problems maneuvering it in the narrow confines, and he cursed comprehensively as two delivery boys on bicycles swerved into his path to avoid a party of rambunctious schoolboys who were throwing snowballs at shop windows.

"You need not stay for me," Madelaine said as Nikolai pulled up in front of the building showing the address he had been given. "I really don't know how long I will be." She did not add that she did not know if James was at home: all she knew was that he was living at this place and was not away from Paris on assignment. "Don't bother with the door," Madelaine told Nikolai as she let herself out of the Minerva.

"You will call Ragoczy's apartment if you need my help?" Nikolai asked, looking back nervously as a delivery van turned into the narrow street.

"Yes, of course. But you had best be on your way now, Rozoh, or that driver will ask you to name your seconds." She motioned him on, stepping onto the narrow sidewalk as she raised the fur-lined hood of her Inverness coat. Nikolai stared at her for an instant as he prepared to drive away, seeing how youthful she was, like one of the young women he occasionally saw hurrying to classes or to work. It was difficult to remember that she was a professor, a woman who had spent several years digging up ruins in harsh faraway lands. He was almost sorry she had not asked him to wait for her.

Just inside the doorway, Madelaine found three flights of stairs, each leading off at its own odd angle. She stood undecided, searching for some indication of which room numbers were where. She had almost made up her mind to try any door and ask for directions when the outer door swung open and a person blundered into her back.

"For God's sake!" the man said in English. "I didn't mean . . ."

Madelaine had turned at the sound of the voice, and the annoyance she had felt evaporated. "James."

James Emmerson Tree almost dropped his two cloth bags of groceries. "Madelaine. *Madelaine*! You're supposed to be in Asia somewhere." He thought he sounded unbearably stupid, but he was sure that the lovely woman in front of him would inform him in the next minute that he was mistaken, that she was not Madelaine, and he would have to mutter an apology and make his way up to his picturesque, inconvenient apartment to battle with the lowering of spirits that would surely claim him.

She touched his face with her gloved hands. "How good to see you. I have missed you."

"I've missed you, too," he said, beginning to believe that she was really in the same room with him. "How did you find me? You did find me, didn't you?"

"Your American colleagues gave me your address. I didn't stumble in here by accident, dearest, dearest James." She stretched out her hands toward his. "Give me one of those: I'll carry it up for you."

"But . . ." He put the bags down, letting them lean against his legs, and impetuously took her into his arms, hugging her with a joyous passion that surprised him. He felt her arms around him, and her response. "Oh, Christ, I love you, Madelaine," he whispered roughly before he kissed her.

Madelaine was secretly ashamed by the intensity of her reaction to this man, and it was she who broke away first. "James. Not here, where someone else might come in with groceries." She reminded herself that Saint-Germain would understand her love for this brash, wonderful man, but she

had never thought that her heart would be so wholly captivated by anyone but her adored first lover.

"And I wouldn't want you to greet anyone else the way you
greeted me." He did not say it as debonairly as he had hoped,
but he did not stop to ponder it. "You were in Asia, weren't
you?"

"Yes. I got back two days ago. If I had had an address, I
would have been here sooner." She bent to pick up one of his
bags. "Which way?"

"It is a maze, isn't it? That one, at the back." He started
toward it, saying, "How long will you be in Paris this time?"

"I'm not entirely sure," she answered evasively.

"Oh?" He had caught the note in her voice that warned him
of her lack of forthrightness.

"What is it? Is something wrong?" He paused on the stairs,
looking back toward her.

"I don't know."

"You don't know. You're not entirely sure. What kind of
runaround is this, Madelaine?" He was fishing in his coat
pocket for his keys and trying to watch her face at the same
time. Some of his light-headed happiness evaporated.

"It isn't a runaround, but . . ." She stopped. "James, don't
look at me that way. I've come to you because I need your
help, yes, I admit it, but it's your love that will help me more
than anything else, and without it . . ." She paused on the
stairs while he opened a door on a triangular landing, her
anxiety returning with more force than it had had before.

He stood aside so that she could enter his apartment. "Without my love, what? You must need something pretty big." He
hated the cynicism in his voice and the jealousy that flared
within him. As he put his bag down by the door to the little
kitchen, he said contritely, "That was unforgivable, even if the
favor is a big one. Give me that bag, Madelaine."

She was still smarting under the sting of his accusation.
"Why?"

"So I can try to make this up to you." His jumbled emotions
were calmer now, and he made up his mind he would not let
them get the best of him again. "You showed up out of nowhere and . . . it all came up again. I was an ass about it. Can
we start over again?" Without waiting for her to speak, he
reached out and took her hand, shaking it warmly. "Hello
there, Madelaine. I'm really happy to see you again, and if I
weren't so surprised to see you, I would have thought of a
proper way to celebrate. Won't you come in and let me make

you some coffee . . . But you don't drink any, don't remind me. Well, maybe you'll watch while I have some." He bent and kissed her hand with something very like flair.

Madelaine was laughing. "James, oh James. How good to be with you again." She went more easily into his arms this time, and if there was less fervor in their kiss, there was also less discomfort. She reveled in his embrace, and grinned at him when he released her.

"There. Better?" He could not bring himself to let her go. He smiled down into her face, loving the contours of it, the violet of her eyes, her well-shaped nose and firm, generous mouth.

"Much better. So much better." She looked over her shoulder. "But it might be best to close the door."

He gave the door a shove, and it slammed shut. "There. Privacy." He looked at her again, taking her face in his hands and kissing her eyelids. "We're going to need privacy, aren't we?"

"Yes. But for more than one reason." She saw the distrust come back into his face and gave a little cry of protest. "No. Don't do this, James. I've come to you for comfort and solace and love. The rest, if you can do it, will help me immeasurably, but if you cannot trust my affection, then I will leave."

"And come back?" He could not keep the apprehension from his voice.

"No." She let her head rest against his shoulder. "And that would break my heart."

"We can't have that," he murmured, holding her tightly.

She let her anxiety rest a bit, hoping that she had not misunderstood him: her first impulse had been to abandon the whole attempt and go at once to Munich in the hope of finding a clue to where Saint-Germain had gone. She did not know how she would convince James to help her, since anything she asked would seem to be a condition of her favor, but she hoped that she could find a way to explain her feelings to him, though she did not understand them entirely herself. "James, come."

"Where?" His hands dropped from her arms.

"I've never seen this apartment. Show it to me. Talk to me." She sighed. "Why must you make this so difficult?"

"You came to me, Madelaine," he reminded her. "That was a cheap shot. I'm sorry."

"At least you admit it," she said, and made herself smile at him. "Where's your sitting room? If we're going to straighten things out, we might as well do it in comfort."

"In the sitting room?" He brushed her cheek with the back of his hand. "Not the bedroom?"

Madelaine bit her lower lip. "If you knew how much I want to lie in your arms, you wouldn't ask that." She read a kind of shock in the back of his eyes. "I'm not supposed to say such things, am I? I should wait and simper and pant until you're convinced I can be told of your desire without swooning. Or am I supposed to tear off my clothes now, overwhelmed at the opportunity? James, have you forgot what it was like together?"

He looked away from her. "I guess I have. It's been more than a year, and there were just the two letters . . ." He broke off. "I thought you didn't want to see me again, or had found someone you wanted more."

"You should have had five letters," she said gently. "I had only one from you, and you mentioned an earlier one which I never received. When I'm on a dig, this can happen. We employ special couriers for the photographs and notes." She took a step away from him. "Which is the sitting room?"

He gave in. "First door on the left. It isn't very big."

She entered the room and looked around, nodding her approval. "You have been reading a great deal," she remarked with a wave at the overflowing bookcases.

"Yes. I want to keep my European assignment, and that means learning a lot more." He indicated one of two shabby armchairs. "Tell me what's on your mind."

Madelaine draped her coat over the back of the chair, then sat down, unmindful of the room's chill. "I have to locate someone."

"Oh? Who?" James took the other chair after lighting the small gas heater under the grimy window. "It'll be warmer in a minute."

"N'importe." She leaned back, hoping to appear more at ease than she was.

"Where is this person? Do you have any idea?" In spite of himself, he was intrigued.

"He was in Munich for a time, but I understand he has left there. Perhaps Vienna now, or Switzerland or Italy." As she said this, she realized how vast the search might be, and it distressed her.

"Any idea how he's—I assume it is a he?—traveling?" The gas meter made a bubbling sound, and he turned to adjust it.

"By train, I think." She put her hand to her forehead. "I know it is probably ridiculous to try, but I must make the attempt."

James felt his hands turn cold, and he stared at her through narrowed eyes. "Saint-Germain?"

"Yes."

He lurched out of his chair and began to pace the crowded, messy room. "Him! By damn, I should have known. You'd offer to sleep with half the devils in hell for him, wouldn't you? And in my case, it isn't all that painful. You have the advantage of being able to like it." His voice rose savagely as he came up behind her. "Doesn't it bother you at all?"

"Yes, it does," she whispered. "But I must do something."

"And you figure I'm enough of a sucker for you that I'll be willing to go along with whatever you ask as long as I get to lay you every night." He was not aware of how wounded he sounded, and so her reaction disarmed him.

"If it were you, and he were in your position, I would do the same thing. How could I come to you, asking for your love, if I deserted him? He's no threat to you. We are no longer lovers, he and I." She twisted in the chair so that she would be able to take his hands in hers.

"Oh, that's right; I forgot. He's a vampire, just like you." His sarcasm was bitter, and he broke away from her, fearing that she would overcome him with her presence.

"He is." Her protest was futile; she knew it.

"Naturally. And you have a blood oath to take care of him." Anger gave his cognac-colored eyes a sulfurous tinge. "What kind of an idiot do you think I am?"

"I don't think you're an idiot at all. I think you are my friend." She smiled blindly, miserably. "There was no one else I wanted to turn to but you. No one else, James."

"To help you find out if—that's the right word, isn't it: *if* —your onetime vampire lover is in Austria or Switzerland or Italy. Well, now, Madelaine, that's a pretty tall order for a country boy like me." He choked suddenly and spun away from her. "God, Madelaine, I didn't mean it. Why do I do this to you?"

She got up slowly and went toward him. "Why do you do this to yourself, James? You hurt yourself as badly as you hurt me." She slipped under his arm and pulled his face down to her. "You think I'm trying to use you. That's a very small part of it."

"I wish I could believe you," he muttered, ignoring the irrational hope that fluttered through him.

"I'm asking you to trust me, as I am trusting you," she told him. "You know what I am, and you are not repulsed." She lifted her shoulder. "It doesn't matter to me that you do not believe me"—this was not entirely accurate, but she did not want to quibble about it now—"but neither do you shun me."

"Shun you? How could I?" It was terrible to feel such desire and such jealousy at the same time. James grabbed her by the shoulders and shook her. "I wish I *could* shun you, for my own peace of mind, but I can't. I don't want to. And if you are using me just to get back to your real lover, I don't want to know about it. All I want is to keep you near me until the end of my life."

"That's not possible, James," Madelaine said gently.

"So you've told me. And you promise me life after death that will not include you. Why would I want to live after death if you will go on to someone else?" Abruptly he pulled her to him, holding her tightly, his features contorted, his heart full of love and anguish. How much he wanted to love her! There was no way to be free of his need for her, but he did not accept his desire, not yet.

For Madelaine there was no refuge in tears, but she trembled with the strength of her dismay and her passion. "James. Please, James, forgive me. I wanted you to understand, and to welcome the only thing I can give you with my love."

He made a sound between a cough and a sob. "What a botched job I've made of this," he said, reluctantly letting her go. "I've been dreaming for months that you'd come back, just like this, just showing up one day, and I'd tell you all the right things. Then, when you do, I muck it up."

"Don't," Madelaine whispered, her fingers against his lips.

"Look, I'll help you as much as I can with finding Saint-Germain. That'll even things up a little. But I can't go into Germany with you." This last was grudging.

"Why not? Saint-Germain would not . . . be rude to you." She could promise that easily, but did not want to say more.

"Who are you worried about, him or me?" He rapped the question out and wished he had bitten off his tongue.

"You," she whispered. "You don't know Saint-Germain."

"As jealous as I am?" He let his hands drop again. "I don't want to talk to you this way. But I can't stop it."

"It's all right," she said, having no idea what she could do to lessen his chagrin.

"It's not," he corrected her sadly. "It's not at all." Then he put one arm around her shoulder. "About Germany," he said, making a determined effort now to speak to her without rancor.

"Yes. There is some difficulty?"

He nodded. "They kicked me out the last time I went there, and told me not to come back." He hitched up his shoulders. "I have contacts there still, but it wouldn't be a good idea for me to go there. For one thing, if you want to do anything that might be . . . private, you couldn't with me around. If I managed to get into the country, you can bet every cop around would be keeping an eye on me. They're afraid of something, but I didn't find out what. I've kept up on what's going on through other newsmen, but it's not the same thing as seeing it for myself."

"I don't want you to expose yourself to any danger," Madelaine said at once, but recalled Saint-Germain's quick, reckless action that had saved her life. This was an entirely different situation, she insisted in her thoughts, and knew that this was so, but could not dismiss the comparison.

"I wouldn't mind, if it would accomplish anything useful, but it would only slow you down. If you find out the man's in Poland or Scandinavia or Italy, then I can do some good, I think, but Germany, and Austria, for that matter, are too risky." He pulled her around to face him. "I'll give you a couple of names, and I'll send wires for you, Madelaine. But you've got to promise me that you won't spend time in futile searching. If my contacts can't turn the man up, it's because he either isn't there or has gone so far underground they'd have to dig a trench to find him." He saw the horror in her eyes, and quickly added, "I didn't mean that the way it sounded. Look, if he has to make an escape, it might be best to let him do it on his own. Trying to help might draw too much attention to what he's doing—do you see that?"

"Yes. You're right." She tried to brighten her outlook. "Well, we don't know for sure that he is in Germany or that he is in trouble. We'll have to wait awhile to find out what your contacts have to say. I've got a few people I can contact as well, professors and other academic colleagues. I've already sent a couple telegrams into Greece. He isn't likely to be there, but there is a chance. He used to have . . . an associate there, and some of Niklos Aulirios' ventures are still going on." Niklos himself had met death uncompromisingly at the hands of a Napoleonic firing squad more than a century ago.

James weighed his next words with care. "If it turns out that your precious Saint-Germain is someplace I can go, I'll go with you."

At last Madelaine's smile was wholly genuine. "Oh, James,

thank you, thank you!" She put her arms around his neck and reached up to kiss him, standing on tiptoe, for he was more than a head taller than she.

"How could I refuse you?" The question was addressed to himself as much as to her, and her light laughter showed how much she understood.

She let her hands slide down his lapels, but she did not move back from him. "I don't want you to think that I say this because I want to give you a reward. I'm afraid you won't believe me, but I must tell you, for myself. I want to love you. I want to feel you on me, within me. Does that make me a hussy?"

"If it does, then I adore hussies," James said, his hands pressing her buttocks through the heavy folds of her woolen dress. "There's no one like you, Madelaine. No one in the world."

It was not in her nature to be coy, and she sought the culmination of passion as ardently as he did, and for a time the doubts were banished and the only thing between them was their winter clothing, which was wonderfully easy to discard.

Text of a letter from Moritz Eis to Hermann Göring.

*NSDAP Headquarters*
*Dresden*
*January 14, 1927*

*Herr Göring:*

*We have heard that you will soon return from Sweden, which fills all of those of us in the SA with joy. Two years is a long time to be away from our important work, but those of us who have had the honor to work directly under your command know how much of your time has been devoted to our concerns and the work of the Vaterland, though you were enduring the rigors of hospitalization. It has been an inspiration to me and to the men I have assigned to the Ragoczy matter to see the extent of your devotion to the SA, the NSDAP, and Deutschland. When you have announced that you are receiving your men, I will take that opportunity to be among the first to visit you, not only to report our progress, great or small, but to extend my heartfelt congratulations at your recovery and return to health.*

*I have put a total of five men on the Ragoczy investigation, and this report should bring our activities up to the present day, so that you will discover all that we have done, and therefore will be able to advise what you wish us to do next. Your personal concern in this matter has shown us all that this is a man of singular importance, and for that reason I have ordered the men assigned to watch Ragoczy to be particularly diligent in their duties so that nothing we do will disappoint you.*

*You were informed of the departure from München, of course, and we provided details on his travels to Wien. He was able to elude two of my men in Wien, and they have surmised that he was aware he was being followed. The men spoke with the staff at his house in Wien and*

*have learned that he has visited the house rarely, even for
the weeks he stayed there, in that he did not entertain at
all and spent most of his evenings at the opera or attending concerts. He also gambled and sought the company of
many of the disreputable women there. As you are aware,
there is a great variety of whores to be had in Wien, of all
nationalities, and many of them the most degraded sorts
of women. Two of these women were closely questioned by
my men there, and their comments are not particularly
surprising. The first woman, a Swiss woman of about
twenty-five, said that she passed two evenings in Ragoczy's
company, meeting him both evenings in the casino attached to the brothel where she is employed. She said that
Ragoczy played negligently and won without much interest. His stakes were high enough and his bearing attractive enough for her to make an effort to attract his attention.
He found her curiosity amusing, and agreed to pass the
better part of the night in her company. They gambled
until some time after three, at which time she invited him
to join her in her chambers, where, she says, he proved
himself an adept lover with a bit more exotic bent than
some she had known. My men claim that she would not
be more specific, saying that a woman of her profession
must not reveal the natures of her clients unless they are
dangerous, because it is not the way a prostitute gets
ahead in the world. The second evening was not unlike
the first, except that she says they were longer at the
gaming tables and that Ragoczy won a fair amount of
money, most of which he gave to her. She claims it was
her superior performance, but as Ragoczy's wealth would
appear to be extensive, it might have been nothing more
than a gesture to demonstrate his superior position. The
Ragoczy family has always had a touch of caprice in
them that is demonstrated in just such actions.*

*The second woman was Hungarian with a spurious claim
to talent as a flautist. It is the policy of her establishment
to offer chamber concerts to the patrons who do not wish to
gamble, drink, or whore. The proprietress fancies herself a
woman of culture instead of the harridan she is, and for
that reason hires only women and staff members who
have some skill on a musical instrument. This woman
told us that Ragoczy attended one of the chamber concerts
and requested her company for the evening, and did not
bother to waste his time or money in gambling. We took*

*the time to investigate the state of his funds, thinking that he might have been temporarily embarrassed, but that was most assuredly not the case. He passed most of the night with this Hungarian woman, and left her after she had fallen asleep. She told our men that she admired his gallantry and found him a tolerable lover. These women, you must understand, are not the sort who have any discernment left to them. Much of the disgusting mingling of races can be traced to these degraded creatures, and the perfidy of the Jews, who are by far the most constant promoters of this immorality. To offer Hungarian women, and worse, to the gentlemen of Wien is a serious affront, and one which must be ended as soon as we have enough influence to show the people what great danger is revealed by the situation.*

*The majordomo of Ragoczy's house in Wien informed us that his employer always kept a small staff at his house, so that it would be ready at any time for his occupancy. He also added that it was not used one year in ten, and although he was more than willing to take his excellent wages for such minimal work, he thought the man to have more money than sense. He also said that Ragoczy kept very irregular hours, communicated little with his staff beyond extending his thanks for the work they had done. Most of his meals, if not all, were taken away from the house, and he brought no company whatever to visit him. This annoyed the majordomo, who said that he did not know why it was important to keep the house so well if no one was going to use it. Under some pressure from my men, he admitted that he occasionally loaned the house out to men needing an elegant place for a week or two, and that once he was paid well by a man in an important government position to keep the wife of one of the foreign ministers there in secrecy for their mutual discretion. He announced that there was no harm in such dealings, as his employer was not being cheated, for the official paid for the extra services and food, with more than sufficient funds. If Ragoczy were to learn of this, the majordomo fears that he would be dismissed without pay or references, and for that reason has indicated that he is willing to cooperate with us in keeping us informed of Ragoczy's movements. In fact, it is through the majordomo that we learned of Ragoczy's intention of going to Praha. Without his comments to our men, Ragoczy might have had more*

*than a day on us, but as it was, we were able to follow
him almost at once. It was a good thing that we were
warned of this, because the men watching him did not
observe him leave the whorehouse he had passed the night
in, and might have lost a great deal of valuable time
waiting for him to emerge. I believe that with a judicious
combination of bribes and pressure we may find the majordomo to be most useful to us, not only where Ragoczy
is concerned but also in regard to other activties in Wien
which are to our advantage to know about.*

*In Praha we did not have much success in following
Ragoczy, though his train arrived only four hours before
our men reached that city. Apparently he stayed with
friends there, for he did not register at any of the inns,
taverns, or hotels of the city. I have one agent still asking
questions in Praha, for I am uneasy, knowing that this
man may have an ally who is unknown to us. For that
reason, we are not entirely certain how long Ragoczy
remained there, but we believe it could not have been
long. He did not visit any of the gaming establishments
or attend the theatre or concerts while in Praha, or if he
did so, they were private performances, where my agent
did not have easy admission. This suggests even more
strongly that he was in the company of a friend or relative who entertained him at home. When we have discovered the identity of the person or persons who did this,
you will be sent a full report.*

*A little over a week ago, one of my agents discovered
Ragoczy in Berlin. Your astonishment can be no greater
than my own, and I did not entirely believe this until I
saw the man for myself, at one of the nightclubs devoted
to the most decadent music and disgusting displays. He
was in the company of a young woman who is known to be
distantly connected to one of the old noble houses, and of
a most rapacious disposition. Her family have died off,
and there are not many left to her. From what I have
learned, she must marry well or find a protector who will
not mind squandering a fortune on her. It is my intention to approach this woman and offer her a reasonably
large sum for passing on to us anything she may learn of
this man. Between what she can get from him and what
we are able to give her, she may do well enough for herself
to allow her to set up house with her brother, which is
what she has indicated she wishes most to do. She is not*

*one to turn away from the service of her country and her
race, no matter how debauched she has become. In a
month we will know a great deal, and then, with your
guidance, we may begin to take those measures which
will assure that Ragoczy does not again leave this country, and that his riches will pass to those who are better
able to appreciate the power such amounts of money
confer.*

*When I have the opportunity to speak with you in person,
I will provide you with all the names of those working on
this venture, as well as those of the persons who have been
questioned and have provided information. In the meantime, I feel it is more discreet to keep that information to
myself, so that if there are difficulties with some of those
Jew-loving figures in government, no one will be cast into
an unfavorable light for the aid they have provided. I am
convinced this is what you will wish.*

*Again, let me offer my congratulations on your return to
health. The physicians who permitted you to become addicted to morphine should be flogged, and it is a tribute to
your great mind that you were not destroyed by the addic-
tion. With you back among us, giving us your thoughts
and your strength, I am confident that the SA will begin
at last to perform near its potential, and demonstrate to
the entire Vaterland what greatness we are capable of,
and how that greatness may be achieved.*

*It is my profound honor to be*

*Most sincerely,
Moritz Eis*

# 6

Frau Bürste's apprehensive expression brought Gudrun out of
her chair, hands clenching before her as she listened to what
her housekeeper had to say. "There is a caller."

"Yes?" She had few of those; since Maximillian's death,
most of the neighbors had stayed away, and there were few
others willing to make the journey to Schliersee, particularly
in winter.

"Helmut Rauch wishes to see you. I have put him in the smaller salon, and built up the fire." She twisted her apron, then smoothed it. "I do not like that man, Frau Ostneige. I have never liked him." So saying, she turned away, plodding back to the kitchen, which was one of the three warm rooms in Wolkighügel.

Gudrun looked around, setting her sewing on the table by her chair. The lamps in the room had been lit, but they burned low, their wicks nothing more than yellow-edged blue crescents. Kerosene was becoming as expensive as the electricity had been. She went around the library and blew out all but one of the lamps, hoping vainly that such a minor economy would ease her current difficulties. That done, she pulled a shawl around her shoulders and started down the hall toward the smaller salon. Her step was slow and reluctant; she liked Helmut Rauch no better than her housekeeper did.

Rauch was standing near the hearth, getting what little warmth he could from the meager fire there. He was dressed in more expensive clothes than the last time Gudrun had seen him. In his lapel he wore a pin with the swastika emblem on it, and he had recently grown a neat mustache. "Ah, Frau Ostneige. What a pleasure."

"I am a little surprised to see you, Herr Rauch," Gudrun said, her voice strained but very polite. "This is a considerable distance to come for a social call."

Helmut's mouth stretched, then assumed its usual stern line. "Yes. And the weather has been bad these last few days. There will be more snow tomorrow, I think."

"Not unusual for Bayern in February," Gudrun remarked, and selected one of the chairs not too far from the fire. "Your journey must have been difficult."

"There were a number of deep drifts," Helmut said, still standing. "They have not been able to keep the roads free."

"Last winter, it was the same." She wanted to scream at him, to force him to tell her at once why he had come, but the years of training that had taught her that no woman should raise her voice to a guest could not be forgotten, and she contained herself, digging her nails into her palms for a distraction.

"I recall a blizzard in late March that did a great deal of damage." He bowed to her as he turned to face her. "It was quite cold, driving out here, and I have not yet entirely warmed myself. I've taken the liberty of speaking to your housekeeper, to request hot wine, or schnapps."

The effrontery of this remark made Gudrun itch to slap him, but she only glared at him. "You must be quite uncomfortable to do such an . . . uncommon thing."

"I was remembering the happy days I spent here with your brother," he confided. "I'm afraid that I got into the habit of regarding Wolkighügel as my second home, and as Maximillian never insisted on formality in his entertaining . . ."

"No, he never did," Gudrun said with asperity. "My brother is dead, however, and as he is not here to act as your host, I hope you will forgive me for being shocked by your cavalier behavior."

"So you can scratch, after all," Helmut said. "I have long thought you were a woman of spirit. I'm pleased I am not disappointed." He came closer to her, leaning one arm on the back of her chair.

"What are you doing here, Herr Rauch?" Gudrun inquired. "I must ask you to choose a chair.

Helmut chuckled, but went along with her. He drew another chair up near hers and dropped into it. "Very well, we will observe the proprieties, my dear. Though why we should bother, when there is only the housekeeper to observe us, I do not entirely understand."

"Persons of quality do not use their good manners only for show, Herr Rauch." She felt rather brave for rebuking him, and thought that she might not have as much to fear as she had anticipated at first.

"And you are giving a demonstration of good manners?" He reached over and patted her arm indulgently. "Women are always falling back on manners as a reason to demand the devotion of the men in their lives, aren't they?"

"I am hardly the person to ask," Gudrun said, and prepared to rise.

"You're not being very wise, my dear," Helmut murmured with an insolent gesture. "You still don't know why I'm here. Are you sure you want to antagonize me before you've learned what the argument is to be?"

Gudrun kept her place. "As you wish, Herr Rauch. What have you come for, other than to gloat?"

He leaned back, then stretched out his legs, crossing them at the ankle. "Why, to see you. I have heard from mutual acquaintances that you have been most isolated here of late, and as your brother was so generous with his friends, I felt that one of them, at least, should take time to see how you go on."

"And now you have seen, and I need not detain you. I imagine you want to be back in München before the snows begin." She tapped her foot impatiently and wished that Frau Bürste would return.

"Or I could remain here until the roads are passable once more, which should be no more than three or four days." He suggested this with a wag of his head, as if he had said something very amusing and witty.

"No!" Gudrun objected, shifting in her chair so that she was as far away from him as possible within its confines.

"So impulsive," Helmut said. "You are reckless, Gudrun, and that—"

"I did not give you permission to use my name," she interrupted at once.

"But you will," he told her. "That was one of the reasons I've come here. There are a great many things you need to know, and to accept. Some of them will not be quite as pleasant as you would like . . ." He looked up as Frau Bürste came into the room bearing a tray with two steaming tankards on it. "Hot wine? Is the schnapps all gone, then? Or would you rather save it for a more fortuitous occasion?"

Gudrun did not dignify his remarks with an answer, but she looked over at Frau Bürste with a significant, minute shake of her head. "I think you will find hot wine as warming as schnapps," she said with meticulous propriety.

"Wirklich?" he asked archly as he took one of the tankards from the tray Frau Bürste offered. "I've developed a taste for schnapps, but I can see why you might not like it, with all the drinking your brother did, especially that last year. Poor Maximillian, he didn't understand what he had become involved in." He took a drink and gave Frau Bürste an approving nod. "Cinnamon goes very well in hot wine. You do well for your employer."

"Danke," Frau Bürste said shortly as she set the tray down. "Do you need anything more from me, Frau Ostneige?" she asked significantly.

"Not at the moment," Gudrun was forced to admit. "But I may, so don't go far."

"I'll be in the kitchen," Frau Bürste said, watching Helmut out of the corner of her eye.

"Is she always such a dragon?" Helmut inquired sarcastically as the housekeeper left the room. "She acted as if I intended to rape and pillage when she let me in."

"Frau Bürste looks after me quite conscientiously," Gudrun

rebuked him. "That is more than I can say for my other servants."

"You mean Otto, I take it?" He drank again, more deeply. "I will want another of these before too much time goes by. Otto was doing what your brother wanted done, and what seemed best in light of all he had been taught. A man who has been in service as long as he has, and to the same family, must be expected to see beyond the immediate pride of the family members. Maximillian may not have been much concerned with you most of the time, but that was because he trusted you to do the right thing, and that Otto would look after you."

"He forgot who paid his wages and he was willing to take Maximillian's word where he should not have." She stopped. "It is not appropriate to be discussing this with you, Herr Rauch. Perhaps you will choose some other subject."

"But I fear this is precisely what I have come about," Helmut said with no trace of discomfort. "I have put it off as long as possible, but things have reached a state where certain matters must be cleared up. You understand that I have obligations to the Bruderschaft that I cannot overlook. Your brother thought he knew the extent of his responsibilities to us, but he conducted them, I am sorry to say, in a most lackadaisical fashion. I believe he thought that much of what we did was a game, or a pretense, such as one indulges in as a child, but he was quite wrong. There is nothing trivial about the Thule Gesellschaft and Bruderschaft. He could not grasp that concept. He felt the rituals were fancy-dress ceremonies designed to give us all a sense of our organization's uniqueness, rather than the formidable focus of forces that they are. Had he ever been able to realize this for himself, he might have gone far with us. As it was, he did a number of foolish things, and attempted to make amends by removing himself from us." Much of his social polish disappeared as he spoke, and the obsessiveness Gudrun had always found so alarming in this man once again became clear.

"He killed himself, Herr Rauch. Was it only for your convenience?" Her tone was no longer courteous.

"In large part, that may have been his thinking. He did not wish to embarrass us, or you, for that matter." He finished the hot wine and set the tankard aside for the moment.

"If that was the case, he did not accomplish his goal," Gudrun said, and got out of the chair. She pulled her shawl more tightly around her shoulders, but it could not thaw the cold within her.

"He did not understand: I told you that." He watched her with something in his eyes that was not quite amusement.

"And for that, he should be what? forgiven? I don't know if that's what he wanted, but I do know that I will not be able to do it for some time. Have you come to tell me that the Thule Bruderschaft is not involved in his death? If you have, you've wasted your breath. It may not be sensible of me, but I cannot convince myself that his association with you was totally unrelated to what became of him. I am not blinding myself to his faults. He was self-indulgent and reckless, but he never became as irresponsible as he was after he became a member of the Thule Gesellschaft. He would come here, spouting the greatest nonsense and telling me that he had found one of the eternal truths. What could I say to him that would not cause an argument, and we already argued about too many other things." She drew nearer to the fire, thinking that it needed more fuel.

"Such as money?" Helmut touched the leather case he brought with him. "That is one of the matters that must be cleared up between us, Frau Ostneige, and you will not find it pleasant, I fear. But nonetheless, it must be attended to, and if we can come to some agreement privately it will not be necessary to take the matter into open court, which I believe you would not like. There is so much that would be brought under scrutiny that would not be a credit to you or your brother."

Gudrun stared at him, no longer capable of being horrified. She found her mind thinking of Maximillian's suicide note, as if it had nothing to do with her, as if it were a footnote in a dull book someone else was reading. Maximillian had all but ordered her to marry Helmut Rauch. What had been wrong with him? Couldn't he see the wickedness of the man, the malice in his face, the greedy shine in his eyes? How could her own brother, no matter what else he deluded himself into believing, wish her to ally herself and her name to a creature like this one, a member of a radical political party, and a disreputable occult organization? No matter how much Maximillian liked Helmut personally—and Gudrun was at a loss to comprehend their friendship—how could he delude himself so about his suitability as her husband? "I am not eager to go to court," she managed to say when she realized he was waiting for her to speak.

"Of course not," Helmut said, so confidently that Gudrun's heart squeezed tight as a fist. "You're a sensible woman, in your way. You will listen to reason and not resist a solution simply because it does not at first appeal to you. Once you see the advantages of a private resolution, you will want to cooperate with me, I am certain."

"What have you in mind, Herr Rauch?" She loathed having to speak to him this way: she wanted to scream at him, order him from the house, and tell him never to return. But she feared that he would take some action against her, whether in court or in some other way, and she dreaded what that action might be. She could not afford to hire a guard for her and Wolkighügel day and night, and she did not want to live in constant apprehension. There must be another way to deal with the man, she told herself. She could not stand the thought of catering to his whims.

"You are not very encouraging, Gudrun. That does not please me." He picked up the tankard, saw that it was empty, and put it down sharply. "I might choose to hold that against you, if you prove to be recalcitrant."

"What is it you want?" She folded her arms, holding her shawl against her like a bandage.

"In a minute. First, I must make it clear to you how matters stand." He reached down for the leather case and opened it, drawing out an untidy bundle of papers. "You will want to look at these, examine them, to satisfy yourself that they are genuine."

"What are they?" She made no move to take them.

"Notes from your brother. Go on. Look at them." He waited until she had accepted the assorted papers. "You'll find they cover a little period, not more than a year, but I don't think there are more of them," he said smugly.

"What are they?" she repeated, opening the first envelope on the stack, noticing that the handwriting was most certainly Maximillian's. She had the note half-out of the envelope and was unfolding the paper when she heard Helmut speak.

"Promissory notes."

The bundle dropped to the floor. "All of them?" she asked weakly.

"Yes. After the inflation was brought under control, Maximillian had very little of his own left, and so he had to use some other means of getting funds." Helmut leaned back. "I would like a second tankard of hot wine, Gudrun. Do you think you could persuade your housekeeper to bring it?"

"Hot wine?" Gudrun said as if the words were in another language.

"Yes. I'm cold." He paused for effect. "I know that is not

exactly your fault, and that if you were not so short of money, this room could be quite comfortable. I have been here when it was. But those days are in the past, aren't they? Unless there is money from somewhere."

"You're being most unkind," Gudrun said with icy reserve. "You are aware that my husband's illness and my brother's habits have done a great deal to bring me to a very bad pass."

"In effect, you are less prosperous than the peasants who keep farms around you. I took a little time to review your financial position before I came—what with having Maximillian's notes of hand, you understand I was curious to know if there was the least chance in recovering any part of the money he owes the Bruderschaft." He cocked his head toward the door. "The hot wine? I don't want to have to ask again."

Gudrun went to the door of the salon and called down the hall in a cracking voice, "Frau Bürste, Herr Rauch would like another tankard of wine." She put her hand to her throat as if the words themselves had burned her as she spoke them.

"I will tend to it," Frau Bürste said from the kitchen door, her face immobile with somber anger.

"Thank you, Frau Bürste," Gudrun said, more softly.

"It will take a few minutes. I will make a little extra, in case he should decide he must have more." She went back into the kitchen, but did not close the door.

"Very good of you, Gudrun," Helmut said magnanimously. He was enjoying himself tremendously, and was able to admit that this time the exercise of power was sweeter than it had ever been before. His face became more animated as he spoke to Gudrun, pointing to the packet of letters on the carpet. "You were not aware of your brother's promissory notes, were you? You thought that he had learned to handle his money with more care, I'd imagine. You thought that he had accepted your burdens and predicaments at last, and was willing to contribute what he could to keeping this estate running. What self-deception! Gudrun, you grew up with Maximillian. How could you believe he was willing or capable of such discretion?" He got out of the chair and retrieved the letters. "You would find these interesting reading, should you care to take the time to peruse them. It might be wise of you to do that."

"You might as well tell me the total," Gudrun said in a lifeless voice. She had waited too long, she thought. Wolkighügel should have been sold last year and the money used to find more modest housing for herself and Frau Bürste. Now the chance was past, and she would be without any resources at all. Her second cousin in Bremen had already said he could not afford to take her in, and her uncle in Kassel was an old man with little money himself. She had a great uncle in Koblenz who had managed to hang on to a small estate, and it might have a place for her, even though it was only a farmer's cottage. Jürgen had an aunt in Trier, but Gudrun had maintained little contact with the woman, and Jürgen's brother Klaus had made only the perfunctory of offers to have her as a guest in his house. Why, she asked herself, had she refused Ragoczy's offer to live at Schloss Saint-Germain as the estate keeper? At the time she had been horrified at the thought of giving up Wolkighügel, but now it seemed to weigh her down more heavily than the stone it was made of.

"Yes, the total." Helmut grinned, relishing the moment. "The total, my dear Gudrun, comes to over fifty-two thousand marks."

"Fifty-two thousand?" Gudrun echoed, her breath catching in her throat. "Are you certain?"

"Oh, very. I'd be happy to go over the figures individually with you, if that would make it any clearer to you. I will show you precisely what he owes, and to whom. Most of it is to the Bruderschaft itself, but about ten thousand of it is personal debts to Bruderschaft members." He shook his head. "I have rarely seen such an obstinately profligate young man as your brother was. Maximillian had an uncanny optimism, and I doubt he ever realized that he could not hope to redeem these notes. I believe he had implicit faith in his own good fortune, and was convinced that he would always have enough money from someone, or something. He regarded Wolkighügel as his own, of course, and not yours."

It took a moment for the implications of that remark to impress Gudrun, and during that time, Frau Bürste came into the room, bearing a large jug of steaming liquid.

"Herr Rauch," she said with a frosty civility, "since you appear to be fond of hot spiced wine, you should find the contents of this sufficient for your needs." She set the jug down in front of the hearth. "The embers will keep it warm," she informed him, and turned away, giving Gudrun a concerned stare.

"I will manage, Frau Bürste," Gudrun said shakily. "It is . . . Herr Rauch has brought me some . . . bad news."

"Should I stay?" She asked it very quietly, but nonetheless, Helmut heard her.

"You need not. When we have need of you, we will send for you." Helmut was pouring hot wine into his tankard, and gave one lofty wave of the hand to dismiss her.

"Herr Rauch," Gudrun said to him, "Frau Bürste is *my* housekeeper. If she is to be dismissed, then it is for me to do, not you. You are an uninvited guest in my home, and your friendship with my late brother requires that I treat you with respect, but it does not mean that I must tolerate your insolence."

"These letters," Helmut remarked affably, "say that you will tolerate anything I wish to do if you intend to remain here." He lifted the tankard and drank. "Your housekeeper had better learn quickly."

Gudrun stared at him, her pale face becoming pasty white. "Just what is it you have in mind, Herr Rauch?" She moved closer to her housekeeper, saying quietly, "Perhaps you had best leave for the moment. If this becomes unpleasant—as I fear it will—it might be wise for the conversation to be as private as possible."

"You are being sensible at last, Gudrun," Helmut said as he took his seat once more.

"I'm not," she countered. "But you have been making such threatening remarks, I thought it might be better to listen to you alone." She was still shocked by the fabulous amount of money Maximillian had promised. *If* he had promised it, she reminded herself darkly, all the while fearing that the figure was correct, for she could recall too many times when Maximillian had shown his belief that he was entitled to half the estate as well as the inheritance he had squandered.

"You're cautious, Gudrun—"

"I would prefer you did not use my name," she interrupted.

"But I want to." He adjusted his necktie, although this was unnecessary. "You're not thinking very far ahead at the moment. You don't want me to believe that you are not willing to clear up this unfortunate situation."

"If you know my financial position, you know that I can't. I have not got anything near fifty-two thousand marks: I barely have two hundred that I can use to pay debts. My settlement is not large, but it is almost enough to keep us going here, with a reduced staff and one automobile." She was determined to be blunt with him, in the hope that he would recognize the futility of her situation.

"I'm aware of that. I also know you have not increased the wages you pay either Frau Bürste or Miroslav in the last two years. You no longer have to support Otto, which is a saving, both in food and wages. But you are undoubtedly aware that inflation is on the rise again, though not as seriously as before. Your allotment from your parents' estate cannot be increased, of course, but I am certain you're cognizant of this." He finished off the hot wine in the tankard, enjoying the glow of it as it spread through him.

"Then why do you bring these to me? Why not go to the court and insist that there be a settlement? This was Maximillian's home and the court would uphold your claim. What do you want? You could take Wolkighügel, I suppose, and you'd find that it is expensive to live in. Does the Bruderschaft want it? Are you doing this for them?" Her voice rose and she had to clamp her teeth together to keep them from chattering. As it was, she trembled violently, though she was able to keep from crying.

"No, not precisely. The Bruderschaft has other plans, for Schloss Saint-Germain, as it happens. With the foreign owner gone, no one knows where, and with his activities under investigation, the government will doubtless grant us access to the place." He was so assured, so complacent, that he was able to laugh once. "We've already discussed matters with the caretaker. These damned Swiss—you know how stiff-necked they can be."

Gudrun closed her eyes tightly. "You have no right to do this. Not to me, and not to Ragoczy. The old nobility have certain rights left, and—"

"They are coming to an end. The Empire is over, and it is now necessary that all the Teutonic people band together to build a modern nation, not one of those imitations of Ancient Rome that have been the models for everyone. We will show the way to the world, Gudrun, and the old privilege will be gone, as it should have been gone a hundred years ago." He got up, poured more of the hot wine, and then came across the carpet to her side. "You have the same fate to look forward to. You will discover that it is no longer enough to be hochgeborn to receive the respect you have grown so used to. No one is willing to pull their forelocks to you, and in a few years, they may well spit on you. It is not as if there is a *von* in your name, but you are known to be landed gentry, and you have long since ceased to behave in the old manner with those around you. You have not given charity to the orphan's school in more than five years, and there was a time when your family paid for more than half of their food and clothing. Do you think they are grateful anymore?" He put his hand on her shoulder, ignoring the flinch. "We of the NSDAP, however, have been doing what we can for those who are as concerned about the fate of the Vaterland as we are. You will notice that we do require agreement with our principles, just as any sensible attorney would. It is to us that the peasants and orphans will turn, not to you, and it is they who will make this country the leader among nations that it must be."

"And for this you need Wolkighügel?" She felt strangely tired and disspirited, as if she had wakened from a long, restless sleep.

"Let us say that I want Wolkighügel. We need other things, such as the remoteness of Schliersee, as well as the road into Osterreich. That is a part of it, and it would be stupid of me to dismiss these advantages. But that is not what I am most interested in." His fingers grew firmer on her shoulder, holding her with a forcefulness that was neither kind nor gentle. "Your brother, I understand, tried in his suicide note to convince you that you should marry me. I gather that he hoped his brother-in-law would not demand payment of his debts, because the hochgebornen don't behave that way to their relatives. I will admit that the idea has a great deal of appeal to me. Men in the NSDAP with well-connected wives go far, and doubtless will go further still once we have consolidated our power and gained the national attention that will make us strong enough to shape the destiny of Deutschland."

"I have no desire to be married again," Gudrun said, her mouth feeling very dry.

"That is because your husband was not a husband to you, and you have forgot the compensations of marriage. In this case, it is more than having another body in the same bed—I would not require you to pay your brother's debts, at least not those to the Thule Bruderschaft itself. For the personal debts, that is another matter, although if I discuss the matter with the other members, they might be willing to forgive the largest part of them. There is a great deal of advantage in accepting my offer, you see. The Thule Gesellschaft and the Bruderschaft might feel that they must prosecute to obtain the money they are owed if you do not ally yourself with me. And the individuals would also be likely to demand settlement. With me, you get a husband, you no longer have to live here as if you were a hermit, you could wear new dresses and get another automobile, one that works well, you could have a larger staff so that the house will not go to ruin around you

. . . you should consider it carefully, Gudrun." He leaned over and brushed her cheek with his lips.

Gudrun was able to keep from screaming, but she could not conceal the repugnance that shook her. What could her answer be, but yes. The very thought of it was disgusting. She was being forced to prostitute herself for a house and her dead brother, but what alternative did she have? Disgrace in court and penury afterward? Death and disgrace? "You are not very diplomatic, Herr Rauch."

"You must call me Helmut. You are going to be my wife, aren't you?" He lifted his tankard as if to toast her, his smile mocking. "You will have Otto back with you, and it will be quite pleasant to live here."

"Otto is your spy." She said it flatly, determined not to let him see how much she despised him and everything he said. With care, she might be able to put him off long enough to find assistance of some sort for herself. She could sell Wolkighügel, and make arrangements with the court to deposit a certain amount against the settlement of the most outrageous of Maximillian's debts. Then she could go . . . somewhere else. Switzerland, or Italy, or even dreadful France. She would be beyond his reach then, and removed from her dishonor.

"Naturally he watches for me. He was not very happy when you decided to keep company with that foreigner, Ragoczy. He was worried that others would learn of your affair, and then you would be completely disgraced. I gave him my word that I would be silent, but, should appearances in court be necessary, I would have no choice but to tell what I know. I think it might make your case more awkward than it already is." He turned his predatory smile on her. "I know that widows do . . . impulsive things. But Ragoczy is gone, and I am here, and I am willing to give you the benefit of my name, which he never offered you."

"You're offensive," Gudrun said, feeling her fatigue deepen.

"Because I tell you the truth? I am willing to marry you, restore your house, and give you the chance to move at the top levels of society. If you would prefer to remain as you are and face poverty and disgrace, then there's nothing I can say." He chucked her under the chin. "You're an attractive woman, Gudrun. There's no reason you shouldn't find it useful to be married to me."

"As I would be *useful* to you?" She did not let him answer or speak. "You've made it impossible for me to reject your offer. Or not quite impossible, but I haven't the strength to kill myself."

"It's not that bad, Gudrun. You will find out that I can be a very accommodating man when I am treated well." He leaned over her and put his mouth against hers.

Gudrun tasted the wine and tobacco that did not surprise her. There was bile at the back of her throat and she had to force herself to keep from striking out at the man. She should never have sent Ragoczy away. She might have learned to sympathize with his grief, she might have been less unwilling to share his loss. Now there was no Ragoczy at Schloss Saint-Germain, and Helmut Rauch was kissing her in the smaller salon of her own home. It was repellent. "Herr Rauch," she said when he broke away from her, "I will need time—"

"Oh, no. You'll start to think of things to outwit me, and that does not suit me at all, Gudrun. I believe that we should be married in a week. Tonight I'll return to München, but tomorrow morning, as soon as the weather is good enough, Otto will be back. And he has your best interests in mind, although you don't believe it. I have had a number of conversations with him, and he is convinced now that the wisest course for you is to marry me and put your fortunes in my hands." He moved away from her, a bit tipsy with hot wine and success. "I will not be too impulsive once we are married. You may have a month before I insist on my marital rights, but after that, I will expect you to be an obedient and complacent wife. Remember that." He reached the door and pulled it open. "I know you'll learn to appreciate me, Gudrun. Your good sense should tell you that."

Gudrun nodded once, not trusting herself to speak or to open her mouth. As soon as the door was closed, she dragged the back of her hand across her mouth as if to wipe away forever the impression of Helmut's kiss. She stood still, listening for the front door to open and close, but instead she heard the salon door swing on its hinges. "What is it?"

Helmut had put on his heavy overcoat and held a long muffler in his gloved hands. "I think I should mention that if you try to leave this country, or this house, for that matter, or make any other attempt to renege on our agreement, I will see that all of Maximillian's letters are published in newspapers all over the country. I can do that, you know. I will also publish all the reports Otto has sent to me, with the details of your affair with Ragoczy. It would make interesting reading, and with journalists what they are, I am willing to wager they would spread the information over most of Europe. It might be that your great-uncle would be moved to stop administering your trust." He put a fur-lined hat on and bowed to her. "Be as realistic as you can, Gudrun. It is the best way." With that parting comment he closed the door, and a few seconds later, the front door opened and closed.

"Oh, Mein Gott! Mein Gott!" Gudrun cried out, then clapped her hands over her mouth, fearing that Helmut could still hear her. She began to sob rather wildly, and when she tried to walk, she shook too badly to get across the room; she held on to the back of the chair Helmut had sat in.

"What is it!" Frau Bürste demanded as she came into the salon. There was flour on her arms and a smudge of butter on her cheek. She came bustling across the room as soon as she saw how distressed Gudrun was. "There, no more tears, my dear. No, no. You must not weep. You will make me cry if you do."

"He insists on marrying me," Gudrun told her in one breathless gasp. "He has letters. Maximillian owed money. So much money. I could not pay it. If I marry him, he will cancel the debts. Oh, why has he done this?" She let herself be wrapped in Frau Bürste's ample arms, her tears no longer held back.

As she sobbed, Frau Bürste stroked her hair and murmured quietly, "No, no, my dearest. Do not be frightened. Do not despair. All will be well. Yes, I promise you, my dove, my angel. All will be well. All will be well."

Text of a letter from James Emmerson Tree to Madelaine de Montalia.

Paris
March 8, 1927

Dear Madelaine;

*I've found him—he's in Berlin, in the Charlottenburg district. He's rented a modernized eighteenth-century house (meaning it has electric lights and indoor plumbing), Number 45, Glänzend Strasse, just off Knobelsdorffstrasse. He paid a year's rent on the place when he hired it, and stocked it with very good antique furniture and a half-dozen servants. He has not yet held a major entertainment there, but he asked a few of the musicians from the opera to join him after a performance of* Die Tote Stadt, *and they have said that they were treated splendidly. I have a friend in Berlin, working for Reuters, who was able to dig most of this up. He's Dutch; I met him in Amsterdam several years ago, and we've done each other a good turn now and again. I'll send him word you're coming, if you like, and you can take advantage of his expertise.*

*You wanted to know if Roger was with Saint-Germain. I understand that he is. He's said to have a manservant of about fifty, sandy hair, blue eyes, lean. That sounds like the man you described to me. He attends to Saint-Germain's personal care and runs confidential errands for him. He also serves as chauffeur now and again, but Saint-Germain often does his own driving. He's bought himself a new Delage, and occasionally goes for long jaunts in the country around Berlin, sometimes with Roger, sometimes alone.*

*There's something I think you should know: my contact there warned me that Hermann Göring has been having Saint-Germain followed. Göring is high up in the NSDAP—*

*that's the National Socialist German Workers Party.
They're very Right-wing, promote the idea that the Germans
are some kind of super race and for that reason are entitled
to rule the world. A couple years ago, Göring's interest
would be nothing more than the whim of a socially-
prominent crackpot, but that's not the case anymore, and
Göring is a chancy man. He comes from an upper-class
family, was something of a war hero, but because of
injuries he received in the Great War, he became addicted
to morphine. He's been in a hospital in Sweden for the
last couple of years, and they've been able to get him off
morphine and onto codeine. They're going to release him
soon, and he'll be back in Germany after that. He's been
running a number of investigations from the hospital,
however, and one of them is on Ragoczy. He has decided
that there is something dangerous about Saint-Germain, or
Graf Ragoczy, as he refers to him. My contact knows that
there have been at least three and maybe more men on the
case, which means that they know most of what he's been
doing in Berlin. He gave them the slip for a while, and
that caused a lot of flurry with the SA types. Those are
the stormtroopers they're training.*

*Madelaine, look, I know you feel you have to go there
and do something or other for him. I'm not jealous of
that. I wish you felt so strongly about me, but I'm not
jealous of him. But I am worried about you. Germany
isn't a very safe place these days, and since you're French,
you're the enemy to them. You know how Germany felt
about the war settlements, and now that they're in the
League of Nations, they're not being very polite about it.
You could get into a lot of trouble if you aren't very
careful. I don't want to see that happen to you. Let me
contact my friend there, and deliver messages to him for
you. I'll make sure he understands how delicate the matter is, and you know that he'll do a good job. You won't
have to get exposed to anything. You said yourself that
they killed his adopted kid, and she was only something
like fifteen. What makes you think they'd hesitate to take
a shot at you? I can't go with you; they won't let me into
the country. I'm worried for you. I don't want anything to
happen to you, and the way some of those extremists are
behaving, it could.*

*If I didn't love you, it wouldn't matter that much to me
that you're undertaking a reckless venture like this, but I*

*do love you, and when I think of you in that lion's
mouth, my breath stops. Promise me that if you can't get
to Saint-Germain, you'll leave Germany as quickly as
possible. Don't linger there in the hope that something may
come of your persistence. You'll attract attention to yourself, and since the NSDAP and Göring himself are after
Saint-Germain, you'll be conspicuous to them, and they'll
make an attempt to find out what you're up to. Those
men are ruthless, and I couldn't stand the thought of you
being around them. You mean too much to me, and it
would hurt too much to lose you, especially to those men.*

*I hope that you do find Saint-Germain, and I hope that
you get him out of there. I mean that, Madelaine. How
could I want you to continue feeling as wounded as you
have these last weeks? You're so dear to me that even if
this man were my rival (and I will believe you when you
say he is not), I would want him to be out of danger and
comforted in his loss, because that is the only way I can
face you honestly. If that's selfish of me, so be it.*

*Be careful, Madelaine. And keep in contact with me as
much as possible. I'm tempted to try to sneak into the
country with you, but if I got caught, then you'd have two
of us to get out of Germany, and one is enough.*

*I love you, I love you, I love you.*

                                                *James*

# 7

Snow had given way to a misty, sullen rain that shrouded the
gray city of Berlin with the same color. The streetlights decked
themselves in shimmering halos at night, and the streets glistened. Traffic was sparse on Knobelsdorffstrasse this midnight,
and few people were on the narrow sidewalks, and the patrol-
ling policeman was heartily bored as he made his rounds. He
passed a couple in evening clothes, the woman tall and slender
as a candle, swathed in a luxurious coat of blue fox. She was
laughing at a comment her escort had made, and the policeman could tell that she was not quite sober. He touched his

forehead as he went past the couple, knowing that it was unwise to bother those who were clearly hochgebornen.

"Did you see that policeman's face?" the woman giggled, pressing close to her companion. "He was scandalized."

"I was looking at you, Nillel, and did not see the policeman," Ragoczy said with automatic courtesy that was as sincere as her smile.

"You're always being so amusing!" she declared, reaching over to tweak his earlobe. "You always make me laugh." She proved this with a demonstration. Nillel was very proud of her laugh, which was watery and musical at once.

"How fortunate," Ragoczy said quietly as he indicated the turning for Glänzend Strasse. "We have almost arrived."

"I'm thrilled!" She turned toward him and put her arms around his neck. "You're so good to me, Mein Graf. I am getting so spoiled by your attentions."

He agreed with her, but gave the protestations that were expected of him. "Nothing could spoil what you are, Nillel."

She kissed him with more enthusiasm than accuracy, and when she had finished, she stepped back from him so that she would be able to see his face. "Isn't it wonderful, how well things have worked out between us?"

Ragoczy knew what was coming next, and so he kept his peace. As they crossed the street, he held her arm firmly, but without too much force. "Be careful. The stones are slippery."

"I'll be careful," she said as she took the opportunity to lean more heavily against him. Her coat was too gorgeously thick to let her press the curve of her breast into his arm, which had been a useful ploy in the past. "I hardly know how to begin," she said with an expression she had been told was adorable.

"At the beginning, perhaps." They entered Glänzend Strasse, which was not as well-lit as Knobelsdorffstrasse. The street had been laid in a time when carriages, not automobiles, frequented the district, and for that reason it was not at all wide. The sounds of their footsteps echoed off the high, imposing fronts of the houses on both sides of the street.

"I like your house, Mein Graf," Nillel whispered in an exaggerated way.

"I'm sure you do," he said, thinking that it was one of the few things she had told him that was unquestionably the truth.

"There's so much in your house that's beautiful. It's remarkable." She clung to his arm as they trod up the steps to the front door.

"Danke," he said as he felt his pockets for the key. He was sorry now that he had told his staff that they need not wait up for him, because he did not want to spend much time alone with this woman. She had been amusing, and her blatant avarice had been mildly entertaining for a time, but he no longer wished to deal with her. The present of a diamond-laden necklace should serve as a proper farewell gift, as the coat had been given in token for her coming to his bed the first time. He turned the key in the lock, and the door swung inward.

"I can't get over how nice your house smells. How do you do it?" She stood in the entry hall, her coat still clutched around her shoulders, her heavily made-up eyes turned greedily on the Sixteenth-Century highboy on the far wall.

"Bowls of dried orange peel and cloves are set out around the house," he said distractedly as he noticed that there was a light on in his study, just down the hall. Roger had not said he intended to be up when he returned, and none of the staff had been interested in using his quarters at any time. He thought of the men who had been following him since the previous autumn and wondered if they had at last gained entrance to his home. If that were the case, he would have to dismiss his servants and hire new ones, which was most annoying. He glanced at Nillel. "Would you like me to take your coat?"

She held it more tightly. "Oh, no. It's a bit chilly here, don't you think?"

Rogoczy knew how little she liked to part with the coat, and so he did not challenge her. "If you will excuse me a moment, there is something I must check on."

"Oh, let me come with you!" She raised her voice to an unpleasant shriek. "I *love* to go sneaking about in the dark."

He would have preferred her to remain where she was, but could not request it without getting into yet another minor dispute with her. "If you like. It may not be amusing, however."

"Do you think it's a thief? My brother once caught his valet taking his best cufflinks. There was a trial and everything." She had not lowered her voice.

"We might do better if we make less noise," he suggested as he preceded her down the hall, half-expecting to see the door open and a figure run off. "Stay behind me, Nillel. If there is a thief in the room, he may be armed. I would not want you to be hurt."

"A thief wouldn't shoot me," she tittered, pretending to tiptoe toward the closed door with the sliver of light at the bottom.

"How trusting you are," he whispered, thinking that whatever element of surprise he might have had was gone. He motioned her to keep back, and moved silently up to the door. He had long ago developed the ability to walk so softly that he was virtually inaudible. Now he was grateful for the skill. Very carefully he reached out and turned the knob, letting the door open on its own weight.

"Oh! Is it a thief!" Nillel crowed, rushing forward eagerly.

"No," Ragoczy said in a strange voice. "No."

On the far side of the room was an overstuffed leather-upholstered chair, and in it sat Madelaine de Montalia in a simple, ravishingly-beautiful dress one or two shades lighter than the violet of her eyes. Her dark hair was swept onto her head in a kind of loose knot and was held in place with three jeweled combs. She looked directly at Ragoczy.

"Mon coeur," he said, his voice so hushed that his breath was louder.

"Saint-Germain," she answered.

"Gracious!" Nillel declared from the door as she pushed into the study. "How deliciously intriguing! Does she want you to give a name to the baby?"

Ragoczy paled at her words, and Madelaine pursed her mouth with distaste. "Has your grief done this to you, my dearest?"

"In part." He spoke in French. "So long as one is lavish with money and gifts, she is more than willing to fulfull any reasonable expectations. She would probably not object too strenuously if we were to lie with her at the same time."

"Saint-Germain!" She sounded more hurt than affronted, and that alone chagrined Ragoczy.

"It isn't fair of you to speak French when I do not know any of it. You're cruel to me, Mein Graf," Nillel pouted as prettily as she could. "Who is this person? Your wife? Your Graffin? You have not mentioned her to me."

"No, not my wife: not my wife." He recovered a bit. "A blood relative."

"How strange!" Nillel stared across the room at Madelaine, her face a mask, her eyes calculating. "Do you want to have him? He's very sensual, my dear. You understand why I'm telling you this? Sensual men, of course, prefer experience. They like a woman who is as sensual as they are." She let herself laugh as she approached Madelaine. "How young you are. You think your youth is enough? You've fallen in love with your disreputable uncle, haven't you. And now you're horrified to see what he's really like, coming in late at night with a woman. He's a good lover, the Graf, but limited, very limited in his way. You have a good grasp of Deutsch, haven't you? You know what I'm telling you."

"I hear you, Fräulein," Madelaine said in heavily French-accented German.

"How charming. Very delightful. And for those with a taste for simplicity, no doubt you would be a rare morsel. It may be that your uncle would be the one to appreciate you." She gave Ragoczy a quick glance. "He's hardly debauched at all, though he is a bit decadent. There are places in Berlin I could show you where he would be thought quaintly naive. And you, well, you would be laughed out of the room."

"I've seen too much decadence to be amused by it, Fräulein," Madelaine said sadly as she looked steadily at Nillel. "Light and dark exist side by side, do they not?"

"You French take such great pride in your sins!" She put a hand out to touch Madelaine's shoulder. "What does a dab of a girl like you know about sins?"

"More than you think," Madelaine answered quietly, her eyes now on Ragoczy.

"From books, no doubt. And your prurient imagination. Did you go to a very strict school? Did the girls all talk about nastiness at night when the lights were out? Did you peek in the showers to see if the other girls had pubic hair yet? So much for your sins." Belatedly Nillel realized her careful facade had slipped and some of the acid in her had been visible. She hastened to repair the damage this might have done. There was no saying how Ragoczy would feel about his pretty French niece. There was something between them; the air was thick with it. She swayed artistically, as if the drinks she had had were catching up with her. "Himmel, Mein Graf. I thought that by now we would have . . . retired for the night. I grow impatient for you." She turned and touched his face. "Never mind about this child. She will be here in the morning, and you may make your explanations then. It is time she learned that grown-ups need to be by themselves." She was not able to resist the urge to look over her shoulder at Madelaine, a smile of malicious satisfaction on her red, red, mouth.

"Nillel," Ragoczy said in a low, even voice, though he now looked only at Madelaine and not at her, "leave us."

"Leave? What?" Her superbly languid eyes were wide with disbelief and irritation. "I won't! You're indulging her for no reason. I'm relaxed, Mein Graf, so . . . relaxed. It would be a shame to waste the night when I feel this way."

At last Ragoczy glanced at her. "You will leave, you know. Roger will see you have a taxi and the proper fare. You do not wish me to carry you from the room, do you?"

When she laughed this time there was no beauty in the sound, only harsh derision. "You couldn't. You're too small and too old. And you wouldn't! It isn't grand enough for you." But she gave him no chance to show her the contrary. She turned on her high, elegant heel and flung out of the room with a shocking curse. The door slammed behind her, and a bit later she could be heard shouting for Roger and screaming insults at Ragoczy.

It was still in the study. Madelaine remained standing by the chair she had been sitting in; Ragoczy kept his place by the door. Neither of them spoke until they heard the front door close.

"Why her?" Madelaine asked. "What did she give you? She is . . ."

"Venal? Greedy? Perverse? Ah, but she does like to think that she is the master and I am her slave. She has the most intense orgasms because she thinks that I cannot, and that serves my purposes very well. I've never told her otherwise." They were speaking French again, with old-fashioned, aristocratic accents.

"Is it enough?" Madelaine asked.

"Of course not. But what else is there? What else can I endure?" He gave the ghost of a sigh. "You should not have come."

"I had no choice." She had known it would be difficult to see him, but she had not anticipated the anguish she would feel at the sight of him, or the tenderness he would rouse in her.

"Why *did* you come? How did you find me? I thought I had been hard to follow." He moved away from the door, but not much closer to her. Both of them avoided the appearance of touching.

"I was worried about you. Irina sent me word a few months ago, and when I read what she had to say, I was afraid for you. So I came back to France and began to make inquiries." She was able to keep her tone flat but not entirely emotionless.

"And how did Irina come to . . . Nikolai! Of course." He touched his forehead and looked down at his elegant dancing shoes. "Do they know where I am?"

"They know you are in Germany. They do not know

specifically where." She followed him with her eyes, but made no move in his direction.

"And how did you find me? You haven't explained that yet." He studied her intently for a few seconds, then gazed down at his shoes once more.

"I didn't. My American friend, the journalist I told you about when we met in Switzerland, wired some of his colleagues, asking about you. One of them located you and sent the information to James, who passed it to me. You haven't been precisely invisible, I hear."

"I see."

She felt her nerves falter, and forced herself to go on. "He learned some other things, as well; they disturbed him."

Ragoczy went to the window and stared out at the street below, seeing the same dark Benz parked at the end of the block that he had seen there every night. A distant streetlight cast a fuzzy blue glare through the Austrian lace curtains, bleaching his features to an unearthly white. One hand was in his pocket; the other lifted one of the curtains so that he could see the automobile more plainly. "You want to tell me that I'm being followed."

"Then you know." She felt so defeated as she said that.

"They have been fairly obvious. There were a few in Bavaria, a few in Vienna. I got away from them in Prague, but here, of course . . ." He jerked one of his shoulders in a shrug.

"Do you know who they are?" She did not dare to ask him if he cared about the danger he was in: she could sense that he did not.

"Probably SA or Thule Bruderschaft. Neither are very pleasant." He saw a tall, pale woman in a fur coat run down the street toward the parked Benz. Unaccountably, he was sorrowed by Nillel's duplicity, although it did not surprise him.

"Why are they following you, do you know?" She strove to be as reasonable as she could, pretending that Ragoczy was her student in need of advice.

"They think that I was responsible for the killing of five SA men in Munich." He frowned as the rear door of the Benz opened and Nillel stepped into it.

"And were you?" Her nails were digging into her palms, bringing her some relief from the deeper pain within her.

"Oh yes," he said rather remotely. "Yes, I killed them. They killed Laisha."

"Saint-Germain," she whispered, wishing she still knew how

to pray so that she could do something, no matter how ineffective, to ease his suffering.

"There were five of them. Five." He let the curtain fall, but continued to look out at the Benz. He could barely make out the pale fur of the blue-fox coat he had given her.

"Do they know it was you?" She wished now that James were here to point out the hazards they both faced. She was annoyed with herself now for leaving James' note behind. If she had brought it, she might have used it to persuade Ragoczy to leave Germany at once. She had not anticipated that he would be so remote from her, separated by a grief that would know no release but the passage of time.

"Not precisely. As I understand it, they are of the opinion that I hired a gang of thugs—either Sparticists or White Russians, depending on who is telling the tale—to come in and do the dirty work for me." He shook his head slightly as he saw the automobile start and drive away down the dark street.

"Did you know that the investigation is under the personal control of Hermann Göring?" Madelaine asked, hoping that she could say something that would startle him out of his reserved state of mind.

"Göring? He's in Sweden." Ragoczy's brows rose and he faced Madelaine. "What makes you think so?"

"James' contact gave him the information." She wanted to scream at him, insisting that he do something to save himself, but was afraid that he would not respond, which would be more unbearable than all the rest.

"Göring," Ragoczy said slowly, looking down at the empty street, staring at the figure in the shadows who thought he was concealed.

"There have been five men on the case, one in Bavaria, two in Vienna, and two here in Berlin. When Göring returns, there may be more men assigned to you. He thinks you're suspicious and dangerous. The man in charge of the investigation is Moritz Eis. James' contact gave me that news when I arrived yesterday." It was not easy to keep from running out of the room, for the desolation of his spirit was growing more daunting.

"Is Eis a member of the SA?" Ragoczy asked lightly.

"Yes." James had told her enough about the SA to make this admission disruptive to her.

Ragoczy nodded calmly, abstractedly. "And the Thule Gesellschaft? Do you know if he belongs to that?"

"No. There was no mention of the Thule Gesellschaft or

Bruderschaft." She felt her hands begin to tremble, and she repressed this sternly.

"That does not mean he isn't part of it. Göring probably is, though I never saw him with the others." He took a half-step back from the window, satisfied now that the man watching the house was fixed there for most of the night.

"Saint-Germain, will you stop that!" Madelaine said, her worry and impatience at last breaking through the tight rein she had held on herself.

"Stop what?" He turned to look at her.

"Do you want to die? Do you? Are you tired of living? You are like one of those idealistic fools who make targets of themselves, taunting their enemies, like those stupid, brave men in Italy. But what are you seeking to prove? What do you think you're accomplishing?" Had she been able to weep, she would have been in tears. As it was, her voice broke and her breath was ragged.

Ragoczy turned his compelling dark eyes on her. "Oh, my heart, my heart. It is bad enough that one of us . . . Please, my heart, don't grieve for me. I could not bear it, with the rest. You must not, Madelaine."

The agony in his words wrung her heart, and she lifted her hand to her mouth so that she would be able to keep silent.

He looked away from her, back through the curtains, down at the street, toward the man in the long overcoat waiting in the shadows of the house at the opposite corner. "I don't know what I want. The true death, yes, perhaps. Why this loss, of all losses?" He thought for a little time, his eyes on his ob-server. "I've never known what it is to have a child. Children of my blood, that is another matter, and not the same thing. Those I have taken in love are . . . different. Laisha was . . . just a child. I never touched her as I touch my lovers. It was not morality, but something else. I could not think of her in that way. I've almost forgot what it is to lead a human life; to age, to marry, perhaps to have children, to grow old, to die. Yet Laisha might have done all those things. I used to imagine what it would be like to hold her child in my arms. Me, a grandfather." He gave a travesty of a chuckle. "I did not want to live *through* her, because that isn't possible. But there are so many things, familial things, that I have never had, or done, and she made me long for them. I used to wait outside the door to the music room when she practiced, to hear her mistakes and improvements. She was learning so much. When she outgrew her clothes, I would marvel at the change, for I have not changed in more than four thousand years. Every day she was different. I felt I was rediscovering the world. She delighted me and maddened me with her intelligence and her willfulness. She would have been headstrong, if she had lived long enough. They cheated her of all the things she wanted most. Her family was lost to her, for they were dead and she could not remember them. And then, when she had a sense of herself again, and was so close to beginning life for herself, they killed her. Oh, no, no," he went on, sensing her desire to interrupt. "I don't think there was any conspiracy against her, or me. I think it was chance. The men who killed her heard a Russian accent, and that was all. The insurgent forces that pillaged the estate where I found her had no idea she was there. I could take some comfort in a conspiracy, because it would mean that there were those in the world other than myself and one or two others who put some value on her. As it was, the police, the judiciary, and the SA officers all regarded the whole thing as an unfortunate accident. Which, in a way, it was. But Laisha is dead, whether from chance or treachery, and everything that she was is gone."

When he had been silent for a few minutes, Madelaine was able to speak to him. "Saint-Germain, what can I do?"

"Nothing. It can't be changed. I suppose in time I will grow used to it. I have before." How weary he looked, standing there in the cold light at the window. The lines and planes of his face were marked as if inked on chalk. The wry curve of his mouth had gone and there was a tragic grimness in its place. He gazed toward the rooftops, as if seeing far into the past, or the future.

Madelaine stood still, mastering herself once again. When she spoke, her voice was very soft, like a caress. "Is that what you want, my dearest love? To be left alone to mourn? Shall I curtsy politely and inquire when the next train leaves for Paris, so that you may continue to look for another chance, another accident that will relieve you of the burden of grief? If you feel that way, why don't you walk in front of a motorbus, and have done with it?"

"Madelaine!" he looked at her as he said it, shocked.

"We are bound to life. You said that to me. You, Saint-Germain, and I have lived by it." Her hands gripped each other as if in battle.

"And you can still live." He said it resignedly enough, but the passion in her voice disturbed him.

"Without you? Why? How?" She took a step toward him. "What am I to do?"

"You do not need me to live," he reprimanded her kindly.

"And you do not need Laisha, but you woo death." It had taken all her strength for her to say that to him, and she waited for the anger that might answer her. Anything he said now, she wondered if she would be able to hear it without being overwhelmed. She looked at the clock on the far wall, caught by the motion of the pendulum, grateful that there was something so ruthlessly, idiotically sane as that clock to hold her attention. If he sent her away, how would she endure it? Better to watch the clock. She was so preoccupied with the pendulum that she did not hear his light tread on the carpet, and jumped slightly as his small hands came to rest on her shoulders.

"Madelaine," he said in her ear, and she could not tell whether he felt love or hatred, so fierce was his whisper.

"What now?" she asked quietly as he turned her around to face him.

"I don't know." He had been tempted to shake her, to make her take back the accusation she had hurled at him, but he knew, in the depths of his soul, that she was right, that he had been searching for the chance to die, to be finally and utterly through with his life. But as he felt the vitality of her under his hands, he could not bring himself to harm her, or give her any more pain than he already had. This was Madelaine, who had loved him with knowledge and acceptance since the first time he kissed her hand at the Hôtel de Ville that September night in 1743. No one had done so before or since. "How could I hurt you this way? How?"

She made a sound in her throat as her arms went around him, and she clung to him in desperate hope. Her face brushed the white silk tie he wore, but neither noticed this. "If you were damned to Hell and I were assured of Heaven, I would rather burn with you than have Paradise alone."

"My heart, don't." He put his hands at the back of her neck and turned her face up toward his. "It is hard enough . . . Don't."

"I will," she responded, her violet eyes meeting his dark ones. "You gave me life, dearest love. I won't let you ruin your gift."

It was strange to kiss her, Ragoczy thought as their lips met. He had never kissed anyone after they had come into his life, not with this passion and yearning. He had never felt what those he loved felt, the need that sought life as well as embraces. He drew back from her. "It's no use," he murmured, his lips near her hair.

"Saint-Germain, please." She held him more tightly, her fear gone.

"Among those of us who have changed, it isn't possible." He touched her face with one finger, outlining the contours he loved so well. "I had heard that there were those who had accomplished it, but never anyone I had met, or knew, or made. They all were optimistic, but in time there was disappointment. You are everything I love, Madelaine, you are all that I could want, but for one thing. And I am the same for you."

She reached up to kiss him again, keeping her mouth on his until she hoped that the words were gone forever. "No. It must be possible. It must."

"How?" His dark eyes were suddenly filled with sorrow and tenderness. "When neither of us has life to give the other?"

"That can't be all that's missing. If it were . . ." She pushed out of his arms, no longer trying to control her emotions. "It isn't fair that that woman you came home with can offer you something I can't!"

"Have you lived so long and not learned that very little is fair?" he asked her gently.

"But that woman, that kind of woman." She folded her arms. "I am not jealous of what you wanted from her, or that you wanted her at all. I am jealous that she had it to give."

"Yes, my heart, I know. I felt something very like that when you told me about your American journalist. The others had not been so . . . protracted or involved. Yet I am glad that you have found him. I hope that he has come to—"

"He hasn't," she said, not letting him finish. "He thinks I'm joking, but he will go along with it because he truly does love me." She did not attempt a laugh, but her eyes were almost as sardonic as his could be. "It doesn't matter to me any longer, or not very much. But that woman, what was the attraction?"

"There was none," he said, taking her in his arms again, seeking the nearness that he knew they could not have. "She gave me release, and I gave her the belief that she had power over me, and, of course, little bribes to keep her cooperative." He could not dismiss the sight of her running to that parked Benz. Her greed was greater than he had credited. "Her intentions, I think, were like a bad opera plot. I was cast as her beneficent protector, I think, or her noble lover. I was supposed to lavish my wealth and goods upon her uncritically and extravagantly, and then, at some appropriate moment, I was to blow my brains out rather than demand anything more of her."

"That sounds horrible," Madelaine said, shaking her head.

"It was, but there are times when it is best if such things are horrible, so that you can leave them behind without regret. That's not always easily learned, Madelaine, my heart. It took me centuries to understand it." How much he loved looking at her. He liked everything about her, the way she stood, the opulent body, the intelligent eyes, her quick mind, her generous heart. "I had too much to regret, Madelaine. I could not add her to the list." And yet, now that he knew what she was, he did regret her.

Madelaine lifted her arms around his neck, leaning against him, taking strength from him. "I have missed you, Saint-Germain."

"And I you, my heart."

Her eyes were luminous. "What can I say to you that will make you want to continue living? I have offered all I have; I can't offer you my blood, although I love you more dearly, more passionately than anyone on this earth. You tell me that it can't be done. I can't take away your hurt, or restore Laisha to you. What am I to do, my dearest? Tell me. Or tell me how to die the true death with you."

"You cannot do that," he protested at once.

"I will. There are plenty of opportunities." She saw the heat in his face, and she tried to step back, but he held her firmly.

"There are always opportunities. You would think that with hunger and poverty and disease to do their part, mankind would not need to look for ways to die. But that's not the case. Hardly; hardly. There is always a new amusement, a new cruelty, a new war. And each time, they deal out death with an enthusiasm that staggers the mind. Yet when a beggar asks for enough bread to stave off starvation for one more day, he is begrudged so little, that troops may be fed before the slaughter. What are you or am I, compared to that?" He let go of her and walked away from her.

"Very well." Her throat was tight and the words came out in painful little clusters. "If that is . . . how it must be . . . tell me when . . . and where. . . . I'll come with you . . . and we will not be alone."

"I don't ask that of you," he said, the remoteness coming back into his voice.

"I am not asking. If you intend to die, then you must be content to take me with you. You are what I love most, and you would leave me here with the wars and starvation and cruelty without your love to mitigate the horror and destruction?" She stared at his back, willing him, without success, to face her.

"Mitigate?" he asked sarcastically, his sorrow sinking its claws into him once more. "When we cannot touch each other with love, no matter how much we wish to? When our lives always take us far apart? When we have nothing but this? Madelaine! Madelaine, I love you to the point of despair. How can it mitigate?"

"Because it must," she answered quietly. She went to him, and standing behind him, took his hand in hers, and leaned on his back, her cheek against his shoulder. "What else is there?"

His fingers tightened on hers. "What indeed."

Text of a note from Roger to Nikolai Rozoh; opened in Germany and read by NSDAP members at the request of Hermann Göring.

*Berlin*
*March 29, 1928*

*Dear Nikolai:*

*As our plans stand at the moment, we will soon be leaving here for Paris, coming by way of Hannover, Bonn, and Luxembourg. We will drive as far as Bonn, and then take the train, for from all we have heard here, the driving becomes hazardous west of Bonn. We have secured first-class compartments and will arrive at the Gare de l'Est on the evening of April 2, at ten-thirty. It would be wise if you will check with the station to be sure that the train is on time. We will expect you to meet us, for it will not be possible to drive the Delage until the customs officials have certified it, which they cannot do until the following morning.*

*My master plans to go on to London as soon as he has settled one or two matters in Paris. There must be arrangements for transportation, which I will attend to as soon as I arrive. Any information you can provide, such as sailing times from Calais and other ports, would be very much appreciated.*

*Madame de Montalia will be traveling with us, and it is her intention to spend one evening at my master's apartment in Paris. There is a bed for her in the attic, which you should, at your earliest convenience, bring down to the second guest bedchamber for her use. It is most important that you do this, for Madame de Montalia does not rest well in most beds.*

*If you would be good enough to notify Madame Timbres of our intended arrival in Paris, it would be most useful to us all. She and her husband are to be invited to a private supper which my master will give in a few weeks to celebrate their marriage and to extend his best wishes to Madame Timbres, who has endured so much, as I am sure you know.*

*Also, Madame de Montalia requests that you visit her friend, the journalist you drove her to meet on one occasion, and tell him that she will be back in Paris shortly. Extend her thanks to him and assure him that she will be looking forward to spending time in his company. It is through his good offices that Madame de Montalia reached my master in Berlin, and so we are all in Mr. Tree's debt. If there is any service Madame de Montalia or my master can perform for him at any time, tell him that both are his to command.*

*Should there be inquiries from the police or those sympathetic to the National Socialists in Germany, you are requested to say only that you have not discussed that matter with my master. It is quite true, which is an advantage, and it will save you from certain unpleasantries. You may tell any who ask that they may speak to my master in person when he returns, but that you are not empowered to speak for him, nor have you been given to understand what his position is on this or any other political matter. It would not be wise to allow yourself to be drawn into conversations with such emissaries, and although this is not an order, it is a request: avoid all such contact until we return. The House of Special Destinations is not the only trap that waits for the unwary in Paris, my good Rozoh. For your own sake as well as ours, be as circumspect as you may.*

*It will be a pleasure to see you again.*

*Sincerely,*
*Roger*

## 8

The Hotel Heiligen Michael was close enough to the Koblenzer Tor to account for the name, since little else about the building did: it was not over fifty years old, done in the most stolid of the Nineteenth-Century modes, with richly overdone decor of rose and deep scarlet and chocolate brown, all highlighted with gold. It was no longer quite at its prime, but being convenient to many of the attractions of Bonn, including the Rhein-Promenade and Universität, it was not unpopular.

Ragoczy was given a suite on the second floor, complete with private sitting room. For propriety's sake, Madelaine was on the floor above, where the management trusted her virtue would be unquestioned. Roger took a room down the hall from Ragoczy, and once their bags had been brought in from the Delage, he went off to the rail station to confirm their reservations on the train the next morning.

"It's a pretty place," Madelaine said to Ragoczy a little while later, when she had got out of her dusty clothes and into a silk evening frock.

"Most of the Rhine country is scenic," he agreed, offering her his arm as they descended to the lobby.

"One day I may see more of it." She had been careful to keep their conversation light since they left Berlin, and was finding it increasingly difficult to think of things to say that would not remind him of his grief. "Would you like to see Beethoven's house?"

"No. Why should I?" The ironic edge was back in his voice again.

"You admire his music so much . . ." She felt flustered, and paused on the next-to-the-last step, her countenance puzzled.

"But his music is not in that house, mon coeur, and it is his music that delights me, not the walls that surrounded the man, who was supremely egotistical and socially boorish, because of, or in spite of, his genius." He smiled faintly. "He did not wash very often."

Madelaine gave half a shrug. "I never saw him, but there was a German Countess in Paris who swore that he was forward with every woman he met. I think it may have inspired him; at least, that was the Countess' opinion. She never said if she gave him inspiration herself, but most of us were encouraged to read between the lines." She came down the last step, confident now that she could keep up the graceful conversation that was so soothing. "There is an excellent library at the Universität here. I've used it once, but not recently. You might like to see their antiquities."

"I have more than enough old books of my own," he said as they crossed the lobby. It was cool and starting to cloud over, promising a spring rain before morning. "I'm happy that we'll be on the train tomorrow. Most of the roads within a day's drive will be little more than troughs of mud by morning."

"The train will be pleasant," she agreed, thinking that she had been spending far too much time on trains recently. They stopped in the narrow porch of the hotel and gazed out at the fading afternoon.

"Are you anxious to see more of Bonn, or would you rather sit and read for a time? I realize that is what you will do most of tomorrow, but the hotel is not moving, and the train will be." He smiled down at her, some of the remoteness gone from his eyes.

"If it would not bother you, it would please me." She looked back into the gloriously stuffy lobby. "There is a bar, but . . ."

"But two of us not drinking would be noticeable. Yes, I agree." He reached over and held the door for her once again. "A few hours in my parlor, if you like, and then some sleep. How much earth did you bring with you?"

"My smaller suitcase is full. It's enough." She thought that anyone overhearing their conversation might well conclude that they were mad, and she was glad that they spoke in French, for no matter how near the border they were, here the language was still German.

"Have you ever run out?" he asked her as he paused in the lobby to purchase a newspaper.

"Only once, and that was a long time ago, in Pamplona. I was able to improvise a box for myself, and remained in a stupor while it was shipped back to Provence. I lived on dogs, for the most part, caught at night while the teamsters put up at inns to sleep. It was not pleasant, but it succeeded, which was all that I could ask."

"I have always thought you're a most resourceful woman, mon coeur." He kissed her hand and would have said something more, but the manager of the hotel came bustling out of his little office just off the lobby.

"Herr Ragoczy, Herr Ragoczy, a moment of your time." He resembled a potbellied rabbit and was given to obsequious gestures, but he was considered a tyrant by his staff, and those guests who had offended him were hectored in strange, irrational ways.

"What is it, Herr Barmherzig?" His brows rose slightly, just enough to discourage socializing.

"There is some difficulty. Ja. Most inconvenient. The police have requested that I inform you that they must have an interview with you. There is an irregularity," he said, as if he were a priest discovering a new heresy.

"How odd," Ragoczy said smoothly. "Then, of course, I will be pleased to await them. The sooner the matter is straightened out, the sooner we may all be at ease again."

Herr Barmherzig folded his arms and dared to say, "We have not had such an occurrence at the Hotel Heiligen Michael for more than twenty years."

"Then you must count yourself fortunate, for in these uncertain times, what business has not been struck by . . . irregularities." He inclined his head in a most distinguished, formidably-polite manner. "Tell them that I am at their disposal."

"What?" Herr Barmherzig was astounded by Ragoczy's imperturbability. It had been his experience that those sought by the police, even in the most innocuous matters, displayed a certain apprehension that was entirely lacking in this man. He decided to try again. "They have said it is a matter of some urgency."

"Since I am planning to leave tomorrow morning, that is not surprising. At what time am I to expect them?" He put one hand over Madelaine's where it rested on his arm, for her fingers were trembling.

"They will be here at the conclusion of their dinners," he said grudgingly, knowing that was at least two hours away.

"Excellent. I am wholly at their disposal. Please let me know when they arrive." He nodded to Herr Barmherzig, and then glanced down at Madelaine. "My dear?"

Madelaine's violet eyes were startled. "What? Oh, of course. I'm ready." She smiled painfully widely, first at Ragoczy and then at Herr Barmherzig. Her legs were rubbery and her palms clammy. "How kind of you, Herr Barmherzig."

"But of course, Madame," the manager answered at once, baffled.

As they went up the stairs from the lobby, Ragoczy said very softly, "This is fortunate. If we had not come down, we would have had no time to prepare. This way, we have almost two hours."

"What do they want?" she asked in a low, thin voice.

"I don't want to speculate. That is a waste of time and thought." They were at the first landing, and he looked down into the lobby one more time. "They'll be watching us, of course, and so we must be very circumspect."

"But the police. You haven't broken any laws, have you?"

She could not envision him doing so, but those weeks in Berlin had been a dark time for him, and she knew that many of the pleasures offered there were not without risks.

"Not that I am aware of. But if they want to detain me, there must be some laws they can use as an excuse. It may be nothing more than taking the Delage out of the country without a special permit. That is becoming popular. It may be that they have found some of my alchemical supplies and have decided that they are not scientific enough. But I told you that speculation was fruitless." They were almost at his door. "Roger will be back shortly, and when he gets here, I must see you both in my parlor. We will speak, I think, in Arabic. That's one language I doubt anyone here understands but us."

"Saint-Germain," she began, then turned her head away.

"Yes, my heart?"

"You . . . you will not use this as an excuse, will you, to die? Not after . . ." She read the answer in his compassionate look. "I didn't—"

Ragoczy interrupted her lightly, but his hands held hers with an unexpected strength. "I have not yet seen Puccini's last opera. I suppose I must live."

"Oh, thank God, my love." She touched his face fleetingly, then said, "Shall I come in now?"

"Yes, if you will." He held the door for her, then followed her in, closing the door sharply as he caught sight of one of the bellmen standing at the end of the hall, watching them.

"This place!" Madelaine said with disgust, referring to the entire country. She took one of the ugly chairs near the fire and unbuttoned her jacket, revealing the lace bodice under it. "There is nothing but trouble here."

"And everywhere else," Ragoczy agreed, and switched from French to Arabic. "We will have to speak to Roger at once. It is imperative that he take you and himself to the train station. You may board the first train for Brussels or Paris, anything that takes you away from here. Do you have a black coat and hat, preferably with a veil?"

"Yes," she said, then went on to protest, "I am not leaving without you, Saint-Germain. I cannot."

"You must. I am fairly confident that the police would separate us in any case, and very likely would not detain you. For Germany to keep a citizen of France without good and sufficient reason would be a most untactful move at this time. Therefore, we will spare them the problem and arrange for you to leave. Wear the black coat and veiled hat. And if you have a very dark dress, wear that as well." He spoke quickly, not pausing to debate with her.

"As if I am in mourning?" she said. "Not very original."

"No, but eminently workable. If there is any question, you are returning suddenly to France, which explains why you will take any accommodations available, because of the unexpected death of your . . . father? brother? sister? perhaps mother? What?"

"Let us say my father. If I must choose one, that may be the best. He collapsed suddenly at . . . at his desk . . . and died two days later of . . ." She shrugged.

"You'd best be sure you have worked out an answer to that question, for you may be asked it." He bent over to put another log on the skimpy fire.

"I don't think I'll know what did it, that it was so sudden and unexpected that no one knows what was wrong. He had been in perfect health, and then, this!" She put a hand to her brow in a flamboyantly theatrical gesture.

"Don't do such things," Ragoczy reprimanded her gently.

"Why not? The Germans expect it of the French and Italians. But I won't. I will be one of the quietly-suffering types, so that my dry eyes will be thought to indicate bravery and self-control instead of heartlessness." She leaned back in the chair. "I don't want to leave you."

"You haven't much choice, Madelaine. We must be prepared to do this properly." He walked across the room. "Two hours isn't much time."

"Should I wait for you to join me at the train station?" She was beginning to enter into the spirit of the occasion, but her apprehension robbed her of any enjoyment she might have experienced.

"No. I won't travel by train." He touched his tie, loosening the knot a bit. "You forget I have the Delage."

"But you said yourself that there is going to be rain, and that means mud . . ." Her eyes were growing wide again, and she started to get up from the chair.

"Yes, but I am assuming that I have a better automobile than what the police here may drive. I will not try to cross the border near here, if they are truly trying to keep me here, but I'll go south, toward Switzerland. There are ways through the mountains, and if the automobile cannot make it, then I will go on foot." He lifted his hand to forestall her arguments. "I have a good supply of earth, and that will serve me well. And I will travel only at night. It should not take me long to reach

France. There is a cache of gold coins in my belt, so you're not to worry about my not having enough money to take a train or buy fuel for the automobile." He had neatly anticipated her various objections to his plan, and she shrugged.

"All right then. You wish me to be a mourning daughter. Is Roger my . . . ?" She looked up at him inquiringly.

"He is, I think, your brother-in-law, who has come to bring you back to Paris. That will account for your marked dissimilarity and the fact that he is traveling at the moment on a Spanish passport." He sighed. "It was easier two or three centuries ago. At the most you needed a travel authorization or a letter of introduction or a business contract, and you could go fairly much where you wished. A patent of arms helped in some cases and was a disadvantage in others. But now there are telegraphs and photographs and passports and visas and . . . all the rest of it. Undoubtedly it will get worse, which disappoints me. I do not want to have to spend decades in out-of-the-way places so that I may keep my credentials credible." He slapped the back of the chair in his annoyance.

"What passport are you using now?" she asked, thinking of her French one tucked into her purse.

"At the moment, I have my Hungarian passport, but in London I have a Czech and a Polish passport, and a set of Russian diplomatic papers as well, not that they are much use anymore." He gave an exasperated shrug. "In time I will grow used to these new complications. It is part of what we must do."

"Have you thought of what you will do next?" she asked. "About your passports, I mean." The rest she did not wish to talk about.

"I believe I will get Canadian papers. It is easily enough arranged. That will make my traveling easier. No one has any idea what Canadians look like or act like. They have a large number of foreigners living there, no mean consideration, and therefore my accent will not be thought unusual. But that is for later." He braced his arm on the back and leaned over her. "Courage, mon coeur. You will come through this well."

"And you?" she shot back at once. "What of you?"

"I will. You have my word on it." The tips of his fingers touched her hair, her cheek, and for some little time neither of them said anything.

"Well, you may wish to change. Get your bags ready and bring them to Roger's room. We might as well begin the deception here." He offered her his hand as she rose from the chair, and they kissed fleetingly.

"I will insist that Roger tell me everything that you do," she warned him, and blinked as the door opened behind them.

"The manager said—" Roger began in his calm voice as he shut the door unhurriedly.

"In Arabic," Ragoczy admonished him. "We're being cautious."

"Oh?" Roger came over to them. "The manager made a strange remark."

"Small wonder," Ragoczy said ironically. "The police are asking questions."

"Questions?" His face was almost without expression, but his faded blue eyes flickered from Ragoczy to Madelaine.

"Yes. Your brother-in-law, Madelaine's father, has just died in Paris and you must escort her back for the funeral."

"A most unfortunate occurrence," Roger said solemnly, waiting to hear the rest.

"Yes, and you will have to be most solicitous of her at the train station. You will take any first-class carriage going in the general direction of Holland, Belgium, or France. You will make whatever arrangements are necessary to get to Paris once you are out of Germany. Wire Nikolai when you have your route established, but not from this country." He did not look at his manservant, knowing that Roger would remember everything he was told and would question if he were dubious about any portion of the strategy.

"And you?"

"For the moment, I am going to have to remain here. Is the Delage at the train station or here?"

Roger coughed delicately. "There is a question about a permit. It is here at present. I had hoped that you would know where the permit might be obtained."

"It isn't necessary. I will take the automobile." He rested his hand on Madelaine's shoulder. "Go change, ma belle, and make yourself ready." He bent to kiss her hand, loving her for her strength that had been his deliverance.

"In Paris?" she asked tenuously.

"Yes. And soon, my heart. Believe this." He did not speak until she had left the room, and then he turned at once to Roger. "I must get ready to see the police. I will need two bottles of schnapps and a glass. Order me a small meal and have it brought to this room." He loosened his collar and unbuttoned his black jacket. "Hurry. I haven't much more than an hour to ready myself, and by then you should be away from here."

"As you wish, my master," Roger said at once, and went from the room quickly. He came back ten minutes later with the two bottles of schnapps, remarking as he closed the door, "Herr Barmherzig was shocked, but I think he liked being shocked."

"Undoubtedly," Ragoczy said quietly. He was seated before the fire, his clothes in disarray, his hair mussed, and his eyes, which he was still rubbing, reddened. "Open one of the bottles and pour it down the sink. Make sure no one sees you. Then bring it here and put it beside my chair, not quite out of sight. I'll take care of the other."

"As you wish." Roger took one of the bottles and tucked it under his arm, then went in to the hall.

While he was gone, Ragoczy opened the second bottle and sluiced a generous mouthful of the stuff, then spat it into the fire, watching the flames rise higher, crackling. A bit more of the liquid was poured onto his hands, and, satisfied at the smell of it, he poured the glass Roger had provided full of the schnapps, letting a little slosh over the rim. By the time Roger came back into the room, it reeked of spirits and Ragoczy himself seemed far gone in drink. He waved vaguely in Roger's direction and slurred out a few words of instruction as his manservant closed the door. "Well?" he asked when they were private again. "Will it serve?"

"To what end?" Roger asked, putting the empty bottle down as Ragoczy had instructed him.

"The police will not have a very coherent conversation with me this evening, and by morning, I will not be here." He rubbed his eyes once more, for good measure. "Take Madelaine out the servants' entrance, and tell anyone who asks that she does not want to have to speak to anyone. I will see that the rooms are paid for, so do not bother about that. We do not want to alert the manager or anyone else that we are leaving." He sniffed at his hands. "I got drunk twice in my life, when I was very young. There was nothing like this, then, just very raw wine. My head pounded for two days after each of them."

"There are worse things to do," Roger said, to indicate that he was listening.

"You're not to let Madelaine worry about me. She will, of course, but keep her from brooding. It will serve no purpose. I have not told her, but I think you should know that I think it may be difficult to cross the border for some distance. If that

is the case, it may take me a few days to leave here. You
know what to do if I am . . . detained." He gave his servant a
long look.

"Yes, my master, I know what to do." He took a deep
breath. "Is there anything else?"

"No, I don't think so. My thanks, but you know that too,
don't you?" He held out his hand to Roger, clasping the other
man's briefly, but with feeling.

"I've never doubted it." He started for the door, but stopped
as he heard Ragoczy say, "You know, a week ago, I would
have welcomed this. I would have let them take me, imprison
me, or execute me, whatever they wished. Now, I am offended by them, and by my own . . . cowardice? I don't know
what it was. I kept thinking of how much I loved Laisha.
Loved! It's absurd to say that. I love her. I will love her
always. Yet I didn't recognize that until Madelaine . . ." He
broke off. "Travel safely, old friend."

"And you, my master," he said as he closed the door.

Ragoczy sat alone for almost an hour. He heard Roger
knock at the door once, a signal they had used for more than
fifteen hundred years. So they were away, he thought, and
felt a rush of gratitude for both Roger and Madelaine. With
them gone, he could turn his attention to the police without
being overwhelmed with concern for them. He tossed the
schnapps from the glass onto the fire and refilled the glass
again as he heard the heavy tread of boots on the stairs.
"Come in," he called out muzzily as a heavy fist pounded the
door. "And be damned to you if you don't cooperate with me
this time," he added with bleary pugnacity.

There were three policemen in the doorway, two of them
constables, one of them an officer. Ragoczy saw that all wore
small swastika pins on their collars. "Herr Ragoczy?"

"What do you want? Did she call you to complain? What
. . ." He reached for the glass, knocked it over, and gazed
at it stupidly. "How'd that . . ." With great concentration he
took the schnapps bottle and poured out a generous amount.
"Join me?" he said to the others as if remembering his manners at last.

"Herr Ragoczy, we have some questions we must ask you,"
said the officer. He was a tall, lean man with strongly-marked
features and an air of worry about him. His brown eyes were
troubled as he looked down at Ragoczy.

"Questions? Don't know why. But ask away, ask away," he

said with an extravagant sweep of his arm that almost knocked over the schnapps bottle.

"I am Inspector Wolfram Spreu of the Bonn police department. I have received a message from Berlin requesting that I detain you." He was unhappy about these orders, for his posture was hesitant and he could not bring himself to stand at full attention.

Ragoczy perceived this, and hoped he could turn it to his advantage. "Berlin? I was there a few days ago. Cold place. It's those Prussians."

Inspector Spreu smiled wanly. "Yes, they are sticklers," he said uncomfortably. "You were there, you say?"

"Been there for several weeks. Had a nice house in Charlottenburg. There was a woman who stayed there with me." He gave a leering wink. "Not the same one with me now. She is with me, isn't she? She's been saying she'll take herself off. Upstairs sulking, no doubt."

"Herr Ragoczy," Inspector Spreu said quietly, "there have been some serious charges laid against you, by a Nillel Schlacke. She claims that you committed indecencies on her body, and that you stole from her."

Ragoczy did not need to pretend to be shocked. He dropped the glass, ignoring it as it broke on the floor. "Nillel says what?"

"It has not been investigated yet, but Berlin would like it if you would return there so that the question may be cleared up." He turned to his two constables and said in an undervoice, "I know that we were warned that he is dangerous, but in this state, I might do better with him alone."

One of the constables hesitated, but the other regarded Ragoczy with a jaundiced eye. "The only thing he's about to attack in the condition he's in is the chamber pot." He chuckled at his rough humor and pulled his fellow constable's sleeve. "Come on. Let the Inspector deal with him. It'll be a thankless job, but . . ."

"He won't tell us much until morning," Inspector Spreu ventured, and ushered the two constables out of the room. He closed it loudly, hoping it would attract the attention of the man in the chair. When he turned, he saw Ragoczy take the mouth of the schnapps bottle from his lips. "Do you think you ought to drink so much?"

"Why not?" Ragoczy asked as he put the bottle down heavily. "In . . . Inspector, you can't . . . I don't like Berlin. Why should I go back there?" He pitched his voice higher than usual, and added a querulous, whining note to it. "What do they want me for? I ask you that."

"There has been a complaint, from Fräulein Nillel Schlacke—" Inspector Spreu said patiently, only to be interrupted by Ragoczy once more.

"Fräulein Nillel Schlacke is a fine one to make accusations. A fine one." He reached for the bottle, then stopped, casting a broad, guilty glance at Inspector Spreu.

"Very wise, Mein Graf," the Inspector said with a sigh. "I know that it is unfortunate to be detained in this way, but you must understand my position. There was a request for my cooperation from those who are very highly placed." He cleared his throat, his mouth curved with distaste. He had not liked his orders, and although he was a loyal member of the NSDAP, he was always reluctant to grant extra privilege to those in exalted positions. He was painfully aware that had Ragoczy also been a member of the NSDAP, no one would have paid any attention to what the woman said, nor would he have been forbidden to cross the border. He looked down at his hands. "Tomorrow, I have been told that I should see that you are on a train to Berlin. I am required to act in this matter, or I would not be willing to do so."

Ragoczy had been peering at him owlishly, measuring the distress in the man's stance. He waggled a finger at him. "You're not making sense, Inspector. You're saying you have to stop me. Why must you do that? Who gave you the orders?"

The Inspector shrank back at the last question, and did not at first try to answer. But than he capitulated, telling himself that it was most unlikely that Ragoczy would remember in the morning, and so embarrass both himself and the Inspector. "It is not the police as much as the NSDAP. Someone in the high command of the party wants to see you. It isn't the woman at all, but some other matter. The woman is an excuse. From what I was told on the telephone, she was working for the NSDAP in any case, being paid to keep an eye on you, so that if they had to come up with some reason to hold you, she could provide one." He felt better now that he had said it. He had missed the solace of confession since leaving the Church, and at moments like this one, he often felt an overwhelming urge to unburden himself. At least on this occasion he had not been indiscreet, and if Ragoczy should remember a few words, no one would believe that a man as drunk as he could make any serious countercharges.

"That's . . . that's pretty corrupt," Ragoczy said, letting

the words roll out of him in long, juicy syllables. He grinned lopsidedly at the Inspector.

"Yes, it is," Inspector Spreu said in a dejected tone.

"Pity." Ragoczy made a lugubrious nod.

"A great pity," the Inspector agreed gravely.

"Now, if you could tell them what to do . . . You're not the sort of man to let them do this thing. . . . See it in your eyes. . . . They're puffed up . . . met a few in Berlin, like grouse . . . strutting around." He laughed with sloppy amusement and paddled the air with one arm. "Don't like Berlin . . . did I tell you that?"

"I believe you did," said the Inspector as he came nearer the fire. There was the first onslaught of a blustery wind slapping at the windows, and a new assortment of drafts scampered across the floor. "I don't relish sending you back there." He had other reasons to feel that way, but was no longer eager to discuss them.

"Well, don't do it, then," Ragoczy said with an overbearing attempt at being reasonable. "Tell them how to use their orders and forget you ever saw me." He leaned back in the chair and propped one heel on the toe of his other shoe, smiling beatifically at this accomplishment.

"I haven't any choice. Even if you did not stop here, there are notices out for you from Meppen to Lindau. Herr Göring does not want you to leave the country." He tried to imagine what it was that had captured Göring's interest in this foreigner. There had been rumors of great industrial discoveries, but unless it was a better way to distill schnapps he could not imagine what the man would have of value.

"Göring again," Ragoczy said with a gargling chortle. "Always Göring. Strange." He picked up the bottle and cradled it against his chest. "I wonder what he wants?"

"You will find out when you arrive in Berlin, no doubt." Inspector Spreu moved away from the wall, his hands joined before him so that he looked for one instant like the choirboy he had been as a youth.

"Tomorrow?" Ragoczy asked. "What time must I leave?" He slurred the question and let his accent grow stronger, so that he was almost unintelligible.

"As soon as you are able." There was a skeptical quality to Spreu's answer, as if he assumed that Ragoczy would have a massive hangover: it was precisely what Ragoczy wished him to think.

"Don't wake me too early, Inspector. . . . Don't want to

. . . you know what morning heads are like." His toe-and-heel balancing came to an abrupt halt, and he sprawled, legs stiff in front of him.

"I sympathize," the Inspector said as he went toward the door. "I am going to leave a man posted in the lobby. If you should try to leave . . ."

Ragoczy laughed far more riotously than the comment merited. "Not tonight, Inspector. Tomorrow. Where's that woman? . . . Oh, well . . . wouldn't do much for her tonight, not now." He brought one hand to his brow in an uncertain salute. "After breakfast, you come to see me. We'll go over all this again then. I'll make more sense of it." He giggled and waved at Inspector Spreu.

"Herr Ragoczy, I feel I should warn you that you may be in a great deal of trouble." The Inspector frowned as he said this, doubt rising in him again. Could this man have the diverse qualities NSDAP headquarters in Berlin attributed to him? It was not likely. Spreu began to think that there were other, more subtle reasons that Hermann Göring was interested in Ragoczy. The man came from a distinguished family if his name was any indication, and he felt free to disgrace that name with impunity. There were a great many well-placed men in Hungary who might be swayed if one of their own nobility were to espouse the philosophy of the NSDAP. That made a degree of sense to Spreu, though he deplored the idea. The NSDAP should not have to wring support out of defunct princes in order to make their cause acceptable. He shook his head and opened the door. "I wouldn't drink any more tonight, Herr Graf," he suggested.

"You aren't me, Spreu, and there's still schnapps in the bottle." He held it up in an unsteady hand. "Another hour, and it will all be gone."

"As you wish," Spreu said, a tinge of resignation in his words. What did it matter to him if the man pickled his brain in alcohol, when he would be little more than a pet on display in Berlin? Yet his reflections cheapened the NSDAP in his mind, and something of the pride he took in his swastika pin was diminished. "Good night, Mein Herr."

"G'night," Ragoczy called after him with farcical cheer, capping his performance with a badly-rendered version of the chorus of one of the lewd songs currently popular in Berlin's underground nightclubs. He repeated it three times until he was certain that Inspector Wolfram Spreu had left the hotel. Then he left his room and swaggered to the top of the stairs,

bellowing down for another bottle of schnapps and demanding
boisterously to know where his manservant and lady-friend
were, and insisting that they join him for a drink.

The bellman who brought up the schnapps told him that
undoubtedly his female companion and his manservant had
retired for the night, it being after nine. Although he was
inured to the boorishness of foreigners, he ventured to suggest that it might be wise for the Graf to retire as well.
Ragoczy cursed him roundly as he fumbled for change, and
tipped him in gold instead of silver. The bellman concealed a
sour smile and hurried from the room to tell the staff that the
Hungarian Graf was drunk as a Cossack and would be impossible in the morning. He boasted a little of his good fortune,
but when he saw the sly, envying looks of the others on the
staff, he became quiet once more.

Almost an hour later, Ragoczy left the hotel, though no one
was aware of his departure. He climbed down the side of the
building, his bags strapped to his back, his compact, deep-
chested figure now in unrelieved black. Inspector Spreu would
not have recognized him, for all the slovenliness that he had
seen was gone. Nothing remained of the miserable, drunken
foreigner who had roused Spreu's pity and contempt: in his
place was a formidable man of commanding presence and utter
competence. His dark eyes were keen, though a little red-
rimmed from the heavy rubbing he had given them, and something of the smell of schnapps still clung to his clothes. He
moved in swift, purposeful silence toward the garage that had
been a stable not so many years before.

There were a number of twenty-liter drums of gasoline
stored on one side of the garage, and Ragoczy appropriated
two of them for his journey, putting them into the backseat of
the powerful automobile and bracing them with his suitcases.
With luck that would give him enough gasoline to cover the
distances he had in mind. There were cities where he could
purchase fuel, he knew that, but he had begun to fear that
such places would be under surveillance. Since detention orders
were out on him from the North Sea to the Swiss border, he
thought it likely that other roads would be watched: with the
rain making a quagmire of all but the main roads, he did not
dare to find his way on the narrow country lanes, and he was
reluctant to risk being spotted on the more heavily-traveled
highways. For the moment, he felt it was safest to drive at
night, not only because he had much less chance of being
recognized or stopped, but because with so little of his native

earth he was not willing to expose himself to daylight any more than necessary.

He got into the driver's seat of his Delage and pulled on his gloves. The front windscreen was raised, but he lowered the one fronting the rear passenger seats. He gave a last-minute inspection to the roof and was satisfied that it would not leak too badly. When the weather cleared, he would take it down.

Ragoczy waited until the clock in the Koblenzer Tor began to chime the hour of eleven; then he depressed the starter and the powerful machine rumbled into life, coughing once or twice with the chill. Slowly Ragoczy backed out of the garage, always looking to see if anyone had noticed his activities. The hotel was quiet, most of the windows dark, and no one stirred as the Delage turned onto the brick-paved streets and accelerated away from the hotel, slipping away toward the south side of the city. There he struck out, not toward the west and the guarded borders, but south-southeast, toward Mainz and Heidelberg and München. The rain that rode on the wind suited his steadily-darkening mood: how fitting, he thought bitterly as he steered around a muddy pothole, that his one escape route should lie through the region he wished most to avoid.

Text of a letter from Enzo DiGottardi to Paul von Hindenburg

*Schloss Saint-Germain*
*Schliersee, Bayern*
*April 2, 1928*

*Presidential Rezidence*
*Berlin*

*My dear President von Hindenburg:*

*I am writing to you because there is no higher author-ity in this country, and your word ought to bear some weight with those who are imposing upon my employer and myself. I am employed by Graf Franchot Ragoczy to be caretaker of his estate, Schloss Saint-Germain, here in Bayern. It is a remote place, of fair acreage, with a Schloss of good size, about four hundred years old. My employer is not in residence, and because of a tragedy in his family, does not expect to be here for some time to come. He has placed the entire estate under my responsi-bility, which I have done my best to discharge well. I am not one to shirk obligations, and I have brought a few family members here to work with me so that the estate and grounds will not suffer during Graf Ragoczy's ab-sence. I have been given a reasonable allowance to draw upon for the upkeep of Schloss Saint-Germain and I have not had to use any of the discretionary funds that have been set aside for me.*

*I tell you this not for my own glory, but so that you will understand that I am not writing to you because of my own incompetence or lack of interest in my employ-er's affairs. For the time I was Graf Ragoczy's cook, he was more than fair with me, giving me excellent pay even when money was so worthless that enough to paper a wall would not have bought a single egg. During those bleak days, Graf Ragoczy paid me in gold coins and in useful necessities, such as food, fuel, blankets, and the like. He*

*is a man who does well by those who work for him, and
expects them to be worthy of his trust.*

*It has happened recently that there have been men,
many of them active in politics and similar endeavors,
who have been interested in Schloss Saint-Germain. There
have been offers from a few of them to purchase this
estate, but I am not at liberty to enter into negotiations
with any of them, and would not do so, even if I had my
employer's permission. I believe that one given the care of
such an extensive holding must be prepared to do a great
deal for it, and to invest the best part of himself in the
place, which precludes any such bargaining, no matter
how opportune such requests and offers may seem. I have
agreed in all instances to inform Graf Ragoczy of the
interest expressed, and have written to his Paris address
with instructions that the information was to be delivered
to him as soon as convenient. Graf Ragoczy has been doing
a goodly amount of traveling recently, and therefore his
responses to these offers have been erratic. In all instances,
however, he has rejected the proposals out of hand and
said that should he change his mind, he will inform me of
it. I have made sure the men who have submitted offers
have learned of Ragoczy's refusal and his continuing
disinclination to sell his estate.*

*I have thought that this settled the question, but appar-
ently I have been wrong. Two days ago I was visited by a
number of armed men in SA uniforms who told me that I
had been instructed by the München court to leave the
premises at once and to relinquish the keys and all access
to the estate to their officers at once. I said that it was
impossible, as I had not been empowered by Graf Ragoczy
to do so. I was then informed that the court had decided to
honor a claim to the estate that had been put before the
bench on behalf of the Thule Bruderschaft. The judge
hearing the case is a member of that organization, and
willingly granted the request of his brother member.*

*I have not yet departed, but I have packed my belong-
ings, and my family and I are prepared to leave within
the hour. I am of the opinion that a gross injustice has
been perpetrated on Graf Ragoczy, and that he is entitled
to redress for the wrongs he has suffered. The men of the
Thule Bruderschaft have said that they will not pay for
their use of the estate and that they will oppose in court
any attempt to recover monies from them. That may be,*

*but I have a duty to my employer, and I cannot abandon him and his Schloss in such a cold-blooded manner. I must voice my protest for this most reprehensible act, and seek the support of those with greater power than the Thule Bruderschaft possesses. I am aware that they are hand-in-glove with the NSDAP and for that reason you may hesitate to dispute title with them. But you are a fair man, President von Hindenburg, and you have been a great hero in war. You know that it is poor strategy to cheat your nobility to oblige a few envious men with money.*

*It is not fitting that Graf Ragoczy should be treated in this way. He has given the fruits of his studies to Farben and he has been called a genius at chemistry. He did not ask for more than what had been granted him at the beginning of his project. When there was no money to continue, he paid for his supplies and materials himself and has never asked that the amounts be returned, although others have profited from his work. To accept so much from Graf Ragoczy and to treat him so meanly is not a credit to you, your country, the NSDAP, the Thule Bruderschaft, or anything else pertaining to Deutschland.*

*If you decide to remain silent on this issue, I will take my case to the League of Nations. It is possible that they will not want to address it, but I will have made my point and it is possible that the Thule Bruderschaft will be shamed into returning that which is not there for them by rights. They have said that one day they will make restitution to Graf Ragoczy, but they do not say when, or what form their restitution will take. The Thule Bruderschaft have an egregious hunger for this estate. Some of the members put a great deal of stock in the name and say that they believe it is associated with an old mystic. Others do not have faith in that, but nonetheless believe that because of its location, it has a few desirable properties for their activities.*

*If there is justice in Deutschland, then this estate must be returned at once to its rightful owner, and compensation for this insult must be forthcoming soon after. If there is no justice, then I am wasting my time in writing this.*

*In the hope that you will stand by the honor you upheld as a soldier, I am*

> *Most sincerely yours,*
> *Enzo DiGottardi*

# 9

A few hours before, there had been rain, but now there was only the drifting mist rising through the trees toward the high peaks, wrapped in snow and clouds. It was dank as the exhalations of flooded mines. The night was densely cold, as if the air itself were heavy with the frigid dampness. Ice lay in the deep ruts in the old lane that led up to Schloss Saint-Germain from the back of the estate, and the Delage churned and groaned with every meter covered. Ragoczy held the wheel steady, fighting the sudden pulls and slithering that threatened to send the automobile into the ditch beside the road. It was his third night of driving, and he was growing tired.

The high section of stone wall that still stood at the back of the Schloss loomed up before his headlights, green with lichen and touched with frosty mist. The stones seemed huge, impregnable, though Ragoczy knew he had only to walk thirty meters or so to come to the end of it. He pulled the Delage into the shadow of a stand of pines and brought the automobile to a halt. When he was satisfied that the brake was properly set and the automobile adequately concealed, he moved away from it, pulling on a hunter's jacket of fur-lined black wool.

Schloss Saint-Germain was draped in gossamer cerements of algid vapor, the building looking as ephemeral as fog, a thing from a dream instead of the solid reality Ragoczy knew it to be.

Ragoczy approached from the south side, coming past the stables and toward the kitchen entrance. If Enzo were awake at this hour, he would undoubtedly be in that room, preparing tomorrow's meals. Using his large iron key, Ragoczy let himself in through the scullery door, prepared to feel the relaxation that came to him when standing on his native earth. He pulled the door closed and locked it again, noticing that he felt no calmer than he had at the wheel of the Delage. He considered this, then decided that fatigue and his own unrelenting grief had blocked the palliation of the good Transylvanian earth lying under the floor. He was mildly surprised to find the kitchen cold, and only the heavy, ancient wood-burning stove giving off the last echoes of heat from dying embers. Ragoczy's tread echoed eerily in the room as he crossed it quickly, not wanting to remember the times he had seen Laisha sit there with Nikolai and Enzo, watching the cook prepare the delicacies he inevitably offered her. Those days were gone. He opened the door to the hall, wondering what rooms Enzo had selected for himself and his relatives; he did not want to rouse the whole house, not at this hour.

He made his way with some caution down the long, empty corridor toward the main staircase. The vague unease that had bothered him was growing more intense. He walked more quickly, more quietly, the first pucker of a frown on his forehead. At the staircase, he looked up to the landing, half-expecting to find his caretaker there with a shotgun, waiting to prevent him from progressing further. When no one spoke to him, he was apprehensive. He could not rid himself of the sensation of being in the midst of the enemy, and it was an effort of will not to leave the place at once.

Ragoczy's study lay under a thin film of dust and smelled of neglect. The empty bookshelves gaped in the dark like tooth-less mouths. The desk, wholly cleared and uncluttered, seemed to be out of place in the oak-paneled room. He trailed his finger along the nearest shelf and left a dark track where it had been. With a sigh, he pulled the Turkish chair around to a better angle and dropped into it. An hour or two of rest should suffice, he told himself, wishing that his malaise would pass so that he might be revived by this place. He propped his feet on a low stool and leaned back, closing his eyes, determined to rest.

But rest eluded him. There was no posture that refreshed him, no restoration of his strength and faculties. The least noise would bring him alert and erect in his chair, a draft was as scathing to his nerves as the sound of a rake on flagstones. After rather more than an hour of vain attempts at repose, he got up, determined to search the place and discover what, if anything, within these walls was the source of his disturbance.

He had reached the study door when he heard a light tread in the hall, and he halted just inside the door, his hand on the knob, waiting.

The person on the other side faltered, then opened the door so quickly that Ragoczy reached out and thrust the shoulder of the person entering the room so that the impetus of movement carried the newcomer forward to sprawl on the old Persian carpet.

"Oh. What . . . !" the voice cried out in a faint shriek, and the figure huddled near the desk, as if trying to disappear.

Ragoczy was astonished. "Gudrun!" he said, shocked, as he came across the carpet toward her, his hands held out to her. "What are you doing here?"

"Graf." She turned her disbelieving eyes on him and shook her head, as if doubting her senses even when his hands closed on hers. "What are *you* doing here?"

He helped her to her feet, smoothing the elaborate velvet robe she wore, and attempting to brush the worst of the dust from its thick, silken pile. He was somewhat startled by her finery, for he knew that she had been making do with a pitifully small trust, hardly enough to permit her to eke out a cloisterish way of life. Yet here she was in his Schloss, dressed in the finest silk velvet. "This is my house, Gudrun," he reminded her kindly, hoping that she would proffer an explanation for her presence.

"Oh, dear." She ran one hand through her fashionably coiffed pale hair, and gave a distracted look to the rest of the room. "I thought I heard, oh, mice in here. I didn't think you would be back, after . . ."

"Laisha's death?" he asked cuttingly. "I had not intended to."

"No. That's not what I meant, but it is a factor, of course. No." She fingered the deep ruffle around her neck. "Didn't they tell you?"

"Tell me what, Gudrun?" He was growing more curious as he listened to her. Clearly there had been developments here of which he was unaware. He had received no warning from Enzo, but his ire at the Italian-Swiss lasted no more than a second. Enzo had not been told where to write to him other than Paris, and had not been given his address in Berlin. He thought that he had been a fool to ignore this place so completely; the negligence had undoubtedly contributed to the difficulties here.

"About the Thule Gesellschaft and Bruderschaft. They petitioned the court to give them title to your estate. Weren't you notified?" She was regarding him with large eyes open wide. She was just beginning to wonder what he was doing here in Schloss Saint-Germain in the middle of the night, unannounced.

"No, I wasn't notified." He doubted the attempt had been made, since he had been followed so much of the time.

"They said that you had, and that there was no response. They claimed that gave them the right to use the estate, since

it was the property of an absent foreigner." She repeated the
words very much as she had heard Helmut say them to her,
and as she said them, she had the same distrust that she had
felt when he had told her, only three days ago, that they
would be living at the Schloss until the Bruderschaft could
send a permanent staff to take care of the estate.

"What did Enzo DiGottardi have to say about this?" He
could not imagine the man would tolerate such action.

"Your cook, you mean?" She saw him nod. "He protested, of
course, but he is a foreigner, too, isn't he? They said that he
could not appeal the matter since the property is not his and
he is not a citizen of Deutschland."

"How convenient," Ragoczy murmured, then asked, "Where
is Enzo, do you know?"

"He's gone. He was told to leave. There were members of
the Bruderschaft who came here with the court documents
and insisted that he be on his way. I was told that he wrote a
number of letters objecting to this, but none of them were
successful in persuading anyone in government to reconsider
the verdict of the court. The judge is part of the Thule Gesellschaft, but I don't know if he is in the Bruderschaft as well."
She knew she was speaking too quickly, that her nervousness
was causing her to chatter in the hope that he would not press
her for more explanation. She used not to do that, she thought,
but since Helmut had forced his way into her life, she had
learned to babble, concealing her fear and disgust in a pleth-
ora of words; endless, senseless words that camouflaged her
deeper feelings.

"I see." He studied her face, then asked with disarming
gentleness, "Rudi, what's wrong?"

"Wrong?" she repeated, almost five notes higher than her
usual speaking level. "Why, nothing. I . . . I don't . . . What
should be wrong?"

"I don't know, but I've never known you to talk like this."
He pressed one hand to her arm. "You're dressing well."

"Oh, yes," she said sadly. "I have a new wardrobe, expensive and impressive. I have new furniture, and Wolkighügel is
filled with painters and plasterers and plumbers and all the
rest of them, being turned back in to the showplace it was.
And I *hate* it."

"Then why . . . ?" He watched her closely as she talked,
noticing her hasty movements, so unlike her usual grace. Her
hands fluttered, her eyes moved restlessly, her body twisted
and shuddered inside her luxurious robe.

"I have married again. I had to. Not for the reason most women claim. I'm not pregnant and I hope that I never am. I don't want his child, not now or ever. He thinks that it is my duty to give him sons, because we're Teutons, and the world is being overrun with racial bastards. He lectures me about it, and claims that it would aid his career if we had children. I don't want his child." Her hands crossed her body and gripped her elbows so tightly that the tendons stood out on the backs in ridges.

"Who is this distressing groom, Rudi? Forgive me, but I was under the impression when I left—although I was not in a particularly observant frame of mind at the time—that you had not accepted any regular suitor and that you had no intention of doing so." His compassion steadied her, and when he offered her his hand, she took it, squeezing his fingers when she was afraid she might break down.

"You see, Saint-Germain, there were debts, and I knew nothing of them. Tremendous debts, for fabulous amounts of money, that I could not pay." She looked away, thinking again of Maximillian's perfidy, torn between despair and fury. "I didn't know about them until recently."

"Your brother?" He was certain of it even before he asked the question, but wanted to hear her say so. Maximillian had been willing to keep living on Gudrun's care.

"Yes. Naturally. Who else could have done it? I knew nothing of it until recently, and when I found out, I had no means of paying the debts. Maximillian had this dream of our life, and thought that as we had lived before, we were entitled to live now. He could not see that the money was gone." She pulled at Ragoczy's fingers, twisting them, unaware of what she was doing. "He promised things he did not have so that he could continue to live . . . He promised Wolkighügel, which was mine—mine!—and when he died, he left no warning, only the suggestion that I should marry Helmut Rauch because he would be able to guide me. Much of the money he borrowed was through Helmut, who must have suspected the truth, but helped Maximillian maintain his fantasy. Not long ago, he brought me the records of Maximillian's debts, and I was overcome. I did not have the money: I haven't got it now. Oh, yes, there are clothes, and my home is being refurbished, but it is nothing. I wish the house were in ashes and that I was dressed in rags!" She stifled her outburst almost at once. "He'll hear. He'll hear."

"Who?" Ragoczy inquired. He was sorry for Gudrun and her

distraught frame of mind. Whatever had convinced her to accept the tokens of wealth had not been sufficient when balanced against its demands.

"Helmut Rauch. I am Frau Rauch now, you know. Oh yes, he married me. He insisted on marrying me. The Thule Bruderschaft canceled the debts that Maximillian owed them and paid those he owed to others. All that was on the condition that I marry Helmut. They are most generous, truly. Their charity is exemplary." She broke away from Ragoczy and paced around the carpet. The ruffled hem whispered as it brushed the carpet, making a sound like the wind through new leaves.

"Helmut Rauch?" Ragoczy demanded. He recalled the man with distaste: the thought of him imposing on Gudrun, who had been forced to endure so much already, made him want to choke the man.

"It was such an impetuous courtship. One afternoon he presented himself at Wolkighügel and showed the letters of debt left by my brother and outlined the alternatives. I could not stand to have the house sold and the estate broken up, and the thought of the disgrace was more than I could tolerate, and so I accepted his handsome offer. We were married not long after. This stay at Schloss Saint-Germain is by way of a honeymoon. Do you know what it is like, finding that repellent man beside me in a room where you slept?" Her voice broke, but she contained herself. "I am learning, you see. I no longer burst into tears for mere unhappiness. Now it takes a great deal more."

"Gudrun, I am truly sorry," he said, putting his arm around her shoulder and holding her gently. "If I had known how things stood with you, I would have done whatever it was in my power to aid you and see that you were not embarrassed again. Perhaps I should have seen it, but when you had refused my assistance and said that you could manage on what you had . . ."—he felt a pang of conscience as he spoke—"and I was not perceptive enough to see that you were only saying what you had been taught to say. I have not made such a serious error in some time. I cannot justify my neglect, but I hope you are willing to forgive me."

She laughed once, not quite hysterically. "I did not tell you. I didn't want you to know. I thought that you would despise me if you knew how badly—"

"Rudi, I have been a beggar and a slave, and though I was born a Prinz, my kingdom is gone. There is no shame in having no money, and no dishonor in being aided. You told me that you wanted to live so that your father and his father would respect what you have done. If they could know anything of how you have been forced to struggle and how poorly your brother behaved, they would commend you in the highest terms." He thought that this was probably a lie, for he had known some of those stiff-necked old aristocrats from the days of the Austro-Hungarian Empire, and they, without exception, would have looked askance on Gudrun for allowing her troubles to reach such an impasse. He said nothing of this to the wretched woman who listened to him with pathetic dependency.

"Oh, I hope so," she whispered, and seemed to go limp with concern. She held on to Ragoczy, and was able to bring herself to a stronger stance. "I don't want to stay here. Your pardon, Graf, but it has become a tomb to me, this Schloss. It is very fine, no doubt, and I am a fool to want to be anywhere else, but I can't remain. If I do, I think it will make me run mad."

Ragoczy's concern for her increased. "Does he abuse you?" he inquired gently, not wishing to reawaken the terror he had heard in her voice a few minutes ago.

"No, not truly. He is brusque and . . . does not much care how I feel when he is with me. When we dine, he praises everything, but in such a way that I shudder with worry and hope to think of something else to give him to eat. Part of it is that he wishes to be rid of Frau Bürste, for he knows she is my confidante and friend, and so he says things to me, snide, cutting things to remind me that I am now the chattel dining at the lord's table, and that this indulgence might be stopped whenever it suits him. He does not want to dismiss her himself, of course. He would prefer I do it, so that I will have to end the only friendship, aside from the one I have had with you, that makes it possible for me to continue." She brought her hands up to her eyes again, and this time she did not stop the tears.

"Do you want to continue in your life? Isn't there somewhere you can go, or someone who would welcome you?" He could not imagine that she would be without family or friends who would be willing to have her with them.

"I have a few relatives, but they are in no position to give me housing or material aid. I considered that, and could not justify it. I have an old friend in Innsbruck who has said that she would like me to visit, but she does not have the means to keep me with her for long, and I could not impose on her." She sniffled and wiped her eyes with the ruffles of her velvet sleeve.

"Do you think she would prefer knowing what has become of you?" Ragoczy suggested more harshly than he wished. "If she has any affection for you, she has to value your happiness to some extent." What was wrong with Gudrun? "What would you like to do?"

Her lips trembled at her attempt to smile. "I would like to live at Wolkighügel with Frau Bürste. It would not matter if it was as it had been. I did not like having no money, no new clothes, and seeing the estate go to ruin, but it was a pleasant life and I miss it." She flushed. "Frau Bürste cares for me, and she is so good to me."

Ragoczy heard the minor shift in her emphasis and thought he guessed the extent of Frau Bürste's involvement with Gudrun, and was not in the least shocked. Gudrun was the sort of woman who would find the empathy of another woman more consoling than sympathy given by a man—which, he realized, included himself. "Is that possible? Is there a way you could arrange to live that way?"

"No," she whispered. "I haven't told Helmut about Frau Bürste, but he is suspicious. He watches me when I am with her, and listens to what he wants to, and reads the orders I write for her. He told me once that he would have none of his household indulging in tribadism. That is why he wants me to be rid of her." She turned to him in supplication. "You won't say anything to him, will you? You won't let anyone know."

"Why should I?" Ragoczy asked, baffled and a bit disappointed that Gudrun should think that of him. "I don't disparage love, my dear."

"But since you've . . ." Her hands waved an explanation, and Ragoczy spoke for her.

"Yes, we have been lovers. You did not wish to continue. For those of my blood, an unwilling lover is . . . useless, to say it callously. There is no purpose in seeking those who are not able to take pleasure from what I do. You know that you were not the first"—he did not remember the first lover he had taken, for it was soon after he had died and walked again; he had been filled with rage and humiliation and a thirst for vengeance which he had not slaked for more than a century of his changed life while he brought the lust of terror to those who had been party to his death—"and you will not be the last. Those I love often seek others as lovers, or accept me in lieu of those they want most. There was a lady in Italy once, whose spirit was widowed when her lover died. Eventually I sought her, and she was willing, because the one she loved most was lost to her and I had been his friend." He could not think of Demetrice without sorrow, for she had been unable to live as those of his blood must, and had died the true death at her own hands when she had discovered what her changed life would be.

"Does it bother you? Don't you care that there might be others?" She had never spoken to him this way, but she felt bolder than she had before.

"Why should I? Do you love me any the less because you love others?" He put his arms around her and held her lightly, without pressure but with affection.

"I . . . I have never known those who . . . It is immoral." She sounded so prim as she gave this halfhearted objection, and Ragoczy could not keep from chuckling at her.

"Gudrun, dear Gudrun, where is the sin? I forsook religion long, long ago, and it has not harmed me. Deity is a fiction, a personification of what we love and fear most in ourselves. There is one God, you say, or are there two? Satan the fallen angel, is he a god? The Trinity—one, or three? Is God a parent, to protect and discipline his children, or a Presence that bestows understanding? What of religions with four gods, or five, or a thousand?" He said it rapidly, with bantering humor.

"They are not true religions," she declared.

"How do you know? Each says that it is, and declares that the rest are in error. Were the gods of Egypt less valid than the Lord God of Israel? Shiva and Krishna, are they false? The Buddha, was he less worthy of veneration than Saint Stephen?" He kissed her forehead. "There is a Power, I don't deny that, but it is without opinions—and morals are only opinions, Gudrun. The fire that warms your hearth and cooks your food is the same fire that burns cities and forests and men. It matters not at all to the fire, whose only purpose is to burn. There. Enough."

She stared at him, a curious twist to her face. "Then you are not . . . What if I left my husband? I hate to call him that. What if I went with Frau Bürste and we lived together as we wish to do? What would you say then?" There was a faint return of spirit in this challenge.

"There would be those who would disapprove, but does that matter to you? Does their approval make your life bearable now?" He saw how worn her face was, how there were deep stains under her eyes and her fragile complexion was chalky; her lips chapped and all but colorless.

"Not . . . not directly." She took a deep breath. "Not at all."

He calculated a moment, then began as reasonably as he could. "I'm trying to get out of Deutschland. There is a writ of detainment issued for me, and from what I have been told, there is not a road on the western or southwestern border of this country where it is safe for me to cross. I must leave: it is imperative. However," he went on as he felt her shrink back from him, "I am willing to take you with me, you and Frau Bürste, and arrange for you to live where you like. You may borrow one of my houses, if that would please you. It would not be Wolkighügel, but you would not have to stay with Helmut Rauch. It might be wise if you put some distance between you and Bayern, but that is up to you."

Gudrun stared at him in complete doubt. "Why will you do this, Graf?"

"Because you have been kind to me, and I have loved you. And because there is nothing else I can do." He was grave now, and did not know if she would believe his concern.

"To live away from here with Frau Bürste . . ." The happiness that had colored her voice was gone. "There is no money."

"I will provide you some. No, don't scowl at me that way. It is not a payment, it is a gift. There is so little joy in life, and we trust it so grudgingly. Do you prefer your misery because it is more concerted than pleasure is?" He dropped his hands and stepped back from her. "It would give me satisfaction to do this for you."

"But . . ." She squared her shoulders. "If I lived with Frau Bürste, I don't think I would want to see you again, except to visit, not . . ."

"You've asked me to go, Gudrun. If you wish me again, you will ask me to return. I don't assume that you will take me to your bed for this. That is not why I suggested it to you. It saddens me to see you in such a state, that is all."

Gudrun gave a watery sigh. "If only it were possible."

"But it *is*," he insisted, wanting to shake her with exasperation. "You have only to go change clothes and take what you need, and I will drive you to Wolkighügel, where you may wake Frau Bürste yourself. But we must be quick and get away at once. If Rauch is here, he will know about the detention writ and it would be . . . awkward to argue with him

about it." On his native earth, within his own walls, Ragoczy
felt slightly more restored, but the improvement was slow,
and he knew the reason now: the building had others in it, and
its ambience had been subtly altered. The virtue of his earth
was still there, but muffled, needing time to work its anneal-
ing benefits. Another hour and his exhaustion would be gone,
but Ragoczy dared not remain there so long. "I cannot stay,
Gudrun, although it is my Schloss. It is too dangerous."

"Because of Helmut?" she asked, knowing the answer as
well as he.

"In large part, yes." He put his hands on her shoulders.
"Hurry. If we fail, you will be no worse off than you are now.
If we succeed, you will have a chance to live as you wish to
live."

A shudder went the length of her body. "It would be much
worse if we fail, but I will help you try. If I don't, I will
always wonder what could have happened, and that would be
more painful than this helplessness is." Her jaw tightened. "I
will be quick. I won't take much. I don't want anything my
husband has given me. They are all chains and cages, even
this." She ran her hand over the sleeve of her robe.

"As you wish. But hurry. I will wait here." He tightened his
hands to encourage her, then released her. "Quickly."

"Yes," she whispered conspiratorially.

"And quietly."

"Yes." She held his eyes with hers, then gathered up her
robe and rushed out of the study, the pad of her feet so quiet
that Ragoczy could not hear her after she had gone a dozen
steps down the hall.

Ragoczy looked around the room and selected a stretch of
floor immediately in front of the cold fireplace. He took his
muffler and wiped the worst of the dust away; then he stretched
out on the chilly stones, letting his thoughts drift, opening his
soul to the potency of his native earth.

In her bedroom, Gudrun gathered up a few items of clothing and two pairs of boots. She was trembling with fear and a
strange exultation as she scurried from closet to dresser,
opening the doors softly, and closing them with excruciating
caution. In the dark, she did not want to risk bumping into
furniture or overturning a lamp or anything else that might
fall to the carpet and make a noise loud enough to wake her
husband, who lay deeply asleep on the bed. That still had the
capacity to surprise her: Helmut slept so profoundly that
he was not easily wakened. This time she did not pause to

marvel over him, but clutched the garments to her and hurried to the bathroom. She closed the door and turned on the light, blinking as the brightness stabbed at her dark-widened eyes. With a shaking hand she slid the bolt on the door, locking herself in, and then she stripped off her robe and her nightgown, shivering as she stood naked. She reached for her riding breeches and pulled them on, hoping she would be able to get underwear from Frau Bürste, for all that she had here was what Helmut had given her, wispy silken things of improbable colors and no practical use. She buttoned the breeches and reached for a lawn shirt. It had a number of buttons and she faltered at the task of closing them all. She was about to pull on her sweater over it when she heard Helmut stumble in the hall.

"Gudrun!" he called out sleepily.

"I'm in the bathroom." She reached over and turned on the faucets in the sink.

"What are you doing?" He had the petulant sound he always did when he was roused unexpectedly.

"Cleaning up." She shoved her sweater under a stack of towels and put her boots behind the radiator. "I am having my woman's friend," she improvised, though it was at least a week before she expected it.

Helmut's comment was not clear to her.

"When I am through, I am going down to the kitchen to heat up some milk and port. It eases the cramps. Go back to sleep, Helmut." She took a washrag and squeezed it out noisily.

"How long—?" he began.

"About five days."

"—will you be in there?"

She covered her hesitation by flushing the toilet. "Not too much longer. Please don't wait for me. I feel so . . . messy." She reached for her velvet robe and pulled it on. It covered her clothes quite well, especially if she raised the neck ruffle a little. It was exhilarating, this deception. The boots were a greater problem, but she hit on the idea of taking her nightgown and a towel and holding the boots under them. She snatched the nightgown from the floor and dropped it in to the sink, running water on it. With the noise of the water as a cover, she took one of the two pairs of boots from behind the radiator and reached for a towel. The results were fairly bulky, but it could not be helped. She took the nightgown out of the sink, wrung it once, and dropped it atop the towel. "I'm coming out," she called as she turned off the water and shot the bolt back. As she opened the door, she turned off the light, hoping that the sudden darkness would be as disorienting to Helmut as it would be to her.

"You're not sick, are you?" Helmut asked suspiciously as Gudrun stepped into the hall. His hair was tousled and his robe was not quite closed over his striped pajamas.

"Of course not," she said with asperity. "This happens to women quite regularly. It is merely an inconvenience." She started past him toward the stairs.

"I'll get the milk for you," he said darkly, or so she thought.

"It's . . . it's not necessary, Helmut. I've been doing this for myself for more than twenty years. Best let me take care of it." She looked at the towel in her hand. "I want to hang this up near the stove so that it will be dry in the morning."

Helmut grunted and rubbed his hair.

The stairs, as she descended them, seemed to go on interminably. She knew that she must not rush, or Helmut, still watching from above, would notice that something was amiss. She checked her impulse to scream and flee. One step at a time, her hand on the bannister, her step measured. If she moved too abruptly, the robe might open and show she was fully dressed but for the boots. She wished she had had a chance to pull on the sweater, but she had a hacking jacket in the sporting room, and that would be some help. At the foot of the stairs she turned toward the kitchen rather than toward the sporting room, on the chance that Helmut was continuing to watch her. Then she heard the bedroom door close, and she turned and ran toward the other wing of the Schloss, her right hand out against the walls to guide her, her left arm holding the towel and nightgown and boots tight against her robe.

The sporting room was small and more devoted to equestrian activities than shooting, though there was a small gun case at one end of the room. Gudrun's hacking jacket was hung over the back of one of the chairs, and she rushed to it, pulling the robe off her shoulders and letting the towel and nightgown drop to the floor. Her jacket was heavy wool and lined in stiff silk twill, designed to keep her warm on cross-country rides in brisk autumn weather. She sat down and reached for her boots, pulling out the thick sock that was rolled in the bottom of each of them. It was a habit her father had taught her, placing clean socks in her boots after polishing them, and never was she more grateful for it. The boots, without the socks, would have blistered her feet in short order. She tugged the boots on as soon as she had donned the socks, and then stood up, buttoning her jacket as she did so. Then she reached for the robe and towel and nightgown, and after an instant's indecision decided to put them in the guncase, which was almost never opened. As she laid them out on the old elm boards, she looked at the guns, and, impulsively, took a .30 calibre Carbine from its rack. She had done target shooting with a similar gun when Jürgen was still well. She doubted she could fire at anyone, but it gave her confidence to hold it in her hand. She opened the ammunition drawer and found a box of cartridges for the rifle. She dropped this into her pocket after loading the Carbine.

As she stepped into the hall, she wondered how long she had been, and if Ragoczy had become impatient and had, perhaps, left her behind. The fear of that turned her to inner ice, but she held it at bay. If he had gone, she told herself, it would make no difference. She would leave Schloss Saint-Germain and walk the distance to Wolkighügel. She would wake Frau Bürste and tell her what she had decided they must do. And Frau Bürste would agree. They would take the Lancia and drive . . . anywhere. They would go to Italy or Yugoslavia or Greece, and live private, frugal, rapturous lives. This resolution banished her fear at last, and she started back toward Ragoczy's study, visions of Aegean islands drowsing in the sun filling her mind.

"And now, Mein Graf, you will explain," Helmut Rauch said as he aimed the pistol directly at Ragoczy's head.

Ragoczy woke abruptly, and stared up at the man in the untidy bathrobe. "How did you find me?"

"My wife thinks she is very clever. I had only to follow the trail of her robe in the dust. I knew that something was the matter when she lied about her woman's friend: Otto told me when she had it last, and it was not yet time." He shook his head. "Not very clever, my wife. She tries, naturally, but like all women, she is at a loss outside of her proper sphere." He motioned with the pistol. "Get up, Herr Ragoczy. I do not like to shoot a man who is lying down."

"If you shoot me, it won't matter, Herr Rauch. I will fall in any case." He turned on his side, propping himself on his elbow. "Would it offend you if I chose to remain on the floor."

"To grovel?" Rauch inquired maliciously. "You foreigners are all like that, aren't you? Cowardly and sly when faced with your superiors. Aren't you?" He was taunting Ragoczy now, wanting to provoke him to some ill-considered action.

"You are Herr Rauch and I am Graf and Prinz, so who is the superior?" Ragoczy responded, suppressing a yawn.

"That is the old order!" Rauch snapped, though from the darkening of his face it was apparent that Ragoczy's jibe had struck home.

"A very old order indeed, Herr Rauch," Ragoczy said as he sat up. "And are you so certain that your new order is any different from it? Is there not the same structure? Or have I misunderstood your remarks of the past few years?" He felt his strength return, and wondered if he could goad Rauch into shooting him where it would do little harm. It was essential that he not be shot in the head or the spine if he were to survive. But a flesh wound in the leg or the arm, while painful, would not present any danger to him. And it would buy him a precious morsel of time in which to attack. If he could reach Rauch without being killed himself, then the other man would be dead.

"Be quiet!" He shouted this, and the room echoed it faintly. "Stand up!"

"Very well." Ragoczy got slowly to his feet, facing Rauch with contempt. "Does this suit you, Herr Rauch?"

"You have come back here like a thief in the night!" Rauch declared unsteadily, a tic in his cheek causing his left eye to jump.

"This is my Schloss, Herr Rauch. I may come here any way I choose. If there is a thief here, it is not I." His words were infuriatingly cool, and he faced the man with unruffled calm.

"It is not yours! The court has awarded it to the Thule Bruderschaft and the SA! We are deserving of it, not you!"

"A thief's excuse," Ragoczy said wryly.

"We are!" Helmut yelled.

"Of course. After all, you hold the pistol." His penetrating eyes were half-closed and his mouth curved in a sardonic smile.

"That means nothing," Helmut muttered.

"If that is the case, then give me the pistol and say the same things." Ragoczy's ironic amusement was more apparent now.

"You call me a thief," Helmut said, not responding to Ragoczy's last barb. "Yet you are the one who seeks to steal my wife. That is why you are here, isn't it, Ragoczy?"

"She seems more of a hostage than a wife, Rauch. Or do you

routinely use blackmail instead of charm to win a woman?" He looked at the other man. "You're despicable, Herr Rauch."

Helmut raised his pistol and aimed it directly at Ragoczy's head. "I have given her my name and my wealth. I have protected her from infamy."

"I gather she did not want any of it." Ragoczy shifted his weight slightly, so that he was balanced on the balls of his feet. He needed one chance, one little opening, and he would deal with Rauch.

"She is foolish. Women do not know how to deal with the world. It is the duty of a man to give them guidance and . . ." Helmut swallowed hard, as if there were an obstruction in his throat.

"Which is why you used her brother's debts to court her? How prudent." His sarcasm was deliberate and heavy, and he waited for Helmut to act. "She would not have had you otherwise, would she?"

"She did not understand!" Helmut bellowed, the barrel of the pistol wavering.

Ragoczy was ready to move. "How could she not? You were the one who threatened her, and you were the one who demanded that she accept you or face ruin. Do you deny that?"

"She is foolish," he repeated loudly. "She is stupid. She has no notion of how she must live! You were one of those who misled her, seduced her with lies and perversions and . . . She is incapable of thought, and without any perspective. It was I—*I*!—who brought her out of disgrace and restored her to the position she was meant to occupy. She could never have done it herself!"

"With you extending loans to her brother which you know he could not repay, she certainly could not," Ragoczy said, hoping this would be sufficient provocation.

"I had to do that! There was no other way to show her. That was why Maximillian had to die! If he had lived, he might have told her what he had done, and then . . . !" He lurched sideways and his pistol went off, the bullet embedding itself in Ragoczy's enormous desk. He reached up one hand, toward a spattering of skin and blood by his ear; then he turned slowly, making a last try to bring up his pistol for a second shot. Quite suddenly his legs collapsed and he fell in a heap, like a puppet with severed strings.

The rifle dropped from Gudrun's hands and she leaned on the wall, her face white. "Mein Gott, Mein Gott!" she shrieked, staring at the crumpled body.

Ragoczy approached her carefully, his arms open to her. "Hush, Gudrun. It is finished."

"He killed Maximillian. I knew it. I *knew* it. He did it deliberately, just killed him." She sobbed deeply twice, three times, gagged and drew herself up. "I will not weep for him. Or for Maximillian." She turned toward Ragoczy, her face severe. "Do not think I did this for you, Graf. It was for myself. For my honor."

"Yes," Ragoczy murmured. "We cannot stay here." He reached for his jacket, blocking her view of Helmut's body.

She looked about rather wildly. "No. This is an evil place. Helmut destroyed it, didn't he?"

"For a time, perhaps," Ragoczy answered her, and took her by the shoulders. "We must not be found here. If we are, you will have done this in vain. Gudrun, do you understand me?"

"I . . ." Her face showed the first immobility of shock, and her eyes no longer held the keen anger that had given her the impetus to shoot. "What am I to do." She tried to pull away from Ragoczy, but his small hands held her with uncanny strength. "They will make me a criminal. And the Thule Bruderschaft, with their policemen and their judges, will condemn me, and I will die. Oh, Christ!" She crossed herself, as she had done as a child, and began to recite the Ave Maria in a low horrified voice.

"Gudrun," Ragoczy said quite firmly to her, "we're going to leave here. Do you understand me? We are going to get into my automobile and I will drive you to Wolkighügel. You will wake Frau Bürste and tell her what has happened. She will aid you in finding a plausible explanation of why you returned to your house this evening. If you act wisely, you will have your wish: you will live at Wolkighügel with Frau Bürste without any taint of suspicion touching you, now or ever. Do you want that, Gudrun?"

"I want that," she said, breaking off her prayers. "Oh, yes."

Ragoczy was relieved to hear this. He looked into her eyes and spoke directly to her. "We will leave here. We will take the rifle and leave. We are going back to Wolkighügel. Frau Bürste is there and she will help you."

"Yes, she will," Gudrun agreed, and the leaden terror began to fade from her features.

"Then come with me, Gudrun." This time when he reached to take her arm, she let him do it. He picked up the rifle and pulled the door open. "You were very brave to . . ." He did not know what next to say.

"Kill my husband?" She stood in the hall while he closed the door to his study. Once more she shivered violently. "I was angry, not brave."

"They're often the same thing," he said as they started down the hall. "Is anyone expected here tomorrow?"

"I think Konrad Natter, but . . . I don't know, Graf." She followed docilely enough, going through the kitchen with mincing steps, as if she expected to be apprehended at any moment. As he opened the rear door, she said, "It isn't tomorrow, it's the day after."

"The longer the better," Ragoczy said, already beginning to concoct a workable story that would account for her absence from Schloss Saint-Germain. He reached into his pocket for the key and locked the door.

"I could send word for him to wait another day," Gudrun suggested with a hopeful smile. Her hands were shaking now, and she told herself it was from the cold.

"No, that would not be wise. If there are any changes, they will be remembered later, when the police enter the picture." He started toward the stables, not allowing her to protest his prohibition.

There was an icy dew on the ground, and both gave their attention to finding their way along the slippery, narrow walkway. When at last they reached the place where his automobile was hidden, he held her briefly before letting her into the passenger's seat.

"Be careful. There is still one drum of gasoline there." He moved his suitcase away from her feet and got into the driver's seat. As he started the Delage, he turned back to her, saying, "You have done very well, Gudrun, and you will continue to do well."

"Danke," she whispered, feeling tired, more tired than she had ever been in her life. As the automobile moved off on the treacherous road, she leaned back on the seat, wishing to sleep, but seeing Helmut on the floor, Jürgen still in his bed, Maximillian dangling from the beam of the gamekeeper's cottage. She moaned once, but it was more in rejection than desolation. Finally, finally, she thought, they were gone from her. They would not touch her again.

Wolkighügel was dark when Ragoczy pulled up to the side of the house. There were neither trucks nor automobiles in the front court, and only the Lancia, with its faded paint and dented fender, waited beside the servants' entrance. Ragoczy got out of the automobile and went quickly to the second window from the door. He tapped the glass once, twice, then waited and tapped again. On the fourth repeat, he saw Frau Bürste's broad, plain face in the darkness of the room, and then the window was opened.

"Herr Ragoczy," she said in surprise as she gathered her plain woolen robe around her and tugged at the nightcap askew on her head.

"I have Frau Ostneige in my automobile. She is very much in need of your help." Neither of them thought it odd that he had not called her Frau Rauch.

"What has happened?" Frau Bürste asked in her forthright way, without any shying away from the question or nervous fidgeting.

"There has been an . . . accident," Ragoczy said, amending his first intention. "Herr Rauch has suffered a . . . mishap . . ."

"Is he alive or dead?" Frau Bürste demanded, dismissing his careful phrases with a nod of her head.

"I fear he is dead." He watched the housekeeper closely. "Frau Ostneige heard a remark he made that she was not intended to hear." He decided to say a little more. "Apparently Herr Rauch was not entirely innocent in Maximillian's death."

"Ah!" She stared at him. "So. It always comes back to her brother. I will be out at once." She closed the window and hurried off through the dark room.

Ragoczy went back to the Delage and opened the passenger-seat door. He shook Gudrun very gently, and when she opened her eyes, he said, "We're at your home, Rudi. Frau Bürste is coming."

"Frau Bürste," she said with such delighted relief that Ragoczy smiled sadly.

"There are a number of things to be done," he told her, hoping that she would wake up enough to be more helpful. "And they must be done quickly."

Gudrun's words were cut short by the opening of the servants' door and the arrival of the stalwart Frau Bürste.

"Frau Ostneige!" she said, opening her arms to Gudrun, and smiling as the other woman hurtled into her arms. "There, my beautiful one, my sweeting. Nothing will harm you now." She looked over Gudrun's shoulder at Ragoczy. "Tell me the rest, Herr Graf."

"Herr Rauch is dead. He is lying on the floor of my study at my Schloss. The gun that killed him is missing, and will be in the deepest part of the lake before another hour goes by." He knew the road to Schliersee well enough to risk driving it in the rising fog. "It will be necessary to account for Frau Ostneige's presence here, and to deny that I was ever about. The police are going to suspect me in any case, but you know nothing of that."

"Of course not. Frau Ostneige was here with me all evening," she declared at once, a glitter in her prominent eyes that was not quite humor.

"And why was she here?" Ragoczy asked, pleased at Frau Bürste's resourceful mind.

"Because there was an emergency. Something has gone wrong with the repairs being made, and since the workers had left, and Otto is at the tavern getting drunk, I had to speak to her at once." She kissed Gudrun's hair, and the younger woman at last began to cry.

"Excellent," Ragoczy approved. "I see I can leave her in capable hands."

"And with my gratitude," Frau Bürste said, with such feeling that Ragoczy bowed his acknowledgment. "I have not seen you, Herr Ragoczy. I have been too busy with the emergency to notice anything."

"Has there been an emergency?" Ragoczy asked, concerned about that one matter.

"There will be a great mishap with the plumbing before morning," she promised him. "Now, I must attend to Frau Ostneige." There was triumph in her plain face as she turned and led Gudrun toward the house. "She has never had anyone to defend her, but she has me now." With this last remark, she closed the door.

Ragoczy shut his eyes, thinking of that indomitable woman, who would be a bulwark against the world for Gudrun. Nothing he could give her could approach that fidelity and utter devotion that Frau Bürste would lavish on her for the rest of her life.

He started the Delage, then took the road to Schliersee. By morning he would be in Austria, and the day after that, Switzerland. Somewhere along the way, he would wire Madelaine in Paris. At the thought of her, he was overwhelmed with his loneliness for her, and for that intimacy they could never again share. His eyes were dry, because he had no tears to shed, but sorrow cut deep within him, relentless and unending, darker and colder than the night.

Text of a letter from James Emmerson Tree to his cousin Audrey.

*Paris*
*May 29, 1928*

*Dear Audrey;*

*Sorry I haven't written sooner, but I've been in Scandinavia, on an assignment, fairly boring, about how the unemployment situation in Germany (it's pretty serious there, with more than 10 percent of the work force without jobs, or that's as much as the government will admit are without jobs) has influenced jobs and money in Sweden and Denmark. I haven't finished the articles yet, and just when I do, you wait, everything will change.*

*Anyway, belatedly, congratulations on your marriage. From what you tell me, Tim sounds like a fine man, and you should do very well together. You say that he's been practicing law for five years and has his feet on the ground. That's very good, and it won't get in the way of all the things you say you want to do. It's a good thing you've moved to Seattle. Things do have a way of turning out, don't they? I'm pleased for you, and I hope that you will both be very happy, this year, next year, and clear on to the end of it all. You'll do just fine, I know you will. And there's a package in the post to you, but I doubt it will get there until late in June, knowing how fast they move those large pieces of mail. I'm sorry Uncle Ned couldn't attend your wedding, but it doesn't entirely surprise me. He's done other foolish things, hasn't he? Don't take it too hard, Audrey. He'll get over it in time, and in the meantime, you have your life to live, and you can't let his pouting spoil what has made you so happy.*

*I haven't had much of a look at American politics until a couple days ago. I've been traveling so much that I haven't seen any newspapers from home, and most of the European papers don't spend much time on the USA.*

*With Italy repealing the vote for women, I'm afraid it might have a bad effect on suffrage here, but it's hard to say what will happen there. You don't know who's going to start looking at these political changes and decide that they'd do well in the USA. It's strange to see how many people are running scared here; if it's that way at home, it could mean there are some drastic changes coming. It probably comes down to money, and if it is anything else, you can bet it ties in to money. I'm sounding cynical, aren't I? But Germany wouldn't be in the mess it's got into if it weren't for money. France has trouble too, and it's hard to say how long they can go on the way they've been without doing something about the national finances. It might happen in America, too. I know that Wall Street is booming, or so they tell me, but one of the British journalists who was over here a couple months ago said that he doesn't like the look of it, and his reasons made pretty good sense to me. It depends on too many things working out just right and he said that things never work out just right. It could be that he's taking too pessimistic a view, but I've got a hunch it would be a good idea to be careful for a while, until things sort themselves out. With you and Tim starting out on your own right now, a little extra caution wouldn't be a bad idea. If it turns out that I'm wrong, you won't be any worse off, but if there's a rough period, you'll be covered. Figure that's the only advice I'm going to give you. I know that after all this time, there isn't much reason for you to put any stock in what I say, but I do listen, and it could be that I hear a little more than a lot of others do.*

*Crandell said that he'll bring me home next year or the year after unless the politics here change drastically, in which case he'll keep me on. I wouldn't mind seeing home again, it's been so long. I've spent almost a third of my life over here, and that's damn sobering. Not that I would have missed it for the world. I'll probably need some time to get used to America again. I haven't heard English regularly in years. We speak it at the office, and when there are British and Americans around, we all use it gratefully. But out in the streets, we hear French, or Spanish, or Italian, or German. That takes getting used to, but now I think it would be strange to hear English all the time. I'm wondering how it will be to see signs in*

*English and ride in American automobiles. Well, I'll
find out in 1929, or so they tell me.*

*Night before last I went to a banquet given by Professor
Simmond Rose for Madelaine de Montalia. She has finished a whole series of translations of some old clay tablets
that are very important in studying the ancient world. It
was one of those very formal affairs, held at an excellent
restaurant in their formal hall. Black tie, long dresses,
jewels, and the best of manners around. It was a fine
evening, and I was very happy that she invited me, because I don't usually see that side of Parisian life. Her
escort for the evening was a man I did not know, but I
think I've seen him once before. He was only half a head
taller than she is—not much above five-five-or-six, with
dark, wavy hair and the most arresting eyes I've ever
seen. He's probably old nobility, judging from the way he
walks and the way everyone defers to him. He's got the
grand manner, no doubt about it. He spent most of the
evening beside her, very proper in how he talked to her
and what he said. Like Madelaine, he did not eat. She
told me once about a very old lover of hers, and I think
this must be the one. I can't imagine who else it could be,
and I can see what it is that he saw in her and she in him.
He's not the kind of man you'd sit around and talk sports
with, unless it was something like fox hunting. Otherwise, he's a fine figure and she does very well by him. A
year ago I would have flung the salad at him for being
with her.*

*I'm going to Lausanne with Madelaine next week, where
we always go, and this time we've got a total of ten days
to spend together. I'm looking forward to it, almost as
much as you looked forward to your honeymoon, I think.
She's the most wonderful woman I've ever known, and
she put up with some terrible temperament from me.*

*The Mors has been traded in, and I haven't yet made
up my mind what I want to buy for my next automobile.
Every now and then I dream about a Bugatti, but it
doesn't look to be possible unless Crandell gives me more
money than he's doing now. I've been driving a Citroën
which I have on loan from a French journalist who is
covering the Cairo office for his paper until January.
Egypt keeps coming back into the news because of all the
antiquities they're digging up all the time. I haven't
much of an interest that way, although Madelaine chides*

me for a lack of historical perspective and warns me that I will need such a thing in the future. It could be. But in the meantime, I am more worried about my transportation than the course of history.

You told me in your letter that you were thinking of traveling to Europe next year. At last! You bring Tim and we'll show you the whole place, top to bottom and sideways. Except for Germany, since they still won't let me in. I applied for entry while I was in Sweden, and they turned me down flat. I don't think I'll make the attempt again for a while, not with the way things are going there. It's worse than Italy, sometimes. But I can get into Italy. You'll like it there. France is beautiful, but you'll have to remember that everything here is on a smaller scale. The cities are small, the houses are small (except for the grand ones, and they're huge), the automobiles are pretty small, and the rest of it is scaled down. The Alps are decent-sized mountains, but if you're used to the distances of Western American states, then you'll find this whole area very tightly packed. Out there you can drive all day and not leave the state, but here, if you work it right, you can go through three countries from breakfast to supper. I think that's one of the things that fascinates me about the place, the diversity. I used to assume I'd get used to it, but I know now that I won't. And that suits me very well.

I've given up on the book idea for the time being. I suppose I don't know how to write fiction. No matter what I do, it comes out like the shopping list of a crazy monarch. You know the kind of thing I mean: all description and a few unreal people wandering around the landscape talking to each other in platitudes. Henry James without the talent, that's me. Maybe later. But I tell you, Audrey, it doesn't bother me anymore. I wanted to be the American journalist with the great novel, but it's fine to be just the American journalist. I've found out I do that well, and that it is not a thing very many people can do at all. In a few years, who knows, I may get a book anyway, but from journalism, not a novel or a play. You have no idea how much that pleases me.

When you've got your travel plans, you let me know what they are and I'll do whatever you want me to do at this end. I can probably get you a break on a hotel room, if you want to stay at a hotel, or I can give you space with

*me. The apartment isn't very fancy, but it is quite pleas-
ant. If that won't do, I'll ask Madelaine if I can borrow
her house, if she's away when you're here. It's not big, but
it's really beautiful. Tell me the kind of money you want
to spend and how long you're going to be here, and I
promise you the best trip you've ever had. It'll be great to
see you again. It's one thing to see your pictures, but it
will be another thing entirely to see you as you are.*

*Until you write, and we get together again, I'll close for
now. There's a lot I want to tell you, but it will wait until
we can see each other face to face.*

*With all my love,
Your cousin James*

# Epilogue

Text of a letter from Madelaine de Montalia to le Comte de
Saint-Germain.

*Athens
September 21, 1928*

*My dearest Saint-Germain;*

*Yes, I will indeed be in Paris by the 2nd of November,
and I am more than delighted to attend the gala with you.
Do you remember the gala given for me in November
when I was still alive? You had written that opera for me,
on Persephone, and they sang it for me. You had that
wonderful castrato Ombrasalice sing Pluton, and he did it
so well, and so elegantly. No one has ever given me such
a gift, and no one ever will again. I have had so much
from you that I cherish with all my heart and that will
give me joy for all the years that I will walk the earth.*

*Yes, James has been much more understanding of late,
and that pleases me. For one thing, I feel less as if I had
done him a disservice in taking him for my lover. Before,
I believed that he would always be torn, but I think now
that he will change and come into our life with appreciation
for what it can be.*

*Always, always I miss you, and I would give almost anything to be able to love you now as I did before I changed, but there is no alteration of our nature, and so I will love you as I have since we met, with all my soul and all my heart, and I will rejoice in your love and your company. At least there is no alienation with us, and we may find that unique friendship, which is more intimate than any lover I have known but James, will sustain us through the long years to come.*

*I would not give up one moment I have spent with you and I will not forsake you, as you have never forsaken me. It might not be faithfulness as much of the world understands it, but it has more genuine trust and whole-hearted care than many other emotions that carry those names.*

*When you move to London, are you taking Nikolai? If you are not, I would not mind hiring him myself. He is loyal and dependable and he drives with some respect for his passengers. Consider it, if you decide you do not need him yourself.*

*With my eternal love, Saint-Germain, and my immortal soul.*

*Your
Madelaine*

## About the Author

Chelsea Quinn Yarbro has written science fiction, detective and occult novels. TEMPTING FATE is the fifth and final book in an historical horror series featuring the Count de Saint-Germain. Ms. Yarbro lives in California.